To June,

with

your birthday and lots

of love,

Norman.

24th June 1974

The Wisest Fool

By the same author

HARSH HERITAGE
MAMMON'S DAUGHTER
TRESPASS
EAGLES FEATHERS
WATERSHED
THE GILDED FLEECE
DELAYED ACTION
TINKER'S PRIDE
MAN'S ESTATE
FLIGHT OF DUTCHMEN
ISLAND TWILIGHT
ROOT AND BRANCH
COLOURS FLYING
THE CHOSEN COURSE
FAIR GAME
HIGH SPIRITS
THE FREEBOOTERS
TIDEWRACK
FAST AND LOOSE
BRIDAL PATH
CHEVIOT CHASE
DUCKS AND DRAKES
THE QUEEN'S GRACE
RUM WEEK
THE NIGHT RIDERS
THERE ARE WORSE JUNGLES
RIO D'ORO
THE LONG COFFIN
MACGREGOR'S GATHERING
THE ENDURING FLAME
BALEFIRE
THE STONE
THE MAN BEHIND THE CURTAIN
THE CLANSMAN
SPANISH GALLEON
THE FLOCKMASTERS
KETTLE OF FISH
THE MASTER OF GRAY
DRUG ON THE MARKET
GOLD FOR PRINCE CHARLIE
THE COURTESAN
CHAIN OF DESTINY
PAST MASTER
A STAKE IN THE KINGDOM
LION LET LOOSE
CABLE FROM KABUL
BLACK DOUGLAS
THE YOUNG MONTROSE
MONTROSE: THE CAPTAIN-GENERAL
ROBERT THE BRUCE: THE STEPS TO THE EMPTY THRONE
ROBERT THE BRUCE: THE PATH OF THE HERO KING
ROBERT THE BRUCE: THE PRICE OF THE KING'S PEACE

THE QUEEN'S SCOTLAND
THE HEARTLAND: CLACKMANNANSHIRE, PERTHSHIRE AND STIRLINGSHIRE
THE EASTERN COUNTIES: ABERDEENSHIRE, ANGUS AND KINCARDINESHIRE
THE NORTH EAST: THE SHIRES OF BANFF, MORAY, NAIRN, WITH EASTER INVERNESS AND EASTER ROSS

LAND OF THE SCOTS

NIGEL TRANTER

The Wisest Fool

A Novel of James the Sixth and First

HODDER AND STOUGHTON
LONDON SYDNEY AUCKLAND TORONTO

 ISBN 0 340 17823 X.
 Filmset and printed in Great Britain for Hodder and Stoughton Limited, St. Paul's House, Warwick Lane, London EC4P 4AH by Thomson Litho, East Kilbride, Scotland.

PRINCIPAL CHARACTERS

IN ORDER OF APPEARANCE

GEORGE HERIOT: Merchant Burgess of Edinburgh. Jeweller and man-of-business to the King.

KING JAMES THE SIXTH OF SCOTS: Son of Mary Queen of Scots, recently succeeded Elizabeth Tudor on the throne of England likewise.

LUDOVICK, SECOND DUKE OF LENNOX: Second cousin of the King. Lord High Admiral of Scotland.

PATRICK, MASTER OF GRAY: Heir of fifth Lord Gray, Sheriff of Forfar, former acting Chancellor of Scotland, the 'handsomest man in Europe'.

LORD HENRY HOWARD: Later Earl of Northampton. Younger brother of executed Duke of Norfolk, member of the most powerful family in England.

MARY GRAY: Illegitimate daughter of the Master of Gray. Mistress of Duke of Lennox.

JEAN, DUCHESS OF LENNOX: Wife of the Duke. Great heiress.

ALISON PRIMROSE: Maid-in-Waiting to the Queen. Eldest of the nineteen children of James Primrose, Clerk to the Scots Privy Council.

QUEEN ANNE: Wife of King James. Daughter of Frederick the Second of Denmark.

HENRIETTA, MARCHIONESS OF HUNTLY: Principal Lady-in-Waiting. Wife of the Catholic Gordon chief, and sister of the Duke of Lennox.

PRINCESS ELIZABETH: Daughter of James and Anne. Later the famous Queen of Bohemia, 'The Winter Queen' and 'Queen of Hearts'.

ANNABEL, COUNTESS OF MAR: Mother of Earl of Mar. Foster-mother of the King.

PRINCE HENRY FREDERICK, DUKE OF ROTHESAY: Later Prince of Wales. Eldest son of James and Anne.

ALEXANDER SETON, LORD FYVIE: Chancellor of Scotland. Later Earl of Dunfermline.

JOHN, EARL OF MAR: Great Scots noble. Foster-brother of the King.

HARRY WRIOTHESLEY, EARL OF SOUTHAMPTON: English courtier and favourite of the King.

SIR ROBERT CECIL: Chief Secretary of State. Later Earl of Salisbury.

PHILIP HERBERT: Brother of the Earl of Pembroke. Favourite of the King, and later Earl of Montgomery.

LADY ARABELLA STEWART: Cousin of the King. Daughter of King Henry Darnley's brother.

THOMAS EGERTON, EARL OF ELLESMERE: Lord Chancellor of England.

PRINCE CHARLES, DUKE OF ALBANY: Second son of the King. Later Duke of York, and eventually King Charles the First.

DUKE ULRIC OF HOLSTEIN: Brother of Queen Anne.

PATRICK, SECOND EARL OF ORKNEY: Eldest son of the King's illegitimate uncle.

HENRY HOWARD, EARL OF NOTTINGHAM: The former Lord Howard of Effingham, Lord High Admiral of England.

THOMAS HOWARD, EARL OF SUFFOLK: Lord Chamberlain. Another brother of the late Duke of Norfolk.

WILLIAM PARKER, LORD MOUNTEAGLE: A Catholic English peer.

GUIDO FAWKES: Catholic adventurer and conspirator.

MARGARET HARTSIDE: A chambermaid to the Queen.

KING CHRISTIAN THE FOURTH OF DENMARK: Brother of Queen Anne.

SIR THOMAS HAMILTON OF BINNING: Lord Advocate. Later first Earl of Melrose, then Earl of Haddington.

THOMAS HOPE: Edinburgh advocate. Later Lord Advocate.

JAMES PRIMROSE: Alison's father, Clerk to the Scots Privy Council.

SIR GEORGE HOME OF MANDERSTON: Favourite of the King. Created Earl of Dunbar and Great Commissioner.

WILL SHAKESPEARE: Actor and playwright.

ANDREW MELVILLE: Presbyterian divine. Leader of the Kirk party in Scotland.

JAMES MELVILLE: Nephew of above. Also noted divine.

RICHARD BANCROFT, Archbishop of Canterbury.

LADY MARIE STEWART: Wife of the Master of Gray. Sister of the Earl of Orkney and niece of the King.

ROBERT KERR, OR CARR: Brother of Kerr of Ferniehirst. King's favourite. Later Earl of Somerset.

JAMES ELPHINSTONE, LORD BALMERINO: Secretary of State for Scotland, and Lord President of the Court of Session.

JAMES HAY, VISCOUNT DONCASTER: An earlier favourite of the King. Later Earl of Carlisle.

PART ONE

I

THE THUNDER OF the cannon from Berwick's castle and walls stopped abruptly—presumably these having run out of powder after nearly two hours of gleeful banging such as the old grey town had not heard since Edward Longshanks' days. In the sudden hush, the chatter of hundreds of tongues, necessarily unpraised previously to counter the din, as hurriedly dropped away, abashed, and only the wailing of the gulls, wheeling everlastingly above the Tweed's estuary, sounded over all the brilliant and colourful throng.

Men and women might stare, even though chatter would probably be considered unseemly—and certain unseemlinesses were frowned upon in no uncertain fashion, though others were not; one could never be quite sure, majesty being an unpredictable quantity and quality. Stare the great company did, then, with varying expressions—and to the keen eye it could have been noteworthy that the variations might be classed under two main heads, the amused and the shaken. Moreover, these categories themselves could be allotted to the two constituent groups, almost exactly. The Scots mainly tittered, and the English looked astonished, alarmed, even appalled. It was as simple as that, on the Spittal shore of Tweed, at the southern end of Berwick Bridge.

One Scot there, watching, neither tittered nor looked shaken, however. A man in his late thirties, dressed richly but not with the extravagance of padding, clashing colour and ornamentation which was prevalent around him, he was stockily built, sandy-haired, with no very distinguished features but shrewd alert eyes which missed nothing, a quietly watching, assessing, steady man whose expression was nevertheless redeemed from anything of stern self-interest by the upturning corners of a firm mouth above a small beard, which hinted at humour never far away. George Heriot was apt to see the amusing side of life, without necessarily bursting into laughter over it all, and sought not to be mocking about it—difficult as this frequently was in his circumstances. But he did not smile now, whatever the attitude of most of his compatriots present, for his sympathies were engaged, strangely enough.

Not that the scene lacked anything to make a cat laugh. To see a knock-kneed, over-dressed, slobbering little man down on the said knees kissing the beaten ground amongst the horse-droppings at the bridge-end, and mumbling wetly, high beribboned hat tipped forward over his nose, was a sight seldom to be seen. And when the individual so engaged was Christ's Vicar here on earth—or so he confidently asserted—the Lord's Anointed, James, by the grace God King, not only of Scots but, since exactly two weeks previously, of England also, the first ever so to be, the thing became the more extraordinary. What added to the general Scots appreciation, of course, was the evident upset and confusion of the English notables most close to the monarch, who, unused to the ways of their new liege lord, did not know whether to get down on the earth with him, pray with him—if that was what he was doing—seek to raise him up, look the other way, or merely wring their hands and look unhappy. When the King stands, all men stand—in England certainly, and presumably in Scotland also. And they were in England now—just. But did it also apply to kneeling, kissing and mumbling? The Earl of Northumberland, representing the Privy Council and both Houses of Parliament, looked at the Bishop of Durham, representing the Archbishops of Canterbury and York before the new Head of the Church of England, but got no help there, and turned to his brother, Sir Charles Percy, who had been escorting their sovereign lord all the way from Edinburgh and ought to know the form. Sir Charles spread his delicate hands helplessly, looking pained in dignified fashion. He had been a courtier of Elizabeth's for thirty years, and never had had to face a problem such as this before.

George Heriot still did not smile, but he scratched his small beard in anticipation.

James Stewart solved the problem in his own way. As abruptly as he had collapsed on his spindly, knobbly knees when he had tottered off the bridge, he stopped his prayers and praise for safe delivery, tipped his very odd and high hat to the back of his head, to look up and around him. And those great lachrymose but lustrous eyes, possibly the only inheritance he had, other than a kingdom, from his beautious mother Mary Queen of Scots, were searching and shrewd as Heriot's own. The Wisest Fool in Christendom missed little of what went on around him.

"Man—have me up, can you no'?" he demanded, at Northumberland. "Standing there gawping like a great gowk! Aye, and you, my lord Bishop—what way's that to bide? Have you no' a word o' thanks to your Maker for winning us ower this Jordan?"

Even as Earl and Bishop burst into comprehensive apology for any seeming neglect, either of their liege lord or their Maker, a score of eager hands hastened to raise Majesty to its feet, each jostling all others in the process.

A voice spoke quietly at Heriot's shoulder. "I swear I am sorry for these English, Master Heriot—tears that I had never thought to shed!" That was Ludovick Stewart, Duke of Lennox, at present the only duke in two kingdoms, the King's far-out cousin and intermittent friend if not favourite. "Their education commences, I think!"

The other shrugged slightly. "Ours also, perhaps, my lord Duke. Who knows? There is change in the air."

"Change, aye. But . . . for the better?"

"We must make it so. If we can. And *we* at least have this advantage—His Grace will not change, whatever else may!"

King James had turned round to face the bridge again, and was pointing, arm and finger still trembling from his alarm and emotion. He spoke thickly—always he spoke thickly, wetly, for his tongue was too large for his mouth and the spittle ran constantly down his straggly beard, as adequate an excuse for a permanent thirst as might be devised. To steady himself, he grabbed Sir Charles Percy's richly padded sleeve, with the other hand.

"Yon's a right shameful brig," he declared. "Your brother, this Northumberland, should have done better for me, man. It's no' right and proper, I tell you. I . . . we are much disappointed. Yon's a disgrace. We might have been submerged in the cruel waters—aye, submerged. It wabbles, sirs—it quakes. It'll no' do, I say."

"To be sure, Sire. As Your Majesty says. But I assure Your Majesty that it is safe. Entirely safe." Northumberland, still clutching the as yet undelivered address of welcome from the Privy Council in London, was earnestly placatory. "It has always been thus. I have ridden across it a hundred times . . ."

"It shoogles, sir—it shoogles. And creaks. Are you contesting my royal word, Englishman?"

"No, Sire—no! I swear! But . . . but . . ."

The Bishop gallantly, if rashly, came to the rescue. "Your Majesty, old wooden bridges *do* creak. In especial long ones. And, er, quiver somewhat. But it has survived a thousand storms . . ."

"Each more weakening it, man—weakening it. Guidsakes, you came here, to bide *this* side, waiting on me, *me* your prince, to take his life in his two hands, and cross yon death-trap to you! What like a people and nation is this I've come amongst?"

"But, Highness—this *is* the English side. Where it was our duty, our joyful duty, to wait and greet you. On setting your royal foot on our, h'm, on *your* English soil. For the first time. Berwick Bridge, therefore, is only half in this realm of England. Your Majesty will not hold us responsible for, for the Scots end . . . ?"

"Na, na, mannie—you'll no' win awa' with that sort o' talk, see you. Yon ill Richard Plantagenet stole Berwick from us lang-syne; 1427 to be precise—aye, 1427, nigh on two centuries past. You've sat snug in our Berwick since then, have you no'? Complain as we would. *North* o' the brig. So you'll no' can jouk your responsibilities. *Incidis in Scyllam cupiens vitare Charybdim.* You, a churchman, will ken what that means?'

"Er, yes Sire." Tobias Mathew was as unused to a monarch who quoted Latin at him, as he was to one who gabbled in almost incomprehensible dialect, dribbled and prayed to his Maker in the public highway. He sought to change the subject. "We have letters for Your Majesty. From the Convocation of Canterbury and York, and from the High Court of Parliament. And, of course, Your Majesty's Privy Council . . ."

"Aye. But this brig," the King said. "It'll no' do. You'll just hae to build a new one. D'you hear? My command—aye, our first royal command on this our English ground. A guid new stout brig o' stone, see you. That'll no' wabble. Forthwith. See you to it, my lords. My . . . my Treasury in London will pay for it."

There was a moment of utter silence. Then a peal of silvery, musical laughter rang out, from the Master of Gray, sheer enjoyment, appreciation; and everywhere the Scots broke into grins and chuckles, while their brand-new fellow-subjects of England, until so recently such proud Elizabethans, exchanged ominous glances.

But James Stewart frowned. He was always suspicious of laughter provoked by himself, even though it came from the Master of his royal Wardrobe and the handsomest man in Europe.

"Hud your wheesht, Patrick Gray!" he commanded. "Every dog his day, aye—but your day's done!"

"Oh, I pray not, Sire," the gallant and debonair Master said, easily. "Who knows—it may just be beginning. Like, h'm, some others!"

"Na, na, Patrick man—no' so like some others!" The King whinnied a laugh of his own, and licked those slobbering lips. "I'm thinking this is where we part company, see you."

Suddenly blank-faced, the brilliant ornament of the Scottish Court stood as though stunned. For once the most eloquent man in two kingdoms found no words—and none other thought to raise his voice.

"I . . . I do not understand, Your Grace," he got out, at length.

"No? Do you no', Patrick? And you sharp o' the wits! Yet it's simple, man—fell simple. I go on to this London-town—and you do not. You turn back. You understand now, my mannie?"

"Your Grace means that you wish me to return to Edinburgh? Meantime. To complete some business of state there, before coming to London?"

"My Grace doesna mean any such thing, no. We left a' things well arranged in Edinburgh, mind. Ooh, aye—Edinburgh'll manage fine."

"Then, Sire, I repeat—I do not understand you."

"It's no' like you, Patrick, to be so dull in the uptak! Most times you're quick enough—aye, ower quick, by far! But since you'll have it so, I needs must discover you the matter. You are a rogue, Master o' Gray—and I've aye kenned you were a rogue! But I needed a rogue, see you. A great rogue, to berogue the lesser rogues around me." James paused, mouthing, his strange glowing glance making a slow half-circuit of all around him, the entire gorgeous throng, English and Scots. "Ooh, aye—it's a great place for rogues, is Scotland. But I intend to leave them there, Patrick man—no' to take them with me. Like a dog shakes off its fleas! The English are honester folk, they tell me—eh, my lord Bishop? Save maybe where Berwick and brigs are concerned! And if they have a rogue or two in London—waesucks, I'll find one o' their ain breed to berogue them! I'll no' need the likes o' you in London, Patrick, Master o' Gray. Now, you understand?"

The handsome elegant with the flashing eyes said nothing. For a long moment he stared his monarch in the eye. Then he bowed, stiffly for so agile and courtly a man, and turning, pushed his way quickly through the throng, to his horse.

The King's laughter was not nearly so musical as the Master of the Wardrobe's and one-time acting-Chancellor's had been.

"Change, my God!" the Duke of Lennox gasped. "This, this is beyond all! The man who put him where he is, no less. Cast aside like a done nag!"

"Quietly, my lord Duke!" George Heriot murmured. "English ears, they say, are long! And they learn quickly."

"But . . . Patrick Gray jettisoned. A rogue, perhaps—but the cleverest head in Scotland. Or in England either, for a wager! I swear my cousin can ill afford to be so nice! And look whom he *does* take with him! The Kerrs. John Bothwell. George Home. Erskine. Ramsay. Hay. The scum of Scotland!"

"Our liege lord has been waiting for this for long, I think. For Queen Elizabeth's death, and all it would mean. A new life. He knows what he is doing, I do believe—having had long enough to consider it. I urge you, my lord Duke, to walk warily—like lesser men, who are wise."

"Like you, Master Heriot?"

"Like me, sir. A tradesman—but with not a little to lose, neverthelesss."

There was a diversion. The King was pushing away the Earl of Northumberland's handsome parchment address from the Council with one hand, and shaking off the Lord Henry Howard, Norfolk's brother, with the other, when the drumming of hooves turned all eyes. Three horsemen came beating down from the higher ground of Spittal and the south road, a young man in fine if travel-stained clothing, and two armed grooms. The newcomers pulled up in a great slithering of hooves and spattering of spume from the horses, to the major alarm of the monarch, who was ready to see dastardly assault and danger in every unannounced development. The young man stared around him, at a loss.

"The King?" he demanded. "Is the King not here?"

Innumerable hands gestured towards the uninspiring if over-dressed person of the shrinking monarch.

Doubtfully the visitor looked, his face grey with dust and lined with fatigue. Then, evidently, deciding that they could not all be wrong or conspiring to hoodwink him, he flung himself down from his mount and sank on one knee before the equally doubtful sovereign.

"Your Majesty—Sire!" he panted, tugging out something metallic from his slashed and padded doublet—and which James Stewart immediately took to be a dagger, and staggered precipitately back into the arms of Northumberland and Howard in consequence, in choking panic.

It proved to be only a great iron key, however, and the young man, licking dusty lips, began again.

"Your most gracious Majesty, serene exemplar of learning, humanity and piety . . ." His voice trailed away.

"Aye, man—aye?" James suddenly was interested, at these indications of percipience.

The other clearly made a major effort to rally his tired wits and remember the rest of his prepared speech. ". . . piety, Sire. The, the hearts' desire of all true Englishmen. Your . . . your devoted subjects. Majesty—I am John Peyton. Son to the Lieutenant of the Tower of London, and the most humble of all your subjects. He, my father, has sent me here hot-foot. Here is the key to the said dread Tower, Majesty—England's citadel. I have ridden without sleep to present it to you. As you set foot on England's devoted soil."

The Scots around the King coughed and looked embarrassed at such unseemly and magniloquent language and behaviour; but James himself appeared to find nothing amiss with it. Smirking and nodding, he took the key.

"Heavy," he commented. "Right weighty. But, then—so is yon Tower. *Parvis componere magna!* Eh, Northumberland, man?"

"Er, no doubt, Your Majesty," the Earl said, blankly.

The young man was commencing to rise, stiffly, from his kneeling posture when, abruptly, the King leaned forward and pushed him back, quite roughly indeed so that the other all but fell over.

"Bide you, laddie," he was commanded, thickly. "Bide where you're at, a wee. Son o' the Lieutenant, eh?" James looked around him. "Vicky? Where's Vicky? I want Vicky Stewart and his bit sword."

"Here, Sire," the Duke of Lennox called, stepping forward.

"Gie's your whinger, man." The King made it a stern rule that no one carried a sword or dirk in his royal presence—but he made an exception in the case of his cousin Ludovick, a strong, loyal and comparatively simple young man, unambitious to a degree, whom the monarch could hardly distrust and whom he tended to look on as a sort of bodyguard and watchdog. "Out with it."

Lennox unsheathed his sword and held it out by the tip. Gingerly his cousin took it, as though it had been red-hot. Of all the royal dreads, cold steel was the sharpest—a legacy no doubt of the stabbing to death before his pregnant mother's eyes of her Italian secretary, David Rizzio, whom so many believed indeed to be the King's true father.

Having to take two hands to the business, for his wrists were less than strong, and having difficulty with the heavy key he was already clutching, James swung the weapon in a highly dangerous swipe at the kneeling man's shoulder, only just hitting it as the other ducked hurriedly.

"Bide still, man!" the King cried. "I canna knight you, jouking about!" He gave another jab. "Arise, good Sir John . . . John . . . eh, what's the laddie's name?" the monarch demanded in a stage whisper, peering round.

"Peyton, Sire—Peyton," Northumberland said hurriedly.

"Aye, well. Arise, Sir John Peyton. Get up, man. Here, Vicky—take it. Aye, and take this key, forby—it's ower heavy. Do something with it . . ."

Young Peyton rose, flushed, blinking, stammering embarrassed thanks, appreciation, his own utter unworthiness for so high and unexpected an honour. He was quite overcome.

James eyed him askance for a moment or two, as though wondering whether he had been wise. Then he cocked an eyebrow eloquently in the direction of George Heriot.

"Geordie—here man. Here, Jinglin' Geordie Heriot. You ken what's what. See to it." And he turned his grotesquely padded royal back on the new knight, Duke of Lennox and most others, to demand of the Mayor of Berwick how long it would be before all his royal train of five hundred would be across his satanic, squeaky and wabbly brig—if indeed the Devil did not have them all in the wicked waters of Tweed in the process.

George Heriot went up to the bewildered and bemused Peyton, took him aside a little, and spoke quietly. "May I be the first to congratulate you, Sir John? A well-deserved honour, I am sure." He leaned forward, and spoke more quietly still. "That will be one thousand pounds, if you please. Sterling, of course."

"E-e-eh!" Like a rabbit startled, the new knight stared at him.

"A thousand sterling, yes. Pounds. It is, h'm, customary."

"But . . . but . . ." The other gobbled. "I do not . . . I cannot . . . A thousand pounds! It is . . . it is not possible, sir. I . . ."

"Hush, you," Heriot urged, but gently, mildly, almost with sympathy. "Not so loud, Sir John. Not in the presence of the King's Grace! His Grace mislikes scenes. Besides, what is a thousand sterling to a son of the Lieutenant of the Tower?"

"I have not got it, sir. I assure you, I do not have so much money. I came but on my father's orders. With the key . . "

"Your note of hand will serve very well, Sir John. A simple matter." As though by sleight of hand, the Scot produced a paper from within his cloak and from the richly-chased silver cylinder which hung from his belt in place of a dirk, a neat quill-pen already wet from the ink-horn within.

Unhappily Peyton wagged his tired head, looking from his monarch's back to Heriot.

"Sir," the latter reminded, with a slight smile. "You have just received an honour without price. Are you, and your father, of insufficient means and gentility to support it? No? This fee but assures his Grace that you are, as is suitable. See, I will write it for you my own self." Using his padded sleeve as a board, he penned, in a firm hand: "At Berwick, 23rd day of Aprile 1603. Promised to the King's Grace One thousand pounds Sterling." He dipped the pen again into the encased ink-horn. "Sign, Sir John. The Duke of Lennox here, will act witness, I have no doubt."

Swallowing, the young man scratched some sort of signature.

Ludovick Stewart, Lord High Admiral of Scotland, a mixture of commiseration and amusement on his blunt features, took the pen and initialled the paper, and George Heriot did the same, and coughed.

Almost immediately King James broke off his converse with the others, and turned round. "Aye, well," he said. "Time we werena here, or we'll no' win to yon place—what was it? Widdrington, aye Widdrington, this night. It's a long gait to London. Johnnie Ramsay—my horse. We'll no' waste more o' our royal time at Berwick Brig . . ."

"Would you say that His Grace had wasted his time here?" Lennox asked his tradesman friend, as they mounted, after the King.

"Does His Grace ever waste his time?" the King's goldsmith, jeweller, banker and creditor, gave back in response.

2

"WEALTH, MAN," JAMES said, low-voiced. "Riches. Beyond telling. More than ever I believed. This England is fat, Vicky—fat!" The King glanced around him in the saddle, warily, those great liquid eyes rolling, to see that none of the English notables riding behind heard him. "Being king o' a' this will serve me right well, I think!"

"Do you think to *spoil* the English as well as reign over them, Cousin?" the Duke of Lennox asked, grimly.

"Not so, Vicky—not so. Hold your tongue, man. But . . . a monarch in a rich land can do more than, than in a poor place, see you. For the folk, you ken—the good o' the folk. Look at those beasts. Have you ever seen cattle the like o' that?"

"They are fat and sleek, Sire. And the folk grow like them, I think! How do you esteem your new subjects, then? Apart from their so evident wealth?"

James eyed the speaker sharply. He never could be quite sure whether or not his cousin was cozening him, mocking—and he was very averse to being mocked. He stood more from Vicky Stewart than he would stand from others only because he knew him to be honest, utterly reliable and quite without ambition—and moreover was the only son of the first man he had ever loved, Esmé Stewart of Aubigny in France, first cousin of his father Darnley. But that did not mean that he could twit him, the Lord's anointed, with impunity.

"They are . . . civil, right civil," he said, cautiously.

"I thought that you must like them passing well."

"Eh? Why?"

"You see fit to honour them, Cousin, in a fashion that you never did at home! I have already lost count of all the gold rings you have bestowed and all the knighthoods created, in seven days, all the offices you have given away, the promises you have made and prisoners freed . . ."

"Houts—knights cost nothing, man. Or, only to themselves!" James tee-heed a whinny of laughter—and then looked round again quickly, in case he had been overheard. "Offices can be taken away, forby. And we'll soon fill the jails again! But, d'you no' see, man—it behoves a liege lord to bind his new subjects to his sacred person wi' stout bonds o' love and gratitude. That he may rule them the easier. Use your wits, Vicky."

"That is not a policy Your Grace made great efforts to follow in Scotland, I think!"

"Scotland? Guidsakes—Scotland's a different kettle o' fish. *You* ken that—you who acted Viceroy for me when I was off in yon Denmark. The Scots are a crabbit, contrary race, man—aye at each others' throats. The only way to rule *them* is to keep them that way, to set one lord against another, one faction against the next. Waesucks—I learned that in a fell hard school!"

"And you think that the English lords and squires are so different? That they have no factions here?"

"They are softer, Vicky. Fatter. Richer. Smoother. Aye, softer. Or that auld besom Elizabeth couldna have kept them in order a' yon time. And frae a sick-bedchamber, these last years."

"She had a nimble and strong mind . . ."

"She was a woman! A weathercock. Like the rest o' them. She blew hot and cauld. Women have no minds to speak of. Reason is the attribute o' men—or *some* men! Logic, logomachy, enthymeme—o' such she kenned nothing, the creature. If *she* could rule these English . . ."

"At least she did not make knights by the score!"

"She had no right to make them, at all, man! A woman canna be a knight. As sovereign, she could appoint, but no' *make*. But—what's a' this havering about knighthoods? A plague on you, Vicky—what's to do?"

"It is that I have always respected the standing and status of knighthood, James. It is a noble order and estate. You made *me* knight once, and I esteem it a higher honour than this dukedom which I but inherited like a house or goods and chattels. But now, you make knights of any and all who come thronging."

"Not all, man—only those who can pay for it!"

"Which, I say, is worse. Selling what should be a cherished honour for base gold and silver!"

"Vicky Stewart—will you hold your ill tongue! I'll no' be preached at by you or any man. I will not."

"I crave Your Grace's pardon."

"Aye—well you may!" James looked at his cousin sidelong from those soulful eyes. "See you—what's the harm in dubbing a wheen knights, man? These English like it fine—for they havena proper lairds and barons like we have. And what for should they no' pay for it? They have the siller—and I need it. Man, each o' these high-nebbit lords has more siller than have I, their liege lord! You ken the state o' the Scots Treasury—empty, man, empty! Would you have me penniless, when I get to London? D'you ken how much I owe Geordie Heriot? Eh . . . some sixty thousand pounds Scots."

"So much?"

"Aye. Or I *did*, when we set out frae Edinburgh! But we're cutting down the score, man—as is only right and proper. Geordie gets half, see you. He keeps the account—he's good at that. Have him up, Vicky—we'll see how it goes. Send for Jinglin' Geordie."

Lennox reined round to call for one of the royal pages to go fetch Master Heriot, His Grace's jeweller—and immediately the Earl of Northumberland and the Lord Henry Howard pressed forward, one on either side of the King, from the rank just behind, both speaking at once in the clipped, authoritative English fashion.

James, slumped like a sack of chaff in his saddle—though, oddly enough he rode well if not handsomely—eyed them unfavourably. "My lords," he said, "you're fine chiels both, I've no doubt. But when I'm needing your lordships' company, I'll ask for it."

Abashed, mumbling hasty apologies, the two proud noblemen fell back.

Lennox returned to say that it might be some time before Heriot could be located and brought forward—for the royal train had swollen to well over a thousand and spread back along the road northwards for well over a mile. He had sent Sir Thomas Erskine to go find him. The Duke announced that with a barely smothered grin; the pampered favourite Erskine would certainly not appreciate being sent to look for a mere Edinburgh burgess like George Heriot. Lennox did not like Erskine, the man who had taken the leading part in the murky Gowrie conspiracy of three years before—any more than he liked most of the King's beautiful young men.

James tut-tutted testily. "A mile you say? De'il tak them! I mislike crowds," he complained. "Folk thronging me. Where have they a' come frae? Guidsakes—I never asked all these!"

"Your loyal English subjects, Sire. Coming to bind themselves to your sacred person in love and gratitude, perhaps? And probably seeking knighthoods!"

"Now see here, Vicky Stewart—enough o' this! What's come ower you, man? You're as crabbit as one o' thae Kirk divines. If you canna keep a respectful tongue in your head in my royal presence, you've my royal permission to leave it! Aye."

"I am only concerned for Your Grace's royal dignity," his cousin assured, earnestly now, low-voiced. "On this your first visit to England. It is entirely necessary for you to make a good impression, before your new people. To cast honours about too freely, to seem to *sell* them, will but lower your kingly dignity in their regard . . ."

"You leave my royal dignity to me, impertinent! What right have you to hector me so?"

"Not hector, Sire—advise. I do so out of love for you. As for right, I am of Your Highness's Privy Council . . ."

"In Scotland, Vicky—in *Scotland*. And we're no' in Scotland, now. Mind it. And, meantime, I have *no* Privy Council in England—until I choose it. Aye—and I'd advise *you*, and others, no' to forget it!"

Lennox bit his lip. He was a pleasantly plain-faced young man, almost boyish-looking for his thirty years, with as little of the great lord about him as his master and kinsman had of regality. But at least he was not laughably overdressed in grossly padded and clashing-coloured magnificence.

The King stole another glance at his friend and sucked in saliva wetly—for he slobbered especially copiously when under any sort of emotion. He spoke more placatingly—for he was a man who required approval of his policies, however little he cared in the matter of personal behaviour.

"As to making an impression, Vicky, I'd remind you that's no' necessary. No' for me. I am the Lord's Anointed, Vicar o' Christ on this earth. Forby I am their *master*, these all my servants now—as are you, Duke Vicky Stewart! Keep it in mind, I say."

Suitably chastened, Lennox held his peace.

George Heriot came riding up, and Sir Thomas Erskine of Dirleton, good-looking in a bland, foppish fashion, looked less than bland when he was waved back whence he had come by the King, with scarcely a glance, while the tradesman was welcomed with a genial grin.

"Geordie—where have you been, man? Hiding away, some

place. Is the company so good, back yonder, that you desert your auld gossip, Jamie Stewart? Is it the English you're after favouring?"

Heriot was careful—as he was wise to be, when the King adopted this wheedling, falsely-familiar tone. "Far from it, Sire—although I find them well enough. A trifle simple, perhaps, after our Scots ways. They seem less . . . devious, than we are! I have been looking to Your Grace's interests, since somebody must!"

"Eh? My interests? How mean you?"

"Hundreds join this your royal train daily, Sire. If this goes on, it will be an army by the time you reach London—thousands. An army that eats and drinks its head off—at Your Grace's expense. I am not Your Grace's Treasurer, nor yet your purse-bearer. But I can add up placks and groats and merks and turn them into pounds sterling! Which is more than some folk seem able to do!"

"But, Geordie—the English will pay for this. Their great Treasury in London. *My* great Treasury! It'll no' come out o' my pouch!"

"Are you so sure, Sire? These English lords do not seem to think so. All consider themselves your guests! It seems that when the late Queen made her progresses about this kingdom, all her train were paid for from her privy purse."

"Guidsakes!"

"Moreover, I hear hints to the effect that the English Treasury is in no very good state. That during the Queen's long ailing, matters have been mismanaged, allowed to go amiss. Taxes left ungathered—or, at least, those who farmed them failing to be brought to account for them. Certain of the Queen's favourites dipping their hands deep into her coffers . . ."

"Waesucks—enough! Enough, I say! You're cozening me, man. I'll not believe it, Geordie Heriot. It's no' what I've been given to understand."

"Likely not, Sire. But that is what I have picked up, by keeping my ears open. These fine lords and gentry will talk in front of me, a mere merchandiser, say things they would not mention to Your Grace."

James groaned, slumped in his saddle, all the brightness suddenly gone out of his day.

Lennox cocked an eye at Heriot. "You reckon we should turn and go home, my friend?"

"Scarce that. But it behoves us all, I think, to gang warily. At this stage."

"Lest the Englishmen spoil *us*! I swear you break His Grace's heart!"

"Be quiet, Vicky Stewart!" James cried loudly—and then glanced quickly, almost furtively behind in case any of the illustrious party riding immediately at his back should have heard. Lowering his voice, he went on, "Man—d'you now see how wrong you were? About the knightings. He's aye complaining Geordie—my lord high and righteous Duke o' Lennox, carping at me for making knights o' ower many o' these English bodies. Sakes—he doesna ken the elementals o' it! You tell him, Geordie. Why I sent for you. How many knights have I made since I crossed yon brig at Berwick, eh? How many, aye—and how much? *You'll* ken."

"How many . . . ? Ah . . . thirty-four, Sire. No, thirty-five, counting that Forester at Widdrington, after the hunt."

"Na, na—forget him. That was just to show yon man Carey that he canna *badger* me into honouring him. He wants to be a Lord o' Parliament. He canna abide his faither—most undutious. The Lord Hunsdon. So Sir Robert wants to be one better—a viscount, no less! Never ceases to deave me for it, the man. A' because he brought me word first o' auld Elizabeth's death. I was for showing him that I can raise up who I will, see you. That I'm no' dependant on the likes o' Robert Carey! Thirty-four, say you? How much, then, man—how much?"

"Well, Sire—*I* have had to gang warily likewise, mind. Your Grace will not want talk, a comparing of costs, as you might say. And I must judge the fleece before I clip it! Not all you have chosen are rich men . . ."

"A pox on you—we ken a' that! Are you failing me, Geordie Heriot? Making excuses? How much, this far? Out with it."

"Twenty-eight thousand, five hundred pounds, Sire. Leastways, notes of hand therefor."

"English money? Sterling?"

"Sterling, yes."

Lennox whistled below his breath.

James grinned, chuckled. "Aye, well. No' bad, Geordie—no' bad. For two-three days. And how much does my Annie owe you now? Can you mind?"

"Seventy-five thousand pounds, Sire, more or less. Pounds Scots, of course."

"Guidsakes—so much as that! Save us—women are the devil! What does she do with it all? Does she *eat* jewels, man? I blame you, Geordie—aye tempting her wi' your gewgaws and trinkets. It's no' right. Vanity it is. There'll be a judgment on such vanities, mark my words."

"Her Grace is generous towards others, Sire . . ."

"Ooh, aye—generous! Fine, that! But—och, well, this will more than pay for it, eh? How much is that in Sterling? Seventy thousand pounds Scots?"

"Seventy-five thousand pounds, Sire. Say six thousand pounds Sterling—since it is Her Grace. But, h'm, may I remind you, Sire, that *Your* Grace owes me more than that? One hundred and eighty thousand pounds Scots, indeed."

"Dear God!"

A single hoot of laughter erupted from the Duke of Lennox.

James glared at his cousin. "Here's no laughing matter. One hundred and eighty thousand pounds Scots! Na, na—you exaggerate, Geordie man. It's no' possible."

"No mistake, Sire. One hundred and eighty-four thousand, seven hundred and fifty pounds to be exact. Or, if you prefer it, fifteen thousand, three hundred and thirty-three pounds Sterling."

The King raised his heavy head with an accession of dignity. "You have the mind o' a huckster, Master Heriot. Pounds, shillings, groats and placks!"

"Precisely, Your Grace. But then, I *am* a huckster!"

"M'mmm. Aye. But, man—it canna be so much as that? But a month past it was little more than half o' that."

"Your Grace perhaps forgets the chestful of rings which you ordered. And give out to all and sundry, on this your royal journey."

"Rings? Them? Och, but they're no' real gold, Geordie. Just *covered* wi' gold."

"Nevertheless, they cost money, Sire. So many. And engraved with your royal sign."

"Aweel, if you say so. But, Geordie—there'll still be *something* left for me, out o' a' these knighthoods, man? You'll no' swallow it a'?"

"To be sure. Even with due and proper interest, Your Highness is five thousand pounds in credit. Sterling."

"There! You see, Vicky? And you berate me. Guidsakes—what would you have? Your king a pauper? Indebted? Aye—and how much does the Duke o' Lennox owe you, Geordie Heriot? Eh? How much our righteous Duke?"

"That, I fear, I am not at liberty to say, Your Grace. You would not have me break the confidence of those who deal with me? But this I can say, that my lord's indebtedness is but a small sum, a mere trifle. Not like many of Your Grace's Court that I could name!"

"Ha! You say so? But—more o' this anon. There's some-to-do ahead. Here's a mannie coming . . ."

A gallant was riding back from the Captain of the Guard's advance party. He doffed his bonnet low.

"Your Grace—a deputation from York. Has Sir Andrew your royal permission to present them?"

"Ooh, aye. York's a fine rich town, they tell me. Have them up."

The magnificent towers of the mighty cathedral, with all the lesser spires and massive walls, had been looming before the cavalcade for long, in this flat, green country, and now they were only some three miles off. A party of richly-robed and bejewelled citizens were brought up to genuflect before the monarch, who considered them assessingly from those knowing gazelle's eyes of his, while the royal trumpeter blew a flourish to halt the mile-long column behind.

"May I present to the King's Grace three gentlemen of the City of York?" young Sir Andrew Kerr of Ferniehirst, Captain of the Royal Guard said. "Sheriffs, they say. And these behind, sergeants or something such."

"Not so," a tall, thin and stately elderly man declared, his bow as dignified as his voice and carriage. "*I* am Sir William Ingleby, High Sheriff of this entire great county and duchy of York. These two are the Sheriffs of the city, George Buck and John Robinson. The Sergeants behind are of, h'm, a different sort. We come to pay our proper respects to Your Majesty, seek your gracious goodwill for duchy and city, and your royal confirmation of our ancient charters and privileges."

James eyed the speaker thoughtfully, plucking at his sagging lower lip. "Is that so?" he said.

The other blinked. "Yes, Sire. We ask you to accept the esteem and support of the greatest county and second greatest city of England. In proof whereof the city Sheriffs present to Your Majesty these tokens."

His Majesty's regard lightened a little at the word tokens—but fell again when the tokens proved to be no more than the Sheriffs' white wands of office held up for him to touch. He tapped their wood distastefully.

"Ooh, aye," he said. "Esteem and support, is it? You could scarce offer your sovereign lord less, I jalouse! Your simple duty, man."

"Yes, to be sure, Your Majesty. Of course." Ingleby looked a little worried. "York will not be found wanting, I assure you. Yes. And these, Sire, are the Sergeants-at-Arms. By name Wood, Damfort and Westrope."

"And what do *they* bring me. More esteem, man?"

"Er, their maces, Sire. Symbols of their authority. To offer you."

"I'ph'mm." James touched the handsome extended jewelled maces, one two, three, as though they might have burned him. "I will consider the matter o' your privileges and charters hereafter," he added, licking thick lips. "After I have tasted the flavour o' your esteem." He raised his voice. "On our way, Dand." And, as the horses moved forward, he jerked his over-large head in a see-you-to-it gesture to George Heriot.

As the distinctly upset representatives of York were all but brushed aside by the resumed royal progress, Heriot fell back, and dismounted, to speak with the High Sheriff.

"Greeting, Sir William," he said pleasantly. "As representatives of your great county and city, you perhaps find His Grace a little . . . unappreciative?"

"I . . . I did not say so, my lord," Ingleby declared hurriedly, caution in every dignified line of him.

"No, sir, But perhaps you thought it. And I am no lord, but a simple tradesman."

"Tradesman? You? At the King's side!"

"Even so. His Grace is a man of . . . simple tastes."

"His tastes, sir, did not appear to embrace the County and City of York!"

"It is too early to say that, Sir William. Newcastle is less fine than York, I am sure. Yet His Grace found Newcastle very much to his royal taste." He paused. "Newcastle, of course, did present His Grace with a purse of gold pieces. Four hundred if I mind aright. As well as their, h'm, esteem and support."

"Ah!" The Sheriff stared.

"Exactly. A pleasing thought, was it not, sir?"

"Yes. Yes, of course."

"Newcastle, to be sure, is a much poorer place than great York. Probably it is not yet too late to prove it."

"You mean . . . ?"

"Only that a fast horse could take you, or one of your friends, back to the city, sir, before His Grace reaches it in his somewhat leisurely progress. You can have my mount, indeed. I will find myself another . . ."

So, in a little, George Heriot, on another horse, spurred up again to the head of the column. But now a very splendid gentleman, the Earl of Cumberland, had moved into the place he had occupied on the King's left—and, not to be out-manoeuvred, the Earl of Northumberland and his brother Sir Charles Percy had edged forward to flank Lennox. Heriot slipped into a position behind, where Lord Henry Howard and the Lord Cobham eyed him with disfavour and urged their mounts a little aside—although the Scots lords and bishops of the train knew better and welcomed him affably enough, most of them owing him money.

At the sound of the name Heriot, called in hearty greeting by the Lord Home, the King turned in his saddle and caught his goldsmith's eye. That man nodded almost imperceptibly and James faced front again.

"What's new, Geordie?" Home asked, low-voiced, reining close. "James has something on his mind, I swear."

"Would he be King if he had not, my lord? He is but concerned for the cost of this ever-lengthening train, I think. As who would not be?"

"Och, the English will pay!" Home said easily—and did not trouble to lower his voice this time, indeed stared round him with a sort of gleeful arrogance.

Heriot did not comment.

Soon, at a mile from the city's Mickle Gate, another deputation awaited the monarch. This consisted of a superior-looking gentleman supporting a tall, thin, mournful-seeming man in richest clothing, who stalked on stick-like legs, resembling a disillusioned heron.

"My Lord Burleigh, Lord President of the North," Cumberland informed him. "And a damned fool!" The Earl of Cumberland was, of course, a Clifford, of ancient line, and despising of Elizabeth's favourites.

"Ha—Cecil's son!" The King peered. "His father wrote me a wheen letters. Aye, kept me well informed."

"No doubt, Sire. But this William Cecil is a very different man from his father, God knows! Her Majesty made him Lord High Treasurer for a time—and lived to regret it! He well earned banishment to the North."

"Eh—Treasurer, you say? You mean that he thieved frae the Treasury? Lined his ain pockets, the man?"

"I scarce think that he had the wits for that, Sire! No, he did nothing so understandable—did nothing at all, indeed. Failed to gather in the taxes. Let others spend as they would. Mismanaged all. A master at inactivity."

The monarch frowned at the earl, for he disapproved of levity on the vital subject of money; but it was as nothing to the darkness of the glare he turned on the second Lord Burleigh, son of Elizabeth's great Secretary of State, who it seemed was responsible for this alleged and most shocking state of the English Treasury, the bright morning-star which had for so long beckoned James Stewart southwards.

Burleigh's jerky bows and equally jerky assertions of loyalty and privilege were cut short.

"Aye, man—no doubt. No doubt. But *facta non verba*, see you. Deeds speak louder than words. We have heard tell o' you, and will reserve our royal judgment. Aye, reserve it."

"But, Majesty, I am your most devoted subject," the other declared, astonished. "Anxious ever to serve you in deed as in word. As Lord President of the North, it is my privilege to bring you the greetings of half Your Highness's kingdom . . ."

"Half, man? I am King of Scots, of England, Ireland and France. Dinna forget it."

"I, ah, meant England, of course, Sire. The greatest, richest, most powerful . . ."

"No' so rich as it should be, as I'm told!"

"Alas, Sire, fortunes vary, fluctuate, with realms as with mere men . . ."

"But it's the mere men that make the realms' fortunes fluctuate, man! *Some* men. *Fortuna favet fortibus—fortuna fortes adjuvat!* You ken what that means? Guidsakes—do they no' give the English *any* education?"

In the profound silence which followed that, James resumed his march on York, the Lord President falling in unhappily with less illustrious but equally shaken folk behind.

With the great city walls rearing their barrier before, they came to the Mickle Gate where a large company waited on a high wooden platform—the Lord Mayor, twelve aldermen and twenty-four councillors in their robes, all kneeling, with the keys of the city, the sword and other tokens. A trumpeter blew a fanfare and the

Mayor launched into a lengthy peroration, rather breathlessly, thanks to the difficult kneeling posture for a man with a notably large belly.

James listened for a little, but fairly quickly lost interest. Because of the height of the platform he would be able to touch the keys and sword without getting off his horse. As the Mayor, Robert Walter by name, gulped and panted on, the King announced that this is what he would do and let them get on into the town, for he was gey hungry. Lord Mayor Walter, preoccupied with memorising his oration, plus maintaining his equilibrium, eyes tight shut, presumably did not hear, and it looked as though there might be some slight dislocation of the proceedings when, from behind, George Heriot gave one of his significant coughs. The King looked round—for he knew that cough of old—and his jeweller jerked his head in a direction slightly left of forward, and raised his eyebrows.

James turned back, peering short-sightedly. A horseman had come hurrying out from the town, dismounted behind the platform and was now pushing through to the front of the official party, something familiar about him. Carrying something under a cloth, he squeezed in between the still-intoning Mayor and the senior alderman, getting down on his own knees in the process. He whispered in the alderman's ear, at some length.

Nodding, the alderman took the covered object, obviously very heavy, and leaned over to nudge the Mayor. At the second nudge, Master Walter opened his eyes and stared, surprised, his voice faltering. There was more whispering.

Oddly, James no longer seemed impatient, but indeed highly interested.

The Mayor got to his feet, smoothed down his robes, and took the covered object, removing the cloth to reveal it as a large silver-gilt chalice.

"Your royal Majesty," he said, stammering a little. "Before we present to you the sword and keys of the city, it is my duty, my pleasant duty, to give you this loving-cup. Filled with gold pieces. As many as it will hold, see you. As mark and token. Token, yes, of the love that this City of York bears to Your Majesty. In promise of further, er, kindness."

The King smiled graciously. Indeed he grinned the sort of boyish leer reserved for highly satisfactory occasions. He actually dismounted and moved forward with his knock-kneed gait to climb the steps of the platform—and perforce everybody else must dismount also, since it would by no means do to be higher than the King.

"Aye, Master Mayor," he said. "This is right kindly." And he held out his beringed hands for the chalice without delay.

Indeed he all but dropped it, as the Mayor handed it over, for, as has been indicated, his wrists were not the strongest of him and the thing was exceedingly heavy.

"Hech, hech—weighty! Aye, right weighty," he observed, juggling with his handful—but in no complaining fashion. He peered in at the contents assessingly, as though to assure himself that they could not have squeezed in another coin or two. "Good, good," he commented. "Angels, eh? Gold angels. They're better than nobles, are they no'?" He raised his voice. "Geordie! Geordie Heriot!"

In anticipation of such call, that man had moved forward. Now he climbed the steps also.

Clutching the chalice to his chest, James picked out a coin. "Angels, Geordie. How many o' them to the pound Sterling?"

"Two, Your Grace. Ten English shillings."

"Aye. There's a peck o' them, here. Take it, Geordie. Aye, but first—the rings. You have some yet?"

Heriot delved into his pocket and produced a handful of gold-plated rings.

James made a quick calculation. "Three'll do. Three'll do fine, man."

There was the Mayor, and the chief alderman and the man who had brought the chalice—who was none other than George Robinson, one of the city sheriffs who had first come out with Sir William Ingleby. The others could be ignored.

So the transfer was made, the gold-filled chalice for three, plated rings stamped with the royal monogram. The King bestowed the latter upon the recipients as though precious beyond rubies.

"We are pleased wi' you, much pleased," he beamed. "We will, ah, see you again. Later."

"But—the sword, Sire. And the keys."

"Ooh, aye. The sword and the keys. Och, well."

From one side a resplendent bearer was waved forward with the city keys gleaming like silver on a gold-tasselled cushion, and on the other, a stalwart individual with a helmet and the usual great two-handed sword. By touching the key and shooing the bearer away from him like an over-eager hen, James got rid of the first, but such tactics did not serve with the second, who seemed determined that the monarch should actually take the sword—unaware of his new liege lord's dire aversion to cold steel. James backed away—but he could not back very far or he would fall over the edge of the platform. Determinedly the other pursued him. Heriot would have taken the weapon for him but he had his arms full of gold angels.

"Awa' wi' you, you muckle limmer!" Majesty cried, in his broadest Doric. As a child he had been brought up in the large and noisy family of the Earl of Mar, hereditary keeper of Stirling Castle, where all spoke the Doric, and it remained his mother-tongue.

The sword-bearer did not appear to understand.

"Your Majesty should take the sword, as symbol that you rule us all," Mayor Walter explained helpfully.

"I dinna want the sword, man!" the sorely-tried monarch snapped at him. "I can rule you a' fine, without yon!"

George Heriot set down the chalice of gold pieces on the boards of the platform. "I will take the sword for His Grace," he said. "Give it to me."

That did not suit the sword-bearer, obviously a man who knew his own mind. The King was the proper and only recipient for York's sword, other than himself its custodian, and no jumped-up Scotchman was going to have it. Heriot came over to take it from him, muttering to the fellow not to be a fool, that the King could not abide naked steel.

James caught sight of his pot of gold sitting abandoned there in the middle of the platform, and letting out a wail, hurried over to stand guard over it. Anybody could have grabbed an angel or two.

"Vicky! Vicky!" he quavered.

In fact, many of the foremost nobles had now recognised that something was amiss, and were hastening to the royal aid—although undoubtedly none of the Englishmen fully understood what was wrong. Lennox did, but he had not been nearest to the steps, and Lord Burleigh it was who arrived first on the platform, however stiffly.

"*I* will take the sword, as His Majesty's due representative," he declared authoritatively.

George Heriot had no objection, but the sword-bearer remained more than doubtful. King James also had his reservations.

"Na, na—who asked *you*?" he demanded. "I cried on Vicky. Vicky Lennox."

"If Your Majesty does not wish to take the sword yourself, then

I, as President of the North, am the proper recipient, as your Deputy, Sire."

"My lord—if His Majesty does not want the sword, it should be returned to *me*." the Mayor announced.

"Who says you're the President o' the North, man?" James asked. "Nae doubt you *were*. But I'd remind you—aye, and a' others—that no man now holds any office o' state lacking my royal appointment. *Any*, d'you hear? I can appoint whosoever I will to be President o' the North. Or none. Mind it." The King looked round, still trembling in his agitation, could not see Lennox, who was in a queue at the bottom of the steps, and found the Earl of Cumberland at his elbow. "Aye—you, man Cumberland. You take it. Yon sword. Take it out o' my sight. Geordie—you got the cuppie wi' the angels? Aye, well. Now—let's awa' out o' this. I've had enough o' this, God kens! And I'm hungry. My belly rumbles. Fetch my horse—you, Northumberland—fetch my horse. I'll climb on frae here. We'll see what they've got for victuals in this York . . ."

The Lord Mayor, aldermen and councillors of the city, left behind on their platform, stared at each other and at the instrumentalists, there to lead the royal procession through the streets, and wrung their hands, rings or none.

* * *

That night, in the fine, lofty, beamed great hall of the Manor of St. Mary, the former Benedictine Abbey now owned by Burleigh, the tables and remains of the banquet cleared away, George Heriot watched the scene from a quiet corner, a faint smile playing about his lips. Dancing was now in progress, the stately sort of dancing which Queen Elizabeth had delighted in, not the more robust Scots variety, and many handsome and finely dressed ladies now graced the royal presence. But James Stewart, up on the dais, was not much of a dancer—knock-knees and unsteady legs ensured that—nor was he very interested in women, young and good-looking men being more to his taste. As a consequence, he had settled down to an evening of hard drinking, abetted by a group of his Scots favourites and cronies, ignoring completely the efforts of sundry English notables to break into the circle, to present their ladies and friends. James, an arm round the neck of young Sir John Ramsay his principal page, a youth of eighteen with the complexion of a girl and the ruthlessness of a wolf, sprawled at the dais table, high hat precariously askew—the only man in the great room covered—paying no attention to host, music, dancing, courtiers, suppliants or anything else than the replenishment of his own and his friends' wine cups. If he had felt any embarrassment when he discovered that his host for the week-end stay at York was not the Mayor and Council, nor the sheriffs, but none other than the Lord Burleigh in this Manor of St. Mary, instead of the Guildhall, he had not let the matter trouble him. Burleigh was finding it just as impossible as were others to approach his royal guest.

Heriot, who knew his place with the monarch as exactly as he knew his debts and credits, was glad to stand aside and watch. By nature and inclination he was a mildly intrigued observer of the human scene rather than an active manipulator, happiest when circumstances allowed him to be an informed spectator. It was not that he was a negative man, any kind of drifter—anyone who suggested anything of the sort in the Scots capital would have been hooted at—but he was of a philosophical and reflective rather than a combative or assertive frame of mind. Observing King James was, in fact, always of absorbing interest to him, sometimes a joy, sometimes almost an agony, sometimes tragi-comedy or high farce, but never dull. The fact that he knew a real affection for and some understanding of his unusual sovereign lord added an element of personal involvement which gave point to all.

He caught the eye of Ludovick Stewart across the room. The Duke did not find it so easy to stand in a corner and watch, however much he would have preferred to, his lofty rank, proximity to the throne and friendly personality ensuring that. A certain innocence about him, in a Court where innocence was scarcely the dominant feature, seemed to attract women, especially the more mature woman, and he was much sought after—which did not please him, for he was deeply in love with Mary Gray, illegitimate daughter of the handsome and dashing Master of Gray, whom he of course, the only duke in two realms, could by no means have married even if he had not been wed already. A young man at odds with his fate was Lennox. Excusing himself to two effusive York ladies who had all but cornered him, he backed out and made his way across the floor to Heriot, circling the dancers.

"You are not dancing, Master Heriot," he said. "Nor yet drinking. Nor even wenching. What do you do for amusement?"

"Some might say I count figures, my lord Duke. Jingle my well-known gold. Jinglin' Geordie Heriot!"

"Then some are fools! I know better. I think your entertainment is to laugh at us all. In that cool, knowing head of yours. Especially at the crowned mountebank up there—yet whom, I swear, you'd give your life for!"

Perturbed at the younger man's percipience, Heriot coughed. "Not laugh *at*, my lord. Laugh with, where I decently may. Otherwise regard, heed—aye, and seek to understand my fellow-men, lofty and less so. Is that not permissable? Even a cat, they do say, may look at a king."

"To be sure. I but envy you your detachment."

"I do not think that I am detached, my lord. Not sufficiently for my comfort."

"Surely when we are alone, man, you can forget the lording and duking! My friends call me Vicky, as you know well."

"But your friends are not . . . tradesmen, I think!"

"Damnation, man—be not so prickly! You, who could buy us all and scarce notice the price!"

"I am sorry if I sound prickly, my lord Duke. I would hope not to be that. Any more than purse-proud. But you will grant me that I have to walk warily? His Grace is kind to me, relies on me much. Too much. That offends many, I know well. And men who lend money are seldom popular—especially to their debtors! I have heard, indeed, that there is a new play written by this English playwright on this very theme—I have forgot his name—set in Venice, I think. Many would pull down a man in my position, should I seem to ride even a little too high."

"So I must remain my lord Duke even when we are alone—lest men think I owe George Heriot more than I do and so he takes liberties!"

Heriot laughed. "Very well, Vicky—as you will. *My* friends, like my enemies, all call me Geordie!"

They stood for a few moments, watching the King.

"As you said, back at Berwick, James does not change," Lennox observed, at length. "These English are shocked. And will be more so."

"Did you expect him to change? When he crossed the Border? He has been a king for thirty-six years, since he was one year old. He is as he has always been, the Lord's Anointed. It is Elizabeth's England which will have to change, not its new liege lord."

"And yet . . . He has been waiting for this for so long, living for it. For the day when he would sit on the dual throne. I would have thought that he would have been concerned to display himself in a more acceptable, more dignified light."

"Once he told me that dignity was for those who required its support. *He* does not. As for being acceptable, it matters still less. He is the King. He must be accepted. So he is himself, only and entirely himself. Perhaps the only man in two realms who may be. We all play a part, or many parts, since we must. But he is James, by the Grace of God—and aware of it!"

Lennox looked at the other curiously. "You have considered it well, I see."

"I have had occasion to do so."

"And you do not blame him? For behaving as he does? Sitting up there drinking. Fondling these odious young men of his. Ignoring, indeed rejecting his host and these English."

"Who am I to blame or withhold blame of my lord the King? But I understand what he is and what he does, I think. He of a purpose holds the English at bay, so that they have no doubts as to who is master. He dallies with his favourites to demonstrate that he, representer on earth of heavenly power, is not bound by the codes which control the acts and behaviour of his subjects. He establishes his position before these new subjects. And though he drinks heavily, he is not drunk. Indeed, I have never seen His Grace drunk. Have you?"

"Now that you remark on it—no. I had not really thought on it. But, no—he is never drunk, however much drink-taken."

"Aye. So there you have him, my lord Vicky. The Lord's Anointed. With one of the cleverest heads in Christendom on those padded shoulders!"

"Eh? You think that? You really think so, Geordie?"

"Can you name any, any at all, whom you deem cleverer, shrewder, more sure of himself and his course?"

"M'mmm. We-e-ell. Only, perhaps, the Master of Gray!"

"Aye. There is the one man who may rival His Grace. This century's Machiavelli! My sorrow that they now are unfriends. That was an unwise move, at Berwick, I think—to send him away, in public mockery. I fear no good can come of it. But perhaps His Grace deemed it absolutely necessary. He must have planned to do it, for long. It was not done on impulse, that I am sure."

"It was folly. But then, James *is* the veriest fool, so frequently. A figure of fun . . ."

"*Seems* so. Acts the fool, perhaps. But is he? My livelihood,

Vicky, depends on judgment of men, of character, or risks to run and trust to be taken. And I assess King James as clever, able, and far from a fool. Strange yes, difficult yes, ruthless yes—but a king. The English will discover it in due course—and perhaps have cause to be thankful for it."

"You surprise me—by God, you do!"

As though James Stewart had realised that they were discussing him—as indeed were many others in that great room—he suddenly pushed Ramsay aside, looked up and directly at them, and grabbing a silver wine flagon, banged it heavily on the dais table, slopping the contents.

Shaken, the dancers came to a halt, the musicians stopped playing and talk and laughter stilled as the banging went on. All eyes turned to the dais and its high chair.

"Hey, Geordie Heriot—here to me, man," the monarch called. "Aye, and you too, Vicky Stewart. To me, I say."

Side by side they obediently made their way to the dais, and bowed before it. James shooed away his drinking companions, and leaned over the table. "A cup o' wine, Geordie? Come closer, man. Come drink a farewell cup wi' me."

'Farewell, Your Grace? So-o-o! I am to go? Back to Scotland?"

"Aye. Back to Scotland. I have been sitting here thinking on it. That it's maybe time. Aye, time."

"I agree, Sire. Your Grace will remember that I asked you to allow me to return, at Newcastle. That my affairs were left hurriedly and in no very good shape . . ."

"It's no' the shape o' *your* affairs I'm concerned wi', man— it's mine! Or my Annie's. Guid kens what she'll be up to! She lacks sense, the woman, in maist things. Och, they a' do! And lacking me to take order wi' her, she'll be fair above hersel'. And there'll be none to cry her down. Yon Seton, Fyvie, hasna the weight for it. She's the Queen! I've thought much on this. She'll heed *you*, Geordie."

"I, I do not see why Her Grace should, Sire . . ."

"Oh aye, she will. She thinks a deal o' Jinglin' Geordie Heriot. Fine I ken it. Forby, she owes you money, much money—and she'll hae to keep the right side o' you or she'll no' get her gewgaws and trinkets, eh? And *you* ken, if anyone does, how much they mean to my Annie! Aye, she'll heed you, Geordie. As she wouldna heed Duke Vicky, here. Or any other. You're to go watch ower her, man. And to bring her, and the bairns, down to me in London. When a's ready and I send for you."

"If you say so, Sire. But I have no authority to control Her Grace . . ."

"Waesucks, you have not, sirrah! Nor has any man, under God, save my ain sel'! She is the Queen. None will control the Queen, by authority."

"I humbly beg Your Grace's pardon. A foolish slip of the tongue . . ."

"Aye, it was, Geordie Heriot. You're going back to Edinburgh to *guide* the Queen, no' to control her. And no' by any authority, but by your wits, honest, decent wits—aye, and the fact that she needs you. Forby, there's the matter o' yon ill limmer, the Master o' Gray." James glanced at Lennox, only too well aware of that man's involvement with Mary Gray and the strange love-hate relationship he had with her father. "I'm feart for what he may be up to, see you. He'll no' be pleased at being sent back. But I wasna having him setting London by the ears the way he's set Scotland. And teaching the English how to be clever—eh? Na, na. There's no room for me and Patrick both, in London. But he'll be up to mischief in Scotland, if I ken him! And *he* kens Annie's weak. So you watch him, Geordie—watch him."

"But, Sire—how can I influence the likes of him? A man with more real power than the Chancellor . . ."

"The same way as you do the Queen—wi' your wits, man. And he'll no' have any power much longer, I promise you! You'll no' can pull him down—but you'll can frustrate his tricks, belike. And keep me informed. I'd send Vicky here wi' you but I'll need him in London, to act for me whiles. Till I can find others I can trust. So you'll off back to Edinburgh, Geordie."

"Very good, Sire, I shall leave in the morning."

"You'll no'. You'll leave the night. *Now*, man. Have you forgot? The morn's the Sabbath. We'll start the way we mean to go on. Elizabeth may have little heeded the Sabbath. But *my* Court will. I'll no' have you leaving for Scotland on the Sabbath day. So go now. Or you'll waste a whole day."

"But of course Master Heriot will have to rest for the Sabbath tomorrow *somewhere*?" Lennox wondered innocently.

"Dinna be impertinent, Vicky Stewart!" the King reproved. "Geordie kens fine what's what. You'll be in Edinburgh on Monday's morn, eh man?"

"If you wish it so, Sire. I will do my best on Your Grace's behalf, in all things. As always. Though this is a, h'm, difficult mission. Have I Your Grace's permission to retire?"

"Aye. Off wi' you. Though—bide a wee. It comes to me that I prefer the *one* English custom to our Scots usage. Aye, prefer it. This o' Majesty instead o' Grace. It's mair . . . suitable, maybe. I'll be Majesty now, no' Grace. Let it be known—both o' you."

"To be sure, Your Majesty . . ."

3

WEARY, STIFF, DUSTY and travel-stained, George Heriot and his two armed grooms trotted round the grassy base of Arthur's Seat in the dusk of the Monday evening, 18th April, two hundred and twenty miles in forty-four hours hard riding. The city gates would be closed for the night—but that did not matter. He had his own apartments in the Palace of Holyroodhouse, outwith the walls, which went with his appointment of Court Jeweller and the Crown's Banker. His private house, in Beith's Wynd above the shop and opposite St. Giles, could wait. Only servants and a step-brother had waited for him there since his wife's death some years before.

Rounding a minor shoulder of the hill his eyes narrowed. The palace, lying under the shadowy heights, had come into view. And it was ablaze with lights. Every window of the great pile seemed to glow and sparkle, almost as though it was afire. Never had Heriot seen it like this. King James was apt to be careful of lights and fuel.

As they neared Holyroodhouse and its ruined abbey, the sounds of music, shouting and laughter seemed to throb through the old grey stonework and set the evening air aquiver. Heriot and his men rode in at the rear gateway from the park. There were no guards on duty. The outer court was full of people and horses, men-at-arms, servitors, kitchen-wenches and women of the town, in loud-tongued, skirling pandemonium, barrels of ale open and spilling, victuals on benches, boxes, even on the flagstones. Horseplay, fisticuffs, near-rape prevailed.

Dismounting with aching bones, and staring about him grimly,

George Heriot left the grooms to take the horses to the stables and pushed his way through the noisy throng to the lower north wing of the palace, part of the original conventual buildings of the Abbey of the Holy Rood, where were his quarters. The door thereto stood open and a couple were grappling on the floor of the vestibule. There was no sign of his servant.

Tight-lipped, he went up the winding turnpike stair and opened the door—to find a large and handsome pair of female breasts as it were staring him in the face from his bed, the owner's head back and laughing, so that only her throat and chin seemed to top them. A hand and arm, somewhat hairy, coming out from the bedclothes, pulled her long fair hair and a dark head was just visible on a pillow.

George Heriot, swallowed, and then cleared his throat loudly.

Two heads rose in indignation and alarm.

"God flay you—how dare you!" an authoritative voice cried.

"I dare for the best of reasons, sir. You are in my bed."

"Damnation! Out with you, fellow! Begone—or I'll have you flogged!"

"For entering my own chamber? I think not, my Lord Lindores."

"Eh . . . ? You know me? So much the worse for you, then! Leave at once, d'you hear?"

"I shall leave this room, yes. But only for sufficiently long for you and this lady to clothe yourselves and leave my house. If you are not gone then, I will call the palace guard and have you thrown out. My lord!"

The other man all but choked, while his paramour clutched her bosom and gasped. "How . . . how . . . who in God's name are you?"

Standing in the doorway, Heriot had been in the shadow. Now he moved forward. "You ought to know, sir—you owe me sufficient! I am George Heriot and these are my quarters. From the King."

"Christ God!" Lindores swore—and his companion promptly leapt out of bed in a flouncing of plump flesh and white limbs, to flee into the dressing-room next door.

"I will leave you, my lord. But when you are, h'm, yourself, I would wish for an explanation."

"But . . . dammit, man—you went away! You should be in London, with the King. How are you here?"

"I am here on my own business. And the King's. It is *you* who should say what you do here. In my bed."

"I was given these quarters. You were gone with the King. No longer needed them . . ."

"*Who* gave them to you, my lord? Not the Queen, I swear."

"Why, my good-brother. The Master of Gray. He is Master of the King's Wardrobe. Holyroodhouse comes under his authority." Lord Lindores and the Master of Gray had married sisters, the Ladies Jean and Marie Stewart, daughters of the King's illegitimate uncle, the Earl of Orkney. The lady who had jumped from the bed, however, was not one of these.

"Ha—I see! The Master of Gray." Heriot looked thoughtful. "I must needs have a word with the Master, then." He nodded. "My clothing and gear, my lord? Where are they? You have not, h'm, inherited all these also?"

"No, no. All are in your garret. On the floor above. All your property. Safe enough . . ."

"All that you did not *require*, shall we say?" Heriot gestured round at the fully furnished bedroom, all therein his own. Then he shrugged. "I suggest that you dress, my lord. You may take a chill. No doubt we shall meet later." Bowing ironically to the naked man, he left him.

Upstairs, amongst a great clutter of his belongings thrust anyhow into the attic room, he found clothing and changed out of his travel-worn riding garb, cleaning himself as best he could. Then he descended and made his way across the outer court to the main building of the palace.

The place was as lively as a fair, and as noisy. Half of the Scotland that mattered seemed to be present, variously enjoying the night. Up in the long Throne Gallery, seething with splendid folk in the blaze of a thousand candles in glittering candelabra, Heriot looked for the Queen—and saw no sign of her. There were women in plenty, many of whom he knew, many holding court in their own way; but none on the scale of a Queen-Consort. A masque was in progress, involving satyrs, shepherdesses, fauns and even a few sheep from the park—but the Queen could not be taking part in that, being seven months' pregnant—one reason why she had not travelled south with the King.

The masque's theme seemed to demand great expanses of bare flesh, male and female, and the lady in his late bed might have strayed therefrom, Arcadian shepherdesses presumably being a hardy breed. The satyrs wore realistic goat's-hair trews, with rather inadequate and flimsy cod-pieces; also very effective small horns, with their faces painted. In this very active charade, it was not difficult to tell the sheep from the goats.

Despite paint and additions, there was no mistaking the most handsome of the satyrs, Patrick, Master of Gray himself. Only in his mid-thirties, despite being a grandfather, and still a year or two younger than Heriot, he had a superb body, beautifully proportioned and kept in perfect condition. Of all the male actors he was the most striking, gracefully vigorous and danced with the most *élan* and brilliance—all with the consequence that the shepherdesses seemed to compete to swoon into his arms, each expertly handled before being abandoned for the next. Undoubtedly the Master of Gray was enjoying himself.

"I was right—it *is* Master George Heriot!" a voice said, at the watcher's shoulder. "Here is a surprise. But a pleasant one."

He turned. A young woman stood there, exceedingly lovely, of a beauty which succeeded in being at the same time ethereal and somehow matter-of-fact, fragile-seeming and yet quietly strong. She was dressed comparatively quietly likewise in that peacock throng, yet beside her most other women faded into insignificance, however gorgeously or provocatively gowned. She was young, still in her twenties, but the directness and serenity of her gaze was ageless.

"Ha—Mistress . . . Lady . . . er, Madam," the man said. "You are kind. And well met. For I have a message for you. From the Duke of Lennox. A letter, in my baggage. A very brief one, for I left York in some haste."

"York? Is that all? Not London? And Vicky? He is well? There is nothing wrong . . . ?"

"No. All is in order, Lady . . . er, ma'am."

"My name is Mary Gray, and Mistress is the only style to which I have claim, sir."

He cleared his throat. This was the young woman whom the Duke would have made Duchess, but who would not marry him though she bore him a son and ran his castle of Methven; because she had known well that the King would have the marriage annulled somehow, as quite unsuitable for royalty and one so close to the throne—even the bastard of such as the Master of Gray. James had, thereafter, indeed married his only duke to a more apt bride—whatever the Lennox protests. Nevertheless, Mary Gray was made an Extra Woman of the Bedchamber to the Queen, on the King's insistence; for though Anne had little love for her, James greatly admired her. She was indeed a very strong-minded and self-sufficient creature, as keen-witted as she was lovely, and quite as much a personality to be reckoned with as her remarkable father himself.

"I shall go get your letter from the Duke," the man said.

"You have but arrived, Master Heriot. There is no hurry. We shall see out this present foolishness," and she nodded at the masquers. "Then you must eat and drink. Refresh yourself. For you look tired. Then I will come with you."

"No need, Mistress Gray . . ."

"When did you last eat, sir? You have the look of a man who has ridden far and fast."

"We snatched a bite at Berwick-on-Tweed . . ."

"Sakes—then no more standing here looking at mummery!" She took his arm. "Come."

"No, no. I can wait, very well. See out the play-acting."

"Nonsense! Watching men old enough to know better enjoying themselves in a public spectacle is no occupation for a hungry belly!" She drew him after her, into the transverse corridor which led through to a twin gallery, with tables laden with food and drink, and all but deserted save for a few determined drinkers, one already on the floor, overcome, and a servitor or two.

"Her Grace—I do not see her?" Heriot asked. "I must make my presence known, pay my respects. It is to her, of course, that I am sent."

"Ha!" She looked at him quickly. "The Queen is not here, sir. She has gone to the Palace of Linlithgow. To be nearer Stirling and her son. And her daughter with the Livingstones. The King—His Grace sends you back to the Queen? He is . . . concerned?"

Noting the sudden change in her tone, the underlying urgency, the man spoke carefully. "He is ever concerned for his wife and consort. Should he have especial reason to be, at this juncture, Mistress?"

"Who knows?" she replied. "See, sir—eat. Here is a capon. Or a duck? Tear me off a leg and I will join you. Wine—do not wait for the servitors. When my father's foolishness in there is over, they will all be in here like a cloud of locusts. Eat while you may."

Nothing loth, he set to, while the young woman bit into cold capon's leg with pearly teeth, cheerfully.

"Mistress Gray," he said, between mouthfuls, "I do not understand. If the Queen is not here, why this present festivity? What is it about? And on whose authority? In the King's royal palace."

"Well may you ask, sir! This is the third such since you left. I fear that you need not look far for the reason. On the contrary. The Master of Gray is still Master of the Wardrobe and in the absence of the King and Queen he is responsible for the palaces."

"But—the cost . . . ?"

"Should the cost concern my father, Master Heriot? Since he does not pay for it!"

"The Master of Gray does naught without reason, I think. He is no foolish spendthrift irresponsible. He must have a purpose in it."

"It may be so. He has not confided it to me! Perhaps you should ask him!"

He chewed in silence for a little.

"The Master of Gray has, I think, a grudge against the King," he said at length. "For sending him back, at Berwick. Not taking him on to London. It was . . . less than kindly done. Could this have to do with it, think you?"

"Spending the King's money on riotous living? I reckon Patrick Gray apt to fly higher than that!"

"M'mmm. You are his daughter, and should know!"

A triumphant burst of music, followed by cheering, heralded the end of the current performance in the Throne Gallery. "Now for the flood!" Mary Gray said.

Sure enough, like pent-up waters released, the noisy, fashionable, over- or under-dressed throng came pouring through. And in the forefront of the first wave came no other than the Master of Gray himself, just as he had left the play-acting, naked but for his goatskin trews, cod-piece and horns, a bevy of laughing women with him—not the shepherdesses these but ladies of the Court and guests, seeming to be anxious not to be denied the experiences of their Arcadian sisters.

Patrick Gray, all lissome, smiling masculinity, came straight to George Heriot and his daughter.

"Jinglin' Geordie Heriot, by all that's wonderful!" he cried, genially. "Welcome to our little celebration! How good to see you. I perceived you when I was cavorting back there. And Mary here carrying you off."

"Then you have sharp eyes, sir. You appeared to me to be fully engaged otherware!"

"Ah, yes. But one can see the hawk as well as the quarry!"

Pleasantly but firmly, effectively, he got rid of the ladies for the moment, playfully smacking sundry silken bottoms and promising later attentions. "And where have you sprung from, Master George?"

"York," the other answered, briefly.

"York? Then you have ridden hard, my friend. For the royal train only arrived there on Saturday."

Heriot's brows rose. "How did you know that, sir? You are well-informed."

Gray made a smilingly dismissive wave of the hand. Despite all his recent very lively activities, his breathing was wholly under control, his splendid torso heaving only the merest fraction more than normal. A man of medium height and slender build, his body was as beautifully proportioned as his features were fine, and clearly at a high pitch of fitness.

"The Master of Gray is always well informed," his daughter said calmly. "It is ever something one has to take into account."

Heriot glanced at her. That was rather curiously put, by a daughter of her father, even in such an unusual relationship as this.

"I did not daunder," he admitted.

"And so your business, in returning, must have been urgent?"

"The King's business is always urgent, is it not, sir?"

The Master eyed him thoughtfully. "His Grace is well? No mishaps? The progress satisfactory—if slow!"

"All satisfactory, yes."

Mary Gray tinkled a little laugh. "Information is of more than one sort," she commented.

"I would be glad to have a little information myself, sir," Heriot said evenly. "I found the Lord Lindores in my bed when I arrived at my rooms here in the Palace. Not alone! He declares that you gave him my quarters."

"Ah, Patrick Leslie does get himself into extraordinary situations," the Master observed easily. "No harm in him—but injudicious, shall we say?" He looked round him, and lowered his voice conspiratorially. "In bed, you say? Hush, then—for one of these delightful creatures who brought me here is the Lady Lindores, my wife's sister. Who knows whether she would . . . approve! But—better that she did not hear of it from us."

"No doubt, sir. She will not hear of it from me. I am only concerned as to why you gave my rooms to her husband."

"Not *gave*, my friend—merely lent. The Palace is greatly

crowded, these days, and all accommodation much in demand. These rooms were presently unoccupied. And, of course, not your property, only lent also. But, to be sure Master Heriot, you shall have them back. Immediately, if you require them. With my regrets if you have been inconvenienced. Are you to be long in Edinburgh?"

"Until His Grace sends for me."

"Ah. Do not say that you also have been turned back from entering the Promised Land? By our somewhat erratic prince? Has he discovered that there are goldsmiths and money-lenders in London also. As well as, h'm, rogues I think it was? Are we companions in rejection, Master Geordie?"

"As to that I know not, sir. Only that His Grace has sent me back to the Queen."

"The Queen, is it?" That was quick. "Her Grace is to go South? Join the King? Even in her present condition?"

"In time, no doubt. That is understood. Just when is a matter for His Grace."

"M'mm." Gray did not look put out or annoyed—seldom indeed he did—but undoubtedly unused to finding himself stalled and baffled, he was slightly less sure of himself than usual. His daughter seemed rather to enjoy his discomfiture.

"Quite," he said. "To be sure. Her Grace is at Linlithgow."

"So Mistress Gray tells me. I am surprised."

"Never be surprised at anything a woman does, Master Heriot—queen or other! That is part of the delight of them. Now, perhaps I should go clothe myself. Let me know how I may serve you, sir—anything." And on that suitably recovered and assured note, the chief satyr sketched a bow and sauntered off. At once he was engulfed by the ladies.

"I admire your aplomb, Master Heriot," Mary Gray said. "Not many can deal so with Patrick Gray! He got little or nothing out of that exchange!"

"And you are not displeased?"

"Far from it. I have a fondness for my sire. Indeed, I love him dearly. But not all his works! You must have heard as much, surely? From the Queen."

"The Queen's confidences towards me are of money, jewellery, Mistress, not as to her ladies."

"I am suitably rebuked, sir! And now, if you are sufficiently refreshed and sustained, perhaps we should go get my letter from the Duke?"

"No need for you to come. I will fetch it . . ."

"It will be my pleasure, sir. Not only to see who Patrick Leslie of Lindores dallies with in your bedchamber!"

"I fear that you may be too late for that, Mistress Gray. I told them to be out of there before I got back—or I would have the palace guard throw them out."

"You did? How splendid!" She laughed cheerfully. "He deserved that—whether the woman did or not. Do you know who she was?"

"She was plump and generously proportioned, fair of hair, and no child. Nimble for her size, too—unencumbered, to be sure."

She looked up at him closely, and actually clapped her hands. "You smile, Master George! A small smile, I swear! You are other than you seem, I think—and I like you. We shall be friends, I hope?" She linked her arm in his, and led him towards the door.

Arm-in-arm they went downstairs and across the crowded and noisy outer court, Mary Gray not seeming to notice the unseemly horseplay and excesses which went on therein. Though, that she was not wholly unheeding was proved when she drew him into a dark corner and asked if there was a back way into his lodging? At his wondering, she said, "You do not think that we will not be followed, do you? When you did not give the Master of Gray the information he desired. And are, moreover, in *my* company. I think you will have to learn to watch where you tread, in Scotland now, Master George!"

Not a little perturbed, he led her inconspicuously round the stable-block, past the wing tenanted by the reprobate Earl of Orkney, and so to the back entrance of his own quarters. Lights still burned therein, but the place seemed to be deserted now.

They went upstairs, and he looked in distaste at his ravaged bedchamber. He shrugged. "King James was always very careful for lights," was all he said.

"As his Master of the Wardrobe is not! Patrick is careful for nothing, save the success of his projects. So—the nest is flown!"

"I will get your letter. It is with my gear in the garret above."

When he brought the paper down, she took it and tucked it into a pocket in the folds of her olive-green gown, a simple garment with none of the extravagance of fashion, padding, slashing, bows and deep-plunging necklines. Yet there was certainly no attempt to hide or make less of the shapely woman's body beneath.

"You will be riding on to Linlithgow, to see the Queen, Master Heriot?" she put to him.

He nodded. "Tomorrow, yes."

The girl hesitated—and it was not often that this capable and clear-minded young woman seemed at anything of a loss. "I think that I must confide in you," she said, after a moment. "And hope that you will be . . . understanding, thereafter. I believe that you are a man I may trust—and God knows, I can think of no other I can dare confide in. With the Duke gone . . ."

"You sound, h'm, concerned, Mistress. I do not seek confidences. But if you wish to tell me aught, I think you can trust me to be discreet. It is to do with the Queen?"

"Yes. The Queen . . . and the Master of Gray!"

He looked at her quickly, but said nothing.

"I cannot speak with certainty," she went on. "You could say that it is all conjecture. That I am a foolish woman imagining dramatics. I cannot prove that it is not so. But I know my father, I know the Queen, and I know the situation. All too well. And I must needs do something to save it, if I may. If I can make you believe me."

"I know, Mistress, how greatly the Duke of Lennox esteems you. Not only in his love, but for your ability and strength. The King himself speaks of you as having wits almost as sharp as the Master of Gray's own—which is saying much! I shall not lightly doubt you."

"Many would. For it is scarce believable. Unless you know my father, and what he can do, has done. I think that he has devised a plot, a most shameful plot. To be even with the King."

"I would not be surprised," Heriot admitted. "He was ever one for plots. And the King treated him most scurvily at Berwick."

"Yes. It was foolish of His Grace. Almost wicked, perhaps. And dangerous. For years the Master has held the King in his hands, guiding him—and the realm with him. Almost more powerful than the Chancellor and the Privy Council, claiming only this position of Master of the Wardrobe, yet in fact holding a balance, moving noble against noble, playing one faction against another, the Catholics against the Protestants, Elizabeth against Spain, the Pope. I have hated it, men are no more than pawns on a board to Patrick Gray. Yet he has served the King and the realm well, in his own way. There has been peace of a sort now, for years—Patrick's peace! The country has been spared the savageries of the great lords. And King James saved from disasters innumerable. For one purpose, to one end. The uniting in his one person of the two thrones, the two kingdoms. This has always been what Patrick worked for, to make sure that it was James who succeeded Elizabeth, against all other claimants. In order that Scotland should enter a new era of peace and prosperity and the endless wars and intrigues between the two should cease. He may have been wrong in this belief—I do not know. But he believed it, worked for it, plotted and all but lived for it, shepherding James to it step by step. And now—this! Cast aside scornfully at the very door of England, while others enter in." She paused, panting, a little with her long declamation, moved obviously, proof if that were needed, that she had indeed a feeling for her extraordinary father.

"I know it. Saw it. And grieved. But the King conceives him a rogue. Has always done so, it seems. And *used* him, in his turn."

"And the King is right. He *is* a rogue. I, his daughter, admit it. But a clever rogue, with a great ability. Not the man to make an enemy of!"

"The King was ill-advised, yes. But no doubt he believes that, in England, on that greater throne, the Master can no longer hurt him."

"And that is where the King is wrong!" She swallowed. "I believe that he, Patrick, intends no other than to unseat James as King of Scots!"

At the man's incredulous stare, she shook her lovely head. "Hear me, before you scoff. The King's eldest child, the Prince Henry, is kept in Stirling Castle under the care of the Earl of Mar, and away from his mother the Queen. You know this—has been these six years. The cause of much bad blood between King and Queen. James does not trust his wife with the children, believes her weak and silly—as, in some truth, she is. He remembers how ill he was served by *his* mother, Mary. Patrick's plan is, now that James has shaken off the dust of Scotland from his shoes, to get Mar, the Prince's keeper and guardian, to proclaim the boy Henry as King of Scots in place of his father and declare no union of the kingdoms."

"God in Heaven!"

"Before you cry impossible, consider. There are many in Scotland who would welcome something such. Many who see the King's departure for England as a blow, a betrayal. Who believe that Scotland will become no more than a mere dependency of England, little better than a great county. That all which has been fought for over the centuries will be wasted, independence gone. Others mislike King James himself and would prefer a child-king who could be swayed to their purposes. Then there are the Catholics—Huntly, Erroll, Angus and the rest—still mighty strong, who had hopes of drawing James back to the old religion—but now, on the throne of Protestant England, they know that to be impossible. They could turn a seven-year-old boy Catholic easily enough!"

"Yes, yes—I see that. I see that it *could* succeed. In the hands of unscrupulous men."

"My father, you will agree, is sufficiently unscrupulous, sir? And remember, but newly on his English throne, James would scarce be in a position to mount any armed invasion of Scotland, to assert his rights. He has left behind in Scotland all the lords he does not like. He should not have spurned the Master of Gray!"

For moments George Heriot stared, fingering his small beard. "The Queen?" he asked. "She is not in this? What of Her Grace? She would never lend herself to such treachery?"

"As to that, I do not know. She is a strange woman and has long held a grudge against her husband over Prince Henry. And the other two children, both of whom he has taken away from her. She sees none of them, her motherhood soured. And now she is pregnant again, and in that state a woman can do strange things. She might prefer her three children, wholly her own, to a husband who shows more interest in pretty young men!"

"Yes—it could conceivably be so. But—Mar? The Earl of Mar is with the King. In England. How could *he* be in this? He has always been the King's trusted friend. They were as good as foster-brothers."

"Patrick may have some hold over him. I know not. But the Countess of Mar, his mother, has the Prince in Stirling Castle and is refusing to allow the Queen to see him. Whether on the King's orders, her son's, or on Patrick's, I know not. But Patrick was at Stirling only three days back. *He* was not kept out!"

Heriot shook his head. "This is beyond all. If it is indeed so. Could it be but conjecture? Would the Master throw over all he has worked for, overturn his policy over England, merely for revenge?"

"I do not know. But Patrick loves power. Power for its own sake. And now, suddenly, he sees his power plucked from him. I think he might do this, to regain it. For of course it would be he, not Mar, who would control the boy-King, and Scotland with him. He might believe that he could then strike some bargain with England, to gain the advantages of the union, but himself still holding the balance, the power. Father and son on the two thrones, and himself in a position to call the tune! It could be . . ."

"It could be. But *is* it? You cannot prove it?"

"No, I cannot prove it, to be sure. The Master of Gray does

not leave his plots open for proof or disproof. But his wife, the Lady Marie Stewart, believes he has some deep plan in hand. We . . . we work together, where we may. To undo some of the evil of his ploys." She wagged her head, almost helplessly for that capable young woman. "And these great entertainments here in the Palace—these are not just to squander the King's money. I am sure that they are arranged so that Patrick can assemble important men here, confer with them. Important men for his plot, and for afterwards. None will suspect anything of huge intrigue amongst all these masques and junketings."

"You make it convincing, Mistress Gray."

"I could wish that I could not! You saw how Patrick was concerned with *your* coming. How he came hastening. Seeking to hear why the King had sent you. He might well be wondering whether, somehow, word of the plot had reached James. And you were sent to spy it out."

"The King is only afraid lest the Queen gets into some foolishness. Spends over-much of his money. Or mine! He has had a fright about the English Treasury—which he esteemed inexhaustible. Also he considers that she behaves indiscreetly with young men. That is all. But this—this is a nightmare, beyond all his fears."

"Yes. A nightmare, in truth. Which I have had to hug to myself for days. Not knowing to whom to turn. Wishing Vicky were here—the Duke. I had no one to turn to, save the Lady Marie. No one who could act . . ."

"The Chancellor—the Lord Fyvie? As head of the King's government here, surely he is the one to tell?"

"My Lord Fyvie is a friend of my father's! Otherwise I think he would not be where he is! He may be honest—but he is new to the task. Not a strong man, as old Maitland was strong. More interested in building castles and palaces, writing poetry, than in statecraft. He is at Dunfermline, building as ever. Would he listen to me, even if I could get to him? As I could not—for I am watched always. My father loves me, in his fashion, I am sure—but trusts me no further than I trust him!"

"So-o-o! What would you have me do?"

"See the Queen. Discover, if you can, whether she is in the plot. If not, warn her. And somehow contrive to get Prince Henry into her hands, and safe away from Stirling. Into England, to his father. Little Prince Charles too, if that is possible. He is at Dunfermline with the Chancellor . . ."

"Save us—here's no light task, Mistress! How can I do this?"

"Somebody must. And quickly. You have authority. A good head, all say. And, money—which might be important! And the Queen heeds you."

"I have no authority in matters of state. Only in private affairs. I am only His Grace's jeweller. I could send an urgent message to the King . . ."

"There is no time, sir. That would take days. Patrick may strike at any moment. What is to be done must be done at once. Do you understand, Master Heriot? At once. Even tomorrow may be too late. My father does not daunder either, when he sets his hand to a venture!"

"I shall ride to Linlithgow tomorrow . . ."

"*Tonight*, sir, I beg you. I know you are weary. But the Master of Gray will have you watched—nothing more sure. If the Queen is in this, he may well seek to prevent you seeing her. Or at least, have her warned against you. He knows that we have been together, knows how I hate his plots. He is not stupid. He will see you as dangerous, I am sure. Ride tonight, Master Heriot—before he has time to make plans for you!"

"This is all too much! So much beyond me, Mistress Gray—this sort of intrigue and plot and treason. For that it is."

"You are the King's loyal subject, servant and friend, are you not? So men say. And he needs such, in this case. Does he not, sir?"

Spreading his hands, he bowed before her urgency. "Very well—if needs I must."

"I would come with you—but that would wholly arouse the Master's suspicions. Force his hand, perhaps. But I shall send messages of aught I hear. Warn you if there seems to be any sudden change. I have a, a helper in Her Grace's household. Even if I cannot be with you, we can *act* in concert."

"So be it, Mistress. And you? Where will I reach you, if I require to?"

"In the Master of Gray's lodging, here in Holyroodhouse."

"Dear Heaven!" he said.

"And, see you, sir—if we are to work thus close together, on His Grace's behalf, we can dispense with this Mistress Gray and Master Heriot, can we not? I have never found the name Mary to displease me."

He smiled. "Your friend, my Lord Duke of Lennox, was

gracious enough to be saying the same two nights ago. I told him that my friends call me Geordie."

"Dear Vicky, he is a good judge. Though, to be sure, it will not be easy to call the richest man in Scotland Geordie!"

"Am I that?"

"So men do say. Are they wrong?"

"Say that more men owe me money than any other in Scotland! I think it is scarce the same thing!"

4

It is eighteen miles from Edinburgh to Linlithgow in West Lothian, on the road to Stirling, and George Heriot and his grooms, getting away from Holyroodhouse again without hindrance, required less than four hours, even in darkness, to reach it. So they halted at the little wayside kirk of Binning, tied their horses to tombstones, and rolled themselves in their cloaks to sleep on the floor within. If the grooms thought it sacriligious, Heriot did not.

In the event, they overslept, despite the hardness of the beaten-earth floor, for they were all bone-weary with long riding. Heriot left a silver groat between the leaves of the pulpit bible to mystify the minister, and moved on to Linlithgow town to breakfast, also to shave, before presenting himself at the gatehouse of the brown stone palace up on its green eminence above the wimpling loch in the sunny, breezy, April mid-afternoon.

He had no difficulty in getting past the guard, for all the Queen's household knew him. He had been the Queen's jeweller since 1597 and only later entered the King's service also. Anne was not the easiest person to deal with, any more than was her husband; but Heriot was grateful to her, for it was undoubtedly through her patronage and influence that he had become not only jeweller but banker to a large part of the aristocracy of Scotland. His father before him, of the Heriots of Trabroun, had been a prosperous Edinburgh goldsmith and burgess, but it was George's connection with the Court which had brought the real wealth.

Queen Anne had her own Court, smaller but almost independent of her husband's—for the truth was that they got on only indifferently well together. It would, indeed, have required the patience and forbearance of a saint to put up with James Stewart, in matrimony—and Anne of Holstein was far from saintly, or even patient. She was moody, extravagant, pleasure-loving and strong-willed—but also she was essentially kind-hearted, even generous, and straightforward. A daughter of the vehement, restless but autocratic Frederick the Second of Denmark, she took but ill to many of James's ideas on both monarchy and matrimony.

In the royal quarters of the handsome, quadrangular palace, much older than Holyroodhouse, Heriot was informed that the Queen was still abed. He was not surprised, for frequently she did not stir before midday—partly it was suggested in protest against the King's habit of rising, and rousing the palace, in the early hours of the morning, to indulge in his passion for hunting. Also, she not infrequently had been dancing or otherwise enjoying herself until much the same hour. Now, of course, she was seven months pregnant and so had ample excuse.

Heriot requested that his presence be made known to her, if she was waking, nevertheless.

A large Junoesque lady with a magnificent figure and a smouldering, sensual look to her, presently swept in to him, in the anteroom. "Why, here is a surprise, Master Heriot!" she cried. "How came you here? We—Her Grace thought you in London. With her husband. As did I, with mine! Have you been dismissed, sent back, like the rest of us? Do not say that Jinglin' Geordie Heriot is no longer required by our odd liege lord?"

The man was careful how he answered that—however used he was becoming to the question. For this woman was thought by many to be a spy for King James. Certainly the Queen so reckoned her and cordially loathed her. But she could not get rid of her. She was indeed, in theory, her principal Lady in Waiting, maintained in that position by the King's direct orders. Nevertheless, Heriot had doubts about whose spy she might be—if any—tending rather to consider her a choice of the Master of Gray, who liked this sort of woman, while James certainly did not.

"Sent back, yes, my lady—but, I think and hope, not dismissed," he said. "His Grace merely entrusted me with a message for the Queen."

"Indeed! An important message, surely, for the King to use the richest man in Scotland as his messenger?"

"That is a title I cannot claim. Indeed, I dare swear that your ladyship could buy me out twice over and scarce notice the cost!"

"You are too modest, sir. But then, you always were almost over-modest-seeming, were you not? I like a man who knows his worth! And I think you are . . . very worthy! In more than just money, Master George!" She came quite close as she said that, and there was no mistaking the hint of conditional promise and invitation in her throaty, deep voice.

"I am flattered, Duchess," he said, meeting her sultry and at the same time overbearing gaze. "I know my worth to within a pound or two! And yours sufficiently to recognise that you have no need for such as me!"

"I said in more than money, friend."

"Knowing my own worth, lady, includes knowing that George Heriot *without* his money, would be worth—that!" And he snapped his fingers. "Even to kindly disposed duchesses!"

She frowned frankly, drawing away a little. Her voice colder, she asked; "The King? He is well? No mischance sent you back?"

"None."

"No tidings disturb His Grace?"

"Should there be, lady?"

"Stop fencing with me, man!" The Duchess of Lennox was not a subtle woman—she did not have to be. "I am not some simpering miss to be foxed with words. Or the lack of them! What brings you back to Scotland, to Linlithgow, so soon? If you are not dismissed? If there is nothing amiss?"

The man thought quickly. Would anyone so devious and careful as the Master of Gray use such a matter-of-fact minion as this? James might—but in that case the Duchess was no danger. Moreover, she was one of the greatest heiresses in the land, a bride found for the Duke of Lennox two or three years before, while they were both under-age; if she was anybody's spy, it was not for payment—at least, not for money. He had no wish to make an enemy of anyone so powerful, and wife of the Duke—although she was only that in name, their marriage forced on them, and his affections wholly centred on Mary Gray.

"The King grew concerned that Her Grace might require aid, guidance, possibly money," he said carefully, but less stiffly. "He chose to send me, with his messages and instructions, as perhaps able to supply such, in some measure."

She eyed him directly, ponderingly, for a moment, and then shrugged. "To be sure. Her Grace always requires money! *And* guidance! As to aid, is there especial need?"

"I hope not. If so, I have yet to discover it. Has your ladyship anything of the sort in mind?"

The tables turned, she shook her head. "She is troubled at not being able to see her son. But that is nothing new. And she is, of course, seven months gone with child . . ." She turned, as a young woman came into the antechamber. "Knock before you enter, girl!" she snapped.

"I would have done, had I known that your ladyship was with the gentleman." The newcomer dipped the merest sketch of a curtsy to the Duchess. There was nothing pert or unsuitable about it, but undoubtedly her answer had been quick and could have borne more than one shade of meaning. She beamed an almost impish smile on the man. "Her Grace is ready to receive you, Master Heriot," she added.

The Duchess drew a deep breath, to raise her splendid bosom, opened her lips to speak and then thought better of it. With a glare at the girl and a mere nod at Heriot, she swept out of the room as proudly as she had entered.

The man cleared his throat, blinking his surprise.

The girl was very young to have got rid of so formidable a lady, little more than a child indeed, of a slim, boyish figure, great lively eyes, not really pretty but with a gamin attractiveness and a most engaging and ready smile.

"This way, if you please," she invited.

"H'mm. You are surprisingly, er, effective, young woman," he said. "You accomplished in two moments what I had been unable to do in ten minutes!"

She grinned widely, showing excellent, regular teeth. "The Duchess is perhaps less successful with her own sex than she is with yours, sir!"

"Indeed!" Absorbing the implications of this, and from a chit of a girl who looked scarcely past school age, Heriot followed her out into the arras-hung corridor. "You are new in the Queen's service, I think? In fact, I am sure of it. I would scarce have overlooked *you*, i' faith!"

"Yes, sir. I am Her Grace's newest Maid-in-Waiting. Alison Primrose by name."

"Primrose? That is not a common name. Are you sib to James Primrose, Clerk to the Privy Council, perhaps?"

"My sire, sir. As he is to eighteen others!" And her laugh rang out along the corridor, clear and uninhibited.

"Ah." Heriot had heard of the little lawyer's abounding brood—no doubt an excellent whetstone on which this child had had to sharpen her wits and polish her assurance.

She seemed to read his thoughts. "After my family, Mistress Gray told the Queen that I would find her service but little trouble," she confided. "Duchesses and countesses the least of it!"

"Mistress Gray? She was in this?"

"Why yes, sir. She is my good friend. And has no little weight with Her Grace."

So this was Mary Gray's contact within the Queen's household? As adept as her father, probably, at gaining information and influencing events—a shrewder choice than the Duchess of Lennox, for sure. He would keep an eye on Alison Primrose—and no great hardship, either.

A blast of hot and distinctly stuffy air met him as the girl threw open the door of the royal bedchamber and announced him cheerfully.

The large room was as untidy as it was overheated, with a huge log fire blazing in a twelve-feet-wide open hearth, despite the warm April morning, clothes, furs and women's things littered everywhere, chests open and spilling, small dogs squabbling and yapping, and the great bed itself a heap of disarranged linen, covers and pillows, in which Anne and two dogs sat.

"Master Geordie, good Master Geordie!" the Queen cried, in the thick and guttural accent she never quite lost. "Why you are come I do not know. But you are welcome. It is good to see an honest man's face, a man I can trust." And she extended a beringed hand to him, over the dogs and bedclothes.

He bowed deeply and moved forward to take and kiss the outstretched hand.

George Heriot was a noticing man, but he did not have to be to wonder what the Queen had been doing while he waited for her to be ready to receive him. For her long hair was still in an uncombed cascade about her shoulders, and under the loose and gaping purple bed-robe she was most evidently entirely naked, her swollen breasts and distended belly very visible and not particularly enticing. Admittedly she wore bracelets as well as the many rings, which flashed with diamonds, rubies and sapphires—of Heriot's own providing—but they might well have been on all night. She was a thin-faced, sharp-eyed, long-nosed and chinned young woman, still only twenty-seven, with a high brow, not beautiful but with a very white alabaster skin, a lively manner and an air of breeding. Heriot noticed something else. The pillows and bedclothes to the Queen's left clearly showed that she had had a bedfellow until very recently. He did not really suspect it to have been a man.

"You may go, Primrose," Anne said, and the girl bowed herself out. There was however a faint hint of movement, of a presence, from an open-doored dressing-room adjoining.

"I rejoice to see Your Grace. And looking well," the man said. "I bring you a letter from the King. Also messages of His Grace's love and warm attachment. His wishes that all should go most well with your affairs."

The Queen took the proffered letter but dropped it on the covers. "His Grace is but little concerned with my well-being, I think," she said briefly. "That is not why he sent you, I swear."

"H'rr'mm. Your Grace must not think that. It is wholly because of his thought and care for you that I am here, I promise you . . ."

"Has he sent orders for my son Frederick to be delivered to me? From that wicked old woman. My first-born. Only if he has will I believe in his love and attachment, Master Geordie."

Heriot cleared his throat. "Er, not yet. Not exactly that, Madam . . ."

"Then his messages are of no interest to me!" Passionately she said it. "He is a cruel and wicked man, and no true husband. How can he separate a mother from her children so? He is a monster, a heartless monster!"

"Your Grace—he is none so ill as that! Because Prince Henry is heir to the throne, the King is concerned lest men of ill will lay hands on him, use him for their own ends, against the Crown. As indeed they did to himself, as a boy. At Ruthven. He cannot have that to happen. So he keeps him in the secure fortress of Stirling, in the care of the Mars. Lady Mar was his own foster-mother, her son, the present Earl, the King's oldest friend, almost as good as a brother . . ."

"And both of them hate me, the Queen! Frederick's mother." It was one of the oddities of the Scottish Court that the Queen insisted that her older son was named Frederick, after her father the King of Denmark, while James named him Henry as gesture towards Elizabeth and her father Henry the Eighth, in his gropings towards the coveted English succession. Which had come first at the christening, only Bishop Cunningham of Aberdeen knew for sure, who had diplomatically mumbled the names.

"Highness—I do believe that you mistake. It is not so . . ."

"You think not? Then why will the woman not allow me to see my son? In Stirling Castle. Deny *me*, the Queen! Her son Mar is with the King, in England. And she forbids me! My little Frederick —in that she-devil's clutch!"

Heriot drew a deep breath, and came to a decision. He lowered his voice, glancing towards the open dressing-room door. "Madam —have you had any word of a move to, er, take your son out of Stirling Castle?"

"What! *Jeg forstär ikke. Hvad er der i den*? Take him? Who? When? What is this?" She leaned forward urgently, uncaring for her more fully displayed nakedness.

Satisfied that Anne, who was no dissembler nor actress, could by no means fabricate this surprise and eagerness, he went on. "Has the Master of Gray had word with Your Grace? Or the Mistress Mary, indeed?"

"Gray? Saints protect us—if that man is in it, then no good will come of it. He is, I believe, the Devil himself!"

"So I have heard others declare. Your Grace knows nothing of this?"

"How should I know? The Master of Gray does not confide his plots to me! What is it? What has my son to do with it?"

"Highness—there is someone in your dressing-room. I can hear it. What I have to say is not for other ears . . ."

"Mercy—it is only Henrietta! My good confidante and bed-fellow." She raised her voice. "Hetty, sweeting—come. I have no secrets from Hetty." A tall, pale young woman came out, rather guiltily, her bed-robe wrapped considerably more tightly around her than was the Queen's, pretty in an anaemic way, Henrietta Stewart, Marchioness of Huntly, sister of the Duke of Lennox.

Heriot bowed. He was not as relieved as he might have been. For this young woman, brought from France to marry Scotland's premier Catholic noble, the Gordon chief, George first Marquis of Huntly, was herself strongly Catholic, a notable entertainer of Jesuits and credited with seeking to turn the Queen to the old religion. And, according to Mary Gray, the Master looked for support for his plot from the Catholics. She had even named Huntly, himself a notorious schemer.

"Hetty—you know Master Heriot?" Anne said. "My true servant and friend."

The other nodded, silent.

"I know her ladyship's husband, my lord of Huntly," the man said. "We have had, h'm, dealings."

"Ha—I swear he owes you money, like all the rest. As do I, indeed!"

"His lordship is, I am sure, an excellent risk, Highness. It is my privilege . . ."

"Save us—you need not be afraid of miscalling Huntly in front of Hetty. She seldom sees him—nor wishes it otherwise! She had no more choice in wedding George Gordon than had I in wedding James Stewart! We are neither of us fortunate in our husbands!"

The man looked uncomfortable. "Your Grace jests. And I am a loyal subject and servant of King James also."

"How loyal?" Anne jerked. "You were *my* servant, my jeweller, before you were James's, do not forget."

He nodded. "I never forget it. And am grateful," he assured.

"Then—tell me of this plot. You may speak out before the Marchioness. She is wholly trustworthy."

"I was a d'Aubigny Stewart's daughter before ever I was a Gordon's wife," that young woman said quietly, her first contribution to the discussion.

"Very well, Highness. There is nothing certain. But Mistress Gray believes that there is a plan to get Mar to yield up the Prince Henry, and to declare him King of Scots in place of his father, gone to England. The Master of Gray and sundry others, to rule the country in the boy's name."

"Sweet Jesu! They would, would *depose* James? Impossible!"

"Not so, I fear. After all, they deposed the King's mother, Mary. And King James is in no state to start his English reign by raising an army against Scotland and going to war."

The women stared at him.

"His Grace has grievously offended the Master of Gray, who so largely built up his succession policy. And he is an ill man to cross. Moreover, there is no strong man, or strong faction, left in Scotland to support the King's cause. Most of his friends are gone south with him. The Catholic lords are here still, and strong, but . . ." He left the rest unsaid.

"Aye—George would take a hand in this, I swear!" the Marchioness averred.

"A mercy! The Master of Gray, it *would* be, to think of this! But—Mar? He is James's friend. No friend of mine, God knows. And an oaf! But would he betray James?"

"This I do not know. It is the one factor which makes me doubt. Mar is with the King now. He was never keen on the English succession, I think—but I have no reason to believe that he would turn against the King. Nevertheless, the Master of Gray seldom misjudges."

"He is an unpleasant man," Lady Huntly observed. "I would not trust him."

"What are we to do?" the Queen demanded.

"I think we must go to Stirling, Your Grace. If you are able to travel? Demand the Prince Henry from the old Countess."

"I wrote a letter to her. Requiring her to deliver up my son to me. She sent reply that she would not. She would give him up only to the King."

"If Your Grace went, in person. I with you. Saying that I came from the King. She might heed us. Lacking her son and the other Erskines."

"If you think it. When? When shall we go?"

"The sooner the better. For the Master may strike at any time."

"Today, then. We shall eat, and then ride. Hetty—my clothes . . ."

"Ah, scarcely so soon, Highness. It is noon, and near twenty miles to Stirling. In Your Grace's present state you dare not ride fast. Tomorrow will serve, I think. Moreover, we need a tail of men. The Queen must ride properly escorted. How many have you here?"

"A score. More."

"Not sufficient, Highness. For this. You must appear strong. With authority."

"Livingstone, the Earl of Linlithgow will find me men. At Haining Castle, but a few miles away. He keeps my daughter Elizabeth—but is no unfriend."

"Good, I shall go speak with him. Tomorrow, then. In the morning. Highness—have I your permission to retire?"

"To be sure. Ring the bell for the Primrose girl, Hetty. She will find you a room and see to your comfort, Master Geordie."

"I thank you. She looks to be a bright lass, that one."

"Over-bright, perhaps. For her years. I do not know, yet, whether I may trust her. I trust few in Scotland, even in my own household."

"Including my lusty good-sister!" the Marchioness said, sniffing.

Alison Primrose appeared, and Heriot bowed himself out.

"Where would you wish to have your bedchamber, Master

Heriot?" the girl asked, innocently, in the cooler corridor. "Near the Duchess's? Or . . . otherwhere?"

"Nearer yours, perhaps," he answered lightly. "Though—would I be any safer there . . . ?"

* * *

The next morning, escorted by the Earl of Linlithgow and sixty men-at-arms, the Queen and her ladies rode for Stirling, Anne carried in a horse-litter slung between two placid jennets, with George Heriot insisting on the most unhurried progress—for the last thing he wanted was for the King to accuse him of causing his wife to miscarry, as she had done once already. They went by the Roman Wall and the great Tor Wood, largely through Livingstone lands. On Heriot's suggestion Lord Linlithgow brought along his charge, the Princess Elizabeth, a lovely and vivacious girl of seven, all spirited grace, extraordinary to be the offspring of James and Anne, although not so extraordinary a granddaughter for Mary Queen of Scots. She elected to ride with Alison Primrose, and together they lightened a dull morning.

George Heriot rode with these two—save when he was summoned to the Queen's side—partly because they were the best company, partly in that he had, as ever, to be careful not to seem to presume on the Queen's friendlieness. He was only an Edinburgh burgess, after all, and in the company of the Earl, Sir Harry Lindsay, Master of the Queen's Household, the Duchess of Lennox, the Marchioness of Huntly and other high-born individuals, he was of very humble status. Admittedly he came of lairdly stock, the Heriots of Trabourn, in Lothian, but that was three generations back, and his father had been a goldsmith, a tradesman, before him. Not infrequently his privileged position close to the Crown was an embarrassment.

They came to the grey, climbing town of Stirling, above the silver coils of the River Forth but crouching beneath its soaring rock-girt citadel, in early afternoon. Queen Anne shook her fist at its lofty battlements.

"My poor Frederick!" she cried.

Through the narrow streets and up the steep hill they rode to the ancient fortress of Scotland's kings where so much of the land's turbulent history had been written. Their approach had been under observation for a long time, inevitably, and at the wide forecourt apron, high above the town and meandering river, the great gatehouse doors were found to be barred against them, the drawbridge up.

"Who comes in armed strength to the King's royal castle of Stirling?" a harsh voice hailed them from the gatehouse parapet.

"The Queen, fool!" Linlithgow shouted back. "Can you not recognise the royal standard of this realm?" And he pointed to the flag carried by one of his men. "Her Grace requires to see her son, the Prince Henry Frederick, Duke of Rothesay." A still larger royal standard than their own floated above the castle's topmost tower.

"Wait you, while I inform the Countess of Mar," the captain of the guard returned.

"Knave! Jackanapes!" the Earl roared. "Think you to keep your Queen waiting like some packman at the door! Lower this bridge and open the gates immediately."

There was no answer from the gatehouse.

As the illustrious company fumed and fretted, the Queen swore that the guard-captain would hang for this.

"He would hang the more promptly had he let us in, Highness," Heriot pointed out. "The Countess Annabel has a notably short way with her, I have heard. She only is of account here."

"In *my* country she would be horsewhipped and then drowned!" Anne snapped.

"She would still have to be caught first, Your Grace!" The Duchess of Lennox pointed out.

Presently, a small shrunken figure appeared at the gatehouse parapet with the guard-commander, rather ridiculous-seeming in a high hat with ostrich feathers and an old tartan plaid hugged about her, Annabel, Countess-Dowager of Mar, who had reared King James with her own family. She made no gesture towards the waiting company.

"Her ladyship says that she listens," the commander called.

As the Queen exploded with something wrathful and presumably Danish, Linlithgow raised his voice.

"Countess of Mar—Her Grace is much displeased to be kept waiting thus. She demands that you punish severely your insolent churl of a guard. And that you order these gates open forthwith, that she may see her royal son."

The Countess spoke to the captain, who began to answer.

"Not you, fool! We do not speak with underlings."

"The Countess says that she does not engage in unmannerly shoutings, sir." And as Linlithgow spluttered, "She says likewise that she will speak only with the Queen—if she is indeed present."

In the ensuing uproar, Heriot moved closer to the Queen. "Wrath will achieve nothing, Your Grace," he said. "I urge that you move nearer to the bridge-end where we can speak without shouting."

Reluctantly the Queen ordered it.

"Countess of Mar," she called clearly, from her litter. "I am Anne of Scotland—as you can see very well, unless age has blinded you! I require you to open these gates and deliver my son to me."

"The Prince Henry is at the hurly-hackit ower the hill, yonder," a thin but strangely forceful voice declared. "It will tak a whilie to fetch him, y'Grace."

"Then do so. At once. And meantime, open to me. I shall no longer wait here like some beggar at your door. Open. Do you understand, Countess?"

"If Your Grace will show me a paper, signed by the King, ordering that I do so, I'll no' refuse, Highness."

"How dare you make conditions to your Queen! Obey my royal commands."

"I dare fine. For, lacking my son, I take instructions only frae the King's Grace, Madam. And his commands are right explicit. Without his written orders, signed and sealed, I deliver the Prince to nonesoever. And none sets foot ower the brig o' this castle!"

"But . . . I am the boy's mother!" Anne all but wailed.

"His Grace kens that, I hae nae doubt!"

"This is outrage . . . !"

"Countess Mar," Linlithgow interjected, "I have the same commission from His Grace. To keep and guard the Princess Elizabeth. But I do not keep her hidden from her royal mother. Nor does the Chancellor, Prince Charles. Here is the Princess."

"Maybe so, Livingstone. You ken your orders, I ken mine. But my laddie's the *heir*. You'll admit there's a difference."

The Queen and Heriot exchanged glances.

"With His Grace in England, Her Grace has the supreme authority in Scotland, woman!"

"No' to overturn King Jamie's commands."

George Heriot took a hand. "I am the King's goldsmith, Heriot, Countess," he called. "I have come straight from His Grace. At York. He sent me to ensure that the Queen and his family were well, and having no troubles. To help prepare them for their journey to London. His Grace said naught of keeping the Queen and her children apart. Indeed he intended otherwise, I swear."

"Sweer awa', mannie—but did he gie you a writing for me, to deliver up his son?"

"No. But His Grace told me to see well to them all. I cannot do that while you keep this Prince hidden away. He said . . ."

"Aye, he *said*! Or you *say* he said! I need mair than that. Aye, and I need mair than any goldsmith to come to me changing the King's express commands."

"It is of no avail!" the Queen cried. "The old witch is beyond all reason. It is insufferable . . ."

Despairingly Heriot tried one last throw. "Countess—His Grace gave me fullest authority to spend all necessary moneys on the Queen and her family's behalf. My purse, therefore is . . . not short! If anything is required, for the Prince's welfare, or in discharge of outlays here—I can deal with it . . ."

"God's death—would you try to *buy* me, Annabel Mar, you huckstering little shopkeeper!" the old woman shrilled. "Get out o' my sight before I hae my guards pistol you like an insolent scullion!"

Strangely enough, George Heriot bowed from the saddle. "I apologise, Countess," he said. "I should not have said that."

Alison Primrose actually clapped her hands—although her royal mistress looked less than approving.

"I will have no more of this," Anne declared. "That I, the Queen, should be repulsed and insulted, kept out of a royal castle, by this woman! She will suffer for it—that I vow before God! We go. At once. I will not stay here another moment."

"The boy, Highness? The Prince, your son? Do you not wait for him?" Linlithgow asked.

"Yes—let us wait for Henry," the Princess Elizabeth cried.

"*Frederick!*" her mother said sharply. "Frederick Henry, child." She set her long chin obstinately. "No. I will wait no longer at this door, like a beggar. To be mocked by this she-devil! Sir Harry—we return to Linlithgow."

* * *

George Heriot was summoned to the royal bedchamber again that night, the Queen having retired, prostrate, on return from

Stirling. He found her recovered somewhat, but very angry.

"What do we do now, sir?" she demanded of him, before he was fully into the room. "It was on your advice I went to Stirling—to be defied and insulted. Have you any more, and better, advice for me?"

"The situation is difficult, Your Grace—but no worse than it was," he told her soothingly. "In the strongest fortress in the realm we cannot *force* the Countess to yield up the Prince. But then, neither can the Master of Gray! All depends on whether or no Lady Mar is in this plot of his. If she is not, then matters may be none so ill. For your son could scarcely be anywhere safer than in Stirling Castle, with that dragon guarding him."

"She will be in it, the horrible creature! The plot. She hates me!"

"I am less sure, Highness. Whether she hates *you* is scarce to the point, in this. What is to the point is—has she turned against the King? She did not sound so. And she has always loved him like a mother—a fierce mother, but still loved him . . ."

"What of it? I want my son."

"To be sure. But Your Grace has managed without him all these years. A week or two more will not try you too sternly. What is important is that the boy does not fall into the hands of the Master of Gray and his friends. To the King's grievous hurt. And your own. If the Countess of Mar is not in the Master's plot, and can remain proof against his pressings and blandishments—then the Prince is probably safer with her than even with Your Grace here. *This* is no fortress. Nor is any other royal palace you might go to. You perceive my point?"

"I perceive that you said nothing of this yesterday, sir, when you urged me to go to get Henry!"

"True. Perhaps I had thought insufficiently deeply myself. But we had to find out whether or no Lady Mar was in the plot. For myself, I do not now think she is."

"Why are you so sure? I believe that you have conceived some shameful liking for the evil old bitch! You . . . you begged her pardon! When she had spat on me, your Queen!"

"Only in that I had made suggestion that she might be bribed. That was a mistake. Let us be glad that she cannot, it seems."

"Why think you she is not in Gray's pocket?" That was the Marchioness of Huntly, pale shadow of the Queen.

"I am not *sure*. But she did not speak and act as I think she would have done had she been concealing complicity. She made overmuch of the *King's* authority, for one about to throw it off. I believe she is still loyal to His Grace. Whether she remains so or not is another matter. Depending on the Master's . . . inducements."

There was silence in the over-heated chamber. The Queen dropped her head into her hands. "Is there nothing, *nothing*, that we can do?" she wailed.

"Two things, I think, Madam. We must send an immediate letter to His Grace, telling him of the plot and requesting written authority to release the Prince. As indeed Lady Mar said . . ."

"He will never give it. He is a cruel, unnatural man! He does not want me to have my son."

"He will not refuse you at the cost of his Scots throne, I think. I shall write also. He commanded me to keep him informed." He could scarcely say that James would pay more attention to his plea than to the Queen's.

"And the other? You said, two things."

"That *I* might go again to Stirling. Myself. Alone, to see the Countess privily. Perhaps she would see me, hear me . . ."

"Go deal with her? My enemy! Behind my back!"

"Scarce that, Highness, surely. Rather to test her. Discover if she knows of the plot. Warn her, if she does not, and seems against it."

"I will not have you having secret talks with that woman! Discussing me and my husband and son. I will not!"

"If you do not trust me, Highness, send one of your ladies with me. Lady Huntly, here . . ."

"I will not have any dealings with that she-devil," that lady declared.

"Then another. Merely to accompany me."

"Not the Duchess, on my soul!"

"No. That might be unwise. The young woman Primrose, perhaps? She would not seem to rival Lady Mar in status, yet could represent Your Grace well enough. It could do no harm, and might achieve something. While we wait for the King's authority. We might even have word with the Prince . . ."

That same night an officer of the Queen's guard, with one of Heriot's grooms, set off for the South, with instructions not to spare themselves, or horseflesh, in getting their letters to the King with all speed. The other groom rode with them as far as Edinburgh, with a message for Mary Gray. And in the morning, their master, with Alison Primrose, headed westwards once more for Stirling at the crossing of Forth.

It was extraordinary how different was their reception from the previous day's. The castle drawbridge was down, and although it was strongly guarded and could have been raised at short notice, a single man and woman represented no threat. They were civilly received and a messenger sent to inform the Countess of their identity.

With no undue delay they were conducted up from the gatehouse to a wing of the palace building on the crown of the rock, where in a small, bright room in a tower they found Annabel of Mar hunched over a fire. Close up, and in the cold morning light, she looked a very old and frail woman.

"Well, Master Heriot! You are a bold man, I think, to return thus to Stirling! And who is this slip of a lassie you have brought to support you against an auld done woman?"

"She is one of the Queen's Maids-in-Waiting, Countess. And I need all the support I can get!"

"Say you so, goldsmith? Perhaps you speak truth. You havena come offering me more o' your Edinburgh gold today, I'm thinking?"

"No. That was badly done. A man may make one mistake, may he not?"

"With me, only one, sirrah."

"He made apology, Lady Mar. Not all men would have done that," Alison Primrose said. "Nor required to, since gold speaks loudly!"

"Ho—so that's the style o' you, minx! The Queen's service must have changed since my day! Aye, then, goldsmith—to what do I owe this courtesy? No' love on Queen Anne's part, I wager."

"It is more on the King's behalf that I come, than the Queen's," Heriot said carefully. "His Grace was uneasy in his mind, and sent me North. I have discovered, with some reason."

"So? But it was his *goldsmith* that he sent North. Not one o' his Council, or lords. Such as my son. So I'm thinking that His Grace wasna just sae greatly concerned."

"I agree that he might have sent a more, er, resounding servant had he known what I now know."

"Come, man—no riddles. I am ower auld for suchlike. Out with it. What have you come for?"

"Seeking the safety of Prince Henry, Countess. That is what."

"Prince Henry is very safe in Stirling Castle." The old woman leaned forward. "Was King Jamie concerned about *that*? In England? Has he been hearing stories?"

"Perhaps. His Court ever seethes with rumours, as your ladyship well knows. And you? Have *you* been hearing stories?"

"What stories would I hear, up on this bit rock halfway to heaven?"

"I should think plenty. At Stirling. Where all men must come to cross Forth. And only thirty-five miles from Edinburgh—where stories start!"

"You'll need to be mair explicit, man. A deal mair explicit." It was not difficult to see where King James had picked up his fashion of speech.

"Very well. But I think that you will know of what I speak. There is a plot to take Prince Henry and declare him King of Scots. In room of his royal father. On the pretext that the King has deserted his Scottish kingdom for another."

She considered him steadily, from beady eyes. "You tell me so? And does King Jamie know o' this supposed fell plot?"

"I think not. Not yet. But . . . I have little doubts that *you* did, Lady."

She made no answer.

"It is a damnable plot. And might well succeed."

"Not while I hold the laddie here in Stirling Castle, goldsmith."

He fingered his little beard thoughtfully.

"Perhaps that is why the Countess would not yield the Prince up yesterday." Alison Primrose put in, smiling. "Perhaps she believes the Queen also to be in this plot!"

They both stared at her.

"Insolent jade!" the old woman said, but as it were automatically, without vehemence.

"Her ladyship would not think that!" Heriot declared, frowning.

"Would she no'?" the Countess snapped swiftly. "I've heard stranger ploys! All ken Anne cares little for her husband. Her sire, in yon Denmark, was a tyrant. She has the same spirit in her, I swear, the woman. She would perhaps prefer to be mother o' a powerless king who would do her will, than wife o' one who will not!"

"But . . ." The man floundered. "You do not truly believe that? That the Queen, in child again, could plot to bring down her own husband!"

"Mary did—James's mother."

Such a thought had just never occurred to George Heriot. Quite shaken for a moment, he groped in his mind. Then he shook his head.

"No. This is, folly. The Queen desires only to win back her children into her own care, have this new baby, and then rejoin her husband in London. She is appalled by word of this plot."

Annabel of Mar said nothing.

"How do you see it, lady? This conspiracy."

"I see it as wholly evil," the old woman said. "And moreover, highest treason. Men should hang for this."

Heriot tried to swallow a sigh of relief. "Then . . . then you will yield up the boy to none? Until the King commands it, in writing?"

"None—the Queen, or other." The Countess hesitated. "Save for my son, to be sure. My Lord of Mar. He is the Prince's lawful guardian, no' myself. I but hold the laddie and castle in his name."

Heriot's intaken breath this time was scarcely of relief. "The Earl's loyalty . . . is not in doubt," he got out.

"I thank you for the expression o' confidence, goldsmith!"

"I but meant, ladyship, that the Prince therefore is in no true danger. Since only the King and the Earl can win into this great fortress without breaking the walls down with cannon. Which even the Master of Gray, I think would scarce contemplate."

"That popinjay!"

"He is no popinjay, Countess—but the most dangerous man in two kingdoms. No to be underestimated." He paused, and considered the other speculatively. "See you, Countess—here is a thought. The Queen's main desire, I know, is to be with her first-born, the Prince Henry. She pines for him. This castle is a royal palace. She has as much right to be here as at Linlithgow or Holyroodhouse. I know that you do not greatly love her, nor she you. But if she was here, biding in this castle with the Prince, she would be better and the King's cause nothing weakened."

"Have her here! Under my feet! That, that . . . Looking at the Primrose girl, Lady Mar all but choked. "No, sir!" she croaked.

"Could you deny her? If she asked. You will not deny that this is a *royal* castle—not an Erskine one? You but *keep* it for the Crown. If the Queen were to demand to stay in one of her husband's houses—as distinct from you yielding up the Prince—could you refuse?"

"Share the same house wi' me? God's death, young man—hae you taken leave o' your wits?"

"That was not my question, Countess. Could you deny admission?"

The other gulped in her scrawny throat. "I'll answer that, goldsmith, when I see Anne o' Holstein come chapping at my door seeking lodging! No' before."

"That means you would, and must, admit her, I think."

"She'd never come."

"Perhaps not. But it would solve some problems. And the King would be relieved, I swear, to have both wife and son—and possibly the other bairns also—under the eye of one whom he can trust absolutely. Yourself."

"Do not seek to cozen me with such syrup, man. I'm ower auld for that!"

"It would also save His Grace the cost of keeping another palace open. Linlithgow. For the lying-in. And he might prefer to have his fourth child borne in his major Scots citadel."

At these shrewd thrusts the other glowered. Then abruptly she rose to her feet, small but imperious. "We have other matters to attend to, goldsmith. You shall be conducted to your horses."

"To be sure. We thank you for your courtesy of this meeting. But—would it be possible for us to see the Prince? For but a moment. That we may inform his royal mother as to how he seemed."

"The laddie's well. Nothing wrong wi' him."

"We do not doubt that you cherish him well, Countess. But no harm in seeing him. To reassure Her Grace."

Muttering something, the old woman stalked stiffly to the door and out. Exchanging glances, the visitors followed.

They did not have far to go. At only the third doorway along the vaulted corridor the Countess turned in, and there was a nine-year-old boy sitting at a table with a young man, at books and papers. The Prince was tall for his age, well-formed and good-looking, delicately featured and intelligent-seeming. Getting down from his chair he ran to the old woman, remembered his manners sufficiently to halt and bow gravely to the two strangers, and then went to take the Countess's hand.

"Here is Master Heriot, the King your father's jeweller, Henry," she said. "And one o' the Queen's ladies." There was something of a sniff about that. "Make your duties to them, lad."

"A good day to you, sir. A good day to you, Mistress. I hope that I see you well." And, in a different voice. "Master Andrew says that my Latin is better today."

"Aye, that'll please your royal father, lad. Master Heriot left him but a day or two agone."

"My royal father is well, sir?"

"Indeed yes, Highness. He sent you his affectionate greetings." That was not precisely a fact, but would bear saying.

"Your royal mother the Queen also sends her fond greetings," Alison Primrose added.

"I thank you, Mistress. And my royal mother. Is she also well?" He still clutched the Countess's hand.

"Well, Highness. And . . . and not far away."

"I do not like Latin much. But Master Andrew says that it is important."

"Yes. The King is a great Latin scholar."

"Greek also, sir. And French. And Spanish. Hebrew also. But . . . he does not know Danish, I think."

"H'rr'mm. Perhaps not . . ."

"Back to your lessons, then lad." Annabel of Mar gave him a little pat on the head before pushing him gently towards the table.

The visitors bowed themselves out.

"I thank you, Countess, for your help," Heriot acknowledged. "He is a fine lad. His parents have reason to be proud of him, I think. We shall tell the Queen how well he does."

"And how content he is?"

"Well—that he does not pine, at least. Also that he is safe here. And will in nowise be given up. To any."

"By me. So long as I command here."

"You mean . . . ?"

"I told you, young man. I am but my son's deputy. He is the Prince's keeper, not myself. Remember it."

George Heriot opened his mouth to speak—and then thought better of it.

They took their leave of the old lady rather less stiffly than when they had greeted each other.

* * *

That evening, George Heriot sought to convince the Queen that it was to her advantage to swallow her pride and go to be with her son at Stirling, assured that Lady Mar could not refuse her, however reluctant she might be. Anne maintained a posture of outrage and shock at the very suggestion. Alison Primrose came to announce that Master Heriot's groom had just ridden in from Edinburgh, and brought this letter.

The man took the paper, and seeking the Queen's permission to scan it, opened the sealed folds. It was only a brief note, obviously hastily penned. "Have just overhead the Master of Gray telling the Lord Sinclair that E. of Mar has left King and on his way back to Scotland. This may be important. M.G."

"So-o-o!" Heriot breathed out.

"Is it news?" Anne demanded. "Ill news? What is it?"

"I cannot think it good news, Highness. The Earl of Mar is on his way back to Scotland." He caught the Primrose girl's eye.

"A coarse oaf of a man! Scotland was sweeter without him! But does it concern us?"

"I think it may. The Countess his mother was at pains to inform us that *he* was the Prince's lawful guardian, not she. He, the Keeper of Stirling Castle. She gave no assurance that the *Earl* would not deliver up the Prince. And Mary Gray, when she told me of this plot, believed that the Earl might be in it. Such was the rumour she had heard. It seemed unlikely, with Mar in England with the King. But now . . . !"

"The King may be sending him. As he sent you," Lady Huntly suggested. "For some reason of his own."

"Our letters cannot have reached him yet?" the Queen asked.

"No, Highness. It cannot be that."

"Mar comes to destroy me! I know it. He has hated me from the first. Ah, God—have mercy upon me!" Anne cried, and burst into tears.

Troubled, the man sought to soothe and console her, but with no avail. The Queen's women hustled him out of the bedchamber. She had been weeping like this for most of the day, fretting herself into a fever, hysterics. It was that Countess of Mar's fault, insulting Her Grace . . .

In the night, Queen Anne miscarried for the second time.

5

"MY LORD OF MAR," the Chancellor said, "I regret it—but it is not possible for you to see the Queen. Her Grace is very ill, and weak . . ."

"I know that, man! God—all Scotland knows it! The more reason that I see her. I have a letter for her from her lord the King."

"I will see that Her Grace gets it, at once . . ."

"No, sir! I will see her. The letter I will give into her ain hands —none other. His Majesty's instructions. And I've messages for her, forby. Frae the King. Take me to her, man."

"I fear not, my lord. Her Grace's own royal commands."

"What! She'll no' see *me*, Mar! Is that what you're after telling me, Seton?" A red-faced, gobbling turkey-cock of a man, John of Mar advanced a threatening step. Only in his early forties, he looked much older, harsh, overbearing, arrogant. "The likes o' Sandy Seton'll no' keep me frae the woman!"

"I must, my lord. I cannot but obey the Queen's direct commands. She said that she would not see you." The Chancellor's voice quavered a little. Sir Alexander Seton of Pluscarden, recently created Lord Fyvie, was a dozen years the other's junior and scarcely a dominant character, slight, slender, modish, good-looking, with the face of an intellectual.

"Christ's Wounds, she did! Well—I have the *King's* commands, Seton, d'you hear? Whose do you obey—heh? The King's Majesty's ain—or his silly bit puling wife's? Tell me that—you that ca's yoursel' Chancellor, *King's* Chancellor—no' his consort's!"

From the background, near the doorway of Linlithgow's Great Hall, the Master of Gray came to his colleague's aid, but calmly, undramatically, as though all was a matter of course. "No call for contest, my lords," he said, coming forward. "Give me His Grace's letter, Johnnie. Her Grace, I hope will not refuse to see *me*. Eh, Sandy? And I can, perhaps, persuade her to give audience to the Earl of Mar later, and hear the King's messages. A woman sick must be humoured, Johnnie."

Mar grunted but no more; and Fyvie agreed eagerly.

The Hall of Linlithgow Palace was crowded as it had not been for long. The Queen's miscarriage and subsequent grievous illness had brought important folk from the four quarters of the kingdom. The Chancellor had hastened from Dunfermline, the Earl of Orkney from the West, the Master of Glamis the Treasurer, from Angus—and now the Earl of Mar, newly arrived from England, from Edinburgh with the Master of Gray. Should the Queen die, a totally new situation would arise, with interesting permutations for those in authority. This was the fourth day after the miscarriage.

In a corner of the huge apartment, Mary Gray slipped away from George Heriot's side. "I will go warn Lady Huntly," she murmured. She had come two days before, as an Extra Woman of the Bedchamber whose services might be required.

A small group, with Fyvie and the Master of Grey, detached themselves and made for the private stairway to the Queen's apartments. Unobtrusively, Heriot followed.

Patrick Gray did not fail to notice it. "Ha, Master Geordie—I heard that you came here. Promptly!"

"I told you, sir, that it was to the Queen that I was sent."

"Quite. You came at a bad moment. I hope that you did not, h'm, worsen it my friend!"

Heriot could have slain the elegant Master for that—for it was precisely that thought which had dogged him for four days and nights. Had he not urged the royal visit to Stirling Castle, might this miscarriage never have occurred? It was a grievous question, and though Mary Gray, Alison Primrose, and even Lady Huntly all united in absolving him, he was not wholly reassured.

At the bedchamber door Sir Harry Lindsay, Master of the Queen's Household would have denied them entry until, in the gloomy stone corridor he recognised the Master of Gray and they exchanged quick glances. Heriot noted that exchange.

In the stifling room, Sir Hugh Herries the royal physician, Lady Huntly, Mary Gray and Margrete Vinster, a Danish Maid-in-

Waiting, stood round the great fourposter bed. The Queen lay flat thereon, eyes closed.

"Your Grace—I deeply regret to disturb you," Fyvie said, low-voiced. But. . . ."

"I . . . will . . . not . . . see . . . Mar!" The words from the bed were weak, but measured and very definite.

"No, Highness. I told him. But this is the Master of Gray. With a letter from the King's Grace."

"I do not want it. Or him."

"My Lady Anne," the Master said, at his silkiest, "as well as the letter, I bring words for your royal ear alone."

A faint negative twitch of the sweat-damp head on the crumpled pillow.

"About your son, the Prince Frederick Henry."

That putting of the name Frederick first had its effect. The red-rimmed, heavy-lidded eyes opened, the pale lips parted just a little.

"It is hot in here, over-crowded," the Master went on pleasantly. "Sir Hugh—I think the room should be cleared. Do not you?"

Herries, who owed much, including his knighthood, to the Master of Gray, nodded, and gestured for all to leave.

The Queen's eyes turned, in sudden alarm and appeal, to George Heriot. He nodded.

As most of the company moved to the door, three remained with the Master and the Chancellor—Lady Huntly, Mary Gray and George Heriot. Coolly Gray eyed each of them in turn. None spoke.

"May I remind all here that there is such a body as the Privy Council," he observed, almost conversationally. "In matters of state, the authority of its members is paramount. The Chancellor, my Lord Fyvie, and my humbler self, are of His Grace's Scots Privy Council. And we would have speech with the Queen. Alone."

"I am Henrietta Stewart, and do not leave the Queen's side, for any man," the Marchioness declared briefly.

"I was sent directly to Her Grace by the King," Heriot said. "I shall leave her presence only if *she* wishes it."

"No!" Anne jerked, surprisingly strongly.

Mary Gray said nothing—but did not move.

"Very well—since it is Her Grace's wish," the Master nodded—and smiled entirely affably at them all. "Here is the letter, Your Grace. As to the Prince Frederick Henry, I know how you wish to have him in your own royal care. His Grace has seen fit to command otherwise. But in the present situation, of your sad sickness and the King's absence, we of the Privy Council who are left in Scotland, deem that His Grace's royal wishes might well bear alteration somewhat, his commands be . . . ameliorated. Perhaps, with your royal permission, I could persuade my friend the Earl of Mar to prevail on his lady mother to deliver to him the Prince, out of Stirling Castle. And he to bring the lad here to Your Grace at Linlithgow. It is admittedly, directly contrary to the King's orders. But I personally, with the Earl of Mar and my lord Chancellor here, would accept responsibility."

The swift indrawing of two breaths, the Queen's and Mary Gray's, drew Heriot's swift glance. With Mary he exchanged meaning looks. When he turned to the Queen, she was eyeing him with an agonised questioning, compounded of both hope and fear. Almost imperceptibly, he shook his head.

There was a tense pause. Then Anne spoke. "No," she whispered. "No. Let him stay . . . where he is." That ended in a sob.

The Master's eyes narrowed, but only for a moment. "As Your Grace wishes of course. But . . . if the Prince knows that you are ill, his mother—and I cannot think that he will not have been told, in merest humanity—then he will be anxious, desirous of seeing Your Highness."

She licked dry lips, her breathing uneven, fevered eyes searching all faces. "No," she got out. "No, no, no! Leave me, Master of Gray. Leave me—in God's name!"

"Go, sir—if you have any humanity of your own!" Lady Huntly cried. "Can you not see how you distress Her Grace?"

The Master bowed deeply. "As you wish, Highness. I but sought your comfort. And that of your family. Should you change your royal mind, I am at your service."

"It was meant for the best, Madam, I assure you," Fyvie asserted—and sounded honest.

Together they backed out of the presence. At the door, the Master's eyes caught George Heriot's, and they were icy cold.

The Queen dissolved into wailing, gulping tears, her weak body racked, and Henrietta threw herself bodily upon her, clutching, kissing, gabbling endearments.

Mary Gray and the man considered each other. "Tell Her Grace that she acted wisely, my lady," Mary said urgently. "For the best. The best for all. I swear it!" Then she gestured with her head towards the door.

Outside in the crowded corridor, with the Master's elegant back disappearing down the far stairway, Mary turned almost as cold a glare as that of her father on Herries the Queen's physician. "Your royal mistress needs your attention, Sir Hugh. I'd counsel you to attend better to Her Grace than to some whom you obey so readily!"

Looking abashed, the plump little doctor bobbed an unhappy bow and hurried within. Alison Primrose, waiting there, was sent in also.

Moving along to a small dressing-room where they could be alone, Mary sighed.

"That was a grievous encounter, Geordie," she said. "And near disaster. A fierce test for the Queen. I esteem her more, I think today, than ever I have done. And it was you she trusted in. Only you."

"We cannot say that. She knows that I am working with you, being guided by you."

"She does not love me. Has always doubted me. Perhaps because the King speaks well of me. So all the greater credit to you. That she trusts you so entirely, on so great an issue."

"The wonder of it—since she *might* well blame me for all her present miscarriage and illness. My advice."

"That would be folly. She may be light-headed but she is not a fool. She proved that."

"Yes. And I fear that I have made a potent enemy of the Master."

She shook her head. "Not of necessity. My father is an ill man to cross. But he does not normally bear grudges. He will fight you, so long as you oppose his plans, fight without scruple. But he will not personally hate you. Indeed he will admire you the more for besting him—and be the more concerned to best you next time! He is a strange man—but not wholly bad."

"It was a cunning move. To get the Prince out of Lady Mar's grip, allegedly into the Queen's but really into his own. This move offers one gleam of hope, I think. It must mean that he is not certain of the old Countess giving up Henry to her son. Else why trouble with this?"

"True. But she told you that she *would*, did she not?"

"She may not have told *him* that. She does not trust him, even though her son does."

The young woman nodded. "And there are more gleams of hope than that, Geordie. This illness of the Queen could be a godsend.

Forcing my father to delay his plot. You have seen the crowds outside the palace. Waiting to hear how the Queen fares. The people. They do not greatly love her, perhaps—for she has never sought their love. But they like her better than the King, for she is gay and generous. And I swear they feel for her as a mother deprived of her children. Now she is ill, they rally to her. No good time, I think, for the Master of Gray to attack her. To pull down her husband and use her son against her. My father will not overlook that—that is partly why he is here today, I am sure. He may not need the people's support, in his plans. But he will not want their opposition, or active wrath. He is far too clever to risk that. So—he seeks to take the Queen with him."

"But this only postpones the issue. Either the Queen gets better, the people forget, and all will be as it was. Or—God forbid—she dies. And his way is clear."

"True. But it gives us time. She will not die, I think. She has recovered from miscarriage before. Time we must use. My father will hold his hand, I believe, while she is gravely sick. So she must seem to remain gravely sick for a time—even if she is truly better."

"While . . . ?"

"While we ask the King to return, with all speed!"

He shook his head. "James will not do that."

"Even if he believes his wife at death's door?"

Heriot spread his hands. "No. I am sure of this. This of the English succession means everything to him. He has lived for it, all these years—as he has *not* lived for Anne of Holstein. He will not turn back, at this stage. For anything."

"Then the man is a monster!"

"Perhaps. Judged in one fashion. But not in another, I think. He is a king. Not as other men. The Lord's Anointed, with the fate of two kingdoms in his hands. He will say 'God's will be done!' and continue on his appointed way. Of that I am sure."

She bowed to his certainty. "Very well. No doubt my father argues likewise. Then we must seek for the next best. To frighten him with the Queen's health, so that he sends a Viceroy back, with complete royal authority to act in all things in the King's name. That could only be Vicky, next heir to the throne after the young princes. He has acted Viceroy before, when James went to Denmark—the only man who has. With Vicky, and a viceroy's authority, we could halt my father."

"Perhaps. But . . . we have already written to the King."

"Not that the Queen is dangerously ill. He surely cannot ignore that altogether. Write to Vicky too. He *wants* to come back. He never wanted to go to London. He would live quietly at Methven with, me, if James would let him."

"That I know is truth. He told me. Very well. We shall write to the King and the Duke. They say that Fyvie has already written. I wonder what *he* said? And we shall seek to keep the Queen feigning illness—even though she betters." He looked at the young woman with mixed feelings, head ashake. "Lord knows where you are leading me, Mary Gray! It is well seen whose daughter you are!"

* * *

It took many days for their urgent courier-borne letters to England to bear fruit, days of anxious waiting, playing a part, fretting—but presumably anxious days for the Master of Gray also, as he waited either for the Queen's state of health to improve, and so not prejudice his programme, or to change her mind about Prince Henry's release. That she seemed to do neither must have been galling in the extreme, as day succeeded day. No signs of betterment emanated from the sick-room, where Anne played her part with a fair realism—and indeed made but slow recovery. What Sir Hugh Herries thought—and told the Master—was not to be known; but he had been joined by two other physicians brought from Edinburgh at Heriot's expense and left in no doubts as to their duty. The Scots people had cause to believe their Queen all but on her death-bed, and discovered for her a new affection and sympathy. Prayers were said for her in every kirk in the land.

Then, late on the evening of 21st May, a hard-riding, spume-flecked, mud-spattered troop of horsemen clattered up the cobbled hill from Linlithgow's Market Square and into the palace courtyard, the royal Lion Rampant of Scotland borne aloft, and Ludovick, Duke of Lennox eased himself wearily out of the saddle, and actually staggered in sheer dizziness on the flagstones, one of his companions indeed falling on one knee in his exhaustion and stiffness. A few moments later, however, Vicky Stewart forgot fatigue, anxiety and certainly dignity, as Mary Gray flung herself into his arms and they clung to each other gasping incoherencies.

It was a while before the Duke was in any state to notice George Heriot standing at his back with a goblet of wine—

although his party was not so slow in perceiving similar proferred restoratives. From an upstairs window the Duchess of Lennox looked down on the scene—but did not seek to intervene at this stage. She and her husband knew precisely where they stood with each other.

"Ha—Geordie!" The Duke took the wine, and gulped a mouthful of it. "I thank you. Good to see you. Am I, am I in time? The Queen . . . ?"

The other nodded.

"And the Prince? And the Master?"

"Nothing yet."

"Thank God! We have killed a dozen horses on our way North."

"Dear Vicky!" Mary murmured. "All but killed yourself, I think! James would not come?"

"No. Did you ever believe that he would? Nothing will turn him back now. I left him at Theobalds, Sir Robert Cecil's house at Hertford. That is the Secretary of State. But a dozen miles out of London. But there is a plague in the city. He will not enter it. He makes for Greenwich, down Thames."

"And have you all necessary authority?"

"The fullest the King could give me. All powers as Viceroy. To see to the Queen. To collect his children. And to conduct them to England just so soon as Anne is able to travel."

"Authority in writing?"

He nodded. "Signed and sealed, my dear. At this moment, I am as good as King in Scotland! Where is your father, Mary Lass?"

"With the Hamiltons, at Kinneil, but three miles away."

"He will know of my arrival here within the hour, then. It would not be beyond him to ride forthwith to Stirling. Tonight. With Mar, or to Mar. As a last throw. To try to take the Prince. Before I can act."

"My thought entirely," Heriot agreed.

"Where is Mar? I do not trust him—never have. At Stirling?"

"He went there, yes. But is now back at Kinneil with my father."

Ludovick nodded, and sighed. "It looks as though I must needs go riding again, Twenty more miles. To Stirling."

"Oh, Vicky!"

"No need," Heriot asserted. "I shall go. Give me a letter. To the Countess. Ordering her, in the King's name, not to give up the Prince to any, even her own son, under pain of highest treason.

Till you come tomorrow. She is a dragon, yes—but with her own honesty. And loyal to King James. She will listen to me, I think—with that authority."

"Very well."

And so, next afternoon, when the King's Viceroy arrived at Stirling Castle, with a great train of nobles, gentry and men-at-arms, the drawbridge was down and at the bridge-end George Heriot stood beside the Dowager Countess of Mar, the Prince Henry and the captain of the guard, to welcome him. Heriot was surprised, to say the least of it, to see the Master of Gray, all gallantry and smiles, close behind the Duke, with the Earl of Mar, less smiling—but then that man seldom smiled, though he could guffaw on occasion. Lord Fyvie was there also; but so were Mary Gray, the Duchess of Lennox, the Earl of Linlithglow and other members of the Queen's household. It was a resplendent company for a notable occasion.

Heriot's rather alarmed glance sought Mary's. She nodded reassuringly.

Considering all the previous contentions and difficulties, everything now went with almost ridiculous smoothness, as though well rehearsed. Trumpeters blew a flourish, the Lord Lyon King of Arms in his gorgeous tabard read out the style and titles of the illustrious Duke of Lennox and declared his viceregal status, and the entire duty of all in the realm, high and low, noble and common, to put themselves under the authority and rule of the said Duke as they would of the King's Grace himself—and held up an impressive parchment with the royal signature and dangling Privy Seal of Scotland as proof. The Master of Gray led the subsequent cheering. Then Ludovick quietly but firmly declared that he had come, on His Grace's express command, to take over the custody and guardianship of Prince Henry Frederick, Duke of Rothesay and heir to the thrones of Scotland, England, Ireland and France, with the Principality of Wales, from the devoted and excellent keeping of the Countess of Mar, acting for her son, John, Earl of Mar here present, Hereditary Keeper of the royal castle and citadel of Stirling, preparatory to his, and Her Grace Queen Anne's departure for London just so soon as Her Grace was fit for the journey. God Save the King!"

When the second round of cheering was over, the Duke dismounted and went to greet the Prince on bended knee, followed by the Chancellor and other great nobles in order of precedence, the Master of Gray coming modestly a long way down the list as mere eldest son of the fifth Lord Gray. This over, and taking the shy boy's hand in his own, Ludovick Stewart held up his other hand and announced that he himself would meantime take up his residence in this castle of Stirling, with the Prince, until the Queen's illness was abated—which, God willing, would not now be long delayed. The trumpeters then blew another fanfare, and Lyon declared that there would be refreshment for all—in the Great Hall for the nobility and gentry, in the inner courtyard for all the others—and pointed to the train of sumpter-horses behind. The cheering developed a new note.

As the entire great company surged on foot up the hill, within the outer ramparts, to the central citadel of the most closely guarded and inviolate fortress in Scotland, almost in wonder, Heriot, well back from the leaders now, found his way to Mary Gray's side.

"The Master?" he demanded. "He has changed his tune, i' faith! Is it some new device? To deceive us?"

"He will deceive us, yes—if he can. But I do not think this to be some cunning new trick. My father has many admirable qualities. One of them is to recognise clearly and swiftly when a tide has turned against him. He does not then waste his time and talents in fruitless pursuit of a lost cause. But promptly acknowledges the position and seeks to make the best of it, to steer it his way if he may. Patrick is no small man—or rogue!"

"So you think that we have won? That the plot is abandoned?"

"Meantime, yes. Only postponed, perhaps. Vicky staying here in the castle will make it impossible for Patrick to contrive anything before the Queen is ready to travel. He will, of course, laugh to scorn any suggestion that there ever was a plot. But that matters nothing, so long as it has failed."

"And the Master goes unscathed?"

"Why, yes. He would not be the Master, otherwise!"

"And you would not be his daughter!"

"Perhaps. I seek to bring to naught his wicked acts—not the man himself."

"You are fortunate in being able so clearly to distinguish one from the other!"

"You blame me? Judge me at fault in this? He is my own flesh and blood." She sounded as though the man's judgment was important to her.

"The good God knows! I do not. What you are saying is that you wish me to go no further in the matter? With the King, or elsewhere?"

"No. Not if you so wish. But I think you would find it . . . difficult. The King will want to hear no more of it, I swear. He is almost as clever as Patrick, you see. He will know when enough is enough. Besides, there will be no proof—Patrick will ensure that. No least hint or whisper to link him with any plot. It could all have been conjecture, could it not? A figment of a woman's foolish imaginings?"

He stared at her, there in the crowd, for a moment, and then smiled. "I pray heaven that I may never fall foul of *both* Grays at the one time!" he said.

In the Hall, with the Duchess present, Mary kept away from the Duke's side and stayed mainly with Heriot. It was not long before her father found his way to them.

"Well, Master Geordie," he said, "This is a happier occasion than at our last meeting. I am only sorry that Her Grace cannot be here. The young Prince is a pleasing child. Good that they will so soon be together again, is it not?"

Heriot was speechless.

"You confuse Master Heriot, Patrick," his daughter said calmly. "We cannot all have your . . . agility!"

"No? I think our friend has his own agility, my dear. Never underestimate quiet, slow-spoken men. What but agility would you name his dash to Stirling here, last night, immediately on Vicky's arrival at Linlithgow. I wonder why he deemed it advisable?"

"Perhaps he feared some plot?"

"Plot? Plots are a thing of the past, Mary. It was James who smelled plots under every bed. Extraordinary! Now he is gone, *we* can forget such childish ploys. It is London's turn!" He shrugged. "But I believe that I know why our friend here made his so urgent dash."

"I dare swear you do!" Heriot agreed firmly.

"Yes. You came because you believed that old Lady Mar might not be prepared to yield up the boy to the Duke. Without some small, h'm, sweetening, shall we say? And so you hurried. And need not have troubled, Master Geordie. For I had already done it for you. Through Johnnie Mar. Knowing that Vicky was coming. A duplication of effort, friend. You should have conferred with me."

"I could describe the situation otherwise, sir!" the other man said shortly. "You say that you *knew* the Duke of Lennox was coming?"

"Why, yes. We wrote to James. At least, I prevailed on Fyvie to do so, for His odd Grace is in no state of mind to pay heed to *me*, at present, I fear. Wrote immediately after the Queen refused to allow the Prince to be brought to her at Linlithgow urging the King to send up Vicky at once in view of the Queen's severe illness and the possibility of a dynastic crisis. Happily His Grace heeded—though not sufficiently to come himself, of course!" He raised his glance. "Now I see the Duchess Jean hungrily seeking whom she may devour. Vicky neglects her shamefully, do you not agree? I shall go placate her, if I may."

As the shapely and assured back moved away from them through the throng, Mary and Heriot eyed each other. And gradually a kind of bemusement gave way to mutual smiles, smiles which grew and broadened to silent laughter.

* * *

It was three weeks later that the royal train entered Edinburgh's West Port to the reverberations of the castle's cannon and the congratulations of the city's Provost and magistrates. The Queen, pale but astonishingly vivacious, sat up in her litter and bowed and waved graciously, Prince Henry and Princess Elizabeth a horse at either side of her—young Charles left behind at Dunfermline with one of his recurring chest troubles. The colourful bevy of the Queen's ladies rode immediately behind, followed by Lennox, the Chancellor and other nobles—but not Mar, whom the Queen still would on no account have anywhere near her. The Master of Gray was there, however, indeed had arranged the entire progress, the mounted musicians and choirs which accompanied it, the tableaux and addresses of loyalty and welcome en route, the excellent commissariat. Even the Queen unbent sufficiently towards him to smile in his direction, devil or none, and admit that he made an excellent master of ceremonies

George Heriot was not in the royal train this time—although he was not far away. With the Queen's affairs now all safely in Lennox's hands he had left Linlithgow a week earlier for Edinburgh to look to his own affairs—and not before time. His half-brother James Heriot was industrious, honest and efficient, but rather lacked the imagination and instinct necessary for really successful dealings with the nobility and aristocracy, where judgment, tact and yet a kind of ruthlessness, were absolutely essential. The move to London, temporary or permanent, on the part of so many of their clients, was making enormous demands on the Heriot's finances, as noble families sought to equip, clothe and adorn themselves to compete at the richer English Court, pay for their long journey, and buy or lease houses in London. A great tide of Scots were flowing southwards, hopeful of making fortunes—but they had to be staked; and the Heriots were themselves having to borrow money on every hand, at high rates of interest, to be able to lend it again at still higher. Disaster could strike so very easily if judgment failed and money was lent to the wrong borrowers. Land, of course, was the great security; and Jinglin' Geordie was in process of becoming one of the great landowners of Lowland Scotland, more by accident than design.

Heriot was waiting at the West Port, behind the Provost and Council—one of whom was brother James, representing the Incorporation of Goldsmiths and Hammermen. Mary Gray spotted him while the address of welcome was going on, and with tableaux to follow and prolonged delay inevitable, dismounted and slipped from her place at the Master's side—she would not ride with Ludovick, of course, the Duchess being present.

"So, Geordie," she greeted, "you came to watch the show. It is good to see you." She had to shout to be heard above the bombilation of the cannon-fire from the castle directly above.

"And you. You are the fairest thing I have seen in seven days!"

"Tut—Geordie Heriot essaying flattery! Why? Do not say that *you* need Mary Gray? Did you get my message? About the new Queen's ladies?"

"Yes. I sent word to have them held at Berwick. Though I think that will scarce be popular! But, if there is to be trouble, let it be over the Border. Where, h'm, trouble-makers cannot add to it!"

"That makes good sense. The Queen is adamant. She will have no more ladies save of her own choosing. Especially English ones."

"It will be difficult. James has sent up the Earls of Sussex and Lincoln with this bevy of countesses and the like. Carefully chosen to play faction against faction, the Cecils against the Howards, Cobham against Raleigh. The old game he learned so well here in Scotland. Nullifying their influence."

"So Vicky told the Queen. But she will have none of it. James can make a political tourney-ground of his own Court, she says—but not of her's. A plague on them all, says Anne! This period away from the King has made her a deal more independent, to be sure. She is a changed woman."

"Scarcely a joyful augury for London!"

They fell silent for the Queen's brief speech of thanks, almost inaudible because of the gunfire. Then the tableaux commenced, angels presenting keys, elves offering gifts, a dragon spewing claret and other typically leaden municipal flights of fancy. At least there were no Latin monologues, *de rigeur* when the King was present.

At last they could move on to Holyrood—although there were further but briefer ceremonies en route, to each of which the Queen listened and responded with unvarying and courteous patience, very different from her royal husband who would have been cursing all angrily long before this.

"Think you that Anne has discovered that perhaps the people's love and esteem can be a thing of value?" Heriot wondered. "She did not used to be so patient."

Holyroodhouse was a different place from Heriot's last experience of it. All was formally correct, decorous, tidy. The guard was evident, punctillious, the staff attendant, discreet. Even Heriot's quarters in the wing had been cleaned up, with some fresh skin rugs and new hangings and items of furniture. The Master of Gray, clearly did not do things by halves. The Lord Lindores seemed to have disappeared.

There followed some days of hectic activity for the royal entourage, in preparation for the great journey to London. Anne was now determined to enjoy the experience and to travel in a style worthy of her position—whatever more modest arrangements Lennox had envisaged, on the King's instructions. The Queen had no idea of economy, and finding herself suddenly in a strong position, with Lennox having a viceroy's powers yet unwilling to say her nay, spent money like water. That it was in the main George Heriot's money, since the Scots Exchequer was emptier than ever after Gray's extravagances, was neither here nor there. That she was egged on to a great spending by the Master of the Wardrobe went almost without saying. She ordered night-and-day work on a most splendid travelling coach to be completed by George Hendry, bought scores of the finest horses to be found in Scotland, and embarked on an orgy of clothes-buying for herself, her children, her ladies and servants. Nothing was too good or too expensive—satins, silks, taffetas, cloth-of-gold and silver, furs, jewellery and accessories. It was all, undoubtedly, partly a counter-gesture after the sorrows of Linlithgow and partly a making of hay while the sun of her husband's absence shone, and his restraining hand was replaced by Cousin Ludovick's easy one.

To be sure, James had partly himself to thank for it all. Queen Elizabeth, parsimonious on most matters to the point of meanness, had been wildly extravagant as to her own personal adornment, and had left behind her, amongst other things, more than two thousand splendid gowns. The King had promptly commandeered a selection of these and sent them up, with his choice of English ladies-in-waiting, for his wife. Anne's reaction had been, perhaps, predictable, exploding in a feminine fury anent cast-off clothing, insults and the like—with the consequence of Heriot's urgent instructions for the English ladies and their escort to be halted at Berwick meantime.

Heriot's own reaction to this spending was ambivalent. He sympathised with his liege lord in the South to some extent, and put in a word of caution now and again, countering the wildest flights of prodigality. On the other hand, he felt for Anne, recognised that to date she had been sorely crimped and held in, and agreed that a queen entering her new and rich domains for the first time should be adequately dressed for the occasion. Also, of course, it was all apt to be good business for himself, a point of view he by no means overlooked. It might be some time before he recovered all his capital—but he would see that it was safe and the interest proportionate.

At last the coach was ready and a start could be made. On a sunny forenoon of early June, the great cavalcade assembled in the forecourt of the palace, with the Chancellor, the Lord Lyon and remaining Privy Councillors and officers of state, the leaders of the Kirk, the city fathers of Edinburgh and a large part of the townsfolk, there to see the Queen and Prince off to a new life in England—the Princess Elizabeth was unfortunately confined to her bed with some sudden childish ailment and would follow on later; while Prince Charles was still at Dunfermline, considered too weakly for the long journey.

It was a felicitous occasion. None would have thought that, only a few weeks before, the country had been in the throes of a dynastic crisis and treasonable plot combined, moreover with all the main characters concerned here foregathered—except the Mars, that is, the Earl having ridden off alone to London, to ensure that he got his own story first into his royal foster-brother's ear.

Lord Fyvie made a valedictory speech, ending with a short poem he had composed especially for the day—it was not every Chancellor who could do the like. Then the Master of Gray presented parting gifts for the Queen and her children, jewellery, loving-cups and silver caskets, expressing in flowing eloquence the warm regards and true love of all, including his most humble self, for their royal mistress and her delightful offspring, and their profoundest good wishes for the future—praying only that in the new-found bliss in the South they would not forget leal and loving Scotland.

"Her Grace perhaps has not got quite such a short memory as your sire implies!" Heriot observed to Mary Gray, as he stood with her and Alison Primrose, watching from a suitably retired position. "I wonder where the money came from for those gifts?"

"Not from Patrick Gray's coffers, you may be sure. Nor yet, this once, from George Heriot's. But it is a good sign—my father covering up any lingering memories of a supposed plot, the royal family's most faithful servant!"

"You think the plot quite abandoned. There is still Prince Charles left in Scotland. Might not *he* serve as puppet King of Scots, instead?"

"I think not. He is too sickly and feeble. Fyvie believes that he will not live. He would be no use for Patrick's purposes—disaster if he died in his hands. No, I believe that plot is dead, and now being effectively buried. But my father will yet have his revenge on the King, if he can—nothing surer. So I will watch closely here in Scotland—and do you so in London, Geordie. Patrick will have his minions there also, you may be sure." Mary was not travelling South with Lennox—of her own sorrowful but sure decision. The Duchess was going, inevitably, part of the Queen's train. Moreover, Mary had her young son to look after at Methven Castle, little John Stewart of Methven, to whom his ducal father had made over his Scottish home and lands—in reality as a gift to his mother. Ludovick would hasten North from London just as frequently as he could, that was certain; and, who knew, once James was well settled on his English throne, he might well have less need of Lennox, and he could come back to Scotland more or less permanently.

And so formal farewells were taken, and amidst more cannonade the royal column set out from Holyroodhouse, the great coach creaking and rumbling, drawn by eight matching white horses, George Heriot and Alison Primrose riding together well in the rear of the brilliant company. The Chancellor and many of the nobles would see the Queen on her way as far as the Border.

But not Patrick Gray, he already had a bellyful of Berwick-upon-Tweed. As they watched the others go, he and his daughter turned and exchanged a long glance.

"As our beloved monarch would say—*absens haeres non erit*!" the man observed conversationally.

"Or again, perhaps—*aut non tentaris aut perfice*!" she capped it.

"My clever daughter!" he acknowledged, bowing. "If you and I could but work in harness, what might not we achieve?"

* * *

After an overnight halt at the Hamilton castle of Innerwick, they came to Berwick on a dove-grey, windless noon, to more cannon-fire—and a confrontation. Here, George Heriot moved up the column discreetly, near to the Queen's side, where Lennox welcomed him thankfully. For here, held back from Edinburgh, waited the already offended Earls of Sussex and Lincoln, with the Countesses of Worcester and Kildare, and the Ladies Scrope, Rich and Walsingham, sent North by King James. With the newly knighted governor, Sir William Selby, they waited in a brilliant group at the Scots Gate of the old grey-walled town.

Anne, who had been at her most gracious all the way, bowing and waving to the people, beaming on loyal demonstrations, kissing children, at sight of this party, and of the canopied horse-litter, splendid with the royal arms, which accompanied them, froze in her saddle—for she had quickly found coach-travel on bumpy, dusty roads uncomfortable in the early June heat, and reverted to horseback like the rest of the company. As they reined up only a short distance in front of the bowing magnificos, she called, in clear, ringing tones, "Who are these, Duke of Lennox? Not Berwickers, I vow! I told you—I will have no more women imposed upon my household by His Grace, or any other. I have had a sufficiency of that!"

"H'rr'mm." Lennox cleared his throat. "It is a welcome, Highness . . ."

The Earl of Sussex intervened smoothly, but authoritatively as befitted one in blood relationship to the late Elizabeth. "We warmly greet Your Majesty, on His Majesty's royal commands, to this your kingdom of England, the fairest jewel of Christendom's crown, opened like a pearl-oyster for your royal delectation. A pearl without price set in a silver sea, to which nothing you have ever seen may compare. To ascend this jewelled throne is a bliss beyond all sublime . . ."

"Your rhapsody, sir, does you credit—but I think you exaggerate!" the Queen broke in briskly. "How know you that your England is so much better than other lands? Have you visited them all? You came to Scotland, yes, for my son's christening—where, I would remind you, I have been Queen for a dozen years! Did you mislike it so? And have you been to Denmark? To Norway, where my brother is King. Speak to that which you know, my lord."

Sussex was far too great an English nobleman to look put out, but he could and did look pained. "I rejoice that at least Your Majesty recognised me, Sussex," he declared stiffly. "And this is my lord Earl of Lincoln, Henry Clinton, member of the Privy Council and valued servant of Her late Majesty. And here is the Countess of Worcester and the Countess of Kildare, appointed Your Majesty's principal Ladies-in-Waiting by King James. And the Ladies Scrope, Rich and Walsingham, also of your new household . . ."

"No, my lord," Anne said briefly.

He stared. They all did.

"I . . . I do not understand, Madam?"

"I would have thought it sufficiently simple, sir. I choose my own ladies."

"But . . . His Majesty . . ."

"I do not seek to help choose the King's gentlemen for him!"

The other earl, Lincoln, an older man, spoke up. "Majesty—these ladies only desire to serve you. They are of the most eminent in England."

"No doubt, sir. Or, leastways, serve the King. I thank them—but have my own ladies. If I wish to add to their number, I shall make my own choice."

The youngest of the waiting ladies, a dark-haired, vivid creature, tried a different approach. "Majesty—I am Frances Howard, daughter to Effingham—or Nottingham, as he now is—the Lord Admiral. Wed formerly to Kildare. We have brought with us a great store of the late Queen's gowns, dresses, robes for your use. Rich clothing of notable worth. I was Her Majesty's Mistress of the Wardrobe."

"Indeed, Countess? And you conceive me, Anne, to be the repository for your late mistress' cast-off clothes?" the Queen asked, coldly. "Must I, your Queen, wear another's discarded wardrobe? 'Fore God, woman—watch how you speak!"

"No, Madam—no! I swear that is not the way of it." The Countess looked shaken. "Believe me, these are not cast-off. Many have never been worn. Her Majesty was, was improvident in this. She ordered great numbers of gowns, three of a kind most frequently. Wore one once and discarded the others . . ."

"So may a queen behave. If Elizabeth, why not Anne? Am I to play the frugal hausfrau of this so rich jewel of Christendom's crown, to make up for Elizabeth's improvidence?"

"Not so, Majesty. But . . ."

"Your Highness," the older Countess of Worcester intervened hurriedly, "these gowns are very splendid. Seeded with pearls, hung with jewels, decked with gold and silver . . ."

"Were they laden with the riches of the Indies, I would not wear another's clothes!" Anne declared. "I am the Queen."

A little back from her side, George Heriot coughed. "Your Grace—these gowns may have their uses," he suggested, in a murmur. "You need not *wear* them. You could bestow them as gifts. Cut up, they might serve many purposes. As at masques and entertainments. The jewels you could have cut off. Used otherwise. Jewels are never at second-hand—as I should know! Indeed, you could perhaps sell them to me! And thereby, h'm, something improve our account!" That was little more than a whisper.

"Ah," Anne said.

"Master Heriot speaks good sense, Cousin," Lennox put in, lightly confidential. "You could start by giving one of the gowns to me! I swear I'd find a use for it! I am not so rich that I could not do with a few English pearls."

"You have a rich wife, Vicky."

Lennox glanced round to see how near was his Duchess. "Jean's riches are her own, Cousin, not mine."

"Very well," the Queen decided. "I accept the gowns. See you to them, Master Geordie. But—I will have no ladies-in-waiting other than my own choice. All understand it."

Sussex bowed. "As you will, Majesty. Now—may I present to

you your Chamberlain, Sir George Carey," and he waved a hand towards a resplendent youngish man, of a pale beauty, standing a little apart. "Son to my Lord Hunsdon, in cousinship to Her late Majesty, and brother to Lady Scrope here . . ."

"God's death, sirrah!" the Queen exploded. "Have you taken leave of your wits! *There* is my Chamberlain, Sir John Kennedy, riding behind me."

"The King, Madam . . ."

"The King is in London—and I am here! Remember it, my lords. Enough of this. Vicky—we have lingered sufficiently long. Have our train move on. Bestow these, these emissaries from His Grace somewhere. They may join us. But not over close to my person! Let us be on our way . . ."

Anne of Denmark's crossing of the Border was almost as dramatic as her husband's own—and just as alarming for her English subjects.

6

THE QUEEN'S SWOOLLEN cavalcade reached Windsor, in the Thames valley, on the last day of June, after a leisurely progress down through England. If King James's entourage had increased on *his* southwards journey to his alarm and disapproval—because of the cost—it was as nothing to Anne's enlarged company. Expanding at York, Worksop, Nottingham, Leicester, Althorp, Grafton and the rest, by the time Amersham was reached the party had become an army, a great sprawling host that covered the land for many miles, its progress inevitably slower and slower. Heriot counted no fewer than two hundred and fifty carriages now, following the Queen's, and assessed those on horseback to be not far off five thousand.

It was largely Anne's own doing. After the contretemps at Berwick, she had apparently decided to change her tune somewhat. Or, more probably, it was always her intention to present a gracious and amiable front to her husband's new subjects, and only James's appointments to her household upset her. At any rate, thereafter, all the long road southwards she was at her kindest and most friendly, delighting all who gathered to greet and entertain her, lavish with gifts, accessible, patient, charming—and obviously welcoming the popularity indicated by the ever-enlarging of her train. If she did not actually urge lords and ladies, knights and squires and their females to follow her to London, she certainly did not discourage them, nor would allow the apprehensive Lennox and Heriot to do so. The Duchess of Lennox declared that she was doing it deliberately to spite her husband, that the King might see how popular she was with the people—and that she might cost him as much as possible of the money he valued so highly.

Admittedly she did not thaw much towards the illustrious group which had met her at Berwick, keeping them rather at arm's length —to their great offence; but that clearly was also more of a gesture to James, that her days of being a pawn for him to move at will, were over. A new start was being made, for her equally with himself. And that the English in general should not be offended, she made much of the Countess of Bedford, Lucy Russell, whom she picked up at Woburn, young, lively and of a ready wit, grand-neice of Sir Philip Sidney, with her protégé Ben Jonson, a notable deviser of plays and masques.

At Amersham in Buckinghamshire, envoys from the King met the entourage, to change its course to Windsor. The hot summer weather was exacerbating the plague in London and people were dying like flies. King James would by no means set royal foot in his new capital in these circumstances and was having to postpone his coronation in consequence. Instead, as a sort of stop-gap, he was going to hold a great investiture of the Order of the Garter at Windsor Castle, the Order's seat. The Queen and her suite were commanded to hasten there with all speed—for His Majesty had expected her to have arrived long ere this—as the Prince Henry was necessary to the occasion, to be installed as one of the new knights.

Anne, nettled that it was apparently her son rather than herself whom the King was anxious to see, agreed to turn the column due southwards to Windsor but firmly refused to hurry; indeed she seemed to go even more slowly, spending more time over wayside receptions and the like—to the increasing concern of Lennox and others.

In this spirit the vast concourse descended upon the lovely and sylvan vale of Thames on an afternoon of scorching heat. Unfortunately, at this stage, James sent to meet them, of all people, John Earl of Mar and young Sir John Ramsay, chief page—a move scarcely well received. Mar at least had the wit not to address the Queen personally, bowing distantly to her from the saddle—and receiving not so much as a flicker of an eyelid in response. Ramsay, one of the King's pretty boys—though a vicious one, who dirked to death the Ruthven brothers at Gowrie House three years before—was left to address flowery greetings to Anne, and got little better acknowledgment.

Mar reined round beside Lennox. "God, man!" he said in his choleric way, "What's this? An invasion? James will take ill out o' it—he will so. Where did you get a' these? This host? Aye—and where have you been? You were expected days back. A week and mair."

Ludovick did not often play the duke, but he did not like Mar and conceived him a bad influence with the King. "I think you forget yourself, my lord," he said stiffly. "Her Grace does not have to account to you for her actions. Nor do I."

"Humph! Hoity-toity!" Mar growled. "You'll no' bide that way long, Lennox. No, nor the Queen either! I warn you, James is right displeased. Hot, he is. You'll discover it."

"Then he ought not to be, sir. Unless someone has been poisoning his mind! He has his wife and son safely here—when she was at death's door, and the boy in danger of being taken and set up as King of Scots against him. James should be a thankful man—and I will tell him so. And small thanks to you!"

"The laddie was held safe in my castle, was he no'?"

"The thing could be described otherwise!"

The Earl of Mar removed himself to more congenial company.

George Heriot and Alison Primrose—who, despite twenty-five years discrepancy in age, had become close allies on the prolonged journey—watched this charade from behind.

"I fear our pleasant easeful dallying is over, Alison," the man said. "Now for the reckoning."

"The reckoning may have its own amusements, Geordie," she pointed out. "The Queen has discovered her hardihood. Aye, and much more. She may hold her own. It will be as good as a play-acting. I vow! Holy Matrimony and the Lord's Anointed!"

"You are an irreverent child!" he asserted. "Is nothing sacred to you?"

"Much," she conceded. "But not this royal comedy of the Lion and the Unicorn!"

"Ha!" he said. "The Lion and the Unicorn! That is an apt title, to be sure. England's lion and Scotland's unicorn—with the unicorn rampant! Yet—which is which, in fact? Which the noble beast and which the laughable creature that never was!"

"Ask His Grace himself, some time," that shrewd juvenile suggested lightly. "Our learned liege might be the only one who could tell you, I think."

As the head of the cavalcade wound its way through the narrow streets of Windsor town, Anne chose to ride a saddle-horse between Lennox and his sister Hetty. Ahead, the huge mass of the castle dominated all, not in soaring aloofness like Stirling or Edinburgh on their rocks, but crowning a slight eminence in sheer, massive bulk and serried, towered masonry. The newcomers could not but be impressed.

At the great new gatehouse to the Lower Ward, built by the late King Henry Eighth, before a large and colourful concourse of fine folk, two thrones had been erected on a dais covered with cloth-of-gold. Higher, behind these on the sloping ramp, were grouped all the English great officers of state, from the Lord Chancellor and Lord Chief Justice to the Garter King of Arms and the principal Secretary of State, Sir Robert Cecil. But the King was not sitting enthroned amongst all this array of resplendent dignity; he was hobbling up and down and around, not on the dais at all, leaning on the shoulder of a long-haired, handsome young man, with the other hand wielding a long white stick, almost as tall as himself, beribboned and with a golden ferule. James was very fond of this stick, despite its donor—the Master of Gray had in fact brought it to him from France—but in the present circumstances it was something of a menace to all concerned, even to its royal wielder, all but tripping him up time and again. But he found it convenient to poke with while he waited—for passive waiting was anethema to James Stewart. So he hobbled about and poked, poked at dignified men's feet, at fine ladies' ankles, even higher on occasion—for he was a man of catholic interests—at the heralds' tabards and Yeomen of the Guard's halberds. He muttered panted pleasantries as he poked, panted because he was puffing and sweating profusely in the heat. Everyone was hot, but James was hottest, his heavily-stuffed and padded clothing ensuring that. Always the King's clothes made him look twice the size he was, so filled were they with padding as protection against the thrusts of cold steel, the thought of which ever haunted him.

He had found an interesting thing to poke at, the loose silver shoe-buckle of a Yeoman of the Guard which made a pleasant clinking sound and delightfully embarrassed its wearer, when the Queen's procession turned into the wide forecourt from the street. At the arranged sign from the Garter King, the ranked trumpeters raised their gleaming instruments and blew a mighty fanfare. James, wholly preoccupied with what he was doing and unprepared, all but leapt out of his bejewelled, slashed and padded doublet at the sudden blast. His high ostrich-feathered hat was knocked askew and the stick fell with a clatter—posing another agonising problem for the unfortunate Yeoman, whether to stoop and pick up the King's staff or to retain a suitably stiff and upright stance. The Earl of Southampton—on whom the King was leaning—it was who retrieved the stick, while in stammering choler James turned and shook his freed fist at the musicians.

The waiting company stood spellbound.

The Queen, with Lennox and Lady Huntly, rode up—with Mar and Ramsay trying to edge in from behind. The trumpets ended with a flourish and fell silent, and for a moment there was no sound but the horses' scraping hooves.

"Yon was a right coarse noise!" the monarch snarled, into the hush. "We are displeased. Right displeased." He still had his trembling back to his newly-arrived royal consort. He turned, making no move either forward to greet his wife or back to his throne. "Annie," he said, "you're late. Fell late."

She inclined her head slightly, with great dignity, and said nothing.

James looked up at her from under down-drawn brows. "You should have been here days agone. We've been waiting on you." Southampton tried to back out from under the royal grip, but could not.

Still the Queen stared straight ahead of her at the ranked notables.

Lennox hurriedly dismounted and bowed low. "Your Majesty's impatience to see your royal consort is very understandable, Sire," he declared, "but Her Grace has been grievously ill. It would have been most unwise to travel more hastily."

"You speak when you're spoken to, Vicky Stewart!" the King said. "We have been kept waiting. It wasna suitable." The rebuke delivered, James was prepared to show generosity. "You look well enough now, Annie. Aye, healthy. I've never see you look weller."

"I thank Your Grace," she answered stiffly.

"Majesty, Annie—I'm Majesty now. Aye, and you too. Yon Grace is done wi'." He peered up at her. "So the bairn died?"

"Miscarried," she corrected him. "It was I who almost died."

"I'ph'mmm. Stravaiging about the country, I'm told, when you should ha' been biding still. To Stirling, heh? Blameworthy, aye blameworthy."

"The blame for my miscarriage lies with the Countess of Mar who refused to let me see my son. On *your* orders, she said!"

"Ooh, aye. Well, we'll no' go into that the now. But—get down, woman! I'm getting a right crick in my craig looking up at you! Down, I say."

There was a hasty dismounting all around, Lennox aiding the Queen to alight, the process drawing James's attention to something of the great size of her following.

"Guidsakes—what's a' this?" he demanded. "This, this multitude and numerosity! Who a God's name are they a'? These folk. What do they want?"

"To present their loyal duty to Your Majesty," Lennox put in hastily. "Your faithful and honest subjects. Er, English ones. Seeking the, h'm, sun of your royal presence. Her Majesty has been picking them up all the way through England . . ."

"Waesucks—then she shouldna! Mouths—mouths to feed! I'm Christ's Vice-Regent, yes—but it's no' for me to feed the five thousand!" James managed a complacent smirk at that example of his quick wit—but quickly reverted to a frown. "It isna right. You'll hae to get rid o' them, Vicky Stewart. A, a plague o' locusts, just."

"I told them, Majesty," the Earl of Mar declared, now well forward. "I said you'd no' be pleased . . ."

"James," Anne intervened coldly, "instead of miscalling your good subjects, who see fit to show their loyalty and affection for your Queen, ought not you to be greeting your own children, Frederick and Elizabeth, who have journeyed all this way to see their father?" Princess Elizabeth had recovered of her ailment and caught up with the rest in the North of England.

"Ummm," the King said. "Och, well. Aye, then—where are they, in a' this clamjamphrie? If you hadna brought sae many folk, I'd see them easier . . ."

Heriot and Alison Primrose brought forward the two children, bowing low.

"Och, is that yoursel', Geordie. Aye, man—it's good to see you. Though mind you, I've a wheen bones to crack wi' you, just the same! But later. And who's this?"

"Your fine son and heir, Sire, the Duke of Rothesay. And his sister, the Princess Elizabeth."

"Sakes, man—d'you think I dinna ken my ain bairns! It's this bit lassie wi' the bold eye. Aye, right bold!"

"The Mistress Alison Primrose, one of Her Majesty's Maids-in-Waiting, daughter of the Clerk to the Privy Council . . ."

"Hech—that cock-sparrow! Jamie Primrose. Aye, and cock's the word, heh, wi' a' the brood he's faithered!" The King hooted. "So—this is one o' *his* gets? Cocky too, eh?" Then Majesty recollected. "But—where's the Kildare woman? I sent her to take charge o' the lassie, Elizabeth. Where is she? Aye, and where's Sussex and Lincoln. And Carey? I dinna see *them* in a' this stramash."

"The Countess of Kildare is somewhere in my royal train, James. I did not require her services," Anne announced thinly. "Nor that of the lords you mention. Now—I humbly suggest that Your Majesty recognises your own royal offspring, the Prince Frederick . . ."

"Och, I recognise them fine. They've grown much—the laddie in especial. Dinna stand gawking there, bairns—come and kiss your daddy's hand. It's the least you can do, in front o' a' these folk." James, in truth, did not greatly like children—unless slightly older boys—finding them embarrassing. However, after the pair had kissed his hand—and involuntarily recoiled at its ingrained dirt, for the King believed water on the skin to be unnatural and dangerous and only permitted an occasional wiping of his fingertips—he patted his son on the head and, having trouble with his stick, picked up the little girl in his arms—so that Southampton escaped at last. "Och, Bessie, eh? No' an ill-favoured wench. Heh—Harry! Harry Wriothesley—you there, man. What think you—she'll outshine her mother one o' these days, eh?"

Southampton coughed. "If she equals Her Majesty some years hence, it will be more, I make bold to say, than any other princess on earth will do!"

James looked at his current favourite pityingly, and turned back to his stiffly-standing wife, setting down the child and shooing her away. "This o' Sussex and Lincoln. And the Kildare. I dinna like the sound o' this."

"Then it can be discussed later, I think, Sire," Anne declared. "Here is scarce the place." She nodded towards the serried ranks of berobed and glittering officers and dignitaries behind the thrones. "Perhaps I should be informed who are all these?"

"Eh?" James turned. He had rather forgotten the welcoming hierarchy, now looking distinctly limp and jaded in the hot sun. "Och, these are a' the English," he said. "Yon's Cecil, wi' the crooked back. And the wee fat man's Popham that they ca' the Lord Chief Justice—as though *I* wasna the Lord Chief Justice o' my realm! And him that's glowering there like a Hielant stot—that's Coke, the Attorney-General. A fell man, yon. Aye, and there's

Egerton, the Lord Chancellor. And Suffolk, another o' thae Howards, that's Lord Chamberlain. And Nottingham, a Howard too, that's the Admiral. Och, and a wheen mair. A' wi' great swollen heads—aye and swollen noses too, to talk through! Auld Elizabeth fair let them get above themsel's. I hae my hands full, wi' these critturs—but, guidsakes, I'll tame them! Think they're the salt o' the earth, stick their bit chins in the air—and havena' the rudiments o' wit and learning. They'd scarce muster a Latin paradigm between them! O' statecraft they've none, and the strategy o' nations no notion. Only of wars wi' Spain and France—war, the resort o' fools! Och, Cecil's got a sort o' cunning and manoeuvre mind and a smooth tongue—*blandae mendacia linguae*! But I'll teach them. Jamie Stewart will be their dominie—ooh aye!" He paused, panting with all this eloquence in the heat, and glancing sidelong at the uncomfortable Southampton to see how he took it. Then, in case these disclosures might seem to imply a weakening of his displeasure with his wife, he frowned. "Och, well—we'd better awa' up to thae chairs. There'll be talking through long noses, and speeches where you ken every next word! Come on, Harry." And resuming Southampton's shoulder, he shambled up towards the twin thrones, leaving Anne to find her own way.

Hurriedly, Lennox moved up to offer his arm and escort the Queen. After a momentary hesitation, Heriot and Alison brought forward the children. Garter King gave the signal for another fanfare.

Belatedly the official welcome proceeded, with addresses, presentations, ceremonial, the Queen gracious, James looking impatient, tapping his shoe-toe and stick on the ground, and the children whispering behind the thrones. The sun beat down.

At last the King could stand it no longer. Abruptly he got to his feet, waving his stick. "Enough!" he cried. "It's ower hot. I'm right tired. Enough's plenty. Ha' done, in God's name!"

"But, Sire!" Garter King, who acted master of ceremonies, protested. "The presentation. To the Prince of Wales, to be . . ."

"Prince o' Wales? Who's that?"

The herald choked. "Why, Sire—your son. The King of England's heir, if a son, is always Prince of Wales . . ."

"No' till I make him so, man!"

"Of course, Sire. Lacking the official ceremony. But in courtesy . . ."

"See you—I've told you all. I'm no' King o' England. Leastways, I am, but that's no' my title and style. My throne is that o' the United Kingdom o' Great Britain and Ireland. Wi' France if you like—though yon's a nonsense. I'll hae no limiting me to this England, d'you hear?"

"Yes, Majesty. To be sure."

"Aye. And the laddie's Prince o' Scotland, Duke o' Rothesay, Earl o' Carrick and Baron Renfrew. Is that no' plenty, at nine years?"

"As Your Majesty wishes. And the Prince's presentation . . . ?"

"Can wait. Harry Wriothesley—where are you? Your arm, man. My lords and gentles—I'll see you later. Aye, later. Or at the Investiture the morn. Annie—come you." And the audience very much over, the monarch stalked off, tap-tapping, uncertain as to footwork but very definite as to purpose, the illustrious, hierarchial ranks parting hastily to give him passage on his way into the castle proper. There was some competition amongst the highest nobles as to who was to be the Queen's escort, Lennox brushed aside.

"There goes the Coadjutor of the Almighty!" that young man observed, low-voiced to his friend Heriot. "By the Grace of God master of us all. Save, perhaps, his Annie!"

"But master of this England, too, I note! I said it would be the English who would have to change, not James. These haughty grandees of Elizabeth's Court will resist and struggle, but they but batter their proud heads against our liege lord's stuffed doublet! They cannot win. For he is entirely sure of his divine right to be master, and so is unshakeably sustained, requiring to concede nothing—therefore conceding only when it pleases him to do so."

"Yet he concedes more to *you* than to most men, Geordie!"

"Only because I require nothing from him. Not even the payment of his debts!"

"A strong position, yes. And Anne? Has she reached that good position also, think you? She is a changed woman, since her illness."

"It may be so. I think that she has chosen, now, to be queen indeed, but no longer wife. And she is a determined woman. James will have to come to some sort of terms with her—the only one he must. Anne is learning, I swear, that she is in a stronger position in England than ever she was in Scotland."

"You think deeply in that long Edinburgh head of yours, Geordie!"

"I must needs sum up my customers, my lord Duke!"

* * *

The Garter Investiture the next day, 2nd July 1603, was a great success, at least as far as King James was concerned—though the Garter King and the Prelate, the Bishop of Winchester, on whom the ceremonial depended, tended to have their brows deep furrowed throughout. But that was a small matter. James had his own ideas, of course, as to how such affairs should be conducted, and if this was apt to clash with the traditional arrangements, that was unfortunate for the upholders of the latter. After all, this was a new dispensation. James enjoyed arranging things.

Garter—and not only he—was shaken from the start by the unexpected inclusion of the young Earl of Southampton in the knights to be invested, but the King insisted. James had only met Harry Wriothesley a few weeks before when, despite the plague in London, he had paid a fleeting visit to the Tower—by river, which he was assured was safer—to see and evaluate the Crown Jewels kept there, a matter much on his mind. While therein, he had received a pathetic plea from the young Southampton to let him glimpse the sun of his royal presence and lighten the gloomy cell to which he was confined on King James's behalf, even for a moment. The Earl had, in fact, been involved in the late Essex's abortive rebellion against Elizabeth, when that disgraced favourite had proposed that James should enter England in 1601, at the head of an army, and insist from strength in being recognised as the Queen's successor—a plot for which Essex lost his head and Southampton went to the Tower. James, not ungrateful and always interested in young men, had acceded, and down in the grim cell was greatly struck, indeed his heart wrung, by the other's pale beauty, delicate air and sad state. On the spot he had ordered a special pardon, coupled with a command to appear forthwith at Court. Progress had been phenomenally rapid thereafter—to the distress of certain young Scots, notably Sir John Ramsay and Dand Kerr. Now the Garter was to compensate him for all his sufferings.

There were other reasons for the King's good humour, on his fine throne in the choir of the magnificent St. George's Chapel. The Duke of Würtemburg, a huge and coarse, red-faced German, was the first foreign royalty to visit the English Court on a tour of Europe since the accession, and James found his bibulous, bawdy company much to his taste. He also must have the Garter; King Christian of Denmark, Anne's brother, was to have it too, but in absentia. The Earl of Pembroke, who had also been imprisoned by Elizabeth—but for getting her Maid of Honour and favourite Mary Fitton with child, not rebellion—was the fourth knight. Then there was Vicky Stewart, who certainly did not deserve the honour, but as the only duke in two kingdoms could hardly be denied it. Finally, there was Henry himself, on the young side perhaps but as heir to the throne not to be outshone by his cousin Vicky.

The King, Würtemburg and Lennox had been hunting in Windsor Great Park from 5.30 that morning—an hour far too early for Southampton who required his beauty-sleep—and had killed no fewer than seventeen fine bucks—a further source of congratulation. James and the German had been drinking steadily in consequence and celebration, since returning, and were now both in excellent trim for services of praise, thanksgiving and initiation, Würtemburg indeed at the singing stage, joining in lustily with the Dean of Windsor's chants and intonations—and not only in the responses—while his host, eye-catching in stuffed cloth-of-gold, scarlet and purple, slapped his padded thigh and hooted, in sheer and hospitable delight. The colourful but slightly stodgy ceremony had never gone so merrily before.

James was particularly pleased with young Henry Frederick's manly behaviour and appearance—even though his Garter robes and feathered bonnet were on the large side, there having been insufficient time for proper measurements and fittings. He made his bows to the high altar, under the enormous stained glass window which filled the entire eastern gable-end of St. George's Chapel, with the greatest dignity—sufficiently for the King to cry out in ringing tones for all concerned to note the fact. At his side, Anne did not know whether to look proud of her son or ashamed of her husband.

The music played by the company of mixed musicians was the King's own addition to the programme, and he felt that it livened things up nicely. James was not really musical, but he could appreciate a well-going rhythm, something with a good beat to it, to which he could thump in time. Beating time here was difficult, the gold ferule of his stick tending to slither on the tesselated marble flooring, and the skreik when that happened set the teeth on edge. The choir of singing boys' contribution was a poor second—and all the priestly yowlings were, of course, a bore.

The procession thereafter, with all the existing Garter knights leaving their splendid heraldic stalls to join their five new colleagues in parade after the hobbling Sovereign of the Order, was perhaps the best of it, with the musicians playing a lively tune, and Würtemburg all but dancing, with rousing hochs-hochs. Not all entered so enthusiastically into the spirit of the thing, but such as could do so declared it the most interesting Investiture they had ever attended.

Unfortunately a good day was spoiled for the King at the end of it when, after the great banquet in St. George's Hall, James settled down to some hard drinking, with a selection of his entourage—nearly all Scots—with Würtemburg already under the table and snoring. The Queen and her ladies retired—and not only her ladies. Quite a number of the men, who knew themselves to be unable or unwilling to keep up with their liege lord's thirst, elected to go with her, including two of the new Knights Garter, Lennox and Southampton. James had been disappointed when the latter asked to be excused, but the young man had clearly already more wine in him than he could comfortably carry; besides, there were plenty of young but hardened topers left available—it seemed to be a fact that the Scots were more seasoned to strong drink than were their southern fellow-subjects. John Ramsay was only too glad to take Southampton's place at the King's side, with James Hay eager to replace him should his capacity fail.

In the Queen's palatial withdrawing-room there was soft music, sweetmeats and dalliance for those not yet ready for bed. Here a suddenly and totally different atmosphere prevailed, feminine, lightsome, though far from innocent. Laughter tinkled instead of hooted, wit became delicate rather than ponderous—although no less spicy—and Anne proceeded to demonstrate that England might well be going to have an alternative Court to the King's.

Oddly enough, it was Anne herself who precipitated the trouble. Undoubtedly, although she pretended to ignore, or at least put up with her husband's fondness for good-looking young men, in fact she resented it fiercely. The latest addition to the string hardly commended himself to her. When she saw Harry Wriothesley, Lord Southampton paying elaborate attentions to Alison Primrose, she rallied him shrewdly—to George Heriot's entire satisfaction.

"Ha—spare my little Scots innocent, my lord," she called, above the liquid notes of a lute. "I vow you are mighty catholic in your affections! Have you not had sufficient for one night?"

"Could I ever have sufficient of so great beauty, wit and kindness, Majesty?" the other returned, nothing abashed if slightly thick in speech.

"With your capacity for, h'm, variety, sirrah, perhaps not. But I must needs watch for my poor lambs of Maids-in-Waiting, since I understand that you have an especial weakness for such!"

A titter of amusement went round the great chamber, at least from the English courtiers—for Southampton had got two of Elizabeth's Maids-of-Honour into trouble, and the old Queen had forced him to marry the second one. The man had the grace to deepen his flush.

"In Your Highness's presence, all other women are safe from Harry Wriothesley," he gave back boldly, nevertheless.

The Queen's eyes narrowed, since that might be interpreted in two ways, in the circumstances. "In that case, my lord, it behoves me to keep good watch on you, does it not? I shall ask my good friend Geordie Heriot, there, to maintain an eye on you. He is good at that—and moreover has an interest in the matter of Mistress Alison, I think!"

That retiring man gulped in surprise and some confusion—first at thus being unexpectedly singled out and brought into the discussion, and secondly at the Queen's casual linking of his name with that of the Primrose girl, and the roguish glance that went with it. He coughed, embarrassed, bowed briefly and said nothing. Alison laughed cheerfully.

The new Knight of the Garter did not so much as spare a glance for Heriot. Goldsmiths and money-lenders only entered his world within very clearly defined limits. "You must take your due precautions, Madam," he said easily. "It will but make the chase the more to my taste!"

"Take care then, sir, lest my precautions follow those of Her late Majesty—who clapped you in the Tower, did she not?"

Southampton forbore to smile at that. "Such would require *His* Majesty's decision—and he has proved that he thinks better of me, has he not?" That was quick, almost sharp. "His Majesty knows his true friends."

"And you are one of these, my lord?"

"I proved it, with my lord of Essex. And others."

"Ah, yes. But my lord of Essex is dead. And the others—where are they?"

"Not here, to be sure." Quite noticeably, suddenly, the atmosphere of idle banter had changed for something more serious.

Southampton looked around the company, and his thin mouth turned down at the corners. "I see none here—or in the hall back there—who elected to aid King James *then*!"

As some quick breaths were indrawn, Heriot exchanged glances with Lennox, these two recognising all too clearly that this was now verging on dangerous politics, certainly not to be advised. The Duke took a step forward, seeking to catch the Queen's eye.

But Anne, amongst her many virtues, counted neither tact nor great forbearance, and once embarked on a course she was hard to stop.

"Who are these good friends, my lord?" she pressed. "And if they exist, indeed, why did they achieve so little. Essex's attempt came to nothing."

"There were not a few. And in high positions. But we were betrayed. The Cecils, Coke . . ."

Lennox interrupted. "My lord—let us have no talk of politics and statecraft here. In the Queen's drawing-room."

"Her Majesty asked me, my lord Duke."

Anne bit her lip, annoyed at the implied rebuke. "I but wished to know why so many great men, as they say, did so little. At the time of the Essex rebellion."

"And I say that if Her late Majesty made a party against the friends of Essex, of course they were bound to submit. Your Majesty may question their zeal. But, I say, none of their *private* enemies durst have expressed themselves so!" That rather incoherent declaration came out in a rush, as the speaker glared round him defiantly.

At the gasps of offence by the Queen's ladies, and others, a new voice spoke up, and in no pacifying tone. "Did you look at *me*, my lord?"

It was the Lord Grey de Wilton, a somewhat older man, prominent in the Cecil-Hatton-Coke faction which had for so long dominated England in Elizabeth's name, violent opponents of Essex the fallen favourite.

"If the cap fits, wear it, Grey!"

"You are saying that honest men dared not to accuse traitors? That we sheltered behind Her late and glorious Majesty?"

"If you so wish to interpret it." Southampton had some difficulty with that word interpret. "But I warn you—watch your words, sirrah!"

"I give you the lie in your teeth, d'you hear!"

"Gentlemen! My lords!" Lennox cried. "This is outrage! A shame—bickering in the Queen's presence. Have done. Seek Her Majesty's pardon."

"This time-server called me a traitor, in the Queen's presence!" Southampton shouted, pointing angrily. "Me—after two years in the Tower for King James!"

"Who do you name time-server, man? There were Greys de Wilton serving England when Wriothesleys were herding sheep for better men than they!"

"God damn you, Grey!" Southampton clapped his hand down to where his sword should have hung—but one of James's first commands to his Court was that, as in Scotland, no man went armed in the royal presence or establishments, save only the Captain of the Guard and the Duke of Lennox.

Grey's own hand groped for a weapon—for he, like his enemy, was somewhat under the influence of drink. Glaring, they approached each other like fighting-cocks.

"My lords!" Anne protested. "Remember where you are."

One of the ladies screamed, but only slightly.

The two protagonists heard nothing, saw nothing but each other and mutual hate. Gone was the veneer of the fine and imperturbable English gentlemen, masters of themselves and all else. Fists were clenched for want of better weapons.

Lennox, Heriot and other men rushed in to keep them apart, upsetting certain furniture in the process. Ladies twittered and cried out—though by no means all of them, the Primrose girl for instance watching in wide-eyed pleasurable anticipation.

Anne was suddenly very angry. Scenes she did not greatly mind and was quite used to; but to have her royal commands completely ignored thus was not to be tolerated. She clapped hands together.

"Vicky!" she ordered. "Send for the Guard. These men to be put in ward. The Guard, I say!"

There was a shocked silence.

"Er . . . Your Grace! Scarce the *Guard*!" Lennox said, in some agitation. "These lords are greatly at fault. They are drink-taken. *I* will escort them to their quarters . . ."

"I said the Guard, my lord Duke. At once."

Bowing, Ludovick went to the door, and brought in two of the scarlet-clad and halberded Yeomen on duty there. "Escort these lords to their quarters," he directed.

"Under ward!" the Queen snapped. And as two peers of the

realm were marched off, one only that day appointed to the highest honour in the land, she turned her back on them and changed tone, expression and carriage. "Hetty, now we are quit of these unmannerly oafs, you and Lucy shall sing us a duet. The ballad Master Jonson taught us at Althorp. Primrose—you will accompany them on the virginial."

As held breaths were released and the illusion of normality returned to the withdrawing-room, Lennox moved over to Heriot's side. He sighed.

"We could have done without that, Geordie, I think!" he said quietly.

"All of it," the other nodded. "I fear the King will not be pleased."

"Aye. Anne has got the bit between her teeth! But . . . James can hobble her. This was folly."

They had not long to wait. The tuneful tinkling ballad was only half finished when the room's double doors were thrown abruptly open by two more of the Yeomen of the Guard, one of whom thumped loudly on the floor with his halberd-staff.

"Silence for the King's gracious Majesty!" he cried.

James came stamping in with stick much in evidence, Mar, Ramsay, Pembroke and others at his back. He was glowering fiercely.

"Here's a fine pickle o' herrings!" he spluttered wetly, thickly, into the sudden hush. "A right stramash! What's this I hear—heh? Answer me—what's this, a God's name? What do I hear?"

"Your Majesty perhaps did *not* hear my ladies singing!" the Queen said, head high. "Else I scarce believe you would interrupt so!"

The monarch ignored that. "You, Annie—I'll hae a word wi' you. Aye, I will. Clear the room."

A notable confusion followed, as men and women eddied to and fro, most only too anxious to get away but others reluctant. The Yeomen were in some doubts as to whom should be shepherded out of this illustrious throng, hesitant to press the loftiest. James stamped up and down, poking at all and sundry impatiently.

At length all were gone save one or two of the Queen's ladies, Lennox, Mar and Pembroke. George Heriot was just slipping through the door when a thick voice halted him.

"No' you, Geordie Heriot. You bide here. I've a flea for your lug, too! Aye and you too, Vicky Stewart. The rest—begone!"

"Hetty—you will stay with me!" the Queen declared clearly.

Recognising possible impasse, James side-stepped skilfully. "Aye, Cousin Hetty—you bide too. Your mistress maybe will need your services! Now—steik that door."

Mar was the last out, making a long face of it, and James was left with his wife, two cousins and his jeweller.

"Aye, well," he said, pointing his stick at Anne. "Did you, or did you no' put Harry Wriothesley under arrest—like I'm told? Wi' yon Grey? And march them off under guard like, like a pair o' cut-purses!"

"I did. And would do so again. They had words, all but came to blows, in my presence."

"You'll no' do so again—d'you hear, woman? I'll no' have it. I dinna care if they piss themsel's in your presence—you'll no' do the likes o' yon! Here's me fair flogging mysel' to keep the peace between my Scots and English lords, and you put two peers o' England in ward on a woman's whim! Before all. One o' whom I've only this day made a Knight o' the Garter!"

"They were half drunk. Would you have your wife insulted in her own drawing-room by boors, English peers or none?"

"Guidsakes, you'll no' ca' Harry Wriothesley a drunken boor, woman! You will not. He's a good laddie, and I like him fine."

"He is a trouble-maker and a lecher and a, a . . ." She swallowed the fatal word. "You know, very well what else he is! But he will not run free with his ill manners in my presence—he or any other."

"What folk may or may not do at my Court is my concern, no' yours—and I'd hae you mind it! Aye, mind it well—frae now on. I've obsairved a right unruly and rebellious spirit in you, Annie, since you cam frae Scotland. Maist unsuitable. And for that I'm no' leaving *you* guiltless, Vicky. I am not. You've been right soft wi' her, I can see. Given in. No' minded my express wishes and instructions. I am right displeased wi' you."

"I am a subject, Sire, and cannot constrain the Queen—even if I would."

"You had my royal powers in Scotland as Viceroy. What d'you think I gave you them for? No' to run after Annie like a lap-dog, to let her spend my siller like burn-water, to parade hersel' shamelessly through the land like some Roman concubine!"

"Sire . . . !"

"James, reserve your ill humours and ill tongue for me, in

private, if you please! Spare Vicky your unworthy strictures. He is blameless of any guilt. He came to my aid when I was direly ill—as you, my husband, should have done! And, with Master Heriot's help, saved me, and *you*, from a most evil plot . . ."

"Tush, woman—havers! There was no plot. Just that lassie Gray's imaginings. It was a' a nonsense. I dinna trust her faither, mind—but this ploy was just blethers frae the start. Yon Mary Gray should ha' had mair sense. Aye, and so should you. Though . . . maybe you were using this o' a plot for your ain bit ends, eh? Was that it? Mair plots than one?"

"I do not know what you mean, James. Can it be that you, Sire, are as drink-taken as your two friends?"

"Na, na—*my* heid's fine and clear, lassie. You'll hae to do better than that! I'm no' sae blate, mind, as maybe I seem—and I hear tell o' maist o' what goes on in Scotland, for a' I'm no' there."

"But innaccurately, it seems. Since you think there was no plot to make our son King of Scots in your room. If the rest you hear is like . . ."

"Johnnie Mar told me the rights o' that. As none should ken better, since he held the laddie."

"Mar! That snake in the grass! That red churl! You believe him before your own wife! Aye, and your cousin here . . ."

"Silence, woman! If you canna open your silly mou' but to miscall my friends, then you'll no' open it at a'! D'you hear? You will remain silent. Until I gie you leave to speak. That's a command. I've had enough o' this—aye, plenties. None here shall speak unless I say so." The King was trembling with anger, slobbering notably and plucking at his cod-piece, as he did when agitated. The other two men at least bowed.

James sucked in saliva. "You have a' failed me, maist grievously. Aye—you too, Geordie Heriot. I'm coming to you! My trust you have abused. Abused and misused. Forby this havers o' a plot, you hae squandered my money, injured my friends, rejected and insulted Sussex and Carey and them I sent to serve you. When I was waiting here for you, you were daundering doon through this England, wasting time and playing the proud fool. Aye, and biding wi' folk who are my enemies. And now you misuse my friends here in my ain house! D'you ken what you do, woman? D'you ken what you do?"

He held up a shaking hand as Anne opened her lips.

"I'll tell you. This England I have to govern, under God. A great and powerful realm full o' proud and arrogant nobles, who hae neither love nor loyalty to me—aye, and conceive me a fool! If it suits me that they do so—guidsakes, they'll learn, the chiels, they'll learn! But meantime, I must play this against that, raise up here, bring doon there, balancing—aye balancing. I'm alone, see you—fell alone." He paused, blinking, licking. "I dinna trust the Cecils—aye, or any o' them. I should expect help frae my family—no' hindrance. I maun play the Cecils against the Howards, the Greys against both, the late Essex's friends against Hatton, that proud crittur Raleigh against a'. Yon Kildare woman you spurned—she's Frances Howard, Nottingham's daughter, the Lord Admiral and the late Norfolk's brother, who died for my mother Mary. He's the powerfulest man in England, and his daughter the apple o' his eye. In your household she could serve me right well. The Lady Scrope—she was Norfolk's sister. Another Howard. And the Lady Rich—Essex's sister, who died in my cause. Eh, Annie—do you ken what you do?"

He drew great gulping breaths. "And you snubbed yon great fat Würtemburg. He's a drunken hog—but frae here he's going to Spain first, then to Rome. The Pope. He can carry my messages—if he will. Fell important messages that I canna risk in writing. No' yet. And nane o' these Englishry maun hear tell o'. Yet. For I'm going to hae peace wi' Spain. Aye, and the Vatican too. War's for fools, and I'll hae nane o' it. The English—they canna see it. Glory, they ca' it, the silly limmers! It cost Elizabeth dear. There'll be nae wars while I reign here, God aiding me. I kept the peace in Scotland—I'll do the same here, some way. *Alea bella incerta*, aye!"

There was silence in the great room for a space, save for the King's heavy breathing and lip-licking. Under royal command of speechlessness, none could make comment.

James took his time, undoubtedly savouring the situation. "I will hae nae mair fools upset to my plans," he went on, at length. "Annie—you will hae your ain Court, and I'll hae mine. You can keep your ain women—but I'll appoint what gentlemen I choose. George Carey will be your Chamberlain, I say—and if yon Johnnie Kennedy tries to say otherwise, I'll break the staff o' his chamberlainship ower his head for him! Tell him so!"

"May I speak?" the Queen asked, voice quivering a little.

"No, you may not! I'm no' finished yet." James swung round, pointing with his stick. "Now you, Geordie Heriot. I'm disappointed in you. You're a man wi' a level head, and some wits to you. No' like these! You ken what's what. And yet you let yon Mary Gray cozen you. You let the Queen spend my siller—when I sent you up to see she didna. You even lent her mair money o' your ain, to waste. Encouraging her—aye, encouraging. You'll no' get that back frae *me*, I promise you! You trailed at her silly heels. Why, man—why?"

"Are you seeking an answer, Sire? Giving me leave to speak?"

"Of course I am. Dinna play the daft laddie wi' James Stewart!"

"Very well, Sire. What I did, I did with good cause, in my own judgment. I believed, and still believe, the Master of Gray's plot to be real. And dangerous. But for the Queen's great help and patient forbearance, and her ill, I believe that by now there would have been a Henry King of Scots proclaimed at the Cross of Edinburgh . . ."

James looked away. "Blethers, man. Enough o' that."

"As Your Majesty wishes. For the rest, I did what seemed best, in the Queen's grave illness. And afterwards, I did not believe that Your Majesty would have your consort enter England in any but fitting style for the wife of a great monarch. Nor was it for me to chide and check Her Majesty—me, a humble tradesman."

"Ooh, aye!"

"And now, Sire, since I have incurred your royal displeasure, I crave your permission to leave this your Court. To go to London to set up my business and trade there. As should have been done ere this. And if Your Highness does not approve of that, then I shall return to Scotland forthwith. And gladly, Sire."

"My, my—so that's the way o' it! Geordie Heriot climbs his high horse wi' Jamie Stewart! The humble tradesman, heh?" The King chuckled, and waggled his stick, mockingly threatening. "Na, na—you'll no' win awa' yet, mannie. I've work for you to do. Plenty. And only you I'd trust to do it. Come to me the morn, Geordie, and I'll gie you a list o' new knights made since I saw you last. I've made a wheen—aye, a wheen. Nigh on two hundred, I'd say. You will ken what to do wi' that, eh? And Vicky can disapprove if he likes—but it will aye help to pay for some o' the debts he let my wife run up!"

James looked round at them all, glowering again. "You've understood me? I've nae wish to speak o' this again. But if I do, you'll ken who's king in this realm! Geordie—to me after hunting, the morn. I've got another ploy to whisper in your lug. Now—a guid night to you—aye, a guid night!" And he swung about and hobbled for the door—which Heriot ran to open for him. The Lord's Anointed stamped back to his interrupted night's drinking.

The Queen collapsed in tears in Henrietta of Huntly's arms, and was led sobbing to the other door, and out.

Lennox and Heriot eyed each other.

"That was . . . a right royal occasion, was it not!" the Duke said, his voice just a little unsteady. "Only James could have achieved it. I will not forget the day I was made Knight of the Garter."

"We were not meant to forget it."

"True. What an astonishment he is! He had me feeling like a whipped child—and deservedly whipped. The royal buffoon—who is anything but!"

"Alison Primrose has a better name for him—the Unicorn Rampant! A strange creature such as never was, which yet supports the crown! Tonight he taught us all a lesson."

"A lesson, yes. And not for the first time. All this of his balancing and playing the factions, Cecils, Howards, Greys and the rest. You think there is any fact in it, Geordie? Or do *they* play him!"

"I have told you. I'd liefer lend my money to James Stewart than to all the English lords and commons lumped together!"

"So-o-o! Perhaps you will do both, then! Since you are not to go back to Scotland, it seems. You believe that James will win, then, Geordie? With the English. But, with the Queen . . . ?"

"Of that I am less certain. But—I shall be a mite surprised if he does not."

"And you would aid him, in this? If you could?"

"I serve them both. But *he* is my sovereign lord. And they are man and wife . . ."

7

IN THE WEEKS and months that followed, the Edinburgh goldsmith's reckoning of the dynastic situation was very largely substantiated. James Stewart, whatever his outrageous behaviour and apparent headstrong bungling, nevertheless was always one step ahead of the forces which would use him, control him, or even unseat him—for there always had been a faction against his accession to Elizabeth's crown who would have put his cousin, the Lady Arabella Stewart, on the throne. Arabella was the only child of the late Charles Stewart, Earl of Lennox, brother of Darnley, James's father. Her line of succession to the English throne therefore was of the same order as his own, in that they were both great-grand-children of Margaret Tudor, Henry the Eighth's sister, married to James the Fourth of Scots—save that James was a great-grandson on *both* his mother and father's sides. But this disadvantage was outweighed, for many in England, by the fact that Arabella was wholly English by birth, residence and outlook, her mother a Cavendish. A month or two of James on the throne had the effect of much reviving and strengthening the Arabella faction.

But the King somehow managed to keep the many groups and factions isolated, to prevent them from coalescing against him. And especially from gravitating towards Arabella. This was no mean feat, for certain conditions did tend to bring the hostile groupings together—in especial the Scots presence. This, in fact, had quickly grown to be one of James's greatest problems. For apart from all those who had come south with the King's, and then the Queen's, trains—these mainly aristocracy—a constant tide of Scots, from the highest to the lowest, thereafter flooded over the Border, all with the same objective of making their fortunes, getting their own back for centuries of English invasion and warfare, and generally demonstrating their undoubted superiority in almost everything—except the superior manner, in which of course the English led the world. Not only so, but they expected their own King Jamie to co-operate and see that good Scots got most of the worthwhile appointments and positions of profit and honour in this newly-united kingdom—profit especially—and at first the King was inclined to concur. Not unnaturally the English, though an easy-going and tolerant people, began to seethe and then to rise in wrath. The Scots soon became a hissing and a booing. Popular songs were composed and sung against them in every inn and market-place; clergy preached on the plague the Lord had sent upon their devoted land; play-actors parodied the Scots accents; lampooners did a roaring trade. There were actually riots and public disturbances. A more unifying factor for the English family and political factions would have been hard to cenceive. And, of course, some of it all rubbed off on James himself, 'the Scotch monkey', and his personal popularity.

Oddly enough, the other plague helped the King in his peculiar battle, in that it kept him and his Court out of London, hot-bed of more troubles than one; had the effect of preventing large gatherings of people and gave him a good excuse for refusing to call a parliament, which might have served as a fulcrum for discontent—James had a typical Stewart dislike for parliaments, much preferring personal rule. Democracy he conceived to be the rule of the Devil—and moreover he could prove it in reason, logic, metaphysics and Holy Writ.

So he survived the first difficult months, even if not all of his Scots compatriots did. But in his personal relationship with the Queen, success was less obvious. In public they preserved a decent façade of conjugality and toleration, but in private they went their own ways. Anne it was, undoubtedly, who maintained the cold front—for whatever else he was, James was not cold, no chilly disapprover or distance-keeper. But the Queen, though gay, laughter-loving, flighty almost, and spreading her wings widely in this warmer, richer, southern ambience, was inflexible as far as James her husband was concerned. He was good at forgiving; she was not.

The Court was split into two distinct households, with little in common; the one concerned with music, dancing, masques, gossip, match-making; and the other with hunting, gambling, drinking and rudery, shot through with political manoeuvring. The two subsisting under the same roof, as it were, led to many a curious and tense situation.

The coronation, with all its mystic and spiritual connotations and concepts might have been a unifying factor—for Anne was at least superficially of a religious nature and tended towards the sacerdotal. But the plague contra-indicated any full and major ceremony in Westminster Abbey—which the English were united in declaring was the only conceivable venue—and only a very brief, truncated and elementary service was held there eventually, attended by a small number of selected witnesses and no contact with the infectious populace, on 25th July. Moreover, the levity with which James treated the entire proceedings further offended the Queen—and not only the Queen—he pointing out that he had been crowned monarch already, thirty-six years before, at the age of one year, and this was merely a homologation. There was actually a scene in the Abbey when his newest favourite, Philip Herbert, responded to one of the King's little kindnesses by kissing him lasciviously before all—to James's chuckles, but the scandal of some.

Thirty thousand Londoners had died of the plague, and were still dying at the rate of one hundred a day. The royal palaces were all either in or too near London for comfort, and there had been an outbreak of the plague in Windsor town. So a prolonged tour of the great country houses of the nobility was indicated—especially those where hunting facilities were available on a major scale, with well-stocked deer-parks—an economical arrangement moreover, where the cost of maintaining the two royal establishments fell upon other than James's purse. A start was made at Losely Park; then Farnham Castle, seat of the Bishop of Winchester; then Thruxton, and on to Wilton in Wiltshire. Wilton was the Earl of Pembroke's palatial seat, where as well as the delights of the chase on Salisbury Plain there was the pleasurable company of the aforementioned Philip Herbert, who was Pembroke's younger brother.

This touring programme had an advantage for George Heriot, allowing him release from Court attendance for a spell, since numbers had to be reduced considerably. Moreover the King's 'new ploy', which he had expounded to his goldsmith and banker, required the latter's sojourn in London for some time—it being nothing less ambitious than the compulsory summoning to receive knighthood of *every* land-holder in England with rental of over forty pounds Sterling; at a price, naturally, and if for any reason this royal honour should be declined, it could be compounded for at a still higher fee. James had concocted this splendid scheme during one of his marathon drinking sessions, using the old feudal-system theory of a knight's fee, whereby all land-holders had to provide armed men for national defence as a condition of the tenure of their lands, the standard being a minimum of one knightly horseman in armour plus a certain number of armed retainers on foot. This military tenure, of course, gave no actual title of knighthood to the land-owner, but James saw how the English love of titles could be utilised thereby, to his own infinite profit. An enormous amount of clerical work would be involved, naturally, in tracing and listing all such land-holders, the country over, assessing their potentialities and sending out the summonses. Geordie Heriot was just the man to supervise this counting-house labour which had to be carried out in London where the English national land-records were stored.

James saw millions of pounds just around the corner. And he was going to need it—for he had discovered that the Exchequer was four hundred thousand pounds in debt over Elizabeth's last Irish campaign alone. And that was but a drop in the horse-trough.

So Heriot at last won free of attendance at Court, to devote at least some of his time to his own affairs. He was not so afraid of the plague as was his royal master and set up business premises, with a modest house above, at the New Exchange, on the Cornhill near Threadneedle Street, a convenient area for his trade. Here he installed craftsmen and clerks to deal with both the jewellery and money-lending branches of his vocation—and was happy to busy himself in the work for which he was trained. There was a vast backlog of arrears to clear up, as well as rich new ground to be broken. Clearly, in time, he could teach the London money-market a thing or two. Not that he enjoyed London as a city; it was too large, stuffy after the sea-breezes of Edinburgh, with no views and prospects, so that a man felt suffocated in the unending narrow streets and lanes. And it stank to highest heaven. But there was money here, to make Edinburgh's a mere pittance. The King's knighthood business was a nuisance but, worked on a commission basis, was like to prove very lucrative.

This was the situation when, one day in mid-October, George Heriot was pacing up and down the central aisle of St. Paul's Church above Ludgate Hill—for much of London's business was in fact conducted here, as a highly convenient and central venue, and moreover, free. Suddenly he halted in his walking, excused himself to Master William Herrick, goldsmith to the late Queen, with whom he was in process of fixing up a working agreement, and hurried through the press of pacers, arguers and bargainers to where he had glimpsed a young and richly-dressed individual, solitary as a peacock amongst a flock of more sober barn-door fowl, and looking somewhat lost.

"My lord Duke—Vicky!" he exclaimed, holding out both hands. "Here is unexpected pleasure, on my soul! What brings so exalted a figure to St. Paul's this autumn day?"

"You do, Geordie. I called at your house in the Exchange, to be told you were here. It seemed an odd time for your devotions!" He shrugged, grinning his boyish smile. "It is good to see you, man. Dammit. I've missed you! Aye and not only myself."

"You are too kind. But I am no courtier, do not belong to your world. Where have you come from? Do not say that King and Court have come to London at last!"

"No, no. Despite being Christ's Vice-Regent, James Stewart is far too frightened of the wrath of God, in the form of this plague! Besides, he's very happy where he is. At Wilton. I've come from there with messages for you."

"For me? From the King? Do not say that Majesty sends the Duke of Lennox with messages for his goldsmith!"

"One from the King, yes. One from my . . . one from Mary Gray. From Scotland."

"Ah. Come—where we may talk privily. Yonder side-chapel."

"I do not know that my tidings is talk for churches and chapels! But, as you will . . ."

"This is England, where they worship a more accommodating God than ours, I think! Your news from Scotland is good?"

"Not very. But first the King's message. It is about some great jewel which he has ordered, some toy. He would have you bring it to Wilton to him, and at the earliest. Claims that you should have had sufficiently long to finish it. Wants it to hang on a double gold chain. He requires it three days from now, no more. You know how he talks."

"Yes. It is a great pendant of St. George and the Dragon. The Garter badge. In enamels. Set with diamonds and sapphires. A costly trinket. I judge it must be for the Queen. A peace-offering, perhaps."

"It may be—I know not. But he is urgent for it. I am to take you back with me to Wilton. James would talk with you on other matters also. This folly of the knightings, I expect."

Heriot frowned. "I have so much to do, here. Work—it ever increases . . ."

"*I* need you at Wilton also, Geordie. I need help. Mary writes from Methven. She has wind of more trouble. A plot . . ."

"Save us—not another!"

"Yes. And this one even more grievous. For the King's very life is threatened, she thinks. She said to tell you, and seek your aid."

"It is here, in England, then?"

"Yes. Though her father is, of course, involved in it, this must be based where the King is. It is, she says, a Catholic conspiracy to kill James and place Arabella Stewart on the throne."

"Arabella! But . . . there has been talk of that for long. Ever since Elizabeth died."

"Yes, talk. But this is more than talk. There are very powerful folk behind it, she says. And not only Catholics."

"And what has the Master of Gray to do with it?"

"That is not clear to me. Mary's letter says only that Patrick insists that Henry and young Elizabeth are not to be harmed. Nor the Queen. And they are to be sent back to Scotland. No doubt for Henry to be proclaimed King of Scots. The old story, with a new turn to it."

"Does she name any names? Here in England?"

"Aye, three. Our friend the Lord Grey de Wilton, Cobham, the Lord Warden of the Cinque Ports, and, of all folks, Sir Walter Raleigh!"

"Phe-e-ew! Raleigh! I scarce can believe that. Not a man of Raleigh's stature. He has not cause to love James, no doubt—who has deprived him of the Captaincy of the Guard. But that is because he advocates war with Spain—it is a madness with the man. But James still allows him to be Governor of Jersey. Cobham is his cousin—but I would have thought that they had little in common. As for Grey de Wilton, he is a Puritan, no Catholic . . ."

"You have not been long, Geordie, in learning what's what, as our liege would say, about the English nobility!"

"My trade demands that sort of knowledge, my lord Duke! Did the letter say aught else?"

"It named one other—Markham. Sir Gervase, I think was the name. I have not heard of him. That, and to watch Mar again."

"So-o-o! And what am *I* to do?"

"The good God knows! She said just to tell Geordie Heriot—he would help."

Exasperatedly the man stared at his younger and so trusting friend, and sighed. He transferred his gaze to the lofty windows of stained glass.

"Myself, I do not know how to begin," Lennox admitted.

"Have you told the King?"

"Not yet. You know what James is—frightened of his own shadow, yet laughing to scorn anything *I* tell him! We'd need more to show him than another letter from my Mary!"

Heriot admitted that. But he did not want to get involved in another thankless exercise in dynastic counter-plottery.

"There is another who looks for your return to Court, Geordie," the Duke went on. "Mistress Primrose. She told me to tell you that Court was a different place, lacking you. That's a lively piece, on my soul! And don't these Englishmen know it! They are round her like flies. Some young lord will snap her up."

"I hope not." The other frowned. "She is little more than a child."

"No child that, but a very knowing young woman. And as bonny as she is bright. Besides, was not Anne, her mistress, wed at fifteen? Myself I was but sixteen. Staveley has just wed a fourteen-year-old. The girl has a fondness for you, all know."

"As an older man. An uncle, perhaps. I am old enough to be her father. Nor, nor am I looking for a wife."

"I but gave you her message. She has the sharpest wits in the Queen's household."

"That I believe—since Mary Gray placed her there! Very well, Vicky—I shall come back with you to Wilton. I must, if the King commands it. For a few days only. But I have affairs to settle here, first . . ."

"We ride tomorrow, then . . ."

* * *

Wilton House, some three miles west of Salisbury, was an experience for George Heriot—indeed, until six months previously, even for James Stewart. Built on the site of a one-time Saxon nunnery, it was not like most of the seats of the new Tudor aristocracy basically conventual buildings, abbeys, priories and the like, taken over from the Church at the Reformation and handed over by Henry the Eighth to his friends and servants. The Herberts had been at Wilton for centuries, and their rambling establishment had grown over the years into what was practically a town of its own, set in an enormous park on the southern skirts of Salisbury Plain. In an atmosphere of vast wealth, almost total security and at least local peace, the need for defence—which cooped up even the greatest Scots lord in strong stone towers—just did not apply; and every whim of the occupying generations had been met and exploited. Seven hundred servants—not men-at-arms—serviced this mighty sprawling domain; and Pembroke himself frequently became lost in his house's labyrinths. Wilton had three great halls as well as eight dining-rooms—apart from the servants' eating-places; three chapels—and five chaplains; four bakeries; a brewery; two theatres, one indoors, one out; an ape-house, a bull-ring, a bear-pit and half-a-dozen cock-fighting-yards. It had its own race-course; a pleasure canal-system, with ornamental lakes, temples and grottoes; and its gardens covered scores of acres. The inner park had a wall twelve miles round; and the outer, stocked with game, extended over whole parishes and included many estate villages. To Wilton frequently came Ben Jonson and Thomas Campion, with their masquers; also William Shakespeare and his Lord Chamberlain's players—Pembroke being Chamberlain. Here Philip Sidney had written much of his *Arcadia*, and Francis Bacon was a frequent visitor.

That all this should be the private establishment of one of his subjects, gave King James much food for thought, more especially in the present state of the national exchequer. George Heriot's reactions were no less assessing, if less predatory.

When Lennox and he arrived, it transpired that the King had been away buck-hunting for hours; while the Queen was off hawking over the heronries of the Avon. Heriot had a room allotted to him in what appeared to be a stable-wing—but found no cause for complaint.

It was there that Alison Primrose came to him, presently, all cheer and welcome. "Duke Vicky told me that you were come," she cried, running up to take his hand. "I am glad, glad."

Although the man had well warned himself that he must watch his step very carefully with this child, that he was in danger of making a fool and spectacle of himself over a slip of a girl much less than half his own age—and worse, possibly damage her good name, precious even in this licentious Court—it was difficult not to respond frankly and in kind to her uninhibited greeting. Especially when he could by no means deny his fondness for the lassie, and would not hurt her for all the wealth of Wilton. He gripped her arms more strongly than he knew—and found nothing to say, by design or otherwise.

"You are so *solid* a person, Master Geordie! Not like most of those I see—not like any of them, to be sure. Even the Duke."

Strangely, despite all his wise resolutions, the man was distinctly cast down at this description of himself as solid. Was that what he seemed to this lightsome bairn—solid, dull, a stodgy old man? No danger to any young woman! He cleared his throat.

"Solidity comes with age—like other things!" he said, a trifle stiffly. "It must be my years weighing me down."

"How old are you?" she asked, matter-of-fact, interested.

"Forty at my next birthday, child!"

"You are older than the *King*?" She gazed at him, big-eyed. "The King is but newly thirty-seven—the Queen says so. And he looks an old man. How strange."

He frowned darkly. "My great age is unfortunate—but need not concern you!" he declared, sourly for George Heriot. "I hope to live for a few years yet!"

She burst into her ready laughter. "Poor, aged Master Geordie! You only look old when you frown! So frown no more on Alison Primrose—who disbelieves in years anyway."

"You do? How is that, pray?"

"Years, I think, have little to do with age. The King, I swear, was born old. As was my father—aged by the time he was thirty. While the Queen now, although nearly thirty, is still a child—younger than I am, in truth! As is the Duke. Ageing is something of the spirit, not of years."

"Indeed." Warily the man eyed this surprising juvenile. "I think that you are possible right. But . . . where does that leave me, child?"

"Old enough to know better than to name *me* child!" she answered him swiftly.

"M'mm. In such case, girl, the sooner we are out from this bedchamber, the better for your name and reputation," he said grimly. "There will be plenty here to watch and whisper, I have no doubt."

"To be sure," she acceded. "Not that I care—since reputations here are the other way quite! Only those who do *not* bed with men are talked about! Conceived to be in some way incomplete, scarce true women. But, come—I will take and show you the water-gardens. They are quite wonderful. And all can dally there, for all others to view!"

Shaken, he opened the door for her. Cheerfully, companionably, she took his arm and led him off, through the maze of corridors and courtyards.

It was a golden October afternoon, with white strutting doves croodling on every roof and arbour, and a faint mellow haze over all. Through the formal Italian gardens, where elegant groups strolled and flirted amidst highly erotic statuary, they came down a terrace to the lower, sunken water-gardens amongst the canals and ponds, where ornamental water-fowl quacked and squattered, and tall reeds, drooping willows and cunningly contrived bowers offered Eros a more active playground for those a stage further than flirtation. Nearly every neuk and corner seemed to be filled with busy couples, at most of which Alison glanced with every appearance of interest—until the man demanded to know whether she had brought him here with the express purpose of displaying this prolonged peep-show.

"Why, yes—in part," she admitted frankly. "That you might perceive what reputations mean at this Court. And likewise age! For you will see grey hairs a-plenty in these bushes, I vow, if you but look! But mainly I came here to row out to one of these many islets. In the lochans. There are gondolas. Where we may talk without fear of being overheard, Master Geordie—of this of the Lady Arabella."

"Eh . . . ? You know of this, then? This new plot?"

"To be sure. Duke Vicky told me of Mistress Mary's letter. We are here to watch over the Queen, you know." This was in the nature of a mild rebuke. "And there are few places, and times, in this Wilton, where one may talk safely."

"I see. The Duke did not tell me that he had confided in you."

"But he does, frequently. Mistress Mary sends me many messages. And I her. But through Duke Vicky—since it would look strange, would it not, for such as Alison Primrose to receive many letters from Scotland?"

"So. You act the spy then, for Mary Gray, in Queen Anne's household! That is the truth of it?"

"Yes," she agreed simply. "But—less loud, if you please! All ears here may not be deafened by houghmagandie!"

He swallowed audibly.

There were many gaily-painted gondolas moored by the waterside paths. Picking one, Alison hitched her skirts high, and stepped in. "My lord of Pembroke is very thoughtful," she remarked. "See—there are kerchiefs here stowed. Cushions. A little wine-flagon in each boat. Sweetmeats. Also towels—most useful. And fishing-lines. There are fish of all sorts and colours. Do you wish to fish?"

"Thank you, no," he said, getting in and taking up the oars.

Alison steered them out to one of the willow-grown islets, where the stones of a moss-grown temple showed through the trees. A tiny inlet screened by weeping branches led in—and as the gondola nosed into this, the girl in the stern opened her mouth, clapped a hand over it, and pointed with the other hand past Heriot's person. He turned, and looked over his shoulder.

Another gondola was already in possession of the inlet. And on the shallow floor of it two large white thighs and bent pink knees were upraised, with a leaner bare bottom vigorous between. Heriot reversed his strokes, and backed out quickly.

Pink also, but with suppressed laughter and far from repressed delight, Alison managed to contain her mirth until they were out into the open water again.

"Lady Carey!" she gurgled. "The superior and pious Lady Carey! Dotes on Jesuit priests. Confession every morning. Her husband out hunting with the King. A plague on it that I could not see from, from—well, who the man was!"

"I should say not!" Heriot reproved. "You are a shameless, er, young woman!"

"Shameless? What have I to be ashamed of? Any shame, surely, is the Lady Carey's."

"I do not see how you can be so certain that it *was* the Lady Carey. I certainly . . . er, h'mm . . ."

Joyous laughter. "Could you not, Master George! But then, perhaps, you suffer under certain disadvantages? Women have their own certainties."

He had the sense not to debate that.

The next islet they came to, they were more wary. But a circuit revealed no other boat. They landed, and moved up to a lichened stone bench beside a marble satyr and a full-breasted nymph.

"Wilton is clearly a place for virile folk," the man commented, sitting. "Are you satisfied with our secrecy, Alison?"

"That is the first time that you have called me only by my given name!" She said.

"Is it? I had not realised it!"

"So I may call you Geordie? Without the Master?"

"Sakes—you could have called me that from the day we met, girl. Most others do."

"But I am so *young*, you see. Little better than a child!"

"Have mercy, lassie! You have proved your point, I swear!" He took her hand, opened it, and pressed a kiss therein. "This is a woman's hand." He leaned over, and lightly brushed her parted lips with his own. "And that is a woman's mouth. From this on, you are a woman to me, Alison Primrose. I promise you."

She took a deep breath, and sat for long moments unspeaking, staring straight ahead of her. Then she turned to smile at him, warmly, glowingly, put her hand back in his, and so sat.

Not a little moved, the man was as silent as she.

At length he spoke, evenly. "About the Lady Arabella? You have something to tell me?"

She sighed a little. "Yes. She is coming here."

"Here? To Wilton? Surely not. The King has kept her from Court. As did Elizabeth. And now—this plot!"

"I heard the Countess of Kildare tell the Countess of Bedford. And she is a Howard and knows all that goes on. Lady Kildare. Although she is not truly Countess of Kildare any more, since she is secretly wed to the Lord Cobham . . ."

"She is? Cobham? He—that is one of those named. In the letter."

"Yes. With Sir Walter Raleigh, who is his cousin. And the Lord Grey de Wilton. Cobham and Grey are here also. But not Raleigh."

"No. He has offended the King. By declaring that there could be no peace with Spain. And declaring that the Scots succoured Philip's Armada in '88. As indeed we did, to some measure. But . . . you say that Lady Cobham, who was Lady Kildare, and before that Frances Howard, daughter of the Lord Admiral, says that Arabella Stewart is coming to Wilton? When?"

"That was not said. But I took it as very soon."

"She would not dare to come without the King's knowledge."

"Of that I know not. But it seems strange. To be coming now. When there is this of a plot. But—there is something else. Yesterday, Lord Cobham's brother, George Brooke, came here. And with him he brought another gentleman, by name of Markham. Sir Gervase

Markham. And Markham was the fourth name written in Mistress Mary's letter. He is a great Catholic, they say. And he has already been to see the Marchioness Hetty of Huntly."

"So-o-o. It looks, then, as though the vultures gather! But—I do not understand this of the Lady Kildare, or Cobham, knowing of Arabella coming—if coming she is. And telling Lady Bedford. The Howards and the Russells are linked with the Cecils—the ruling faction, and very much against the Catholics. Here is something strange indeed. If they know of it all . . ."

"They may not know of the plot. Only of the Lady Arabella's coming to Court. Perhaps . . . perhaps they it was who gained her summons?"

"For what purpose?"

"I have no notion. But the Lord Admiral, and Secretary Cecil, so close to the King, might have their own reasons. For a change of policy, with regard to Arabella."

He frowned. "She was kept all but a prisoner, during Queen Elizabeth's later years. As a possible claimant of Elizabeth's throne. That was the Cecils' policy then. Why should they change it now . . . ?"

They could between them produce no answer to these questions; and presently Alison said that she ought to go back to the Queen's quarters, to prepare for the royal return from hawking. For there was to be a great masque that night, in which the Queen was herself taking part—as indeed was she, Alison—and there would be much to-do with costumes and dressing.

They rowed ashore.

"I shall see you at the masque—or after it," the girl said.

"Not before? When we eat?"

"No. The King's and Queen's households are now almost wholly separate. They no longer eat together. Only when there is some especial banquet. But—you could choose to belong to the *Queen's* household, Geordie, could you not? You were her royal jeweller, before you were the King's."

"True. But I am here on the King's summons. I fear that I must grace *his* table, however lowly the place."

* * *

James's hunting-party came straggling in in the late afternoon, after having been in the saddle since sunrise, a weary, dusty, dishevelled crew, fine hunting greens soiled. Heriot watched from his stable-wing window—and marvelled anew at his sovereign lord. For the King, slumped like a sack of chaff in his saddle—oddly, always he rode like that, despite being one of the best horsemen in two kingdoms—seemed to be almost the freshest there. The man who wearied after hobbling a hundred yards, who grew impatient with any ceremony lasting longer than ten minutes, who was terrified of loud noises, violent action and the sight of human blood, would spend twelve hours in strenuous hunting, slay game by the score, even on occasion gleefully gralloch his own deer in a slaister of blood and guts, and return in highest spirits. Today a long string of sumpter-horses, each bearing a head-dangling buck, seemed to ensure that the King would be in excellent mood.

A thoughtful host further improved the occasion by announcing that the royal repast would be served alfresco and out-of-doors, or at least under a tented canopy as to the King's own table, at the circular banking of the open-air bear-pit, where a great bear-baiting would take place throughout the meal, an especial performance with a notably fierce bear kept starved for the purpose, and some of the stoutest-hearted dogs in England—all arranged by his brother Philip, who was an expert in all such matters. James was graciously pleased to express entire appreciation.

Philip Herbert was, apparently, not just good-looking but an asset to any Court.

And so, to a strong and musky smell of live bear, sawdust and long-spilled blood, the great company of the King's household and Pembroke's guests sat down to laden trestle-tables set up on the grass terracing around the central pit, and were plied with victuals hot and cold, fish, from congers to creatures so rare that they had been brought in ice from Russia; poultry, from peacocks and swans to godwits and cocks' combs; meats, from Polonian sausage to venison seethed in wine; in all, two dozen dishes, all served on silver-gilt plate by an army of liveried attendants.

George Heriot found an inconspicuous place for himself as far as he decently could get from the sanded floor of the arena. A large and shaggy brown bear, lean to the point of gauntness, was led in, shackled by one leg, grunting and growling and chained to a central post. Then Philip Herbert took charge of the proceedings.

He was rather different from the general run of James's favourites, tall, well-built and muscled, handsome but not in the least effeminate-seeming. He wore a thin, down-turning scimitar of moustache and no beard, and with it an arrogant, hot-tempered manner. He lived for horses, dogs, sport and gambling, and it was his expertise as a huntsman which had first drawn the King to him. Whether he satisfied James in other respects seemed open to doubt, but the monarch meantime would find little fault in him.

He had a hunting-horn sounded for silence, and then, in ringing tones, announced that he was prepared to wager one hundred pounds that his black mastiff Diablo would outlast any other dog soever against this fine Muscovy bear. What takers?

There was no lack of these. Many lordlings shouted the claims of their animals; but Herbert declared that only three other dogs should be engaged at one time, as a sporting proposition. The others' turn would come.

And so a large mastiff, two terriers and a wicked, slinking grey lurcher cross were brought and let loose in the arena, to a low rumbling from the chained bear. The dogs, all trained for this activity, had their own methods. The big mastiff sat down at once on all fours, and then began to inch forward thus, slowly, with infinite menace; the two terriers went yapping into the attack without a preamble, leaping and dancing as though on springs; while the lurcher loped and circled, teeth bared. There were great shouts of enthusiasm and advice from the high-born diners. The bear, up on its hind legs, weaved its tall shaggy body to and fro gently, but otherwise appeared to pay little heed.

Like lightning the lurcher suddenly made a viscious bound for the throat—and the click of its teeth meeting sounded across the arena, short of the bear's fur by barely an inch when, scarcely to be discerned, the brute flicked head and shoulders a mere fraction sideways. As incredibly swiftly, a great claw-armed paw lashed out, and a long scarlet score appeared down the lurcher's side. The yell of the watchers drowned the animal's scream.

Like a missile from a catapult the mastiff sprang direct from its crouching position, just as a terrier nipped in low. The bear stooped to cuff with its other paw and was hit at the shoulder, as by a bolt, by the heavy larger dog, staggering to the impact. The terrier was tossed into the air, yelping high, but the mastiff sank its teeth in just behind the bear's shoulder.

Roaring with pain, the bear tried to throw off the big dog. But it was too far round for the lethal claws to reach. Then it tried to shake off its attacker, but the teeth were clenched firm in the flesh. The lurcher, despite all, leapt in again to the now unprotected belly—

and with a snarl the bear dropped on all fours, then crushed down with all its great weight. All heard the life go out of the slender dog with a choked-off howl.

With great swiftness for its bulk, and the entangling tendency of its chain, the bear rolled over on its back. The mastiff had to fling itself clear or be crushed in turn. As it leapt away, a single three-inch claw ripped a rent in its black flank.

Then the barking terriers were in like shrill small furies. The bear flicked one off in red ruin, as it would a fly; but the other clung, worrying at the throat.

Wagers were now being shouted all over the enclosure, women's voices upraised as well as men's. As the bear, seeking to dislodge the terrier, rolled over again to get up on his hind legs, the mastiff bored in low. And the long, barbed hind foot that was not hampered by the chain, scooped up, and gutted the big dog as cleanly as a gralloch, coming away in a tangle of smoking entrails and skin. The mastiff hung there kicking, but did not unclench its teeth.

"You've lost your siller, Philip—you've lost your siller!" the King cried. "Man—you're dog's deid! But, never heed, laddie—I'll make it up to you. I will so."

"Dammit—the brute's not dead yet!" Herbert denied. "It's hanging on. Another fifty pounds, Staveley—to outlive your terrier!"

"Done, shrive me!"

The bear dropped on all fours once more and shook itself mightily. The terrier was almost, but not quite detached, flung half round. And there a great forepaw flashed over and caught its hind-quarters, all but tearing them off in bloody collops. The thin shriek bubbled to silence.

The bear stood up again to its full height, reddened paws waving gently. The disembowelled mastiff, eyes closed, jaws still clamped, jerked its hind legs feebly.

"By God, I win!" Herbert yelled. "See it! One hundred and fifty pounds you owe me, Staveley, d'you hear? A pretty sport! You spoke too soon, Majesty! Now—another three dogs, heh? I have a second brute I'll wager . . ."

With slow dignity the bear stooped, and with fore-paws tore the twitching mastiff bodily from itself, some of its own shaggy hide coming away with the teeth, and tossed it far, so to stand, red tongue lolling, to stare around on its tormentors.

Sickened, Heriot pushed away the plateful of beef before him, appetite gone.

The bear, sadly weakened now, with strips of its hide hanging off, was attempting to beat off its third quartet of dogs, the torn carcases of the others strewn around it on the bloody sand, when Lennox found his way to his friend's side, to discover him drinking more deeply than usual. Glancing at the scarcely touched dishes, he grinned.

"Do not say that you find Wilton's hospitality not to your taste, Geordie?" he commented. "Or is it this traditional English sport which palls on you?"

"Say that I have a delicate stomach," the other answered briefly.

"Ah—you should have been born a nobleman, my friend. Then such pastimes would not trouble your belly! Though, I must confess, I prefer my eating . . . otherwise!" He shrugged. "But the sport flags somewhat, and Majesty's attention wanders. He would have a word with you."

"Now?"

"Now. For a short-sighted man, James misses little. He saw you sitting alone here and sent me."

They made their way to the King's table, where James had obviously lost interest in the entertainment—and as clearly was annoyed that young Herbert had not perceived the fact. He turned the more affably to the newcomers.

"Ha—Geordie Heriot!" he greeted. "Man—it's good to see your honest face. Though glowering! So you've survived yon London! The pest—does it lessen a mite?"

"Undoubtedly, Sire. With the cooler days. They believe that it will soon be gone. God grant it true."

"Amen to that—aye, Amen, Geordie. It's been a right inconvenience. Sit in, man. Join me in a goblet." James lowered his voice to a thick whisper. "You hae the toy I ordered? It's finished? I'll hae a peek at it, under this table. I dinna want them a' seeing it."

"I have it, Sire. But not here. Not on my person. It is a mite heavy to carry in a pocket. And valuable! I have it in my room, locked in my kist . . ."

"Your room, heh? Heavy? No' too heavy, man?"

"Solid gold, Sire. And all those jewels. And a double chain. Shall I go fetch it?"

"Na, na. I'll come see it."

"But—Your Majesty! Not *you*—to my quarters! I will bring it. In but a minute or two . . ."

"Och, wheesht you, Geordie man—I'll come. I'd rather see it privily, ony gait. Gie me my stick . . ."

And so, to the consternation of all, Majesty rose from the table—so that everyone else must do the same—and went tottering off on Heriot's arm, stick poking a route through, while still dogs yelped and snarled round the flagging bear. Inevitably, Lords Pembroke, Nottingham, Southampton, Mar and a number of others came hurrying after, wiping lips and greasy fingers.

"Bide where you are!" James barked round at them. "When I'm needing you, I'll tell you. Aye, you too, Philip Herbert. Bide you wi' your bit dogs! But, Vicky—*you'd* better come."

Much embarrassed to be thus leading off the monarch before the entire Court to his humble quarters in the stable-wing, Heriot bit his lip. This sort of prominence was the last thing he sought. "If Your Majesty will go to one of your own private chambers, I will bring it . . ."

"Hud your wheesht, man. Heh—unless you dinna *want* me in your room? Eh? Maybe you've got someone there? A quean, belike? Och, maybe the lassie Primrose, that I'm hearing you've got a notion for? A smart one, that!"

"No, Sire—no! Nothing of that sort. Mistress Primrose is, is safe from me. We are friends. No more. She is very young . . ."

"Och, aye—young! But that'll mend, man. Forby, the young ones are the sweetest, eh? Dinna tell me you havena discovered that! Eh, Vicky—*you'll* bear that out, I've nae doubt. Wi' yon Mary Gray."

"As Your Majesty says . . ."

Past astonished servitors they came to the stable-wing and mounted the stairs, James peering interestedly into every room they passed. At his own apartment, Heriot offered the only chair to the King and went to unlock the small iron-bound chest which he had chained to the bed.

"Aye, you're canny, Geordie," James nodded approvingly. "As well you might be. What else hae you got in yon wee kist? Besides my trinket?"

"Some papers to show Your Highness, anent the knighthoods. And some private items."

"Private, eh? No' private frae *me*, Geordie?"

"Not if Your Majesty commands otherwise, of course."

"Aye, well. We'll see. First the jewel. The medallion. You'd ca' it a medallion, Geordie?"

"Something of that ilk, Sire. A pendant, a gaud. An ornature."

He drew the chamois-leather-wrapped parcel out and unwrapped it.

Immediately the humdrum little room became a different place, indeed was lost, erased, in the flashing, coruscating beauty of the glittering jewel, its diamonds sparkling with a thousand lights, its sapphires glowing deeply, the shining gold a rich mirror to reflect the rays of the sinking sun, its enamels' colours brilliantly enhanced.

"Bonny! Bonny!" the King exclaimed, taking it. "Right handsome. Guidsakes—look at yon dragon! And flames o' fire! Maist delectable. See, Vicky—is it no' beautious?"

"Very, Sire. And costly, I would think!"

"Ooh, aye—costly? Is it gey costly, Geordie?"

"I fear so, Sire. Inevitably. I warned Your Majesty . . ."

"Aye, well. Uh-huh. Maybe it will be worth the siller, man. Maybe. It's heavy, though—heavy. It's no' ower heavy? For a woman to wear, man?"

"I think not. It would not be worn for long periods."

"She's no' ower robustious, mind. Och, well—we canna change it now." James wrapped the precious contrivance in its leather, and bestowed it in a capacious pocket of his over-stuffed doublet—one of the advantages of such. "Now—this o' the knights. How goes it, Geordie?"

"It is a great labour, Sire—and goes almost too well! The papers are all here—so far as we have got. There are seven thousand, eight hundred land-holders listed, thus far, holding lands worth forty pounds and more. And we have not yet got further north than Northamptonshire. . . . ."

"Sink me! So many? A mercy—near eight thousand!"

"Sire—you cannot possibly think to confer the honour of knighthood on all these!" Lennox cried. "It would make a supreme mockery of the entire . . ."

"I'm no' thinking to confer an honour, Vicky—I'm summoning to a degree, rank and status, aye status. I'll make o' knighthood what it used to be, in this country, in a' Christendom. Knights' service to the throne, for lands held. Only, the service will be in siller instead o' armed men. Aye, I'll make a whole new order o' landed men knights—and fine they'll thank me for it! Their wives mair especially. See you, in Scotland every bit laird is ca'd by his lands—Heriothill, Dumbiedykes, Cowcaddens. Even if they're scarce mair'n a bit field or two and a doocot! Aye, and his wife's the Lady Cowcaddens, see you—a' Lady this or that. And do they no' delight in it? Much mair the English, who love titles mair'n they love meat and drink—and that's plenties! Yet they hae nothing o' the like. The rich squire may hae a thousand acres o' prime land, but they are plain Maister Rich or Maister Green. And worse, their wives are only Mistress Rich and Mistress Green. Will they no' thank me for making them Sir and Lady? And pay for the privilege! As they ought."

Lennox could not gainsay that logic.

"How much to pay, Geordie? Hae you worked it out? The rate."

"Not fully, Sire. We all conceive that the thousand pounds you sought, for every forty pound land, is too much. Many could not produce you such, without having to sell much land. We reckoned six hundred pounds for each forty pound rental."

"M'mmm. And what to pay if they refuse it.?"

"That is for you, Sire. We suggest a level fee of one thousand pounds."

"Sweet Mercy—for refusing knighthood!" Lennox cried.

"That was His Majesty's instructions."

James was clearly calculating busily; but though none could question his learning, arithmetic was not his strongest subject. "It's gey hard to assess," he announced. "It depends on how many o' the eight thousand are *only* forty pound men. And how many above it. A wheen will hae ten times that, and mair."

"True, Sire. But, let me say that one third were forty pounds only, another third twice that, and the remainder variously higher—say three times. Then, of this seven thousand, eight hundred you would garner in, if all paid, nearly thirteen million pounds."

"Guid God in Heaven!" Christ's Vice-Regent observed, eyes goggling.

"That is but a crude calculation," Heriot pointed out. "Nothing of that order could be relied upon. Perhaps half would be more true counting . . ."

"Half? Even so! Och, man, man." The monarch was lost in roseate dreams. He turned to Lennox. "Vicky—d'you no' see what this means? Here's the Exchequer empty—thanks to Elizabeth's Irish and Spanish wars, and that fool Burleigh. This realm's taxation is a' farmed out, to third, fourth and fifth collectors—who a' tak their skelb o' the cheese! A right damnable system. I canna win new taxations lacking an English parliament's leave—the insolence o' it! And even then, the siller doesna come into *my* hands, but the Lord Treasurer's, and him accountable to the said parliament. We do things better in Scotland! But here, man—

here's a right excellent ploy, you'll no' deny? I needna ask the permission o' any—and the siller comes direct to me. It's *my* privilege to create knights. And, you hear—there's millions in it! Save us—it's a godsend!"

"I might call it something else, James—but you will have it your own way, no doubt."

"Aye, I will so. God be praised it's no Vicky but Jamie Stewart that sits on this throne! Aye, nor Arabella Stewart either!"

Both his companions stared at him.

The King leered at them, but did not amplify. "I'll see these papers later, Geordie. Now—what else hae you got in your kist?"

"Only some money. Notes of hand. And a few pieces of jewellery—nothing of real worth." He looked at Lennox significantly. That man nodded.

"James—you mentioned just now our cousin Arabella," the Duke said. "Did you, h'm, do so advisedly?"

"Can I no' speak *inadvisedly* alone wi' you and Geordie Heriot, Vicky?"

"To be sure. But . . . this of Arabella. I have not heard you speak of her, for long. And to do so now, when . . ."

"Aye—when, Vicky? When what?"

"When there is talk about her. When her name is whispered . . ."

"Whispers, eh? And what do they whisper about Arabella, our bit cousin? She's no' sick? Or bedding wi' some loon? Or wi' child? What's the whisper?"

Lennox looked at Heriot for help—and got little. "There is talk of a plot, Sire," he blurted out. "Another plot."

"A plot, eh? Waesucks—no' again!" The King sighed extravagantly, in simulated weariness—but he did not sound really surprised.

"Yes, Sire. This time to put Arabella on your throne."

"You say so? Then they'd need to dispose o' me first, would they no'?"

"Exactly so."

"And who utters siclike whispers, Vicky Stewart?"

The Duke smoothed a hand over mouth and chin. "We hear it here and there, James. From here and there."

"Aye—here and there, just. Man, you'll hae to do better than that!"

"Yet, Sire—you did name Arabella. When she's not been at Court for long."

"She's my faither's brother's daughter, is she no'? A quiet bit lassie, frae a' accounts. Am I no' to speak her name?" James got to his feet. "Plots are a right pastime for idle folk, Vicky. Now—I'll awa' back to my ain quarters. Annie's got another o' her pestilent masques, the night—she should ha' been a mummer, no' a queen! Gie's your arm, man. Half thirteen million did you say, Geordie? And you're only at Northampton? Guidsakes!"

* * *

Even the largest of the halls at Wilton was scarcely large enough to hold both Courts, plus the raised dais platform and the area roped off for the Queen's masque. In consequence, a lesser hall nearby was brought into use also, and the passageways between festooned with evergreens and coloured lamps—a satisfactory arrangement for many, for there was no lack of rooms off betwixt, where folk who sought to provide their own entertainment could do so in approximate privacy—although privacy was by no means a prerequisite for not a few, it seemed.

James was late in arriving—which caused some upset, since even Anne could scarcely order a start on the masque before the monarch and their host appeared. When the King's train approached it was heralded through the long corridors by singing—not the sweet melody of choirs or singing boys, but the bibulous chorus of drink-taken men. A lively evening seemed to be assured.

The royal dais table was well stocked with flagons, bottles, tankards and beakers, and James, himself supporting rather than leaning on the shoulder of an already reeling Philip Herbert, but in high good humour, wasted no time on preliminary courtesies, but reaching for a flagon promptly got down to the serious business of the evening. There was the usual unseemly tussle amongst the Scots and English lords as to who should share the limited space of the dais table—the Scots, being on the whole less drunk, doing best. Heriot noted that the Lords Grey de Wilton and Cobham both managed to find a place up there, and neither seemed inebriated. Lennox took up his stance carefully nearby. Heriot had had George Brooke and Sir Gervase Markham pointed out to him. They stood together in the main part of the hall, where of course the vast majority of the company waited, and Heriot moved discreetly to a position quite close behind them.

A trumpet's almost immediate and peremptory flourish intimated

Anne's impatience, and Master Jonson's stage-sets and backcloths came trundling out before ever the seating of the dais table was resolved. These were highly elaborate representations of tall trees in a grove, a flower-girt pool, and the broken white pillars of a ruined temple. In the centre of all, a cunningly devised natural staircase, seemingly of mossy stone steps, led up to a yawning cave in a ferny cliff, with a shelf-like ledge at its entrance. Birds twittered in the background, and a flight of doves were released—which however preferred to fly off to the far end of the hall and there try to get out of a window.

There was loud cheering, and Lord Southampton shouted that hawks should be brought in to deal with the pigeons.

An odd figure emerged from behind a central bush, clad in wide green breeches right up to the neck, with a loose cap above pulled down over the face to meet the breeches-top, small slits left for the eyes. This curiosity announced, in a high treble, that its name was Nobody, and that its privilege was to introduce the Masque of the Goddesses, set in the Temple of Peace of the peerless Pallas Athene.

Philip Herbert, hiccuping a little, intervened with a cry that he would lay fifty pounds with all takers that the creature was male—although it might be with the testicles removed. To which the King countered that this was nonsense, for you could see two paps poking against the green if you looked right closely—not that he would wager good money on it.

Some who would have hissed, or hushed for quiet at young Herbert, hastily desisted at the monarch's reaction. But another trumpet blast gained the required silence. A dark curtain was rung back from the cave mouth, and therein was to be seen a masked black lady—there was no doubt about the sex here, for she was naked to the waist and well-endowed—in the process of wakening a white and recumbent youth, and intoning in a sing-song voice: "Awake, awake dark sleep, arouse thee from the cave!"

The oddity Nobody announced helpfully that this was Night arousing her son Somnus.

"It is Mary Harington—I'd know her breasts anywhere, black or no'!" the irrepressible Herbert declared. "And that's Tom Henniker. The first time he's lain *under* her, I'll be bound!"

"Wheesht, Philip—here's Annie!"

To the simulation of a cock crowing, Pallas Athene emerged from behind the trees, a fine martial figure in a gilt helmet starred with jewels, a white tunic embroidered with cannon, spears and swords, representing civilised war, a glittering corslet seeded with pearls, and a short kilt-like skirt above gold-strapped calves and sandals. She bore a golden zigzag spear, as thunderbolt, and a round aegis or shield, showing the Gorgon's head and studded with red rubies. From her throat hung a long cloak-like train, also jewelled, borne up behind by a slender masked attendant in short, silver shirt-of-mail, whose legs were more shapely than any boy's—or, for that matter, the Queen's—although the clinging chain-mail outlined very frankly a fairly boyish figure. The red-gold hair peeping from under the smaller helmet, however, was undoubtedly that of Alison Primrose.

There was a loud cheer and even young Herbert forbore to comment. Only James himself remarked, "Scanty! Scanty!"—although to just what he referred was not clear.

Pallas Athene stalked with great dignity around the roped-off area, and then mounted the rustic steps with deliberate and regal poise—less easy for the train-bearer who could not see where she was putting her sandalled feet—to the cave-mouth shelf, where she turned to address the company:

> Warlike Pallas in her helmet dressed,
> With lance of winning, target of defence,
> In whom both wit and courage are expressed,
> To get with glory, hold with providence.

She declaimed that in something of a hurry, as though before she might forget the words, but none found any fault, and the King nodded sagely.

"Aye, well said," he commended, loudly. "Only—gain would ha' been better than get, mind. Aye, *gain* the glory."

Ignoring his helpful suggestion, Pallas Athene turned graciously to greet the rising Somnus and with zigzag spear banished black Night into the deepest corner of the cave. Somnus made some answering statement, but with insufficient volume to be heard.

"Speak up!" resounded from various parts of the hall.

A stirring trumpet voluntary broke in, just a little on the fast side, and out from both flanks of the wings came two lively corps of goddesses, six on each side, one golden-clad the other silver. All wore the short kilted skirts and sandals, and all were helmeted and masked. They pranced round amongst the trees, the music more or less dictating the antic pace, and came together around the pool, to sing in distinctly breathless chorus with much heaving of divine corslets. The singing was scarcely audible amidst the shouted debate of the audience as to who was who, going by shape, busts, legs and general carriage, with more wagers placed.

Master Ben Jonson had been very busy, and had written a verse or two for each goddess to recite—and voices gave away identification where other attributes failed. The first two declaimers were accepted as Lady Bedford and Lady Rich, as Vesta and Venus respectively, amongst some spirited argument as to their entire suitability for these parts, with Lady Kildare or Cobham following on. But twelve soliloquies, however refined, cannot be guaranteed to hold the fullest attention of even the most patient assembly, and long before the end the audience was contributing a deal more to the entertainment than was the cast.

It was at this stage that Chief Secretary Cecil, never addicted either to entertainment or drinking, came limping through the crowd to mount the dais and whisper in the ear of the King who nodded.

A stately dance of the goddesses brought to an end the first half of the masque, and Nobody announced an interval.

Hardly had the Queen retired from the scene when Sir Robert Cecil raised a hand, and over at the far door two of the King's tabarded trumpeters blew a prolonged and splendid fanfare. Then Yeomen of the Guard threw open the door and Garter King of Arms strode in, to announce in ringing tones, "By His Gracious Majesty's royal command—the Lady Arabella Stewart!"

There was a gasping reaction, and then a profound silence. Into the hall stepped a slight figure dressed all in virginal white. Three paces in, she halted, and sank in deepest curtsy—and remained down.

"Aye," James called, over all the heads. "Welcome, Cousin, to my Court. Come, you."

She rose, bowed again, and then commenced her long walk across the crowded floor, the four Yeoman clearing a passage for her, Garter King pacing behind.

Arabella Stewart was aged twenty-eight, with a natural dignity, pale, fair-haired but rather plain, with a firm mouth and determined chin but no especial physical attractions. She had good eyes, however—all the Stewarts had—and a serious, almost studious expression. She was as flat about the chest as a boy.

That walk across the hall, under the battery of assessing, critical, wondering eyes, must have been an ordeal for a woman who was obviously not of a bold nature. But she performed it well, head held high yet modestly, looking neither right nor left. She carried a folded and sealed letter in her hand.

It was deformed Cecil himself who came forward to hand her up the dais steps, and lead her round the table to the King, who was on his unsteady feet to receive her—as of course were all the others there, who could stand, though one or two were sprawled out witless and one was actually on the floor. She curtsied again over the hand held out for her to kiss.

"So, Cousin," James said, and leaned forward to plant a wet kiss approximately above her left eyebrow. "You've come. Ooh, aye—you're here. And looking fine and well. We are pleased to see you."

"I thank Your Majesty for your gracious summons," she answered, low-voiced, but clear. "Your very humble, grateful and entirely loyal servant." And she held out the paper in her hand.

"And this, Cousin?"

"A letter. Addressed to me, Sire. And unopened. Another I received, under the same seal—and considered treasonable."

There was a great in-taking of breath throughout the hall.

"Say you so?" The King peered at the seals, and then cracked them open and spread the paper on the wine-soaked table. "Ha!" he said, allowing himself time to have read only the first few words. "Here is an ill matter, indeed. Maist improper. Treasonable, as you say—right treasonable. This letter seeks for you to approach the King o' Spain, the Archdukes in the Netherlands, and the Duke o' Savoy, to assist you to become Queen in this realm, in return for tolerating the Catholic faith and making peace wi' Spain. And you no' to marry without the King o' Spain's consent. Guidsakes—and it says Sir Gervase Markham will carry your message. Aye, and it's signed by George Brooke. That'll be him that's brother to my Lord Cobham here, Warden o' my Cinque Ports. Heh?"

There was a deathly hush throughout the great apartment, broken only by a snore or two.

James looked slowly round the great company. His strange, glowing eyes slid past where Cobham stood as though turned to stone, and Grey de Wilton beside him nibbled his lip anxiously, and on in unhurried survey. Then he spoke.

"If George Brooke and Sir Gervase Markham be in this room," he rasped, "arrest them! On charge of treason against my realm and person."

Into the stir Sir Robert Cecil raised his precise voice, to the stab of a pointing finger. "There! And there! Guard!"

The four Yeomen of the Guard, who clearly knew just what to do and who the victims were, marched straight over to the two men named, conveniently close to them and clamped stern hands on their shoulders. They offered no resistance, made no protest, and were marched off, men and women drawing aside to give them passage-way as though they were plague-stricken.

James tossed the paper across the table to Cecil, who picked it up, and went through the process of reading it.

"This letter contains the names of others besides these," he announced thinly. "Two Jesuit priests, to act as intermediaries. And . . . others of more note!" He paused, ominously. "With Your Majesty's gracious permission, this might be best enquired into hereafter."

"To be sure, Cecil, man," Majesty agreed genially. "Waesucks—is this no' meant to be an evening o' entertainment! Forby, Her Majesty will be getting right impatient again! And that'll no' do. But, before thae goddesses tak ower again, I've a bit word for the Lady Arabella, here. Aye." He turned to the young woman still standing there. "Cousin—I thank you for this notable and leal service for our weal, the realm's weal. And I'm right glad to hae you grace our Court. In proof o' which I ordain you a pension o' one thousand pounds sterling each year—frae the Exchequer. Forby a diet frae our royal table—that's eighteen dishes *per diem*, you ken. And now, I present you wi' this token o' our cousinly affection and regard. Aye, regard." And groping in his doublet pocket, he brought out the chamois-wrapped jewel and handed it to her. Surprised and fumbling, Arabella all but dropped the substantial affair.

"Mind, woman—it's heavy! It's a pendant, gaud or ornature, see you."

As she gasped at the sudden revealed magnificence of the jewel, James grinned delightedly—at it, rather than at her. "It's real bonny, is it no'? And costly—gey costly." He snatched it from her again, stroked its brilliant surface lovingly for a moment, and then, almost reluctantly, leaned over and hung it round the young woman's neck, planting another slobbering kiss on her cheek. "Aye," he said, "that's it, then." And stepping back, made a shooing-away gesture with his hands.

Cecil stepped forward, touched Arabella's elbow, and bowed. Obviously bewildered at it all, this abrupt dismissal not the least, she curtsied hurriedly again, and was led off, supporting the heavy trinket in both hands.

James waved vaguely towards the roped-off masque enclosure and sat down heavily to reach for his tankard. His own masque over, his wife's might now recommence.

Wilton's hall buzzed like a hive of bees disturbed.

The second half of the Masque of the Goddesses suffered rather from anticlimax, not unnaturally. The performers seemed hardly to have their minds on what they were doing, Pallas Athene especially. Moreover, some of the goddesses had most evidently been sustaining themselves during the interval with the divine juice of the grape and there was rather less nervousness but also less co-ordination, in consequence. The audience, too, had become not a little preoccupied with other things; likewise the dais table imbibings were having cumulative effect. Many in the hall clearly decided that this would be a good time to be otherwhere, and, not always unobtrusively, slipped away.

Anne, with some dramatic sense, perceived that a winding-up was called for, and in the midst of a rather disconnected dialogue between Venus—who was finding it difficult to stand upright—and an even more skittish if substantial Jupiter preferring mime to recitative, possibly because his deep-set male voice unaccountably kept breaking through into the contralto, despatched her attendant to order the musicians to move on to the final dance sequence. This, after a little initial confusion, was achieved, to the relief of all; and the goddesses set themselves to prove the superiority of action over words. Led by Jupiter, a lively abandon prevailed. Not a few of the divinities began to beckon gentlemen of the audience to come and join them, particular and general.

"I say one hundred pounds on Jupiter being woman—and Alethea Talbot at that!" Philip Herbert shouted.

"Taken!" Southampton replied. "I say it's the boy Cavendish."

"It's young Paget . . ."

"Na, na—it's a woman. It's Jean Lennox. I ken her shape fine!" That was the Earl of Mar.

"We'll prove it!" Herbert yelled, and tossing his still half-full tankard over towards a corner, leapt down from the dais platform and went weaving towards the dancers.

Half-a-dozen young and not-so-young bloods followed his example—although not all completed the course, equilibrium being at a premium. Pallas Athene, perceiving the way that things were going, abandoned her nominal control of the dance and made a fairly expeditious exit.

Herbert reached the posturing Jupiter and reached out to remove the mask. As the god put hands up to protect it, the young man, with remarkable swiftness considering his state, stooped instead and grabbed the kilted white skirt—worn apparently by Olympians of both sexes—and wrenched. It came away in his hands—to reveal undoubted femininity in the shape of a major golden triangle above choice thighs.

"Jean Lennox as I said!" Mar bellowed. "That's one hundred pounds you owe me, Herbert! Aye, and you shall hae half o' it, Jeannie."

The buxom Duchess continued to dance.

After that, the situation developed rapidly and predictably. Certain ladies fled—but more remained. Southampton, having lost one bet, tried to recoup himself by chasing the curious Nobody around the enclosure. Hampered by the odd garb and limited visibility, this character was fairly quickly caught, upended and more or less efficiently de-breeched—proving to be another female, to royal shouts of satisfaction from the dais.

The more prudent of the residual ladies decided to flee, squealing, and the sportive remainder accepted the progressive removal of their skirts philosophically. The musicians, not having been commanded otherwise, played on, James thumping on the table-top with his tankard.

Lennox, abandoning his self-appointed watch over the Lords Cobham and Grey de Wilton who had taken no part in these proceedings, jumped from the dais, snatched up one of the many discarded draperies and ran to wrap it forcibly round his still capering spouse. She protested vigorously, but for once her husband was concerned, and with an accession of strength he dragged her, resisting all the way, off behind the wings, and out.

George Heriot was also in some concern about Alison Primrose. Admittedly she had followed the Queen out in good time, but she might not have gone far, or might even have come back—and in the present climate of behaviour, even so self-possessed a young woman was unsafe in this part of Wilton House, chain-mail or none. He pushed through the cavorting, laughing, shrieking throng, to hurry after the Duke and Duchess of Lennox.

Chaos to music reigned behind, as James Stewart watched, smiled a little, sipped, and beat time.

Out in the long back corridor, where a mixture of dramatics, frolics and hysterics prevailed amongst players, guests and servitors, Heriot heard upraised Scots voices coming from an anteroom. He strode in at the open door to find Lennox, his wife, the Earl of Mar and Alison, the first three all very vocal. The newcomer's appearance had an effect. Voices dropped somewhat, and Alison ran to his side, to take his hand.

With an obvious effort, the Duke mastered himself and spoke more quietly. "My lord of Mar—kindly return to the King's side. In this folly, he may require aid. Aye, and keep an eye on Cobham and Grey. Master Heriot and I will conduct the Duchess to her quarters." He turned to Alison. "Where is the Queen?"

"She has gone back. To her own part of the house. With the Marchioness of Huntly and Margrete Vinster. And two of the Guard. She is well—but angry."

"No doubt! Well, my lord?"

Mar, redder-faced even than usual, and perspiring, bowed stiffly and left.

"Jean, come with us. And no more fuss, if you please."

Jupiter, with a discarded toga wrapped round the middle and not a little drunk, was escorted to Wilton's west wing.

After handing the Duchess over to her tiring-woman, Alison adopting the toga for herself, the trio repaired to the Queen's music-room, empty now and there sat down, to look at each other, silent for the moment.

"So-o-o!" Lennox said, at length. "A notable evening's entertainment! Right notable, as our lord would undoubtedly declare! A right royal occasion. What do you make of it all, Geordie?"

"Which? This drunken cantrip and what followed? Or what went before?"

"The last will be forgotten in a day or two at this Court. The other, no."

Heriot nodded. "To me it proves once again that we have a cleverer sovereign lord than we are apt to remember."

"Aye—so think I. Clearly James knew of this plot, yet said nothing. For how long?"

"It is a full month since he ordered me to make that jewel. I believed that it was for the Queen. Now we know differently. It was made for a purpose. Only this afternoon he said that maybe it would be worth its great cost. He has arranged all for this night."

"But why thus? This charade?"

"That I do not know. Save that he is James and has a mind of much subtlety."

"I think that he would have no more plots built around the Lady Arabella," Alison put in. "Therefore, instead of locking her up in the Tower, as Queen Elizabeth would have done, he binds her to his side thus—and lets all the world see that he does so. It would be a bold faction, would it not, that now sought to use Arabella against the King?"

"M'mmm. Yes, that could be . . ."

"You heard it all, then?" Heriot asked.

"Yes. We were behind the side-scenes. Watching through slits. The Queen. The Duchess. Many ladies. The Queen was very wrath. Over the Lady Arabella. In especial the jewel. She all but issued forth . . ."

"That would have been foolish. The letter, that was strange. Think you it was a forgery? Planted to embroil the plotters. Brooke and the others?"

"I think not," Lennox said. "I would not doubt that James would use forgery, if need be. Or Cecil. But if what Arabella said was true, that she had received another such letter, it might not be necessary. And forgeries are chancy things—they can be two-edged, when it comes to trial. A sealed and signed letter, displayed before all, would make dangerous evidence, forged."

"How much do the seals mean? Clearly that letter had been opened before. James and Cecil had both read it."

"Seals can be softened, opened, and hardened again, yes. All it means is that Arabella received it earlier, handed it over to James, or Cecil, but then was given it back to present to the King thus strikingly. For better effect."

"What I do not understand is why the Lords Cobham and Grey were not arrested with the other two?" Alison wondered. "We know that they were in the plot. They were there—and Sir Robert Cecil said that there were other names in the letter. Of more note. Why not arrest them then?"

"There would be a reason," Heriot assured. "Those two know what they are at. Possibly they are baiting their hook to catch still larger fish?"

"You mean . . . Raleigh?" Lennox asked.

"It could be. Raleigh, if indeed he is implicated, could be hard to catch. A clever man, of notable fame. Idol of the people. Cecil hates him, they say—although he used to be his friend, profited from his enterprises. They could be laying a trap for Raleigh."

"Are they sufficiently clever for that?"

"Who knows? But I believe they may be. It seems the King scarce needed *our* good offices!"

Alison laughed, with her unfailing enjoyment of most situations. "It is the English plotters who need help! They need the Master of Gray, I vow, to teach them how to plot! He would never have bungled it thus."

Her companions did not contest that.

PART TWO

8

"VICKY," Queen Anne exclaimed, "of God's mercy, go get him! This is beyond all! I vow, if he does not come back forthwith, I shall return to Whitehall by boat! Now. Tell him so. It is cold. I will not wait here, thus. Aye, and as you go, have that woman Arabella's coach moved further back. I will not have her coming immediately behind myself, as though she was some great one. Tell Cecil he must change it."

Lennox began to speak, checked himself, and sighing, shrugged. "As Your Majesty says." Signing to a groom to hold his horse, he bowed and strode off down the lengthy column. He did not catch his cousin Arabella's eye as he passed her white and gold open coach directly behind the Queen's. That was not difficult, for she looked at the Duke as little as possible, resenting the fact that he now held the Lennox lands in Scotland which she conceived should be hers.

He had to pass numerous other coaches and actually turned a corner from Tower Hill before he could find Cecil who stood, frowning impatiently, with a group of other notables—for the Tower of London was scarcely the best place conveniently to assemble a mile-long procession, with open space at a premium, no length of straight streeting and the strung-out but stationary cavalcade winding away through a network of side-streets and lanes most awkwardly.

"My lord," he said—for Sir Robert had been created Baron Cecil of Essendine and Viscount Cranborne—"Her Majesty commands that the Lady Arabella's coach be removed further back. Will you see to it?"

"But I cannot do that, my lord Duke," the Secretary of State objected. "She is there on His Majesty's express order. Next to the Queen's coach," he said.

"It is difficult," Lennox admitted. "But . . . you could try to move the coach back a little way, to insert some of the Guard to march between, perhaps? That might serve."

Cranborne inclined a large but disapproving head barely perceptibly.

Sir Edward Coke, the Attorney-General, and related by marriage to Cecil, stood beside him, a brilliant but irascible man. "This is intolerable—this delay!" he snapped. "We have been waiting here fully an hour, already. What in God's good name is the King doing?"

"That, sir, the Queen commands me to go see. But—His Majesty will conduct matters his own way, I have no doubt!"

Coke muttered something probably treasonable for anyone other than the Attorney-General.

Lennox retraced his steps, and turned in at the main gatehouse of the Tower—as indeed had James himself an hour before, when he also wearied of the waiting involved in marshalling the procession. Where was His Majesty, he demanded of the guard-captain of Yeomen?

"The Menagerie, sir," he was told. "He is gone to the lions. You can hear them roaring."

Hurrying across the outer and inner baileys, the Duke came to the pit, surrounded by cages, in which the royal lions and other animals were kept. James had been relieved to hear that the creatures had survived the plague without loss, even producing a couple of lion cubs. He was now, apparently, investigating their condition.

The noise of angry roars and screaming yelps brought him to the King, with young Prince Henry, leaning over the rail round the pit, and experimenting to discover how different varieties of dog reacted to being pushed into the lions' dens. At sight of Lennox, he hailed him happily.

"Come you, Vicky, and see. The little dog is best. Mair spry and spirited. And lasts longest. Yon mastiff was no good. Humpit there in a corner, and had its back broke with the first whang o' a paw. The bulldog wasna much better. It attacked but was picked up like a kitten and the life shaken out o' it. Yon's it the lioness is eating. But the little sma' terrier, now, is still alive and jumping around like a flea. It has agility and wit, baith—as well as muscle and teeth, see. There's a lesson for you there, Henry laddie—aye, a moral."

"Let it out, Sire," the boy pleaded. "It has done sufficient well. The terrier. If you please. Look, it bleeds . . ."

"Na, na—there's spirit in it yet. The danger brings out the spirit, see you. This is the high moment o' the bit dog's life, Henry. Facing and outleaping lions. You'd no' deprive it o' its moment? There is much to be learned here, boy."

"Please, Sire—save it now . . ."

"Quiet, boy! Be a man. Sir Edward," James turned to the Lieutenant-Governor of the Tower, Peyton, father of the young man so dramatically knighted at Berwick Bridge, "hae you nae mair dogs?"

"Alas, Majesty—these are all my dogs. Or were!" the other said sadly. "A bear, perhaps? Or a wolf . . . ?"

"No sport wi' a bear. A wolf, maybe . . ."

"Sire," Lennox intervened, "may I ask that this entertainment be left, meantime? Taken up again later, perhaps. All wait. Hundreds. Thousands. And it is cold. This March wind. The Queen asks that you will deliver her out of it. That you will allow the procession to move off. All is long ready."

"Nae doubt, Vicky. But there is mair to life than processions provided for the rascal multitude. *Belua multorum capitum!*"

"Your loyal London subjects, Sire. Who have suffered greatly. And now would welcome you."

"Ooh, aye. Crowds. Vulgar, ignorant folk. Unlettered, untutored. *Odi profanum vulgus!* I'll no' hurry for the likes o' them."

"Perhaps not, Sire. But the Queen talks of returning to Whitehall Palace. By river, as you came. Now. She is chilled with waiting in this March wind. Cecil—or Cranborne—and Coke also urge a move. Much is planned en route, for your state entry into your English capital . . ."

"I ken better than you what's planned en route," James interrupted. "It's *my* entry, man—and they'll no' can start without me!" He chuckled. "Eh, Vicky—be not so concerned for what doesna signify—you that might ha' been a king."

"I thank God that was *your* fate, not mine, James!"

"Sire—look! The terrier—another wound. Oh, Sire—save it! It cannot last much longer, I swear. It tires. Save it, Sire—and, and may I have it if it lives? It is a brave dog."

"Och well, laddie," James relented. "If Sir Edward says so. It's his bit tyke."

So the terrier was rescued on the end of a hooked pole, and with Henry clutching it, panting and bleeding, to his fine white satin, pearl-seeded breast, an unhurried return was made to the waiting parade.

James noticed that Arabella's carriage now had a posse of Yeomen of the Guard between it and that of the Queen and ordered this to be removed. Anne pointedly looked the other way as her husband passed.

The procession was most carefully marshalled, in theory, according to precedence, in the English fashion. The Earl Marshal, the Duke of Norfolk, having been proscribed and executed by Elizabeth in 1572, his brother the Lord Henry Howard, now Earl of Northampton, took his place and organised it all, assisted by his great-nephew the Earl of Arundel, rightful Duke of Norfolk. First of all came the King's judges, splendid in their robes—and glad of them in the wind—led by the Lord Chief Justice Popham. Then the great officers of state, under the new Lord Chamberlain, another Howard, the Earl of Suffolk, and still another, the Lord Admiral, Earl of Nottingham. Then the Privy Council behind the Lord Chancellor Egerton, newly created Lord Ellesmere for the occasion. There followed the Knights of the Garter, then the mass of the nobility, four by four in seemingly endless ranks, succeeded by the Knights of the Bath. Then the bishops, mitred and chasubled in coped glory behind Archbishop Whitgift of Canterbury. There followed the royal household under Captain of the Bodyguard, Sir Thomas Erskine of Dirleton, a kinsman of Mar's, replacing Sir Walter Raleigh who remained at the Tower—in a cell. The heralds under Garter, Clarencieux and Norroy Kings of Arms, brilliant in colour, came next, before the royal group.

All this enormous column had to move off in as orderly a fashion as was possible, at the same time, westwards, interspersed with trumpeters, many bands of instrumentalists, choirs of singers and the like. This was to be effected by trumpet-call signals, but owing to the long delay certain constituent groups had become dispersed—even into wine-shops—and much trumpeting and toing and froing of couriers was necessary before any consistent forward movement could be achieved. James had something to say about that.

When eventually the start was accomplished, the royal party came almost two-thirds of the way down the lengthy column.

First young Henry rode, alone on a white Barbary mare, small back straight, upright, bowing gravely right and left, his fine white satin only slightly sprinkled with terrier's blood. Two scarlet Yeomen marched at his horse's head. Then yards behind came the King, on a white jennet, scowling rather, in orange, purple and green, so padded and stuffed as to seem as broad as he was high, his lofty-crowned hat with its diamond-studded band sprouting multi-coloured ostrich plumes. Over his head was borne a handsome canopy embroidered with the royal arms and carried on ribboned poles by eight Gentlemen of the Bedchamber, all looking daggers at one another, Herbert—now Sir Philip and a Knight of the Bath—Southampton and six Scots including Sir John Ramsay, Sir George Home and James Hay, newly created Viscount Doncaster, the King having been busy filling up the House of Lords, for financial and personal as well as political reasons. Large contingents of Yeomen of the Guard flanked this group on either side, three deep, to ensure that the populace was kept at a suitable distance.

Immediately behind came a band of musicians consisting entirely of drummers—James's own arrangement; on the whole he preferred percussion to harmony, providing always that he was prepared for the outbreak, it being only sudden noise which upset him. This company certainly gave of their best, decibel-wise—and if they flagged, the monarch turned round in his saddle and apostrophised them as to their duty and privilege in no uncertain style.

The Queen's white-and-gold carriage, drawn by two snow-white mules, followed, with Anne frequently clapping hands over her ears to seek to temper the thunderous beat from in front on over-sensitive ears. She was blue with cold, for, though mercifully dry, the March wind off the Essex marshes was particularly chilly, and she was dressed in silks and satins more apt for the boudoir, with a notably low neckline, the extravagant starched ruff round her throat being neither comfortable nor warming. Her own ostrich plumes, inserted with such pains into her elaborate coiffure by Alison Primrose and Margrete Vinster, had succumbed rather to the breeze and long wait and required constant adjustment. Nevertheless, Anne smiled and bowed and waved with great amiability and royal beneficence. But she never turned her head fully either right or left, in case she should glimpse, out of the corner of an eye, Arabella Stewart in the identical carriage behind, now close up again.

The Duke of Lennox, as vaguely royal, rated a horse, the only other in the entire cavalcade—and he kept as far behind his monarch, consort and cousin and those drums, as he decently could. Thereafter came carriage after carriage of the Court and well-bred hangers-on, forming the most cheerful section of the entire procession—for they had had the foresight to bring considerable liquid refreshment with them, and moreover had three choirs of boys from London churches accompanying them, who vied with each other in the ribald wording they could contribute to selected stately melodies, with the courtiers joining in with mounting enthusiasm and invention.

Seven-year-old Princess Elizabeth had measles at Coombe Abbey, where she had been placed in the care of Lord and Lady Harington.

The so-called state entry took a three-mile route westwards from Tower Hill, by the Byward where, from the churchyard of All Hallows by the Tower, three hundred boys from Christ's Hospital sang sweetly; and some dislocation was caused by James pressing on up Mark Lane, after only a brief pause and a nod, to the resumption of drumming, while Anne waited to hear out the chorus. The coach drivers thereafter, concerned to catch up, went rocketing up Mark Lane and down Fenchurch Street at a spanking pace, the carriages lurching and heaving, despite their occupants' cries—and the choirboys behind raced, leaping and hallooing in joy, to the alarm of many lieges who, assuming the procession was over, had started to stream homewards. However, at the foot of Fenchurch Street was erected the first of no fewer than seven triumphal arches, where a speech of welcome from the city guilds had had the effect of holding up the King, so that continuity was more or less re-established. This arch had a cunningly devised model of the entire City of London balanced on its apex, a contrivance which so intrigued James that he all but cricked his neck in peering up and trying to identify the various buildings represented, moving his horse from this side of the arch to that in the process, much lessening the tedium of the speeches.

The next archway, at Gracechurch Street, was still finer, quite splendid indeed, as became the work of London's Italian colony—although James pointed out roguishly that it might be said to be something Papistical, and might not find favour with all of his Council. Anne again got delayed here, admiring the artwork and priceless pictures of saints—and with her, of course, the second half of the column—so that there had to be another tally-ho along Cornhill, passing the third arch at the canter—much to the indignation of the apprentices' body which had erected it.

At the Royal Exchange the powerful Dutch trading community, representing some of the richest men in the city, had still another arch, symbolising the seventeen provinces of the Netherlands; and here there were more speeches, lightened however by being in Latin, to which James at least was prepared to pay consideration—and indeed to put right the orators on one or two occasions, drawing Prince Henry's attention to slips and alternative usages. Here George Heriot watched from amongst the crowd and was interested to hear the comments of London's loyal citizenry on their new monarch.

In Cheapside, a reunion was effected with the first half of the company, Justiciary, Privy Council, Church and the rest, who, not having had to listen to speeches, had made much more expeditious progress, and indeed had not seen the sovereign for some time. Here an elaborate Fountain of Virtue actually ran wine, of fair quality, and moreover was serviced by scantily-robed virgins who, in the chill wind and waiting, were to be excused a certain amount of previous ware-sampling, so that the virtue demonstrated was hearty rather than chaste. This well suited the processionists, even the majority of the bishops—amongst whom Puritans were not prominent—and enabled the crowned heads to catch up. Gold cups—empty, by some mischance—were here presented to King, Queen and Prince, and the marathon was restarted in better fettle. Unfortunately the drummers and choirboys got left behind at the wine fountain, by an oversight.

Fleet Street delighted the Queen, at least, by producing an orchestra playing traditional Danish airs, at the sixth triumphal arch, so that there was another disjunction, resulting in Anne arriving late, with the majority of the Court, at the Temple Bar final archway, where James was being presented with the city sword by the Lord Mayor, plus a jugful of gold coins, which someone had had the good sense to arrange. James was much displeased at this interruption of the most serious part of the programme, but managed to contain himself sufficiently to knight there and then the Lord Mayor, the two Sheriffs and, by chance, the Master of the Soapmakers Livery who had somehow got pushed into a forward position—all without further financial arrangement. Thereafter, suddenly becoming weary of the entire proceedings, he announced, to nobody in particular, that he was going back to his bed at Whitehall, and that his Annie and the laddie could continue with the remainder of the programme—seeing they seemed to be enjoying it. Himself, he had a bellyache and enough was plenties.

Some disorganisation ensued, as processionists tried to decide who went with whom, or at all. James resolved this by digging spurs into his jennet's flanks and setting off riverwards at a rousing half gallop. Being the only man mounted, save for Lennox and the Prince, he had the occasion to himself, and clattered off down The Strand. Recognising this probably to be unsuitable, after a little hesitation, the Duke spurred after him. At least the citizenry here were treated to a display of royal horsemanship such as they had never seen before.

Anne, now the centre of attention and attraction, and in her element, continued on her regal way, the epitome of queenly charm and benevolence, indicating however to Arabella that her attendance was no longer required, and choosing not to notice the gradual dropping off of a large part of the retinue. The waiting crowds, starved of royal pomp and display—for Elizabeth in her later years had given up the popular street parades of her glorious heyday—cheered themselves hoarse, and, being still queen conscious, scarcely noticed the lack of the King, especially with the first princely heir to the throne for fifty years, riding, like Prince Charming in white, through their midst. West London at least was conquered for the Stewarts.

* * *

"Maister Heriot! Maister Heriot!" Tom Henderson cried, head thrust round the door of Heriot's office. "It's himsel'! Come you down. My Goad—it's himsel'! Here, I tell you." Henderson was the foreman goldsmith, brought down from Edinburgh. He was a man of sterling worth—and knew it—was no respecter of persons, and had taught Heriot much of his trade.

"Himself, Tom? Who is himself? What's the steer . . . ?"

"Himsel'—the King, man! He's here. In the shop."

"Save us! What can this be . . . ? Who is with him?"

"Naebody. He's alone. There's a puckle guards left oot in the street."

"And you've left him alone! In the work-room, man!" Pushing past the other, Heriot hurried out of the office and down the stairs.

He did not trust James Stewart left alone in a jeweller's workshop.

He found the King admiring a finely-engraved silver-gilt chalice, and was relieved that this had caught the royal eye, since it by no means could be stowed away in even the most capacious doublet pocket.

"Sire!" he cried. "This is too much! Too great an honour. That Your Majesty should come in person to my humble shop . . ."

"Eh, Geordie man? I used to come to you in Edinburgh, did I no'? Yon bit booth at St. Giles. Many's the crack we've had yonder."

"But—this is different, Sire. London. They do not understand such, such familiarity between monarch and tradesman, here in England. Their habits are a deal more . . . rigid . . ."

"Rigid! Aye, rigid's a good word, Geordie. *Rigidus, rigor*. A good word—but a bad quality, eh? Rigid things break, see you—mair supple things bend. I'd aye liefer bend than break, man! How much is this bit cup?"

"I have had it made for the Earl of Shrewsbury, Sire. It will cost him twelve pounds."

"I like it fine. I'll hae it, Geordie."

"But, Sire, it is ordered. And it has Shrewsbury's arms engraved. I will make you another . . ."

"I'll hae this one. Shrewsbury can wait, the man. You can wipe off his arms, easy and put in mine. His talbot beasties will change into a lion and a unicorn, fine."

"As you will, Sire." Heriot inclined his head. "To what do I owe the honour of this visit, this unprecedented visit?"

"Och, I just want a bit word wi' you, Geordie."

"Your Majesty could have summoned me to Whitehall Palace."

"There's aye folk about, yonder—folk wi' long ears! What I hae to say is for your lugs alone, man."

"Then Your Majesty had better come up to my room. Where we can be alone."

Upstairs, James looked around Heriot's office with interest, poking and prying. "Books, papers, ledgers," he commented. "You'll hae a wheen secrets in a' yon books. Debts. Notes o' hand. Title-deeds, belike."

"Secret, Sire—yes."

"But no' secret frae me. Eh, Geordie?"

Heriot said nothing.

"There might be papers there could tell me much. Ooh, aye—

about some folk I'd be as well to ken about! For my ain and the realm's good."

"In such case, Sire, you must trust me to inform you. Of anything dangerous or treasonable."

"Och, I trust you, man. As I dinna trust many. But your judgment might be faulty. Aye, faulty."

"Has Your Majesty found it so hitherto?"

"No. No' yet. Though, in the matter o' plots, I'm no' sure that you're a' that fly!" The King looked round him. "It's gey cold in here. I'd hae thought you'd had a better fire, man." He tottered over to peer into an open deed box. "I'm hearing you lent Rutland ten thousand pounds. Yon's a lot of money. Sterling. I'm no' sure Rutland's a friend o' mine."

"I am interested that Your Highness should have come to hear of it! But my lord of Rutland is adding to his castle of Belvoir—where you have hunted. And will no doubt hunt again! I understand that is what the money is for. And he offers excellent security. I cannot think that there is any cause for Your Majesty's . . . concern!"

"I am relieved to hear it, Geordie!" James said dryly. He sat down abruptly. "This o' loans and property—aye, and hunting," he observed casually. "I'm thinking that it's maybe no' just suitable that the monarch should aye hae to go hunting in other folk's parks. The monarch should hae a bit park o' his ain. Nearby. Would you agree, Geordie?"

"You have Windsor Great Park . . ."

"Ooh, aye. But Windsor's no' to be compared wi' some I'd name. It's no' right hunting country." He shot a glance at his jeweller. "I was thinking o' Royston. In Hertfordshire. Royston, aye."

"H'mm. A large place, Sire, I'm told. Very fine—but expensive."

"Is your king to hae some wretched bit house so much poorer than his subjects', man?"

"No, Sire—no. But the price is high just now, for all such. So many Scots lords have come South, to be near your Court. Buying properties around London. Many will have to sell again all too soon, I fear . . ."

"And *you* have lent them money?"

"Some Sire, yes. Too many, I fear. I may well have over-lent—may not get it all back . . ."

"You'll no' tell me that Jinglin' Geordie Heriot hasna covered himsel'! Wi' holding the title deeds to a' these properties?"

"To be sure. But if too many are forced to sell, owing to the high cost of London living, the market will fall badly."

"That'll no' apply to *me*, I'm thinking! Gie me twenty thousand pounds, to help buy this Royston, Geordie."

The other drew a deep breath. "That is a lot of money, Sire. In . . . in the circumstances."

"Can you no' find it for me?"

"It will be difficult . . ."

"Difficult, eh? Then—there are other usurers in London, Geordie Heriot, let me tell you! There's John Spilman—aye, and William Herrick. Both jewellers to Elizabeth. Aye, and both anxious to be jewellers to *me*! Rich men, wi' big lands. They'd maybe no' find it sae difficult to lend a few pounds to their liege lord!"

"To be sure, Sire," Heriot shrugged. "But they might charge Your Majesty interest! And expect to see their money back rather more quickly than I have done! No doubt you will sound them out—if you have not already done so!"

"H'mmm. Ooh, aye." James looked at his companion from under down-drawn brows. "It's no' that I'm wanting to go past you, Geordie, Guid kens. You and I hae done business for a long whilie. Our friendship is of auld standing, eh?"

"Your Majesty greatly honours me. Old standing, yes—like some of your bills of hand which I hold!"

"Houts, man—what way's that to speak! To your auld gossip Jamie Stewart. And I dinna owe you that much?"

"Thirty-eight thousand pounds, Sire—not counting the jewel for the Lady Arabella. Since you said to keep that separate. Sterling."

"Waesucks—sae much as that, still! Och, you'll likely no' be adding it up right, man."

"Add them yourself, Sire, if you doubt me. Your notes-of-hand are all here, in this box. Here is the key . . ."

"Och, never heed. Aye, but here's my note for the two thousand pounds, man. For Arabella's bit gaud. I've brought it wi' me. It was gey expensive, mind."

"I warned that it would be, Sire." Heriot took the crumpled note-of-hand which James had fished out of one of his unsavoury pockets, smoothed it out and laid it down. "I thank you." He cleared his throat. "And might I remind Your Majesty that the Queen's indebtedness to me amounts to nine thousand pounds."

"Guidsakes! A' that? My Annie? Hech, hech—this is no' to be

borne. She is fell extravagant, the woman. Her faither, yon Frederick o' Denmark, was just the same. Extravagance is a right sin—especially in women. Here have I gotten her a jointure o' six thousand, three hundred and seventy-six pounds a year, frae that Cecil. Like winning blood frae a stone! Mind you, like a' the rest in this ill-run realm it falls to be sanctioned by the parliament. Parliament, mark you—deciding on how much it's Queen has in her pouch! Is that no' *my* business? It's a right scandal. But I'll teach them—I will so! The morn's morn I'm opening this first parliament o' my reign in England. They'll hear a thing or twa, these English squires and merchants, I promise you! It's them that's making a pauper out o' their sovereign, wi' their insolent rules and customs. It's no' to be borne, I say. It's them that's keeping me frae my millions. My bonny ploy. But you ken that."

All too well, George Heriot knew how the English parliamentarians had objected to the wonderful knighthoods scheme, claiming it to be a form of revenue-raising, and as such the responsibility of parliament. All financial matters, they insisted, came under the purview and authority of parliament—and this was indubitably financial. Cecil had strongly advised against any offending of parliament, even before its first meeting of the reign, holding that to go ahead with the scheme meantime would be almost unthinkable. Knighting might be the King's prerogative, but sanctioning compulsory payment therefor was parliament's. So the money-spinning was held up and James grew the more disenchanted with his English subjects.

"Your Majesty will, I have no doubt, give parliament something to think about!" Heriot acceded. "But since it decides on the amount of your royal revenues, in this country, it is in a strong position. You will, probably, decide to gang warily with them." He could scarcely say more than that.

"We'll see." James rubbed his hands together. "Man, it's fell cold. Can you no' do better wi' your bit fire? It's colder in here than in the street, I do declare. Sakes—I'd expect a rich man the likes o' Jinglin' Geordie Heriot to hae a better fire than this. Scented logs, at least, like I burn in my palaces—no two-three bits o' deid coal!"

"I am sorry that my fire is too poor for Your Majesty. If I had known that you were coming . . ." He shrugged again, and leaning over, picked up the King's note-of-hand for two thousand pounds. He glanced at it, and then tossed it on to the smouldering embers. "That will make a little blaze, at least. Scarce as rich as scented logs, perhaps . . . !"

James stared, from him to the burning paper and back again, and drew a jerky, wet-sounding breath. "Man!" he got out, licking lips with busy tongue. "Och, Geordie man! My goodness to God! That was . . . that was two thousand pounds! Sterling!"

There was silence in the office while the smoke of the note-of-hand went up the chimney, the monarch watching the process with something like awe.

"On the knighthoods matter, Sire," Heriot went on, "I have some information which perhaps may have escaped you. It seems that some of your, h'm, gentlemen not infrequently introduce candidates for knighthood to Your Majesty. And in your kindness you may oblige them. I have heard that this has become a recognised source of profit for some of the said favoured gentlemen. They it is who charge the fee—and keep it. This would seem to me a form of robbery which Your Highness might wish to halt."

James actually flushed, something Heriot would not have thought possible. He looked away. "You tell me that? Who? Who man—do you know?"

The other had no doubts as to who was involved. But suddenly he was sorry for the man before him and shook his head. "No names, Sire. I know only that it is done, by some whom you favour. *You* will know who bring you men to knight."

"Aye, well—maybe. I'll see to it. I, h'm, thank you, Geordie. Thank you for this . . . and for the other. Yon two thousand pounds. It was kindly done, right kindly. I'll no' forget it. But—the loan for Royston, man? You'll gie it to me, will you no'? Until this ill-begotten parliament finds me some siller." And, when the other still puckered his brows, "A knighthood for yoursel', Geordie? Would you no' maybe like to be Sir George Heriot, Knight? It sounds well enough."

"Thank you, Sire—but no. Not for me. I am not of the stuff of knights, I think. Calling me sir will not make me other than I am. A goldsmith and, and usurer! I pray to be excused."

"I jaloused you'd say that, mind. It's your pride, see you. Sinfu' pride in you. Geordie Heriot, the pridefullest man in my two kingdoms!"

The other smiled. "Not for me to say that my liege lord is wrong! But . . . I will find you your twenty thousand pounds, Sire. Give me two days, or perhaps three."

James sighed with relief. "Uh-huh. Good. I ken't I could rely on Geordie Heriot. I'll pay you back right soon, never fear. Next to Spain, this is the richest realm in Christendom. There's a mite wrong if its monarch canna pay his debts. Or buy a bit house! But, see you, man—a word in your lug. I'm thinking you're ower kind to my Annie. You're maybe a wee thing soft wi' her. Now she's got yon Somerset House for her own, here in London. And Hatfield and Nonsuch—aye, and Pontefract in Yorkshire—she is getting right costly notions. You've no' to encourage her. No, nor in this silly ploy she's at about founding a university. At Ripon. A *university*, see you—my Annie! I ken who put that in her heid! But I'm no' having it, mind. So dinna go wasting any o' your siller that airt, Geordie!"

"As Your Majesty wishes. But I would remind you that I am *Her* Majesty's jeweller also, and have been for many years. You will understand my position, Sire."

"Aye, fine I understand it. I'm just warning you." James rubbed his hands again. "Man—you've nae mair bit notes-o'-hand for this fire o' yours? It's still gey cold!"

"I hope Your Majesty is not unwell? I do not feel it so cold," But, perceiving that the King was presumably intending to stay longer yet, Heriot put more coals on the fire.

"Aye, well—there's another matter I want a word wi' you about, Geordie. On this o' siller, likewise. It's to do wi' yon man Raleigh. D'you ken him?"

"I met him but the once, Sire. A tall and goodly man, noble seeming. I was grieved . . ."

"Ooh, aye—we were a' grieved! But he's in the Tower now—and bides there! But, the point is—he was a gey rich man. And we canna just find out where his money is. It's no' a' in lands, by any means. Cecil's sniffing after it—for the man's forfeit for treasonable activities mind, and his riches wi' him. If we could but lay hands on them, it would be naething to do wi' parliament, Cecil says. It's a judiciary matter, and Cecil has Coke and yon Popham in his pocket! So maybe *you* could do a bit sniffing around, too, Geordie? You ken a' about money, and where it hides itsel'. Hae a bit sniff, man."

Heriot's features stiffened. "I would wish nothing to do with that business Sire," he said levelly. "To be honest with you, I think it smells badly. I would prefer to do my sniffing elsewhere!"

"Oh-ho—so your nose has become ower delicate, has it! Well, *I* canna afford to be sae nice in what I smell, man! Of course it stinks—but in statecraft a wise man uses his neb for sniffing out, no' for turning up! Raleigh was playing wi' fire, and burned his fingers. He maun pay for it."

"It is surely absurd to say that a man of Raleigh's stature was in this fool plot against you, Sire. If he had been, it would have been a deal better managed, I swear! I would conceive his name to have been dragged in by Cecil, who now hates him. And possibly has designs on his wealth!"

"So! Geordie Heriot would conceive that, would he? I'll note it, aye—even though it was no' the opinion o' this realm's judges, at the trial!"

"You have already said that Lord Chief Justice Popham and Attorney-General Coke—who prosecuted viciously—are in Cecil's pocket."

"Dinna bicker wi' me, Geordie. Forby, Walter Raleigh knew o' the plot. He admitted it. Even if he didna tak part. And he didna inform me o't—as was his leal duty. Whether or no' he'd have raised up Arabella, he wouldna hae minded to see *me* down, yon man. I see him as less noble than do you. But yet I was merciful—aye, merciful."

"Do you call it merciful, Sire, to lock up in the Tower one of the greatest Englishmen of the day? A valiant venturer and soldier, discoverer of new lands and dominions . . ."

"Great, d'you ca' him? The man who brought the filthy tobacco-weed to this land, taught this pestilential habit of smoking, to defile men's mouth's and lungs?"

"I do not affect the weed myself—but I see little harm in it . . ."

"If the good God had intended us to burn deid vegetation in our heids, Geordie Heriot, He'd hae provided us wi' lums, chimneys! It's an unnatural and pernicious habit, man, and will rot the bodies o' them that partake o' it, mark my words. *Hostis humani generis!* I'm thinking I might mak it unlawfu'."

"Would parliament agree, Sire?"

James glared at him—and then recollected that he had not yet got what he wanted. "We'll see. But . . . I was mercifu', as I say. I only locked him in the Tower—where Elizabeth would have had his head. Aye, and only executed the twa Jesuits and yon Brooke. Cobham and Grey and Markham, I spared. Was that no' a great mercy?"

"Since you ask me, spared after a fashion, Majesty. You had them through the pains of hell, first!"

"I didna lay a finger upon them, Geordie. I gave them a bit fright, aye—but that was for their ain good, mind. They'll no' do the like again."

After the December trial at Winchester, and the condemning to death of all the alleged conspirators, James had in fact personally ordained that Markham first should be brought to the place of execution, bid his friends farewell, ordered to say his last prayers, then lay his head on the block. With the axe actually upraised a King's messenger came running, to say that the execution was stayed for two hours, for unannounced reasons—and the wretched man hustled away. Exactly the same procedure was followed with the Lord Grey de Wilton. When Lord Cobham was brought out, in turn, he had come more cheerfully—and indeed had indulged in ringing prayer for half an hour—for he had been promised his life secretly in return for implicating Raleigh and the others. Finally the other two were brought back to the scaffold and only then informed that the King, in his great clemency, had granted a pardon. All this performance James had watched with interest from a window—and moreover arranged that Raleigh should see it also, from another room, before being taken off to London Tower. England was beginning to learn that she had acquired a monarch with imagination as well as erudition.

"But I'm no' accountable to you, Geordie Heriot, for my acts and judgments," the King went on. "I'm just asking that you keep your lugs open as to Raleigh's siller. What he's done wi' it. And there's another thing. Elizabeth, the silly auld fool, gave Raleigh the monopoly for the licensing o' a' taverns. In a' England. Guid kens how much he made out o' it! Properly farmed it should make much. I want it looked into. What like it's worth. How it had best be worked. Who farmed it for Raleigh. Discover me this, Geordie, and you'll no' be the loser."

"A large task, Sire."

"Wi' commensurate rewards, man. And I ken none better to do it." He rose. "Now—gie's your arm down yon stair. It's steep. Aye—and you'll be at the opening o' the parliament the morn's morn. It will be worth attending, I'm thinking. There will be a place for you wi' the royal household . . ."

* * *

The Duke of Lennox should have been sitting in his own House of Lords stall—for he had been given a peerage of the United Kingdom in addition to his purely Scottish dukedom—but he preferred to sit with George Heriot and the Queen's ladies behind the Throne Gallery, even though it meant being also in the proximity of his duchess. The Lords' hall of Westminster Palace was crowded already, even before the Commons arrived, and a great air of expectancy prevailed. It was the first parliament for five years, the first of the new reign, and it might well prove a momentous session. Queen Elizabeth had tended to alienate her later parliaments, and there was a strong feeling amongst many members that it would be wise to show the new monarch what the true position was, from the start.

The King was late, probably deliberately. Much trumpeting eventually heralded his arrival. Preceded by the Yeomen of the Guard and Gentlemen at Arms, the entire College of Heralds and the great officers of state, these last bearing the crown, sceptre, orb, sword and spurs of the regalia, James came in at a sort of purposeful shamble, tall stick clicking and clacking. At his side, Anne started out with a hand on his arm, but quickly found his odd and unpredictable gait impossible to approximate to, and detached herself to move along with dignity half a pace behind, leaving wary room for that waving stick. Prince Henry walked just behind, handsome in his Garter robes, self-possessed but grave.

The Lord Chancellor, now Earl of Ellesmere, in his capacity of Lord Keeper and Speaker of the House of Lords, received them up at the Woolsack, and conducted the royal pair to their twin thrones, with a stool for the heir to the throne a little to the side. James seated himself, with the usual difficulty of disposing of the long staff, and turned round to peer behind his chair to see who was there who might be entrusted with it. He was having a tiff with Sir Philip Herbert about a horse race, where the favourite had said unkind things about Scots horse-copers and horse-leeches, and there had been something of a riot; Sir John Ramsay was in disgrace over an amour with the Venetian ambassador's son, and Southampton and Doncaster were duly occupying their seats on the Lords' benches. Sir George Home seemed to be the only depository—and was beckoned forward and given the staff. Then, settling back in his throne, James took off his high hat, gave it to Anne to hold, and beckoned for his crown to be brought from its cushion. He clapped it on. The Queen was already wearing her smaller one. Well content, the monarch beamed round on all.

Clearing his throat, Ellesmere came forward, to bend and whisper. "The Commons, Sire. The faithful Commons."

"Ooh, aye—the Commons. Have them in, man."

"His Majesty, James, by the Grace of God, King and Defender of the Faith, summons his faithful Commons to this place," the Chancellor declared in ringing tones. "My lords, you may be seated."

As officials went in search of the members of the Lower House, who normally met in the Chapter-house of Westminster Abbey, James stared about him with interest, pointing out features of the building to the Queen and his son and comparing it unfavourably with the Parliament House in Edinburgh—which of course had to be sufficiently large to hold all three estates of Church, Lords, and burgh and landward representatives, met therein together in session, not separately as here. The King made these points in loud tones, for the edification of all.

When at length, led by their Speaker, the Commons made their somewhat belated entrance—no doubt they likewise sought to establish their position and privileges—and the bowing process to the Throne commenced, the monarch smiled on them benignly, and waved a beringed hand.

"James is in good fettle," Lennox observed. "He intends to enjoy his day, I can see. Whoever else does."

"You think that there will be trouble?"

"The possibility is never absent when our liege lord is about! But he is in a good humour. All may be well."

Before all three hundred-odd Commons finished shuffling into position in ranks at the back of the hall—there was no seating for most of them—James had had enough of waiting. He fished under his magnificent robe of state and found the speech which Cecil had prepared for him, straightened the crown on his head—he had a large head, as he said himself most apt for wearing a crown—and cleared his throat vehemently. When that failed to quell the hubbub and stir, he hawked again—Heriot feared for a moment that he was going to spit on the floor, as he had seen him do before this—and banged on the arm of his throne. This had the required effect. Of the firm conviction that wearying ceremonial should be cut to a minimum, he decided that Loyal Addresses and the like could be dispensed with and the meat of the business got down to. He licked moist lips and launched forthwith into action.

"My Lord Chancellor, honourable representatives o' foreign princes and powers, my lords and faithful Commons," he declared thickly. "We salute and greet you warmly, on this the opening o' the first parliament o' our reign." That was as far as he read from Cecil's paper—which he then laid firmly aside by tossing it on the floor. "Aye, it's a new reign, to be sure," he went on, "but it's a deal mair'n that, see you. It's a new dispensation, no less. A milestane, aye, a milestane in history. And a fingerpost, forby. To point the way in this new situation. Much that's auld is by wi'—and well by wi'. Much o' enmity and bloodshed and foolish bickers. We mak a fresh start. *Experientia docet stultos.*"

That was received in a wary silence.

"Aye, well—here is a new kingdom, see you. No longer the Kingdom o' England. Nor yet o' Scotland. But the United Kingdom o' Great Britain, united in dynastic union in my royal person. And to be united hereafter in state, governmental and political union, indissoluble and for a' time coming."

"No! You'll no' do it. No, I say!" a single voice cried loudly from the back of the hall—and it was a distinctly Scots voice, so that it could scarcely have been a Member of Parliament.

There was a horrified silence, and then uproar. Some applauded, some shouted at the interrupter; others, especially Puritan M.Ps, equally appalled at what the King had said about there being no longer a Kingdom of England, yelled their agreement with the protester; still others, upset at this wholesale departure from traditional ceremony into the realm of policy, exclaimed to each other. The Lord Chancellor, much agitated, held up his hands for silence and when that failed wrung them instead.

James Stewart, to whom controversy, debate, argument, were as meat and drink, leaned forward eagerly in his chair, great eyes alight, letting the hubbub ride. Then, when he esteemed it sufficient, he flicked a quick glance and nod at his principal trumpeter, who stood nearby at the ready. The subsequent bugle-blast brought down dust from the hammer-beam roof and stilled every voice.

Into the hush James spoke genially enough. "I'll do it, to be sure. Ooh, aye—I'll do it. As is right and proper and my Christian duty, in Church as in State. Aye, we'll hae an end to disorders. This my realm maun be one realm. You canna hae me, the King and Christ's Vice-Regent, reigning at the one time ower twa warring and divided kingdoms. I am the husband, see you, and this whole island is my wife. I am the heid and it is my body. I the shepherd and it my flock. And flocks and bodies—aye, and wives too, should be dutifu'." He cast a roguish glance at the Queen, and leaned over to poke her in the ribs with his padded elbow.

Anne managed to retain an admirable impassivity of appearance.

Warming to this pleasing and vital theme, James went on, saliva copious. "I'm hoping, therefore, nae man will be sae unreasonable, aye unreasonable, as to jalouse that I, who am a Christian king under the Gospel, should be a polygamist and husband o' twa wives! Or that I, being the heid, shall hae a monstrous and divided body. Or that, being the shepherd to sae fair a flock—whose worth hath nae wall to hedge it in but the four seas—should hae my flock pairted in twa! Na, na—that wouldna do. A union there'll hae to be. One state, one church, one parliament, one law. You'll proceed to establish this great matter in this your first parliament, my lords and Commons. That's the first thing."

There was a spontaneous outcry now from all sides of the hall, as the shaken legislators took in what was being commanded. Having just learned how to upraise their voices in the royal presence—a thing they would never have dared hitherto—they gave tongue vigorously.

"Sakes—had you any notion that he was going to do this?" Heriot demanded of the Duke.

"No. He has talked often of the need for a union, a political union. But to thrust it down their throats, thus . . . ! He'll have them all against him, all the factions, English and Scots both. Look at Cecil there—he's fit to burst! Look at old Nottingham—aye, look at all the Howards! And the Chancellor . . ."

"It is the Commons I'm looking at! They are not going to like this. Any of them. They don't want to be tied to Scotland. They will not share their privileges and wealth with us—in trade and colonies and monopolies. They consider us beggars, paupers, all but savages! And the Puritans will never agree with the Presbyterians, any more than with James's bishops. He may win over or bribe a sufficiency of the lords—but he'll never cudgel the Commons into doing his will. Certainly not by telling them what they must do and they must not, like this."

"Yet—look what he has already achieved. The man is impregnable. Knows that he is right . . ."

James stopped the noise again, with his trumpeter. Now he wagged a minatory finger, the diamonds of his rings catching the light. "Ower much noise," he said. "I'll no' have it. Debate is good and right. But *aequam memento rebus in arduis servare mentem*! A' this din isna suitable. Like the braying o' asses! Your turn to speak will come. Meantime, you hear me, James."

Despite the drooling and the slobbers and the flapping hand, the sheer authority in that was extraordinary. None raised voice to contest it.

"Aye, well. You've mair'n the union to see to, this session—plenties mair. There's to be peace wi' Spain. Aye, peace. I'll hae nae mair wars and bickers wi' my princely neighbours in Christendom. Or elsewhere, forby. War is no' only wicked, it's the business o' fools! And costly—aye, right costly, as *you* should ken! My Treasury is empty—empty, d'you hear? Its siller squandered on wars wi' Spain and Ireland. This England's bled white—aye, white as well as red! That's to end. Scotland's no' at war wi' either, nor yet wi' France. My United Kingdom willna be—and you'll a' profit in your pockets, I promise you! I've given orders, as is my divine right, that a' hostilities at sea cease forthwith—there's nane on land the now, anyway—for I've never been at war wi' Spain, and couldna become so by merely inheriting this English throne. Aye, and a Spanish ambassador is being received at my Court o' St. James—as at my Court o' Holyroodhouse. And one frae the Pope o' Rome, too. Aye, and the Earl o' Tyrone, the Irish leader-mannie, will grace my Court also. Parliament will draw up a' the necessar papers and the like."

The stir this time was more in the nature of a long, low growl—in fact more frightening. But clearly James Stewart did not find it so. Licking his lips he proceeded on his appointed way.

"Anent matters o' the Church you here assembled hae nae business. That's *my* affair, as heid o' the Church, in consultation wi' my bishops. You'll hae heard tell I had a bit conference at yon Hampton Court—I dinna like the name Nonsuch—wi' the churchmen. That's a' by wi'—but it is fitting aye fitting, that you ken what's what, and that in matters spiritual this realm is now in guid hands. The bishops and mysel' are agreed right well." And he waved a conciliatory hand towards the benches of the Lords Spiritual. "There will be one Church in this United Kingdom, of which Christ is the Heid and I am His Regent—as is right and proper. I will settle bishops in Scotland—for the Scots Presbytery as well agrees wi' a monarch as God and the Devil! If they had their way then Jack and Tom and Will and Dick shall meet and at their pleasure censure *me* and my Council, and say it maun be this or that! Ooh, aye—we'll put an end to that! But here there's bickering and unseemly strife too, see you, wi' the Puritans and Novelists on the ane hand, and the Catholics and Jesuits on the other. Aye, even in your parliament, so they tell me. Weel—that's to cease. I'll no' have it. Quiet, you! I hae just put down a Catholic plot against my life and crown—aye, and what did parliament or my faithfu' Commons do to save me, heh? I may procure peace wi' the Pope, and welcome a Papal ambassador—but there will be no Catholic faction and cabal in my realms, no nor Catholic *public* worship either. But nor will there be Puritan. In *private*, see you, it's different, aye different. A man must can follow his conscience in matters o' religion—let there be nae doubt about that. But public worship is otherwise. Persecution is one o' the infallible notes o' a false Kirk, and I will never agree that any should die for error in faith—as distinct frae treasonable attempts on my royal person, you'll ken. But one Church there shall be. The Holy Scriptures will be written oot again, plainly in guid English for a' to read and understand. And I'll expect this parliament to aid me in a', as is its bounden duty, nae less."

The commotion which followed differed from the earlier interruptions, as no doubt was intended, with men starting to argue with each other rather than railing at the King.

"That was cunning," Lennox said. "There was no call to introduce religion here. He did that of a purpose, I swear, to set man against man, Catholic against Puritan, Puritan against churchman, Scots against English. So they are less able to unite against himself. He has not forgotten what he learned in Scotland. This is as good as a play-acting!"

"But dangerous," Heriot averred.

James gave this particular dose of his medicine more time to act, and then raised his hand for quiet. "I hae one final matter to express my royal will upon," he declared, jabbing an accusatory finger before him. "I am displeased, maist displeased, at the lack o' proper provision, in moneys and funds, made for mysel' and my family and household. I came frae Scotland to this England, as your due liege lord and sovereign prince—and find the Treasury empty, the realm in debt and no right maintenance, purvey and resource made for my sustenance and upkeep, and the support o' my Court and household. This was ill done. Och, a wheen great lords hae put their hands in their pouches—their *deep* pouches, aye—to our royal aid. But—would you hae your monarch a pauper in this rich land? Living on the charity o' lords? And Sir Robert Cecil, whom it has been my pleasure to create the Viscount o' Cranborne for leal service, has done much, right worthily. But it is parliament, they tell me, which *insists*, aye insists, that a' matters o' money and supply are its affair. And parliament has done nary a thing! I have been near a year here in England—and parliament hasna even met. Ooh, aye—for fear o' the plague, you tell me! But if my parliament insists on keeping a grip o' the purse strings—and, and interfering in plans o' my ain for the provision o' moneys by knighthoods—then my parliament will hae to recollect its duties. We are displeased."

The silence was now profound.

The King sat back, as though he had said his piece, with no more to add, straightened his crown again, crossed his legs, fiddled with his cod-piece beneath his robe and considered the golden buckle of his shoe. Then, almost as an afterthought he added, "Mind, parliament canna insist on *anything*, wi' me, James. Any authority, right and privilege it has, to meet, pronounce or even to exist, depends on *my* royal permission, good will and favour. Naught else. If you doubt me, consult your judges o' the courts, *my* courts. Under God, I am King, absolute and without contradiction. *Aut Caesar aut nullus!* The King reigns, and the King-in-parliament rules, aye. But tak the King out o' parliament and what is left? Whereas the King can rule lacking parliament—aye, and has done these five years. So—my revenues are the prerogative o' none save mysel'. If I permit that parliament arranges them for me, then parliament must mak them adequate. Aye, adequate." James nodded, found it difficult with his crown, and took it off. "My stick," he said. Then he smiled round, with a sort of qualified benevolence. "Aye, then. Enough's enough. My faithfu' Commons can go back to their ain place."

There was considerable agitation at this abrupt ending of a unique interlude. The Speaker of the House of Commons was due to deliver an address of grateful thanks to the Throne for a gracious opening speech. But what he had come prepared to say hardly corresponded with the realities of the royal lecture received; moreover, the King, stick recovered, had already clapped on his high hat again and was obviously about to leave. Catching the Lord Chancellor's eye, the Speaker hurried a few steps forward, bowed deeply, and launched into a brief and entirely formal vote-of-thanks, courteous and restrained though somewhat gabbled.

James, on his feet, nodded agreeably, told his Annie to come on, and set off for the door at a fair pace. Hastily the Yeomen of the Guard raced, passing through the midst of all and sundry unceremoniously to get there first. The parliament of 1604 was opened.

"God save the King!" the Duke of Lennox, in the Throne Gallery, declared. "Although, to tell truth, I do not know that divine aid is necessary! God save the parliament might be more apt."

But Heriot shook his head. "They will have to come to terms, these two," he said. "King and parliament. This will not serve. James will never browbeat parliament for long. In Scotland that was possible. There the King was *part* of parliament, sat in it, debated with it, could dominate it—as well as arrange that his own men controlled it. Here that is not possible. He can only open and prorogue parliament—he cannot sit in it. He may dominate the Lords. But, his person removed from the company, he cannot control the English parliament for long."

"You may be right. But it is also true what James said. That without him parliament had no authority. It is King-in-parliament that rules."

"Authority, no. But influence, a vast deal. That is what I say—they need each the other, and so must come to terms, one day."

"Not this session, I swear!"

9

THE HILLS WERE hazy blue on every hand in the early August sunshine, the heather was beginning to purple, and the corn to yellow in the valley floors as the two friends rode pleasantly up the wide and fertile vale of Strathearn, with a trio of armed grooms well behind, all the Highland Line ahead of them. The swallows darted, the bees hummed amongst the meadow-sweet, a pair of buzzards circled on seemingly motionless pinions high above, and all was for the moment well with their world. London and the Court seemed very far away, almost in another life—and one which neither by any means pined for. Had they asked themselves seriously why indeed they continued to put up with such a life, when they both could, in fact, have opted out of it, defying royal displeasure, undoubtedly each would have been hard put to it to answer adequately. Mere men are all too apt to find themselves in such a position, when they pause for a moment to think about it.

George Heriot had been up in Scotland for nearly a month. His business in Edinburgh was still large and demanding of periodic visits, with his half-brother James only a competent but unimaginative manager. With hundreds of thousands of pounds Scots on loan, and many estates held as security, most careful vigilance and over-sight was necessary. James Heriot was well enough for looking after the jewellery and small loan side of the enterprise; but the estate and nobility side of it had him floundering.

Ludovick of Lennox, on the other hand, had only just arrived from England, sent up by the King—or, more truly, only allowed to come up, as he was ever wishing to do, by James, as suitable escort to bring South the little Prince Charles, now considered sufficiently strong to stand the journey and join his parents. A doctor and an apothecary had been sent up with him, to minister to the prince, and these had been dispatched directly to the Lord Fyvie's house at Dunfermline Abbey while the Duke made a detour to Methven to see Mary Gray and his son. In Edinburgh, he had persuaded Heriot to accompany him.

Methven Castle stood on a green shelf above the cattle-dotted water-meadows of the Cowgask Water six miles west of Perth, a tall, commodious and pleasant house of mellow brown stone, all towers, turrets and crowstepped gables, a fortified mansion rather than a true castle, and a fine place and large property to be the demesne of so small a laird—for the Duke had made over the entire estate to his infant illegitimate son John, in free gift, mainly as a device for providing a suitable home, station and income for the mother, Mary Gray, and such as that independent young woman could bring herself to accept. So Mary Gray was chatelaine at Methven, in the name of the ten-year-old John Stewart of Methven.

Mary Gray, informed of their coming, met them at the ornamental bridge over the burn from Methven Loch built by Queen Margaret Tudor, during her third marriage, to Henry Stewart, Lord Methven. She looked a picture of wholesome, healthy yet delicate loveliness, essentially modest and without artifice—which was, of course, as misleading as any Court lady's painted façade. Jumping from his horse, Ludovick ran to her and picked her up in his arms and went dancing around with her thus, in significantly unducal fashion, Heriot grinning his pleasure but concerned lest his presence cramped their style.

He need not have been, for these two were for a little quite lost in each other. When Mary eventually detached herself and came laughing to the other man, she was quite unabashed and entirely natural.

"Dear Geordie Heriot!" she cried, if a little breathlessly. "How good to see you. Welcome to Methven—and forgive your hosts who have not seen each other for so many months. It has seemed so long. You are well? You are scarcely ruddy, either of you!"

"London is scarcely the place to win ruddy cheeks, Mary . . ."

"Blushes, now—that is different!" the Duke put in.

"So I hear. Alison sends me notably full letters—a deal better than yours, Vicky! I learn much of what goes on—and even some of your own ongoings, gentlemen! You would be surprised how knowledgeable I am."

"About you, my love, nothing could surprise me!" the Duke

declared. And on that note, asking for their son, a move was made to the house.

The boy John was found, helping with a late sheep-shearing at the farmery, a sturdy, level-eyed, self-reliant lad, most obvious son of his father, who made dutious greeting to his parent but clearly preferred to continue with his task amongst the oily fleeces meantime, none constraining him. The newcomers were very quickly absorbed into the quite busy domestic rhythm of a country household, a small self-supporting kingdom—or queendom—and found nothing to complain about. Ludovick in especial metamorphosed into his true self of landed laird and practical farmer.

There was, of course, much to be related, on both sides, much discussed and debated, personal as well as political and dynastic; but it was not until evening, round an aromatic birch-log fire in Mary's sitting-room, that the young woman broached the subject which she had hinted at once or twice previously.

"How secure sits the King on his English throne?" she asked.

"For but sixteen months on it, more secure than I would have expected," Ludovick replied. "He has thrown down the gauntlet to parliament and has a fight on his hands, there. He will not achieve this union which he seeks, I think—and for that, I for one rejoice—but he has the Church and the nobility accepting him as master. And less apt to call him fool and buffoon than they did a year past."

"And the people? Do they love him?"

"No-o-o. He makes little effort that they should. But they are coming to love Anne, I think. At least the Londoners are."

"That is what Alison writes, also—and though she is young she lacks nothing in shrewdness." Mary plied her needle for a few moments. "If, then, there should be trouble between King and Queen, James's position would suffer? Grievously?"

"Always there has been trouble between James and Anne," Lennox said. "They are as unsuited as man and woman can be. But they know that they must put a face on it. For their own sakes, for the realm's sake. They will go their own ways—but will not break their ultimate compact, I think."

"I agree," Heriot nodded.

"*They* may not will it so. But others might. Others might contrive to break that compact. For their own purposes. Might not that conceivably bring down the King? Or injure him greatly?"

"Patrick?" Lennox jerked.

"Who else? Patrick still has to achieve his vengeance. Moreover, he is much against this incorporating union. He says that it would ruin Scotland. He worked for a union of the crowns, worked as few others did. But not for this other, this union of states. He will stop it if he can."

"I think he may not need to stop it. The English parliament will perhaps do that for him."

"But you suggest that the Master of Gray will seek to do it by breaking up the royal marriage?" Heriot asked. "If he can."

"I think so. With my father it is always difficult to be sure. He covers himself so well. But others with whom he must work are sometimes less discreet. And, as you know, his wife the Lady Marie confides in me. With a view to lessening something of the harm he may do."

"Not another plot, lass . . . !"

"Scarcely a plot, this time. More a slow campaign of destroying. Did you know that he has written to the Queen, informing her that when she was so greatly sick after the miscarriage at Linlithgow, had she died the King was all prepared to wed the Lady Arabella Stewart? At once."

The two men stared at each other, minds boggling.

"How long since he wrote it, I do not know," Mary went on. "Even if it is really true, I do not know. His wife found the draft of his letter, undated in a doublet pocket. It may have gone weeks ago—or but recently. *Is* it true, think you?"

"I do not know. I do not know. This is the first I have heard of it. But . . . with James, who can tell?"

"The Queen has disliked the Lady Arabella from the first," Heriot said. "I wonder . . . ?"

"This new pregnancy of Anne's brings the issue to the fore again. She has miscarried twice now. And been gravely ill . . ."

"Pregnancy! Anne—she is pregnant? But . . . !" The Duke turned to Heriot. "Is it possible? You knew naught of this, Geordie? It cannot be true. We have heard nothing."

"You men! I have known of this a month and more. She expects in March. Ah, I can see you counting! June it means—conceived in June, or thereabouts."

"But . . . but Anne and James scarce ever spend a night together. They have separate palaces, he at Whitehall, she at Somerset House. She told him at Windsor, in our presence, that she would be a queen but no wife to him. Because of his young men . . ."

"Yes, Vicky—and so you play Patrick's game! As will others. This is what he wants—doubts as to the paternity of the child. If the King himself so doubts—or pretends to. And now Anne believes him ready to wed Arabella should she die. If such is the talk of the Court—as it will be—then the royal marriage can scarcely be said to flourish."

"But . . . but . . ."

"There are many buts, yes. Patrick will not have failed to think of them all, you may be sure. And planned accordingly."

"There must be more to this than you have told us, nevertheless," Heriot put in. "To declare that the child is not the King's is not enough. He requires a named father, does he not? And that, I think, would be difficult for even the Master of Gray to provide! In such circumstances. Moreover, one who will not himself deny it—or deny it sufficiently lukewarmly to leave grave doubts. I can think of none who might fit. Or fit the timing."

"But then, Geordie, you have not Patrick Gray's mind! His *kind* of mind. Whereas—God forgive me—in some degree I have! What think you of Patrick, Earl of Orkney?"

Lennox drew a sudden long breath; and his friend opened his mouth to speak, and then shut it again almost with a click. They sat silent.

"June, you will recollect, was the month for this child to be conceived, or thereabouts. Late May would serve. And, as you know, the Earl of Orkney was in London in May—indeed, near fought a duel with the King's Sir Philip Herbert. Some drunken escapade. Did not you speak for him, with the King, Vicky?"

Lennox's swallowing was audible. "Yes," he admitted. "Yes. He is a distant kinsman of my own. Not a man I love. But . . . nor is Herbert! They came to blows over some horse race . . ."

"But he did appear at the Queen's Court for some days?"

"Yes. He had been to France. Where we Stewarts have estates, as you know. On his way home, he came to London . . ."

Patrick Stewart, second Earl of Orkney, was brother-in-law to Patrick Gray, the Lady Marie's brother. He was eldest son of the late Robert Stewart, first Bishop and then Earl of Orkney, the King's uncle, one of the many bastards of James the Fifth. He was a youngish man of smouldering if heavy good looks, violent passions and utter lack of scruple—that, and a notorious ladies' man. He loathed his cousin James with a well-known and undisguised hatred—for sufficient reason.

Mary's hearers had ceased to interject buts. They gazed at her with a sort of reluctant and unhappy fascination, perceiving now something of the implications of her suggestions.

"You recollect, in '96, eight years past, that the King had the Master of Orkney, as then he was, tried on a charge of consulting with witches? Ten witnesses died under James's questioning, in his attempts to convict his cousin. Only my father saved him—on Lady Marie's beseechings. But we all knew that it was not truly witchcraft that James held against him—that was but a convenient device to which it was possible to produce ignorant witnesses who could be persuaded to swear anything under torture. The true reason was because the King suspected dalliance between the Master and the Queen."

"Aye—but the King suspected many of dalliance with the Queen. Myself included!" Lennox exclaimed. "As you know, Anne was indiscreet. A neglected wife. The Earl of Moray, too. That bad business at Donibristle . . ."

"Yes, Vicky. But the Earl of Moray is dead. And the King now trusts *you*. But Patrick of Orkney is still . . . available! I do not say that there was ever any truth in the tale of dalliance at that time, any more than in yours—although he has no good reputation. But *James* believed it. Which is all that matters—then or now—for my father's purposes."

"He will prevail on Orkney to say the Queen's child is his?" Heriot said.

"I believe that to be his intention—so Marie fears. The Queen and he have been much together of late. And this new visit to London is altogether to the point . . ."

"New visit to London?" the Duke repeated. "What is this? Orkney?"

"Have you not heard? The Earl of Orkney and his brothers are to pay a visit to his cousin's Court at Whitehall, by royal invitation, in October. At the same time as Duke Ulric of Holstein, from Denmark—the Queen's brother. It appears that the Duke and Orkney are friendly. There are to be high doings."

"I knew of Ulric's coming—but not this of Orkney. You think Patrick has contrived it? Your father?"

"Either contrived it, or is using it. What will happen in London I do not know. But I think it will not be to the King's benefit."

Lennox rose, to pace the floor. "This is damnable!" he said. "To seek to hurt James by destroying Anne's good name and reputation. But—what can we do? It is like the other, only more difficult. The plot over young Henry. It is all a matter of rumour, conjecture, supposition. No proofs, nothing we may grip."

"At least you can warn the King. And the Queen."

Heriot spoke. "James will not thank us for telling him this. As it now stands. He conceives us fearful at shadows, scaremongers—or pretends to. He ever demands proofs, sureties. And the Earl of Orkney is, after all, his own cousin."

"You are fortunate to have even conjectures to go upon, where Patrick is concerned," the young woman pointed out. "I cannot swear to you that all this is planned just as I have told it. Or, indeed, that there is not *more* to it than this! But the Earl of Orkney is to travel to Court in October and his brothers with him. And Patrick Stewart, like Patrick Gray, has an account to settle with the King!"

"We must warn James, yes, and Anne too," Lennox acceded. "But whether they will heed, or what they can do . . . ?"

"The King is no fool—as we all know," Heriot said. "He may seem to scorn us—but may pay some heed, in fact, and take his own precautions."

"It will not be easy to broach the matter to Anne, either!" Lennox pointed out. "To suggest to her that there are doubts as to the paternity of her unborn child!"

They considered each other unspeaking, for a while, as the birch logs hissed and spluttered.

* * *

After the precious stolen few days at Methven, reluctantly they left to ride south by east the thirty miles to Dunfermline, and duty. Mary rode with them so far, to gain a little longer with her Duke.

The grey climbing town above the northern shores of Forth was loud with the sounds of busy hammers and saws and stone-masons' malls, as Chancellor Seton, Lord Fyvie, added a fine new wing to the ancient palace of Malcolm Canmore, beside the abbey founded by Malcolm's English queen, where the hero Bruce and his wife lay buried. The Chancellor had a passion for building, and somehow the funds for indulging it—where the money all came from was something of a mystery, even though he had married a rich wife. Admittedly Dunfermline had been the richest Church property in all Scotland at the glorious Reformation of fifty years before—which was why Patrick Gray himself had managed to procure it during the years in which he was acting-Chancellor; but it was not in fact wholly Fyvie's property, for in theory it still belonged to Queen Anne, as part of her jointure, and he was only Hereditary Keeper.

The newcomers found all in readiness for them, indeed waiting. And they quickly perceived why it was that the Master of Grey had made no attempt to use little Prince Charles as a pawn against his royal father. The child, now four years old, was in fact a poor creature physically; as to mentally, this was not entirely clear, for although he could speak, he scarcely ever did so—although his eyes were bright enough, large and lustrous like the King's. Otherwise, he was undersized, feeble, the legs so weak that he could scarcely stand alone much less walk. Whether he had an actual impediment in his speech was uncertain at this stage—although James had given his doctors instructions as to how to cut the string of the boy's tongue the better to bring him to eloquence, which however Fyvie had refused to allow while the child was in his care. This, then, was the shrunken, big-eyed mite who waited for them at Dunfermline—and who would by no means have served the Master of Gray as puppet-king.

The doctor and apothecary sent up for the journey agreed with the resident physician, Atkins, that the child, carefully cherished and not overtired, was fit to travel. The Chancellor was only too glad to get the little creature off his hands—although he had treated the prince kindly enough.

And so, on a misty morning, a start was made by boat for Edinburgh; and farewell taken of Mary Gray on the quayside at North Queensferry. Ludovick of Lennox was a silent man thereafter all the way to the capital.

The boy was no trouble, at least. Two nurses and the physicians looked after him adequately, carrying him everywhere. He cried little, ate little, slept a lot, and seemed interested in what went on; but he spoke not at all—although one of his nurses swore that he could speak, that he spoke to himself quite lucidly when he was asleep.

Despite not hurrying or taking over-long journeys each day, Prince Charles took considerably less long to reach London than had either of his parents—this because they had no entertainments, no receptions, no hunting, to detain them. Ten days after leaving Edinburgh Lennox delivered the child into his mother's hands at

Somerset House—the King was away hare-hunting at his new estate of Royston in North Hertfordshire. Anne wept at the sight of him. They left her trying to coax him to speak.

Between them, Lennox and Heriot had agreed that one should approach the King and the other the Queen on the subject of Mary Gray's suspicions. While the obvious choice seemed to be for Heriot to speak to his 'auld gossip Jamie', Lennox would not hear of telling Anne. The Queen and he had never been the best of friends, he said, since the unfortunate business which had led to James's accusation of dalliance between them. He would prefer not to open this most delicate subject with her. He would deal with the King.

So George Heriot, tradesman, was left with the awkward task. He could not feel that the right moment for it was the mother's reunion with her handicapped child after more than a year's parting, so he sought Alison Primrose's advice. She said that the Queen was going to watch an archery contest at Hampton Court the following afternoon, and when she came back a quiet talk with her probably could be contrived. She also confirmed that Anne was indeed pregnant.

Next afternnon, then, the man presented himself again at Somerset House, to find that the royal party was not yet back from the archery. Alison was prepared to act hostess meantime, however, and conducted him to a rose arbour overlooking the palace orchard where, as she observed frankly, tongues might clack about them but at least ears would not overhear them.

A little troubled, Heriot considered that, and her. "Lassie," he said, "do you have to suffer a deal of talk and raillery on account of me? Of our . . . friendship? A man old enough to be your father."

"None that I cannot deal with," she answered lightly.

"That is beside the point. You should not have to suffer any. It is wrong, unsuitable. At my age . . ."

"Your age again! Your great age appears to worry you, sir. Years. So old a man! Did we not finish with this matter before? At Wilton?"

"Talk will not alter the twenty-five years between us—our own talk, any more than others'."

"I grow older every day. But, goodness—by *your* talk you grow older every minute! And yet, you look not a day older than Duke Vicky, who is ten years younger. What must I do to wipe out those twenty-five years, Geordie?"

He smiled—and certainly his grin could be very boyish. "Even the nimble-witted Alison Primrose would have difficulty in doing that! Perhaps, if you found an entirely suitable young Scots laird to bestow your affections upon, and went back to Scotland, out of my ken, I might start forgetting about my great age, lass."

"You would wish me to do that?"

"No," he said.

She tucked her arm in his companionably.

"I spoke with your father when I was in Edinburgh," he told her, after a pause. "He sent you his affectionate greetings."

"He could have sent me that, by letter, many a time," she observed. "After all, he *can* write! He is Clerk to the Scots Privy Council, is he not? Never a letter has he sent me."

"M'mm." Heriot did not mention that it had not been his daughter in London that James Primrose had been mainly concerned about, but the possibilities of raising a loan, and the lowest figure King James would be prepared to accept for a knighthood. "He is a busy man. With much on his mind—including your eighteen brothers and sisters! But he spoke warmly of you, and is much concerned for your welfare at this scarcely moral Court. He asked me to, h'm, keep an eye on you."

"Ah! And you told him that you were much too old for such an onerous task?"

"What I told your father is not for your ears, young woman! But . . ." He paused, to a stir and the clatter of hooves from behind them. "Ah—here comes Her Majesty, I think. As well, perhaps." But he sighed a little. "Will you convey my humble duty to the Queen, my dear?"

"If I must!" the girl said shortly, and stalked off.

The man, waiting to be summoned to the royal presence, was surprised when quite soon, Alison returned to the rose arbour with the Queen in person.

"Primrose tells me that you wish private word with me, Master Geordie," Anne said, accepting his salutations. "Here is as secure from prying ears as anywhere, I vow. Come—sit here by me. Girl—go yonder by the pear tree and watch. None to disturb us."

"You are gracious, Majesty. It is not my wish to detain you for long."

The Queen sighed. "No doubt it is my debt to you," she said. "I am sorry. I know well that it is far too large. I spend over-much, yes. But what am I to do? James keeps me shamefully short of money. I have three houses to maintain. I must pay for my own household. I spend much on masques, yes . . ."

"Madam," Heriot dared to interrupt, "do not concern yourself. I am not here to speak of money, believe me. I understand Your Majesty's difficulties, have always understood them." He coughed. "Far from dunning Your Highness for money, I have here brought you a little gift. From my booth in Edinburgh. If you will do me the honour to accept it." And he produced from a pocket a small crucifix on a chain, gold studded with sapphires and Tay pearls the Christ-figure in silver.

Anne was entranced. She was inclined towards devotionalism, some calling her a secret practising Catholic, and Lady Huntly her confessor—amongst other things. When she had sufficiently exclaimed over the gift, the man coughed once more.

"Majesty—may I further trespass on your kindness and goodwill? It is presumptuous, I know. But you will perhaps bear with me?" He drew out another trinket, a slender gold bracelet bearing a curling feather contrived in turquoise. "Could I prevail on you to give this toy to Mistress Alison, one day? Not now. As a gift from *you*, not from me. It is unsuitable that such as I should offer gifts to a young woman. But she is kind, friendly, a pleasing child. And she has no jewellery, in this Court where all wear it. Her father is much pressed for money, with his over-large family. I think that she would like this."

The Queen looked from the bracelet to the man, interestedly. "You are a strange man, Master Geordie. She will like it very well, I swear! As well she might. But—give it to her yourself, sir. Why not?"

"No, Majesty—of your pardon, no. There would be talk, unkind talk. She would be asked whence it came. A young woman must not receive gifts of this sort from a man of my years. From Your Highness it would be different. She is your good servant, deserving of reward."

"Very well. If so you will have it." Anne hid the bracelet away in her bodice. "You have no small liking for my Maid-in-Waiting, I think, my friend?"

The man was very stiff. "She is very young. But true. And kind. I promised her father that I would look to her welfare . . ."

"To be sure." The Queen smiled. "How long is it since your wife died, Master Geordie? I have forgot."

"That has naught to do with it," he said, all but snapped.

Then recalled, "I crave your royal pardon, Madam. Forgive me. My wife died eight years ago. We were wed young."

"As was I, to be sure. I was little older than this Primrose. Would you wed her?"

"At my age? Dear heaven—no! Not to be thought of."

"And yet you think of it, I swear! Not infrequently, eh? I think that you are too modest, too concerned with what others say, Master Geordie. You would make a good husband for any woman, young or not so young, I do vow. Better than most, I think!"

"Your Majesty is too kind." Heriot drew himself up, sought to change his tone of voice. Having got the Queen into a suitable and grateful frame of mind for his difficult task, with his gift and intimate request, he was now in danger of throwing all away, indeed coming almost to verbal blows over this unfortunate and unprofitable subject. "I have something other to speak to Your Majesty on. With your gracious permission?"

"Ah, yes. You would change the subject, sir! Very well."

Now that he was faced with it, he did not know how to begin. He made three or four false starts, and Anne, amused now, helped him nothing. At last he blurted it out. "I understand, Highness, that I have to congratulate you. On being . . . on having . . . on going to have another child. Another royal prince. Or princess, to be sure. I . . . ah . . . yes."

Raising her brows, she considered him, and then nodded. "I must admit it," she conceded. "Do you consider it cause for congratulation?"

"M'mm. To be sure." That might have sounded a little doubtful, so he added, "Of course. What else, Majesty?"

"Yes, what else, Master Geordie?" she returned. "For there is something else than congratulations, I am certain."

"Yes. Your Majesty must bear with me. What I have to say is difficult, unpleasant. But you have unfriends. Not many perhaps, but potent. Although, to be sure, they are the *King's* unfriends rather than your own. These can say ill things, evil things, in their endeavours to hurt His Majesty." He paused.

"Go on," she said.

"There are, Highness, rumours to be spread, wicked tales. That this child which Your Majesty carries is not the King's. But . . . but another's." He was sweating, but he had got it out.

"Ah," the Queen said.

He stole a quick sidelong glance at the woman beside him. She had sounded calm, unshocked. He nodded, unspeaking.

"You are but newly back from Scotland," she said. "This rumour, then—it comes from there?"

"Yes. It is damnable."

"Do not look so unhappy, my friend Heriot. This is but part of the price of being Queen. There are other prices—worse, on my soul! My unfriends in Scotland who contrive this, and so quickly, would be . . . whom? The Master of Gray and the Earl of Mar?"

"Of Mar I know nothing. Nor indeed do I *know* anything of Gray. It is all supposition, hearsay. But it was Mistress Mary Gray who told us. The Duke and myself. As before."

"Yes. She is a strange young woman, that. You trust her? Vicky does, of course. But you?"

"I do, yes. Wholly."

"And does she say whom rumour makes my lover?"

"Yes, Majesty. The Earl of Orkney."

He heard her breath catch. But when she spoke her voice was still cool, unflurried—and she was not a cool-tempered woman. "Clever," she said. "Shrewd. Patrick Stewart!"

"A careful choice, yes."

They sat silent for a few moments. The man could by no means probe.

"Patrick Stewart would not declare that, to my hurt, I think," the Queen went on, at length.

"Perhaps not, Madam. Though Mary Gray thinks him a man who would stop at nothing. He has a bad name."

"Yet good enough to link with mine own, thus?"

He did not answer.

"You believe that he would stoop to this? Make such a statement?"

"He would not require to, Highness. Enough for him not to deny it. A mere rumour. Or to do so in such fashion that folk were scarcely convinced. It is cleverly thought on."

"No doubt. I see that full well. Many might believe it, yes. But not James, I think—not the King."

He did not comment.

She turned to look at him directly. "You, *you* do not think that the King would heed such a tale? Could doubt the matter?"

Embarrassed, he eyed the ground. "The King must know the truth," he muttered. "He *should* not have any doubts. But . . . ?"

She did not respond to his implied question. "I will speak with James."

"Yes, Madam, to be sure. That is the most important of the matter. That Your Majesties are at one in this. None can stop rumour and talk. But that may not greatly harm you, I think. The object of it all is to harm the King, to cause his marriage to seem to fail, to lose him the respect and esteem of his people. The English still have not forgotten their Henry the Eighth, and his marital troubles. They want no more of that. They esteem *you* greatly. And, any seeming break between Your Majesty and the King could greatly injure the throne. And therefore the realm."

"And that is what our enemies seek?"

"So Mary Gray believes. Revenge."

"I would trust that one better were she anyone but her father's daughter."

"Yet she considers herself Your Majesty's faithful servant still. An Extra Woman of the Bedchamber. And she was right, about the plot concerning Prince Henry. She looks for trouble when the Earl of Orkney comes to London in the autumn."

"*He* is coming?"

"She says it. With his brothers."

"I knew not that he was coming." The Queen rose suddenly, seeming more concerned, almost agitated. He jumped up.

"I shall speak with the King," she repeated, "He could perhaps forbid Patrick Stewart to leave Scotland."

"That might not be the wisest course, Majesty. Cause for added talk . . ."

"You think it? We shall see. I thank you, Master Geordie, for your good-will. Kindly intentions. And also for the jewel. That was most friendly, amiable. I shall not forget." Quickly she gave him her hand to kiss, and turning, hurried away.

Surprised, he gazed after her, saw Alison start up from her seat under the pear tree, hesitate, raise a hand to him, and then hasten dutifully after her mistress.

Thoughtfully he made his own way out of Somerset House, and back to the Exchange.

10

THE PALACE OF Whitehall seethed like a pot on the boil, crowded to overflowing. Not only was it Christmastide, with all its attendant activities, and both the King's and Queen's households were for the occasion joined, but Duke Ulric of Holstein's Danish entourage was also in residence. Add to that, the Earl of Orkney and his party of Scots was making a delayed appearance in London—having been held up hitherto at Royston, hunting buck, coursing hares and carousing, with the King. And the installation of Prince Charles, as Duke of York, was on the programme. Moreover, this day, 27th December 1604, Sir Philip Herbert had actually been married, in the palace chapel, to Lady Susan Vere, grand-daughter of Elizabeth's William Cecil, first Lord Burleigh, and the banquet now to be held was in the nature of a wedding feast, with all the wedding guests present also. Whitehall was by no means the largest of the royal homes, and its resources were strained to the utmost.

Herbert's wedding might have caused a great uproar. Apparently he had been secretly betrothed to Susan Vere, daughter of the Earl of Oxford, for months, and was planning to be as secretly married, when Lennox got to hear of it and warned him that such a thing would grievously offend the King. James was a little strange about his favourites; he did not mind them having relations with women as long as they told him all about it, and indeed regaled him with choice and intimate details—and of course granted their favours to no other *men*. Philip Herbert was not the man normally to listen to good advice, but in this instance he had taken heed, and gone and confided his romance to his loving monarch and sought blessing on the match—with the required revelations and embellishments. The Lady Susan was a bold piece inevitably—or Herbert would not have been involved. James had been intrigued and delighted, and had insisted on naming the wedding day, providing the venue, giving the bride away, donating the marriage bed and contributing the wedding feast. That was James Stewart, a man of large affections.

George Heriot was present. It would have been strange had he not been, since he it was who was paying for all. Parliament, still at odds with the King, had not yet agreed to any increase in James's income, and the royal finances had got quite out-of-hand, money even having to be sent from Scotland. Duke Ulric's visit was costing a lot, for he was a man who liked to do things in style; as was the suitable entertainment and accommodation for the new ambassadors of Spain and the Vatican, and James's general efforts to spread amity and concord around Christendom. Peace had its expenses as well as war—only parliament was less prepared to pay for them. In theory, of course, Heriot was only making one more large loan, for this day's activities; but he doubted very much whether he would ever see any repayment.

That did not mean, to be sure, that he might himself sit anywhere up near the dais end of the palace hall, amongst the seats of rank and privilege, even had he wished to do so. This being an official occasion, Duke Ludovick would have to be up at the royal table, unfortunately. Heriot would have liked to sit beside Alison Primrose, in a modest place amongst the Queen's junior staff, but restrained himself firmly, sufficiently to select only a seat directly across the left hand long table, where he could look at the girl and smile occasionally—although he quickly recognised that smiles were likely to be in short supply, on his part at least, owing to the antics of the two young bloods, pages, who sat on either side of Alison, vying with each other for her attentions and favours. The tables were disposed in a great inverted U, with the long wings stretching down each side of the hall from the dais table and twin thrones at the top, leaving an open space in the centre for displays and entertainment.

For once James was not late; at least, although not openly present as yet, he could be observed by the keener-eyed, hiding not very effectively behind curtains at the back of the minstrels' gallery half way to the roof, tankard in hand, watching what went on below. He would not make his entry until all others were in their places, of course.

Trumpet flourishes heralded each of the official entries, when all more ordinary guests stood—if they could. The first entry consisted of the eleven young nobles who were tonight to be created Knights of the Bath—an important group, for they and their parents had had to pay dearly for the honour, although unfortunately the proceeds were already long spent. According to the laws and rules of knighthood and chivalry, these should have spent the day, indeed the entire previous night, in prayerful vigil and vow-taking; but James, Sovereign of the Order, although a bishops' man, was less sacerdotally inclined than his wife, had declared that attendance at a religious service—namely Philip Herbert's wedding—would do excellently well for preparation. Having spent the interim since noon wassailing and celebrating, this party made a spirited entry, some riding on each other's shoulders, others leap-frogging—although two required Yeomen of the Guard to support them. They made their round-about way towards a special table near the top of the hall, to hooting and cheering, Bath King-of-Arms and the Dean of Westminster, Dean of the Order, following on in full fig and looking distinctly disapproving.

The next arrivals could be heard coming from some distance through the palace corridors, to the tune of sweet fiddle music. The trumpeters drowned this, of course, as the doors were flung open—but the heavy man in the lead quickly silenced them with a gesture of sheerest authority, and the two fiddlers, drunk both of them but playing divinely, proceeded into the hall in their stained and ragged tartans. Many guests ostentatiously held their noses. Behind the musicians, light-footed despite his weight, almost tripping to the jigging metre, came this stocky individual, with seven others at his back of the same sort but of a great diversity of ages, plus a pack of perhaps a dozen graceful deer hounds, loping, long-limbed and shaggy. The leader was swarthily handsome in a ravaged way, in his mid-thirties, with a scarred cheek which drew up one corner of his mouth in a permanent leer, odd under the thin down-turning long moustaches. But it was the eyes which held the attention, steel-grey, level, unwinking, utterly assured, peremptory, intolerant, with no sort of leer about them. He was oddly dressed also, in what had been the height of fashion some dozen years before, all black and silver, but with a tartan plaid wrapped across the chest and pinned on a wide shoulder by a great, gleaming jewelled clasp of Celtic ornament—Patrick, second Earl of Orkney and Lord of Zetland, son of one of Mary Queen of Scots' half-brothers and illegitimate son of James the Fifth, and therefore the King's cousin.

His seven followers were all his brothers, some lawfully begotten, some otherwise, but without any distinction of identity or style, a notable assortment, ranging in age between twelve and thirty, dressed in every style known to fashion, or mixtures of styles, from Highland to hunting rig, or no style at all. They all carried themselves like antique princes, and all were quite drunk, like their brother—Patrick Stewart was always drunk—but unlike the embryo Knights of the Bath, none of them showed it, even the youngest. They strode on towards their places at another special table, the King's kin, as though Whitehall and all else belonged to them, only they were too much lost in contemplation of fine fiddling to notice it. They did not swagger; there was no need for that. These, however povery-stricken, were the Stewarts. Their deer hounds, which never left their heels, bore the same stamp.

The succeeding party required no heralding either, for they did their own trumpeting in roaring bibulous song and laughter. At entry, the first, an enormous, youngish man, built like an ox, clad in yellow satin slashed with green, grabbed one of the trumpeters' instruments, and raising it to his lips blew a mighty and discordant blast of noise from vast lungs, before hurling the trumpet with a clatter to the floor and staggering onwards, a train of belching, cheering Danish notables after him—His Serene Highness Ulric, Duke of Holstein, Bishop of Schwerin and Schleswig, brother of Christian the Fourth of Denmark and of Queen Anne. He bore no resemblance to his sister, a man of unpredictable moods and large appetites—he boasted that he was the biggest eater in Christendom, and seldom sat down to less than eighteen courses at a meal. He made his unsteady way towards the dais table, scowling at something suddenly.

This noisy eruption safely disposed of, a more grave and dignified group made its appearance, escorted by the Captain of the Gentlemen-at-Arms as marshal and led by Signor Molin, the Venetian envoy. This was the corps of ambassadors, including the new representatives of Spain and the Vatican, attending their first large-scale Court function. Magnificently dressed, their ruffs fresh-starched, their stars and Orders glittering, they made an impressive sight. They had some difficulty, however, in maintaining their sober dignity when they had to pass through a sort of tournament of would-be Knights of the Bath, mounted on each others' backs and jousting with table cutlery, while the Bath King flapped his tabard at them like a hen-wife with recalcitrant poultry. The deer hounds also, now decently settled on the floor, had to be stepped over.

There followed a pause. James, it could be seen, had left his vantage-point. Then a rather longer flourish of trumpets introduced a very small party indeed, no more than two persons, one carrying the other. This was Henry Howard, Earl of Nottingham, Lord High Admiral of England, bearing in his arms the four-year-old Prince Charles. The latter was decked out in splendid purple and ermine robes, his small wizened features and big eyes peering out like a monkey's. There was a dutiful cheer at this, drowning some sounds of altercation up at the dais.

Still louder trumpeting ushered in Prince Henry, all in white and gold as usual, an upright, heartening figure, ten years old this day, full of life and youthful grace with the Garter round his slim, left silken leg. Escorting him was another Lord High Admiral, that of Scotland, the Duke of Lennox. The cheering for the popular Henry was loud and prolonged.

A resounding fanfare cut it short, and produced the monarch and consort. But not only these two. Flanking the King were the day's bride and bridegroom, each supporting a royal arm, while Anne, a little to one side, had to carry her husband's stick for him—managing to do so in entirely regal fashion, despite being somewhat over-dressed and over-feathered. The Queen's taste in clothes tended towards the flashy side and tonight she was wearing more jewellery even than usual. George Heriot had had to deliver a casketful to Somerset House that morning, on loan for the day from his stock, most of it now decorating Anne's person wherever room could be found for it.

The Lady Susan scarcely could be accused of over-dressing, at least. The bodice of her pearl-seeded gown was so low as to be practically non-existent and her already prominent breasts underpinned with whalebone to thrust them up and out, the currently fashionable blue veins thereupon enthusiastically inked in, the nipples' aureoles painted scarlet. King James rather rolled expressive eyes in some distate at this colourful display so close under his royal nose and tended to lean more to the other side on the resplendent but distinctly dishevelled bridegroom in the azure, crimson and white of his house. It was hard to say who was supporting whom.

The knightly tournament, still proceeding, was forcibly stilled by Yeomen of the Guard to allow the royal party passage to the dais table. Up at the head of the hall, Orkney's fiddlers started to play a lively measure, to which their lord beat time with a flagon on the table—but to which his cousin found difficulty in fitting his own and his supporters' somewhat unsteady steps, although he nodded his large, high-hatted head in genial approval.

But, beyond the Bath postulents the ranks of dignified couchant deer hounds posed a problem and one which even the Yeomen of the Guard were a little doubtful of clearing a way through. James gave his attention to this, paused thoughtfully, and suddenly turning, disentangled himself from the clutches of the so-blooming bride with some appearance of relief—whom Anne promptly and efficiently shouldered aside—and pushed Philip Herbert away with a sort of playful exasperation.

"Man, Philip," he said wetly. "Bide a wee. We'll get rid o' these laddies. We might as well get this by wi'. They're getting gey rough. Aye, it's been a long day, mind." He raised his voice. "Vicky! Vicky Stewart—your bit sword, man."

It was not Lennox's Scots accent which answered him however but the louder and thicker Germanic accents of his brother-in-law of Holstein. Ulric complained, and vehemently. He had been insulted. The ambassadors' party had come in *after* his own, according them precedence over himself. And now the wretched Venetian envoy was in a seat nearer to the thrones than was his own. It was not to be borne. At least, that seemed to be the gist of his complaint; Ulric's English was not good at the best of times.

James looked somewhat taken aback, opening his mouth and licking slobbering lips. He peered at Anne, suspiciously. She it was, indeed, who, having quickly become tired of her brother's manners, habits and conversation, had ordered that the Venetian Nicolo Molin, whom she found witty and amusing, should be inserted between Ulric's seat and her own. She could hardly explain this there and then. The King muttered something placatory and gestured vaguely.

This would by no means do for Ulric who was drum-full of wine. He raised his unclear voice higher.

The royal party exchanged accusatory glances and looked unhappy.

"Quiet, man! Sit doon!" A great roar suddenly exploded upon the company. "Doon, I say. The King's Grace commands it." Surprisingly, that was the Earl of Orkney, pointing a forceful finger at the Serene Highness. And at the pure and simple menace in that order, Ulric gulped to silence and sat down heavily—before recalling that one did not sit in the presence of a standing monarch, and heaved himself to his feet again, but unspeaking.

James cast a doubtfully grateful glance at his cousin. "Aye, well." he said, and turned to find Lennox at his shoulder with the drawn sword. The Duke was still the only man allowed to draw a sword—even though it was a specially blunted one—in the royal presence indoors. Gingerly the King took it, and swung on the candidates for knighthood.

But the interlude with Duke Ulric had allowed these high-spirited and semi-intoxicated sprigs of nobility to revert to their playful antics. In anticipation of their new status they were now busy knighting each other with knives and forks, and making an increasing noise about it, assured of the well-known forbearance of their liege lord where young men were concerned. The King's genial injunction that they should come and kneel before him went unheeded, probably unheard.

James repeated his summons, waving the sword about unhandily—but to scant effect.

Abruptly, without warning, the entire situation seemed to explode in their faces. A bellow from the dais was followed immediately by a paralysing crash as a full flagon of wine, hurled with accuracy, smashed into the midst of the posturing postulents, shattering into a hundred fragments and splashing the contents over them all. And promptly the deer-hounds rose in savage baying threat.

"Silence, bairns—for the King's Grace!" the Earl of Orkney yelled. "Doon, I say! Doon, by God!"

Whether the last command was to his hounds or to the knights-to-be was not clear—but complete silence and stillness descended forthwith on man and beast alike.

All but holding their breaths, everyone including the monarch stared up at Orkney. In two brief gestures, Patrick Stewart had established himself as master of the great unruly gathering. He flicked a stubby finger at his cousin to continue.

"Ooh, aye," James said, goggling at his shaken and wine-splattered young friends. "Just so. You're no' hurt? Any o' you? Kneel you, then."

All eyes warily on the dreadful ogre from the North, and his dogs, the eleven candidates hurriedly knelt in a ragged row, nervously dabbing wine from faces and persons, evidently much sobered. Taking the sword in both hands, James tottered down the line not so much striking blows on each bent shoulder as dragging the blade indiscriminately over heads and bodies muttering 'Dub thee knight, dub thee knight, dub thee knight,' as he went. He said it approximately a dozen times, and it is probable that most if not all of the postulants received some touch of the steel, some to their dire danger. At the end of the row, panting, the King added, "Arise—aye, arise, all o' you. Guid knights . . . to life's end. Up wi' you. Now—where's our Charlie?"

The Dean of Westminster stepped forward, fine in his Bath robes, bowing, with an open book, to proceed with the rest of the ceremony—for there was a great deal more to the investiture of Knights of this ancient Order than merely bestowing the accolade upon them. But James had other things on his mind and was in a mood for dispensing with unnecessary ceremonial. He shooed the Dean away, and then turned to do the same for the now standing eleven.

"Off wi' you," he said. "That's it. Awa' wi' you. I want Charlie."

"He is here, Sire," Lennox assured, from behind.

The new members of the Most Honourable Order of the Bath, finding themselves no longer the centre of attention, and thus dismissed, were only too glad to escape. Making a variety of bows to Majesty's padded back, they hurried away. However, both Bath and Garter King-of-Arms perceived difficulty, and exchanging glances, hastened after the new but departing knights, gesturing for them to halt. They managed to stop them near the door.

Meanwhile James found the Earl of Nottingham behind him, bearing his small wide-eyed son. He grinned at the mite, tweaking its ear.

"So there you are, my mannie. Bide you still, now—and we'll get this by wi'. Nae bother, mind. Toby, man, are you there?"

"Here, Sire."

"Aye, well. You got a guid hold o' him, man Nottingham?"

"I have, yes," the Lord Admiral declared stiffly.

James, who had been using the sword to lean on, now brought it up to waver about his little son's head. Nottingham jerked his own grey head back sharply, with the point only an inch or two from his eye.

"Stand still, man," his lord commanded. "This is fell difficult. Dinna jink about, that way. Now—Charles Stewart, Duke o' Albany, my son, I do dub thee knight o' this maist Honourable Order o' the Bath, preparatory, aye preparatory, to your investiture as Duke o' York." By this time he was resting the sword partly on the child and partly on Nottingham's shoulder. "Arise, Sir Charles Stewart—and be thou a guid, true and proper knight until thy life's end. Aye." Thankfully he lowered the blade—and Lennox had to be quick to catch it before it fell altogether. "Now, you, Toby Mathew, man. And guidsakes, be short about it!"

Dr. Tobias Mathew, Bishop of Durham, deputising for the Archbishop of York who was old and ill, was a genial and witty cleric—the same who had greeted James at Berwick Bridge. He recognised that prolonged histrionics and the normal ceremony of investiture were contra-indicated here and now. Nevertheless the occasion called for certain form and dignity, however abbreviated. He raised a beringed hand, therefore, and launched into prayer, with a fine cathedral intonation. Not everyone was prepared for this, and there was some background noise, especially from the new knights held up near the door, and also from a group near the head of the right hand table, where Philip Herbert had abandoned his bride to get involved in a card game with certain other courtiers. Fearing that Orkney might feel called upon to intervene again, James coughed loudly—and the Bishop, assuming this signal to be aimed at himself, brought his invocation to an even swifter close than intended, and proceeded in a more conversational tone to the next and indispensable stage of the programme. This consisted of a number of formal questions put to the new duke anent his good intentions towards the people and province of York, his support for the archepiscopal see, his stewardship of the secular revenues thereof—large, which was why James was in such haste for this investiture of his second son, when the first was not yet created Prince of Wales—and so on. To all which questions the Lord Admiral answered in the affirmative, for the child, in a bored voice, Finally, he repeated the ducal oath, made to dukedom and monarch, after the Bishop.

This over, James himself took the ducal coronet, gold-studded with gems, and placed it on the little boy's head, where it settled to rest on his ears. "Geordie's made it ower big," he observed—to add jocularly, "Och, but you'll grow into it! There you are now, laddie—you're Duke o' York."

"Hail, Duke of York!" Bishop Toby cried—though only one or two took up the salutation.

The child, who had been entirely docile throughout, smiled

beatifically when his mother gave him a kiss—however much the Lord Admiral puffed disapproval.

At a sign from Garter King, the trumpeters blew a fanfare, and to the notes of this the Admiral paced away with his charge, flanked by Yeomen, to join the other waiting Knights of the Bath, and so to march out of the hall in some sort of procession.

The King sighed his relief, and grabbing his stick from Anne, used it to poke a route through the deer-hounds on his way, at last, to his seat up at the dais table, where the flagons stood ranked.

He took off his high hat and sat down—and everybody else was thankfully looking forward to doing so likewise once the Queen was seated, when Anne, escorted through the dogs by Lennox, reached her husband's side and stooped to whisper in his ear.

"Eh? Eh? Waesucks—to be sure. It had escaped me—aye, clean escaped me." James looked round for something convenient to bang on the table, but his queen tapped his shoulder and pointed to the trumpeter behind his chair. "Blow, man—blow," he commanded.

So once again the imperative summons to attention rang out—and retained everyone on their feet. Lolling in his chair, the monarch waved a vague hand. "See you," he announced, "there's another matter. Important. It's my royal pleasure to welcome to this my Court a man you'll hae heard tell o'—aye, a notable man. Frae Ireland. Hugh O'Neil, Earl o' Tyrone. He that would ca' himsel' *King* o' Tyrone, if I would let him!" He chuckled, and raised his voice. "Enter, Tyrone," he called. "Wi' another."

A side-door opened at the foot of the hall, and, from where they had been waiting all this time, two men marched in, arm-in-arm. They made an odd pair, for one was a red-headed giant with a bushy beard flecked with grey, and a wild eye, his clothes hung about him anyhow—the principal leader of the long Irish campaign against domination by Elizabeth's England; the other, a slender, dapper dandy of a man half his age, in the extreme of fashion, with a supercilious cast to his pale features—Charles Blount, eighth Lord Mountjoy, Elizabeth's Lord Deputy of Ireland, who had succeeded the ill-fated Essex. They had difficulty in adjusting to each other's step, these two—as to much else, indubitably—but continued to pace forward arms linked nevertheless, by royal command.

Astonished, enthralled, the huge company stared at the great and terrible rebel of the line of Ulster, bogey for so long to the English, destroyer of cities and armies, slayer of the innocent; and at the elegant who had gained eventual victory over him, where Essex and all others had failed.

Stalking unevenly, they came up to the dais, and bowed in approximate unison.

James put on his hat again, and nodded to them genially. "Aye," he said. "Right satisfactory. A symbol o' happier times. *Cedant arma togae.* Welcome, Hughie. Welcome, my Lord Mountjoy. Here you see the kindly fruits o' peace and amity. *Sic volo, sic jubeo!* For thirty years there has been stupid war in Ireland, wi' thousands dead. Now, on my royal command, that's by wi'. There'll be nae mair o' it, I tell you. And these twa are the sign and seal o' it. Loving each other!" Even James himself could not but grin at that interpretation of the pair's attitude before him. "Aye, love we'll hae, no' hate and bicker, in my realms. Mind it. Wars and bloodshed I'll no' abide. In token whereof I make proclamation, proclamation d'you hear, that Hugh O'Neil, Earl o' Tyrone, has my fullest, freest pardon and remission, and a' styles, titles and lands declared forfeit are restored to him. A' men will show him fullest respect—on penalty o' my wrath. Aye, and Charles, Lord Mountjoy—you I hereby appoint and create Earl o' Devonshire, for your guid services. Your patent and bit belt you'll get later." He took off his hat once more. "Aye, then—that's it. Awa' to your places. God be thankit, that's done. We can now set to. This is by way o' being a wedding feast, mind. For my honest gossip and guid friend, aye *amicus usque ad aras,* Philip Herbert, and his bit lassie. We'll set him on his way, and right warmly. Bring on the meats . . ."

* * *

As a banquet, perhaps it was less successful than some—whatever else it was. The prolonged delay had not improved the cookery; moreover it was possibly a mistake to have had the wines on the tables beforehand, for hungry folk had had to fill in the time and put something into empty bellies. As a result, many had lost interest in the food by the time it arrived, and some were not in the best state to appreciate the good things to come. And there were very good things to come, undoubtedly.

It was a fairly late hour before the last of the twenty-odd courses was over, and not a few, including James himself, would have been glad to forgo the masque to get down to the final climax. But this was Anne's contribution to the evening, and she had spent upwards of three thousand pounds upon it, with the newcomer Inigo Jones, talented protégé of the Earl of Pembroke, designing the setting and decor for Ben Jonson's theme. Moreover, there had already been something of an upset about it all, for the Earl, a man with cultural leanings, had himself written and designed a masque for his brother's wedding, called *Juno and Hymenaeus,* unaware that the Queen was intending the other for this night. It was unthinkable that all should be abandoned now—especially as it was important that royal marital harmony should be seen to be maintained, at present.

Towards the end of the feasting, then, with performing bears dancing to the music of a gipsy band, the Queen and some of her ladies, who were to take part in the masque, slipped away.

James had been waiting for this. After a little he obtained approximate quiet by the usual methods. "My friends," he said, "it is my pleasure and satisfaction to mak twa pronouncements. One is that the Queen and mysel' are to be blessed wi' another bairn, to be born, God willing, in the month o' March, to our notable joy, aye joy. The bairn was conceived between us here, in this England, in this very house o' Whitehall—and so is your very ain prince, or again princess. It is our royal wish and intention suitably to mark the occasion some fashion. Aye, in some fashion no' yet decided. Accordingly, my friends, I therefore seek your kindly suggestions to that end. In due course. You will pleasure me and the Queen by thinking o' some worthy design, mark or employ, to grace the occasion o' this notable birth o' the first prince o' our Great Britain. Think on it, and inform me."

Far apart as they were placed, Duke Ludovick and George Heriot managed to exchange glances, of mixed admiration, relief and amusement. However uncouth, it was no fumbling hand which steered this so doubtfully united ship of state.

When the cheering died down, James went on. "My second pronounce concerns my guid and loving cousin Patrick, Earl o' Orkney," and he waved a cousinly hand towards the Stewart table, "and his brothers, forby. It pleases me much to gie them welcome to this my Court in London. Mind, they're no' a' here—the brothers. I canna just mind how mony there are!" He chuckled, to emphasise the genial tenor of his remarks.

"Ower mony!" Patrick Stewart interpolated briefly, into the laughter.

"Eh? You say so, Pate? Aye, well—maybe. We can a' hae too much o' a guid thing, even. My Cousin Pate—he's a swack lad, as you'll see. And guid on a horse or a woman! He'll maybe teach you a thing or twa, Philip!" He paused. "But it grieves me right notably to say that I've got something against the guid Pate, aye. A small matter, just—that maybe needs put to the test. My Council in Scotland, see you, is getting fair deluged, aye deluged, wi' complaints and protests frae the guid folk o' Orkney and Zetland anent oppressions, extortions and depredations—aye, and rapes too, mighty rapes—committed they do say by my said Cousin Pate, Earl thereof. Och, unpleasant, unpleasant! It's maybe a' lees, mind—untruths. But it will hae to be enquired into."

The sudden silence was dramatic. All sober enough to recognise what was happening, sat up in various stages of alertness.

"What is this?" Orkney demanded slowly, quietly.

"A small matter, Cousin," the King answered easily. "We'll hae my Scots Privy Council investigate. Och, they will likely assure me there's nae truth in it. Or no' much. Or you'll can explain, to our royal satisfaction. But we maun enquire, see you—when so mony complain. You'll no' think ill o' me for that, will you, Patrick man? It'll no' tak that long."

The Earl's ravaged features were set like stone, his cold eyes icy.

"Meantime," James went on affably, "I'll need to keep you under watch and ward, eh? To show your island folk that they've still got a king to look after them—though six hundred miles awa'! Ooh, aye—my duty, nae less. We'll no' ward you right straitly, mind, Pate—no' in the Tower, or the like! But you'll consider yoursel' under my royal care and keeping. Aye—and you'll no' return to Orkney, nor yet Zetland, until I say so—as precaution, just. But, man—you'll be gey little inconvenienced."

Patrick Stewart was entirely still, motionless—and, strangely, infinitely more dangerous-seeming, menacing, than if he had risen and stormed in wrath. There was dead silence for long moments. Then he gave a single nod. "We will speak with Your Grace on this, after," he said evenly, authoritative still.

"Do that, my lord," James agreed. "Meanwhile, hold yoursel' in ward, just. Answerable to our cousin the Duke o' Lennox. That's best." He smiled round on all, a man entirely at his ease. "Well—that's my twa pronouncements. The Queen's bit masque will be starting—and we'll need to gie it due attention, mind. But the night's young yet. So drink up, my lords and gentles. Eh, Philip—the night's young yet, man?"

"I am at Your Majesty's disposal, any hour," the bridegroom called back, hiccuping, amidst relieved laughter.

"Aye—you're time will come . . ."

Tension eased as it became apparent that the Earl of Orkney had a firm grip on himself and his brothers, and obviously intended that there should be no scenes or trouble meantime. None doubted his capacity to make such trouble, in his own time. That superficial harmony was not in fact achieved there and then was not his fault, the trouble starting elsewhere. Attendants were now wheeling in scenery and backcloths for the entertainment to follow. Master Inigo Jones, a serious and rather self-important young man, who had learned his craft of painter in Italy, where he had had the Medicis as patrons, came hurrying in to speak to the Garter King, as Master of Ceremonies, declaring that they must have more room, and that at least one of the lengthy side-tables would have to be cleared away if the masque was to be properly staged. Also a corner of the dais itself, if that was possible.

Good-naturedly the King agreed, and there followed a major upheaval, for a while, as furniture was moved about, and guests likewise. The deer-hounds presented a problem, and had to be manoeuvred into a corner with much tact. Various new groupings formed amongst the company, and Heriot found himself able to stand at Alison's side, where Lennox presently joined them. They had just begun to exchange appreciative comments on James's remarkable handling of the Queen-Orkney situation, when high words drew all eyes to the dais again. The table there had been moved back and sideways, and a rearrangement of seats became necessary—various dais guests being already on the floor and no longer requiring chairs. The Duke of Holstein had apparently come rather poorly out of this readjustment, precedence-wise, and now was placed further from the King's chair than heretofore—although in the same position relative to the Queen's empty throne. The fact was that James was getting to that stage of the evening when he liked to have his especial hard-drinking favourites close around him, regardless of rank and precedence—and although Ulric was sufficiently hard-drinking, the King was getting a little tired of his brother-in-law, more especially with the labour of conversation in a mixture of Danish-English-Latin-Doric. So now Ulric was on his feet, making protest loud and long, assisted by his Danish aides, all roaring drunk anyway. Ludovick hurried away again, fairly certain that the monarch would soon be calling upon him to pour oil on troubled waters.

"That Ulric is a fat stot!" Alison observed succintly. "The sooner he sails back to Denmark, the better. The Queen has had quite enough of him. What would the King do without Duke Vicky?"

"He has been doing notably well without him, or anyone else, this evening, I swear!" the man returned. "James has achieved more than I would have believed possible, since coming into this room."

"Yes. But when aught goes amiss, he calls for the Duke. Or you. This masque will never succeed tonight. It is too late. Folk are too drunk. Too much has gone before. Moreover, Master Jonson and Master Jones are at each others throats. It will come to grief. Heigho—there will be worse upsets than Duke Ulric's ruffled pride, for Duke Vicky and you to deal with, before the night is out!"

"You do not sound unduly cast down at the prospect!"

She laughed. "Should I? This Court itself is a better show than any masque! I am sorry for the Queen. But she ought to have let Lord Pembroke have *his* masque tonight, for his brother's wedding. Sakes—look at yon bullock from Denmark!"

James was not greatly trying to placate his brother-in-law. His suggestion that Ulric should sit in his sister's throne, since she would not be requiring it, apparently did not commend itself; and thereafter, with a wave of his hand, the monarch left the matter to Lennox and the Garter King. In a lull in the general hubbub, the former could be heard explaining soothingly that if His Serene Highness would draw his chair in just behind the King's own, he would be sufficiently close for converse and dignity both—to which Ulric declared in conglomerate eloquence that if he was denied his due and proper seating, he would be forced to stand throughout, in protest.

It was at this awkward juncture that the clash of cymbals drowned all other sounds, and a large blackamoor emerged from the scenery at the foot of the banqueting-hall to announce in a deep bellow that the Masque of Blackness now commended, by order of her Imperial Majesty the Empress of the Niger. Let all be silent.

Duke Ulric, caught at something of a disadvantage, had either to swallow his words or remain standing. He stood, if not firm at least stubbornly. Unfortunately his aides from Denmark felt bound to stand with him.

A painted curtain drew back to reveal a cunningly devised lake, real water in front, held in shallow trays, magnified by mirrors and merging into a painted background of meres, woods and mountains, all flanked by growing reeds and potted palms which rippled in a fan-made breeze, most realistic. On to this lake, to the sound of wierd and barbaric music never before heard in the land, thin fluting and wild jangling and clanging, came a great scallop-shell which seemed to float on the water, drawn by white sea-horses, setting up an effective splashing. Escorting this were six swimming sea-monsters, very terrible and spouting steam, each bearing on its back two torch-bearers, naked but for loin-cloths, from which torches, at intervals, spouted firework stars. Within the scallop, on a throne of shells, sat the black Empress Euphoria—Anne herself—ablaze with jewels on turban and corsage. Behind her stood the Countess of Bedford as slave, clad only in a breastplate and loin-fringe, both of threaded pearls, and waving above her mistress a great fan made of two entire peacocks' tails. Around them were grouped half-a-dozen more ladies, all, like the Queen, blackened on all visible parts of their bodies—which was most of them, for they were in the main scantily clad.

Loud cheering and stamping greeted this vision, mixed with guffaws, and also a certain amount of censorious outcry from those who disapproved of the highest in the land demeaning themselves as naked blackamoors. Duke Ulric was the most vehement of these. It was a considerable time before quiet could be restored, though the cymbals achieved it in the end.

At a signal Yeomen of the Guard now extinguished the candles and torches in the main part of the hall—which, although it certainly highlighted the masquers, was probably a mistake in the circumstances, since all else was left in darkness. This, coinciding with the start of recitation, poetic declamation and singing, not all of it of a professional standard to match Inigo Jones's decor, soon produced stir, catcalls and anonymous goings-on amongst a high-spirited, drink-taken audience which had been waiting for too long. When young Prince Henry came on the scene, as a white slave in clanking chains and little else, to dance for the black ladies, there was a certain restraint for the heir to the throne. But after his part was over, all quickly degenerated into pandemonium and licence in the darkness of the banqueting hall. Everywhere women began to squeal and yelp as they found themselves being kissed, embraced, man-handled and their clothing interfered with. A shout that sounded suspiciously like the bridegroom's called for skirts to be removed—echo of the other occasion at Wilton—and nothing loth, no lack of others took up the cry.

Heriot found Alison being assailed by two youths—whether the pages who had flanked her at table or others he could not be sure in the gloom—and laid about him with clenched fists and no little fury. Lennox, the Garter King, and others shouted for the candles to be lit again—but this was a much slower process than the extinguishing. Chaos reigned, with no attention paid to the masque any longer.

The deer-hounds bayed loudly—but no peremoptory masters' voice cried them down.

Light was eventually produced, to reveal an extraordinary scene. Chairs and even tables were overturned, dishes, wine flagons and beakers strewed the floor, amidst spilt liquor and clothing. Young men were waving women's garments in triumph, some actually wearing them—while their owners screamed, wept or giggled, sought to flee the hall, hide in corners or boldly strut, according to temperament. Many ladies, however, discovered more serious losses than their clothing or modesty—jewellery, necklaces, chains, purses had been stolen. Deafening was the outcry.

Only one oasis of calm and normality was there in all the turmoil. Up on the dais the King and his close companions sat drinking methodically, watching, interested, amused but unconcerned. And at their nearby table the Orkney Stewarts eyed all with unconcealed contempt, disdain. Ulric of Holstein still stood, prominent eyes goggling.

In this chaotic situation Queen Anne, perhaps recognising that her orders to extinguish the lights might have been responsible for touching off the ferment, made a gallant effort to retrieve the situation. Abandoning the remainder of the masque, she summoned her musicians from the wings, and ordering them to play a quadrille, led the better clad of her ladies out on to the main hall floor to seek partners for the dance, assured that her royal presence there would tone down the wilder excesses. She herself perceived the new Spanish ambassador, Don Juan de Tassis, standing alone and distinctly bemused, and went to him offering her hand. He kissed it, thereby obtaining a blackened face, and found himself whisked away in somewhat feverish romp.

In some degree Anne was justified, for the worst horseplay died away, and many followed her lead. Others took the opportunity to slip away, improper as this was while King and Queen remained. But nothing could restore the evening to anything like order now—especially as the monarch himself made no attempt to do so. Bowing to the inevitable, the Queen took leave of her partner, and beckoning to her ladies to follow her, swept doorwards.

Alison Primrose grimaced at George Heriot, and reluctantly trailed after her mistress. Heriot was wondering whether to accompany them as escort when he saw that some of the Yeomen had detached themselves for that duty.

Only as they were disappearing through the doorway, with Master Inigo Jones appearing weeping therein, did a trumpeter sound a belated and perfunctory flourish for the Queen's retiral.

It was as though James had been waiting for this moment. Hardly had Anne passed out of sight than he raised hands above his head, to stretch largely. Then he clapped on his feathered hat.

"Aye, then," he announced. "Enough's enough. Time for the bedding. Philip lad—you in guid fettle?"

"Never better," that stalwart declared thickly. "Ready for aught!"

"Let us hope the lassie can say the same, then!"

"Susan will do very well," Southampton called out. "I can vouch for her!"

There was a shout of laughter, in which the Lady Susan's high-pitched whinny overtopped all.

The King got to his feet. "We'll see," he said. "Gie's your arm, Philip. And you too, girl. Tut—pu' up your bodice, woman. We're no' in the bedchamber yet! Now Cousin Pate—your fiddlers, heh?"

Orkney stared for a moment bleakly, and then nodded, but shortly. He jerked a hand at his two musicians. They could now hardly stand—but they could still fiddle. They moved unsteadily foward to pace before the King. The Earl and his brothers, however, remained unmoving, sitting at their table, tankards in hand. Everyone else left in the hall, and sufficiently sober to be so, was upstanding.

Ignoring his peculiar cousins, arm-in-arm with bride and bridegroom as before, James started on his tottering way to the door, fiddlers ahead, courtiers falling in behind. He seemed in a state of entire felicity, but as he passed where Heriot stood, he nodded his head at him.

"Come, Geordie," he said.

"Pray to be excused, Majesty," that man requested, bowing.

"Nonsense, man—be no' so delicate! Come you." And as he passed on, he threw a word or two over his shoulder to Lennox, who came close behind.

Heriot, following on unenthusiastically after the noisy crew, found the Duke at his side.

"This may not be to your taste, Geordie," he murmured, "but James says you had better be there. The bride, it seems, is wearing certain jewellery belonging to you. When she takes it off, James thinks that you had better be there to claim it, or it will vanish away!"

"He thought of that? In this ploy!" As he went, Heriot marvelled anew at a monarch who could, and would, consider one of his servant's interests at such a time.

They wound, shouting and singing, along corridors and up stairs, to one of the great state bedrooms prepared for the occasion. Here, all looked like degenerating into complete riot, when James obtained a partial quiet by someone beating one of the cymbals from the masque. He declared that all must be done decently and in order, for his friend Philip, in the proper tradition—which might have seemed a curious way of describing such proceedings.

The company divided roughly into two, according to taste, to undress the bride and groom, although in scarcely orderly fashion. The women—and quite a few had survived the evening—not unnaturally gravitated towards Sir Philip, as of course did the King; but Lady Susan's disrobers undoubtedly outnumbered them, the bride wisely assisting. George Heriot managed to grab a string of pearls, warm from the flesh, and two gemmed bracelets, before anybody else could do so, and then stood back.

Quickly, amidst much acclaim, the two protagonists were reduced to a state of mother-nakedness—although they did not appear quite, perhaps, as on the day they were born, the man's highly positive masculinity rather remarkable in the circumstances, and the woman's slight improvements on nature much commented upon. Then they were picked up by such of their supporters as could manage to get a hand upon their persons anywhere, and carried to the great bed. There was some argument here as to who should be set down on top of whom, the principals proclaiming the matter immaterial—but James's plea for natural seemliness prevailed, and Lady Susan was lowered first on the bed.

Thereafter no urgings, counsel or guidance as to the next stage was necessary, or indeed could have been found time for, as Sir Philip settled himself into his due and effective position, for these two were obviously experienced practitioners, possibly more so than most of their assistants. In one way, perhaps, it was a little disappointing for habitual attenders at wedding-beddings, since the encouragement, schooling and manipulation of less confident performers could on occasion provide considerable interest, not to say hilarity. These two went at it, from the start, with expertise and enthusiasm—to their own very evident satisfaction, whatever else. It was all over before the best epigrams and flights of wit had really got going—and Philip Herbert had disproved that a surplus of wine was necessarily any handicap to bedtime prowess—and his bride that an audience need be an inhibiting factor.

"Aye—very guid," King James commented, although perhaps just a little doubtfully. "Expeditious. Aye, right prompt."

"That is one hundred pounds you owe me, Sire." came a contentedly languorous voice from the bed.

"Ooh, aye. But I'll might get it back yet, man. An hour later, you said? We'll be back up in the hour, then, to see if you can keep my hundred—or you can make another fifty! Come you, then, my lords and gentles—gie them a bit peace, for they hae a heavy night ahead o' them, I'll wager! Gie's your arm, Vicky. Geordie—you got what's your ain? Well—doon wi' us. There's plenty wine yet—unless yon Patrick o' Orkney and his crew hae drunk it a' while we've been doing our duty by these innocents! Come, you . . ."

II

His cloak tight around him against the chill November drizzle, George Heriot presented himself at the gatehouse of Whitehall Palace, and waited while it was checked whether he should be admitted or not—for, unlike the Queen's Somerset House where almost anyone could walk in and out, entry here was strictly controlled. It was an odd time for an urgent summons to the presence—just before three in the afternoon—for when he was not out hunting, the King liked to take a nap after his midday meal. It was scarcely his time for discussing money matters or ordering jewellery.

The Duke of Lennox himself came down to the gatehouse to conduct his friend to the King. "A strange business, Geordie," he declared. "Some sort of conspiracy, it seems. To do with the Catholics again. Thank God our slippery Patrick Gray does not seem as yet to have a hand in this one—there seems to be no connection with Scotland. James has a letter—very mysterious, just after his own heart! Whether there is any truth in it is another matter."

"But what is this to do with me? Why bring *me* hurrying from the Exchange? I am no plot-breaker—as the King has not failed to tell me!"

"There is talk of money—much money. It is seemingly a large matter—no mere plot but a great conspiracy. Or so Cecil thinks . . ."

"Cecil? Is he in this? Then it becomes serious, one way or the other! Serious for somebody!"

"No doubt. The Catholics, I would think. Such as we all were, not so long ago!"

Heriot looked at the other quickly. The Duke's sister, the Lady Hetty of Huntly, was a fervent Catholic, as had been his father—as had been most fathers, indeed, with the Reformation not more than fifty years old, in Scotland at least. Until the age of thirteen Ludovick had been brought up in Catholic France, then taken to Scotland and put largely in the care of the Master of Gray—whose Protestantism was notoriously of the suspect sort. In theory, the Duke was firmly in the Protestant camp; but in fact . . . ? Heriot believed that a man's religion was his own business; but in a situation such as this it was wise to tread warily.

There was no time to pursue their discussion. Past the Yeomen on duty they came to the King's own bedchamber. In the anteroom thereof they found James, in a bed-robe but wearing his hat; Cecil, recently promoted, once more, to be Earl of Salisbury; the youngish Howard, Earl of Suffolk, Lord Chamberlain; and a tall, thin, dark man whom Heriot knew to be the Lord Mounteagle, a moderate Catholic peer. The King was sitting at a table, poring over a letter, Cecil was watching him tight-lipped, Suffolk looking bored and William Parker, Lord Mounteagle distinctly agitated and unhappy, all standing.

"Ha, Geordie," James cried, "Here, man, and cast your eye ower this. Here is a letter. Sent to the Lord Mounteagle. A fell strange letter. Warning him o' danger. Frae ill men, gey ill. Wicked treasons. Danger to my royal person. Aye, and to this parliament I'm to open the morn. You've a guid canny heid on your shoulders, Geordie. What d'you mak o' it?"

Heriot took the paper, and scanned the ill-spelled epistle, watched by the others, Salisbury and Suffolk with ill-concealed impatience and disapproval at this waste of their time over a mere tradesman's views, however wealthy he might be.

> My lord—out of the love i beare to some of youer friends, i have a caer of youer preservacion, therefor i would advyse yowe as yowe tender youer lyft, to devyse some exscuse to shift of youer attendance at this parliament, for God and man hathe concurred to punish the wickednes of this tyme, and think not slightlye of this advertisement, but retyere youre self into youre countrie wheare yowe maye expect the event in safti, for thowghe theare be no apparance of anni stir, yet i say they shall receyve a terrible blowe this parleament, and yet they shall not seie who hurts them; this councel is not to be contemned, because it maye do

yoew good, and can do yowe no harme, for the danger is past as soon as yowe have burnt the letter, and i hope God will give yowe the grace to make good use of it, to whose holy protection i commend yowe.

Heriot looked up, smoothing mouth and small beard. "A very curious document, Sire," he commented slowly, thoughtfully. "Which presents more questions than it answers. Wicked, shameful —but curious."

"We discovered that for ourselves, man!" Cecil said testily.

"Let him be, my lord," the King observed, raising a grimy finger. "Geordie Heriot's no' a new-made earl! Nor yet slightly aulder one!" Suffolk although a son of the former Duke of Norfolk, had only been created earl in 1603. "But he's got mair siller to jingle in his pouch than the twa o' you together, I vow! And he's no' made a' that by failing to ken what's what! He kens how mony maks four, does Geordie Heriot! And he has a quick eye. Well, Geordie—what say you? These questions?"

"I take it, Sire, that this is warning of the threat of an attack upon yourself at the opening of parliament tomorrow? But more than yourself—the entire parliament in assembly. The writer does not mention Your Majesty—but if the whole of parliament is threatened, it can only be when both houses are together assembled, in the Lord's chamber. For the opening. When you and Her Majesty and the Prince are present. An attack on the King in parliament all but takes the breath away! The first question then, is—is this to be taken as serious? Or is it some folly, some prank? Or the work of someone light in his wits?"

"Think you that such as ourselves would be here, sir, troubling His Majesty, if we did not conceive it serious?" Suffolk demanded.

"As to that, my lord, I know not. But I agree that it probably should be taken as serious. Any prankster, hoaxer or scatterpate would, I think, have used names, the King's or others. Where he aims his threats. This does not. Moreover, he says to burn the letter. Were it a hoax, would he not rather wish many to read it? Else his satisfaction is limited to cozening one man only—my Lord Mounteagle."

"I hadna thought o' that," James admitted. "I daresay you're right. But that's no' important, since we're taking it fell seriously onyway. But what d'you think o' the matter itsel', man. The threat? Quiet, my lords—I wish to hear Master Geordie's ain impressions."

Glancing at the letter again, Heriot put his finger on a line midway. "These words, Sire, seem to me of the most import. '. . . they shall not see who hurts them.' To threaten an entire parliament with destruction, and then to say that they shall not see who hurts them, seems to rule out armed attack, many men making assault. Some cataclysm, then—devastation. Fire, perhaps. To burn down the House of Lords. Or smoke, suffocation . . ."

"Or gunpowder, man—gunpowder!" James could not hold back his own theory. He slapped his bare knee excitedly. "Man—your mind works the same way as my ain! I was telling these lords—only gunpowder would serve. To destroy all, so that nane kenned what slew them. I say it's gunpowder."

"Your Majesty may recollect that I also mentioned gunpowder amongst the possibilities," Cecil put in stiffly.

James ignored that, "Man—think o' it! In one michty displosion and discharge, to dispose o' the entire realm—or a' that matters in the realm. King, Queen, heir to the throne, great officers o' state, ambassadors, bishops, Privy Council, judges, lords and commons. Waesucks—what a contrive! What an excogitation! Worthy o' the mind o' auld Satan himsel'!" Quite carried away by the magnificence, enormity and comprehensive scope of the entire conception, Majesty gobbled, goggled and dripped saliva.

"It would require a deal of gunpowder," the practical Lennox remarked, "to bring down the whole House of Lords. It would not serve to bring down only part. And it is costly stuff. Even one barrel costs a deal of money. As Admiral, in Scotland, I know."

"That is one reason why I brought Geordie in. My lords, here, compute that it would tak maybe a score o' barrels o' powder to blow up yon building—more, belike. And to move so much through the city wouldna be easy, unkenned. It would hae to be by boat, I'm saying. A ship in the Thames. A' this means much siller. Who has that much siller—who would wish to do the likes o' this? Catholics? It's the sort o' ploy yon man Raleigh might devise. And he has the money. But he's safe lockit up in the Tower."

"You are sure that it is a Catholic plot, Sire?"

"Who else? My Lord Mounteagle, here is a Catholic—forby a leal one and he believes it so. What other party would wish to get rid o' the entire rule, rule, in Crown, Church and State, this way? Eh, Mounteagle, man?"

"I fear that it must be so, Sire," the tall, thin individual acceded unhappily. "Else why warn myself?"

"Do you *know* that you are the only one to be warned, my lord?" Heriot asked. "That was the third of my questions."

The other eyed him quickly. "What do you mean, sir?"

"Merely that you are not the only Catholic peer, my lord. There are many. Someone in the plot has sent you this letter, because they say they love you and do not wish you to die in the holocaust. You may, or may not, have a notion who the writer might me. But surely it is conceivable that other plotters—or the same man, indeed—may wish to save some other Catholics also? Members of both Houses, perhaps. So there may be other letters. Or if not letters, other warnings. Such as might tell us more."

"Sakes, Geordie—you have a point there. Cecil, man—you should ha' thought o' that."

"It had indeed occurred to me, Sire. But I did not see that it would take us greatly forward."

"It might, my lord." Heriot asserted. "A swift enquiry amongst Catholic lords and Members . . ."

"We do not want this trouble bruited abroad, Master Heriot. The fewer who know, the better. It is not good for His Majesty's name and repute that any should consider such outrage. Moreover, we do not *know*, as yet, that there is any truth in it."

"But you believe there is. And must act for the King's safety. Surely certain Catholic noblemen can be approached secretly? This day. If there is naught in it, they will scarcely spread the rumour, to the hurt of their own people?"

"Geordie's right," the King declared. "And we've no' that long to act. Hae you anyone in mind, man? In especial?"

"I thought of the young Earl of Arundel, Sire. Kinsman of my lord Earl of Suffolk, here. He is only a youth, too young to take his seat in the Lords—but he will be at the opening ceremony, will he not? He is the head of your great family of Howard, is he not, my lord? Who would be Duke of Norfolk and Earl Marshal of England were it not for the forfeiture of his late father, your brother? Surely Catholic conspirators would not wish to destroy the highest-born Catholic in England?"

Suffolk looked uncomfortable. His own Protestantism was undoubtedly political rather than of conviction. "If my nephew had received such a letter, be sure that he would have brought it to me, sirrah. Or to the Lord Admiral. Or to Northampton."

"He might not. He might be too frightened. Or believed it but a jest. Not understanding the importance of it. It would be worth asking."

"It would so," the King decided. "See you to it, Suffolk. Anything else, Geordie?"

"You mentioned ambassadors, Majesty—when you spoke of those who would be destroyed if—and God forbid—this evil conspiracy had not come to light. But surely the last thing that Catholic rebels would wish would be to slay the ambassadors of the Catholic states—the Vatican, Spain and France, Venice and the rest. It would be of interest to know whether *they* have been warned not to attend."

"Well thought on. We'll find out frae Don Juan. He's right friendly wi' my Annie—she's even given him a bit wing in her Somerset House. Vicky—can you make shift to find out if the Spanish ambassador will be going to the opening the morn? As invited."

"Sire, I would strongly advise care in this matter of ambassadors," Cecil put in. "Such cannot be questioned as can other men. Moreover, we want no alarming messages sent to Madrid or Rome or Paris, declaring England to be in a state of revolt, and Catholics ready to destroy the realm. I crave your royal leave to attend to this of the ambassadors myself."

"He doesna trust you, Vicky! But—as you will. So long as it is done."

"A further matter, Sire. Although no doubt my lord of Salisabury has already thought of it also!" Heriot said. "As well as the question of the cost and bulk of sufficient gunpowder, there is that of where it would, or could, be bestowed. Without being seen. Difficult, I would think."

"I have indeed thought of it," the Secretary said. "Nor would it be so difficult. There are many cellars under the House of Lords."

"You'll hae to search them, man. Instanter."

"With your permission, Sire, any such search should be postponed for as long as possible. So that the dastards do not take fright. We want to catch them—not merely frighten them off, to make their wicked attempt on some other occasion. We must capture some of them. To put to the question. For this conspiracy must have wide ramifications. If these assassins intend to blow up the King, parliament and government, they must have plans for taking over the rule of the realm thereafter. It does not end but only begins, with the gunpowder, or other means. I believe that there must be a great many involved. Men of note and riches, prepared to govern. Otherwise all is a foolishness."

"Aye—the mind which conceived this satanic ploy, to destroy a' at one fell blast, wouldna fail to think on what would hae to follow," James nodded. "Much will hae to be wheasled oot. Aye, it's right diabolical to think on such base ingratitude and unkindness to their sovereign lord—waesucks, it is. You'll need to catch some o' them, to question, right enough. Maist severely. Naething's ower bad for the likes o' these."

"Agreed, Sire. Therefore they must not take fright and abandon all. Disperse before we can lay hands on them."

"But we havena long, Cecil man. Only the night. The morn's the opening."

"We have twenty hours, Majesty. Much may be done in that time—and we have much to do. I suggest that we waste no more time in talk. That knowing, or at least conjecturing, what we do, we each now go our several ways, and make all enquiries that we may. In discretion and circumspection, I must insist." Salisbury looked pointedly at Heriot, whom obviously he considered quite unfit to be mixed up in anything so delicate and important. "No alarm must reach the conspirators. We should reassemble, to report to Your Majesty, and further discuss the situation—or such of us as have any true contribution to make—in, say four hours. Shall we make it seven o' the clock, Sire?"

"That sounds right enough. But can you find oot that much in four hours?"

"I think that we can, yes."

"Aye, you're a right beagle, man, once on the scent! Off wi' you, then. Vicky—go you wi' Geordie Heriot. In case he needs authority—aye, my royal authority, to mak ony investigation he thinks fit. Find oot, Geordie, if you can, if ony Catholics o' means and substance hae been borrowing money, or pawning or selling jewellery or plate. Aye, and hiring shipping. Find who sells gunpowder, and who they've been selling it to. *You* can mak siclike enquiries a deal better and mair quietly than these lords amongst your city acquaintance."

"Shall I search the cellars of the House of Lords?" Suffolk asked.

"Not yet," Cecil said. "Too soon. Wait until we next assemble. Monteagle, you will know well many Catholic lords and gentlemen.

Find out what they know. You can, h'm, remind them discreetly that their heads may be at stake, in this! Here is opportunity to make proof of their loyalty."

Unhappily Monteagle nodded.

* * *

Four hours later they were all back in Whitehall Palace, with an addition—Sir Thomas Knevett, magistrate responsible for this section of Westminster. The King was as eager and impatient as a schoolboy with a new game.

"Well?" he demanded. "What have you discovered? A' the pack o' you. Out with it. What's new? Monteagle—you first."

"I have learned but little, Sire. Not for want of will, I assure Your Majesty. I have found only the one other who has been warned not to attend the opening. My own brother-in-law, the Lord Stourton. But not warned by letter. Only by a message. Spoken to his manservant. By a stranger, he says. In the street. The message only that if he valued his life, he would not go to the House of Lords tomorrow."

"Stranger? What sort o' stranger? Complete strangers dinna gie that sort o' warning to lords' servants and expect to be heeded, man."

"I know not, Sire. Stourton said that his servant had never seen the man before. He was waiting outside his lodging . . ."

"It seems at least as though the stranger had an especial love for your family, my lord!" Cecil put in dryly. "Interesting."

"More than interesting," Lennox added. "For Stourton's name came up in *our* investigations, likewise. Eh, Geordie."

"Only indirectly," that careful man pointed out. "His name given only as a reference. We were seeking the identities of any Catholic borrowers of moneys, or large sellers of goods, as Your Majesty suggested. There were none in my books, of any significance. None that I know to be Catholics. Then we went to my fellow money-lender and jeweller, Sir William Herrick, who was also the late Queen's goldsmith. He had received, in pawn, almost a year ago, considerable plate. On which he had advanced three thousand pounds. Two thousand pounds to one party and one thousand pounds to another—both known Catholics. The first was Mr. Francis Tresham, who gave the name of Lord Stourton for his security. The second was Sir Everard Digby. The pawnings were within a week of each other."

The quick indrawing of three different breaths, at the emunciation of these names, clearly was significant. The King looked round them all.

"Well, my lords—what o' it?"

Monteagle moistened his lips. "Francis Tresham, Sire, is also my brother-in-law. His two sisters are wed to myself and Stourton."

"Ha! You say so? Now we could be moving!"

"Further to which, Sire, Tresham was involved in Essex's rebellion," Cecil put in. "He is a plotter. Moreover his father, Sir Thomas Tresham, is well known as a man aggrieved, much fined for recusancy in the late Queen's day."

"Aye—so they hae a grudge against the Crown! We progress. And you, Suffolk? Hae *you* no' something to tell us?"

"Only, Majesty, that my nephew Arundel had been asked if he was to attend the parliament opening—*asked*, that is all. He had said no—for he has a distemper of the bladder, it seems. He is a sickly youth, as you know. It was Sir Everard Digby who asked him!"

"So-o-o! Digby, eh? He's o' a namely family. Is that a', man?"

"Yes. When Arundel said that he would not be going, Digby said no more. It may mean nothing."

"It's fell coincidental. Byordinar!"

"There is another matter, Sire. Relating to Tresham, not Digby," Heriot mentioned. "A month ago, Tresham hired a three-masted barque from Ebenezer Willison, trader, of Duck Wharf. It was said to be for trading to the Low Countries. But it is still lying in the Thames."

"Did I no' tell you!" James crowed. "This Tresham is in it deep as the neck. Aye—we'll hae him talking. And then dangling on the end o' a rope! Aught else, Geordie?"

"No, Sire. Save for one small matter perhaps. Amongst the plate pawned by Tresham was some engraved with the arms of Catesby—or so says Herrick. It need not signify."

"Sir William Catesby is a kinsman of Tresham's," Monteagle observed.

"And was also in the Essex business," Cecil added. "He has a wild son, Robert, who has been in some trouble." He cleared his throat. "You have done well, Master Heriot." That was scarcely warm, but it was a major acknowledgment.

"I told you Geordie kens what's what," the King said, beaming. "What o' yoursel', my lord? Did you no' discover aught?"

"Little to the point, Sire. Save that the Earl of Northumberland had been advised by his kinsman and steward, one Thomas Percy, against attending the opening. Strangely, on the grounds that he might be put to the question, at the parliament, by your royal self, Sire, regarding your Commission of Ten, sent up to settle the problem of the Border disputes. Presumably the Percys have uneasy consciences over the Borderland situation!"

"That I can believe! And you reckon this nothing to the point? A different matter, forby?"

"I would not like to say, for sure. Northumberland is not a Catholic—or not a *known* one! But this Thomas Percy may be, and in the plot. And wishes to save his chief. So tells this story. I have not had time yet to enquire as to his religion. But he is a gentleman-pensioner of your own, with duties around this palace."

"You say so? Waesucks—we're getting a wheen names now! Aye, plenties. What o' the ambassadors, man?"

"It was there that I wasted most of my time, Majesty. At Somerset House, with Don Juan de Tassos. It seems that he has not been warned. Nor has the Pope's envoy. Both declare that they are coming to tomorrow's ceremony. So the plotters, it seems, are not depending on foreign aid. Or greatly concerned for the envoys. Which makes me wonder, Sire. Gives me cause for some doubts."

"Doubts, man? At this hour? After a' that's been uncovered. What mair do you want?"

"It is still so much supposition, Your Majesty. A tall structure, yes—but built on but scanty foundations. A plot there probably is. But whether it is to blow up the House of Lords, or no, is but conjecture."

"Then put it to the test, man. Arrest a' these named men forthwith—Tresham, Digby, Catesby, Percy. For questioning. I wager we'll soon find out what they ken. Bring them before *me*. If they ken anything, I'll mak them talk! And I'll swear yon Tresham kens something."

"Too soon, Sire. We must have something to confront them with. More than conjectures. Some fact."

"These cellars? Under the House of Lords?" Heriot said. "They seem the likeliest place to put gunpowder. You could search these. If there is nothing there, we must consider further. But if there is . . ."

"Exactly," James agreed.

"Dangerous," Cecil objected. "In that they might take fright.

Believe that all was discovered, and flee. The main plotters. Be sure *these* will not all be hiding in some cellar under Westminster! And it is the leaders we want."

Suffolk spoke. "See you, it is my duty as Chamberlain and acting Earl Marshal, to ensure the proper ordering of parliaments. To arrange all ceremony. I could make a round of inspection of the building. Alone, or with an officer. Look into the cellars in the by-going. None could take fright from that. It is my simple duty."

"What if you stumble on them? The conspirators?"

"I must needs ask them what they do there. They will have some story to tell, for sure. If I can, I must seem to believe it. And leave. Pass on, without affrighting them. To give you time to make the arrests . . ."

"I still do not like it. If I were one of these men—which God forbid—I would then conceive all lost. They might even seek to slay you, Suffolk!"

"Not so. Slay the Lord Chamberlain, knowing that I would be missed immediately? Search be made for me, and all discovered? All thrown away. No, no."

"Why not take the Lord Monteagle with you, my lord?" Heriot suggested. "Since he is a Catholic. His presence with you might soothe the conspirators' fears—if you find any."

"A right guid notion, Geordie. That's it, Suffolk, you and Monteagle, go. Forthwith, aye. We've wasted time enough. Be expeditious about it, mind—we've no' that long to act. And back here wi' your report. We'll hae a bit refreshment while you're awa'."

"If you will permit my withdrawal—I will make certain arrangements," Salisbury said, "whilst we wait. Alert certain, er, henchmen of mine. And some of the Guard. To be prepared to make arrests. So that no time is lost."

"Aye, Cecil—off wi' you. And you, Knevett, go wi' him. Be back within the hour . . ."

The three Scots left in the anteroom considered each other. James winked heavily.

"We could ha' dealt wi' this fine and well, lacking them a'!" he said, confidentially. "They need it a' spelled out for them! Whereas *dictum sapienti sat est*! But in England we maun humour the English! Och, but they can be wearisome stiff. That's the worst o' them, I do declare. Stiffness. Cast-iron! Mysel', I like a bit quick-silver! Like we hae in Scotland."

"Such as the Master of Gray?" Lennox enquired, smiling.

"Even so, Vicky. Even in roguery there's lightsome ways o' doing things. I miss it—aye, I miss it."

"I doubt if even the Master of Gray would have considered blowing up King, parliament and everyone in authority, men, women and children, with gunpowder!" Heriot observed. "If this is indeed the facts of it. Sire—there is one point which troubles me still. This of Tresham and Digby—that money they gained by the pawning. This was done a full year ago. The plate has not been redeemed, admittedly—but a year ago! If it had been a month, two months even . . ."

"That's nae difficulty, Geordie," the King assured. "The plot could ha' been a year back, just as well as today. The parliament *was* to ha' been a year ago. But I put off the opening for six months—and then another six. Och, they'll no' gie me my money. Nor yet will they agree my terms for the uniting o' the kingdoms. They're fell obstinate—right contumacious. The Commons. They canna meet forby I summon them. So I've been teaching them a lesson, eye. Now, I need them to pass these laws I've made for a regulation o' the Borders. You ken—to bring to an end a' the strife and rieving and feuding and moss-trooping. I'll no' have it, in my united kingdom o' Britain. I've sent up this Commission o' Ten, to do the work, half Scots, half English. But it will cost money—grants-in-aid, compensations, bounties. And that means parliament's approval, God damn them! So—I open parliament the morn." James got to his feet. "But—come you into my bit cabinet. There's cauld meats and wine. As well be comfortable while we wait."

Cecil and the magistrate Knevett were the first back. Then, somewhat later than the suggested hour, Suffolk and Monteagle arrived, both obviously much excited.

"We have it, Sire—I swear we have it!" the Earl cried, almost as soon as he entered the room. "In one of the cellars. A man. Called Johnson. A desperate fellow, I vow! A wild eye. With a lantern. Much coals . . ."

"Aye, aye, my lord—tak your time. Let's hear it in some order. And no need to shout, man."

"Your pardon, Sire. I . . . we made circuit of the hall and galleries. All in order there. Then the cellars. Starting from the river end. We had an officer, with keys. But two we could not enter—the locks so rusted with disuse. Another empty but for the rats—faugh, a hundred rats! Big as cats. And the stench! Then a larger one. Locked. But we could not get the key in. Another key on the *inside*! So we beat on the door. In time, this man came. He had a lantern. He called through. Asked if it was Thomas. Or John. I said, aye, Thomas. My own name. He opened. A wild man. But no ruffian. Good clothes. A sword. A gentleman of sorts. We did not challenge him. I said I was Thomas, Earl of Suffolk, seeing that all was well for tomorrow's opening. Monteagle named himself . . ."

"I had never seen the fellow before," that man put in. "But he seemed to know my name."

"Not to alarm him, we but glanced into the cellar. There was a great heap of coals and wood. Going far back. No other men that we could see. We asked him what he did there, and at this hour of night. He said that he was servant to Master Thomas Percy, who rented the cellar from the Crown . . ."

"Ha—Percy!" James exclaimed. "We come to it!"

"Yes, Sire. He said that this Percy used the cellar for storage of his coals and billets. For his house nearby. And others. The gentlemen-pensioners' houses. The man—he said his name was John Johnson—was sorting his master's coals, for a new load was coming in a day or two. For the winter. I said his master must like to keep himself warm, for he had a good supply there already. And he said this Percy let other pensioners use it also. A thin story. But we wished him a good night, and left him. We heard him lock the door behind us. And came straight to Your Majesty."

"Mercy on us! And you dinna think he took fright?"

Both lords thought not.

"Waesucks—are you satisfied now, man Cecil? Wi' our conjectures and suppositions?"

Grimly the Secretary of State nodded. "Yes, Sire. I think that we can safely try to make the arrests now. This Percy, Tresham and the rest. Although, to be sure, they may be in hiding."

"We'll get the man Johnson, at the least. If he hasna bolted already. Then question him as to the others."

"Sire—with respect, no! There is this ship, in the river. The others might be aboard her. Or would flee to her, on the first hint of trouble. And get clean away to sea, in the dark. We must not have them alarmed one moment before it is necessary. I will have the watermen see to the ship, to prevent it sailing. And watch other shipping at the quays. But this will take time. We must place guard on the cellar, yes—but not take this man Johnson before need be. I want all these conspirators—*all*!"

"Aye—you're right, man. But we darena lose this one sure capture. If he's still there."

"I suggest, Sire, that Knevett here, with a party, goes down. To watch the cellar door. Ascertain that the fellow is still within. Remain nearby to guard it. Not challenge or enter, unless forced to, by being discovered or by the man leaving. Then, when we have the ship, and have arrested the others—in, and take Johnson. Others may come to join him. This must be handled with much care."

"Aye, well. It's your business, Cecil. You'll ken what you're at."

"I have my methods, Sire. Sir Thomas Knevett—collect a party of the Guard. Not too many—for they must remain hidden. Six or eight will serve. Cover them in cloaks—we want no interest or outcry from citizens. Take up position opposite or near the cellar door. There are merchants' warehouses there, for the quays. And wait. You understand?"

"Yes, my lord."

"You others, my lords—and Master Heriot—need not be further detained. I will now handle this matter . . ."

"Not so, Salisbury!" Suffolk exclaimed. "I am acting Earl Marshal. This is as much my responsibility as yours. I'm damned if I'll be pushed out at this pass! I'm going back with Knevett. He may require guidance . . ."

"So am I!" Lennox declared. "I'm certainly not going quietly to my lodging and bed, now! Eh, Geordie?"

"You will find it a cold, wet vigil, I think, my lords!" Cecil said thinly. "But so long as you abide by what I have said . . ."

"Och, man—we're no' a' bairns!" the King reproved. "We've a' done well this night—we'll see it out. I'd come doon there mysel'—but it wouldna look right. No' right. But you'll a' keep me right well informed, mind. For I'll no' sleep until I hear the outcome. And I want to see this man Johnson, when you tak him. Bring him here. I ken how to deal wi' his like!"

In the end, Monteagle went off with Cecil; and Suffolk, Lennox and Heriot, heavily cloaked, accompanied the magistrate down to Westminster, picking up half-a-dozen Yeomen of the Guard as they went.

The thin drizzle of the day continued, cold and raw—for it was nearly midnight. The damp, earthy smell of the Thames permeated all these riverside streets. Without the usual link-bearers, they hurried anonymously through the narrow, dark lanes—and such very few people as were about gave them wide and wary berth. Coming to the old Palace of Westminster, they moved cautiously round the riverward side of it, a deserted area of docks and storehouses, and Suffolk pointed out the significant cellar. Fortunately there was a warehouse almost opposite, with a pend through its basement. This pend was blocked by a gate, locked, but it was set far enough inside to leave a space where men could huddle in cover and darkness.

Before settling to their vigil, Suffolk and Knevett went over quietly, to the cellar door, to look and listen. They came back, heads ashake.

"Not a whisper of a sound. Or a chink of light," the Earl said anxiously. "He may have gone. Taken fright, after all. God's eyes—we should have taken him when we had the chance! All this caution of Cecil's! He's an old woman . . . !"

"He may still be inside," Lennox said. "Maybe asleep. If he is but on guard, waiting, he needs no light, need not move about . . ."

They settled to wait, since there seemed nothing else to be done.

It was cold and uncomfortable, as the Secretary of State had prophesied.

Midnight chimed from a score of church clocks—the 5th of November. About half an hour later, footsteps sounded on the wet cobblestones—one man's. They huddled back.

It was difficult to see anything in the gloom, but it was evident that the newcomer was on the other side of the street. He halted, opposite—and distinctly they all heard a key fit and turn in a lock, the faint creak of a door opening and shutting, then silence.

"You heard that?" Suffolk whispered. "That was a key turned on the *outside*. Therefore there cannot have been one on the inside. So the cellar was empty, locked from without. Our man must have gone away, and come back. No doubt to warn his fellows, of my visit. Now he's back. Or another is."

"So at least we have *someone* to capture, and question," Lennox said.

They waited again. One o' clock struck. Nobody else came. The watchers shivered in their cloaks, all excitement gone out of the business, the gentry all but deciding that they had had enough. Two o' clock. Parliament would be opening in nine hours.

Then there were sounds of the key turning in the lock again. There had been no more footsteps. The door creaked.

"Quick!" Heriot jerked. "He's coming out. If he's going away, we'll have to take him. Cannot let him get away again . . ."

They heard the door close and the lock click again. That was enough. The man was leaving, locking the door behind him.

Lennox leading, they rushed out, dividing right and left to prevent escape either way. Hemmed in the narrow street, taken completely by surprise, their man had no chance. One against ten, he put up little struggle. Knevett declared that he arrested him in the King's name.

Heriot delved into the fellow's pocket and found the key. He went to open the cellar-door once more, and they all hustled within, shutting and locking it again. Someone struck a light and the tinder flared. The lantern, still warm, stood on a shelf near the door. They lit it.

"It's the same man," Suffolk declared. "Johnson. Aye—we would like a further look at Master Percy's coals, Master Johnson!"

The man was swarthy, with an Italianate look to him, slender, wiry, keen-featured, with long, flowing hair and a small black beard. He glared at his captors, certainly did not cringe, and held his tongue.

The cellar proved to be larger than had seemed likely from the outside, and very deep. Coals and timber were heaped up to form a barrier, but it could be seen that the chamber went far beyond that. One of the Guard, clambering over the coals, shouted.

"Barrels!" he cried.

There were no fewer than thirty-six barrels of gunpowder stacked in the long probing cellar, two of them great hogsheads—sufficient explosive to demolish an even larger and stronger building than this old palace. According to Suffolk, they were directly under the Lord's chamber.

Leaving most of the Yeomen to guard the cellar, and to arrest anyone coming to it, they took the man Johnson back with them to Whitehall.

King James was in his great bed, nightcap on, but very much awake. He insisted on the captive being brought in for his personal interrogation, there and then. They would see what they could get out of him, before Cecil got his hands on the crittur, he declared.

James, in fact, was not without experience in this matter of questioning. When younger, he had taken an enormous interest in witchcraft—and had actually written a book on the subject. In his enquiries and investigations he had put to the question literally hundreds of his subjects—and since all were accused of an offence against both Church and State, he had not required to be over-delicate in his methods. He had presided personally over these sessions, and often declared that the most efficacious way of getting quickly to the root of things, even with the most obdurate, was to tie a rope round their temples, apply a lever, and twist until the scalp was lifted off. Seldom, apparently, was it necessary to go quite to this length, before the truth came flooding out.

John Johnson, before his monarch, was prepared to talk, after a fashion. He admitted his guilt—he could scarcely do otherwise—and his intention to blow up the King and parliament. For reason, he gave only his belief that it was the will of God that they should be destroyed, on account of sins innumerable. He had no accomplices, he said. It was all his own notion. He was the servant of Master Thomas Percy—but his master knew nothing of the project.

His hearers scoffed at this. If he was only a servant, how had he got the money to buy all the gunpowder? How had he conveyed it, single-handed, into the cellar? Moreover, how came it that he spoke with a gentleman's voice if he was but a servant?

He had been a soldier in the foreign wars, he said. He was gently born, yes, but with no means. Most of the powder he had stolen from ships at the quaysides. Barrel by barrel. Rolling each barrel to the cellar at night. For over a year.

Getting angry, James declared that he was lying. To him, the King. That he, the King, had means of making men talk the truth. He described his rope speciality, in detail.

Johnson did not blanch. On the contrary, he grew the more defiant. That sounded like the barbarities which might be looked for from Scotland, he declared. He had never found the Scots to his taste—hypocrites and savages all. One of his objects in this employment was to blow all the Scotchmen back to Scotland!

The King, gobbling and gasping, was bereft of speech. Suffolk hit the man twice across the face, so that his nose began to bleed. James had never liked blood at close quarters and drew back on his bed almost primly. But he forced himself to nod approvingly.

"Aye—suitable!" he said. "Suitable for an ill-mouthed limmer. A right opprobrious scoundrel. We'll mak him sing another tune. You'll hang, my mannie—but first you'll talk! And civilly."

Just then Cecil returned, with the Lord Admiral, Ellesmere the Chancellor, Coke the Attorney-General, and other members of the Council.

"All is in train, Sire," he announced. "Percy is flown, but we found an older man, Keyes, in his house. He will not tell us what we wish—yet. But a servant of Percy's, one Kempson, has talked to some effect. We have now many more names. Is this the man Fawkes, from the cellar . . . ?"

"Fox? No. He ca's himsel' Johnson. An ill loon, if ever I saw one! He'll no' tell us anything. Just unseemly abuse. To me—the King!"

"You should have left him to me, Sire. Scarcely work for Your Majesty. We'll stretch his tongue for him—like other parts! His true name is Fawkes—Guido Fawkes. So Kempson says. A fanatic Catholic, associator with Jesuits, and daring adventurer. Kempson turned evidence, to save his skin. As I guessed, there was a major conspiracy amongst certain Catholic squires, mainly from the Midlands. No great names yet. A few knights and men of means. But we will get them all, never fear."

The prisoner stared round at them all, unwinking, blood dripping from his nose.

"Fawkes, eh?" the King said. "*Guido* Fawkes! A queer-like name. A man who would ha' murdered the Lord's Anointed! Disgraceful!"

"And near one thousand others, Sire!" Lennox reminded. "Including all here!"

"Ooh, aye. Regrettable. But we'll mak them pay for their fell design, on my royal word! Tak him awa', Cecil man—and do your worst wi' him. He's an ill limmer, and I'll no' further soil my hands wi' him. Get his masters' names out o' him."

"We shall not spare him, Sire, be assured. But we have already got many names from this servant, Kempson—Thomas Winter, Robert, John and Christopher Wright, Ambrose Rookwood of Coldham Hall, and Robert Catesby, son to Sir William. And we shall get others, I promise you. The ship is held, and we have all now well in hand."

"Nae doubt. But, mind—you wouldna ha' had onything in hand, man, if I hadna put you right on it. Anent the gunpowder. And the ship, and a'. Aye, wi' Geordie Heriot's help. You kenned naething o' it. I am right displeased wi' you, Cecil, Earl of Salisbury. My royal person could ha' been disploded and dissolved, just, for a' you were like to do about it. This great wicked conspiracy against me, in this England—and my English Secretary and Council hadna hint nor hair o' it! A fair disgrace. You'll hae to do better than this—or there will be changes in this realm o' England. Aye, changes!"

Majesty drooped one heavy lid over a deeply lustrous eye in the direction of George Heriot. "Off wi' you, now—and I'll maybe get some sleep. I've a right heavy day, the morn." James took off his high hat and tossed it down the bed, as token that the audience was over, nightcap retained.

Hastily all started to bow themselves out, the prisoner being dragged with them. Fervently expressed desires for the monarch to have a good night, and praise to the Almighty for his great deliverance, came in a volley—even Cecil muttering something of the sort.

Before all were out and the doors shut, Majesty had a parting shot. "I will expect to see you a' in your places at the parliament-opening in a wheen hours—aye, you too, Knevett, and you Geordie Heriot. Just to be fell sure that if there's any mair attempts on our royal person that you havena heard tell o' yet, you'll a' be there to share the danger wi' your liege lord! Off wi' you!"

And so, seven hours later, and a little late, the second parliament of the reign was duly opened, with pomp and ceremony, and the Archbishop of Canterbury offering urgent and agitated thanks to God for the preservation of their beloved and esteemed sovereign—to the mystification of the vast majority of those present. Wild rumours did not fail to circulate, of course—but displosions by gunpowder, to use the monarch's own phrase, was by no means one of the whispered suggestions. Catholic threats, yes—that was a foregone conclusion, with dire prognostications as to retribution and reprisals to come.

It was five hours before the full story was allowed to leak out—by which time a great haul of conspirators had been made in Staffordshire and thereabouts, from whence most of the ringleaders seemed to come and where most had fled; although a number, including Robert Catesby, who appeared to be the master-mind, were slain resisting capture. The feared general Catholic uprising did not materialise—indeed many of the Catholic nobility and gentry drove refugees from their doors with bitter reproaches that they had brought disgrace on all who professed the ancient faith. To the surprise of his English ministers, if not of the Scots, James forbade any consequent witch-hunts or campaigns of terror, pointing out reasonably that though he deemed them mistaken in their views, some of his best friends were Catholics; and hinting that an alternative party in the realm was an excellent means of keeping his good Protestant servants on their toes. Almost a dozen unfortunates fell to be hanged, of course, after the normal preliminaries—amongst them Guido Fawkes, defiant to the end despite his tortured state, Sir Everard Digby, Ambrose Rookwood and others, these all claiming repentance for their desperate intention against the monarch and parliament but professing unalterable attachment to their Romish faith.

The venue chosen for this epilogue to a most curious drama was none other than the west end of the same St. Paul's church where George Heriot was wont to prosecute his daily ambulations, business exchanges and social gossipings—a most useful edifice. King James watched all, from a hidden corner, with lively interest.

12

The warm and humid July day was one of those in which George Heriot asked himself why he stayed in this airless London, amongst people he did not particularly love, dealing in and amassing money for which he had no particular use, and serving an oddity of a monarch who could get along all too well without him, when he could go back to his native Scotland, with its fresh winds and great skies, and live at ease and leisure amongst his own folk as a country laird with as much substance as a modest man would ever require. Frequently he asked this of himself, and had so far discovered no very convincing answer. Especially on stifling days of summer, when London stank to high heaven. They had smells in Scotland, admittedly, but always, as he remembered it, there was sufficient breeze to blow them away.

He was considering locking up his ledgers, with the secrets of so many proud and lofty folk in them, and walking over to St. Paul's to see if company and the latest news of the city and its follies might stir him out of his mood of discontent, when his foreman goldsmith mounted the stairs to his office to inform him that they had visitors —and young ladies, at that. Scots voices behind him amplified his announcement.

Alison Primrose stood there, a picture of fresh and winsome delight, heat or none, another young woman at her side, somewhat older, more heavily built but of a sonsy and buxom good looks nevertheless. Heriot sprang to his feet, temperature like gloom—and years—forgotten, and hurried forward, hands outstretched.

"Here's a joy!" he exclaimed. "I have not seen you this whole month. How come you here? I believed you were at Greenwich, with the Queen?"

"We took opportunity to come up the river in one of the King's barges, Geordie. In all the to-do of King Christian's coming, we will scarce be missed, I think. The barge was coming for more wines! Wines are in great demand at Greenwich these days! The barge will take us back in two hours time. Meg—this is Master Heriot, a good friend. And Mistress Margaret Hartside, from Kirkwall, one of Her Majesty's chambermaids."

"Kirkwall, eh?" Heriot said, as the other girl sketched a curtsy. "I think that I have seen Mistress Hartside around Somerset House, but we have not spoken. Greetings, Mistress—I am pleasured."

"And I honoured, sir. All know of Master George Heriot, the King's friend." She cast a sly glance at her companion. "And Alison's!"

"H'rr'mm. I am much privileged, yes. And how is the Queen? Better, I hope?"

"A deal better, yes—with her brother's coming. King Christian makes a new woman of her. He is very . . . rousing. But less of an oaf than Duke Ulric. The Queen is venturing from her room for the first time since the child died," Alison informed. "That is why we have been able to get away. We have been kept close tied, for long."

"Yes." Queen Anne had given birth, at Greenwich, to her seventh child in June of that year, 1606, a weakly infant, hastily christened Sophia, which had died after only a few hours. Anne had been plunged into depression since—for the previous child, the Princess Mary, born the year before, was almost equally sickly and only just holding on to life. At least there had been no alarms and rumours about the parentage of little Sophia. But the Queen was grievously cast down, and swearing that she would have no more children. She was aged but thirty-three.

"I rejoice to hear that King Christian is an improvement on his brother," Heriot said. "Since we are to have him with us for some time, it seems. King James will be pleased. He has worked hard for this visit. It is to show Christendom that he is a power amongst princes—but a power for peace and goodwill, his realm to be courted rather than feared. England is no longer to be an island, living within itself, as Elizabeth would have it, but part of Europe and the comity of nations. The King is far-sighted. This visit is more than just brothers-in-law forgathering." He paused, conceiving that this sort of talk was hardly suitable for young women callers. "Come—sit you down."

Alison found no fault with what he had said. "He came two days ago. The Danish king. In great style. In a great ship called the *Three Crowns,* with seven ships-of-war as escort, no less. Greenwich is now full of Danes. They outnumber even the Scots, I swear! Some of them are very handsome, in a pale, golden way. Are they not, Meg?"

"No doubt," the man commented, without enthusiasm. "We heard the great cannon-firing at Tilbury even here in London, on the east breeze. Would God there was still some breeze! This heat!"

"Yes. King James and Prince Henry went down to Tilbury in a fine barge, all banners and awnings and painted work, with musicians, to bring the other king back to Greenwich . . ."

"And wine-casks!" Margaret Hartside put in. "They were all drunk by the time they got back—the musicians too. I never heard such noise!"

"Not King James, surely? I have never known him drunk."

"No-o-o. But he and the other king were supporting each other. And both were singing. Ours does not usually sing, I think?"

"M'mmm."

Alison changed the subject. "I have brought Meg to see you, Geordie, for an especial purpose. She has something to show you. Something to *sell* to you, if you will consider buying."

The girls were dressed in light summery gowns, with much of bare arm and throat and little scope for pockets, but out from a bundled, silken shawl the other brought a little leather bag, which she opened and emptied on to the table before the man.

Heriot drew a quick breath, used as he was to fine jewellery. Cascading on to the table fell a shower of gems and pieces of gold and silver-work, a dozen items at least. Outstanding amongst them was a single great pearl on a chain, pear-shaped, pinkish, glowing warmly. He did not speak.

Alison did. "Meg is desirous of selling these. For so high a price as she may obtain. I believed that you would either buy them, or advise her. Since it is your trade, Geordie."

"My trade, yes," Heriot said slowly. "But . . . there are problems, perhaps. Questions, you understand? These are notable pieces. This great pearl in especial. I, h'm know it. Indeed, I know some of these others also. One was made in this house."

There was a pause, the young women apparently each waiting for the other to speak.

"May I ask, Mistress Hartside, whether you are selling these for yourself? Or for another?" the man went on carefully.

The girl hesitated. "For myself," she said, at length. "In order for me to return to Scotland. I have no money. I wish to return to Kirkwall, my home in Orkney." That sounded like a lesson learnt.

Heriot looked at Alison. "Before I may buy valuables such as these, I must know something of whence they came. Do not misunderstand me. Jewels are a strange and very special merchandise. They are *known* by many. And therefore it may be known who previously owned them. That pearl you see, I bought for the Queen, some years ago. In Scotland. And made that brooch for her, likewise."

"Are they so . . . so kenspeckle?" the older girl all but whispered.

"I fear so, yes. A queen's gems in especial."

She looked at Alison.

"You must tell him," that more forthright young woman said. "All that you told me. Master Heriot is good, kind. He will not betray you."

"You tell him."

"Very well. Meg is wed, secretly, to John Buchanan of Scotscraig. Also in Orkney. One of the Earl of Orkney's gentlemen. An Elymosinar of the King's. They have known each other long—but wed only when the Earl and his brothers were at Court a year back. The match had to be kept secret, or Meg could not have remained chambermaid to the Queen. None married may so serve her. And they have insufficient means to set up house together."

"I see. Orkney!" Heriot's eyes had narrowed and he tapped the table with one finger. "And these jewels?"

"Her husband, who is gone back to Scotland with the Earl, gave her them to sell. For him. For them both. So that they should have enough money. For Meg to leave Court, so that they might settle, back in Orkney. At Scotscraig. Together. As they would wish to be."

"Aye—but where did this Buchanan get the jewels?"

"The Earl gave them to him. In free gift," Margaret Hartside put in. "For his good services. Part of a casketful, given to my lord by the Queen."

The man half rose from his chair, but sank back again, biting his lip. "The Queen *gave* Orkney these?" he demanded.

"Yes. And many more. When he was at Court, a year back."

He whistled beneath his breath. "This is . . . extraordinary!" He turned to Alison. "Did *you* know of this?"

"Not until three or four days ago. And Meg swore me to secrecy."

"As well she might! You see what it means? Or what it *could* mean! For, to be sure, Orkney might have lied about the gift."

"How then would he have got the jewels? The Queen's jewels?"

"God knows! This smells rank. There is ill work here, somewhere. The question is, where does the evil lie?"

"Not with Meg, at least, Geordie. Or her husband. He received the gifts in all honesty. From his lord."

"Must it be evil?" the other girl faltered. "John, my husband, conceived no ill in it. The Queen has many jewels. The Earl of Orkney is her kinsman by marriage is he not? He may have served her well. Might she not seek to reward him with these?"

The other two exchanged glances.

"I fear that it is less simple than that," Heriot said. "Orkney is . . . no ordinary man. And he is at odds with the King. If the Queen did indeed give him these jewels . . ."

"But she did. How else could he have gained them? She might even have done it to spite the King! Because he took a hard line with my lord. She has done things to spite His Majesty before this."

"I accept that she must have given them to him, yes. But how willingly? That is the question. These things are valuable. And she is much in need of money."

"How mean you, sir? Willingly?"

"I do not know myself, to tell truth. I but try to think. Have you any notion what these things are worth?"

"No-o-o. Not truly. One hundred pounds perhaps?" She said it almost breathlessly.

"That fine pearl is worth over one hundred pounds Sterling itself. Twelve times that in pounds Scots. I know—for I bought it once, the greatest pearl ever brought out of the Tay. These other pieces—especially this diamond—add up to another three or four hundred pounds Sterling, at least. Say five hundred pounds Sterling altogether. Six thousand pounds Scots. A lot of money. And you say that this was only *part* of a casketful given by the Queen? Why should she give so much to the Earl of Orkney?"

No answer was offered.

"But these are *ours*. My husband's. The money for us to live together. As man and wife. In Orkney . . ."

"Yes. I understand. But you must understand *my* position also, Mistress. I am the King's jeweller. The Queen's also. Knowing these to be the Queen's jewels—or to have been—I cannot just buy them, in ordinary trade. What would His Majesty say? Or the Queen herself?"

"Then can I sell them to some other man? Can you tell me whom?"

"That is almost equally difficult. I cannot send you to any jeweller of repute in this city. They would all see it much as I do. Some crooked cut-purse trader down amongst the quays might take them—but give you not a tenth of their worth. And I could not advise such fate for the Queen's so excellent jewellery."

"What *can* we do, then?" That was a quaver.

He looked at them unhappily.

"I blame myself," Alison put in. "I confess, I feared something of this. Feared that there might be trouble in it. That is why I proposed coming to you, Geordie. Perhaps I was wrong—should not have brought you into it. But I thought that you would know best. Would advise and *help*." She emphasised that last word.

He nodded acceptance of her appeal. "You did not do wrong. See you, Mistress—I shall not buy them. But shall take them from you, and hold them. Not in pawn, but in trust. I will give you money for them, such as you need. Not what they are worth. But sufficient for your need. If all is well and I may dispose of them in true trade, I will pay the remainder . . ."

"Oh, Geordie—you are good!" Alison exclaimed.

"Yes, indeed. That is most kind, sir. But . . . how much?"

"You thought of one hundred pounds? I will give you two hundred and fifty pounds—if that will serve?"

"Two hundred and fifty! Sakes—so much?"

"Only one half of their true value, I'd remind you."

"What of that! In Orkney, two hundred and fifty pounds will make us almost rich! You are good."

"Scarcely that. But, it must be understood—I may deal with these jewels hereafter as I think best. When I have made enquiries. It may be that they will go back to the Queen. I do not know. I must do what seems best for all."

"Yes, yes. To be sure. We want nothing more to do with them, I swear!"

"I hope that it may prove as simple as that! See—leave them with me. You cannot carry two hundred and fifty pounds in gold and silver coin. I will give you fifty pounds Sterling now for your journey to Scotland. And my note-of-hand for two hundred pounds, to be drawn at my house in Edinburgh. My brother James will pay it, at your convenience. Will that do?"

"It is better far than I had dared to hope, sir."

"Very well." He gathered up the jewels into their bag and went to unlock his strong box.

When, presently, he left to escort them back to the quay and the wine barge, with Margaret Hartside going down the steps ahead of them, Alison took the opportunity to murmur in Heriot's ear. "I came to you, for more than helping Meg. I thought you should know of this. I misliked the sound of it. There is something wrong, somewhere. You may discover what it is . . ."

"Perhaps it would be better *not* to discover!" he returned. "It could be awkward knowledge."

Amidst heartfelt expressions of gratitude, he handed over the two young women to the King's watermen and turned back for the Exchange. Deep in thought, he scarcely noticed the heat and the stinks.

* * *

Although George Heriot saw both King and Queen the very next day, it was only as one of London's citizens, and he had no opportunity for speech with either. James brought his royal brother-in-law up to town to see the sights, and Anne felt sufficiently recovered to accompany them with the royal children. They made a state ride through the city and attended a banquet, ending up at Somerset House—which was renamed Denmark House to mark the occasion. King Christian was a fine upstanding figure of a man, of a ruddy countenance, inclining to stoutness but with the height to carry it, a great eater, drinker and laugher, but with a marked capacity for enjoyment, in contrast to his brother Ulric's prickly temperament. He quickly became immensely popular in London, particularly as he gave presents on a truly regal scale and threw money about like water. King James became not a little concerned.

The second day, the royal sightseers repaired to the Tower, where they inspected the crown jewels, the coronation robes and the torture machinery. Also the Mint, housed there. Still more to Christian's taste was the bear pit, where quick thinking on James's part provided an unusual spectacle. The keeper informed his lord that only the day before a child had died there, having been, it seemed, accidentally left in the bear house. No satisfying explanation of how this had transpired being forthcoming, Anne—who had brought Henry, Elizabeth and little Charles with her as a treat—shed a tear for the poor innocent and declared that the parents must have been careless. James, although he did not weep, was less censorious and more practical. He left the keeper twenty pounds for the bereaved mother—and condemned the offending bear to death. Moreover, he stipulated the method of execution, the bear was to have the most savage of the lions set upon it, watched judicially by the entire royal party. Unfortunately the lion, when brought amidst great excitement, and assured to be ferocious, confronted with the bear in the pit, merely sat down and yawned in the heat, while the other animal busily searched for fleas. No amount of stimulation having any effect, two large mastiffs were brought and substituted for the lion. These proved by no means keen either, and when spurred on to the attack, went about it so half-heartedly that they were cuffed away into a corner where they cowered and sulked. Much offended, James demanded half-a-dozen dogs of mixed breeds and sizes, with a young lion and lioness, all in together, with darts thrown to prick all into suitable activity. In the subsequent mêlée and hullabaloo, it was not very clear just what went on, much fur flew and blood and entrails came into evidence. King Christian, who had fallen asleep, was wakened up by Elizabeth screaming, and hurrahed vociferously in true Viking fashion, while James took the opportunity to improve on the situation by expounding to his children the moral lessons of what they saw, with Latin interpolations. The bear was almost certainly dead when the royal party left, and most of the dogs likewise, with the lion and lioness satisfactorily crunching up the remains indiscriminately. All agreed that the child had been suitably commemorated, in the end.

A move was then made to Westminster Abbey, to inspect the progress of the magnificent tomb James was having erected therein for his mother, the executed Mary Queen of Scots—which was to be the finest in the establishment, bar none, he declared. Not to seem to neglect her executioner and his predecessor altogether, he had the effigy on Elizabeth's tomb dressed up in mourning garments, very unusual.

In none of all this had George Heriot, tradesman, any part.

He did, however, receive a summons to attend on the King personally, about three weeks later, the page who brought the message adding that he was to bring his kist and keys with him—clearly an indication that the King was requiring money again. This was not entirely unexpected, for most evidently entertaining and keeping up with King Christian was an expensive business. The two monarchs were presently at Theobalds Park, Cecil's seat in Hertfordshire, for the buck hunting. The Queen certainly would not be there, for she hated Cecil and would not darken his door. Heriot learned from the page that she had, in fact, returned to Greenwich—which she preferred in high summer to London. The man decided that, before he had his interview with the monarch, who was almost certainly wanting something from him and therefore amenable perhaps to a little pressure, he ought to inform himself as far as possible as to the Queen's position. Accordingly, that very afternoon, he took boat down-river for Greenwich.

He was less warmly received at the great palace than was his usual. He learned that the Queen was indeed there, in her private apartments; but though he sent his humble duties and the request that Her Majesty might graciously receive him for a brief interview he was kept waiting an unconscionable time. Nor did Alison Primrose appear to lighten the tedium. When at length he was ushered into the royal sitting-room, it was to find both Hetty, Marchioness of Huntly and Lucy, Countess of Bedford, with the Queen. Neither made any move to leave at his entry.

Anne was apparently in a lofty mood. "A good day to you, Master Heriot," she said cooly. "I understand that you wish some speech with me?"

"Yes, Majesty—if you will be so kind. I would humbly say how grieved I was to hear of your recent great loss and sad sickness. And how rejoiced I am now to see you so well restored."

"I thank you. But I cannot think that you came all the way to Greenwich to tell me that, sir!"

"Perhaps not, Madam. I had hoped that I might be permitted to have a word with Your Highness alone. On a matter of importance."

"I have no secrets from these my good friends, sir. And I hope that you have not come to talk about the tiresome matter of moneys, again. For I cannot help you in this. Until parliament sees fit to do its duty, and settle our royal revenues, I am quite unable to make repayments. You must needs apply to my husband, the King."

Heriot sought to make both features and voice expressionless.

"That is not the purpose of my visit, Madam. I know the position, passing well. My concern is otherwise. But . . . I hesitate to speak before these ladies."

"Then do not speak at all, sir. If it is unfit for their ears, it is unfit for mine, I vow!"

"If I may say so, not necessarily, Madam. But—as you will."

"In fact, Master Heriot, I think I know very well what brings you here. If it is not the money. It is the matter of that Primrose baggage, of whom you are so unsuitably enamoured! And of the other wretch, Hartside!"

He drew a quick breath, but said nothing.

"I am much displeased," the Queen went on—sounding, for once, rather like her husband. "It is quite disgraceful. And that you, sir, should aid and assist these wicked young women in their designs against their queen and yours, is a like shame. I would not have believed it of you!" That came out in a rush.

Staring at her, he shook his head. "I do not understand Your Majesty. Not fully. Yet, it seems you *have* believed it of me—whatever it is! Without seeking my explanation . . ."

"What explanation can you offer, sir, to meet the occasion! My property is stolen by my own servant—valuable property. And you, in collusion with another of my servants, Primrose, buy it, knowing it mine. Here is the work of an unprincipled huckster, I think!"

"Stolen . . . ! Madam—can you mean what you say? Are you accusing Mistress Hartside of *stealing* your jewels?"

"Naturally. How else should my chambermaid have in her possession all these riches? She is a thief, sir. And her friend Primrose little better. And you abetted them, they told me. When I examined them."

"But . . . that is not how I was told it, Majesty. There is something far amiss here. I cannot vouch for Margaret Hartside's honesty—although I believed her honest. But Alison Primrose I do know. She could never injure or despoil Your Majesty. She is honest as the day. She wholly believed the other's story, I swear. As did I."

"Aye—we all know how crazed you are over that pert jade! Despite being sufficiently old to know better, sir! I accept that *you* would believe anything she said! Apparently in preference to your queen's own word!"

He began to speak hotly, and checked himself with an effort.

"Your Majesty may consider me foolish. But not dishonest. Mistress Primrose brought Mistress Hartside to me with these jewels. Believing that I could best advise her. There was no talk of theft. The story she told was quite other . . ."

"I do not wish to hear the stories of a lying, thieving minx, sir!" the Queen interrupted strongly. "Spare me that. The fact remains—my jewels were stolen. And *must* have been stolen, to be in a chambermaid's possession. As you should have known. And you bought them. Scarcely the act of my loyal jeweller—for whom I have done much!"

"With respect, Madam—no. I did not buy them, I took them, in trust. Until I had ascertained the true position . . ."

"So you did doubt? Yet you paid her money for them—much money. Is that not buying them? Do not bandy words with me, sir!"

"I would not do so, Majesty. I respect Your Highness's esteem too much for that. Acknowledge all that your influence has achieved for me." He almost pointed out to her however that her debt to him now stood at eighteen thousand pounds Sterling—but managed to forbear. "I but assure you that Mistress Hartside's account of this matter of the Earl of Orkney was . . ."

"Silence, sir! I will not hear you! I have heard more than sufficient of Orkney, and all concerned with him. Including this wretched woman. You will not name that name again in my presence." Her bosom heaving, Anne was most obviously in an unusually agitated state. "Is there anything else, Master Heriot?"

"Only that I must ask Your Majesty, whatever else, to absolve Mistress Primrose from all blame in this. She brought the other to me believing that I would know best what to do . . ."

"She could have come to *me*, her mistress!"

"That might have been less easy! In the circumstances."

"Just so! *That* I agree! At all events, whether she is guilty of dishonesty, or only of folly and error, she will have time and opportunity to repent of it. In Scotland!"

He swallowed. "In Scotland! You mean . . . ?"

"I mean, sir, that I have sent her home to her father. Where she will perhaps learn wiser behaviour. And Hartside also—only she is under close ward as a felon. And will in due course be tried for her crime."

"But . . . but . . ."

"Do not but *me*, sirrah! These young women were greatly

privileged to serve in my household, close to my royal person. They have betrayed my trust. And must pay for it."

"You have sent them both back to Scotland, Madam? Hartside also?"

"Yes. I will not have them near me, further."

"Your Majesty said trial? That Mistress Hartside is under arrest. Why send *her* to Scotland? Will you bring her back for trial?"

"She will be tried in Scotland. In due course."

He eyed her thoughtfully. "That seems a curious arrangement," he said.

"She is a Scotswoman. And will be tried according to Scotland's law."

"When the offence—or the supposed offence—was committed here in England?"

"Sir—this is unbearable! I will not be questioned and harried thus. By you, or any subject. I have stood more than enough. You will leave us."

"Yes, Majesty—if it is your royal will. But before I go, you may be glad to have these." And drawing the little leather bag from his doublet pocket, he placed it on a table. "You will find all your jewels there, I think—or, at least, all that were given to Mistress Hartside!"

It was Anne's turn to gulp. She took a step towards the table, then drew back again, biting her lip.

When she did not speak, he went on. "Your own returned to you. At my charges. With my compliments and loyal duty. That is why I came," he said.

"I . . . I thank you," she said shakily, unsure of herself now.

"It is my privilege, as Your Majesty's faithful servant. I would but plead that, now you have the jewels back, you will withdraw the charges against Mistress Hartside, and order her release. Of your charity. And allow Mistress Primrose to return to your services."

The Queen's features hardened. "So that is it! You are a rich man, Master Heriot, and would buy back your inamorata's presence here by this gesture. It cannot be. It is too late. And I do not bargain with subjects. Take your jewels, sir—and begone!"

"*Your* jewels, Madam. Not mine. Have you not said so? Stolen from you. I do bargain, frequently—but not with my sovereign lord or his lady. I leave them with you." He bowed deeply, and backed to the door. As he opened it, he added, as afterthought,

"I would be so bold as to remind Your Highness that a trial might be injudicious. For your own interests. Even in Scotland. Talk, Majesty—talk!"

* * *

It was almost evening next day before George Heriot could cover the distance to Theobalds. He arrived to a great stir and to-do, as Robert Cecil, Earl of Salisbury, mounted a splendid masque to entertain the two monarchs his guests, and to outdo, if possible, anything that the Queen might have put on. The fact that King James found masques tedious did not appear to weigh with him; perhaps Cecil's sights were set on impressing King Christian, whose Danish navy was a major factor on the European scene.

At any rate, no expense was spared, hundreds of workmen had been for days erecting the huge open-air theatre around a grassy hollow, actors and musicians by the score milled around, women abounded, and all was in readiness for the opening of the performance. Heriot perceived that his interview with the King would have to wait.

He found Ludovick of Lennox dressing for the evening, after a hard day's hunting—and that friendly duke insisted that he shared the room with him, for he would not find so much as a corner unoccupied in all the great house. Two Courts and all the hangers-on taxed even Cecil's resources.

The two kings made an exhausting partnership, Lennox complained. They were all up with the larks each day, hunting and hawking, and up all night carousing, wenching, singing and playing practical jokes—to which the Danes seemed distressingly partial. That is, when anyone was sober enough to play them. Christian's appetities were enormous, like his capacity for every aspect of living; and James, who normally could make do with but little sleep, was beginning to wilt under the strain. As for the rest of them, they were all but foundered. The Danes, who were as preoccupied with women as they were with food and drink, had somehow collected vast numbers of females from far and near, and the house positively hotched with unattached and eager ladies of all ages, shapes, sizes and categories—much to Cecil's displeasure, who was something of an old maid. It was all just too much. Perhaps it would have been better if the Queen had been present.

Heriot was only half-hearted in his sympathy. He had other things on his mind. He told the Duke about the jewels, the Queen's reaction, and what had happened to Alison Primrose and Margaret Hartside—and the questions all this raised.

Lennox was suitably perturbed. "What does it mean?" he demanded. "What *can* it mean? Is Anne lying? Or could the jewels indeed have been stolen? Perhaps not by this Hartside woman, but by another. Her husband, perhaps? Even Orkney himself. And given to her to sell."

"It is many months since Orkney and his party went back to Scotland—as you know, who are in a fashion responsible for him! Almost a year. And there has been no word of stolen jewels until now. If they *were* stolen, the Queen made no protest. I cannot believe it so."

"Then you think that she did *give* them to Orkney?"

"If Hartside's story was not a pack of lies—and it did not sound to be—then I can think of no other answer. Though she may well have given them unwillingly."

"You mean that he forced them from her? As the price for keeping his mouth shut?"

"Something after that fashion."

"Which could mean that Patrick Gray was right!"

"Possibly. But not necessarily There could have been some other . . . indiscretion."

"Ah!"

"Not necessarily her own."

"You mean—James's?"

"It is the King whom Orkney seeks to hurt. And the Queen might fight for her husband's name and honour equally with her own. Even though she does not see eye to eye with him always."

"I suppose it could be so. How might we find out?"

"I am not greatly concerned with finding out. Save insofar as Alison Primrose be reinstated and given recompence. And Hartside's name cleared—if she is innocent. Also, Orkney prevented from doing the like again—if indeed he did it!"

"So many ifs, my friend . . . !"

In order to have the masque over before darkness fell, if possible, Cecil had arranged for the evening's banquet to proceed, out-of-doors, while the staged entertainment was going on. Heriot found a modest place in the great grassy amphitheatre amongst a group of Danish officers in blue velvet and silver lace, now somewhat soiled, who were already tipsy enough to have brought their uninvited women to the tables with them, where the ladies, dispensing with chairs and benches, stood, sat on knees, on the grass, even under the tables amongst the hunting dogs, screeching and skirling. It was as well that it was a warm night, for many of them were spectacularly underclad.

There was not much rising and bowing when the two monarchs made their belated appearance. Christian was a magnificent figure, and managed to hold himself markedly upright, even though he staggered somewhat. James always staggered, and never troubled about standing upright. Arm-in-arm they lurched to their places, whilst the instrumentalists played stirring music.

Trumpeters blew, and then announced that the Masque of Solomon and Sheba would now be presented before their esteemed present-day Solomon and his guest, the noble warrior-king Christian. Let all be silent and give due attention.

Silence and attention were scarcely easy of attainment in the circumstances. Men shouted for food, drink, at each other and at performers; women squealed and whinnied; servitors hurried to and fro, banging flagons, clattering dishes, and cursing; dogs barked, stole viands and squabbled over their hauls. Moreover, King Christian started immediately on a round of bellowed toasts, the first to his 'goot broder Chames, the best bock honter in the vorld', after each of which toasts he embraced his fellow-monarch lovingly, a progressively more difficult operation as the series extended. His innumerable Danish henchmen roared, hooted and stamped approval, and loyally followed their master's example by embracing all in sight. Heriot found himself breathless, battered but surprisingly popular.

Throughout, the masque proceeded, in the centre of the arena. King Solomon, majestic in his pillared Temple, received the dusky Sheba, who brought gifts such as a dromedary, a pure white deer-fawn, apes dressed as Nubian chieftains, and cages of brilliantly-coloured birds, all led in by black slaves. The sight and smell of some of these rarities upset many of the dogs present, and Solomon's Court and Temple suffered to some extent; but with remarkable aplomb the Biblical monarch took it all in his gorgeously berobed stride, and, in answer to the cheers, sent Sheba with a large tray of special sweetmeats to present to the two latter-day monarchs on their canopied platform opposite.

Sheba, on this occasion, was the statuesque Countess of Worcester—who had most evidently been fortifying herself for the event in a major way. With the black slaves supporting her, she managed very well until she came to the steps up to the royal platform, even seeking to skip a little to the lively air provided by the musicians. But her slaves modestly held back at the steps, and, silver tray before her swelling profile, she mounted alone, tripped over the top step, and hurtled forward all her length and shapeliness, to collapse at King Christian's feet. Unfortunately, the tray being in front of her, emptied all its contents over the great Dane's lap and person, cream, jellies, spirits, cakes and the like. Spectacular was the ruin.

Christian was nothing if not gallant, and a good man in an emergency. Shouting commiserations to the lady, he struggled to his unsteady feet, wiping mixed delicacies off his clothing and beard, and stooping, sought to raise the Countess. But this was too much for his own precarious equilibrium and he collapsed in turn, part over James and part over Sheba—for there was a lot of him.

James yelped and gesticulated, and courtiers rushed forward to the rescue. Somehow they got both Christian and the lady to their feet, and tried to press the Dane back into his chair and lead the Countess off. But they reckoned without the Viking spirit. The music continuing even more urgently, Christian decided that he must put the unfortunate Sheba fully at ease by dancing with her—although by this time she was in fact giggling in helpless abandon. Possibly the monarch might have achieved his laudable aim to some extent, had it not been for the wretched steps down from the platform—for there was no room to dance thereon. Steps are awkward things at the best of times, and these, although berugged with fine Persian carpeting, were none the more negotiable therefor. Down them King and Countess fell in mighty prostration, to crash headlong on the grass. And there, although Sheba crawled off in sobbing hysterics, Christian lay outstretched, breathing stertorously.

Swiftly, eager hands hurried to raise him up once more. But this time the King of Denmark was temporarily not interested in the upright, or in anything else; and his supporters, not all stone-cold-sober themselves, found themselves with a weighty problem on their hands. What to do with a slack-jointed would-be-recumbent monarch?

King James, apostrophising the Deity, took charge. With royal swipes he personally cleared everything off the top of the monarchial table, flagons, beakers, dishes, sent them all crashing to the ground, and ordered His Scandinavian Majesty to be laid thereon, amongst the spilt wines and residues. There Christian snored, while Solomon continued unperturbed to expound wisdom from his Temple—wisdom as little appreciated by the rest of the somewhat bemused company as it had been down the ages.

Concerned for his friend, who seemed to have settled for the night, James muttering about dews and chill vapours, with Latin allusions, commanded Christian to be removed to his bedchamber forthwith. He himself, having had enough of the masque, escorted the cortège, recollecting to clap on his high hat before leaving the scene.

Solomon, although lacking Sheba and much of his entourage, continued. Cecil cancelled the fireworks display.

George Heriot, knowing his own monarch of old, disentangled himself from his new Danish friends and their ladies and sought out the Duke of Lennox. Sure enough, they found King James already esconced in the anteroom to his bedchamber, with a few of his Scots intimates and Sir Philip Herbert, recently created Earl of Montgomery, settling down to a more profitable evening's entertainment with new bottles and flagons. At Lennox's representations, James looked over to where Heriot stood, frowned, shrugged and finally rose to totter through to his bedroom. The Duke waved his friend over, and together they followed their liege lord, and shut the door.

"Aye, Geordie—so you've come! You've taken your time to heed my call, I'm thinking!"

"I am ever at your service, Sire. I dropped my other commitments as swiftly as I might."

"Ooh, aye—maybe. Yon was a right stramash, tonight."

"It was, Sire. I hope that His Majesty of Denmark will be none the worse."

"No' him. He's got a heid like a cannon-ba'. But yon Worcester woman was fell lacking in discretion."

"It was scarcely a discreet performance, in any way!" Lennox commented.

The King chuckled. "Cecil will be fair whammled! Now—this o' the Master o' Gray."

Surprised, the two men considered their unpredictable sovereign.

"You ken what that limb o' Satan has the effrontery to be up to now? He is suing me, in the High Court o' Scotland, for fifty thousand pounds Scots! Me, the Crown! In my ain courts! Fifty thousand pounds!"

They could only stare.

"Hae you ever heard the like? The brazen insolence o' the man!"

"But suing you for what, Sire. What is his case?"

"God kens!"

"But this is impossible. To sue you, to sue *anyone*, in the courts, the case must be accepted as having some basis for debate. In law. *Has* his case been so accepted? For hearing? In the High Court?"

"Well, sort o' Geordie—sort o' accepted. I'm right displeased about that. Wi' Seton. I made him Chancellor and Earl o' Dunfermline—and this is how he serves me. And Tam Hamilton o' the Coogate, the Advocate. He's a kind o' cousin o' yours, Geordie, is he no'? *He* should ha' kent better."

"There must be some sort of case, then. You must have some notion, Sire?"

"Och, well—the man says I owe him some siller. For some ploy or other. Something long by wi'. When he was acting Chancellor," James said vaguely.

"*Can* he sue the King? In court?" Lennox demanded.

"They tell me he can—a plague on them a'! It's wicked. Unsuitable."

"It will be Your Majesty's Scottish Exchequer that he is suing, Sire. Not you personally."

"No, it's mysel'. Me, the King. The Lord's Anointed! It's beyond belief."

"And *do* you owe him fifty thousand pounds, James?" Lennox asked. "Or did you?"

"Waesucks—no! It's a' havers. Och, maybe a pound or twa, here and there. Nae mair."

"But you did owe him something?"

"Dinna harry me, Vicky—I'll no' have it'. It's a' by wi'—long ago."

"But you remember the issue, Sire?" That was Heriot. "If you wish us to help Your Majesty in this, we must know the facts. What was the occasion, do you recollect?"

"Och, it was yon ill business o' Patrick Stewart. When he was Master o' Orkney. But it wasna onything like fifty thousand pounds. That's a' interest he's claiming, the man. Wicked! Besides, I didna *borrow* the siller. Gray gave it."

"How much, Sire?"

"I canna mind. You've no' to keep at me, this way. Or I'll get some other body to do my business for me!"

"What do you wish me to do, Sire?"

"Go up to Scotland. Search out what Patrick Gray's at. Stop the case being tried. I'm no' wanting talk. And I'm no' wanting Orkney brought into it either—that's for sure!"

"But the money was connected with Orkney in the first place?"

"I've said so, have I no!? Orkney's an ill limmer. But he's my cousin. I'll no' hae him brought into this."

Perplexed, the other two exchanged glances.

"My mission is less than clear, Sire," Heriot complained. "I am at a loss to know what I am to do."

"Use your wits, man—that's what. Find oot Gray's case. Discover its weaknesses. Come to terms wi' the wretch, if you must. But keep it oot o' court. And keep Orkney oot o' it. Is that no' simple enough?"

The other considered. There was a deal more in this than met the eye, obviously. And a murky deal, probably. But equally obviously, it would be better handled by himself than by officials. Moreover, he had come to Theobalds with the intention of trying to press James into letting him go to Scotland, to see Alison Primrose and try to clear up the other business, in which Orkney also was involved. He had been prepared to pay for that permission—and now he was being presented with it free. And without having to involve James in talk about the Queen's jewels—which he did not want to do. He should probably be thankful, relieved. He decided, however, that he might as well make the most of his opportunity, while he had it, in his friend's interest.

"Majesty—you put the Earl of Orkney under a suspended sentence, for good behaviour. Under the supervision of my lord Duke here. Would it not be wise to send him up to Scotland likewise, if the Earl is to be kept out of this affair? My lord of Orkney will pay little attention to *me*, I fear. But my lord Duke could speak with authority, strength." Looking over at Lennox, he saw that man's eyes light up. He was ever longing to get away back to Scotland and Mary Gray— and James knew it, but was markedly loth to allow it.

"Ooh, aye—I ken you twa!" the King said, eyeing them shrewdly. "You play each other's hands. I'm no' sure I can aye trust you, together! But maybe you're right, on this ploy. Aye, you go too, Vicky—and see your Gray lassie! In case there's trouble wi' Orkney. You deal wi' him."

"To be sure, James. It will be my pleasure."

"When do you wish us to leave, Sire?"

"So soon as you may. Settle your affairs in London, and then off wi' you. But—bide a wee, bide a wee, man. I'm no' finished wi' you. Geordie. I'm needing some siller, see you. This good-brother o' mine, King Christian, is a right expense. And he's here for a month, yet. Parliament's no nearer a proper settlement. I'm saving them millions on sojers and ships and guns and the like—but d'you think they thank me? They bicker and argue ower my royal moneys. I've made a' the knights I can, o' everyone that wants to be a knight—and a wheen that didna! Aye, and lords, too. Can you let me hae twenty thousand pounds Sterling, Geordie?"

Heriot groaned with himself. He was not to get off cheaply, after all. "Could Your Majesty not do with less, meantime?" he asked. "It will stretch me to the utmost. Already I am outlaid more than that, on your royal behalf. And the Queen . . ."

"No, I couldna, sir. That's the least I can get by wi', until King Christian goes. You'd no' hae me begging frae *him*, would you?"

"No, Sire. Very well. I have five hundred pounds with me, in my box. The rest I shall bring here, as we pass on our way North to Scotland . . ."

"Do that, Geordie. And, see you, one Sir Amyas Ramsden, who had the customs o' Harwich haven to farm, has died. George Heriot, jeweller, shall hae them in his place. And I swear he'll mak mair oot o' them than ever Ramsden did! Off wi' you both . . ."

13

The bell-heather was glowing richly purple on all the Border hillsides as the two friends rode into Scotland, their hearts lifting to the unfailing vehemence, vigour and challenge of their own land after the softer atmospheres and attitudes of the South.

In Edinburgh, however, they did not find overmuch to maintain the uplift of their hearts. They were not long in discovering that none of the principal actors in the dramas, personal and political, with which they were presently concerned, were in fact in the city. Mary Gray and Alison Primrose were both in Perthshire, the former at Methven, the latter at her father's small lairdship of Burnbrae, near Culross, James Primrose's duties with the Scots Privy Council not requiring him to be in the capital at this season. Indeed Edinburgh was empty of much of its gentry and nobility, for this was the harvest season and almost all that class were still closely enough linked with the soil to be returned to their lands for this busy and important period. The Master of Gray was at Broughty Castle in Angus; the Earl of Orkney was said to be away in Orkney itself once more, despite the royal ban put upon such return; and the Chancellor, now Earl of Dunfermline, was at that town, still apparently palace-building.

As for Margaret Hartside, she was not in Edinburgh either. According to James Heriot, she was confined captive in Blackness Castle, the state prison near Linlithgow in West Lothian. No, she had not come to him for any moneys, as his brother's letter had said she would; she had not been free to do so, indeed taken straight to Dunfermline, under guard, where she had been questioned, and then confined in Blackness.

"Dunfermline?" George Heriot repeated. "Why Dunfermline?

Not because the Chancellor is there, surely? This is not so great a matter that the Chancellor must attend to it? Do you mean that she was put to trial at Dunfermline, for some reason?"

"Not trial, no. She has not been tried. Only examined. Questioned. And is now being held. I can only think that she was taken to Dunfermline because it is the Queen's own bailiwick, and this was her servant, accused of hurt to Her Grace."

"Strange. Who then examined her? Not the Chancellor?"

"No. Sir Henry Wardlaw, they say. Chamberlain to the Queen, in Scotland."

"And he had the power to imprison her in Blackness Castle? Without trial?"

"That I do not know. But Blackness is where she is kept."

James Heriot did not know, either, anything of the Master of Gray's demands on the Crown. This was the first he had heard of it.

The enquirers were fortunate in running to earth one notability of some significance in their quest, however, in his town house in the Cowgate of Edinburgh—Sir Thomas Hamilton of Binning, the Lord Advocate. He was laid up with the gout and so unable to travel to his estates meantime. A coarse-looking, red-faced bull of a man, with nevertheless, one of the sharpest minds in Scotland, he was a cousin of the Heriots, his mother having been a daughter of Heriot of Trabourn, the head of the family. Tam o' the Coogate, as he was known, was not a little surprised to see the Duke of Lennox and his cousin from London, but he greeted them, in his bedchamber, with a sort of wary joviality.

They asked about the Hartside case first, and Hamilton, after a keen glance disclaimed much knowledge of the matter. "I am the King's Advocate," he explained, "and this seems to be a private matter o' the Queen's. It doesna come into my responsibilities—God be thankit, for I've plenty!"

"But if she is to be tried, surely you, or your people, would come into it? You are responsible for all prosecutions by the Crown, are you not? And the Queen is part of the Crown, surely?"

"That is arguable, man Geordie. If the Queen chooses to mak *private* prosecution on her ain behoof, then the Crown needna come into it. Nor my Crown Office. And as to trial—*is* there to be a trial?"

"She is locked up in Blackness, I understand, awaiting trial."

"I'ph'mm. Awaiting something, maybe. But maybe no' a trial! I heard tell, see you, just between me and you, that the Queen was now very much against a trial, in this matter."

"But . . . what does that mean? This young woman is arrested, charged with stealing the Queen's jewels—and charged privately, mind you, by the Queen. She denies it—but is sent up to Scotland under guard, examined at Dunfermline, so I hear, not *tried*. And clapped in Blackness Castle, untried. For an offence allegedly committed in *England*. This is contrary to all justice, surely? Is there a law in this land, or is there not?"

"Aye, aye, there's a law right enough. But maybe no' quite so convenient a law for Mistress Hartside as that for the Queen's Grace! At the moment she's but taking order wi' her ain servant, making enquiries and the like. It's no' reached the stage o' law, man."

"But if there's to be no trial, what is to happen to the woman?"

"Dinna ask me, Geordie. It's nae concern o' mine, as Advocate. *You're* the Queen's jeweller, straight frae her Court. You should ken mair than I do."

Lennox intervened. "But if there *is* a trial, Sir Thomas, you will be concerned?"

"If the Crown prosecutes, yes. But the Queen still has her ain jurisdiction in the regality o' Dunfermline, her jointure lands. She would have the woman tried there. Without bringing the Crown into it."

"That is why she was sent there, for examination? There is strange work here, I think. But Blackness Castle is a state prison. *That* is not within the Queen's prerogative, is it?"

"No, my lord Duke. But it *is* within the King's!"

"I do not know that the King is aware of any of this."

"I wonder? The King, I jalouse, is aware o' mair than maist folk reckon—eh, Geordie? Even you, maybe! But I'm no' wanting to ken! What's between, or no' between the King and his lady wife is no concern o' mine. Forby, Blackness Castle doesna come under the Crown Office. You'd hae to see either Dunfermline, the Chancellor, or Erroll, the High Constable. If see you must! I'm thinking there's drumly waters here, best left undisturbed, maybe. By wise men!"

"I cannot do that. I am involved. Mistress Hartside is alleged to have sold the jewels to me."

"And did she?"

"No. Not sold. I took them from her. On trust. Gave her half the value. And have given them back to the Queen, free of charge."

"But you did gie the young woman money for them? A nice point in law, Geordie. You exchanged stolen jewels for money. It might be hard to prove you didna *buy* them. I'd let yon flea stick to the wa', if I were you, man!"

"I believe the jewels were never stolen."

"Ah, well—that's no' concern o' mine. As yet. But it might be, Geordie—it might be. In which case, as Lord Advocate, the less you say to me about it the better. We'll change the subject, by your leave! Hae you ever suffered frae the gout, my lord Duke . . . ?"

"There is another matter, Sir Thomas," Lennox said, presently. "On which we would value your guidance. This is the *King's* business—his private business. But we ask on his behalf. It is this of the Master of Gray's claim against His Majesty for a large sum of money. A claim in court, we understand."

"Aye—I jaloused we'd be coming round to that, when I saw you! It's an ill business."

"It seems to be more than that! It appears more of a mystery to me. What moneys are these? And how can Patrick Gray sue James for them?"

The big man on the bed stroked his thin beard. "That's a large question my lord Duke. And a long story. One *I* dinna ken a' the answers to. But the Master can sue, in law. He has proofs, evidences, witnesses, papers. And a right before the Court o' Session. It seems we canna refuse him."

"But how—what is it? Some old debt, apparently?"

"Debts dinna just fade awa' because they're auld, my lord!" the Advocate pointed out dryly.

"No. But this must be *very* old. Why has Gray waited until now to bring it up? And why sue the King, rather than the Scots Exchequer?"

"Because, as I understand it, the King's personal bond is involved. It was something between James and Gray. And his counsel assures that he has papers to prove it. Why he waited a' these years, your guess is as guid as mine."

"And you have no details?"

"Not at this stage, no. My Crown Office has to be satisfied that there is a case to hear. Beyond that, you canna expect the pursuer to gie awa' details o' his case to me, who will be defending. It's *me* who will hae to be asking you—or leastways, the King—for details. To mak a defence!"

"His Majesty does not want this matter brought to court," Heriot said. "Indeed, he is determined that it must not be."

"So-o-o? That sounds bad. And easier said than done, now the case has been entered."

"Well, that *is* your business!" his cousin pointed out grimly. "You are the King's chief law officer. He commands that there be no court hearings on the subject."

"So His Grace has something to hide, eh?"

"No doubt. But he is the King."

"Aye. So he'd settle out o' court? Pay for silence?"

"Not necessarily. Only if he must. And only the minimum. He will certainly not give Gray all he asks."

"Well, that's no business o' mine, either. I'm the Advocate. I'll fight the King's case in court. But it's nae part o' my duties to bargain and haggle wi' such as Patrick Gray about how much he wants to keep his mouth shut! That's a task for others—I rather think you two gentlemen! Is that no' what you were sent up for?"

They stared at each other, at a stalemate.

"It would be a help to us if we only knew where to begin!" Heriot declared, frustratedly. "James would tell us nothing. And now you!"

"Because I *ken* nothing—or practically nothing, Geordie. But I'll tell you where you can begin, man. Go you and see Tom Hope. He's Gray's counsel. Next to Gray himself, he'll ken mair o' this ploy than anyone, I reckon. He'll maybe no' tell *you* much—for he's a hard bargainer is Tom. But he has the papers—or some o' them. Unless you want to go to the Master himself? You hae links with Gray, have you no', my lord Duke?"

"Yes. But I see no advantage in approaching Patrick himself, before we have found out a great deal more, sir. You know him—he will talk us under the table! Tie us in knots. A man has to know just what he is at, when he deals with Patrick Gray!"

"Aye. With Tom Hope too, mind. He's the hardest man at the Scots bar—and will hae *my* office one day, or I'll be surprised! And dinna reckon you can frighten him wi' the King's name. For he's challenged a royal case already. He defended those six thrawn divines, back in January just, who claimed that the King had no authority in the Kirk o' Scotland. No one else would take up their case, but Tom Hope did—and near won. Would have won, too, if I hadna carefully picked the judges—though I say it as shouldna'!"

Hamilton chuckled. "He's a clever limmer, forby—so watch how you tread wi' Tom Hope. And dinna say I sent you . . ."

* * *

They had difficulty running Master Thomas Hope, advocate, to earth; but eventually they found him down at his new property of Prestongrange, near the Salt-pans of Preston, nine miles down the Forth coast from Edinburgh. He proved to be a younger man than they had anticipated, still only in his late twenties, far from handsome and with an ungainly body, sallow features and dark piercing eyes. He was the son of a rich Edinburgh merchant-burgess, with neither pretence to, nor any affectation of much in the way of gentility. But his shrewdness, strength and striking personality were self-evident. He seemed more impressed by a visit from George Heriot than by the Duke of Lennox.

Clearly, no beating about the bush was necessary, or advisable, with this young man. Heriot stated their case plainly and without preamble. He did not over-emphasise the King's authority, but indicated that where the royal prerogative was concerned, the pros and cons of a case were by no means as straightforward as in normal litigation. It would probably be to both parties' advantage to talk, he suggested.

"What do you want from me, Master Heriot?" Hope asked bluntly.

"We wish to know, in broad terms, what is the case against His Majesty. So that we can judge whether there are any grounds for settlement."

"So you wish to pre-judge my principal's case?"

"No, sir. But we represent the King, privately—the Duke, His Majesty's cousin, I his man-of-business. We cannot talk about the case, to you or to any other go-between, because we do not know what is at stake—what the Master of Gray sues for, or why."

"You would learn in court, gentlemen!"

"No doubt. But to whose advantage would that be? Scarcely the King's, certainly. But not, I think, the Master's. Nor yours, sir—to seem to act against your lawful sovereign's interests?"

"I am prepared to bear that burden, in the interests of justice, Master Heriot."

"Perhaps. But it cannot be beneficial to your career, sir."

"Are you seeking to threaten me? With the royal displeasure?"

"No. Merely reminding you that you also have something to gain by this matter not coming to court. Like the two principals."

"I am unaware that the Master of Gray has anything to gain."

"No?" Lennox interpolated. "Yet you must be aware, sir, that the Master's father, the Lord Gray, is very old, and a sick man. He could die at any time. And the King, with sufficient cause, could declare the Master infamous, to have spoken and acted publicly against his royal person, and so be unfit to succeed his father as a Lord of Parliament."

"Ha! Now we have it!" Hope took a turn to his window, to look over the water to Fife. He came back. "Perhaps the Master has considered such royal reaction, and will make it part of his submissions that no such reprisal should follow the winning of his case!"

"Perhaps. But the judges would probably not dare so to limit the royal authority, sir," Heriot said conversationally. "Not all necessarily being so bold as yourself! "So—I think that you should tell us something of the case against His Majesty!"

The other gave a wintery smile. "You are very persuasive, Master Heriot. But then, I always heard that you were a man of parts! Perhaps I may inform you, to some small extent—in my principal's interests." He paused. "This action goes back to events of ten years ago and more. When King James was, shall we say, indiscreet. He was concerned that Queen Elizabeth of England, although obviously failing of health, had not named him as her successor on the English throne. He was afraid that there was a strong party in England which was against his claims, advocating the rights of the Lady Arabella Stewart, and others. So, perhaps in a rash moment, His Grace decided that he must have an army ready to substantiate his claims. To march into England whenever Elizabeth died, and ensure by strength of arms what should be his, as he believed, by right of birth."

"All this we know," Lennox declared. "James tried to raise the soldiers on the Borders. I, as Lord Admiral, was in some way concerned."

"No doubt, my lord Duke. But did you know of the Danish venture!"

"Danish? No."

"I thought not. This was, it seems, a close secret. As well it might be. James wanted ten thousand regular trained troops from King Christian, for six months. Only six months. He wrote that he had reason to believe that Elizabeth would die within six months. And so he would need them for no longer."

Lennox whistled, and Heriot looked appalled. Neither required to be informed what that sort of statement could do to upset English susceptibilities—especially parliament's. There had, as usual, been rumours that Elizabeth had eventually died of poison—such were commonplace and had largely been forgotten. But if it was stated in court that James had actually prophesied such a thing, in 1590, it would sound exceedingly bad. Especially with himself as the beneficiary. Together with projected armed invasion by foreigners of England's sacred soil. King Christian's present visit would hardly end in felicity.

"Did James put that in writing?" Lennox demanded.

"Unfortunately for him, yes. And the Master of Gray, who was acting as his go-between, has the letter. The Earl of Orkney, then only Master, was the bearer of the letter." Hope shrugged. "I see that you take the point, gentlemen. But there is more to it than that. The Danish king agreed to send the troops—but, being then in need of money for his wars, required that they be paid for. And some payment in advance. James also, as ever, lacked money. And so it had to be found elsewhere. It is his outlays in this matter, never repaid, which the Master of Gray sues for now."

Taking a great breath, Heriot stared at his friend. If Guido Fawkes had threatened James Stewart with gunpowder, this was almost as explosive a mixture.

"The Master of Gray must well know that any such disclosures could greatly harm his liege lord, indeed the whole realm," he declared. "Although it was kept secret, this was state business—however misguided. And the Master, you say, was involved in it. In a matter of much confidence, to reveal it now, in furthering a private claim for moneys, would be shameful. Indeed, to produce such a letter in court, an exchange between monarchs, could be treason, I think."

"I do not require you to instruct me in matters of law, Master Heriot. I would not produce such letter in court, as evidence; only indicate its existence beforehand, to the Crown, as proof that there is a case to answer. There are other papers which will serve."

"You must be aware that Gray does this only to spite the King, sir? To strike at him, for not having taken him to England with him."

"I am aware of no such thing. I am assured by my principal that he brings the action only to recover moneys owed to him by the King, privately, and refused of repayment. Moneys and interest. It is on such grounds that I act for him, on a perfectly lawful issue."

"You will not deny, Master Hope, that if this is so, the matter could infinitely better be settled out of court?"

"Supposing the King is prepared to pay the sum claimed—which hitherto he has steadfastly refused to do." The other raised thick eyebrows. "Have you two gentlemen powers so to settle, on the King's behalf?"

They were silent.

"Until you are in such position, I must retain freedom to press my principal's case with all vigour and expedition," Hope went on. "If His Grace wishes otherwise, he has the remedy to hand."

"So you will do nothing to aid your monarch in this, sir? *Your* monarch as well as ours—and Gray's!" Lennox accused.

"Not for me to make any move in the matter, my lord Duke. I am merely the Master's counsel, in receipt of his instructions. He it is you should approach. He is presently at his house of Broughty, I understand." Hope bowed and moved towards the door, the interview evidently over as far as he was concerned.

Heriot took a risk. "Sir—since clearly you are a man of strong principles, not readily deterred by opposition in high places, it may be that you would consider aiding me in another matter? Again in your capacity as counsel. But on *my* behalf—or leastways, paid by me. For I require guidance in law."

The other looked at him curiously, but made no comment.

"It is the matter of Mistress Hartside, chambermaid to the Queen. Accused of stealing the Queen's jewels, and now held without trial in Blackness Castle. You may have heard of the case?"

"Heard, yes sir—but little of detail. Enough, however to assure me that it stinks to heaven! I would not wish to be concerned in any such case of manifest injustice."

"Even on Mistress Hartside's behalf?"

"Eh . . . ?" Hope peered at his visitor. "Did I hear you aright, sir?"

"You need not doubt your hearing, Master Hope. The fact is that, although I am the Queen's jeweller—and, greatly presuming, might even call myself her friend—yet I am against her, in this. Or against whatever it is that makes her act so, so much against her usual good nature. There is something wrong here, I know not what, but conceive it to have to do with the Earl of Orkney."

I

"An ill man to meddle with!"

"Perhaps. But under the King's displeasure meantime—indeed, under the caution and authority of my lord Duke, here . . ."

"Little as *that* seems to affect him!" Ludovick put in, wryly.

"My sympathies are with Mistress Hartside," Heriot went on. "I think that she is the innocent victim of some Court intrigue. It is my desire to see that she is aided, cleared of this charge, if may be, and freed from ward."

"Against the Queen's wishes?"

"If need be, yes. I would not harm the Queen. But I would seek prevent her further harming this young woman."

"And the King?"

"The King, so far, is not concerned in this. If he knows of it, at all. The Queen dismissed this woman, sent her under guard to Scotland—although the stealing, if such it was, took place in England—has had her examined by her own Chamberlain in her bailiwick of Dunfermline, and now committed to Blackness. I conceive her rights as a citizen to have been sorely violated."

"With that I concur. What do you want of me?"

"I want you to discover what her rights may be, in law. What the Chamberlain now intends. If possible, get her out of Blackness Castle. And, if it seems best, insist on her being brought to proper trial."

"You would risk that? It could be dangerous."

"The Queen does not want a trial, we now know. Therefore, it could be to Hartside's benefit. It would force the Queen to state her case, at least. Let us know what we fight against. For my own name is involved. The woman is accused of selling the jewels to me."

"I see. This might be a costly business, Master Heriot. For a chambermaid's honour!"

"And my own, sir. The cost will be met, never fear."

"Very well. Tell me all you know, if you please . . ."

* * *

In a corner of the walled garden of Methven Castle, Lennox and Mary Gray sat on a rustic bench, arms linked and watched their son Johnnie clamber amongst the old apple tree branches, while George Heriot stood nearby.

"Think you, then, that there is any profit in us going to see the Master, your father?" he asked.

"I do not see what you will achieve by it," the young woman admitted. "You will not turn Patrick from his course, save by outwitting him, Geordie. And for all the esteem I have for you and Vicky, I do not think that you will achieve that, face to face. I have never yet met anyone who could."

"Except perhaps his daughter!" Lennox put in.

"Nonsense! He can run around me in rings. Only on occasion can I cut across his entanglements—and that is because I can sometimes think as he does, and so can anticipate his next move. Not that I am proud of it . . ."

"Come you with us to Broughty Castle, then, my love."

"I see no advantage in it, Vicky. For any of us—or for the King. As I understand it, Patrick holds all the cards in this sorry game. My only wonder is—why he has not played them before this. Is not this debt a dozen years old, and more? Ever since James threw him over, there at Berwick Bridge in 1603, he could have done this. Why wait until now?"

"Is he greatly in need of the moneys, think you?"

"I have not heard so. The Lady Marie has not said so. But, who knows with Patrick?"

"You have not heard of him being especially concerned in any new plots or ploys, meantime? It is unlike Patrick *not* to be!"

"Nothing important. Although Marie says that there are constant letters and messengers, coming and going, with her brother, the Earl of Orkney."

"Ah!" Heriot said.

"In regard to what?"

"I do not know. Nor did Marie. She has no great love for most of her brothers, and Orkney does not confide in her."

"You think there may be some ploy between them? Orkney and Patrick? Which requires money?"

"Orkney, all know, is building a great new palace at Kirkwall—even though he has not yet finished his new castle at Scalloway in Shetland. The Kirkwall palace is said to be a wonder, with French architects and craftsmen. It must be costing a great deal of money—and by now he must have squeezed his unfortunate Orkney folk dry! But I do not see why Patrick should find him the money for these. They are none such great friends. But Orkney *was* at Broughty, two weeks past."

"He was? We were told that he was back in his islands—although forbidden by the King to go there."

"Marie was here, at Methven, to see me, then. She had left her brother at Broughty, with Patrick."

"If there was a link, in this, between the Master and Orkney," Heriot mused, "it might help to explain the other business, of the jewels. Think you they could both be part of the same ploy?"

"I do not know, Geordie. I see no connection. It is not impossible, I suppose. But—none of this explains why Patrick has waited until now to assail the King for this money."

"It could be that he kept it in reserve. For a special occasion. He well knows that the King has been ever short of money. And so might despair of ever getting it out of him. But now, the King of Denmark is here—and involved in this business. The Master could argue that the last thing which James would wish would be for it all to come to light *now*, during the state visit. He might conceive that James would do anything, pay anything to keep it quiet meantime."

"And James will not?"

"I do not know. He was very strange. Close. He is almost as cunning as your father, I think. But clearly he does not want to pay the money. Considers that he may avoid it. Nor yet will he have it all brought into open court, however."

"Then I think that you have a notable task on your hands, Geordie!"

"I know it! And you can offer no help? No good counsel? We hoped that you could, Mary. With your quick wits. And knowledge of your father."

"I told you. As I see it, Patrick holds all the cards. The King, I think, must needs settle, if he would not have it all shouted from the roof tops." She paused. "If he will not pay the full sum, there is only one venture, which I can see, that you might try. Instead of having the case in the public court, it might be arranged to hear it in commission. A special panel of judges. The King could so order—on a matter of state concern. I do not see that Patrick could lawfully object. I do not know the law—but there *are* special cases tried so. The judges would be sworn to secrecy. So the secrets would go no further."

"Dammit—quick wits indeed!" Ludovick cried. "Not the first time I've said it! Why did we never think of that?"

"It would mean that the King would almost certainly have to pay *something*," Mary pointed out. "If Master Hope is so sure of

Patrick's case, the judges could scarcely throw it out altogether. Without Patrick shouting all abroad again, and secrecy lost once more."

"True," Heriot nodded. "But if the debt *is* a just one, however ill the ploy, a just payment should be made. I, for one, am not concerned to save King James from paying his just debts. He owes *me* too much, for that! My concern is to prevent roguery, and harm to the Crown and realm. To prevent all this getting to the ears of the English parliament and the King's ill-wishers there. A commission of judges, sitting in private, is an excellent notion. I do not see that Hope could refuse to accept it, or the Master either. We must get Tom Hamilton on to this."

"As to the other matter, the Hartside case," the Duke went on. "Do you think that Patrick could have anything to do with that?"

"I do not see why he should. But nor would I swear that he had not! With my peculiar sire, one can never tell." She shook her fair head. "My heart goes out to this Margaret Hartside. And to Alison Primrose, in lesser degree. I have seen Alison since she came back to Scotland. She told me all that she knew, and of your kindness, Geordie."

"Kindness!" he snorted. "I was not kind. Nor, in the end, befriended either of them. I much blame myself. I should have perceived the trap."

"Do you really think the Queen planned it all?"

"Not the Queen, no. She is not of that sort. But somebody did. And the Queen concurred. Or was forced to concur."

"Orkney? Or some friend of Orkney's?"

"I would reckon so. Although, again, I would not have thought *him* to be of that sort, either. A rogue, yes, and quite without scruple. But a far subtler hand than Orkney's seems to have contrived all this."

Eyeing each other, they considered that in silence, while the Master of Gray's grandson swung and laughed, carefree, amongst the tree branches.

Heriot stayed only one night at Methven, for he was anxious to be elsewhere—and Mary Gray did not restrain him. Arranging to meet Lennox in Dunfermline in two days' time—for they could spare no longer—he rode off south-eastwards again the following morning, alone, for Culross, leaving his friends to their brief interlude of bliss.

The Stewartry of Culross, with its ancient abbey, lay on the north shore of Forth, in the small and detached portion of the shire of Perth which thrust eastwards into the shire of Fife and Fothrif—and looked, in fact, slantwise across the narrowing estuary to Blackness Castle on its headland on the West Lothian shore. Riding by Muthill and the steep Glen Eagles pass through the green Ochils and down Glen Devon to the plain of Forth, Heriot reached the salt water at Kincardine and turned eastwards along the shore road. In four or so miles he came to his destination, the small lairdship of Burnbrae on the outskirts of the former abbey lands of Culross, where the Primrose family had been settled for a few generations. It was not a very impressive property, with a somewhat tumbledown house and offices, a few fields and some straggling woodlands; but the situation was very fair, crowning a steep high bank above the shoreline, where a stream plunged down through a deep wooded ravine almost as a prolonged waterfall, giving the place its name—and with superb views southwards over the firth to the Lothian coast and the hills beyond.

The shouts of children greeted the newcomer even before the house in its trees came into sight. Leading-in the harvest seemed to be in progress—as it was all over Lowland Scotland—and it appeared to be a noisy and exhilarating process at Burnbrae. Horse-drawn sleds, or slipes, laden or unladen, were coming and going from field to stackyard, each in charge of a group of young folk, all of whom seemed to find it necessary to yell at the pitch of their lungs—a heartening scene, but one which might well become wearing. Whether all these were Primroses remained to be seen—but with eighteen others besides Alison, the Privy Council Clerk could muster quite a labour force without hired men.

The visitor had to rein his mount round to avoid a careering empty slipe on which balanced precariously two girls of perhaps eight or nine years and a boy slightly younger, who nevertheless kept whipping up the shaggy garron to its fastest pace, the whole unwieldy contrivance lurching and skidding over ruts and unevennesses in alarming style, while the children stared at the horseman in frankest interest, the boy continuing to shout joyfully. Heriot nodded to them, grinning, and was about to ride past the field gate when something about the stance of one of the field workers caught his further attention. Jerking his beast's head round abruptly, he rode in after the slipe.

Alison was dressed for the task in a skirt which was either very short or kilted up for the occasion, with a wide-necked, halterthroated and sleeveless blouse of white linen above and apparently nothing else. Barefoot, tousle-headed, flushed, but gleaming-eyed and the picture of radiant healthy young-womanhood, she stood leaning on a hay-fork and laughing at the antics of a chubby three-year-old with a collie pup. At sight of the horseman she straightened up and began to run a hand through her hair, detaching straws. Then suddenly her hand stopped in mid-air, and dropping her fork, she came racing across the stubble, arms extended, hair streaming, lips wide. The contrast with the last time Heriot had seen her, dressed as one of the Queen's ladies in his office at the Exchange, London, was extraordinary enough to bemuse the man considerably. Nevertheless, he mustered his wits sufficiently to jump down from the saddle and so was able to catch her as she hurled herself bodily into his arms—catch and hold her heaving, warm, rounded and so very evident person, and clutch her to him.

"Geordie! Geordie! Geordie!" she cried, into his chest. "You have come! You have come! Geordie, my heart—my own Geordie!"

"Yes," he said. "Yes." He was grinning stupidly. He could think of nothing else relevant to say. "Yes, lass."

Then she was kissing him, a flurry of kisses, at random at first on cheeks and chin and brow, until she settled on his lips, and there clung, mouth opening. He did not discipline himself to any suitable restraint there and then, it is to be feared.

So they stood, there amongst the stooks and oat stubble, while a notably interested band of children gathered round, to stare and point, comment and giggle.

Awareness dawned—but Alison at least was not the one to be overcome by proprieties or conventions, especially in a corn field. Loosing herself from his clasp, she stood back—but still held him by the forearms—and gazed at him. "Master George Heriot," she panted, "your devoted . . . servant . . . Alison Primrose! This is . . . I think . . . the happiest day of my life!"

He shook his head, helplessly. "Och, lassie," he said, "you must not speak so. It's it's—och, Alison, my dearest!"

"You came. Came to me. Alison Primrose. All the way from London. Dear God—I can scarcely believe it!"

"Why not? What has London that I'd rather have than this Culross?"

"You mean that, Geordie?" That was a whisper.

"Aye, I mean it. Though, God knows—I fear I should not!"

"Wheesht, wheesht! Is it your great age again!" She laughed

aloud, joyously, and swung around, him as well as herself. "Bairns—here is Master Geordie, I've told you about. The King's own man-of-business, no less—and the brawest gentleman at Court, dukes and earls or none! Master Heriot, come all the way to Culross to see us. What do you say to that?"

They said nothing very coherent to that, but laughed and shouted and jigged, while their eldest sister beamed on them all and on her capture. Then she recollected her attire.

"And here's me barefoot, and dressed like a tink!" she exclaimed—but did not sound greatly oppressed by the thought. "Heigho—the truth will out, Geordie! This, I fear, is the true me—and no Court lady."

"Heaven be praised for that!" he said fervently. "I've had my bellyful of Court ladies! But you lass—I've never seen you looking more lovely, and that's a fact. A joy to behold."

She bobbed a mocking bow—and her firm young breasts were entirely and bewitchingly evident within her loose white linen. "You can say courtly things, for one who is no courtier, sir! Even though quite untrue! But, come—wherever you have travelled from, you will have ridden far to get here. Yonder is the house, in the trees. No palace—but all yours to command. No, bairns—not you. Stay you all here. Get on with the work, now. This field to be clear before any of you eat a bite of supper! Master Geordie is *my* friend, and I'll take him to the house. Alone. Away with you . . ."

Leading Heriot's horse, they walked to Burnbrae House, Alison explaining that her father had business in Dunfermline and her stepmother had ridden pillion with him to attend to some marketing. They would be back before supper. Meantime there was cold fowl, oatcakes, honey, canary wine, ale, for a hungry traveller. And a room to get ready for him.

He told her that could wait. They had so much to say, to discuss. He would have a bite and a beaker of ale, while they talked.

The house, a tall L-planned fortalice with a corbelled stair-turret and crowstepped gables, its whitewashed harling flaking off, appeared very much the same within as it did outside, rather the worse for wear, the hall untidy above vaulted basements, its hangings shabby, its furnishings plain and well-worn. But all was clean and comfortable enough—though it was very obvious that there was a lack of money, and that it was inhabited by a tribe of careless children. The single serving-woman was elderly but strong as a horse, and cheerful in a masterful way. Heriot was installed in a crow's-nest of a room at the top of a narrow turnpike stair—which clearly was Alison's own, for he found on the top of the bed-post the gold bracelet with the turquoise feather which he himself had given her, via Queen Anne—a sight that moved him.

It was warmer out than indoors, that late summer's day, and to get away from the interested servitor, Alison—who had miraculously managed to tidy herself notably in a short time, as well as don shoes—led him out, with the viands on a tray, to a grassy terrace looking out over the Forth, where, in an evergreen arbour beside a headless and moss-grown marble nymph, they could sit in privacy.

"Blackness Castle!" the man said, nodding his head in that south-easterly direction. "Where your friend is a prisoner. An ill business. Three miles? Four? But far as London—or Orkney—in truth!"

"Yes. A wicked shame. A sin! How often I look across to her, and wish and wish! Poor Margaret. She is not a thief, you know, Geordie. It is all false, untrue. She would not steal, the Queen's jewels, or anything else."

"I never believed that she did. Or I would not have taken the jewels. She is, I think, being made the scapegoat for others. And you also, to some extent." He paused. "I knew nothing of your dismissal from Court, and being sent back to Scotland, until weeks after you were gone," he assured her. "When the Queen herself told me. And roughly! I cannot remember when I was so angry. It was a shameful thing—and well the Queen knew it. But she made herself adamant, would hear no excuses, listen to no reason. She would not see me alone—dared not, I think. She was set against me. As against you and Margaret Hartside."

"Yes. By bringing Margaret and those jewels to you, Geordie, I caused the Queen to turn against you. You who have always been her good friend. I did you a great hurt. Oh, I am sorry, my dear!"

He took her hand. "No blame to you. It was the right course you took. The fault is all otherwise. Perhaps I should have been more careful. In accepting the jewels, not questioning the story deeper. If I had refused them, you at least might have been spared banishment from Court. It was your friendship with me, you linking Mistress Hartside with me, which caused your dismissal, I am sure."

"But it was because of *me* that you accepted Margaret's tale, and gave her the money so readily, was it not? So in that I *am* to blame."

He could not deny it. "We should not be debating blame, lass.

But what to do to right matters. If only we knew what was behind it all. Have you no notion?"

"Only that it has to do with the Earl of Orkney—that I am sure. He is an evil, hard man. And the Queen is frightened of him, I swear. I have seen her with him. He treats her without respect—and she accepts it from him. There is something between them—and the jewels are part of it."

"You believe it true? That Anne did indeed give all that casket of jewels to Orkney?"

"Why not? Margaret's husband, Buchanan of Scotscraig, believed it so—and he is one of Orkney's gentleman. The Earl, at least, must have told him so. And given him these jewels."

"And what is Buchanan doing to aid his secret wife?"

"I know not. He is, I suppose, in Orkney. I wrote him a letter. But travellers to Orkney are few, and he may not have received it."

"The Earl, his master, may not wish Buchanan to do anything. For his wife. If this is some ploy of Orkney's . . . ?"

At a loss, they fell silent, hand-in-hand—until Heriot perceived it, reckoned it ridiculous for a man of his years, and disengaged. He began to tell her all that he had done, or tried to do, so far. Also of the Master of Gray's demands on the King.

"This man Hope?" she asked. "He is to be concerned in both matters? Do you believe that he can do anything to help Margaret?"

"My cousin Hamilton, the Advocate, thinks highly of him—although they are often opposed. And he should know. If anyone can aid her, I think he is the man. He is to try to get her out of Blackness meantime, whether or not there is to be a trial. I will stand surety for any sum required—although I told Hope not to give my name, since I am in some degree implicated, and *my* surety might not be acceptable. He will arrange it in some other's name."

"You are good, Geordie."

"Good, no. But money I know how to use. It is my trade. And has its uses. But, again, there is much that money cannot do. And I think it makes me more enemies than friends!"

"It frightens me," she said. "Your money."

"Why, child? Why—a God's name?"

"All those riches. You so rich a man. We, here, so poor. Not that I mind being poor. But, but . . ." She jerked away from him, abruptly. "And you are calling me child, again!"

"I am sorry, Alison lass. A slip. I do not think of you as child, believe me—wholly as woman, now. Too much as woman, I fear!"

"Since I *am* a woman, how can that be? I sometimes think that you are *afraid* of me being woman grown, Geordie."

"Perhaps you are right," he said soberly.

Two small Primroses put a stop to this unprofitable conversation by appearing round the corner of the arbour, with smirks, to announce that their father was back from Dunfermline, and Alison had better come out of there if she did not want to be in trouble!

Guiltily Heriot started up—but it did not escape him that it was their father, with no mention of the mother, or stepmother, whose arrival was announced.

This was explained, very shortly thereafter, when Alison brought him to James Primrose and his second wife. Her father was a pink, pot-bellied, self-important little man, round-featured, purse-lipped and strutting—an unlikely sire for his daughter, indeed for his entire lively and uninhibited brood. Lady Burnbrae was small too, but thin, meek, apologetic and self-effacing. It was not to be supposed that her life was of the happiest in that household.

Primrose greeted his unexpected guest with an uneasy mixture of doubt and respect, indicating that he often had cause to hear of Master George Heriot; indeed in the Privy Council, they had had occasion to take note of certain of his activities. He paused, at that, and gave a penetrating stare, implying unspoken volumes. But he welcomed him under his poor roof—which might not be all that Jinglin' Geordie was used to these days, but was at least an honest man's house. If he had notified them of his coming, they might have been better prepared to entertain him suitably. The gudewife would do what she could—but his, of course was not a courtier's table. He himself had been away on important business at Dunfermline, it must be understood. Etcetera.

Lady Burnbrae scurried away in evident agitation, while the laird's eldest daughter eyed her father in a sort of amused exasperation.

The repast which followed was adequate enough, if plain and distinctly noisy. Primrose conversed solely with his guest, ignoring the presence of his family; and his lady, at the foot of the necessarily lengthy table, made no attempt to control the vociferous household. Heriot counted only sixteen of them, so presumably three were either dead or living elsewhere. Alison, every now and again, sought to quell the worst squabbling or other outbreaks of high spirits, but out of a sense of duty, it seemed, rather than any conviction. The visitor found it all rather amusing if somewhat distracting.

That is, until James Primrose, in his best pontifical Privy Council fashion, felt it incumbent on him to impress on his guest the importance of the day's visit to Dunfermline, where he had been to confer with the Chancellor, no less. This, he emphasised, was a frequent occurrence—the Chancellor, of course, acted chairman of the Council. But today's had been a rather special occasion—but very privy, of course. The laird pursed his lips still further, and nodded portentously.

When Heriot did not only forbear to press for details, but actually allowed himself to be entertained by ongoings further down the table, his host saw it as necessary to elaborate, and so to bring the other to a due recognition of the responsibilities and weighty issues resting on the shoulders of the Clerk of the Council. Logan of Restalrig had fairly recently died, it seemed, in drunken squalor and poverty in a house in Edinburgh's Canongate, and developments were coming to light such as to flutter many a doocot in Scotland, and outwith it.

Heriot pricked up his ears, then. Logan of Restalrig he knew, as did most others, to have been an unscrupulous adventurer in a very big way, allegedly deeply involved in the notorious Gowrie Conspiracy of 1600, as well as in innumerable other unsavoury developments in Scotland over the last score of years. But Heriot knew also that he was a kinsman of the Master of Gray's, and had acted for that Machiavelli of Scottish politics on many an occasion. He had had to withdraw from public life rather hastily after the Gowrie business—but Fast Castle, his eagle's-nest of a stronghold on the Berwickshire cliffs, was sufficiently impregnable a refuge for even King James to give up the pursuit of winkling him out.

"Died in poverty, you say? How can that be? He was ever a man of means, with large estates. And if Logan could not line his pockets in a long life time, no man could!"

"Nevertheless, he died in poverty," the other insisted, at least gratified that he now had the visitor's full attention. "And has left debts. But not only debts, sir—problems. Many problems. And most delicate."

"Which concern the Chancellor and Privy Council?"

"Just that. His papers are, h'm, highly dangerous. And some have already got into wrong hands. Wrong hands, sir."

"I see. Yes, I agree that if Logan of Restalrig kept papers, they might well prove awkward for some folk. But why the Privy Council?"

"Because, Master Heriot, certain members of the Council are much involved. Even His Grace the King! And the Lord Home, who is one of Logan's heirs at law, a kinsman and a member of the Council, is for suing certain other members, who are, it seems, Logan's debtors. The Master of Gray, once a member, and also a kinsman, likewise."

"The Master does keep cropping up," Heriot observed. "A man of much initiative! And a friend of Fyvie's—or rather, Dunfermline's, the Chancellor!"

"Precisely, sir. But then, so is the Lord Balmerino and the Earl of Dunbar, the King's former and present Secretaries of State."

"And they come into it?"

"Unhappily, they do. The Earl of Dunbar it was—as Sir George Home of Manderston—who bought Fast Castle from Logan. Also Gunsgreen and Flemington estates. And has not paid eighteen thousand merks of the purchase price. And Lord Balmerino, who as Secretary Elphinstone bought Restalrig itself, and still owes fifteen thousand merks."

"Whe-e-ew! I did not know that Logan had sold his estates. Why should he have done that? A rich man?"

"That interests the Privy Council, sir, likewise. For the Lord Home claims that Logan was forced to it by these two friends of the King. On pain of them divulging some informations against him. And that they then refused to pay most of the purchase moneys. Moreover, the King's own name is said to come into it. His Grace is said also to have received some of Logan's moneys. Lord Home and the Master of Gray have these papers, and wish for . . . restitution!"

Heriot was silent, as his mind sought to cope with all this, and all that it implied. Primrose glanced at him, almost anxiously.

"You do not believe me, sir? I assure you that it is absolute truth, and greatly distressing the Chancellor. Logan, it seems, left his papers in care of a notary in Eyemouth, near Fast Castle. One George Sprott. And he has handed over some, at least, to Lord Home and the Master."

"I do not disbelieve you, sir. I but perceive that Scotland is in sore need of a strong hand to govern it—not an absent one, four hundred miles away in London!"

"As to that, sir, I do believe that the King's accession to Elizabeth's throne was . . . unfortunate. But my lord of Dunfermline is quite capable of governing the country, with the aid of the Secretary of State and the Privy Council. Quite capable, sir."

"I rejoice to hear it." Heriot shrugged. "The Earl of Orkney does not, by any chance, come into all this?"

"The Earl of Orkney?" Startled, the little man stared at his guest, and then away. "The Earl of Orkney, sir—I cannot say aught of the Earl of Orkney. That is a, a different matter. My lips are sealed—sealed, do you hear? Moreover, the Earl of Orkney is the King's cousin."

"The King has a number of cousins!" Heriot mentioned. "His grandsire, James the Fifth, being a very potent prince! I but wondered, since the Master of Gray was concerned, whether Orkney might not be also? They are brothers-in-law."

"I can say nothing about the Earl of Orkney, Master Heriot," Primrose jerked, and pushed back his chair. "I . . . I have no knowledge of his affairs."

His guest inclined his head—but looked keenly at the laird as he did so. The man was suddenly frightened. He had been eager enough to talk, before; had all but babbled, and of matters which some might have considered secret to the Privy Council. Orkney's name had changed all that. Thoughtfully Heriot followed his host out to inspect the new doocot being built, with its hundreds of stone nests.

Later that evening, with the children, even Alison banished to bed, and the diffident Lady Burnbrae retired also, Heriot was on his way upstairs likewise when James Primrose summoned him into the little withdrawing-room off the hall, where a log fire smouldered, convenient for the laird—who had contracted the unpleasant new West Indian habit of burning tobacco weed in a pipe and sucking the smoke—to light and relight the evidently not very combustible mixture.

"Master Heriot," he said, settling down, and puffing with considerable determination. "I presume that you have come to my house with the purpose of seeking from me my daughter Alison's hand in marriage?"

Heriot swallowed audibly. "I . . . er . . . ah," he said. "Well, sir. I, see you—I am so very much older than she is . . ."

"Yes, she is very young, sir. In my opinion, as yet too young to marry. Although a man of your mature years would no doubt make the best husband for her. I am prepared to consider it, sir. But not for a year or so."

"Indeed. Yes. I see. You will understand, Burnbrae, that I have not spoken of this. Said anything of the sort. To Alison."

"Quite right. Proper. As her father, I should expect you to approach me first. Now—as to the matter of dowry. You will not be expecting any large sum, Master Heriot, I am sure? I am not a rich man. And have many daughters to provide for."

Distinctly bemused by his sudden translation towards marriage status and negotiation, Heriot wagged his head. "No, no. Of course not, sir. I had not thought of it. The matter had not occurred to me."

"Aye. Well, then—no doubt we can come to a satisfactory arrangement." He pursed his lips. "I shall, of course, expect you to settle a substantial jointure upon my Alison, sir. A man in your situation could do no less. Substantial."

"Oh, quite. Quite."

"Have you any figure, or properties, in mind?"

"Well, no. The fact is, sir, I have scarcely considered anything of the sort."

"But it is most necessary, Master Heriot. You are a man of affairs, of means. These important matters must be given due thought, and dealt with in good time. Beforehand. A proper marriage settlement is the basis of every satisfactory match, none will deny."

The other opened his mouth to speak and thought better of it. He drank a gulp of canary instead.

"Consider it well, then, my friend," Primrose went on, "so that I may draw up proper settlement papers, as is right and due. Meantime, sir, I drink to your betrothal." He raised his tankard.

"You are, h'm, very kind. Very. Be assured, Burnbrae, that I shall give this matter much and suitable thought."

"Aye, do. Then I give you goodnight, sir. And shall look to see you my good-son in a year or so. I hope that our association may be to our satisfaction and profit, aye profit, sir."

As George Heriot stumbled up the narrow, winding stairway to his lofty bedchamber under the roof, he had already begun the process of deep and extended thought. Indeed his contemplations extended far into the night, in that bed which was Alison's—of which he was much aware—his head seething, his doubts questioning, his judgment seesawing—but his heart singing.

* * *

In the morning, the man found himself loth to meet Alison's eye across the breakfast table. But the girl was her usual cheerful, laughing self, and no constraint was long possible. Certainly no serious discussion did or could take place in such circumstances and company. His host was silent, preoccupied, frowning, presumably ruminating on matters of state. Heriot contented himself with trivialities.

It seemed to be taken for granted by all concerned that the harvest leading-in process should continue at full strength—as indeed would be happening all over the land, with good weather therefor a by no means normal state of affairs. Heriot was far from averse to a day's hearty and healthy labour in the harvest field, in good company—especially when he realised that the laird, with a mind above such matters, would be otherwise engaged. In shirt and breeches, sleeves uprolled and hay-fork over shoulder, he sallied out with Alison and the rest of the Primrose clan, equipped with baskets of cold meats, pitchers of milk and flagons of home-brewed cider—and, in fact, thereafter enjoyed one of the happiest and most satisfying days of his life, a day of wholesome and essential physical effort, sunshine, laughter and companionship. His back ached and his arms were limp before the end of it, and the sheaves grew heavier and heavier, but that was a small price to pay for those well-spent hours, hours wherein his mind quietly settled itself, and he came, without any cudgelling of wits, to see his way reasonably straight before him, his good way.

It was evening before he had a chance to be alone with Alison, when, shaking off the last of her ever-present family, the young woman led him, walking, down to the shore of the Forth. And now he found himself strangely reluctant to broach the subject which so closely affected them both. There was a risk, he felt, that it might alter, mar, the day's happy companionship.

It was the girl herself who brought it up, presently. "Geordie," she said, as they picked their way over the rounded pebbles of the beach, "last night my father packed me off to bed with the others, as though I had been a child. He does not usually do so. I took it that he wished to speak with you, alone. He has spoken openly to you, at the suppertable, about his precious Privy Council affairs, caring for none of us. So it could not be that. I wondered if it could be about *me*?" She wrinkled her nose. "If I had been sleeping in my own room, I would have crept down the stairs to listen at the door! But I was in a room with four of my sisters—and they would have come with me, you may be sure! *Did* he speak about me?"

"He did, yes."

"To what purpose?"

"He . . . ah . . . well, spoke of your future."

She drew a deep breath. "That is what I feared. Geordie—I do not know what he said—but I know my father. You are not to pay any heed to what he said, do you hear? He is a good man, but trying at times. And, and very full of himself. Forby, a lawyer—and he *thinks* like a lawyer! You are not to consider what he said about me and my, my future. You understand?"

"I am sorry about that, my dear!" he told her, smiling a little. "For he told me much that was good to hear."

"He did? I can scarce believe that! Oh, he loves me well enough—but I swear that is not what he would tell you, of me. Did he, did he . . . ?"

"He did for me, lass, what I think I would never have had the courage and wit to decide for myself! He, h'm, suggested that I should ask you to marry me. In a year or two's time."

They had both halted, there on the shingly beach, gazing at each other. The girl was absolutely silent—but her breathing was heightened, her lips parted, her eyes bright.

"Well, my dear?" he asked.

Still she stared at him. A pink tongue-tip came out to moisten those lips. "You mean it?" she whispered.

"To be sure, I mean it. I mean it, I hope for it, I pray for it, lass."

"Oh, Geordie—at last! At last!" And she flung herself into his arms.

On the open shore they embraced, oblivious of who might be watching. It was some considerable time before anything like coherent and rational converse was resumed between them.

"I do not think . . . I doubt whether . . . it comes to me that you did not answer my question, young woman!" the man declared, at length, somewhat breathlessly. "I asked, you may recollect, whether you would marry me."

"Think you that I would say no, sir? When I have been seeking to bring you to the asking, this year and more! Never fear, I shall not let you go now that I have you! Now, or ever. I would wed you tomorrow, if I might!"

"Scarce so soon, my love," Heriot demurred. "Your father's condition of agreement is that we must wait a year or so. As indeed the wiser part of me accepts as best—the part I *think* with, not the part I feel with!"

"Why?"

"Your father conceives you too young . . ."

"That again! Mercy—you men! You judge all by years and months. As though that was important. What do you know of women and how their age should be judged?"

"I do not claim deep knowledge of your sex, no. But this I do know—that *I* was wed too young, before."

"Oh," she said. "Yes, of course." That brought her up short. "I am sorry."

"No need to be. Christian and myself—Christian Marjoribanks—were wed when she was little more than a child in years—and I, though turned twenty, was young, young. The match was arranged by my father and her guardian—for she was an orphan. We scarce knew each other. Nor ever did learn to know each other, properly, as we ought. Perhaps I did not try sufficiently hard. If our marriage lacked much, the fault, no doubt, was mine—for she was fair and good and should have made what is called an excellent wife. But I was young. I thought that I knew all . . ."

"So that is why you were ever so concerned about my age—or lack of it, Geordie? I understand now. But we are not all the same at similar years."

"No. But marriages are for life. And a man that a girl of your age might think to wed, joyfully, she might find intolerable when she is older. And that, my dear, I think I could not bear!"

"Geordie—how can I convince you that I know my own mind? Have done, since ever I met you that day in Linlithgow Palace. I am no child—and have considered a plentitude of young men. And not so young. You know what it is like at Court. Many would have wed me—apart from those who merely wanted my body. And some were what, no doubt, my father would name a good match. But I kept myself for *you*. I knew that you were the man for me, Geordie—although I dreaded your riches. So—why wait months and years now?"

"Because your father would have it so, lass—and, however little of a child you may be in truth, you are far from of due age. And, to speak fair, I also would have to wait, Alison lass—the wiser side of me. For me to take you back to London and the Court as bride, now, would serve neither of us well. It would seem a defiance of the Queen. And though I might care little for that, in one respect—it would mean that you would not be received at Court. That would be difficult, since I must be at Court myself, as the Queen's jeweller and the King's man-of-business. It would come between us. In time, this folly will be resolved, or will subside. A year or so, my heart—it would be best. Meanwhile, we are betrothed—which is a joy . . ."

"Betrothed? Are we?"

"Your father says so. He drank to our betrothal last night!"

"Ah! He did? Geordie—did he . . . did he talk about money?"

The man cleared his throat. "A little. As was to be expected. A father has duties in this respect . . ."

"Do not seek to spare him, or me!" she charged. "I know him. He will see you as a rich catch, I swear! A source of siller, to bind to him! This is what I had feared, dreaded. I will have none of it—do you hear? I will not be sold, chaffered over, like a heifer at a market!"

"Sakes, lass—never think it! When you are my wife, you will receive a jointure, as is suitable. So that should I die, you would have a sufficiency. Think you I would not insist on that?"

"And that was all? No shameful bargaining?"

"None. You are your own woman, Alison Primrose—and always will be, as far as George Heriot is concerned. That I promise you."

"Dear Geordie! Why are you so good to me?"

"I could tell you that, perhaps. But it would take a long time, girl. You would have to be very patient, to hear it all. Are you a patient young woman? I think—I think it might be better if I told you while sitting down! Less . . . wearying. You see yonder bushes, and the grassy bank between? As good a place for a long accounting of your attractions to me, attributes and delights—do you not agree? Retired. It would be a pity to be disturbed, in such a matter. Sakes—no need to *run*, my betrothed!"

14

The day following, George Heriot duly met the Duke of Lennox at Dunfermline. As expected, and as before, Ludovick had brought Mary Gray with him, that they might have this extra day together—which was an excellent excuse for Alison Primrose also to accompany her new betrothed so far on the start of his long journey to London. Much joy and excitement developed when the other pair heard the glad tidings; and thereafter a celebration was called for in the town's best inn—which had the effect of interfering with the men's fullest preoccupation with the raison d'être for their visit to Dunfermline. They were, in fact, there to see the Chancellor.

They did send a message, presently, to the old Palace—where, as Heritable Bailie of the Regality, for the Queen whose property it was, the Earl of Dunfermline had his quarters while he built his fine new house—to inform him that the Duke of Lennox and Master George Heriot were in town on the King's business and would be grateful for an interview with the Chancellor at his convenience. Unfortunately for them, convenience brought the Earl, all too speedily, in person to the inn, to welcome his distinguished guests—or at least, the Duke of Lennox, the King's cousin and occasional viceroy. This rather interrupted the betrothal celebration.

However, Alexander Seton was a pleasant and courtly character, as well as a poet and architect, unlikely a chief minister as he seemed for unruly Scotland, and he greeted both young women with gallantry and honeyed phrases. Indeed he seemed almost as reluctant as the two principals to drag himself away presently to attend to the

King's business. Leaving the girls to their own devices for a little, he led the other two across the street and through the Pended Tower, to the Constable's House, where, in a private room, he produced more wine, and enquired as to their business.

On the way thither, Lennox had rather mystified his friend by muttering hastily in his ear, twice, the phrase 'The Queen's Casket Letters'; but no opportunity presented itself to elaborate on this, and Heriot did not know whether the Duke was referring to letters connected with Queen Anne's missing casket of jewels, or to the more famous and mysterious Casket Letters which had contributed so greatly to the downfall of the King's mother, Queen Mary. He wished that Lennox had thought to inform him of the meaning and significance of this before the Chancellor arrived. Admittedly their minds had been on other matters.

Heriot did most of the explaining as to the reason for their visit to Scotland on the King's behalf, with Dunfermline looking ever more uneasy. But when he came out with the suggestion that, to avoid any public trial, the Master of Gray's suit might be heard in private before a special commission of judges, the Chancellor seized on it with obvious relief. Clearly he knew quite a lot about the background to the case, and was torn between his duty as the King's chief minister in Scotland and his friendship with Patrick Gray. But this seemed a suitable solution, he agreed—although it almost inevitably *would* imply that some sum would in fact accrue to the Master, for the indications were that the case was a genuine one. Yet, from all that he could gather, the King was unwilling to pay anything at all.

"His Majesty is not anxious to pay for so old a debt, occasioned on state business," Heriot said carefully. "But, on the other hand, he would not wish to fail in what was just and due. He will never agree to fifty thousand pounds—which, we believe, is the size of the Master's claim; but that, it is thought, is mainly a charge for interest. Some lesser sum, consonant with the original loan, might be proposed by the judges and accepted by both sides."

"To be sure. That would be the wisest solution, Master Heriot. But, it would have to be substantial, for the Master to agree. Have you any sum in view?"

"That would depend on the Master's case—which, of course, we do not know. And also, h'm, how much he needs this money which he has been so notably long in claiming."

The Chancellor cleared his throat and took a few paces about the room. "That I cannot tell you," he declared, after a pause. "But—I think it possible that he might require the money . . . somewhat urgently."

"Why?" asked the blunt Lennox.

"I do not know that I am at liberty to answer you in much detail, my lord Duke. For this is a close matter, to be put before the Privy Council. But since you are still a member thereof, and Master Heriot is here on the King's business, perhaps in confidence I may say *something*. The fact is that the unsavoury Logan of Restalrig has died—and the Master of Gray, his cousin, is an heir. He left no close kin, and indeed was still under the King's forfeiture when he died—which much complicates the situation. The Lord Home is another heir-general. You will perceive the problems? Especially as certain aspects of Logan's estate are very difficult, not to say dangerous. I fear that there will be much trouble before all is resolved. And more suits at court, perhaps! To the distress of the realm, it may be."

"And this may have to do with Patrick Gray's demands on the King?"

"Indirectly, yes. I am not in the Master's confidence, you will understand. But it is my belief that he requires much money, in order to gain something of, of notable cost. Which Logan's papers, now in his possession, reveal. Reveal the whereabouts of. Hitherto unknown, a secret . . ."

"My God—the Casket Letters!" Lennox exclaimed.

Dunfermline stared. "How did you know?"

The Duke glanced over at Heriot. "A whisper my lord—no more. But—this is extraordinary. And dangerous."

The Chancellor nodded grimly.

"You mean the so-called Casket Letters of the late Queen Mary?" Heriot put in. "Were they not destroyed?"

"Copies were destroyed. Those used against the Queen at her trial in England. But the originals never left Scotland. They have been lost—or thought to have been lost—for many years. And apparently are not! In fact are in, shall we say, dangerous hands!"

"Orkney's?" Lennox demanded.

"Yes. I see that you know not a little of this, my lord Duke? The last known holder was the Earl of Gowrie—the first Earl, Lord Treasurer. After his execution, in 1584, they disappeared. It was thought that much of the trouble between the King and young Gowrie, at the Conspiracy of 1600, was on their account—for they could be very damaging towards His Grace. Now it appears that the Lord Robert got them. Robert Stewart, the King's uncle, first Earl of Orkney. His name appeared in certain of the letters, it seems. Logan of Restalrig appears to have been the go-between, carrying them to Orkney. So that Patrick Stewart, the present Orkney, inherited them. And now . . . !"

"Now Patrick Gray seeks to buy them from Orkney?"

"That is my belief, my lord Duke. Orkney is in sore need of money. He is grievously in debt, forfeited, and has not yet finished building his great palace at Kirkwall. Nor yet his castle at Scalloway. Both magnificent buildings. And building is an expensive business—as I know to my cost! Moreover he, Orkney, in trouble with the King as you know, has returned to Orkney against the royal commands. We may well have to outlaw him, King's cousin as he is. We fear that he will seek to defy King and Council from the islands—set up, in truth, a small kingdom of his own in Orkney and Shetland. This would require much money—which he has not got. So he seeks to raise it, wherever he may."

"And he has had these Casket Letters all the time?"

"It seems so."

Heriot looked at Lennox. "This could account for much. If they are so, so grievous as rumour makes them!"

The Duke cleared his throat. "They could be more explosive than Guido Fawkes's gunpowder, I think! They could even, it is said, throw doubts on James's right to the English throne. Or the Scots one, itself!"

"Scarcely that, surely!" the Chancellor protested, but without conviction.

"What are they?" Heriot asked. "Letters from the Mary Queen to Bothwell? Could such be so damaging?"

"There are, it is believed, at least twenty-two documents, not all letters," Dunfermline told him. "There are said to be two marriage contracts, some love sonnets, and sundry proofs of various sorts. Nobody knows—other than Orkney, perhaps—just what the Casket contained. It is a silver-gilt box, a foot in length they say, bearing the Crown of France and the initials of King Francis the Second, Mary's first husband. She gave it to her lover, the Earl of Bothwell, before they were wed, before King Henry Darnley's death at Kirk o' Field. And Bothwell, when he fled in haste from

Edinburgh Castle in 1567, left it behind. He sought to get it back, later—but he was too late. Morton had got it—and used it to damn the Queen. At Morton's execution, Gowrie got it, he being Treasurer."

"And now the Master of Gray wants it—and is willing to pledge his all to get it!"

"Better in the Master's hands than Orkney's!" the Chancellor said. "At least he would not use its contents against the realm."

Heriot looked at the Earl curiously, but did not comment on that. "What is so dangerous to the King, in this?" he asked. "You say it could endanger his throne? Why?"

Lennox shrugged. "The letters may be false, forgeries. But it is said that one of them throws doubt on James's legitimacy."

"Good God!"

"That, I am sure, is folly!" the Chancellor declared. But he looked agitated and less than sure of himself.

"You believe, then, that Patrick Gray did not know that Orkney had these letters—like other folk—and only learned of it from the late Logan of Restalrig's papers, which he inherited, but, having discovered it, and knowing that Orkney needs money, he is seeking to purchase them?" Lennox asked.

"Exactly."

"To what purpose?"

Dunfermline took a long breath. "That I do *not* know. But . . . I would liefer see the Casket Letters in Gray's hands than in Orkney's."

"And yet Orkney has not used them?"

"Do we *know* that he has not?" Heriot put in.

There was silence.

"I think that he may have done. But . . . perhaps less subtly than Gray would do!"

Again neither of the others commented.

"What, then, is to be done?" Lennox demanded.

"I would say, encourage Gray to get the letters. Or—do not hinder him. At least, then, we would know where they were. We might be able to get them from him—which we can never do with Orkney," the Chancellor said. "Gray is a man who has served the realm well, many a time—Orkney never. Who knows—he may only wish to sell them to the King, at a higher price."

It was Heriot's turn to remain silent.

"I think that I agree with my lord," Lennox said. "Better that

Patrick should have the Casket Letters—if indeed they still exist—than Orkney. But must *either* have them? If Orkney would sell them to Gray, would he not sell them, for a better price, to others? Acting for the King?"

"Not, I think, if he *knew* they were for the King," Heriot said slowly. "As I see it, he will give the Master the originals, and keep copies for himself. If the King has the originals, such copies would be almost valueless. But if not, he might still use them against His Majesty."

The others nodded acceptance of that.

"It is a damnable fix!" the Duke declared. "But I think that we should allow Patrick to get them—if he can. And then seek to deal with *him*. It puts him in a strong position, yes—but at least he is a man we can negotiate with. And possibly counter. Whereas Orkney . . . !"

"My view entirely," Dunfermline nodded.

"Therefore we should not advise the King wholly to resist Gray's claim, before a commission of judges."

"What sum do you suggest, gentlemen?"

The Duke looked at Heriot.

"Twenty thousand pounds," that man said. "No more."

"Yes. Suitable. Fair."

"I think that it could be . . . arranged."

Before they left the Chancellor, Heriot asked if there was anything the other could do to aid Margaret Hartside—and found himself up against a stone wall. This was entirely a matter between the Queen and her officers, he was told. The woman was Her Grace's private servant, concerned in a private offence against her, and being examined by her officers. There was nothing that he, or other, could do, unless Hartside was actually charged in open court. Blackness Castle was admittedly a state prison; objection might be taken to her presence therein. But she could be held in any of the royal properties—and would she be any better off?

On that note his visitors returned to their ladies.

* * *

"I think it is clear to me now what is behind all this mystery," Heriot declared to his friends. "Behind possibly both of the matters we are concerned with. Orkney has been using these Casket Letters to threaten the King, his cousin, to extort mail, blackmail. Likewise the Queen. That is how he got the jewels—by threatening to deliver the letters, or copies of them, to the King's enemies, those who would unseat him and put Arabella on the throne. If there are doubts as to the King's legitimacy, then his tenure of both thrones could be at risk. This is the hold Orkney has had over both James and Anne. They have been paying him to keep silence."

"But," Mary objected, "if Elizabeth and her Council had copies of these letters—as they did in 1568, when they shamefully tried and executed Queen Mary—they would *know* about this. About the King's possible illegitimacy. Or, at least, proofs thereof—for always it has been suggested, by some, that he was Riccio's son. If they knew, would James ever have been allowed to succeed Elizabeth?"

"I thought of that, yes. But we need not suppose that *all* the letters, or copies, were sent to Elizabeth and Cecil. Moray, the half-brother of both Queen Mary and of old Orkney, it was who arranged it. The eldest of James the Fifth's bastards. He wanted his sister condemned—shame on him! But he would not want his nephew James put aside, for Arabella or other. He wanted to—and did—rule Scotland in the name of his nephew, as Regent. After Morton. The Good Regent Moray! No advantage to him if Arabella had become Queen. Or any other, in Scotland or England. He himself was illegitimate, so he could not have the throne himself. James, so long as he remained youthful and could be dominated by Moray, was *his* card to play. So he would not send South any letter which questioned James's legitimacy. Even though there may have been one."

"It hangs well together," Lennox admitted.

Mary nodded. "Yes. That was the only flaw I saw in it all. No doubt you are right, Geordie. And now my father, through Logan's papers, has discovered the secret of who has the Casket Letters—and wants them! And Orkney will sell—for a sufficiently high price—now that he is outlawed and greatly needing money. So Patrick revives this ancient debt of the King's with interest. And who knows what other sources he seeks, to gain the money?"

"And the Earl of Orkney seeks to sell the Queen's jewels, for so much as they will fetch," Alison put in. "Those that Margaret tried to sell to you, Geordie, perhaps were just the first. A test and trial, to see if they would sell in London. At higher price than they would in Scotland. With poor Margaret duped as seller. If she had succeeded with those, others would have followed—for she says that the Queen gave Orkney a whole casketful."

"No doubt. But why then did the Queen turn against this Margaret and you?" Mary asked. "If she knew very well that the jewels were not stolen. Why put the blame on Margaret?"

Heriot answered that. "She did not do so until the jewels turned up, to be sold. She must have given them to Orkney a year before, but made no move before Hartside and Alison brought them to *me*. She, the Queen, knew that I would recognise them as hers—since I had provided them for her. And so the secret was out. She dared not accuse Orkney of the blackmail, while he still held the letters. But she could hit back at Margaret—whom, no doubt, she believes to be Orkney's minion. As warning not to try her further."

They considered that. It seemed to answer the case—or most of it.

"And now," Lennox went on, "we seem to be going to have Patrick Gray to extort the blackmail, instead of his brother-in-law! Is the King any way advantaged? For Patrick is a much cleverer man than Orkney. I feel in my bones it is better, somehow. But . . ."

"I would say yes," Mary answered, slowly. "Patrick is a rogue—but a rogue with principles! He is at war, meantime, with James personally. But I believe that he loves his country, in his own way. Would do nothing to hurt the realm. Orkney is otherwise—cares nothing for the realm, or any other save himself. Patrick may charge the King dear for those letters—but he will not bring down the throne, and Scotland with it, I believe."

"It seems that James will have to pay heavily for leaving behind the Master at Berwick, that day!" Lennox said. "It was an ill-advised move."

"Even he would not deny that now, I think," Heriot agreed. "But at least the King will now know where these letters are. And, who can tell, may even be able to lay hands on them. Which he could not do in the Isles of Orkney."

"That might be to underestimate Patrick's ability to look after his own interests," Mary pointed out, warningly.

"Perhaps. What think you the Master's price will be?"

"Who knows?" the Master's daughter said. "Almost certainly not money. Perhaps the Chancellorship of Scotland. Or even a call to the Court in London, after all—and power there. It is ever power that Patrick seeks—not mere money."

"Nothing that we may do about it, now," the Duke declared. "The question is, where do we go now? What *our* next move?"

"Return to Edinburgh," Heriot said. "See both Hope and Hamilton again. About Margaret Hartside's court case, as well as the Master's claim. Then back to London and the King. Lay all before him, advise that he settles with Gray. Further decision is his, not ours. We have done what he sent us to do—or as much as we might. We have, we believe, found out what is behind it all. What remains is for the King to choose."

"It is a bad business—like so much else," Mary Gray commented. "Unfinished business, too. But—heigho! that is the one satisfaction of it! At least, for you and for me, Alison, my dear. For it will not be so very long, I think, before these two men of ours will be coming back to Scotland once more, on this the King's unfinished and tangled business! To our joy."

They all drank to that.

So, that early evening, six miles to the south-east, at the North Queensferry, the two strong-minded young women waved goodbye to their chosen men, on the boat for the Lothian shore. If they swallowed a tear or two, they did not do so until the others were beyond perceiving it.

In Edinburgh next day, the travellers were surprised to discover that Master Thomas Hope had already extracted Margaret Hartside from Blackness Castle. She was now in the care of one of her husband's Buchanan kinsmen in Stirlingshire. This had been achieved by Hope's knowledgeable pressure, legal expertise, and by a surety of ten thousand merks being paid on the woman's behalf, in the name of one John Dalziel, an Edinburgh burgess under some obligation to the advocate. They, and the woman, undertook to appear before any properly constituted court, whenever summoned, as was lawfully correct. Meanwhile she was not to leave Stirlingshire.

George Heriot wrote his note-of-hand for ten thousand merks there and then, much pleased with their counsel. Hope, for his part, put forward no objection to the idea of hearing the Master of Gray's case before a special judicial commission, in private—since it implied royal recognition that there was a case to answer. He would advise his principal to concur.

Later, they saw Sir Thomas Hamilton, and he also agreed to the commission, saying that it was a reasonable move, and promising to make the necessary arrangements. Like the Chancellor, he also wondered about a target figure for settlement, and again Heriot mentioned the sum of twenty thousand pounds. The other seemed to accept that as fair and practical, in the circumstances. But would the Master of Gray?

They set off on their long ride to London, the following morning.

15

THE TRAVELLERS ARRIVED at Theobalds to discover that the two monarchs had moved back to Greenwich, preparatory to Christian's departure for his own Denmark in a few days' time. Lennox pressed on to Court, therefore, to make his report, while his companion delayed for a day in London to deal with his own business problems which had accumulated during his absence.

When Heriot took boat down the five miles of Thames to Greenwich the day following, it was to discover stirring ongoings at the great palace when he arrived—a tournament, no less. This seemed to be in the nature of a valedictory flourish towards the foreign guests—and London had been ransacked for ancient suits of armour for the contestants, for all was to be done in true, colourful, medieval style, in the interests of chivalry and honour: or approximately true. The riverside park had been turned into a great tilting-ground, with wooden terracing for the spectators, a gorgeously decorated royal box, with the Lion and Unicorn competing above it and the Danish and Holstein banners alongside. The entire scene was a riot of colour, with striped pavilions and awnings for the great nobles and ambassadors, standards and flags everywhere, the lists adorned with the competitors' coats-of-arms, horse-trappings of striking hues, helmet-plumes, surcoats and heraldic favours, a chromatic spectacle in themselves—so that the ladies, although spectacularly enough clad, could by no means compete with all this male flamboyance. It was a no-expense-spared occasion, most evidently—and George Heriot was spoil-sport enough to wonder where all the money was to come from this time. How much of his latest twenty thousand Sterling remained? Fortunately the August weather remained excellent.

It transpired that even the newly-returned Duke of Lennox had been dragooned into the jousting, along with King Christian himself and nobles innumerable. The clash of armoured knights already resounded when Heriot arrived, and almost the first sight to greet him was two unconscious individuals being carried off on biers, one of whom he recognised, behind all the nose-bleed, as a customer of his own, the Earl of Rutland. He hoped that he would not die—for the Earl owed him money. According to bystanders, Rutland had actually been the victor of his joust—but his horse had collapsed under him, with a burst heart, soon after he had unseated his opponent with his lance, and any fall from the saddle, in armour, was apt to knock the encased knight unconscious. These riding horses, or course, were totally unsuited for carrying the weight of knight plus almost a hundredweight of steel-plating; but the heavy destriers of the age of chivalry were no longer bred. Heriot thanked his Maker that humble tradesmen, at least, were not expected to make fools of themselves in this fashion. Clearly it was no time to approach King James who, excellent horseman as he was, had more wits than to adventure himself in any uncomfortable suit of iron for others to poke at, preferring to fill the role of judge up in the royal box amongst a bevy of ladies around Anne—who, of course, was Queen of the Tournament. He had, however, donned a special and gorgeous heraldic tabard for the occasion—although it was noted and complained of by many that the Lion Rampant of Scotland was worn to the front, and the Leopards and Tudor Roses of England only at the back.

Heriot found a seat for himself amongst the noisy crowd of courtiers and guests on the timber scaffolding near the entrance to the lists.

There, however, he quickly had had enough—for one joust was very like another, with a trumpet being blown, one high-sounding name shouted in challenge to another, then two colourfully-caparisoned but totally steel-encased horsemen lumbering heavily towards each other, lances out-thrust, to collide, with a clash and clatter as of kitchen pots tumbling, and one, or both, falling to the grass and being carried off. A little of this went a long way, for those not educated up to it; and Heriot would have slept there and then, in the sun and warmth—for he was still tired from his long journey South—had it not been for the incessant noise, trumpeting, shouting of encouragement and abuse, wagering on the outcomes, squabbles over identities and over non-payment of bets, unhappy horses whinnying, dogs barking and pedlars hawking their sweet-meats, ales and watered wines. One spectator at least wished that he had stayed in London. For some reason, he was not in the mood.

There came a diversion. Four magnificently arrayed knights rode up together to the mouth of the lists, to a tremendous flourish of trumpets, each with a mounted esquire bearing a great banner. It was only the banner with the Stewart blue-and-white fess chequey on gold, surmounted by a ducal coronet, which revealed to Heriot that one of the quartet was his friend Lennox. The Garter King came to announce, through a speaking-trumpet, that these four champions of Christendom, Ludovick, Duke of Lennox, Thomas, Earl of Arundel, William, Earl of Pembroke and Philip, Earl of Montgomery, hereby challenged the whole world to deny four chivalric and traditional propositions. One: That in service of a lady no knight has free will. Two: That it is Beauty which maintains the world in valour. Three: That no fair lady was ever false. Four: That none can be perfectly wise but lovers. Let any who would contest such indisputable truths, in the presence of Beauty personified by the Queen's most excellent Majesty, and before these most puissant champions, now declare it—if they dared!

There followed a loud groaning, catcalls, whistles and stamping, Kings James and Christian leading the racket. Then out from the far end of the arena rode four anonymous knights in wholly black armour, without caparison, heraldry or banners, mounted on coal-black horses. A bellow greeted their appearance—drowned by another blast of trumpets, all deliberate discords and rasping, from black-clad minions. Without a word declared, the four black knights rode forward.

To the cheers of the company, the noble champions dug in their great spurs, and moved to meet them.

It would be good to record that they galloped gallantly to the fray. But alas, that was not possible on horses grossly overburdened, and with riders so stiffly encumbered with metal that they could by no means have stayed in the saddle had they done so. They lumbered out at something less than a canter—and even at that the young Earl of Arundel, perhaps still suffering from his bladder-trouble, swayed about in his saddle alarmingly and twice all but fell off. The older men were better, but none appeared as to the manner born; and Pembroke, who was the oldest and heaviest, fell quite noticeably behind, vehemently as he beat his steel gauntlet on his beast's cloth-of-gold-covered croup.

The black knights, in fact, seemed to be rather more effective.

In these circumstances, it was as well perhaps that when the clash came it was theoretical rather than actual. Lances crossed and clattered—and one of the blacks had to lean dangerously far over to make contact at all with Arundel. But it was the moral power of good over evil which was so strong that promptly, and all but in unison, all four sinister figures were unseated, to fall to the ground. Admittedly they all managed to land on their feet, before keeling over and lying still—where Arundel and Pembroke almost joined them, as they reined round their staggering steeds. But it was a highly complete and unanimous victory; and as the valiant champions trotted round the perimeter, to pause and raise their lances before the royal box, they were cheered to the echo—despite some of the comments enunciated around George Heriot.

That man moved over to the splendid pavilions from which the noble knights had emerged, and so was able to be close by when Lennox dismounted. The paladin perceived him, and opening his visor with some difficulty, revealed a very red, indeed sweating face.

"Folly!" he spluttered. "Damned foolish bairns'-play! Did ever you see the like? I am sore in every bone. Half my skin rubbed off! Heaven defend us from crazed monarchs!"

"At least you triumphed gloriously—and in upright posture!" his friend commented gravely. "You appeared very handsome—in especial with your visor closed. You would seem to fill your armour nicely, my lord Duke!"

"It is not *my* armour—that is part the trouble. It was made for some walking deformity, I swear! Nothing fits, or bends, where it should. As bad as the rack, the boot and the thumbikins combined! To provide sport for fools!"

"Hush—that verges on treason! And have I not heard you glorifying knighthood and chivalry? And berating the King for debasing it?"

"Knighthood! This rattling about like loose peas in an iron pod has little to do with knighthood and chivalry, man. It is mummery, play-acting. I refused to take part, until James commanded me. *He* is not so daft, you will note!"

"His Majesty indulges in daftness by proxy! Have you spoken with him yet? As to our mission, our findings?

"Only the briefest. I have not seen him alone. He says that it is *you* he sent North. I was but a ducal appendage! You it is must report."

"When?"

"God knows! I will tell him that you are here, now, to be sure. There is another of these deplorable banquets tonight. And to-morrow a review of ships, if you please! Off Chatham. Slaistering about in boats and barges, eating in tarry, smelly bottoms! As Lord Admiral of Scotland, for my sins, I must be present. I know not a forecastle from a poop!"

More trumpets, loud and prolonged, interrupted the Duke, and cursing, he went stamping and clanking off to receive some sort of chaplet from the Queen of the Tournament, whilst Heriot returned to his seat, to watch King Christian himself, resplendent in bright blue armour, and young Prince Henry in pure white, ride a circuit of the ring, and then seek to pick up on their lance points a wreath-like favour of flowers sent down by Anne. Neither came within inches of achieving this, until attendants set it up on edge, supported by a pair of their caps—whereupon both royal contestants managed to spear it simultaneously, and bore it in triumph between them to the royal box, to the hearty applause of all, Christian hooting hollowly from within his helm.

This seemed to represent the climax of the day, and James was prompt in leading the way back to his palace.

Heriot discovered no provision made for his reception, but as usual, found accommodation in Duke Ludovick's quarters, even huge Greenwich Palace being packed to the doors.

No royal audience was forthcoming that evening, although Heriot saw James looking directly at him during the interminable feast, with its innumerable courses and relays of entertainment—jugglers, tumblers, dancing-bears, wrestlers and the like. It was not that the King was too deeply involved with his principal guests to have time for a word with his man-of-business—for King Christian was asleep by half-way through the banquet and was in due course carried ceremoniously to bed; and Queen Anne retired early from the scene. Heriot would have like to have an interview with the Queen also—but recognised that it was necessary to see her husband first.

Later, Lennox came down to declare that James was evidently

playing some game of his own. He had ignored suggestions that he should see Heriot and himself that night, but at the last moment had commanded that his goldsmith should accompany them on the river excursion the next day—and to bring what he had called a kist of geegaws with him, for gifts. This news caused not a little upset—for of course, Heriot did not travel around with a supply of such heavy and expensive toys, and had, in consequence, there and then, to set off up-river for London again, in a royal barge, to the disgust of the watermen and a general fraying of tempers. It was two a.m. before that much-tried jeweller reached his premises at the Exchange—and thereafter had much difficulty in rousing his foreman, who slept above the shop and office, to open up, all to the grave offence of sundry disturbed neighbours and the suspicions of the Watch. It was breakfast-time before he got back to Greenwich with the jewellery—although King James, with Lennox and some others of his unenthusiastic courtiers, was already out hawking for herons in the Thames-side marshes. They would sail two hours before noon, for Chatham, he was informed—and he repaired for the hour or so to the Duke's bed, commiserating with himself on the disadvantages of being a close servant of Christ's Vice-Regent here on earth.

He was but little rested when Lennox stormed in, to change, in a flood of new cursings, from his hunting-rig into something more suitable for a naval review. Not that James himself would bother to change, but he certainly would expect others to do so. The Duke was already pining for Scotland. All he wanted was to be a simple country laird at Methven. His friend sympathised, but tersely.

Almost an hour late, a string of royal barges, highly decorated and with coloured awnings, flags and bunting, some full of busy musicians, and towing huge artificial swans and whales crewed by scantily-dressed maidens and youths, set off on the twenty-mile voyage down-river—for Rochester, surprisingly, where there was a cathedral service, for some unexplained reason; whereat James interrupted the proceedings to declare that this great kirk had been built out of the stricken consciences of the English of the thirteenth century, on account of a good Scot being murdered here, St. William of Perth, a decent baker, on his way to the Holy Land in pilgrimage—a matter for the moral musings of all. A little later he complained loudly that there were bat-droppings falling from the roof on his royal head, and so clapped on his high hat in consequence, keeping it on thereafter. The Bishop was much distressed, but was not permitted to absent himself from the further proceedings.

Thereafter, the two monarchs hurried out to cannon-fire from the line of Elizabethan forts flanking the dockyard, an employment after James's own heart—so much so that the entire review was held up for another unscheduled hour while the monarchs rivalled each other in applying fuses and matches, and continuous explosions shook land and water, and deafened courtiers and citizens clutched their ears. Even Christian looked slightly wan before eventually they ran out of powder—James, of course, having had the forsight to bring ear-plugs along for himself.

Relief thereafter was very brief, for as they rowed out into the Medway the entire fleet opened up with incessant salvoes, and thereafter it was gunfire, at close quarters, for the entire day, the ships seemingly having an inexhaustible supply of saltpetre; and the inspection was accomplished up and down the lanes of Elizabeth's vaunted navy amidst clouds of billowing, choking smoke, lit by orange flashes and a noise as of the end of the dispensation. Queen Anne and certain of her ladies had a form of hysterics and James, berating them with apt Latin apologues, had weak women and bubbling bairns—for the Princess Elizabeth and little Prince Charles were in tears—transferred to another barge and taken to the flagship *Elizabeth Jonas* moored at a pontoon bridge from the dockyard, where eventually there would be the necessary banquet.

The bombardment continued.

George Heriot's was not the only sore head and short temper when, at last, he climbed wearily aboard the said flagship, with his box of trinkets. But James was in high spirits and good hunour—so much so that he knighted several naval captains on the deck, without so much as an enquiry into their financial capabilities—Lennox growled, presumably the ones who had made the loudest bangs.

The repast which followed was held in a kind of silken saloon on deck, under a vast awning with cloth-of-gold hangings—for no cabin could have contained a tenth of the company. To counter the smells of tar, bilge-water, smoke and gunpowder, the area was sprayed with perfume for the ladies; but the Queen nevertheless excused herself, and remained below. There was a suitably nautical flavour to the feast, with many kinds of shellfish, including Rochester oysters with a pearl inserted for each guest; lobsters, some cooked but others still alive and waving their claws on the tables, giant sturgeon cooked in a piece, whitebait in wine, steaks of seal—very tough-roasted swans, and a life-sized mermaid sweetmeat, sculped in icing, each of the monarchs getting a breast. Christian who ate all set before him, declared that *his* navy was never fed so. Before the serious drinking started, James bestowed farewell gifts from Heriot's box on all the Danish party, and sundry others, rings, bracelets, medallions, necklaces and choice pearls, indiscriminately. King Christian, now very drunk, hiccupped that he would beat that, on the morrow.

Since the evening's entertainment seemed to be interminable, and Heriot had neither royal permission nor means to leave the ship, he presently found his yawning way below, eventually discovered a cabin of sorts not occupied by love-makers of one kind or another, and flung himself down to sleep—if his aching head would let him. And there he was, at some stage of the night, roused by the Duke of Lennox, summoned to attend forthwith on his liege lord. Protests, grumbles and mutinous threats availed nothing—the King's command was imperious and immediate.

The Duke led his disgruntled friend to the captain's cabin, amidst scenes of some disorder, where they found James preparing for bed, being assisted out of his clothing by the Earl of Dunbar, recently Sir George Home, and Viscount Haddington who had been Sir John Ramsay, two old and tried favourites who could drink beaker for beaker with their monarch—despite the fact that the new Viscount was still only twenty-three. Disrobing in public never worried James.

"Ha—Geordie!" he greeted, wagging a minatory finger. "There you are, then. Where ha' you been hiding yoursel', man? Wenching in some bit corner, I'll be bound. A man o' your years should be fell ashamed!" The King chuckled, and made rude signs with his fingers.

Heriot's bow was curt, and he made no reply.

James cocked a lustrous eye at him. "Eh—so that's the way o' it, is it? Jinglin' Geordie Heriot has no word o' greeting for his liege—nor yet for his auld gossip Jamie Stewart, forby! That's no' right and suitable, man. Is it, my friends?"

The two courtiers made the required noises.

Heriot spoke through tight lips. "Your Majesty no doubt has more important matters to disclose to me than the state of my manners. To have roused me from sleep at this hour of the night."

"Hech, hech—hoity-toity! Hear you that, Doddie Home? And you, Johnnie? Frae an Edinburgh goldsmith!"

"Insolent, Sire," Dunbar averred.

"Your Majesty has all along been over-kind to this upjumped usurer!" Ramsay, who had never got on with Heriot, said.

"Maybe, maybe. You think so, Johnnie? What do *you* say, Vicky? Hae I been at fault wi' Geordie Heriot?"

"If you have, Sire, it is not in being over-kind to him!" the Duke gave back. "Your Majesty knows a deal better than Ramsay does what you owe, what we all owe, what the realm owes, to Master Heriot."

That man coughed. He was grateful to his friend—but this harping on debts and owing was scarcely calculated to improve the situation. "I am sorry, Sire, if you consider me lacking in proper respect," he said. "You know that my duty and regard for Your Majesty is of old standing, and has always been of the greatest. If I am less forthcoming than sometimes, it may be because I am but new wakened from sleep . . ."

"Sleep, heh? You weary o' our royal bounty and hospitality, Geordie? We feed and wine and entertain you right royally, and then you go hiding awa' and sleeping, before we oursel' hae retired. And waken crabbit as a bear! Shame on you, man!"

"That is one way to describe my case, Highness. Another would be to point out that I have been on a long and tiring journey to Scotland and back, on Your Majesty's affairs, and returned to much labour, having to remain in London overnight to deal with my own affairs. Then hasten down to Greenwich, only to be sent back to London overnight to obtain gifts for Your Majesty's bestowal, so that I lost another night's sleep. And have all this day been all but deafened by cannon-fire on shipboard. If I am weary, Sire, it is in your service."

"My heart bleeds for you!" James observed. "But where were you, man, twa nights ago? Vicky here managed to win back to his sovereign lord's side, and his duty—but no' Geordie Heriot."

"My lord Duke does not have the oversight of a trade and business of much weight and complexity, Sire—a trade which, though humble, enables Your Majesty to entertain me, my lords here, and the King of Denmark, thus!"

The monarch, now in a state of complete nudity save for his hat—from which he was always loth to part—narrowed his great eyes, drew a deep breath—and then burst into hooting laughter.

"Sakes—guid for you, Geordie!" he cried. "A right stout answer. Aye—*audaces fortuna juvat timidosque repellit,* eh? Did you hear that, Johnnie? Frae your upjumped usurer? Tak note—as an upjumped viscount! Ah, weel, Geordie—if that's the way o' it, it becomes us to mak the best o' it while you *are* wi' us—and be gratefu', eh? What hae you to tell me, then? Out wi' it."

Heriot frowned. "Sire—what I have to say, relative to the business you sent us on, is highly personal to your royal self." And he looked meaningly at Dunbar and Haddington.

"No' suitable for the ears o' these friends o' mine, Geordie?" James asked, being eased into a bed-robe.

"No, Sire," the other said firmly.

"So be it. Off wi' you, then," the King ordered, waving his hands in shooing gesture to the others. "Master Usurer, here, doesna cherish your company, my lords! But you'll let our Vicky stay, Geordie—will you no'?"

Looking daggers, the earl and viscount withdrew.

"Aye, now—we'll have it," James said, in a different voice, as the door closed. He sat down on the bunk bed.

"Yes, Sire. I do not know how much my lord Duke has told you. But, to be brief, we discovered the reason and terms of the Master of Gray's claim upon you. And the steps to take to come to a suitable arrangement, on Your Majesty's behalf. As instructed."

"You did, did you!" James looked wary. "Suitable, eh? How suitable?"

"Twenty thousand pounds Scots, Sire. To be found for the Master by a special commission of judges, sitting in private. No open trial."

James licked thick lips, and did not speak.

"We strongly advise that you agree such a settlement, Sire. For your own advantage. As does the Lord Advocate Hamilton, and the Chancellor."

"You say so? When I desire the advice o' my Advocate and my Chancellor I'll spier at them," the King declared. "I didna send you up to Scotland to collogue wi' *them.*"

"We were in some doubt, James, as to what you *did* send us up for!" the Duke put in, grimly. "It was less than clear."

"You speak when you're spoken to, Vicky Lennox! And you, Geordie Heriot, tell my why I should pay twenty thousand pounds to that fell Patrick Gray?"

"Because, Sire, it appears that you lawfully owe him the moneys. And if you do not pay it, he will make public much which would serve your present case very ill. About the proposed Danish troops to invade England from Scotland when Queen Elizabeth was ill—which was what the money was for, was it not? Parliament, the English parliament, would not like to hear of that. Or, perhaps, *would* like it, to your cost!"

The monarch fiddled amongst his private parts. "Twenty thousand pounds is a lot o' siller," he said.

"Less than half what Gray is asking."

"This is mail, just—blackmail, man Geordie."

Heriot and Lennox exchanged glances. The first waited for his friend to speak—but when he did not do so, coughed, and went on.

"I fear that there is more blackmail than that, Sire."

"Eh?" The look shot at him was sharp, calculating, vigilant. "You say so? Gray?"

"Not . . . yet! No, Sire—the Earl of Orkney."

A long sigh escaped from the none so slack royal lips. "So-o-o! You've been right busy, eh? Wheaseling oot a foul, stinking commerce! The evil nundinations o' lying men!"

"Was not that what you sent us to do, Sire? That you might be freed from their toils?"

James did not answer that directly. He considered his unwashed person thoughtfully for a space—and then looked up. "What hae you discovered?"

"That Logan of Restalrig is dead—died in poverty, strangely. That the Master and the Lord Home, cousins, are amongst his heirs general—and likely to cause trouble. That the ill-spoken-of Casket Letters of the Queen, your royal mother, were at some time delivered by Logan to the Lord Robert Stewart, late Earl of Orkney, and are now in his son Patrick's possession. That Earl Patrick is now in dire need of money, much money—and the Master of Gray has learned of the Letters, and is seeking to buy them. Hence requires this old debt of Your Majesty's repaid."

"Aye." Clearly none of this was unknown to James Stewart. "Filthy, stinking commerce, as I said. And you'd hae me to pay, man?"

"Yes, Sire. Weighing the bad against the worse, yes. It will be no new thing, I think? To pay?"

"That is as may be. You believe I'd do better wi' Patrick Gray than Patrick Stewart?"

"I . . . I think so, Sire. Gray would not wish to bring down the Crown—although he might wish to change the wearer! Stewart might!"

"That is my opinion, James," Lennox said. "And Dunfermline's."

"*He* kens o' this? You told Seton, man . . . ?"

"He knew of it. From . . . other sources. And, of course, much else."

"Much else? What?"

Lennox hesitated. "Of more stinking commerce, James. Which you may, or may not, know of. Concerning Logan. And his poverty. A rich man, if a rogue—and suddenly poor. His estates sold. Sold, Sire, to friends of yours. Last year. To George Home, who has just left us—Lord High Treasurer of Scotland, as you have made him. He bought Fast Castle and Flemington. But did not pay for them—or fifteen thousand merks of the price. And James Elphinstone, Lord Balmerino, your Chief Secretary of State, bought Restalrig and Gunsgreen. And still owes eighteen thousand merks. Why should Logan sell all his patrimony? To *your* ministers? And not be paid for it? There was more blackmail than one going on in Scotland!"

"You tell me that, Vicky? Bad. Aye, bad. Unsuitable. Shamefu', even. But no concern o' mine, mind. I'll hae a bit word wi' Doddie Home."

"I suggest, James, that a word will scarce be enough! As you heard, Patrick Gray and the Lord Home, George Home's cousin, are amongst Logan's heirs. They make an ill pair to tangle with. They are going to want that money—and any more amissing likewise. Or know why not. And, it is likely, shout aloud until they get it! Not pleasing, for two so close to yourself, your ministers."

"You're no' suggesting, Vicky Lennox, that *I* had a hand in this?"

"I did not suggest that, Sire," his cousin said carefully.

"As well, man—as well." James was up, hobbling about the wooden decking on his bare feet. "But . . . see you now. A man forfeit in law has no *rights* in law. Is that no' a fact? And if no rights, then no credit. Debts wouldna need to be repaid to him. Or his heirs."

"But Logan was not forfeit in law when he died."

"No-o-o. But he could still be tried. For yon ill Gowrie business. And found guilty—as he was, you may be sure. And so forfeited. Is that not so?"

"Lord!" Lennox whispered. "Try a dead man? And forfeit him thereafter? To save . . . your friends money!"

"Why not? He was a scoundrel, yon Logan, and well deserves it! I've been keeping my eye on his attorney. Another ill rogue. A notary o' Eyemouth, one George Sprott. Up to the neck in Logan's villainies. He'll serve us nicely. We'll squeeze Master Sprott—and Logan, late o' Restalrig, wi' him. And see justice done—and save a bit siller!"

"Then . . . then you *knew* of all this! You knew of this man Sprott. Nothing of it all came unknown to you?"

"I ken a wheen things going on in Scotland, although I'm no' there in my royal person, Vicky. Ooh, aye—I'm still King o' Scots. And no' so blate as some folks reckon."

His cousin could find no words.

Heriot could. "Sire—it seems that little or nothing which we have told you is news to you. But it makes ill telling, ill hearing. It but confirms what we saw and learned—that matters are in a poor way in Scotland. The country is, in fact, ill governed. My lord of Dunfermline is a good man enough, but not strong. And I fear there are rogues about him. You said, when you left to come South, that you would return at least every three years. It is now three years since 1603. I believe that you should return to your own country. For a space. Let men see that it still has a King. Put matters to rights. My lord Duke and I are in agreement that this is very necessary."

"Yes, indeed," Lennox substantiated.

"You are, eh? In your wisdom, you agree, the pair o' you? To teach me my God-appointed task and duty! Right fortunate I am! But, see you, I've got a wheen wits o' my ain! And twa Privy Councils to advise me, forby. I ken the state Scotland is in. And meantime, I prefer to govern it frae here. Aye, frae here. By your leave! Yon's an unchancy realm, wi' ower many rogues in it, lawless rogues such as I've had to deal wi' all my days. I had my bellyfu' o' them, waesucks! I'll deal wi' them through others, now, see you. And if some o' the dealers I maun use are rogues too—well, Scotland's a great place for the like. And they can maybe best deal wi' their ain kind. Forby, the English need my presence here yet awhile—aye they do so. I'll return to Scotland in my ain time, Geordie Heriot."

"As you say, Sire. Forgive me if I seemed to take a liberty. But we saw many signs of misgovernment there. And your ministers scarcely in good control."

"Aweel—Vicky at least will hae the opportunity to put that to rights," the King declared, chuckling suddenly. "For he's going right back to Scotland, forthwith. My royal representative, wi' ample powers to disrogue the rogues! I've called a parliament, see you—a meeting o' the Estates. Moreover, for your especial convenience, Vicky, I've called it for Perth. So that you can bide wi' your bit whoor, Mary Gray, at yon Methven! Aye—you will open and preside ower the parliament, as my viceroy, Cousin, and guide it to good decisions, guide it well."

Lennox began to speak, but thought better of it.

"Mind, you'll hae some help in the matter, forby Seton and Elphinstone and the others. Doddie Home will go up wi' you, to lead the debates on this matter o' bishops. So you can see he pays his just debts, eh? And Elphinstone too. It should be a right righteous and reforming parliament, wi' Vicky Stewart in the chair—for you'll likewise hae the comfort and support o' a wheen bishops and twa archbishops I've made. The Lord's Spiritual. As is right and proper."

"Bishops . . . ?" Lennox repeated. "How, bishops? There are no bishops in Scotland now—at least, none who rule as such. No bishops have sat in the Scots parliament for forty years and more."

"But they will, frae now on, man. In my united kingdoms of Great Britain shall I have Lords Spiritual in England and no' in Scotland? Am I no' head o' both kirk and state in both, and my powers and rights no' to be limited by a wheen arrogant presbyters and so-called divines? Bishops will be restored in Scotland forthwith, as the proper leaders o' Christ's flock, for whom I deputise here on earth. And this parliament which you will preside ower will establish it. Dinna stand there shaking your head, man—this is my royal will, edict and command. I hae appointed the said archbishops and bishops, and they will attend the said parliament. To be sure, you'll find them a right help in your worthy efforts to improve the state o' my auld realm o' Scotland!"

While his hearers digested that, the monarch climbed into his bunk, as an indication that the audience was all but over.

"To say that you surprise me, Sire, scarce meets the case," the Duke got out, after a pause. "The wisdom of this policy is highly doubtful, I think."

"The wisdom o' my policies is for *my* decision, no' yours, Vicky Stewart. And God be thankit for that! Now—awa to your beds. We've a lang and busy day ahead o' us the morn, wi' yon Christian awa at last, praise be! And Geordie is fair yawning his heid off!"

"Do I go North again with my lord Duke?" that man enquired.

"Na, na—you do not. You've got the oversight o' weighty trade and business you'll mind, on which so muckle depends—which Vicky hasna! You'll bide in London. But, nae doubt Vicky will carry a bit letter for you to the lassie Primrose!"

"We are betrothed to wed, Sire."

"Hech—you are? Waesucks—she's catched you then! Och, but you could do worse, man Geordie. Much worse. I'll maybe come to your wedding! But—watch you yon wee Primrose man. He'll mak an unchancy gudesire, I'm thinking, him!"

"I thank Your Majesty for your interest. But the wedding will not be for a year or so. Alison is young, yet."

"Is that a fact? You're no' that hot, then! Why wait? For she's ready, that one—ooh aye, she's ready. I've watched her. But—maybe you're getting a' you want without the waiting? Eh, Jinglin' Geordie?"

"Sire, Mistress Primrose is a young woman of virtue and honour . . ."

"To be sure—they a' are! When it comes to marriage. And so is Mistress Gray, eh, Vicky? Oh, I agree, I agree—but *varium et mutabile semper femina*! Mind, I'm no sure my Annie is going to like this, Geordie."

"I see no reason why not, Sire," Heriot said stiffly. "Alison has served Her Majesty well and faithfully. The business of her dismissal was ill-judged, unkindly done. We know now why . . ."

"You do, heh? Then that's mair than I do. Why, man? What was at the back o' yon stramash?"

The other cleared his throat. "It is a difficult matter to speak of, Sire. But we believe that the Queen has also been paying this blackmail to the Earl of Orkney—whether with Your Majesty's knowledge, or without."

"Ooh, aye—you believe so? Go on," the King said, non-committally.

"She has been forced to give the Earl jewels. Presumably to buy his silence. Over these unhappy Letters, we do presume. When Margaret Hartside brought those pieces to me, to sell, Her Majesty believed she was acting for the Earl—which she was not. Mistress Hartside is secretly wed to Buchanan of Scotscraig, who was your Almoner and is one of the Earl's gentlemen. He gave her these jewels, saying that they were a gift from his master. To sell them for *him*, Buchanan. That they might set up house in Orkney."

"Maybe aye, and maybe hooch-aye!" the monarch observed. "I commend your simple faith in the lassies, Geordie! I kent o' the marriage—but I didna let on to Annie. Yon Buchanan had his uses! But the bringing o' the gewgaws to you was fell stupid! Annie couldna do otherwise than she did."

"Her Majesty wrongfully punished two innocent young women."

The King leered at him. "You think so? Och, awa to your bed, man. You are a right bairn in some matters, Geordie Heriot! And yet you presume to advise me, the King, on how to deal wi' my subjects! Forget the whole business, man."

"I would wish to speak with the Queen on the subject, Sire, before I do," the other said stubbornly. "Have I your permission?"

"No, you havena! You will say nothing more o' this. I will hae a bit word wi' her, mysel'. Now—be off. You did nane so badly up in Scotland, the pair o' you—but there's a lot you dinna ken, nor are like to ken. Aye—and Vicky, when you go North, you can agree that twenty thousand pounds Scots for the limmer Patrick Gray. But no' a plack mair, mind. Begone, then—and a guid night to you both. What's left o' it!"

* * *

The next day's activities were to centre on Gravesend, where the Lord Mayor, aldermen and city company representatives of London came down to bid farewell to the Danish monarch whose squadron of ships was brought up-river thus far to anchor. Great play was made by the city deputation, in lengthy speeches, on the fact that it was from Gravesend, considered to be the seaward limit of the Port of London, that many illustrious sailors had ventured forth in the past, Willoughby, Frobisher and so on. All this, and the prodigal present-giving from Christian which followed, too much longer than James at least found suitable; and by the time that the royal party embarked to be rowed out to the Danish flagship, *The Three Crowns*, amidst more cannonading, His Britannic Majesty's patience had worn very thin. Farewells, he indicated, in a loud whisper, could be over-extended. George Heriot still accompanied his royal master, although his box was now nearly empty.

On the Danish ship there was to be another banquet; and Christian, probably realising that if he delayed until the meal was over, or even well-established, he would almost certainly be in no state to present anything, plunged straight into present-giving. Every one of James's gentlemen, like the foreign ambassadors, got a jewel—even Heriot found himself the recipient of a handsome ring, not gilded this one, with a strange coat-of-arms. There followed the gifts to his hosts, his sister, her husband and their son, the Prince Henry. Anne was presented with a smacking kiss, and Christian's portrait set in diamonds, a princely gift indeed. James was delighted to get a copper cannon, especially cast in Helsingborg in Sweden, and bearing the British royal arms—and nothing would do but that it should be tried out there and then, powder produced and the gun fired, not once but many times. Happily for the less enthusiastic, practically all the flagship's gunpowder had been expended the day before, otherwise Prince Henry might have had to wait a long time before getting *his* gift. The Danish monarch had taken a great fancy to his nephew, and now displayed the scale of his affection in truly majestic fashion. Apparently the boy, asked earlier what he most desired in all the world, had declared that he would like a boat all of his own. And now his Uncle Christian took Henry's shoulder and pointed to a full-rigged naval sloop-of-war, moored next to the flagship, one of the Danish squadron. It was his, he shouted, bellowing his laughter and beating his nephew almost to the deck with avuncular affection, all his own, with all its crew, all its armament, ammunition, equipment and furnishings, down to the ship's cat. At least, that is what he seemed to be declaring, for Christian's English was uncertain. Utterly overwhelmed, the boy could only stare open-mouthed, wordless—and try to remain upright.

Over the side they all went again, necessarily, to go inspect this astonishing gift, Anne distinctly tight-lipped and disapproving, forseeing all sorts of complications and disasters hereafter, and even James somewhat put out. He had been very pleased with his cannon, admittedly—but this sloop for his son had, he counted, *eighteen* cannon, and was in fact a more modern warship than any he could show in the fleet inherited from Elizabeth. Moderation, he muttered to Ludovick of Lennox as they were rowed out, moderation was in all things most necessar'. Christian and Henry, however, were in transports of enthusiasm.

The sloop, thereafter, was explored from stem to stern, above and below decks, forecastle and quarter-galleries such as no English vessel boasted, displayed and explained, and the officers introduced to their new young master. All this took a long time, and King James, very much supernumerary, grew ever more fretful and disgruntled. He was, of course, hungry as well as slightly put out, and he feared that the banquet back on the flagship would be ruined. Christian was impervious to all hints. James therefore summoned his Lord High Admiral, who seemed to be the right man for the occasion, and ordered him to do something, anything, to get them off this wretched sloop.

Charles, formerly Lord Howard of Effingham, now Earl of Nottingham, who had outfaced Elizabeth Tudor on more than one occasion, to say nothing of defeating the Spanish Armada, was not the man to be diffident with monarchs especially foreign ones. A crusty old sea-dog, he had already lost all patience with the proceedings, and was only too glad to go up to Christian tap him on the shoulder and tell him that it was time that they returned to the flagship for the meal, otherwise they would miss the four o'clock tide to get back into Gravesend. King Christian was not interested in getting into Gravesend; he was concerned with showing his favourite nephew this ship—and said so. The Admiral was so bold as to insist, under the eye of his own monarch. Knowing that the Dane's English was doubtful, he shouted—in typical British fashion, with wretched foreigners—emphasising that four o'clock tide. Christian at least got the four o'clock bit, and delving into a capacious pocket, produced the fine round, gold watch which had been James's present to him, via George Heriot. It said two o'clock. Grinning widely, the Dane raised two fingers of his right hand, in a distinctly rude gesture, and continuing with the upward movement, brought the fingers up to his royal forehead, where he wiggled them at the Lord Admiral, hooting his accustomed laughter.

It was unfortunate perhaps that Nottingham, tough as he was, was nevertheless particularly thin-skinned over only one matter—the fact that he had fairly recently married, at the age of seventy, a new wife young enough to be his grand-daughter; and the

Countess was not only exceedingly goodlooking but of a renowned generosity of nature. He took Christian's waving fingers to represent horns. Queen Anne's tinkling laughter nearby—she did not like the Countess of Nottingham—did not help matters. The Admiral exploded into nautical language, and shook his gnarled fist in the monarch's face.

James looked in the other direction and declared plaintively that he wanted his dinner.

Lennox and other courtiers rushed to come between Nottingham and King Christian—who appeared to be more astonished than outraged. All perceived now that a prompt move back to *The Three Crowns* was probably advisable, James leading the way down into the barges, despite his usual horror of water. Prince Henry pleaded to be left behind with his new acquisition—but his mother called him smartly back to her side.

The banquet on the Danish flagship thereafter was less than usually successful. A certain preoccupation was evident all round, with tensions, both on the deck and in the cabin. Christian himself was probably the least affected—of course, with the flagon his unfailing consolation.

James brought matters to an abrupt close by again referring to the four o' clock tide, pointing out that his admirals assured him that if they let the ebb get too well established, the royal barges would be stuck in the mud off Gravesend. This got the Queen quickly to her feet, as it was intended to do; and though Christian protested that he had a fine fireworks display arranged for dusk, and that therefore all should pass the night on board, his brother-in-law, for once supported by Anne, declared that they had had enough of ships and bunks and water, and that he, for one, intended to sleep secure in Greenwich that night. Besides, the Danish squadron was to sail at first light, and that was an unchancy time for leave-taking.

So the fireworks were let off there and then, in very hurried and abortive fashion, and not even the ebullient Dane could raise much enthusiasm over what was inevitably something of a damp squib, with rockets pale in the sunshine and bangs much less satisfactory than real cannon-fire.

With the tide ebbing inexorably and James becoming agitated, things were rounded off at speed, and a distinctly final farewell taken of the Danish guests, Christian looking bewildered as to why and where his splendid leave-taking day had gone wrong. James, as a final gesture, handed over what remained in George Heriot's box for his brother-in-law to distribute to any of his people who might have been missed out, patting his fellow-monarch on the shoulder. Then he was hurrying down the steeply-sloping gangway to his barge, when abruptly the proximity of the sea below him seemed to strike him, and he waited until watermen came up to conduct him safely down, the while calling on his Maker to preserve him from the perils of the deep. Anne, a sea-king's daughter, laughed unkindly, but was not far behind. Only young Henry lingered, and had to be brought off in the last barge, by Lennox, along with the servitors and other nonentities, tears in his eyes at losing his new hero and kindred spirit. Christian wept too.

Heriot was also in the last barge, his usefulness now over for the time-being.

"Thank God that's all by with!" Lennox confided to his friend, in a corner of the barge. "Christian is all very well, but his visit has gone on for too long. I, for one, am exhausted. As are you, I swear. Not to mention our liege lord."

"No doubt," the other agreed. "But it is not *our* exhaustion, nor yet the King's, which concerns me so much as the exhaustion of the Exchequer! Funds, siller, pounds Sterling. This visit has cost a mint of money—and where it is all to come from, even to pay me back *my* share, the Lord knows. Even at the end there, King James threw away three-hundred pounds and more, in jewels. For nothing. The folly of it!"

"At least he got a whole ship in return—and that's worth a deal, I'd say! Have you ever seen the like? They say it cost twenty-five thousand pounds just to build that ship. What worth is a sloop-of-war, manned, armed and provisioned?"

"Worth little or nothing to a king who does not go to war!" Heriot asserted. "He can scarcely sell it—and parliament will not give him money in exchange for an addition to the realm's navy, I think. Besides, it is the Prince's ship—whatever he can find to do with it! I am interested in hard money, gold, silver, jewels—not ships and cannon. I am, to be sure, a tradesman and huckster, and no nobleman with a mind above such things!"

The Duke grinned. "Spoken like Geordie Heriot and none other! But you need not concern yourself overmuch about James's purse now, my friend—nor your loans to him. He told me, while we were waiting on yon ship, that he has won part of his battle with parliament—the English parliament. They have agreed to grant him four hundred thousand pounds immediately, for his personal expenditure—although they refuse to give him a fixed annual income in return for his surrender of his feudal dues. In exchange for the four hundred thousand pounds, they claim that he may no longer levy customs duties personally but must hand all such over to parliament—although the judges declare that he is entitled to do this, in law. So you ought to get your money back now, Geordie, never fear." Lennox sighed. "Would that my problems were as nearly solved."

"You think mine solved? I have yet to get the money out of the King's pocket. And if parliament is to take to itself customs duties, then I lose the customs of Harwich haven which James granted me before we went to Scotland. I have been arranging their efficient collection—at cost to myself. The Lord giveth—perhaps—and the Lord taketh away, certainly! Blessed be the name of the Lord!" Heriot smiled then, at his friend, for the first time for a while. "Forgive me, Vicky—I am a gloomy dog these days. And selfish. I am finding it hard to be so far away from my Alison. To be denied . . . what my being longs for. Yet you, I know well, are likewise so denied. I ask your pardon."

"Aye, Geordie—we are a sorry pair! For our ladies to shake their fair heads over! At least I shall be seeing mine soon again. And I shall require all Mary's wits and good offices to get me through this parliament at Perth, I fear. I am not happy about this imposition of bishops that James is set on. For myself, I care not whether we have bishops or presbyters or the Pope himself! But can you see Scotland lying down to this? Even though James has prepared the way, it seems."

"He has?"

"Oh, yes. James is cunning. He has been winning over this lord and that, giving his bishoprics to carefully chosen folk. Aye, and setting Glasgow against St. Andrews, Aberdeen against Brechin, and the like."

"He will not win over Andrew Melville and his like-minded friends, for all that."

"Ha—but here is more of his cunning. He has summoned Melville, and six others of the most prominent of the Kirk party, down here to London. A royal command. To explain to him their views. So that they will not be there to rouse the parliament. If they refuse to come, he can banish them. Possibly he hopes for that. Either way, he gains. You must agree, for a fool, he is not backward at getting his own way!"

"Who says James Stewart is a fool? Never George Heriot—only those who look on the surface, do not truly know the man. As he says himself, he's nane so blate and kens what's what! And that, I think, is putting it modestly. I find him a sore trial, yes—but, by God, I prefer to be his friend than his enemy! If sometimes, foolishly, I forget it!"

PART THREE

16

GEORGE HERIOT was at his promenading in St. Paul's Church, discussing the state of quite a number of prominent folks' credit with Sir William Herrick, now also Court jeweller, and alleged to be the richest money-lender in London, when a stranger approached them and rather diffidently requested the favour of a word or two with Master Heriot. He did not look, nor sound, like any sort of prosperous client, was modestly dressed, but had a certain air about him which appeared to be compounded of an odd mixture of demonstrative if superficial self-denigration, contained force and down-damped humour. Heriot had seen him before somewhere. Excusing himself to Herrick, he led the newcomer aside, into the same side-chapel where he had once taken the Duke of Lennox.

"I should know your face, sir," he said—and that was true, for apart altogether from the demeanour and bearing, the countenance was unusual, with a great swelling brow which seemed to dominate all, and receding hair, above keen, almost foxy features, with a long nose and chin and pointed little auburn beard. The eyes were deep, dark, and rather sad. He was approximately Heriot's own age.

"You will have seen me at certain Court masques, Master Heriot—since I think that you are not a play-goer? My name is Shakespeare—Will Shakespeare, of the Globe Playhouse, in Southwark. And of His Majesty's Players."

"Ah—to be sure. That is it. I saw you at Wilton once, I think. With my Lord Southhampton's company."

"My lord has been sufficiently kind to advance my poor offerings, in what we are assured are the right directions!" the other agreed gravely—although Heriot did not miss the faint mockery behind the words.

"Your offerings, as you name them sir, are their own best patron. You have, I believe, written many plays and sonnets and masques, all well-spoken of by those knowledgeable in such matters. I have heard that you have not failed even to write of the sad plight of money-lenders and usurers! Her Majesty indeed, for a little, took to calling me Shylock!"

"My Merchant was of Venice, sir, not of Scotland—but a man of parts, nevertheless. He had a long memory, a strong sense of justice and a grim humour. I am told that the Scots very generally display the same? Even His Majesty's royal self!"

"H'mm. Perhaps. And what can I do for you, Master Shakespeare? You now have no lack of wealthy patrons, I understand. It cannot be that you wish to borrow money, I think?"

"No—on that I can set your mind at rest, Master Heriot, at least! As well as counselling you never lend to folk of the play and theatre anyway—for their own good! I come to you because His Majesty sends me."

"The King? To me? Here's a strange charge, surely? I know nothing of plays or playwrights, nor yet of masques or costume either . . ."

"But you do of Scotland, sir—which is to the point." The other looked around him. "I come of a sacrilegious, not to say impious profession, I fear, and I find a church scarce the place for discussion of my craft. I did call at your premises at the Exchange, and your man sent me here. Perhaps we could speak more freely there?" The man had a Midland countryman's accent, overlaid by an actor's emphasis and intonations.

"As you will. It took some time for me to accustom myself to doing business in this church, I assure you. It is not so in Scotland. Let us move out, yes—but better than my shop, there is an ale-house just beyond the churchyard here . . ."

Seated in a corner of a dark, low-ceiled tavern, with beakers of ale before them, the man Shakespeare came to the point. "King James is concerned to improve—or perhaps I should say, correct—the view, the notion, of the Scots and Scotland held here in England," he said, picking his words. "You, I have no doubt, know well that in truth your fellow-countrymen are scarcely loved, sir! The fault may not all be their own, but there is little question but that most Englishmen would fain see them all back in Scotland tomorrow—and rejoice! This is unfortunate, lamentable—but a fact, whatever the reasons."

"I know it well, never fear," Heriot nodded. "I could scarcely help doing so. But I am interested to hear that the King is so concerned. I had not thought that it would much trouble him."

"It seems that it does. Sufficiently for him to seek the aid of such as myself. He would have me to write a play, which would make folk here see Scotland and the Scots in a kinder light, make them better aware of the virtues of your nation, its antiquity and history. He believes that this would benefit his united kingdom."

"You surprise me, sir—or at least, His Majesty does. But then, he seldom fails to do that! A monarch who would think of such a thing is something new! Could a *play* have such effect?"

"I know not. But the King believes it so. I have never written one with such an object. But staged and enacted, many see and speak of such productions. Who knows what their influence might be? Who am I to refute our illustrious and so erudite sovereign?"

Heriot ignored the thinly veiled mockery in that. "This play, then, is to be about Scotland's history? That, I fear, is a bloody one, sir, from first to last. I do not know whether this is the stuff of plays and entertainment!"

"Tragedy can be as entertaining as comedy, Master Heriot—I can move people to tears more easily than I can make them laugh! And they will remember the sorrow long after they have forgot the merriment."

"As to theme—has the King any notions for you, Master Shakespeare?"

"Yes, indeed. He would wish me to magnify and extol the antiquity of his own royal line, as is to be expected. But he is concerned to emphasise the *nobility* of the Scots—since he perceives that the impression made here in England by many who have come South in the royal train is scarce of that quality!"

"That I can understand. I fear my countrymen, as a whole, who have followed the King, make but a poor showing. But then, it is seldom the best who leave their own land. Nor who form princes' courts. I sometimes think that I myself should have remained in Scotland."

"If the others were all like you, sir, I think King James would have little need of my services! No—I do not flatter you. Your reputation stands high in this city for honest dealing, shrewd wits and a modest bearing and civility, less than usual in such of your compatriots as we find amongst us."

"You exaggerate, Master Shakespeare—as perhaps playwrights

will tend to do! Both the good and the ill. But—how can this paragon of shrewdness and modesty aid you, since I know nothing of your craft?"

"It is the King's belief that you can help me to know the *Scots*, the true Scots. He says that I will learn little of them, or of Scotland, from the nobles and courtiers that flock around him. But Geordie Heriot, as he names you, is different, it seems. A man of the people, who has yet his roots deep in the soil of Scotland—for I understand that you come of a landed family, sir? The King thinks most highly of you."

"Sometimes you would scarcely suspect it! But I will help you if I can. What is required?"

"Guidance, first as to theme, and then as to scene and character. For I am all too well aware of my own ignorance in this matter. We need a dramatic situation, where a great evil is committed, but by a man for whom the playgoers may feel some sympathy, some understanding of his lapse and fall into temptation. It must be an ancestor of His Majesty. And there must be a strong part for a woman, or women—this all insist upon. Though not the King! Moreover, as you will understand, since it is to please and edify the English, battle and intrigue against England will not serve—and, to my mind, most of Scottish history seems to be concerned with that! So the great Bruce and his successors, or any of the Jameses until this one, tend to fail us . . ."

"The death of James the First? *Our* James the First. Murdered by the Graham, before his English Queen's eyes—Joan Beaufort? At Perth. With Catherine Douglas barring the door against his assassins with her arm, broken to try save her liege. That has nothing to do with England."

"Aye—that would make notable drama. The King did indeed suggest it. But assassination of monarchs by their subjects is scarce suitable theme, he feels! After Guido Fawkes his plot. Moreover, he is greatly interested, it seems, in witchcraft. He has written a volume upon it—as you will know. He believes that Scots witches are of an especial sort, with great power of divination. He would have me to bring this in—indeed purposes to instruct me in the matter! The which I hope to escape! He therefore suggests the case of King MacBeda the usurper—he who, it seems, slew King Duncan whose general he was, and ruled in his stead. Witchcraft, King James claims, was partly responsible. His wife, Grula or some such name, was closer to the throne than was MacBeda himself, and spurred on her husband's ambition. The chronicler Holinshed tells of this, the King says. It seems a likely theme. You know of this MacBeda, Master Heriot?"

"To be sure. Though most in Scotland call him MacBeth. And his wife was Gruach, grand-daughter of Kenneth—Kenneth the Third. I would not call MacBeth usurper, any more than half the kings before him. He was of the royal line, as was his wife, and strong where Duncan was weak. Scotland has always needed strong kings. And he reigned well, for many years. As to witchcraft, I know not."

"All that is nothing harmful to the drama of it. King James sees it not as a subject slaying his lawful monarch so much as a fellow prince replacing another, under the dominance of an evil woman. He is strong on this—the sin of women dominating men, especially in the rule of a state. Only ill can come of women with overmuch power, he says—which will scarce please those who loved the late Gloriana, I fear! So the murderer must die—but the woman to suffer the worse fate. And at the hands of the murdered King's son. From which son, of course, our liege lord claims descent."

"In somewhat round-about fashion! But the throne descends from that Malcolm, yes. If you think this so old a story—for it was five hundred years ago and more—will make a play to cause the English better to love the Scots, then I will aid you the best of my poor ability. But, sir—I do not see in what I may be of use?"

"You can keep me right on matters Scottish, customs, titles, lands. And the King says that, perchance, we might go to Scotland hereafter, so that I may learn something of the true scene and setting."

"Ah! Now, sir, you speak to the point! I ever seek excuse to return to my native land. Or royal permission to do so, which is something different."

"So His Majesty indicated! He said that I would find you nothing backward."

"When do we go?"

"That I know not. The King did not make it clear, for certain. I am acting, myself, just now, in a comedy at The Globe—*Love's Labour's Lost*. You may have heard of it? It would not be convenient to go until the run is ended. Besides, King James, I think, has the Scots virtue of thrift well developed! He does not wish me to travel to Scotland at any great cost to himself. His suggestion is that I take the company of the King's Players with me and that we play in Edinburgh and other Scottish cities, and so earn the price of our journey!"

"That certainly sounds like James Stewart!" Heriot admitted. "When will this be, think you?"

"Our comedy should run for six weeks yet. Mid-autumn—October. Would that be too late for travel to Scotland? Snow? Ice?"

"Scotland is not Muscovy, sir—nor yet the Arctic wastes! Our West has a gentler winter than you have here in London, our East drier. October will serve very well."

"I learn, Master Heriot—I learn! And where should I best go, then, to learn of this MacBeda? To set the scene of the play?"

"That I shall have to think on. As I mind it, Perth, Dunsinane, Birnam, come to mind. Lumphanan on the Dee. MacBeth was Mormaor of Moray, and Elgin his capital, I think. I must refresh my memory."

"Very well. And if you can think of aught wherein I may read more of all this ancient story, pray inform me. Meantime, I shall seek out the chronicles of Holinshed. I thank you for your courtesy, Master Heriot."

"Another mug of ale, sir?"

* * *

The anticipated summons came some ten days later, and Heriot duly repaired to Hampton Court, the vast palace which Cardinal Wolsey had built a century before and presented to his monarch—who had repaid him by execution. He found Will Shakespeare there already; but when the call to the presence came, it was for Heriot only, with the playwright left in the anteroom.

James was tottering alone about a great gallery lit by many windows, hung with crystal candelabra, the walls adorned with hangings and rows of stiff-looking portraits which had the appearance of being all painted by the same hand. There was a long central table, with many chairs drawn up to it, paper, books and scrolls spread, as though for a meeting.

"Aye, Geordie—it's yoursel'?" James greeted. "Shut the door behind you, man, and come here." He was moving over to the far corner of the gallery. "See this, now. Easy seen this house was built by a churchman! It's a squint, see. Right cunning." He had pulled aside a tapestry of gods and goddesses beside a waterfall, to show behind it a narrow door contrived in the panelling, unnoticeable save to one who knew of its presence. Opening this, the King revealed a small dark chamber, cut in the thickness of the walling, only about six feet square, furnished but with a bench. Beckoning the other in, James pointed to the back of the door on which hung a sort of sliding shutter-device. Drawing this to one side, a series of oddly-placed holes, perhaps half-an-inch in diameter, were uncovered. Letting the tapestry fall back into place, amidst a puff of dust, and closing the door on them, he pointed. The darkness of the garderobe was illuminated by rays of light coming through these holes which the shutter had covered. "Have a peek through there, Geordie."

Peering, the other could see, through the various holes, about two-thirds of the gallery, including almost all of the central table.

"Holes cut in the arras," James went on. "Where the eyes o' thae shameless hussies are—so's they'll no' be noticed. *I* noticed it, mind. The holes. One time at a meeting. I kent it couldna be moths—no' just there. That's how I found this bit convenience. Right handy, on occasion. I use it now and again. So this gallery makes a suitable place for some meetings, see you!"

"Very interesting, Sire," Heriot acknowledged, warily.

"You can hear, too—och, fine and clear. There must be some kind o' laird's lug some place—though I havena found it." The King opened the door very quietly, and peered round the side of the tapestry, to make sure that no one had entered the gallery. "Out wi' you—quickly! Aye, then. You'll ken where to go, Geordie. You'll no' have to cough or sneeze, mind. That wouldna doo." As an afterthought, he added, "The Privy Council whiles meet here. When I so order. Other meetings, forby."

"Ah—I see! Convenient, as Your Majesty says. And my Lord Salisbury and his spies have not yet smelt this out?"

"Eh? Cecil? Na, na—he kens naething o' it. Or he wouldna have said some o' the things he has done at yon table! When he's been left to preside in place o' my royal sel'!"

"H'mmm. And why me, Sire? Where do I come into this? You do not wish me to spy on Master Shakespeare, do you?"

"Sakes, no! But I dinna want him seeing it, mind. I can trust *you*, Geordie—but others havena to ken o' this. No—there's a Privy Council to be held here in an hour frae now. No' an ordinary meeting. I've commanded that limmer Andra Melville, and his Kirk cronies frae Scotland, to compear before me and the Privy Council here. He's a proud, upstuck and arrogant deevil, yon, as I ken well.

I want him to deliver himsel' o' his sentiments and treasons before these English lords and bishops—so maybe they'll ken better what I have to contend wi' in Scotland frae these black corbies o' divines, and accord me the better support. But they'll no' ken one-half o' what he's at, being only English. And the *Scots* members o' this Council, Vicky Lennox and Geordie Home, are up at Perth for the parliament. I canna invite the likes o' you, Geordie, to attend at a Privy Council, or any no' sworn into it. So you'll bide in yon bit squint-hole, and watch and listen. And there'll be *twa* o' us who'll understand what Maister Melville and his crew are at! You've sharp wits for some things, Geordie, and just the man for this."

"I do not know that I like the notion, Sire. Of spying on my fellow-countrymen . . ."

"I didna ask you if you *liked* it, man—I'm commanding it! A leal duty you owe to your monarch. I whiles wonder if you're no' developing ower delicate a stomach for an Edinburgh money-lender, Geordie Heriot! You'll look and listen, in there, and afterwards we'll have a bit crack about it. For the weal o' the realm o' Scotland! You understand? Aye—well, now go and tell yon guard to have the man Shakespeare in."

With the playwright bowed in, and obviously somewhat over-awed by the company and surroundings, they had a further discussion on the proposed Scottish play. James was quite decided now that it should be on the theme of MacBeda—as he called him—Duncan and Gruath. He dismissed Heriot's suggestion that Malcolm Canmore, Duncan's son, and his Saxon-English Queen Margaret, might provide a more cheerful and profitable subject, as representing Scottish-English co-operation, on the grounds that tragedy was the real stuff of drama; moreover, Margaret had been much too strong-willed a woman, and had largely ruled Scotland through her husband and sons thereafter—an ill thing and unsuitable to be published abroad. Had she not well-nigh imposed Popery on Scotland, in place of their own good native Celtic Church? Well, then.

Will Shakespeare seemed quite happy with MacBeth and Duncan, delating a little on some of the scenes he proposed to introduce. He was not so sure about the witchcraft aspect, however, having no real knowledge of the subject, and not seeing how it was to be fitted in.

James allowed him to get no further than that, but plunged forthwith into a deep and lengthy exposition of witchcraft and warlockry, satanism and demonology, in all their branches, with illustrations back to the Witch of Endor and other Biblical references, quotations, largely from his own works on the subject, Latin interpolations and classical parallels. In a spate, a flood, this continued—and since subject could by no means interrupt monarch, and there was no pause, the thing developed into a major discourse and dissertation to an increasingly dazed and lost audience of two.

Their ordeal was only terminated by a knocking at the door and the entry of the Earl of Salisbury himself—who looked distinctly disapproving at finding the King closeted with two such low-born nonentities—coming to inform that the Privy Councillors were now assembled, as were the Scotch presbyters, and awaiting His Majesty's summons to the table.

Frowning, James flapped an unwashed hand at the newcomer. "Aye, well—they can just wait," he declared. "Awa' and tell them so, Cecil man. I'll have them in when I'm ready, and no' before. You're interrupting me, sir—aye, intercluding and anteverting me, the King! I'm expounding a serious matter. You should ken better. *Experientia docet stultos!* When I want you, I'll send for you."

Shaken, the Principal Secretary of State, and earl, tip-toed out—but he got in a venomous glance at the monarch's companions in the by-going.

"A right tiresome limmer, that!" Majesty commented. "And crabbit, too. Now—where was I?"

Heriot cleared his throat, greatly daring. "Sire—do you not think . . . would it not be wise . . . in the circumstances, to leave this subject meantime? I swear Master Shakespeare and myself have been given as much, and more, than our poor wits can take in, on this deep matter of witchcraft. For the time being. We have not Your Majesty's profound and long-standing familiarity with the subject. We are but babes at this . . ."

"Aye—I can well believe that!" the King said severely. "I've been watching the pair o' you—and you've no' shown the interest and comprehension, aye the apperception and perpension I'd have expected frae men o' proper wits. But maybe you're right—and it would be wasting time to gie you mair, the now. Forby, there's the other matter," and he glanced conspiratorially from Heriot to the corner of the gallery where was the hidden chamber. "Maister Shakespeare—you have our royal permission to leave. I'll see you again, on this."

"Yes, Your Majesty. To be sure. I thank Your Majesty, I, ah, bid Your Majesty good-day and godspeed. If, if I may be so bold. With my deep thanks for your, your disquisition of these occult and difficult matters."

"Aye—then see you mak guid use o' what I've told you, man, in this stagery and dramaturgy. Our witches, mind, are to be maist notable and horrid, of a right powerfu' and diabolic quality. Nane o' your auld wifies wi' simples and herbs, drying up coo's udders and lassies' maidenheids, such as your dweebly English beldames go in for. Ours are otherwise in Scotland, Satan's ain sisterhood! So see you to it. Now—off wi' you. Geordie—you bide here."

When the playwright had bowed himself out, Heriot was hustled to the hidden garderobe behind the tapestry, with much shushing and adjurations as to no coughing, sneezing or coming out until he, James, came for him. Then the door was shut, and he was left in darkness save for the dusty lances of light coming through from the gallery windows opposite.

Sighing—not audibly, he hoped—the man sat on the bench, immured in the cause of duty.

He had not long to wait, at any rate. In only a minute or two the Privy Councillors came trooping into the gallery—and the King was proved right about a watcher being able to hear clearly as well as see, for Heriot was promptly regaled by the sight and sound of the highest in England's church, state and court manoeuvring and squabbling over precedency and who was to occupy the best seats round the table. Clearly, the Howards and Cecils were most adept as this endeavour. The head of the table was just opposite Heriot's squint-holes, but the rightmost aperture was so aligned that he could see the bottom also, where two secretaries sat. James's throne-like seat at the head was flanked by two lesser chairs, whereon sat the Lord Chancellor Ellesmere and the Principal Secretary of State, with the new Archbishop of Canterbury, Dr. Richard Bancroft on the former's right and Thomas Howard, Earl of Suffolk, Lord Chamberlain and Treasurer on the latter's left. When the King had sat down, all others did likewise, save for Salisbury, who, hunched and crooked of back, addressed His Majesty and Council. They were met together, he declared, not for any normal meeting but as His Majesty's command, to hear certain views and assertions put forward by prominent members of Christ's Church in Scotland, which views impinged upon and affected the processes of government in the state. Admittedly that state was the realm of Scotland; but since their kingdoms were now in measure united, in the person of their gracious and respected monarch, and would, it was to be expected, be further united hereafter; and moreover their Church of England was concerned—it was deemed proper that these views should be heard by the Council, from the mouths of spokesmen of the Presbyterian persuasion, in particular Master Andrew Melville, Principal and Rector of the University of St. Andrews. Master Melville and his colleagues had already been given opportunity to address sundry assemblies and parties, including some of their Spiritual lordships here present. This occasion was for a general exchange of views on policies, all attending entitled to hear and question the Scotchmen. With His Majesty's permission, he would call them in.

Yeomen of the Guard had barely got the door open when eight black-garbed figures strode in, as though to battle, heads high, led by a white-haired and bearded man of noble features, stern expression and flashing eye. He, and they all, were dressed in ordinary clothing, not Geneva gowns but noticeably plain and all black, relieved only by deep white linen collars—very different from the rich and colourful dress of the Privy Councillors—the few Puritan lords thereof had not been summoned, naturally—and the splendid canonicals and rochets worn by the bishops. Their leader marched half way up the chamber and then halted, to jerk his head towards the throne, in what would better be described as a curt nod rather than any bow. His colleagues did not even do as much. They were all men of middle years.

"Aye, Maister Andra—it's yoursel'," the King greeted genially. "And you, Maister Jamie. Yon's his nephew, wi' the big belly," he added, for the benefit of the assembled councillors. "I dinna mind a' the names o' the rest. But come up a bittie further, Andra—so's I can have a right sight o' you, man." James darted a quick glance towards the important tapestry to ensure that all would be within its range. "Aye, then—that'll do, that'll do."

"Sire—before aught else, I hereby do mak protest!" Andrew Melville cried strongly, in a clear but rich and powerful voice that contrasted notably with the monarch's thick and wetly conversational delivery. "We have been subjected to notable folly and intolerable affront. We have been forced to attend and listen to nae fewer than four sermons in what they ca' your Chapel Royal, a right scandalous place filled wi' shamefu' Popish mummery, altars, idols and superstitious imagery. Aye, sermons of a puerility and

L

extravagance and inordinate length, submitted by men as lacking in a' knowledge o' God's revealed Word and purpose as, it appears, they were in any decent education! And this, we were told, on Your Grace's direct command."

James's voice rose somewhat squeakily above the gasps and exclamations of his outraged councillors—but not in any evident disapprobation. "I wouldna have thought that *you* would object to sermons, Andra—or the length o' them! I've had to listen to some right dingers frae yoursel', man. Hours and hours, aye—at St. Giles and Holyrood. I jaloused they'd put you a' at ease—your ain coin o' exchange, just. Moreover, *fas est et ab hoste doceri*, eh? Aye, and it was fitting that you should be informed on the doctrines o' the supremacy o' the Crown and the rights o' the Episcopate, which we're a' here to decide on. I'd no' have you ignorant o' the case contrar to your ain, Maister Andra."

"Doctrines! Yon werena doctrines—they were sacrilegious encroachments on the prerogatives o' Almighty God, sir! The mouthings o' vain and uninformed profaners . . . !"

"Sire!" Archbishop Bancroft of Canterbury jumped to his feet. "This is beyond all bearing! This, this ranting demagogue must be silenced! To abuse Your Majesty and the leaders of Christ's Church in this fashion is utterly without precedent, and, and . . ." His voice was drowned in the angry agreement of the rest of the Privy Council.

"No' exactly without precedent, my lord Archbishop—no' for Maister Melville! I've heard him at it before—ooh, aye. And you mauna ca' him a ranting demagogue, mind—for he's the Principal o' a great university, and former Moderator o' the General Assembly. And no' only in Scotland, forby—he was Professor o' the Humanities at Geneva, one time. Is that not so, Andra?" James was smiling happily—as well he might.

Melville drew breath, as well *he* might—for he was far from a fool, and could be playing into the King's hands. "I have made my protest, Sire," he answered, more quietly, "as I was in duty bound. On a matter of principle. *Liberavi animum meum.* As Your Grace will agree is wise."

"Ooh, aye. But principles can be mistaken, man. *Hominis est errare*. And again, *graviora quaedam sunt remedia periculis!* Eh, my lords?" The King looked around him, beaming.

The Privy Councillors considered each other, at a loss, and stirred and coughed uncomfortably in their seats.

"Aye well, Andra—we'll let thae fleas stick to the wa', meantime.

But there's some points need clearing up, see you. In matters o' policy, no' principle. You and your like refuse and deny the office o' bishop. Yet you found a' on the Word, the Word o' God as revealed in Holy Writ. Is that no' so? Well, then—tell you me any place in Holy Writ where the presbyter or presbytery is named without above it a bishop? Tell me that, Andra Melville!"

"The word bishop, Sire, is not such as you interpret it. In Holy Writ. The word bishop and angel were aye interchangeable in the early Church. And angel but means messenger. Messengers we'd accept!" Melville actually smiled, if thinly. "But would you? I dinna see even your prelatical friends genuflecting before the Archangel Richard, here!"

That at least exchanged grins for frowns on some non-ecclesiastical faces.

James hooted. "I'll mind that one, Andra! But you're wrang, man—wrang! Angel and bishop are the same, aye—but the angels o' the New Testament were no' just messengers. They were men in high authority in the Church. In the Blessed Revelation didna John write to the Angels o' the Seven Churches in Asia? The Angel o' the Church in Sardis, the Angel o' the Church in Thyatira, the Angel o' the Church in Philadelphia and so on. They were the men in authority ower those churches. Bishops. John didna write to the Presbytery o' Sardis, nor yet the General Assembly o' Philadelphia! Is Holy Writ, and John wrang then?"

"Holy Writ is never wrong. Only the interpretation o' it."

"And *your* interpretation is the only right one? A' else wrang? Have I no' the finest scholars in Europe, some frae Scotland, working on Holy Writ to mak it intelligible to a' men? Even my lords, here! And you claim misinterpretation, Andra Melville!"

"I spoke of interpretation, no' translation, Sire. There is a difference. Name me Your Grace's authority to create and impose bishops in Holy Writ."

"Guidsakes, man—you question my divine right as the Lord's Anointed! God's Vice-Regent here on earth in these kingdoms?"

"In matters secular, no. In such, I am your subject. But in matters divine and religious—yes! I have said before, and to your face, that there are two kings and two kingdoms. There is King James, the heid o' this Commonwealth, and there is Christ Jesus the King o' His Kirk and people, whose subject James is, and of whose kingdom he is not a king, nor a lord, nor a head, but a member, God's vassal! I say . . ."

There was a great outcry from the Council, drowning out that thundered assertion, led by the prelates. James allowed the uproar ample scope, licking his lips and toying with his cod-piece.

He raised a hand, at length. "Aye, well—you've heard Maister Andra's interpretation o' Holy Writ as applied to the Lord's Anointed, my lords. But even he grants me some small authority, in matters secular just. I ask him, then, as relevant to our discussion and exercitation, whether the assembling together o' my subjects, in one o' my burghs o' regality, contrar to my royal command, is or isna lawfu'?"

Melville shot a quick glance at his nephew. Both knew what was coming, and perceived the trap sent for them.

"A court of Christ's Kirk may meet where it will on Christ's earth, Sire," the nephew said reasonably. James Melville was a thick-set man of around fifty, plump, with rubicund features and of a more gentle disposition than his fiery uncle—but of proved equal determination.

"When the courts o' Christ's Kirk are made up o' subjects o' mine, sir, they are bound to obey my express commands in matters secular—that you'll no' deny? I commanded that they didna meet in General Assembly in my royal burgh o' Aberdeen a year past—but meet they did. And you, James Melville, led them in that defiance! Do you say that Assembly, therefore, was lawfu' or unlawfu'?"

"In God's law, lawful, sir."

"You claim, then, to ken God's law better than do I, His Anointed?"

"I do."

Into the rumble from the Council, his uncle raised his tremendous voice. "We all do. We are the ordained ministers o' Almighty God!"

James pointed a finger. "And you rate ordination higher than anointing man?"

"We do. We must. Or the Gospel is meaningless."

"You will note that, my lords—note well," James said, glancing round. "We are right notably instructed this day o' Our Lord! Maister Melville declares that any minister, any ordained minister soever, rates above the King! You heard him? That means every minister soever—Catholic priest, Puritan preacher, vicar, curate and Dissenter, in this land or other, is above the King's Majesty. And above the realm's law. A' he needs to do, mind, is to interpret

God's law otherwise, and he is supreme, safe. Ower *me*! Ower your lordships, too. Aye, and ower the General Assembly o' the Kirk o' Scotland, likewise! Think on it, my friends—think on it."

Uproar filled the Hampton Court gallery. James took the opportunity to cast a triumphant glance in the direction of the tapestry.

Andrew Melville's lion-like roar eventually brought quiet. "Sire—I do protest!" he cried. "I made no sic like claim. My claim is that the highest court o' the Kirk, the Assembly, must be free to mak its ain decisions. In the light o' God's laws. The civil power isna inferior but irrelevant thereto . . ."

More clamour. Archbishop Bancroft got to his feet again. "Your Majesty—this is both open heresy and lese-majesty, if not highest treason! Must your Privy Council sit here and listen to both Your Majesty and its members being insulted and decried? I say it is too much . . . !"

"If *I* can thole it, so can you, Bancroft man! We asked these guid presbyters here that we might be informed. Well, we're being informed, are we no'? Right fully and remarkably! You'll no' deny that?"

"I have received sufficient information, Sire, to assure myself that these men have no other thought in them but arrogantly to declare their own rectitude and to abuse Your Majesty's generosity and mercy. I myself see no advantage to be gained by further hearing them. I urge you, therefore, to dismiss them, Sire. And thereafter to make this Master Andrew Melville pay for his unlawful statements and . . ."

"Unlawfu', sirrah!" Melville interrupted powerfully. "You, a churchman, chairge *me* with unlawfu' speech! I was summoned here to explain why bishops shouldna be imposed upon Christ's Kirk in Scotland. I have done so. If you canna bear the truth when you hear it, then I chairge *you—aut non tentaris aut perfice!*"

"Truth—from your prejudiced and proud lips, sir? You, Melville, who are so fond of Latin, heed this simple Latinity—*scandalum magnatum!* Do you know what *that* means, sir? For I do hereby charge you with it, before His Majesty and this high Council."

Melville raised both hands, and snapped his fingers twice, thrice. "That for your *scandalum magnatum!* The miscalling and denigration o' magnates. It isna possible to misca' and denigrate such as you, sirrah! For it would imply lowering you frae a standard to which you havena yet risen!"

"How dare you, you insolent profaner! Your Majesty—I demand your royal protection from the outrageous attacks upon me by this, this . . ."

"Profaner, you name me? *You!* You, who of a' men profane the Sabbath, silence faithfu' ministers o' the Gospel, encourage Popery! You, the very fount o' superstition in this land!" Beside himself, Melville strode forward to the Archbishop—and though Bancroft was a bigger man, he shrank back before the sheer fury of the burning-eyed Scot. Grabbing the lace-edged sleeves of the archiepiscopal rochet, Melville shook them and their owner vigorously, violently, and went on shaking. "You are . . . a foe o' Christ Crucified!" he panted. "The capital enemy . . . o' a' the Reformed Churches in Christendom! You . . . you whited sepulchre! You and yours, I will oppose . . . to the last drop o' my blood—so help me God!"

By the time that he reached the Deity's name, half-a-dozen councillors had leapt up and rushed to the help of the unfortunate Primate, and were dragging Melville off. Practically all there in the gallery were standing now, in vehement outcry, shouting for the guard, demanding dire judgment and the wrath of Heaven. Only King James sat still, fingering his wispy beard, a half-smile about his slack mouth. He uttered not a word.

The Lord Chancellor took charge, as was his duty. "Take him away!" he commanded. "Away! Attacking a member of this Council! Intimidating the lieges. Brawling and violence in the presence of the King. All indictable offences against the realm. Off with him, to ward. The guard to hold him close."

James let them hustle his struggling countryman to the end of the room, before holding up his hand. "Bide a wee, bide a wee," he ordered. "Man, Andra—yon was injudicious!" he complained, shaking his head. "Right precipitate and no' seemly, at a'. We canna have this sort o' behaviour in our royal presence. Och, man—what are we to do wi' you? What'll they say at St. Andra's, man?"

The Archbishop, collapsed in his chair, babbled something incoherent. Ellesmere signed to him to be quiet.

"Sire—this man may be a dignitary in his own country but he has broken the laws of England, here before all, and cannot be excused. I . . ."

"Cannot, my lord Chancellor—*cannot?* Who says cannot to the King?"

"Your pardon, Sire—a slip of the tongue. *Should* not, is better.

More seemly. Master Melville should be punished, or the law becomes a mockery. *Your* law."

"Aye, maybe. But he's an auld man getting. And learned, mind. Fu' o' years and learning. Eh, Andra?"

"Sire—then he should be taught to join wisdom and gravity—aye, and some modesty and discretion—to his years and learning!" the Chancellor declared—and had the loud support of almost all present. "I say that he should be sent to the Tower!"

"Na, na—no' the Tower, man. No' yet, leastways. Have you no regard for siller hairs, my lord? You'll have some o' your ain soon enough! Andra'll do fine in the chairge o' the Dean o' St. Paul's, meantime, decent man. See you to it, my lord. The Dean o' St. Paul's, To be kept close until I say otherwise. Tak him awa'."

Protesting angrily, Andrew Melville was led out.

James turned to the nephew and his colleagues, who stood looking appalled and at a loss. "Aye, Maister Jamie—a bad business, eh?" he sympathised. "Och, that was fell untoward. Aye, untoward and intempestive. But never heed—you're a man o' mair sense, I'm thinking?"

James Melville took a deep breath. "I agree with all that my uncle said, Sire—if not the way he said it!" he declared.

The King held up a hand to still the noise from the now thoroughly roused Council. "Is that so? I'm right sorry about that, man. I was hoping for better things frae a mair reasonable chiel the likes o' yoursel'. We'll maybe win some guid out o' this day yet, though."

The other looked unhappy and unsure—for he was indeed a more reasonable man. "I would wish it also, Your Grace," he admitted.

"Aye. I was thinking you'd maybe mak a fair bishop yoursel', Jamie. Dunkeld is vacant. How would you like to be Bishop o' Dunkeld, Jamie Melville? And help wi' the bringing together o' the warring factions in the Kirk? As is but your simple duty, forby."

James Melville swallowed audibly. He raised his head high. "I . . . no, Sire."

"No? You'll no' be Bishop o' Dunkeld?"

"No, Sire—I will not."

"Gie me a guid reason why not—a *guid* reason, mind. Nane o' your uncle's ranting havers!"

"Very well, Sire. There are, I say, three sorts of bishops—divine, human and devilish! Of these, I am already, by the grace of God, one of the first . . ."

He got no further before the outrage of the English bishops drowned his words.

But James was interested. "Quiet you, my lords," he ordered. "We'll hear what the other sort o' bishops are—to our edification, nae doubt. Proceed, Maister Jamie. The second sort . . . ?"

"The second sort are those set up by human, not divine authority, Sire. These daily incline to the third, the devilish and satanical, with which in substance they are at one . . ."

Even James could not keep the Council quiet now—and did not indeed try very hard. He sat back.

"Sire!" Salisbury exclaimed. "This one is as bad as the other. Have him in ward, likewise! All of them. They are rebel rogues all. A danger to Your Majesty's realms."

"Yes—away with them!"

"To the Tower with the scurrilous dogs!"

"Hush you, my lords. It is for me to say how these shall be disposed," the monarch declared. "And six o' them have committed nae offence yet, have they? They havena opened their mouths. Be no' so thin-skinned, my lords. Mind, in Scotland we have a mair outspoken custom and usage—aye, mair debative and controvertible. So I'll send these gentry back hame—since I reckon we are now sufficiently informed as to their views! Unless any o' you lords o' my Privy Council are anxious further to question them? No? Then back they shall go. But no' Maister Jamie, I think. In case he felt moved to convene another General Assembly on his ain! He doesna want to be Bishop o' Dunkeld, and *I* dinna want him back Moderating the Assembly, nor yet ministering at Anster and Kilrenny. He'll do fine at yon Newcastle, aye Newcastle—until I gie him leave to go back to Scotland. Aye, Jamie Melville—you pleased yoursel' fine at Newcastle once before, did you no'? When you chose to act pastor there to yon arrogant lords I exiled there? Ooh, aye. So that's it, my lords. This Council is closed. We are a' the wiser, are we no'? You have my permission to retire."

Majesty waves them all away.

When, after an interval, James, alone, came tip-toeing back into the gallery, closing the door carefully behind him, and coming to release Heriot from confinement, he was positively gleeful.

"Man, Geordie—was that no' just prime!" he demanded. "Couldna have been better arranged, though I say it mysel'. Thae Melvilles cooked their ain goose, eh? I didna need you, in here. A' just went maist excellent well. Nae trouble at a'."

"There seemed to be trouble in plenty, Sire!"

"Not so. Yon wisna *trouble*, Geordie—yon was the working out o' my purpose. In better fashion that I expected, mind. I'm right gratefu' to Andra Melville. I dinna need your testimony now, to help lock him up."

"You mean, Sire, that you planned all this in order to get the Melvilles to trap themselves?"

"To be sure, I did. I wanted them out o' Scotland. And to bide out. So's this business o' my bishops is settled decently. Och, without the Melvilles Vicky and Doddie Home will have little bother, at all. The Kirk's been a thorn in my flesh for lang. It'll no' be, now."

"You intend to keep Andrew Melville here? As good as prisoner?"

"Ooh, aye. For a year or so. The Privy Council will no doubt advise me strongly to put him in the Tower. Where there's better men than he is!"

"He's an old man for the Tower, Your Majesty . . ."

"He's an auld man for ca'ing the lugs off archbishops o' my Privy Council! But, och—I'll see he's comfortable. He'll no' dee there, man—I'm no' for making martyrs for the Kirk, see you! And, whiles, I'll maybe go along and have a bit crack wi' him, anent sundry doctrines and dogmas. He'll be fine. And in a year or two I'll pack him off to France or Geneva, where he was before. But, mind this—I'll no' have Andra Melville back in Scotland again, and that's a fact!"

Heriot inclined his head, silent.

Before he took leave of the King, the goldsmith reverted to the subject of the projected Scottish dramatic production. "When does Your Majesty wish me to take Master Shakespeare to Scotland?" he asked.

"Aye, you're keen, heh? Eager, Geordie man! To get your hands on yon lassie Primrose again! At your years you shouldna be so hot, I tell you. Forby, though she's ready enough, she'll be a' the better for waiting a wee. Ripening nicely, aye—nicely!"

"Does that mean that Your Majesty is having second thoughts about sending us up?"

"Nothing o' the sort. Touchy, eh? You'll go in my guid time, and no' before, Geordie Heriot. So keep your manhood between your twa legs, meantime, and remember you're a decent London tradesman o' middle years!"

17

IT WAS, in fact, late the following Spring before George Heriot got away on his jaunt to the North. His position as Court Jeweller, with all its additional banking and financial ramifications, was one of considerable advantage and influence; but it had its drawbacks, one of which undoubtedly was that, like all other Court appointments, no major travel or absence beyond the King's ready call was allowed without express royal permission. And James kept a notably close grip on his entire entourage—extraordinarily so for so apparently haphazard and casual an individual—and especially on his banker.

There was another aspect of the position. Heriot was still in the Queen's black books over Alison Primrose and Margaret Hartside, the more so, it seemed, in that he had discovered the blackmail by Orkney. Whether that particular situation was improved, or no, he was given no indication; but he was no longer summoned to Somerset (or Denmark) House, and Anne had bestowed her custom and favour on Sir William Herrick. This was a veritable financial relief to Heriot—but the man regretted his estrangement from the Queen, with whom he had had great sympathy in the past and whom he had served for long. Whether Anne positively intrigued to keep him from going to Scotland was not to be known; but he suspected it. How much influence she had, in fact, on the King these days was a doubtful quantity, for the Courts were almost entirely separate, and there were many days when James did not see his wife.

Will Shakespeare got up to Scotland before Heriot did, he and his King's Players company travelling North to present a series of plays at Edinburgh, Perth, Dundee and Aberdeen. Whether this would result in the financial profit James fondly hoped for remained to be seen; for the Presbyterian climate in the northern kingdom was less than favourable towards play-acting, except against a good religious background. The King's Players ransacked their repertoire for suitable themes, but departed doubtful.

Heriot's permission to depart, as he had expected, coincided with his involvement in another errand for James Stewart. The Master of Gray's case had been heard before a secret commission of judges, and he had been awarded nineteen thousand, nine hundred and three pounds against the King. Admittedly this was within the suggested sum for settlement—but the fact of having to pay at all rankled with James. The judges had been much too open-handed with other folk's money, he contended—especially as one of them was James Elphinstone, Lord Balmerino, Lord President of the Court of Session as well as Chief Secretary for Scotland. The same Balmerino was holding back eighteen thousand merks, or twelve thousand pounds Scots, of the price of Robert Logan's estates he had bought, was he not? Patrick Gray was one of Logan's heirs general, as a first cousin, and the King strongly suspected that his Chief Secretary and Gray had done a deal—and at the royal expense. This would by no means do. Gray was a proven scoundrel, of course; but it looked as though Balmerino might well be one also. Moreover, there was another matter. There was a complaint to the King, personally, from the old Lord Gray, the Master's father—a donnert auld fool by all accounts, but one who had served the Crown in his time. He declared that his eldest son had violently entered his house of Castle Huntly and cruelly driven him out, dismissed his servants and consumed all his victuals and fodder, with the intent shamefully to bring his grey hairs to the grave that he might inherit the sooner. He had appealed to the Scots Privy Council, but to no avail. Now as a last resort, he sought the royal intervention.

When Heriot demurred that this did not sound in the least like Patrick Gray's style of behaviour, a man of infinite subtlety, James overbore him. The old lord would not be likely to write so if he had *not* been evicted from his castle. And if the Scots Privy Council were refusing to do anything about it, might it not be because they were looking after the Master's interests in more than the nineteen thousand, nine hundred and eighty-three pounds! Indeed, might not Patrick Gray be getting a grip on more than Balmerino? What about Sandy Seton himself, Chancellor Dunfermline? They had ever been friends. He had asked Vicky Stewart about that—but his ducal cousin could see no further than a mole in sunlight! So Geordie Heriot was to go to Scotland, and make quiet enquiries. Find out what he could about Balmerino, and Dunfermline too. Search out what was at the back of the eviction of the old Lord Gray. Discover whether the nineteen thousand, nine hundred and eighty-three pounds need in fact be paid—to a possible felon who might conveniently be outlawed! And while he was at it, see if he could learn whether those fell Casket Letters were indeed now in the Master's hands.

No protests on the part of the reluctant enquirer that this was turning him into little better than a spy and secret agent, had any effect on the monarch, who did not fail to invoke the sacred ties of friendship, as well as the simple duty of a loyal subject, throwing in the royal command when the other looked unconvinced.

Before heading northwards, Heriot went to see the Duke of Lennox, not long returned from his quite prolonged vice-regal stay in Scotland settling the new bishops into their places in the state, if not in the Church. Lennox was full of the oddity of this situation, and very doubtful as to the wisdom of it all—for James was antagonising much of the nobility, by taking back from them the bishopric lands they had gained at the Reformation land-grab to bestow again on the restored prelates. Moreover, the Kirk would have none of them. Nor did the strong Catholic influence, which still remained a force, consider these bishops as anything but frauds. So, according to the Duke, James was uniting the three warring factions of nobles, Kirk and Catholics against himself, by this episcopal imposition, and gaining nothing save a superficial appearance of unified church polity as with England—a concordat, James called it—and of course the important matter of the bishops' votes in the Scots parliament.

"And, do not forget, a totally reliable, educated and continuing corps of leadership in Scottish affairs," his friend pointed out. "From whom the King may choose ministers of government, high officials, secretaries of state, to carry out *his* policies, nominated by himself, wholly dependent on his goodwill. The bishops are only an instrument in that policy. However unpopular and ineffective as churchmen, they will be an enduring tool in the King's hands."

"You may be right," Lennox admitted. "James has no interest in popularity. Or indeed in doctrine, I think—although he likes to argue and debate dogma. Efficacy is all he is concerned with, I swear! Divide to rule has always been his policy. Religion, I think, does not come into the matter, so far as James is concerned. Myself, I have little use for doctrine—but I mislike being so unpopular as I am now, in Scotland. I have spent months settling and imposing these bishops—and ended up being hooted at in the streets! George Home does not appear to care—but I mislike it, Geordie."

"At least you are an *open* agent of the Crown—not a spy, as I am to be! I had rather be hooted at than considered an underhand informer!"

"We are all spies for James. It is his method of government. He does not go to war, slay men by the thousand. He is the first king to use wits, intelligence and the weaknesses of men, instead of the sword and the axe. Mountebank Royal—with, I am coming to believe, the keenest wits in his two realms!"

They contemplated that proposition for a little, in silence. Then Heriot mentioned the King's suspicions of Secretary Elphinstone, Lord Balmerino, and, to a lesser extent, Dunfermline the Chancellor, and the charge to himself to discover what he could.

"I have never trusted Elphinstone," Lennox conceded. "He is cunning and able, but I think crooked. And, of course, a Catholic but thinly disguised. He pays only the barest lip-service to the Kirk. Dunfermline is Catholic also, of course—all the Setons are—though he makes a show of conforming. But he is otherwise fairly honest, I believe. Indeed, Patrick Gray too is a Catholic at heart—if he is anything! Perhaps James fears those three, and others, overturning Reformed Scotland and his throne!"

"Some call *you* Catholic!" his friend reminded.

The other smiled. "I say a man's religion is his own business! I do not, and will never, make mine a matter of the state's."

"Would all were so wise." Heriot changed the subject. "What of Margaret Hartside?"

"There has still been no trial. The Queen is playing cat-and-mouse with her. She is living quietly in Stirlingshire, as ordered. But they say that her husband visits her secretly from Orkney—and makes no attempt to take her back with him, as he might, where she could be beyond Anne's clutches. And so saves you your surety money!"

"Which means, then, that the Earl of Orkney still believes that he can make use of her?"

"So I would think."

"And the Casket Letters?"

"Of those I learned nothing. Or whether Orkney is still being paid mail."

"The King wishes to know if Gray has them. So he is still concerned, on that score. Moreover, he is seeking to avoid payment of the moneys awarded by the judges."

"That is folly. He should not make more of an enemy of Patrick Gray than he must."

"My own opinion." Heriot sighed. "Well—have you the letter for me to carry to your Mary?"

* * *

George Heriot arrived in Edinburgh, to discover that Will Shakespeare and his company were meantime playing in the city of Perth. Before proceeding thither, however, he had other fish to fry. He sought out James Primrose, in his town house at the top of a high tenement of the Lawnmarket, but was part disappointed, part pleased, to learn that Alison was not with him there, but was staying with Mary Gray at Methven—which, he knew from her letters, she often did. Primrose, although his visitor pumped him gently, discreetly, revealed nothing of interest regarding Balmerino, Dunfermline or other members of the Scots Privy Council, nor why nothing had been done about the old Lord Gray's complaint—save to mention that the Master of Gray was still Sheriff of Forfar, the county in which Castle Huntly was situated, and so, in theory and possibly practise also, was the law there. Heriot could get little more out of him; perhaps he recognised that he had been somewhat indiscreet previously. He was, however, prepared to talk about his daughter's wedding. He proposed that the ceremony might be held at the very least a year hence when, he considered, Alison would be of a fit age—and before which he could by no means spare her. Nor would he be in a position to produce her dowry before then. The bridegroom-to-be could not have been less interested in the proposed five thousand merks dowry, but recognised that the decencies had to be observed. Moreover, although his heart, like his whole body, wanted Alison *now*, his head told him that he would have had to have made his peace with the Queen before he could bring the young woman back to London—or, at least, to Court circles; and he was not going to put her in any position where she was likely to be slighted or snubbed. If this Scottish mission of his was in any degree successful, he ought to be able to make overtures to Anne from a position of some strength. Next summer, then, let it be.

His brother James was not of much use to Heriot regarding hints and rumours of what went on below the surface in Scottish affairs; but the lawyer, Adam Lawtie, his Edinburgh 'doer', was a shrewd and busy little man with an ear very close to the ground, and from him the enquirer gained some relevant information, or at least the avenues to explore. For instance, that the Earl of Dunbar, still in Scotland as Lord Treasurer and commissioner, and Lord Balmerino the Secretary, had reputedly fallen out, and that the Chancellor Dunfermline was taking part with Balmerino. That these two crypto-Catholics were, strangely enough, in ever closer touch with the Calvinist leaders of the Kirk. That Balmerino was said to have arrested the Eyemouth lawyer George Sprott, 'doer' for the late Logan of Restalrig, and was holding him hidden away secret somewhere. That the Master of Gray was very active visiting and being visited by a great many of the nobility. And that the King's proposed Act of Union between Scotland and England, together with the bishops who were thought to be the main instruments for bringing it about, were likely to be resisted by a for once almost united Scotland.

Thoughtfully, Heriot went seeking his cousin, the Lord Advocate.

He found Sir Thomas Hamilton in better health, entirely affable, but less forthcoming as to confidences even than previously. It seemed obvious to Heriot that he was being more than habitually close and careful—and therefore presumably had something to hide. This was reasonable enough for a man in his high office; but he knew that his cousin came straight from the King, however unofficially. Even Heriot's suggestion that James might possibly be considering making a peer of him did not open the King's Advocate's thick lips to any extent.

Disappointed in this, the discreet enquirer sought out Master Thomas Hope, the advocate not of the King but, men said, of the King's enemies. He found him more difficult of access than the other, for he had become the busiest practitioner in the Scottish High Court, with everywhere his ability, independence of mind and fearlessness recognised. The caller had to wait almost two hours at the Court of Session, and took the opportunity to sit-in on a couple of cases in which the advocate was involved—being left with an enhanced respect for Hope and a recognition that this was a man whom he could much prefer to have for than against him. He gained the impression that the judges in the cases felt the same way.

When eventually Hope had time to see him, it was to find the tables turned rather, and Heriot himself in the role of examinee and witness.

"I played my part, Master Heriot, and convinced my client, the Master of Gray, to agree to a private commission of judges, and to accept their award. Within the twenty thousand pounds limitation. That award has not yet been paid. That would be a serious defraudment, besides being extremely dangerous, I think. Moreover, a failure in confidence and good faith towards myself, sir."

"But . . . I think that you go too fast, Master Hope," the other answered, carefully. "The payment of large sums is ever apt to be slow—as I know to my cost. Would it were only nineteen thousand pounds Scots wherein *I* was outlaid, on the royal account! There is no reason, is there, to believe that it will not be paid in due course?"

"Is there not, sir? Then why has the Lord Scone, Comptroller, whom the Lord President Balmerino authorised to pay the award, been stopped from making the payment? Presumably by the Lord High Treasurer, the Earl of Dunbar, on the King's command."

"He has? I knew nothing of this. His Majesty did not say so. It may be, perhaps, that this is a matter between Dunbar and Balmerino? I am told that they are at odds."

"All Scotland knows that. But I scarce think that even Dunbar would halt payment of the court's award without royal sanction."

"I do not know. I am sorry, sir. The Duke of Lennox and I approached you in all good faith. The King acceded to it all. This must be looked into . . ."

"It must indeed, Master Heriot—and swiftly. Or I, for one, will not be responsible for the consequences. I need not tell you that the Master of Gray is an ill man to cross. And there is much in Scotland today for ill-will to harness and exploit. The realm needs a resident king and government—not one four hundred miles away, dealing through venial underlings!"

Heriot did not attempt to deny that. "Might not the Master of Gray use the moneys awarded to further stir up that ill-will, Master Hope?" he countered.

"That is no concern of mine, sir. Nor of yours, I say. The award has been made by the King's judges, and accepted. It must be paid.

Any further delay, I warn you, could result in most serious consequences. Consequences much more expensive than twenty thousand pounds Scots!"

"You have reason to state that?"

"I have my God-given wits, sir! As, I swear, have you! Do not tell me that you are unaware of the fire that could blaze in Scotland today—requiring only a spark!"

"And you conceive the Master of Gray to be ready to strike that spark?"

"I have not said so. Others may strike it. But my client has just grievances. And much influence in Scotland. As he has shown in the past."

"And as his father, it seems, has recently discovered to his cost! He has, I understand, turned him out of his own house. And he a Lord of Parliament."

"As to that, I am not informed, sir. But . . . I advise that the Master be paid. And forthwith."

"I shall inform the King of your advice, Master Hope."

"That, I fear, may be too late."

Quickly Heriot searched his face. "You think so?" he asked, after a pause.

"I do. I have no wish, sir, to see this realm in any disturbances. There are follies enough lacking that. And the King cannot plead either ignorance nor lack of money. The English parliament has given him four hundred thousand pounds for his personal use, I understand."

"So you knew of that?"

"It is my business to know things. The Master of Gray knows of it also! Twenty thousand pounds Scots is a very small sum compared with four hundred thousand pounds Sterling. Is it worth Scotland aflame?"

"You judge it as serious as that?"

"In present circumstances, yes."

"If I knew just what those circumstances were, sir . . .?"

"I advise that you find out, then, Master Heriot. But—not from me! I am my client's advocate, nothing more."

"I see." Heriot perceived that he would get nothing more from this man. He changed the subject, and asked about the Hartside case in which, since it was his money that was retaining Hope's interest, he had every right to enquire. But the advocate could tell him little that he did not know already. The next move was up to the Queen, either to call for trial or to declare the charges abandoned —as was advisable.

With that, George Heriot had to be content. But he left the Court of Session premises in the High Street with much on his mind.

Next morning he rode off, west by north, for Linlithgow, Stirling and Perth.

* * *

The arrival at Methven Castle the day following was such as to banish all his anxieties, national and personal, from his mind—at least for the moment. Colour, young, verdant greenery and blossom was just beginning to paint the land after the long winter, although the snow still coated in gleaming white all over two thousand feet, to add depth and contrast and challenge to every vista. Strathearn was an utterly different world from London, or even Edinburgh, not only in its scene but in its values and tempo. Here was little of power and authority, of destiny, intrigue and momentous events; here, however, were the enduring verities, the essential rhythm of the seasons, the unchanging land, simple but basic things. As ever when the man entered into this ambience, he asked himself why he did not resign his Court appointments, sell his business and responsibilities to others, come up here and buy himself a landed property, to settle down as a country laird. He could well afford it, for he was by any standards a rich man. He could put up with the royal disapproval. And he had no ambitions, that he was aware of, to fulfil. Why not, then?

At the castle, he discovered that Mistress Gray and her guests had gone riding to the ravaged Inchaffray Abbey, some five miles to the west, with young John Stewart; and in no mood to sit waiting for them, Heriot went spurring on. Half-an-hour later he found them amongst the roofless aisles, seeking to unearth from the rubble fine carved work cast down by the over-zealous Reformers of half a century earlier, his unannounced appearance on the scene setting off an eruption as overwhelming as it was joyous and incoherent. At sight of him, Alison emitted a yell of sheer delight, and abandoning all pretence at ladylike behaviour, came racing, bounding over fallen masonry, blackened timbering and weeds, setting scores of pigeons into alarmed, flapping flight from the broken clerestoreys and wallheads, laughing aloud as she came. Mary Gray began to follow her, then restrained herself, and also her son who had started to run also, and turned instead to the fourth member of the party, in explanation.

Heriot had only time to jump from the saddle before his betrothed was upon him, a vehement, uninhibited assembly of urgent limbs, fluttering clothing and streaming hair, to be caught, lifted high, whirled round and hugged close, all in one continuous, sweeping motion, amidst a breathless and disconnected babblement of words and exclamations, until lips met lips and at least the noise was stilled—scarcely behaviour apt for the Master-Elect of the Worshipful Company of Hammermen of the City of London, and in consecrated premises, moreover.

Mary and the boy came to present themselves in smiling welcome, after a due interval, while Alison, clutching the man's doublet sleeve wove to and fro on tip-toe at his side, unable to stand still and blinking tears of joy from her eyes, still seeking an intelligible pattern of words. It was Mary Gray however, who enunciated the required phrases of greeting, gladness, affection and question, after bestowing her own generous kiss full on Heriot's fortunate lips. John Stewart of Methven had difficulty in obtaining a hand to shake.

The newcomer, less than fluently, was commencing to explain his arrival on the scene when he perceived that there was another person present, lingering behind a little, a tall, flaxen-haired and serenely beautiful older woman, in her late thirties, grey-eyed, fine-featured, dressed in notably rich riding-clothes, who waited with a half-smile and a calm dignity. He paused.

Noting the look, Mary turned. "Marie," she called, "here is Master George Heriot, Alison's betrothed and the King's man of business. Geordie—the Lady Marie Stewart, Mistress of Gray. Whom I suppose you might name my step-mother!"

Heriot contrived a bow of sorts, his wits for the moment all agley. This was the Master's wife, Orkney's sister, the King's cousin, and Mary Queen of Scots' niece—in the circumstances hardly the person he was best prepared to meet.

The other effortlessly put him more at ease. "The famous Master Geordie himself!" she said, in a voice melodious as it was warmly assured. She came forward. "My loss that I have never met you until this. But I feel that I know you well—and like what I know! These two never fail to sing your praises, sir."

"My lady," he said. "I . . . ah . . . am greatly privileged. Your servant. I, I know your husband . . ."

"Ah, yes. Who does not? And Patrick ever speaks of you with great respect—which he does not of all men! Moreover, Patrick, whatever else, is a shrewd judge of character. As, I think, is our Alison here, in different fashion! I understand that she wanted only you, of the whole King's Court!"

"And had a mighty task to convince him that he was not altogether too far gone in years for this babe-in-arms!" The girl had found her voice again—although still she clung to him.

"You have not brought *my* man with you, Geordie?" Mary Gray asked. "That is too much to hope for."

"Only a letter, I fear . . ."

"Have you come to wed me, Geordie?"

He swallowed. "Not this time, lass. Next year. I have seen your father. Next year . . ."

"A year!" That was a wail. "Another whole year! Oh, Geordie, how can you say that? How could you?" Alison flung away from him. "I believe that you do not truly love me, at all!"

"I do, I do! Am I not here, to prove it, my dear? But . . . your father would have it so. And I agree that it would be wiser . . ."

"Wiser! Is that the kind of betrothed I have! Is it wisdom that I've to wed?"

He bit his lip.

Mary took his arm, instead of the other. "Look not so cast down, Geordie." She smiled. "Women are ever thus. Give them the world, and they want the moon and stars! Alison would count the days, rather than the weeks and months. Were she quite content to put off for your year—then, I say, you might well look glum!"

"Yes. Perhaps. But it is necessary. I do not wish this delay, God knows. But . . . in London, the Court . . . where we must live . . . the Queen . . . it would be difficult."

"Difficult. Is it for ease that you would wed me?" Alison demanded. "I have waited all these long months already. Must the Queen's spleen date our marriage?"

"It was *your* misjudgment which roused the Queen, Alison my dear," Mary reminded. "And caused Geordie to fall from her favour—to his much cost, I am sure. If you would wed the King's jeweller you cannot *afford* the Queen's spleen, deserved or other."

"You *would* take his part! It is easy for you . . .' Alison stopped, and drew a deep breath. "Ah, well—at least he is here! And did not say, this once, that I was too young!" And she came back to the man's side.

He put his arm around her. "Forgive me, lass. Would that we might be wed tomorrow! Nothing in this world would rejoice me so much. But this, I fear, is part of the price I have to ask you to pay, in marrying an older man—only a part, indeed. I cannot throw responsibilities to the winds, as once I might—my responsibility towards *you*, most of all."

"Yes, but . . ." She looked up at him, and smiled again. "I am sorry, Geordie. No more of this. For I am happy, truly—very happy. And proud, too."

"You should be." That was the Lady Marie. She came over and kissed the girl on the cheek. "I think that you are the most fortunate young woman in all Scotland, my dear!"

"When are we going home?" the bored John Stewart of Methven asked. "I am hungry."

The laughter provided the necessary and welcome break. Mary Gray took charge. They would be on their way, she decided. But the Lady Marie and Johnnie and herself would ride ahead, with the grooms—for the two betrothed would wish to be alone together, with much to say to each other after the months of parting. Let them follow on to Methven in their own good time.

And so, presently Alison Primrose was riding pillion on Heriot's horse, her arms tightly round the man, in fact singing liltingly if somewhat jouncily in his right ear to the rhythm of the trot, as they followed a bridle-path along the alder-grown banks of the Pow Burn, a quiet route eastwards advised by the young woman as unlikely to yield any fellow-travellers.

"The Lady Marie?" the man said, presently. "I had not thought to encounter the Master of Gray's wife here. I had hoped to speak with Mary about him, her father. Having the wife present may prove difficult."

"I think not," Alison said. "The Lady Marie is not difficult. She is good, understanding. She and Mary are like sisters—better friends than most sisters."

"Aye—but this of her husband. I can scarce speak of it before her. His relations with the King . . ."

"I think that you may. She is fond of the Master—but so is Mary. They have long united in seeking to keep him from the worst of his mischiefs. Or what they consider so. He is a strange man, with much good to him as well as ill, they say. These two are at one in seeking to counter that ill. Neither, I swear, will ever *betray* him. But they will strive to prevent his wickedness where they can. For his own sake, I do believe, rather than the King's, or others'."

"I still would be loth to speak freely of him, before her."

"Yet she knows more of the Master's affairs than anyone else, of necessity, Geordie." She jerked at him, from behind. "Is *that* what you came for? I had hoped that it was to see me!"

"As you know very well, my dear, I need excuse to leave the Court. I could not be come to see you had I not an errand to fulfil for the King. But . . . I am here, to see *you*, first and foremost. The rest is but the price I have to pay for that joy." He pointed. "See yonder trees? I will prove what I came for, there. By your leave!"

Her laughter trilled at his ear. "Remember your age—and mine—sir! A man of great responsibilities. And, and wisdom!"

"Wait you!" he told her.

There was not much of waiting on the part of either of them, indeed, when they reached the little copse of wind-blown pines and whins and bracken at the west end of Methven Moss. They were into each other's arms almost from the moment their feet touched the ground, Heriot's horse left to its own devices. With mutual eagerness they clutched each other, lips and hands busy, bodies urgent, words all but dispensed with, in compensation for the weary months of parting. Last year's bracken offered all the couch they sought, and Methven Moss and Tippermuir were transformed for these two, thereafter, into the very anteroom of paradise. Time, like everything else extraneous to themselves, was no longer relevant.

They had much to say to each other, in more eloquent language than mere speech.

When eventually they rode on eastwards across the moorland, both were equally silent, lost in the aftermath of delight, savouring, sifting, sounding but by no means satiated, glowing with a foretaste of the promise of deeper fulfilment so richly promised back there. It was going to be all right, better even that they had hoped, a splendour. They could wait now, assured, certain, however superficially impatient. Every now and again they squeezed each other, and sometimes the man looked back over his shoulder into her shining eyes, unspeaking.

That evening in Methven Castle, Heriot's mission with Will Shakespeare, the actor and playwright, greatly intrigued the women. Mary and Alison had recently been to nearby Perth to see the King's Players in a comedy called *Love's Labour's Lost*, and though they had not particularly noticed Master Shakespeare, they were full of the excellence and delights of the entertainment, and enthusiastic over the idea of a Scottish play. As for the Lady Marie, she proved to be very knowledgeable about King MacBeth and his period—he was an ancestor of her own, of course. She was able to advise Heriot as to locations which the man Shakespeare ought to visit, in the Perth area at Dunsinane and Collace and Forteviot and Birnam, up in Moray at Forres and Elgin, and in Aberdeenshire at Lumphanan and Kildrummy. Only, she did introduce a complication when she pointed out that the tradition of the witches, who were so prominent in the MacBeth story, had an alternative location to the Hardmuir of Forres—namely, a heath much nearer at hand, only some ten miles away from Methven indeed, across Tay and west of the Dunsinane area. This was the Eastmuir of Cairnbeddie—the Beddie but a corruption of Beda or Beth—and there they would find the Witches' Stone and other named relics of MacBeth a hundred miles from the Forres scene. The man promised to investigate. Presumably King James had not known about this, for in his preoccupation with the witches, he had mentioned only Forres.

From James and Shakespeare the talk moved to Margaret Hartside's case and the Queen's attitude and intentions. The Earl of Orkney, behind it all, inevitably came into this; but Mary Gray made no bones about referring to him as an unscrupulous and very potent firebrand, which the Earl's sister not only did not contest but implied full agreement. Not that she had any suggestions as to what his ultimate intentions were, or how he might be countered. She did indicate, however, that her husband's constant traffic with his brother-in-law seemed to have stopped, meantime.

This brought them to the verge of Heriot's more secret mission, which he was in grave doubts about airing in front of the Mistress of Gray. But, whether or no Alison had had a word with her, Mary Gray clearly had no such doubts. As the man cleared his throat, preparatory to a complete change of subject, she spoke.

"Geordie—the Lady Marie is no stranger to many of the problems which concern you, on the King's behalf. She is as anxious as am I that Patrick Gray should not be involved in further plots or actions against the Crown—we have had more than sufficient of such! She is entirely to be trusted, I do assure you. You may speak freely before her."

"That is so, Master Geordie," the older woman agreed, quietly. "I love and cherish my husband—but that makes me the more concerned for his welfare and best interests. He is an inveterate and most skilful plotter—always I have known this, and have worked to save him from the worst consequences of his plotting. To save the victims also, if I might. That makes my fondness for him none the less. I shall not reveal any secrets."

He still hesitated. Obviously this woman already knew much of his own part in the affairs of the King versus her husband, with Mary evidently confiding in her entirely. But if it came to a vital clash of interests, a matter of life and death—as it easily could do, with treason in the air—where would her ultimate sympathies lie? Where Mary's also?

As though she read his thoughts, Mary added, "The Lady Marie and I will ever seek to save Patrick from the most grievous effects of his activities. Where that is possible. But we prefer that we do so by helping to halt such activities before they go too far, rather than afterwards! Which, I think, is your own intent, Geordie?"

He nodded. "Which means, does it not, that you believe that the Master is indeed at present planning some new devilment?"

"We fear so, yes."

"And do you know what it is?"

"Only in part. We think that he intends to oppose the King's policy of setting up one realm, a United Kingdom to replace the ancient kingdoms of Scotland and England."

"Many oppose that. I do not know that I myself favour it."

"But not many are prepared to go as far as Patrick in opposing it, I warrant." That was the Mistress of Gray. "My husband seldom merely expresses his disfavours. He acts upon them. And in no small fashion."

"And in thise case, he has started to act?"

"Yes. How far he has gone, I cannot tell. But he believes this policy to be the probable ruin of Scotland as an independent realm, the betrayal of all that Scots have fought for since the great Bruce. And, God knows, he may be right! He has I believe three principal fields of action. Here in Scotland—where he is forming a party, a strong party, to oppose union. In England, where he seeks to stir up the English parliament against it. And in France, where he has friends in places of much influence."

"So much? For one man to attempt?"

"Patrick ruled Scotland more than once, you will recollect. The power behind James's throne. And he does nothing by halves."

"What can he gain from France?"

"James sees himself the peace-maker of Christendom. He requires the good will of France. And France is Catholic. Patrick would use Catholic support for maintaining the separate kingdoms."

"Ah!"

"Yes. If Scotland could be turned Catholic again, even only in name, there would be no support for James's policy in England, where they fear Catholics like Satan himself!"

"I see. And you think this is possible?"

"It matters not what *I* think. Or others. It is what Patrick thinks that is important. And few know what goes on below the surface, in matters of governance and rule, as does he."

"Does the Earl of Orkney come into this?"

"My brother? No. Such affairs concern him no whit. He is interested only in his own advantage. To be left to rule Orkney and Shetland as a small king—or *misrule* them. Untramelled by law or aught else."

"It is not Patrick Stewart you need concern yourself with, Geordie," Mary put in. "But Patrick Gray. He is as a rapier to a woodman's axe! Do you realise how strong the Catholic faction has become since the King went to London? James used it to keep the Kirk in its place—and now it holds the real power here. And indeed works with the extreme Kirk ministers. It dominates both the Privy Council and the Court of Session—Dunfermline, Balmerino, Montrose the former Chancellor, Argyll, Linlithgow, Crawford, Glamis, Ogilvy. These do not call themselves Catholic, but are. Then there are the true Catholics, who never renounced the Papacy—Huntly, the Lieutenant of the North, Erroll, the High Constable, Angus, Maxwell, Sanquhar, Fleming, Seton, the Chancellor's brother, and many more. And all the Highland chiefs. Many of these hate each other. Some are at feud. Few have ever worked together. But if Patrick can unite them, even for a little . . . !"

"And is he in touch with English Catholics also?"

"No—not so, I think," the Lady Marie said. "It is the English *Protestants* he is concerned with. Particularly those in parliament. To some he sends money . . ."

"Money! The Master does? To bribe English parliament men will cost him dear! Pounds Scots will not go far with them!"

"That is true. Patrick is spending money like water! Getting it wherever he may. Selling lands, raising loans . . ."

"This is why he wanted the King's debt repaid, after so long? To bring low the King's policy!"

"Yes. That is but one small source. He needs a deal more than that—for this is costly work, with more than the English parliament votes to buy! He needs money—and, being Patrick, does not scruple overmuch how he gets it, I fear. Many in Scotland owe place, position, lands, titles to him, when he stood at the King's right hand. Now they must pay for it—for he knows secrets without number."

"Ha—more of the black mail! It is not only my lord of Orkney, then, who knows how to use such! The Casket Letters? Does the Master have them now? Are they also for use in his campaign?"

The Lady Marie shook her head. "I do not know. I know nothing of these, save what Mary has told me. Patrick has never spoken of them—though they were in my father's care once, I understand."

"But . . . if he has them, would the Master use them also?"

"How can I tell? I think not, perhaps. If they endanger the King's right to his thrones. That might not serve Patrick's purpose, I think."

"I agree," Mary said. "Moreover, I believe he would be loth to assail the King *in person*, too hard, as yet. Until, until he succeeds his father. As a Lord of Parliament. It is within the King's power to declare him infamous, and to forfeit him from this, his birthright. He will not wish for that—for to be a peer of Scotland would give him more power. James has dropped him from the Privy Council. But as a Lord of Parliament, and Sheriff of Forfar, he would be entitled to a seat again. He could then dominate the Council, as he used to do."

"I see. So you would expect the old Lord Gray, your grandfather, not to live for much longer? But while he does, the King is safe from the worst of the Casket Letters?"

"Something of the sort. Granlord—I have called him that since a child—has been a sick and ailing man for long. He is very old, all but witless now. This last year he is so much the worse . . ."

"And so the Master, his son, turns him out of his own house! To speed his father's passing!"

"It is not quite so," the Lady Marie declared, quietly but firmly. "Although Patrick's enemies so represent it. My good-father has been but a poor creature these many years, living close in Broughty

Castle, seeing none but members of the family, attended to at Patrick's charges. He and my husband have little love for each other, I admit—but there has been no mistreatment. Now Patrick needs Broughty Castle—no doubt for this campaign of his. It stands on a headland on the coast, with its own secure haven, convenient for the coming and going of ships and messengers, secretly, by sea. From England and France. It has a ferry to Fife. Meetings can be held therein, with none knowing. Unlike Castle Huntly, our home. The old lord's presence there became difficult, an embarrassment. Not so much for his own sake, but in that his other sons visit him. And one of them, in especial, hates Patrick, and would do him disservice. So Patrick removed his father to another house inland—the House of Gray, indeed, near to Liff. A smaller place, but a deal more comfortable. That is all."

"And the letter? To the King. Complaining that the Master is bringing his grey hairs to the grave! Denying him his shelter and his servants?"

"Written by the brother, James Gray of Bandirran. Only signed by the old lord—who could be made to sign anything. If Patrick was to be forfeited and declared infamous, then, now that Gilbert is dead, James would be sixth Lord Gray when his father goes!"

"I see. I thank you. All this explains why the Privy Council took no action."

"I do not seek to make my husband seem greatly better than he is," the other concluded. "But nor will I keep silent when he is misjudged, or there is good to be said of him."

"You could do no less," the man acknowledged.

"There is one matter where you should tell *us* the truth of it, Geordie—not we you," Mary put to him. "We have heard it whispered that the King does not intend to pay the nineteen thousand pounds agreed upon and awarded by the judges. Certainly it is not yet paid, although the Lord Scone was ordered to give Patrick the moneys. Is this a fact?"

Heriot coughed. "The King is in two minds," he said. "This is part reason why I am here. He also hears rumours, see you . . .!"

"But, Geordie—that would be the greatest folly! After all was arranged. Nothing is more like to make Patrick angry, truly angry. And Patrick angry is dangerous indeed! Nothing more calculated to cause him to hit at the King, in person. To the danger of the whole realm. Patrick calm, plotting yes, but cool, is one matter. But Patrick angry at broken faith is another. All for nineteen thousand pounds

Scots! A nothing, where the King is concerned. Do you not see it?"

"I see it, yes. A folly, I agree. And to lower my own name and credit, who acted for the King."

"That too. Is it worth it? Geordie—you are the King's man of business. Can you not do something?"

"Twenty thousand pounds Scots is less than three thousand pounds Sterling," Alison mentioned, her first contribution for long. "The Queen would spend as much on a single masque. And out of *your* pocket, Geordie!"

Looking at her thoughtfully, he nodded, point taken. "But—if the money is to be spent to counter the King's policies—should the King then pay it?" he asked. "James is no fool, see you, however many think he is."

"That is not the point," Mary contended. "What matters in this is that the King should not make a dangerous situation worse. For himself, as well as others. Think of the effect on all Scotland, when it is known—as known it will be. The King, in London, in a breach of faith. Defrauding his former servant and Privy Councillor. Overturning the decision of his appointed judges. Will this serve the King's cause? It could blow up, like gunpowder. And time is important, surely?"

"You are right. I will do what I can . . ."

That night, Mary and the Lady Marie retired, not early but sufficiently so to allow the other two an hour or so by themselves, undisturbed. Intrigue, plotting and affairs of state were forgotten, for the time being. It was late before they parted, reluctantly, at Alison's bedroom door.

* * *

Heriot spent two full and happy days at Methven. Then the Lady Marie left, to return to Castle Huntly at the other side of Perthshire, near Dundee; and the man surrendered to the pull of duty, to go in search of Master Will Shakespeare and his locations. Perth was only five miles east of Methven, and nothing would do but that the two young women should come with him, eager to inspect the actors as they were to traipse round the countryside sight-seeing.

There was no theatre or playhouse, of course, in St. Johnstoun of Perth, and the plays were being performed in what had been the refectory of the former Blackfriars Monastery, a large building now semi-ruinous and much the worse for the attentions of the Reforming mob of forty years previously. Here the visitors found rehearsals proceeding for another of Master Shakespeare's productions, called *Hamlet, Prince of Denmark,* with the playwright both acting and directing, a performance which greatly intrigued the ladies, who pleaded to be allowed to stay and watch. Heriot, who was not much of a play-taster, perceiving that there might be a couple of hours of this, mentioned that he had business of his own to see to in the Perth district, and if he might be excused, would come back for them presently. Wide-eyed at all that was going on in the refectory, they scarcely appeared to notice his desertion.

Scone, the former abbey and home of Scotland's famed palladium, the Stone of Destiny, had, since the Gowrie Conspiracy of 1600, been the seat of Sir David Murray of Gospetrie, Cup-Bearer to the King, and two years earlier created Lord Scone. It lay barely two miles north by east of Perth. Heriot was asking the best route thereto, across Tay, when the citizen he had accosted pointed out that if it was the Lord Scone himself who was sought, there was no need to go all that way, for his lordship had a town house in Perth—and in fact the speaker had seen him in the street that very morning. So Heriot found his way the short distance eastwards from Blackfriars, beyond the huddle of vennels and wynds of the craftsmen's sector of the walled town, to the wider North Port, where there was something of a cluster of Murray town houses, belonging to the Earl of Tullibardine and the lairds of Balvaird, Arngask, Abercairny and others.

The Lord Scone, who was meantime next door drinking claret with his kinsman Tullibardine, was not long in appearing when he heard the identity of his caller. As well as being Cup-Bearer and Master of the Horse to the King, in Scotland, he held the office of Comptroller of the Privy Purse, all offices of more honour than substance in the present circumstances. He was an old crony of James's, a man of middle years and no presence, with a curiously wide head and narrow chin, scanty hair and little twinkling foxy eyes, his carriage round-shouldered and paunchy. But Heriot did not mistake the shrewdness of the man.

"My lord," he said, "I crave pardon for coming upon you an-announced. But my business is something private, and were better not blazed abroad. You will understand, I am sure?"

"Is that a fact, sir? Come awa' in, then, Maister Heriot. Aye, I've heard tell o' you, mind. Och, aye—often. And what sort o' private business have you for Davie Murray, eh? Frae London?"

"Yes, from London, my lord. I am His Grace's jeweller and man of business, as you will know. And am come north on certain business of the King's own. My visit to you is in your capacity of Comptroller to His Grace." Heriot glanced around him, and lowered his voice in suitably conspirational style. "In connection with the matter of the Master of Gray."

"Ha—that limmer!"

"Precisely, my lord. You have, I understand, withheld payment to him of the nineteen thousand, nine hundred and eighty-three pounds Scots awarded to him against the King's Privy Purse by the Court of Session in commission? On the instructions of the Lord Treasurer?"

"That is so, sir. Acting on King Jamie's behoof and command."

"Yes. Well—the situation has changed. It is now to the King's benefit that this sum be paid, and promptly. And, I may say, secretly."

"Sakes—what's this? Here's a right strange turn-around, Maister Heriot. Pay after a'?"

"Just that, my lord. For reasons of state, this money should be handed over, quietly, privily—but forthwith. To the Master of Gray, at Castle Huntly."

The other looked at him keenly. "On *your* say so, Maister Heriot? Against the orders o' Doddie Home, the Treasurer?"

"The Earl of Dunbar will no doubt be notified in due course. I have seen the King since he has—and have come straight to you, my lord. For this is a matter of some urgency. In the light of . . . developments." Heriot reached into his doublet-pocket and brought out a paper. "Here is my personal note-of-hand for twenty-one thousand pounds Scots—which will suffice, I think, to cover the payment—plus any small outlays your lordship is put to in the matter."

There was a pregnant silence in the stuffy little room, as Scone picked up and examined the paper. The sounds of the street were suddenly evident.

"Ooh, aye," the Comptroller said, at length. "To be sure. Uh-huh." He carefully folded and pocketed the paper. "Very good, Maister Heriot."

"Yes. You will have the payment made swiftly, my lord?"

"Yes, yes. The siller is here. It will be at yon Castle Huntly before this hour the morn."

"That will serve very well. And the King well served in it."

"Mmmm. You're no' telling me *why* this change o' tune, sir?"

"Policy, my lord. In connection with certain moves that are afoot. To contain certain Catholic ambitions!" Scone was a fervent Protestant. "Hence the secrecy."

"Ah!" The other nodded. "I have heard tales, mysel'. Very good, Maister Heriot. Leave the matter to me. Aye. Now—a glass o' wine . . .?"

Walking his horse back to the Blackfriars thereafter, George Heriot felt somehow cold about the back of his neck. James Stewart had not actually executed anyone for some time—but the Tower of London loomed with a chilly presence.

Will Shakespeare proved to be getting on famously with the ladies, and they were drinking ale and eating sweetmeats with him and certain others of the players when Heriot returned. It turned out that the playwright had been using his own initiative during his time in Perth, and had already visited Birnam Wood, Dunsinane and sundry other locations relevant to the theme of MacBeth, and was bubbling over with enthusiasm for the scale and wildness of the scenes, so much more dramatic than anything he had experienced hitherto. He had the entire tragedy all but plotted out in his mind, and had seen many curious and colourful characters here in Scotland on whom he might base his protagonists. He had but to see Elgin, Forres and the witches' moor there, and he would have sufficient for his purposes.

Heriot pointed out that there was more to the MacBeth story than these locations. He explained about the alternative witches's moor in the St. Martins-Dunsinane area, MacBeth's Castle at Cairnbeddie, and the fact that MacBeth's final defeat and slaying was at Lumphanan in Aberdeenshire; but while the other agreed that he ought to see these nearby sites, unless they were infinitely superior to the Moray ones, for the play's purposes, he would prefer to hold to the ones the King had suggested, as a matter of policy. Moreover, it would complicate matters to introduce an entirely new location for the final battle—for a playwright had to consider the number of acts and scenes, with their backcloths, for his production, and discipline himself strictly. His duty was to entertain and instruct by demonstrating the spirit and essence of historical drama rather than by seeking to portray exact detail and sequence of historical events. His listeners accepted that.

It was agreed, then, that they would all go to look at Cairnbeddie and the Eastmuir of Dunsinane, in Gowrie, only seven miles away, the next day; and then, in two weeks time, when the season at Perth was finished, Shakespeare would take his company north, to Elgin and Inverness. Whether they would have time to visit Aberdeen and this Lumphanan, would depend on developments. Heriot mentioned that he was doubtful about the profitability of play-acting in the North, which was in the main an Erse-speaking area—although Elgin, where the Old Church had been so strong, might provide audiences capable of understanding English actors.

So the day following, the young women once again very much present, they picked up the playwright at Perth, and rode on, over Tay, east by north into Gowrie, towards the northern foothills of the Sidlaw Hills, a territory verging on the Angus border. There they saw the green mound rising out of an apron of broom-clad hillside, which was all that was left of MacBeth's Castle, his southern stronghold after he became king. They climbed Dunsinane Hill, and exclaimed at the magnificence of the far-flung vista, pointing out the Birnam and Dunkeld wooded hills to the north-west; and after much searching, and at grave risk of becoming bogged in a swampy, scrub-grown heath, discovered the extraordinarily-shaped Witches' Stone, like a great anvil, with its neighbouring stone-circles and standing-stones, a pleasant enough spot on a sunny May day with the gorse blooming golden, but undoubtedly eerie, even grim, of a winter's dusk. That was all that they had time for, as Shakespeare had to be back for the evening performance. This his companions thereafter attended, with much enjoyment; even Heriot, with Alison at his side to share in and savour the experience, found the evening a delight.

Thereafter, in the long gloaming of May in Scotland, the trio rode back to Methven in the shadowy yet shadowless half-light, wherein outlines had no certainty and distances no measurement, a world of jetty black, dove greys, sepia and the sheen of pewter, tired but happy. It was not often that King James's service proved so much to Heriot's taste.

Shakespeare clearly no longer required his assistance. It had been his original intention to visit Castle Huntly and seek interview with the Master of Gray himself. But in the circumstances, and on Mary Gray's advice, this was unlikely to be productive of advantage, face to face confrontations with Patrick Gray being seldom of satisfaction to other than himself. Better to be content, and let what had been set in train work its own results—with the Lady Marie's aid.

After two more halcyon days, the man took his grudging, heavy-hearted departure from Methven. Alison, at first, had thought to accompany him at least as far as her father's house in Edinburgh; but on consideration, despite the extra day or so it would give them, they decided that it was better to part here, on the scene of their happiness, than in the crowded city, where James Primrose and the thronging family inevitably would come between them, in some measure, and spoil the quality of their farewells. This did not make the parting any easier—but at least it was all their own.

The bridegroom-to-be rode off southwards, and the counting of the months could begin.

18

The morning after his arrival back in London, George Heriot duly repaired to Whitehall Palace to report to his liege lord. He observed his normal wise precaution, however, of first seeking out the Duke of Lennox, in his private quarters of the great rambling establishment, to ascertain the royal availability and mood.

He found Ludovick at a belated breakfast, after a hard night in the King's company, entertaining in typical style the Landgrave of Hesse in the interests of European peace, the sun having been rising down-Thames before they got to bed. For all that, Geordie could not see the monarch yet awhile—not because he was still abed or incommunicado but because of the new daily routine. A bright new star had arisen over the land, and the Court, like all else, must worship—however awkward the hour! All was changed, and London upside-down.

"I have been gone but three weeks," Heriot pointed out. "Do not say that the King has become a new man in the interval?"

"James does not change, no—only changes others. We have a new master, Geordie—as you will learn to your cost. A mere boy, at that—a stripling. But a stripling cuckoo in our nest, I think, with strong wings, beak and claws! Young Rob Kerr of Ferniehirst—though he is now calling himself Carr, as the English spell it."

"You mean, the page? The fumbling one, who was dismissed? Ferniehirst's younger son? From Jedburgh?"

"The same. The laddie who came south with us four years ago. Whom Anne got rid of as incompetent—who dropped the wine-cup over her gown, tripped over James's train and could not recite the Latin grace! It seems that James Hay, now my lord Viscount Doncaster, some kin of his, sent him to France thereafter—where he has learned a lot! Learned notably to be less of a fumbler. Now he is back, aged eighteen, and has us all by the ears. Or, it may be, the balls!"

"But . . . how can this be? Dand Kerr's young brother . . .?"

"You will learn. He is beautiful—oh, a young Adonis! All flowing locks, swan's-down cheeks, a girl's red lips and melting blue eyes—only they melt not the ice behind them! Yet well made, a manly body, long slender limbs—even with one of them broke! Made to our Jamie's measure—and withal, having a most fetching French intonation, grace and manner, with all most modest insolence! Rob Carr aims higher than the Border peel-tower he came out of, I swear!"

"And he has got so far in three weeks?"

"He has had the Devil's own aid—or Hay has! Doncaster. As you know, Hay has been a fading favourite for long—ever since leaving Scotland. He grows fat on southron fare! So he needs look to his . . . assets! He was over in France as an ambassador in James's new pacifications, saw his young kinsman—and perceived the gift of the gods! So he brought him back, to put in the King's way. After you left, there was the usual annual folly to celebrate James's Coronation-day, and one of these stupid tourneys and tiltings. Thank God I was excused this once! Hay dressed this young sprig in white armour and the red-and-white colours, set him on a magnificent black Barbary stallion assured to catch the King's eye, and sent him into the lists with the Lord Dingwall. By the most extraordinary chance, the Devil's work as I say, just as they were passing the royal box, a fanfare sounded, and the stallion took fright. It reared high, the boy overdid the correction, pulling the brute's head too far round while still it reared, and with the weight of his armour, it overturned. Fell on its back—and the youth beneath. Right under James's royal nose!"

"And the King's heart was touched?"

"Whether his heart or other parts, who knows! But he halted all, there and then, hurried down to the fallen Carr, had the helmet removed—and fell in love with the beautiful unconscious! The youth had his leg broke. James, tears in his eyes, had him removed with the utmost care to the Master Rider's house in Charing Cross nearby, sent for all the royal physicians and went there after him, cancelling the tournament, all solicitude. Now, every morning, he attends the dressing of the leg in person, and kisses the pains away. Hunting has to wait until later—would you believe it? That is where he is now. Carr is already made an extra Gentleman of the Bedchamber, with six hundred pounds Sterling a year! James will speak of little else than the excellences, of mind and spirit and body, of this youthful paragon—who, it seems, has an intellect, but awaiting the King's awakening, to flourish and astound us all! We must needs all go worship at the shrine, daily. No doubt *your* turn will come."

"A nine-days-wonder, let us hope."

"Would that it were. But I think not. Others think not, to be sure. They say the youth is clever. Or, at the least, cunning. I reckon Hay will gain but little out of his investment—for others are taking Carr over. Folk with keener wits than Hay. There is a battle for him, already, between the factions. The Howards, in especial, are amove. See you, the Countess of Suffolk herself goes early each morning to this house, before James arrives, to curl Carr's hair, perfume his breath, paint his lips and anoint his body! Old enough to be his mother, no doubt she obtains her reward—but the entire Howard clan are abetting her. They usually know well what they do. Even Cecil pays court. It sickens *me*. As it does Anne."

"The Queen mislikes it? Seriously? More than her husband's other . . . weaknesses?"

"Aye. She is angry. Bitter. For this Carr has already said ill things of her. He so soon conceives himself secure enough to do so. She it was who had him dismissed for incompetence, mind—and he has not forgot, it seems. And he has already snubbed young Henry, whom James insisted must go visit him, bearing gifts. As you know, Anne is a tigress where her bairns are concerned! She is in a great state."

Thoughtfully Heriot scratched his chin. "James has ever had a great need, and capacity, for affection," he said. "The pity that he must needs turn for it, thus . . ."

When, presently, a commotion heralded the King's return from Charing Cross and his mission of mercy, the Duke took his friend to see if he could gain audience. James proved to be in a glowing and expansive humour, at one with his world. He allowed Heriot into his presence at once, greeted him warmly, declared that Geordie and Vicky must accompany him there and then, for he had a ploy on, a justifying of justifiers, which might well hold some good sport—and they must not keep Philip waiting, must they?

Mystified, the pair fell in behind their happy sovereign lord who, preceded by a posse of Yeomen of the Guard and followed by sundry dignatories, hobbled off forthwith along the lengthy corridors of Whitehall, tall white stick waving and clacking.

"I'm new come frae Robbie's bedside, Geordie man," Majesty announced, over a padded shoulder. "Robbie Carr. You'll mind Robbie? Him my Annie put aside, yon time—the mair fool her! Och, he's a guid lad is Robbie. And I owe him something, mind you, for Annie's unkind extrusion—aye, her fustigation. A right martyrdom, no less! But he's doing fine, now—och, just fine."

When Heriot made no comment, James turned and looked at him, the stick coming up to jab.

"You said, Geordie . . .?"

"Nothing, Sire. I, ah, had scarce time to express my, my felicitations."

"Aye. Well." The march was resumed. "I've great hopes for Robbie, see you. He's got wits in his bonnie heid—oh, aye, notable wits. And wi' me for his tutor, he'll go far, far."

Behind the royal back, Heriot and Lennox exchanged glances.

They came to a large chamber overlooking the river, where were assembled quite a group of people of both sexes, and varied types and classes. Standing apart from the others, and looking distinctly chilly and offended, was Philip Herbert, Earl of Montgomery, dressed in the exaggerated height of fashion. He had been drifting from favour ever since his marriage—James had come to the conclusion that he did not like the wife—and now the new favourite's meteoric rise would be the last straw. He sketched the briefest of bows at the royal entry, while all others genuflucted deeply.

The King did not appear to notice, all genial attention on Montgomery. "Ha, Philip lad!" he cried, "It's yoursel'? A right bonnie morning, is it no'? Fine for the work in hand, eh? If we're a wee thing late, I couldna help it. Man, you're looking fine and swack. Getting fat, on my soul!"

"Your Majesty is pleased to jest!" the other returned, sulkily.

"Na, na—nae jesting in it, Philip. It's work, the day. And I've got a right suitable and worthy ploy for you, lad—and a' in the interests o' justice and good governance. You'll thank me, I swear!" James made his way to the head of a central table, and sat down, laying his stick along the board, and beckoning to a clerk for papers. "Aye, well." He cleared his throat, and tipped his hat forward over his brow to signify that utterance was now official.

"We are here assembled and forgathered, my lords and friends, on a matter o' much concern to this realm, lords o' justiciary, magistrates, appellants and witnesses—or, shall we say, deponents and evidenters. Aye. The subject is witchcraft. Or, leastways, the matter o' misclaims and misjudgments thereanent. A right serious matter that has been brought to our royal notice. See you, it's this way—there has been a notable onset and increase o' claims for the punishment o' witches, and the compensation o' the victims thereof, such as I did stipulate when I ascended this throne o' England. Notable." He smirked complacently. "No' unconnected wi' the publication o' my ain work on Demonology, I'm thinking! Aye. But no' a' folk are so enquirous and single-minded in the matter as their liege lord, mind. There's ill-conditioned folk who jalouse they can profit frae my kind care for my subjects by making *false* claims. Accusing their unfriends o' witchcraft, and claiming in law upon their goods and properties, in compensation. A maist deplorable defraud. My justices are no' ay o' the ability and penetration to discern the truth in such misclaims. They havena a' studied the matter as hae I. Is that no' the case, my lord Chancellor?"

Ellesmere, who with Coke, the Attorney-General, was standing by, bowed warily.

"Aye, then. I have, therefore, summoned to my presence two contested cases, for my ain judgement this day. As demonstration and test. *Experimentum crucis.* Two right different cases." James consulted the paper. "Item—the case o' Samuel Colt, yeoman, and his wife Deborah Vance, o' Ware in the county o' Hertford, against one Suzanna Gaffney, spinster, goose-wife, likewise o' Ware, their neighbour. Alleged that the said Suzanna, being reputed a witch, did bewitch the said Deborah, out of ill-will and spleen, by crossing fingers and eyes at her, caused close her secret parts, to the end that she, although a mother of two children, may no longer enjoy proper wifely communion wi' the said Samuel her husband, nor can bear further children on the said account. And so they petition for the due punishment o' the said Suzanna, as notour witch, and the arrestment o' her property for payment o' the sum o' thirty pounds Sterling, in sloatium for the said grievous deprivation in bodily comforts and marital bed."

Something between a snigger and a snort came from the Earl of Montgomery and sundry others smiled. James cocked an eyebrow.

"Aye, Philip—I reckoned you'd be interested! But it's no matter for mirth, mind. Samuel Colt and Deborah Vance to stand forward."

From the group at the foot of the table, a long-featured, stooping man of early middle years shuffled out, bobbing continously and turning his hat round and round in his hands, the picture of discomfort. And with him a red-cheeked, buxom woman, considerably younger, who, though flushed, kept her head high.

The King eyed them thoughtfully, especially the woman. "Ooh, aye," he said.

There was a lengthy pause, wherein the yeoman Colt became increasingly unhappy, and his wife, although she endeavoured to maintain her pose, bit her lips, plucked at her gown, her ample bosom beginning to heave.

"I've no' ca'd the alleged witch, Gaffney, to be present," James went on presently, "until I acquaint mysel' wi' the details and rightness o' the chairge. As I have it, Samuel Colt, it's no' *you* that's bewitched, but your wife? You can still do it, can you?"

Stammering and nodding, the man indicated that he was still a capable husband.

"Aye, then—it's you that canna, Mistress Deborah? You canna what?"

"I . . . may it please your High and Mightiness . . . I cannot . . . cannot . . ." Gulping, and red as a beetroot, the lady spread shaking hands.

"Be mair specific, woman," her monarch commanded.

"I cannot . . . take him. Take him in. Sam'l. Not as 'ow I used to, as you might say, sir. My lord. Mightiness."

"Is that so? You canna tak him in. And you, sirrah—you canna *get* in?"

"Y'yes, sir. N'no, sir. I . . . I . . . no, Highness."

"Mak up your mind, man. We maun get to the bottom o' this!" James glanced over at Heriot and Lennox, to see if they had caught the allusion.

"Your case is that you're no' gravelled, nor yet impotent, but that since Suzanna bewitched your wife you canna get in? She canna tak you, she says. Canna—or winna?"

"Cannot, lord. She goes . . . stiff. Closed up."

"Stiff, man? That's fell interesting. The boot on the wrang foot, heh? And you, Mistress—how do we ken you've no' just taken a scunner at your husband? He's getting auld, I see. It's happened before now. Maybe that's the cause o' your stiffness and closeness downby? Maybe you've your eye on another lad—wi' mair smeddum to him?"

"Oh, no, sir—no! King, sir. Not so. As God's my witness . . .!"

"Aye, well. You claim that you're bewitched, woman, so that you canna tak a man in? And you claim thirty pounds Sterling in compensation. See you, that's an unverified statement, just. I'll need verification before I can pronounce a right judgment. Aye, verification. I therefore command, Mistress Deborah, that you go ben the next room, while test is made o' your assertion. Wi' a man other than this Samuel Colt. To wit, Philip, Earl o' Montgomery, who, besides being a peer o' this realm is a right notable lover and performer on women! If *he* canna get in, then I'd likely accept your claim. You have it, Philip lad? Nae raping and roaring, mind—just a decent bit haughmagandie. To your, h'm, mutual comfort! I'll gie you a half-hour. The bit room's a' ready, wi' a bed and a flagon o' wine. You'll no need mair than that, I'm thinking—a man o' your prowess?"

There was a chorus of exclamation, wails and protest from the husband, little controlled squeals from the wife, chuckles from Philip Herbert, and varied reactions from judges, magistrates and lookers-on.

James held up his hand for quiet. "Silence in my royal presence!" he reproved. "This is a court o' law, I'd remind you a'. The highest in the land, forby. Guard—tak them ben. A half-hour—nae mair, mind. Now—next case?"

Consulting his paper, as the Earl gallantly took the lady's arm and escorted her somewhat reluctant person to the door, behind two Yeomen of the Guard, all assured if somewhat lofty and patronising charm, the King went on:

"Item—the case o' the young woman, Kate Selby, o' Brentwood in the county o' Essex, against one Nell Carter or Hives, alleged witch. A right interesting case, this, wi' mair o' meat to it. The lassie Kate, or her faither Matthew Selby, saddler, avers that she is bewitched by the said Nell Carter or Hives, in that whenever the first verse o' the first chapter o' St. John's Gospel is read in her presence she is cast into a fit. Whereby she is held askance by the hale community o' this Brentwood in general and her betrothed husband Peter Lukes in particular. The said Peter Lukes being minded, on this account, to withdraw frae marriage, the said Matthew Selby claims the sum o' nineteen pounds Sterling in salatium for himsel' and five pounds Sterling for his daughter Kate, making twenty-four pounds Sterling against the person and property o' the said alleged witch, Nell Carter or Hives. Aye, an interesting case, you'll a' agree?"

There was only a comparatively modest murmur of concurrence, most of the company's thoughts being rather obviously elsewhere —next door to be exact.

"Aye. Some questions arise," the monarch went on. "Kate Selby and Matthew Selby to stand forward. Aye. I have stated your claim correctly? Now—these fits the lassie taks? What form do they tak, man Matthew?"

The father, a stout and rubicund character, lacking nothing in confidence spoke in a rich, broad accent. "Bad, bad, Sir King. She be took bad, with jerks and twitches, something cruel. Stiff she goes, and falls down. Very bad."

"Indeed. And only when this verse o' St. John's blessed Gospel is recited? She hasna been subject to these fits before?"

"No, Sir King—never before. This scurvy witch, Nell Carter, is an evil woman. She be sold to the Devil, as all do know. She put the Evil Eye on my Kate, sitting behind her in the church, when this 'ere reading was being read, see. Three weeks back. My Kate did fall in a fit. And since does be doing the same whenever this 'ere verse is read, Sir King. To her sore hurt and the scandal of all, I say."

"Is that a fact? But, Matthew man, the first verse o' the first chapter o' St. John will no' be read that often, I'm thinking? In the Kirk, or elsewhere. Now I think on it, I havena heard it read this past six month, my ain sel'. So your Kate will no' be just ay falling doon in fits, eh?"

"We put it to the test, my lord King, seeing as how we must be sure, like. We have had Vicar to read it to Kate many times— and allus she do take this fit."

"And does the Vicar read other verses? Or only this?"

"To be sure—many verses. But only on this one does the witch be striking her."

"M'mm. Very strange." James felt deep into his much-padded doublet and drew out what looked like a chapbook or pamphlet. "This is a copy of the Gospel according to the blessed St. John, as translated by my ain scholars presently at work on my command to translate all Holy Writ to your English tongue," he explained. "Maybe it will no' be precisely the same wording as your Vicar's version, mind—but och, likely it will be near enough." Opening the pamphlet, James cleared his throat, and read: "'There was a man sent from God, whose name was John. The same came for a witness, to bear witness of the Light, that all men through him might believe.'"

Everyone in the room but the King and her father, watched the slight, pale-faced and rather plain young woman. She revealed no reaction.

"My lord—may it please Your Worship, that is not the same words as Vicar reads," the saddler declared, in some agitation now.

"No? Och—you're right, man. You're right. Waesucks—by a mischance I read the wrang bit. Yon's the *sixth* verse, no' the first. Aye, well—here's the first: "'In the beginning was the Word, and the Word was with God, and the Word was God . . .'"

The King got thus far when the girl uttered a high moaning noise through her clenched teeth. Rising on her toes, her eyes upturned so that only the whites showed, she began to shake, with great sobbing spasms, arms and legs twitching. Her father caught her as she commenced to keel over and others came to her aid. James stopped reading.

"Maist interesting," he observed. "Och aye, very sad. Lay the lassie on this table, so I can hae a bit look at her."

Held upright between a Yeoman and her father, the young woman had stopped moaning, and her eyes came back to normal.

"Sir King," Selby said, "she will be herself again in a moment. No need to lie her down."

As though to prove her father's knowledge, the girl seemed to relax, then stood upright and looked about her, paler than ever but seemingly herself again.

"Sakes—that was right expeditious!" the monarch exclaimed, as though highly impressed. "She's a' right, the lassie? Nane the waur? Yon's remarkable." And without pause or any change of intonation, he went on reading the Gospel, the same verse as previously.

Promptly Kate Selby's moanings and twitchings and shakings started again, and she went rigid more swiftly.

The King stopped. "A notable possession," he commented. "Possession, aye. But the question is—whose possession? The Devil's. This Nell Carter's? Or the lassie's ain?" That was a general enquiry, which no one apparently felt competent to answer.

The young woman took a little longer to recover, this time. James looked rather anxiously at the timepiece on the wall.

As soon as the sufferer seemed approximately in her right mind again, the King addressed her. "You a' right, lassie? You need to sit doon? No? Right trying for you, heh? Aye—trying!" He chuckled. Well, now—let me see." And again without pause, having turned over the pamphlet in his hands, he read something written in ink on the back. This turned out to be a mere babblement of strange words. All stared, eyed him askance.

The rigmarole ended and the King looked up, great eyes gleaming. "*Sure* you are a' right, lassie?" he repeated. "Nae mair dwaums, nor yet pains? You're fine, again? Good. Aye, very good." He rose to his feet. "Then that is a' my lords and friends. Case dismissed. The lassie's no' bewitched. She's just fell clever—like her faither! But no' clever enough. Nae Devil possession there—save maybe the devil o' greed and malice! For I've just read the first verse o' the first chapter o' the Gospel o' St. John in Greek—and she didna turn a hair! Dinna tell me that Auld Horny doesna ken the Greek, when he hears it! Na, na—I'm no' to be made a fool o' by the likes o' these. Tak them awa!—their ain magistrate to reward them suitably, aye suitably. For disponing fause evidence and wasting my royal time. Aye—and release yon puir crittur, Nell Carter or Hives, and gie *her* the solatium o' twenty-four pounds against this Selby, see you. Now—your airm, Geordie. And your's, Vicky. My lords, we'll leave you for a space. Two-three minutes just. Bide you here—and we'll hae the outcome o' the other case to consider. O' the closed up Mistress Colt!"

Although supported on his two friends' arms, his stick left on the table, there was no question but that it was James who was conducting—and hastening—the Duke and Heriot out of the chamber, along the corridor, down a short passage and into another and smaller room. "Yon took longer than I jaloused," he confided, in a stage whisper. He detached one arm, put a grimy finger to his lips, and began to tip-toe totteringly, a picture of elaborate secrecy and conspiracy.

They all heard the sound of feminine giggling.

"Ha!" the monarch said.

The little room was panelled, but the far wall was hung with arras. James tip-toed over to this and with great care drew aside a fold of the hanging. A slant of light was revealed. There was another hanging or curtain behind, beyond which was daylight.

Clearly here was a doorway, open, between one room and another, screened only by double arras. Drawing the cloth further, the King peered round, at an angle.

"A-a-ah! We're no' too late, after a'," he whispered. "My, oh my—interesting!"

The giggling rose to a whinnying, punctuated by a series of breathless but distinctly formal protests.

"Philip's doing fine—even if he's been a mite slow," Majesty reported. "He's got one hand up, and one doon. Aye—she's well formed, the crittur. Plump. Hae a bit look, Geordie."

James did not move aside from his viewpoint, so Heriot had to crouch down and peer from below. He saw a bedchamber in some disorder, clothing scattered on the floor, wine and flagons on a table, with one beaker spilt, one of Montgomery's high-heeled shoes beside it. The owner thereof was stark naked, sitting on the edge of the bed, with Mistress Colt lying slantwise half-across him, on her back. The clothes on the floor were certainly mostly his, for the lady had managed to retain hers, even though less than staidly arranged. Her skirts in fact were rucked high, displaying lengths of well-rounded white thighs, distinctly massive, and her bodice was open to the waist, large breasts escaped—though not from her companion's attentions.

"They appear . . . fairly well matched. Scarce at odds," Heriot commented, straightening up.

"No' right sorely bewitched? Vicky—how think you? As a magistrate, mind."

The Duke bent down, to peer. "So-o-o! Very nice," he said. "But—why Philip Herbert, James? Though, I confess, he looks well up to the business."

"You'd rather I'd chosen yoursel', Vicky? Och, well—I jaloused Philip to be mair experienced in the matter. Mair like to win quick results. Forby, I dinna like yon wife o' his."

"I scarce see the connection . . ."

"You will—any moment now! He's got her right on the bed now, Geordie. Och, aye—Philip kens what he's at. See there—prying and probing like a ferret at a warren! I'm no' wagering man, mind, but . . ."

"No call for wagering," Lennox reported. "See—she spreads herself."

"A-a-ah! Shrive me—he's in! Guidsakes—*aut amat aut odit mulier, nihil est tertium!* And nae fight, as you might say, at the latter end! Latter end, see you. A surrender, just. A right capitulation! There they go, post and spur and stirrups short! Merry work!"

Lennox rose. "That's it, then. Only the run-in, now. Another glimp, Geordie?"

"I will accept your word for it. The matter seems to be decided."

"Aye—but bide a wee," James directed. "We'll wait for her squeal. Witnessed, wi' oral and enunciate proof. We hae our lawfu' duties to complete, mind. My, oh my—up she goes! Heels red as apples! There fa's Samuel Colt's case! Solved by simple practice. *Solvitur ambulando,* after a manner o' speaking! *Sine ira et studio.*"

A high whickering gasping laughter from the bed served instead of the hoped-for squeal, and James, careless now about silence, grabbed arms for support and led the way back to the main apartment.

In the doorway thereof, he halted, as all turned to bow again. "This case dismissed likewise," he announced. "Disproven and witnessed. The woman Deborah isna closed up, as libelled, nor yet bewitched. Sam'l Colt to be fined in the sum o' thirty-five pounds Sterling, o' which thirty pounds to be given to the aforesaid Suzanna Gaffney, in compensation for wrongous accusation o' witchcraft, five pounds cost for wasting the time o' this and other o' my royal courts o' justice. Failing payment, the said Samuel to be put in ward—though nae doubt Mistress Deborah could well earn the siller as a talented whore! Aye, well—that's it, my lords and gentlemen. A guid day to you a'." Nodding, the King turned his companions around, and hobbled off.

Heriot recollected. "Your stick, Sire. Your staff. On the table." He disengaged himself and hurried back into the chamber, amongst the bemused judiciary and litigants.

When he returned the stick to its royal owner, he took the opportunity to introduce the object of his presence there. "The Master of Gray gave you this stick, I understand, Sire. Brought from France. I have certain information for you, about both."

"Ooh, aye. France, eh? Is that the airt the wind blows? Man, our Patrick's ower active for his ain guid! But, bide a wee. Philip Herbert's no' the only one who has earned a beaker o' wine this morning. Forby, if we're going to discuss yon limmer Gray, we'll be needing something to wash the ill taste o' him frae our mou's. This Whitehall's a gey comfortless house, but I've got a bit corner, wi' a decent fire o' holly logs I keep for mysel'—deid holly's the stuff for a right cheery blaze mind. Though it doesna heat sae well as a guid-going note-o'-hand for pounds Sterling—eh Geordie? Come you—we'll hae a jug o' frontiniak I've got."

In a distinctly overheated study thereafter, Heriot recounted the results of his mission to Scotland—or such of them as he deemed James ought to know. As ever, it was difficult to tell what was news to the King and what he already knew or suspected from undisclosed sources. One item which he was sure that his liege lord did *not* know, however, and which he was notably loth to enlighten him upon, he had to divulge at length.

"Finding affairs in such state, and perceiving danger to your Majesty's and the realm's interests growing the more serious, I decided that it was necessary to pay the Master of Gray the sum adjudged to him by your Commissioners, Sire," he informed, slowly at first, but ending in something of a rush. "This nineteen thousand pounds-odd Scots. As a matter of urgency."

"Eh . . . ? Pay? You did? *You* decided!"

"Yes, Sire, I did. You had sent me up there to look to your interests. It was clear that delay in the payment was greatly harming those interests. And Your Majesty's credit. I therefore took it upon myself to pay the moneys, there and then. Before worse harm was done . . ."

"You *paid* the money. Precious soul o' God—you paid siller! To Gray?"

"To your Comptroller, the Lord Scone, yes. For Gray."

There was a silence which all but throbbed, in that stuffy room. James Stewart glared, licking away the saliva which dribbled from both corners of his slack mouth and breathing heavily.

Greatly daring, Lennox spoke up. "Wise," he said, though a little thickly himself. "You are fortunate, James, in having someone there who *could* pay money on such a scale . . ."

"Quiet, Vicky Stewart! When I require your sage guidance, I'll ask for it!" The King swung on Heriot. "I'll need an explanation for this, Geordie," he said, in a quite different voice, quietly, sibilantly. "Aye, an explanation."

The very quiet and brevity of that was in itself alarming, so different a reaction from the monarch's usual garrulity. Heriot drew a deep breath of his own. "The explanation is simple, Sire—my love for Your Majesty. The Master of Gray is the cleverest man in Scotland—now that you are no longer there in person. He already conceives you to have injured him in refusing him leave to come to London, and dispensing with his services. He plots against your policy—but the menace of his plans is later, not yet. Your Majesty, and your ministers, have time. To counter him, it is thought. Grievously to offend him further, and he could well strike now, in his anger. That time I judged to be precious, for your cause. Therefore I bought time, with that money. I paid Your Majesty's adjudged debt, that you might not have to pay a deal more dearly."

"You paid what wasna yours to pay! I adjudge that dishonest as it was insolent, sir!"

"With respect, Sire, not so. I paid what was my own. The note-of-hand I gave Lord Scone was mine, and mine only. That money he will draw from *my* account. Whether you repay me hereafter is for Your Majesty's own decision. I shall not ask you for it."

"So-o-o! That's the way o' it? Geordie Heriot plays high and mighty—and no' for the first time! To his liege. That's pride, man—the wicked pride o' riches, o' worldly gear. Insolent, as I said. You think that you can buy your liege lord wi' siller!"

"No, Sire. But I think that I can buy time against a notable Catholic plot with siller—if not yours, then my own. Am I at fault in that?"

"You are at fault. In overturning my policies, man. By your ain showing, Patrick Gray seeks to turn my realm o' Scotland Catholic again. And to turn my parliament o' England against me, to my hurt. A fell ambitious and expensive scheme, for which he needs money, much money. And you hae given him near twenty thousand pounds Scots to aid him in this, kenning it against my wishes. Think you I hadna heard something o' this plot, and wasna taking my precautions?"

"All of which I guessed, Sire—although you did not confide in me. Yet you sent me to Scotland to act for you, and to gain information. I acted in what I believed the best interests of the Crown, overturned no policy—but bought you time."

"Aye, you're a right eloquent advocate, Geordie Heriot—for your ain case! You ken how to look to your ain business."

"And yours, I hope, Sire—since I am still Your Majesty's man-of-business. But if you would be quit of me in this, I am at your entire disposal."

"I might tak you at your word, Geordie."

"Then, Sire, I should gladly sell my business here in London, return to Scotland, marry, and set up as a small laird in Strathearn. I might even be the better off!"

Thoughtfully monarch looked at subject. "That you will never do, my friend," he said softly. "I promise you that." After a pause, he shrugged. "Aye, well—what o' the man Shakespeare and this MacBeda ploy? How does he fare?"

On this safer topic Heriot could relax somewhat. He recounted progress, and assured that the playwright was full of enthusiasm, and quite enamoured of Scotland and the Scots, at least in dramatic terms. James pooh-poohed any ideas that the witches might be located on the Eastmuir of Dunsinane instead of the Hardmuir of Forres. The North was the most truly wild and barbarous area, he contended, where old hags and beldames most aptly belonged.

"Why are your witches always *old?*" Lennox demanded. "To my mind, young queans are much more like to bewitch successfully than old crones. Surely, witches must be born, not made? So should they not manifest their witchery at all ages?"

"Na, na, Vicky—Satan finds auld dames o' mair use to him, auld in wickedness. Even Holy Writ says it."

"Holy Writ? I claim no great knowledge of the Scriptures, James—but I'd like to hear you give chapter and verse for that!"

"You would? What o' this? 'The Devil walketh in dry places . . .'?" The King tee-heed loudly at his sally. "Matthew 12, verse 43, if I mistake not. Mind, I could do better, given time." Suddenly, he frowned. "Time—aye, time I wasna here. I've yon French ambassador to see, before we eat. He'll hae been waiting this hour—and the French are fell important, in my policy o' peace. Especially wi' yon Maister o' Gray at work—and wi' siller to burn! Eh, Geordie?" James raised an eyebrow, and tapped his goldsmith's arm. "See my new Purse-bearer, Geordie—he'll gie you your money. Nineteen thousand pounds Scots, mind—that only. I'm no' paying any interest, Guidsakes . . . ! Your airm, Vicky."

19

THE ELEGANT GENTLEMAN looked around George Heriot's modest premises with a strange mixture of hauteur and embarrassment. "My name is Dewsbury. Sir Asher Dewsbury," he declared. "And I, ah, come on a matter of business." That last was enunciated in a tone which made it clear that he would not be seen entering such a place were the business not highly important.

"As do most who come here," Heriot acknowledged, gravely. "How can I help you, Sir Asher?"

"I do not seek *help*, sir!" the other said sharply. "A matter of business as I say. No doubt to your advantage." That 'your' was stressed.

"Ah. Then I should be grateful, Sir Asher—should I?"

"H'm. So I would judge. My man is outside. He has, ah, certain items for your consideration. Items of value, you understand. Have him in, Master Heriot."

"*You* have him in, sir."

The knight frowned, then went to the door, and beckoned a servant in from the Exchange. The man carried a large and obviously heavy bag. "You will understand, sir, that the circumstances are unusual. Very unusual. And that this entire proceeding is distasteful to me."

"Ah. If I can lessen the distaste for you, I shall do so, Sir Asher. You wish to pawn something? It can happen to any man."

"Good God—*pawn*, sir? No! I do not . . . pawn! I have come to *sell* you certain items of great value. A simple matter of sale. The items are no longer required by me. They might as well be made use of, by others."

"I see. A worthy attitude, sir. May I see . . . ?"

Dewsbury, looking detached but pained, gestured to his man to open the bag, and then stalked over to investigate some jewellery on display as though with a view to purchase on some suitable occasion. He kept his beautifully-garbed back stiffly turned while Heriot examined the contents of the bag.

"Very nice," his back was told, in due course. "The silver of good quality, the plate fair, the jewellery excellent, if old-fashioned . . ."

"Old-fashioned, sir! What do you mean? These things have been in my family for generations."

"Exactly. As I say, old-fashioned though of fine quality. Fashions change in jewellery as in other matters, Sir Asher. You desire me to buy these?"

"I desire to dispose of them. If your price is sufficient."

"I perceive the difference, sir. Let me see, then." Heriot examined the pieces more closely, took the jewellery over to the light, scratched the plate a little, and weighed all in his hands. "Shall we say seventy pounds, and one hundred pounds, and another seventy pounds? Two hundred and forty pounds Sterling in all. Or . . . make it two hundred and fifty pounds as a comfortable figure."

"But . . . 'fore God, man—this is ridiculous! Not half their worth. You are insulting, sir. I want six hundred pounds, at least."

"Ah. Then I am sorry, Sir Asher. I fear that you must take them otherwhere."

"I shall, sirrah—I shall. But—probably you are making a joke? Testing my wits? I am no pigeon to be plucked, Master Heriot. Come, sir—give me an honest price."

"An *honest* price, sir, would be two hundred and forty pounds. But I will repeat my two hundred and fifty. If it is insufficient, go otherwhere, by all means. But I would advise you that you will not get ten pounds more in all London—and most like be offered less."

"But—the quality, man! You said yourself that the silver was good quality. In weight alone . . ."

"Unfortunately, it has your arms engraved on all, sir. One of the disadvantages of your rank and status. Before I could sell it for use by others, I must remove that. Otherwise, merely melt all down."

Dewsbury looked shaken. "You swear on your word as a gentleman, Master Heriot, that I will get little more elsewhere?"

"I am a tradesman and no gentleman, Sir Asher—so I cannot swear as one. But I will swear as the King's jeweller that it is so. If that will serve."

"Ah. Yes—to be sure. But . . . I need six hundred pounds, sir. And quickly. I can spare no more such items." The knight took a turn up and down the shop. "Master Heriot—I believe that you also *lend* money upon usury?"

"Aye—I am a usurer, sir. I lend—where the credit is good."

"I have two thousand, four hundred good acres in Dorset, sir. Two manors. Will you lend me the remainder of the six hundred pounds?"

"I shall consider it, Sir Asher."

"I require it at once. Today. I shall repay you, shortly."

"How shortly? My interest is twelve per centum. For three months. For folk in a hurry!"

"You shall have it back before three months."

"Sir Asher—are you a wagering man? For I am chary of lending to such. Wagers can fail—and my repayment with them."

"No. No such thing. Never fear, sir—your money will be safe enough. Entirely safe. I have an office of profit in the Queen's household."

"Ah. Indeed. Now you interest me, Sir Asher."

"Yes." The other seemed to recover something of his assurance. "I am to be one of Her Majesty's Almoners. Now—will you let me have the six hundred pounds, sir? Today?"

"Is there such haste? Will tomorrow not serve?"

"No. I must pay it tonight. To Sir Robert Carr."

"Carr? You have been borrowing from young Carr?"

"I have not, sir. I have never borrowed aught in my life! At least, h'm, until today. But I must pay Sir Robert six hundred pounds by tonight—or fail to gain the office of Queen's Almoner."

Heriot drew a long breath. "I see. So . . . Sir Robert Carr is *selling* you the office? Is that it?"

"In a fashion, yes. He uses his influence with the King to gain such appointments. And, and charges for his services."

"Six hundred pounds is a large charge, Sir Asher! See you, I had heard rumours of this practice—but doubted the truth of it. There have been other such . . . arrangements?"

"To be sure. Carr can gain anyone a place, they say. But he is damned expensive!"

"Very well. I think that I may just be able to raise your six hundred pounds on the premises. Two hundred and fifty pounds to buy these items. And three hundred and fifty pounds at twelve per centum. I shall write the papers . . ."

After Dewsbury had gone, George Heriot sat very thoughtful, for a while.

* * *

Two days later, on a grey November afternoon, he presented himself at Denmark House, a thing he had not done for two years, and sought audience of the Queen. He had not to wait for so long as he expected, before being conducted to a pleasant small boudoir where Anne and the Marchioness of Huntly sat before a fire of scented logs, stitching embroidery. His welcome was stiffly wary—but at least the Queen called him Master Geordie, not Master Heriot, and managed a hint of a smile as he bowed low.

"You have not found occasion to call on us these many months," she declared, after the formal greetings. "In consequence, I have had to purchase my jewelley from Sir William Herrick." That was distinctly tart.

"An excellent gentleman," Heriot said. "I am sure that he will serve Your Majesty passing well."

"No doubt," she answered, frowning a little. "His prices are fair. But he is mighty mean in the giving of credit."

Heriot sought to look sympathetic, but did not comment.

They eyed each other heedfully.

"What have you come for?" the Queen asked, at length.

"I have been desirous of coming, for long," the man declared then, frankly. "Wishful to end this . . . estrangement. I still consider myself Your Majesty's servant. I have been much grieved that I no longer had your trust and confidence."

"I have never refused you audience, sir. You have never come."

"Because I did not believe my coming welcome, Madam."

"And you do now?"

"Who knows? But now, at least, I have reason to come. A matter to speak of."

"A favour to ask, perhaps?"

"No. Or, perhaps, that too. But not firstly. My main concern, indeed my duty, is to inform Your Majesty of a matter which has come to my notice—and which I cannot believe you to be aware of. I believe that you *ought* to be aware of it. I have learned that appointments are being made to your household—one appointment, at least—for payment of moneys. Payment to a person at Court. Large payment."

"To *my* household? Not the King's? How dare they? Are you sure, Master Geordie? Have you proof?"

"Yes. I think I have."

"My new Master of Hawks? Strickland?"

"No. Or, it may be so. But that is not the one I learned of. It is Sir Asher Dewsbury, Almoner."

"But—he is not yet appointed. I have but heard his name mentioned."

"He has already *paid* for the office, Madam! Whether or no you have appointed him. And paid sweetly."

"To whom?"

"To Sir Robert Carr."

"That . . . that insufferable youth! That insolent catamite! Great God—can this be true?"

"I fear it is. For I lent Dewsbury money only two days ago. For the payment."

"Infamous! Shameful! Hetty—do you hear? How I am misused, mocked! By that puppy! Oh, it is beyond all bearing. *Carr's* minions in my household! How long has this been going on?"

"I do not know, Madam. I heard only two days ago. Have you made many new appointments?"

"*I* do not make them, sir! I have scarce any say in the matter. It is James who appoints. Sweet Jesu—*he* who humiliates me, at every turn! But yes—there have been new appointments of late. Are they all . . . Carr's?"

"Who knows? Perhaps not . . ."

"They shall all be dismissed! Every one! I will not be served by creatures of that depraved boy! And this Dewsbury shall never start. I will teach them!"

"Your Majesty's wrath is just and understandable," Heriot observed. "But see you—that might not be the wisest course. After all, the fault lies not with these, so much. The men so appointed. They may be honest enough, in their way. They may even love and desire to serve you well—sufficiently so to pay hundreds of pounds for the privilege! Although I doubt the worth and results of such a system. The fault lies elsewhere . . ."

"The greatest fault lies with James!"

"H'm. If His Majesty knows."

"You did not go to *him?* First? To tell him. You came to me. Why?"

Heriot chose his words carefully. "Before I spoke with His Majesty, I believed that *you* should hear of it. In case there was aught I did not know. In which the King might be . . . concerned."

"You mean . . . ? You do not suggest, sir, that James might himself be in this, this wickedness? Dear Christ—that the money goes to *him?* Or part of it?"

That was exactly what the man did mean. But he could not admit to it. "Scarce that, Madam. But . . . His Majesty, I have learned, knows more of what goes on, in things great and small, than might be expected. It could be that he is aware of this of Carr—since there have been rumours—and has some purpose in permitting it meantime. I wished to discover this from Your Majesty."

"How should *I* know? James tells me nothing. You are his man-of-business, are you not? Have you been aware of him gaining large moneys, knowing not whence they came?"

"No. But I might never hear of it. I am not His Majesty's treasurer or purse-bearer. And I have not spoken with him these three weeks."

They discussed the subject for some time, the Queen outraged, seeing the hands of all against her, Heriot seeking now to limit his involvement, to soothe and parry. He even made a plea on behalf of Sir Asher Dewsbury, indicating that as Almoner he should be watched, in the distribution of the Queen's charities—but pointing out ruefully that, if the man was actually refused the appointment now, after paying for it, he, Heriot, might never get his loan back!

When he deemed the moment ripe, even more carefully the visitor introduced his second subject. "I have this other matter, Madam, on which to seek your good offices. The same sorry matter on which we disagreed heretofore."

"Ha!" the Queen said, stiffening.

"I am, I hope, a wiser man now than I was then," he went on, placatingly. "I have learned much of the constraint and difficulties under which Your Majesty laboured at that time—and could by no means tell me. In, h'm, the matter of the Earl of Orkney."

Anne sat up straight, eyes widened, wary—but did not speak.

"I regret my . . . intransigence then," he went on. "Not understanding Your Highness's difficult position. With regard to the King, and his cousin Orkney. Now, I know better, seek your royal pardon, and make bold to suggest how an unfortunate situation could be improved."

"The Letters, sir? You mean that you know how we might gain those evil Letters?"

"Not that, Madam, I fear. I do not know just where these Casket Letters may be now—although I think that my lord of Orkney no longer has them, and may have given them to the Master of Gray."

"Which is worse, I say—for he is the cleverer man! That I knew, anyway."

"Not necessarily worse, Majesty, I think. The Master is cleverer, yes—but has scruples which the other has not. But that is not what I would speak of. It is rather the consequences of that trouble. The case of Mistress Hartside."

"That creature of Orkney's! She deserved all that she got, sir!"

"Perhaps. Though I still believe her innocent of intent against Your Majesty, and used by others. But whatever the rights of it, the present situation is not good. Your Highness has always been held in love and esteem by the folk of Scotland. But your credit and fair name is being impaired by the holding of this unfortunate woman without trial for so long."

"How can I bring her to trial, without all that evil business of Orkney and the Letters and the blackmail being brought to light? Before all?" Anne cried. "You must know very well my difficulty. That is why I sent her away, to Scotland. Where I have my own jurisdiction of Dunfermline."

"I know it, yes, and understand. But I believe that now the girl can be brought to trial, and safely. The Earl of Orkney will no longer have reason to try to use her . . ."

"But she will still *deny* all. Hartside will. And so it will all come out."

"Not necessarily, Madam. That would depend on what was the accusation. If you, or the Crown, accuses her of theft, of *stealing* those jewels, then to be sure she will deny it. But if a lesser charge is brought, it might be otherwise. She might well be brought not to deny such. Or only make token resistance. So that the court appearance is only brief and formal, and no unhappy disclosures necessary."

"How could I make so small a charge? When Hartside has been kept under ward all this time? Would not I seem harsh? My credit suffer as badly, sir?"

"The charge would have to be carefully considered. I am no lawyer, but I believe it could be arranged. Suppose the charge was not stealing but misappropriation—a lesser offence. Or depositing jewels in her care with the Queen's jeweller—myself—without your royal permission? With no intent to defraud. Might that not serve?"

"Would she admit to that?"

"She might well. With . . . guidance! She could admit that the jewels were in her care. That she brought them to me. And I would testify that I restored them to Your Majesty."

"And the moneys you paid her? What of that? She took it. Was that not stealing?"

"Not, perhaps, if she intended to devote it to some good purpose in Your Majesty's service. In fact, she wanted it to give to her husband, so that they might settle in Orkney. You also, in fact, gave these jewels to the Earl of Orkney, and he gave some to his gentleman, Buchanan, Hartside's husband. So, it would be near enough the truth to say that she intended to give the money to one of the Earl's gentlemen, on your royal behalf, for services rendered to Your Highness."

Anne clutched her head. "This is too deep for me, Master Geordie! Too complicated. You spin a veritable spider's web!"

"Only that I may lift Your Majesty off the horns of this dilemna. And restore this young woman to her liberty, at minimum cost to all. A trial there must be, now. And a verdict which is not a mockery. But . . . no disclosures of the true cause. Can you think of better?"

"No. No, I cannot. You say that there must be a verdict. What would this verdict be?"

"It would be guilty, to preserve Your Majesty's credit. But guilty of what would not too greatly hurt Margaret Hartside. With able counsel—such as Master Thomas Hope whom I have already retained, and discreet judges, the penalty would be no more than perhaps the repayment of the price of the jewels taken. With, say, perpetual banishment from Your Majesty's Court—to Orkney!"

"Ha! But—would she, *could* she pay?"

"*I* would pay, Highness. In her name. It is little enough price to clear up so grevious a matter. A few hundred pounds Sterling."

"I see. You are exceeding noble in all this, Geordie Heriot! Why, I wonder?"

"For my love for Your Majesty. And the King. That is all . . ."

"Aye—and your care for one, Mistress Alison Primrose! That

she might be invited back to my Court and household, I think!" the Queen said shrewdly. "I am not a fool, my friend!"

A little put out—for it was near enough the mark; and a large part of the man's manoeuvring had been to ensure that Alison would not have to be implicated in the trial or called as witness, and so seem to oppose the Queen's interests—Heriot shook his head, perhaps too positively. "No, Madam—not that. Alison and I are to wed—as you will know. But it is the wish of neither of us that she should have any appointment at Court. Only, that as the wife of Your Majesty's jeweller, she should not be forever denied to come into your royal presence."

"I see. Very well, Master Geordie—that I might permit. If you can so arrange all this complicate matter, then you have my agreement to it. And, indeed, my thanks. When will it be done, think you?"

"It will all take some time to effect, I fear. Many letters to Scotland. Possibly a visit there again. And lawyers work but slowly. But, by the late spring, no doubt . . ."

Reasonably satisfied, George Heriot took his leave thereafter—and with the royal assurance that he was now, once again, welcome at Denmark House, on both professional and personal business, or no business at all. With this last, especially, he was genuinely pleased.

His satisfaction, however, went for the moment into suspension when he got back to the Royal Exchange to find that during his absence no less a visitor than the monarch himself had called—and sounded not a little put out at finding his so-honoured tradesman from home. He had left commands with Heriot's foreman goldsmith that his master was to report at Whitehall Palace forthwith. Such summonses were by no means always productive of joy.

* * *

But at Whitehall, the urgency was not so apparent. James was actually at table when Heriot arrived, not so much at a meal as at what might be described as an intellectual drinking exercise. It was held in the same gallery as that in which the judicial bewitchment-enquiry had taken place, but now the long table was littered with bottles and flagons instead of documents—although there were one or two dishes of cold meats and the like for those who felt that they required solids with their wine. And the company was very different, legal luminaries and litigants being equally and conspicuously absent. Only courtiers were present, reinforced with a few selected divines of the rubicund and genial English sort, and no women. James, at the head of the table, was in full flood—although his preoccupation with the expounding and elaboration of his syllogisms and propositions did not prevent him from stroking, fondling and occasionally turning to kiss the gorgeous youth who sprawled at his side. He perceived Heriot's entrance, even so, and waved him to a chair near the foot of the table without pausing in his peroration.

The newcomer found himself seated between the former favourite, the Earl of Southampton, Knight of the Garter, and Sir Andrew Kerr of Ferniehirst, elder brother of the young man at the head of the table. Kerr, a cheerful if unscrupulous extrovert, greeted him with a grin, and pushed a flagon and beaker towards him. Southampton was asleep and snoring gently. Directly across the table, while seeming to pay rapt attention to their liege lord's lengthy abstractions, two clients of Heriot's own, the Earl of Rutland and the Viscount Doncaster, were playing cards with miniatures behind an elaborate screen of feathered hats and bottles. From further up the table the Duke of Lennox drooped an eyelid at his friend and yawned carefully behind a hand.

The King was partial to these debating and syllogism sessions, in which he could display his learning and agility of mind. They were less popular with his courtiers—but very good excuses had to be tendered for non-attendance. The churchmen were there to provide the necessary vocal reactions—since the Court gentlemen, save for a few Scots, were almost without exception out of their depth from the first proposition. Also the divines were able sometimes to applaud the frequent Latin comments or aphorisms that fell from the salivating royal lips.

The present monologue—since it was that rather than any debate, at the moment—appeared to be concerned with the nature and identity of the language spoken in the Garden of Eden, James declaiming with an authority rivalled only by its lack of clarity. It seemed that his illustrious great-grandfather, James the Fourth of hallowed memory, had had similar conjectures, and for experiment had deposited two newborn infants, with a deaf-and-dumb wet-nurse, plus a large supply of food and drink, on the otherwise uninhabited islet of Inchkeith in the Firth of Forth, in the confident expectation that they would grow up, uncontaminated by the rest of the world, to speak the basic language of all humanity—which inevitably would be that of Adam and Eve, and therefore of Heaven itself. Unfortunately the second winter later prolonged gales prevented food being landed for the experiment for a couple of awkward months, and an excellent piece of research was spoiled through the death of all concerned. James, it transpired, had frequently thought of making a scientific investigation of his own, on similar lines—and might well do so yet. But meantime, his confident contention was that Gaelic was undoubtedly the language of Eden, and Heaven itself.

This averment aroused not a little doubt around the table, even from some who had appeared to be elsewhere in spirit. Nobody actually was so unwise as to challenge the statement, of course, at this early stage; but not a few eyebrows rose.

James nodded happily—and proceeded to prove his point. The Gaels of Scotland had migrated over long centuries to their present home in the north-west extremity of Europe, via the Mediterranean lands, and Spain, France and Ireland, leaving the names of Galicia, in Spain and Gaul, for France, behind them in the process. But they had first come from the very cradle of mankind, in Asia Minor. The Garden of Eden was known to have been sited, not in the Holy Land but to the north-east thereof, in the heart of Asia Minor, where the great River, the Euphrates rose. And what was the name of that heartland? Galatia. Galatia, whence came the Gaels. The same to whom St. Paul wrote his epistle. The Gaelic-speaking people of Scotland, therefore, were the true and most direct heirs of Adam and Eve, and their language the mother-tongue of all other languages on earth. If any doubted this, let them consider—take the simple word *cuibhle*, pronounced cooyul, Gaelic for circular. From this came the English wheel and whirl and curl. From the same root came *wirren*, to twist, in German; *virer*, to turn, in French; *vermis*, a worm and *verter*, to turn, in Latin; *vermicelli*, in Italian, *Krimi* in Sanskrit. And so on. Could any doubt, then, that the Gaelic was the language of Heaven, the Scots the heirs of Adam, and he the heir of Scotland—and so well-suited to be Vice-Regent of Christ Himself? He would be interested to hear any who contested his reasoning.

While, after a somewhat stunned silence, all disclaimed any such presumptuous assertion, and one of the divines launched into a fulsome eulogy of this resounding proposition, which explained so much of the heavenly wisdom which fell from the royal lips, James took the opportunity to use the said lips to plant a slobbering kiss on those of young Carr, and obviously to fiddle about with him below the table. The youth smiled lazily.

Carr was beautiful, there was no denying that. From a rather awkward boy he had blossomed into a fair and graceful young man, tallish, broad of shoulder and narrow of hip, with curling auburn hair, worn long, above a wide brow, long-lashed and rather prominent eyes, a straight nose and full pouting lips, moistly red. Dressed all in cloth-of-silver, seeded with pearls, beribboned in blue, with cheeks and finger-nails as red as his lips, he lounged at amiable ease. Heriot, looking, wondered how much financial astuteness could lie beneath that complacently immature exterior—and, if little, who was "managing" him?

"Your brother rides high, Sir Andrew," he murmured to Kerr at his side. "He has learned how to butter his bread since he went to France!"

"*Is* he my brother?" Dand Kerr asked. "Damme, sometimes I wonder! Leastways, he scarce acknowledges *me*, now! He never looks the road I'm on."

"Whose road does he look, then? Other than his own? My Lord Doncaster's, there?"

"Jamie Hay's? Not him. He is as little heeded as am I. Robin finds his kin tiresome. It seems he can do without us."

"I give him twelve months." That was Southampton, who seemed to have wakened up, at the other side of Heriot. "No more. Unless Overbury is less greedy."

"Overbury? You mean Sir Thomas? The poet, my lord?"

"Poet? I'd call him otherwise, Master Heriot. But that's the man. He, h'm, advises our Robin. Did you not know?"

James suddenly was banging on the table with his tankard. It had seemingly occurred to him that Master John Donne, theologian, was implying, in his otherwise adulatory remarks, that he, the monarch had more or less imbibed knowledge of the heavenly language by divine right and godly connection, and had not had to learn it the hard way like other scholars. Much incensed, he announced that he had indeed had to study the Gaelic, along with Sanskrit, Hebrew, Greek, Latin and French, with the help of his tutor Geordie Buchanan's wicked tongue and ready belt. Many a sore ear and ringing head he had suffered, etcetera.

Heriot was not listening, his mind busy. This of Overbury interested him. Sir Thomas Overbury was quite famous, a politician rather than a courtier, an academic of some renown who had travelled widely abroad, an intimate of Ben Jonson and something of a protégé of the Howards. But he was seldom seen at Court, and seemed an unlikely 'manager' for young Carr.

James had got back to the subject of language, and was demanding of Philip Herbert, Earl of Montgomery whether he agreed that Aramaic predated Sanskrit—for it was his wont to keep his courtiers on their toes in these sessions by descending on individuals for opinions without warning; moreover, he made a point of seeking to retain the goodwill of his displaced favourites and keeping them by his side. Montgomery, for instance, had been appointed to the profitable office of Keeper of the New Forest, coincident with Carr's rise. The Earl now declared that, being as a new-born babe in the matter of languages, having enough trouble with English and Welsh, he was well content to accept a master's ruling, namely His Majesty's.

The King reproved him for mental laziness, but was evidently well enough pleased. He went on exploring by-ways of the subject for a little longer, impervious to the growing weight of boredom around him, then suddenly appeared to become aware of the passage of time and brought the session to an abrupt close. He turned, and tweaked Carr's ear.

"It is late," he declared. "Just time for your Latin lesson, before we eat, Robin lad. Eh?" And when the youth groaned audibly, James took it to indicate pain in the said ear and leaned over to lavish kisses upon the organ. The he rose, and personally aided the other out of his chair.

It was Heriot's turn to groan. He had heard about these daily hour-long Latin sessions with which the sovereign honoured his new favourite. It looked as though he himself would have a long wait yet.

But, as so often, James Stewart surprised. As he was hobbling to the door, on Carr's arm, amidst the relieved bows of all but his goldsmith, he paused and pointed down the chamber.

"Geordie," he commanded, "come you."

Hurrying after the pair, Heriot came to the royal den, or study, with its lining of bookshelves, its blazing fire of holly-logs and table covered with wine-flagons and papers.

"Aye, Robin—here's Geordie Heriot," James said, turning. "A canny chiel who kens what's what. Kens how to mak siller grow, forby—which is something that interests yoursel', if I'm no' mistaken, heh? This is Robin Carr, Geordie. Is he no bonnie?"

The other two bowed stiffly to each other, without any extravagant warmth.

"Aye." The King glanced keenly from one to the other. "You'll get on fine, I see! Waesucks—you'll hae to!" There was just a hint of asperity behind that. "Now, Robin—awa' you and empty that bladder o' yours. You're ay needing, at the wrang moment! I want a word wi' Geordie. Back in five minutes just, and we'll get on wi' the Latinity."

As the door closed behind the young man, James put a finger to thick lips, and tip-toed to the door. Opening it suddenly, he peered out. Satisfied, he closed it again. "He's a great one for listening behind doors, is our Robin," he confided, with a chuckle. "And I want this to be a surprise."

"Indeed, Sire?"

"Aye, Geordie—indeed. I want you to contrive a bit present for me, see you. For Robin. Another medallion, or ornature, like you made for the woman Arabella. But no' a pendant, mind—something mair suitable for a man. Square, I'd say, no' round. Here's what I want—a bit tablet o' gold, set wi' diamonds, wi' the Kerr's arms in the front—that's red and white so it'll need to be rubies and pearls—supported by a lion and a unicorn. That's me, see? And just the plain gold at the back. But it's no' to be just what it seems. It's to be able to open, see—a wee case. Two sides, hinged thegither, and wi' a cleek to shut it. Inside there's to be a bit mirror on one side—for Robin's right keen on admiring himsel' in mirrors—and a depicture o' mysel' on the other. A miniature, just. I'm getting yon Dutchman Hendriks to paint it for me. So you'll need to get the size right, mind. Is that no' a right cunning notion, Geordie?"

Heriot swallowed. "Cunning, Sire—but expensive!"

"Och, well, we'll no' fret about a bit expense, man, you and me! What's a few pounds to a man who writes notes-o'-hand for twenty thousand pounds Scots, and doesna care if he gets it back? Forby, I'm working on a new scheme to mak siller. In right substantial style. Och, a notable scheme."

The other's heart sank. "Still *another* scheme, Sire?"

"Aye—and a bonnie one. I canna mak that many mair knights. The market is near overgorged, as you might say. *Eheu iam satis!* But there's plenty siller yet in a' yon new knights' pouches. I could be doing wi' some o' it. Maybe I can mak them pay twice! Supposing I was to offer to mak their knighthoods hereditary? So they could leave them to their sons! Like lords can. They'd be willing to pay for that, eh? How think you o' that for a ploy, Geordie man?"

"But—Sire, the whole notion and principle of knighthood is that it is gained by only one man. For himself. A personal accolade and honour. It is not something which can be passed on, to a son or anyone else."

"No, knighthood itsel' isna. But the title o' Sir to their names. We'd hae to ca' it something else. A totally new order. Higher than knight, but below the peers. Hereditary sirs. Folk would be right clamouring for the like, eh? Is it no' a notion?"

"I suppose . . . yes, I suppose it is, Sire." Even though Heriot sounded doubtful, he was much relieved that this was the new money-making device rather than what he had feared, the selling of appointments at Court, through Carr. Though he had still to ascertain that was not, in fact, also in process. He brought the subject back to that young man. "But that is for the future, Your Majesty. This jewel, for young Robert Carr, will be very costly *now*. Must it be so handsome? Plain silver, with the mirror and miniature, would serve equally well, would it not?"

"No, it wouldna. What ails you at Robin Carr?

"Just that I would wish Your Majesty to save your money. When this young man is already making so much out of your royal kindness."

"Meaning—what, sir?" That was rapped out.

"Meaning, Sire, that Sir Robert seems in no need for expensive presents from yourself, when he is making so much out of selling positions at Court to the highest bidder. With or without your royal knowledge."

There was silence in that book-lined room for long moments. Then the door opened, and Robert Carr came strolling in.

"Out!" the King snapped, stabbing a pointing finger. "Awa' wi' you! When I want you, I'll cry on you! And dinna stand listening at the door."

Shocked, the young man gaped, but withdrew hurriedly.

"So you, Geordie Heriot, would teach me my business, eh?" James said, rounding on the other. "You believe you ken better than your lord. And no' for the first time. D'you think I dinna ken every last thing about that laddie oot there, man?"

Heriot cleared his throat. "I did not conceive . . . that Your

Majesty could know . . . and be unconcerned. Of this scandal of the selling of appointments . . ."

"I ken fine. And am watching it."

"But . . ."

"But nothing! Credit me wi' a mite o' sense, will you? You're no' the only man can add two and two. When Robin goes ower far, I'll check him."

"Six hundred pounds Sterling for an Almoner's position in the Queen's household, strikes me as sufficiently far, Sire! Even if the system is accepted as, as respectable, that sum, equal to seven thousand pounds Scots, seems to me . . . exorbitant! And the youth who demands it, both unscrupulous and grasping." Heriot paused, blinking, himself alarmed at his own rashness in making the charge.

Oddly enough, James only chuckled. "Unscrupulous and grasping!" he repeated. "So that's Geordie Heriot's considered opinion? Hech, man—you're a right judge o' character. For Robin Carr *is* unscrupulous and grasping. And other things, forby. He's sort of cunning, but no' really intelligent. He has a gift for survival, though sae young. And he kens how far he can go—oh, aye, he kens that fine. And that's important. But he's bonnie, bonnie. And has . . . other attributes. Aye, attributes."

"I fear I do not understand, Your Majesty, in this matter," Heriot was genuinely bewildered. "You perceive all these dangerous failings in this young man. Yet you cherish him, and wink at his, his extortions?"

"Who said they were *dangerous* failings, Geordie? Failings, aye, maybe—but no' dangerous. No' to me, anyway! Which is what matters. I can use them—fine I can use them." James moved quietly back, to listen at the door. "See you," he went on, voice lowered. "I wouldna tell this to a'body but yoursel', Geordie—for you can keep your mou' shut. Aye—and you'd better! I'm for training that laddie up. For a purpose. A right usefu' purpose. I'm training him, and testing him oot. And he's doing fine. What d'you think I'm wasting an hour every day teaching him Latin for? He'll need to ken Latin, presently—and a wheen other things—for my purposes. The realm's purposes."

"The realm's, Sire? Young Carr . . . ?"

"Just that, Geordie. Here's the way o' it. The man Cecil's getting auld and done. Forby, he's mair crabbit each day! I've never liked the man—but he was necessar. He isna, any longer! I've had enough o' Robert Cecil. Fortunately the man's sick, and will soon die, God willing! So my physicians tell me. I'm going to rule this realm, Geordie, *without* any poking, prying, arrogant Secretary o' State telling me what I can do and what I canna. I'll rule it fine, lacking any such, I do assure you! Cecil will go—and no' be replaced."

Heriot was careful now to keep his tongue between his teeth.

"Now—this damned English parliament, aye and the Council too, they're no' like our Scots ones. They reckon they hae a God-given *right* to interfere in a' concerned wi' the rule o' this realm, *my* realm. I'm told that a principal Secretary o' State is *necessary*, part o' the machinery o' the state. between the monarch and themsel's. Very well—I'll appoint a new Secretary o' State, when I'm ready. But nae mair clever, ambitious, masterfu' and high-born limmers like Cecil! Nae mair nominees o' the Howards, or other great pridefu' English houses, who think to control *me*, their lord, through their watch-dog at the Secretary's desk! Na, na—I aim to appoint Robin Carr. Who'll do what I tell him and naething mair—or I'll ken the reason why!"

Licking his lips, the other shook his head, wordless.

"D'you no' see it, Geordie man? Use your wits. I've been looking for such a one, for long now. Young Robin will owe *a'* to me—no highborn lordling wi' powerfu' relatives behind him. And I'll ken every thought in his heid! You ca' him unscrupulous and grasping—and so he is. But a Secretary o' State needs to be that—under control. Rule and governance demands methods that maybe wouldna do for a shopkeeper nor yet a minister o' religion! Ooh, aye—and Robin will manage a' such for me, fine. He thinks he's got a' these folk appointed to office in his wee bit pocket! Fine, fine—but it's *my* pocket they're in, no' his! They'll likely a' come in right usefu', one day. And meantime, they pay up! They're right carefully chosen, these, mind, afore the whisper reaches them that Robin's the lad to approach!"

"I . . . I am lost in wonder!" Heriot got out.

"Aye, well—I must needs see to the proper ordering o' this realm the guid God has put in my care. One way or the other," James added complacently.

"And Sir Thomas Overbury, Sire? Does *he* fit into this, this proper order?"

"Overbury? What ken you o' Tam Overbury, man?.. That was sharp."

"Only that I have heard his name linked with Carr's. And it seemed an . . . unlikely pairing."

"Overbury is a fell clever man," the King said, slowly. "He is in my confidence. Where did you hear this, Geordie? He keeps awa' frae Court. I dinna want him brought into it."

"It was my lord of Southampton mentioned the name. Casually enough."

"Harry Wriothesley did, eh? I'll hae to look into this. Overbury maun be discreet—or he goes! Aye—and that applies to mair than Tam Overbury, Geordie Heriot. You understand that fine, I am sure?"

"Your Majesty has had long experience of *my* discretion."

"Aye, well. Mind it. Now—it's time for Robin's Latin. Fetch the laddie in, man . . ."

20

THE TOLBOOTH AT Linlithgow was not really apt for major or state trials, being comparatively small, with no apartment large enough for any sort of elaboration or display; certainly no room for any spectators, over and above the necessary judges, assessors, counsel, witnesses and accused. Which was one of the reasons why the affair was being held here, rather than in Edinburgh, in the interests of discretion. Also, of course, Blackness Castle, where Margaret Hartside was for the moment installed once more, for the look of things, was only three miles away and within Linlithgow's jurisdiction. But at least the place was comfortable, almost cosy, with hangings brought to cover the grey stone walls, a good coal fire burning on the hearth, wine on the table, and all bright with the late May sunlight, little of the atmosphere of trial or legalities evident.

There were twelve people in the room—eleven men and the accused young woman. The four judges were James Elphinstone, Lord Balmerino, Lord President of the Court of Session as well as Chief Secretary; James Hamilton, first Earl of Abercorn; Alexander Livingstone, first Earl of Linlithgow, in whose jurisdiction the trial was taking place—the former guardian of Princess Elizabeth; and Sir Peter Young, one-time tutor and preceptor to the King. All were extraordinary Lords of Session. Crown counsel and prosecutor was the Lord Advocate, Sir Thomas Hamilton of Binning, Heriot's cousin; and counsel for the defence Master Thomas Hope, advocate, assisted by Master John Russell—who was there mainly to look after George Heriot's interests. In addition, there were two reverend gentlemen, the ministers of Methven and Ceres, there in the capacity of sureties for Margaret Hartside, who had been lodging with one or other of them since her release from Blackness, both being in fact uncles of her husband and both called Buchanan. John Dalziel, the Edinburgh burgess in whose name the necessary deposit of ten thousand merks had been made, was there. Heriot himself was the only witness likely to be required. Finally there was Margaret Hartside herself, subdued, wary but suspicious.

It took a while for proceedings to get started, amidst all the sociability. Balmerino in particular seemed loth to commence, being apparently more interested in making himself agreeable to Heriot—no doubt in the hope that some of the affability might rub off eventually on King James in London, for he knew very well that his star was far from in the ascendant, and that his former colleague George Home, Earl of Dunbar and Lord Treasurer, was seeking to pull him down, and had the ear of the King. Abercorn and Linlithgow knew it equally well and were careful not to seem too friendly with Balmerino—and were in consequence the more patronisingly genial with everybody else, save the accused.

Hope it was, a man not notably sociable, who eventually got proceedings under way by crisply reminding the Lord Advocate that time was passing and that there was the Deacon-Convener's Dinner in Edinburgh, eighteen miles away, that evening. Sighing, and reluctantly putting down his tankard, Hamilton shrugged and bowed to their lordships across the table. All sat down, with the exception of Hamilton himself.

Clearing his throat, the Lord Advocate read out the dittay, an abbreviated version of the original charge, which outlined the case and ended by accusing Margaret Hartside, former Chambermaid to the Queen, of stealing and/or misappropriating certain jewellery, namely one diamond valued one hundred and ten pounds Sterling, other pearls, precious stones and goldsmith work to the value of three hundred pounds Sterling, all in London, and selling it to one George Heriot, jeweller at the Royal Exchange, London. The said jewellery had since been recovered; but this could by no means be held to homologate or compound the offence.

The judges nodded sagely, and Balmerino, finding the charges relevant, enquired whether the panel pleaded guilty or no?

Thomas Hope stood up, and declared that before pleading, he

would make formal objection to the presence of Sir Peter Young as one of the judges in this instance. He had every respect for Sir Peter, but would point out that he had long been a domestic servitor and pensioner of the Crown, and therefore in no position to sit in judgment on another domestic servitor in what was inevitably a domestic action within the Queen's household.

This agitated the judges not a little, spoiling the rather artificially genial atmosphere—as it was meant to do—and after an uncomfortable pause for whispering, Sir Peter, a venerable, white-bearded old gentleman, rose and bowed, said that he accepted the objection and sought their lordships' permission to retire from the case. But, if their lordships agreed, and the Lord Advocate and other counsel had no objection, he would like to remain purely as an observer, since the case interested him. The advocates intimating no objection, Young moved round and sat beside Heriot at the other side of the table.

Hope then declared that his client pleaded not guilty to the charge of theft or stealing, but was prepared to plead guilty to one of misappropriation of jewellery in her care and of offering them to Master Heriot.

Hamilton announced that, in the circumstances, he was prepared to abandon the charges of theft or stealing and to rely on that of misappropriation.

Balmerino, hardly glancing at his colleagues, said that he thought that, all things considered, such was a wise decision, and that they would be prepared to proceed on that basis.

Linlithgow nodded, but Abercorn held up his hand. Would learned counsel kindly define the difference between stealing and misappropriation where the goods taken were then sold to a third party and the money retained by the thief or misappropriator?

A sigh escaped from Balmerino, Hamilton and one or two others—but not from Hope, who had foreseen this as inevitable. Abercorn had been almost bound to take up a contrary attitude from the other two judges. He was a Protestant—very much so, since his whole fortune and rise to power was based on the grant of the rich abbey lands of Paisley, after the Reformation and he had been created Lord Paisley before becoming Earl of Abercorn. Balmerino and Linlithgow were Catholics. The judges had, as ever, been carefully balanced out by the Lord Advocate, Sir Peter Young being a staunch Protestant—which was the main reason for Hope's objection to his sitting. Now the judgment would almost certainly be two-to-one—for Linlithgow, even though uneasy about being too friendly with Balmerino, would not disagree in law with the Lord President. The required explanation to Abercorn was a small price to pay for a favourable verdict.

Hamilton left Hope to make the explanation. He informed concisely that misappropriation was a lesser offence, concerned with intent and ameliorating circumstances, a putting to wrong use rather than an actual theft. In this case he could show that his client had no intent to steal; indeed she would have scarcely have taken the items to the Queen's jeweller had she so intended. The defence case, in essence, was that the accused did not in fact sell the jewels to Master Heriot but merely deposited them with him, in return for a sum of money manifestly much less than the saleable worth. Misappropriation, therefore, was a suitable indictment, to which they would plead guilty.

Balmerino asked if Abercorn was satisfied. The Earl declared that he was not.

A form of trial therefore had to proceed. Hamilton described the accused position as a trusted member of the Queen's domestic entourage, concurred that the said jewellery was put in her care, mentioned her secret marriage to one of the Earl of Orkney's gentlemen and recounted her visit to George Heriot's shop with some of the items in her care, where she deposited them and received in exchange the sum of two hundred and fifty pounds. It was the Crown's case that this was a sale, not a pawning, whatever the sum received—even though Master Heriot later gave the jewels back to Her Majesty without charge. This was in no way to the credit of the accused. The panel Hartside was, therefore, guilty of, at the least, a charge of misappropriation, a grievous putting to wrong use of items entrusted to her care. A charge of outright theft, admittedly, would be less simple to sustain, in view of the especially trusted position of the accused, and therefore he was prepared to accept the plea of guilty to the lesser charge.

Abercorn looked bull-like, and declared that he was unconvinced. It seemed to him that it was the duty of a Lord Advocate to prosecute, not to defend the accused, as he appeared to be doing this day.

Bridling, Hamilton pointed out that it was, in fact, the Lord Advocate's duty and privilege, and *solely* his, to decide on charges levelled. And certainly not the judges, whose duty was to decide on whether or not the said charges had been proved. That only, with sentence.

Balmerino hurriedly agreed that this was so. But he suggested that, for the Earl of Abercorn's benefit, they might hear Master Hope's defence of the panel, despite the plea of guilty.

Hope was nothing loth. He declared that Her Majesty had entrusted the said jewels, with others, to the care of the panel, as he could establish by a letter from the Queen's own hand, had thereupon *forgotten* them. The items were therefore, at the time of the alleged offence, *pro derelictus*. To dispose of them, by depositing them, for a token payment, with the Queen's jeweller—which the defence declared firmly to be no sale—could not be a theft, since the jewels were in truth lawfully in the accused's possession. The fact that it was to Master Heriot that the accused took them, and that she did by no means flee with the money or otherwise absent herself from her duties thereafter, substantiated that the panel felt no guilt. She was now, however, prepared to plead guilty to the lesser charge, out of her love and duty to Her Majesty, recognising that her action had been foolish without being criminal. Witness and productions could be brought to all these averments. There the defence confidently rested.

Everybody looked at Abercorn, who frowned, puffed, shrugged and intimated that he accepted the situation, especially as it seemed to be the Queen's own wish.

Balmerino nodded relievedly, muttered something to Linlithgow, and then announced that His Majesty's Court of Session found the accused Margaret Hartside guilty of the charge stipulated. In view of the fact that she had already served a considerable period in ward, however, they would limit sentence, in mercy. The panel would pay the full sum of the jewels' worth, even though they had already been restored, namely four hundred and ten pounds Sterling, by way of amercement and fine. And she would be condemned to perpetual exile in the Isles of Orkney, in the care of her husband. This for judgment. God Save the King!

As they all stood up, Heriot permitted himself a sigh of relief.

"Who pays the fine?" old Sir Peter Young murmured in his ear, with a chuckle. "You needna have unseated me, Geordie! I'd have agreed the judgment."

"Perhaps, sir. But we could not be sure."

"And you're willing to pay twice ower for those gewgaws, eh?

And smile to do so! There's mair to this than meets the eye, I'm thinking."

"The motto of my house is 'I Distribute Cheerfullie'," George Heriot pointed out, mildly.

* * *

When Heriot had engineered this Hartside trial for the month of May 1608, his main preoccupation had been to create an excuse and official reason for getting away from Court, for a much more personal concern—his own wedding. James's odd finances, and desire to have his banker constantly at hand, made such escapes to Scotland difficult to arrange. On this occasion the King, needless to say, had found some other services for his friend to engage in while he was at it—his unconcern with the Queen's problems being remarkable. Unfortunately the monarch was not the only one in a position to be awkward about George Heriot's affairs, however. James Primrose meantime was also a factor to reckon with. Alison had written tearfully more than a month earlier, to say that her father had gone back on his word—or, at least, that he was now insisting that the marriage be postponed for still another year. He said that he could not meantime dispense with his daughter's services; that he found himself in no position to raise the five thousand merks dowry for another year, and that anyway, in his judgment, Alison was still too young for marriage. The fact was that his wife was ill and he required the girl's attendance at home to look after the invalid, his house and the enormous brood. And he was in a position to enforce this delay, unhappily, since his daughter was still under the legal age of consent. So, however little Heriot cared about the dowry, wedded bliss was still not yet.

His beloved, therefore, was no longer to be sought, with Mary Gray, in pleasant Strathearn, but skied and tied in frustrating domesticity at the top of the tall tenement town house in Edinburgh's Lawnmarket, nursing an ailing stepmother and seeking to manage an unruly household of high-spirited children, while she coped with the moods of a preoccupied sire, who, by the very nature of his office and employment was going through a most difficult period. He was not really an ill-natured or particularly selfish man, although inclined to pomposity; but, with some reason, he felt, and proclaimed, that her problems, though real enough, were truly minor, ephemeral, and in no sense comparable with his own.

The fact was that Scotland was falling into a condition bordering on anarchy—the rot stemming from the top, not the bottom. And this was not so much reflected as concentrated in the Privy Council, of which Primrose was the unfortunate secretary and factotum. The ancient kingdom had undergone many crises in its long history; but never before had it suffered by having no resident monarch or regent, no undoubted voice of authority nearer than four hundred miles away—a vital matter in a highly monarchial form of government. Long-range control just did not suit Scotland, either its institutions or the character of its people. Added to this, the Reformation, later here than anywhere else in Christendom, was still not settled and secure. Lacking decisive on-the-spot direction, it could, and looked as though it might, suffer overturn, and Catholicism be re-established. A large part of the nobility and aristocracy had never changed; many who had, had done so only in name, to gain former Church lands—and some of these were now frankly turning back to the old religion; and the vast Highland area, with certain Lowland hegemonies also, were still predominatly Catholic. The Kirk, deliberately weakened and riven by James's policy, and the imposition of bishops again, was split, and its aggresively left-wing Presbyterian faction harsh and out-of-sympathy with most of the people, and therefore not the bastion of Protestantism it could have been. In consequence, the Privy Council, made up so largely on a herediary basis, but with the bishops an added and uneasy dimension, was split, not so much down the middle as in three warring sections. And, as it happened, its presently most influential members were on the Catholic side—the Chancellor, Dunfermline, and Secretary of State and Lord President Balmerino—to Protestant James Primrose's discomfort and distress. Moreover, in all this ferment, the dark hand of the Master of Gray was at work, skilfully stirring, subborning, dividing, a hidden hand but with much gold in it, most evidently. Small wonder if Alison's father was in no frame of mind for domestic distractions.

There was no room for Heriot in the already overcrowded Primrose house in the Lawnmarket, and he had long given up his grace-and-favour quarters in Holyroodhouse. So he lodged meantime with his half-brother James, above the shop in Beith's Wynd opposite the Lesser Kirk of St. Giles. The ancient walled city of

Edinburgh was a positive warren of tall tenements, lands, closes, wynds and beetling masonry, all huddled together on the narrow spine which ran down from the castle to Holyrood, with deep valleys on either side. James Heriot's house was, in fact, no more than two hundred yards from James Primrose's—although there were some dozen storeys of difference.

To gain any privacy the betrothed couple found a problem, in these circumstances. In Alison's own house there was never a room unoccupied; and James Heriot's was smaller, and little better. His brother rapidly had enough of sitting amidst the noise of the Lawnmarket house's cooped-up, racketing children, and when the girl could escape for a little, they took to meeting in the unromantic and constricted ambience of the little office behind the Beith's Wynd goldsmith's booth. Admittedly it had on many occasions in the past been graced by the monarch's presence; but it was scarcely a lovers' nest.

These all too brief interludes were not wholly taken up with dalliance and matters of no concern to other than the parties involved, however. Alison was well versed in current affairs, had sharp ears and shrewd wits. Although scarcely so keen an interpreter of matters politic as was Mary Gray, she was an able observer of the scene, and because of her father's employment and friends, in a position to overhear much and gather more. From her, Heriot learned that Lord Balmerino was thought to be tottering to a fall. Dunbar, it was said, was determined to bring down his former friend, coveting the complete rule in Scotland. To bring down the Chancellor also—but this was considered secondary. The odd circumstance was that the Master of Gray appeared to be abetting Dunbar in this—even though Balmerino was a Catholic and Dunbar a Protestant. The now commonly spoken of Catholic resurgence, master-minded by Gray—it was not so much a plot as a movement—appeared, strangely enough, to be going to jettison the most powerfully-placed Catholic of all, Balmerino, the Chief Secretary. No doubt Patrick Gray had his reasons—one of which might well be the unpaid fifteen thousand merks due to the late Robert Logan's estate; but then, equally, Dunbar's eighteen thousand was likewise unpaid, and Gray, an heir-general, was, if not actually working with Dunbar, seemingly on a parallel course. It was all a great mystery.

Heriot informed that the King also seemed to be turning against his Chief Secretary and Lord President. There must be something to bring these unlikely forces together, something devious but very potent. It could all be a policy of divide and rule—with three dividers at work! In an academic sense it would be interesting to see which actually did the ruling in the end—although, since one was their sovereign lord, there was no question as to where their duties and hopes should lie.

Alison's opinion of her sovereign lord was not of the highest, and her betrothed found himself, not for the first time, standing up for his peculiar monarch and seeking to explain away some of his manoeuvres for the greater good of his two kingdoms. He was less successful in this than in some of his endeavours with the girl.

She went on to expound upon the King's extraordinary methods and notions of justice, by instancing the case of George Sprott, the late Logan's notary and doer. Balmerino, allegedly on instructions from London, had arrested the Eyemouth lawyer and subjected him to a series of questioning sessions, by torture and otherwise—with the object, it seemed, of proving that Logan, Sprott's client and friend, had been one of the main instigators of the notorious Gowrie Conspiracy of eight years before. All the principal actors in that mysterious drama had been extravagantly dealt with, those who supported the King's peculiar story most handsomely rewarded, those on the other side forfeited, slain, executed, even their very names banished. Two figures only, connected therewith by rumour, however persistently, had escaped—Robert Logan of Restalrig and his cousin Patrick, Master of Gray. Poor Sprott was something of a substitute, a scapegoat.

Heriot declared that Logan was a rogue, whether or no he was involved in the Gowrie business. He had long been employed to do the Master of Gray's dirty work—or some of it. And his lawyer and close associate was likely to be tarred with the same stick. He would be apt to deserve his uncomfortable questionings.

Perhaps, Alison conceded. But did he deserve hanging? It was surely the first time a lawyer had been hanged for his client's offence!

Brought up short, the man stared at her. She informed him that George Sprott was indeed dead. The Lord Treasurer, the Earl of Dunbar, had gone over the heads of Balmerino, the Chancellor and the Privy Council—therefore, presumably, on the King's direct authority—had taken Sprott out of the Tolbooth, treated him kindly in his own house, ordered a new and gentler questioning by Sir Thomas Hamilton in his own presence—and then, having evidently got what he wanted, set up a swift secret trial and had the lawyer hanged at the Cross the next day. None doubted but so that he could not speak further. The charge was high treason and forgery.

Heriot was not a little shaken. What all this meant he had little idea. But certain implications were clear. Dunbar would never have dared to do it all, over-riding the Chief Secretary, Chancellor and Privy Council, without King James's specific agreement. Therefore it was to the *King's* advantage that Sprott should be silenced for good. But Balmerino had questioned him at length, earlier—so Balmerino probably now had the same information. It would be a rash man, in the circumstances, who gave the Chief Secretary a long life and fortune.

One phrase worked in Heriot's mind—high treason and forgery. Treason was the obvious blanket-charge, to cover practically all activities of which the Crown did not approve. But forgery was different, on another level altogether. In this context, what did it mean? To use the word in the same breath as high treason? What forgery could be important enough for that—and linked presumably with Logan of Restalrig, the only point at which poor Sprott inpinged on national affairs? It was Logan's papers which had revealed the whereabouts of the Casket Letters—at least to all but the King, Queen and Orkney. Logan's papers would have been in the care of his notary. Forgery, then—it could be that! The Casket Letters, the most damning and dangerous papers in all Scotland's story, which had already brought a queen to the block? Was this the answer to the riddle—a copy of the Letters, or some of them? It could explain much—including why the Master of Gray was apparently presently supporting Dunbar against Balmerino. If he held the originals, he would be much concerned about copies, extracts or forgeries. Was this, in fact, what the Gowrie Conspiracy had been about? The Gowrie family had also, at one time, held these fateful Letters—and had paid the penalty. Had George Sprott been just too clever a lawyer and kept a copy?

Alison had more than that to tell. The rumour in Edinburgh was that the Earl of Dunfermline was as likely to fall as was Balmerino. He was, strangely enough, Provost of the city as well as Chancellor—multiplicity of offices being a feature of the regime—and it was being whispered in the wynds and closes that Dunbar's spies were watching the Earl's every move, bailies being secretly questioned and threatened, and so on. The girl said that her father did not give the Chancellor six months. Small wonder if he, and all the Council of which Dunfermline was chairman, were worried men. A kind of quiet terror was beginning to reign in high places in Scotland.

When, after a few days, George Heriot took reluctant farewell of his bride-to-be, promising that, though the heavens should fall, he would be up to marry her next summer—having now actually got the marriage-contract signed by her father—he too was a worried man. Clearly crisis point was rapidly being reached in the affairs of his native land, and he did not at all like the way that crisis appeared to be shaping. Everything pointed to the most intricate, unscrupulous, not to say Machiavellian plotting, and all emanating from the ultimate source of power, the King himself. Admittedly the Master of Gray was undoubtedly engaged in equally elaborate and dangerous plotting; in fact the whole Scottish situation was almost certainly a personal duel between these two so different but equally subtle and devious protagonists, a long-drawn-out chess game, with ministers of state as well as lesser men, governments, parliaments, even religions, as mere pawns to be moved and manipulated and sacrificed at will. Clearly the game was reaching a decisive stage—and Heriot misliked being one of the pawns, misliked being connected in any way with the entire ominous and alarming affair. Especially just when the greatest personal happiness of his life was imminent—and might conceivably be put in jeopardy.

As he rode southwards, in uneasy frame of mind, he asked himself—as so often before—what it was the King wanted from him in these errands and commissions? When there were obviously so many other spies, agents and informers in action already. James did not need *him*, his goldsmith and banker, for underground probings when he had Dunbar and all his minions, besides God alone knew what other secret informants. Yet there must be a reason. Could it be that James *trusted* him, where he did not fully trust Dunbar or any of the others? Knew him to have no ambition, as regards power, position or more wealth than he had already? If friendship was the word, they had been friends for a long time, near twenty years now—and by the very nature of things, James could have few friends. Indeed, apart from Ludovick Stewart, he could think of none—since favourites and courtiers could never be classed as friends. A reigning monarch's position was the acme of loneliness—and perhaps James Stewart needed friends? However little these might affect his behaviour and policies. That might be the answer.

The thought did not make the man any more joyful.

21

BACK IN LONDON, no atmosphere of crisis, or indeed of urgency, was detectable. James appeared to be wholly engrossed in young Carr, and each day hinged on the Latin lesson—with the King now said actually to be using a rod to chastise his pupil, when necessary, with kisses to counter any ill effects. Not that this was allowed to interfere too greatly with James's other activities, the Court spending most of its time in Hertfordshire, either at Royston or at Salisbury's house of Theobalds, hunting, feasting, gambling, debating philosophy and theology, or just drinking.

Finding the monarch absent, Heriot went first to Denmark House, to report to the Queen. Anne was relieved by his account of the proceedings at Linlithgow, and thankful that the wretched and embarrassing business of Margaret Hartside was finally disposed of without further distress. Her gratitude took the form of ordering a large supply of jewellery and plate—on credit, of course—and of borrowing a considerable sum of money in order to pay off indebtedness to Sir William Herrick, interim jeweller. Master Geordie was once again firmly restored to the position of Queen's man-of-business.

Learning that Anne was going to Theobalds next day, to join her husband from not-far-distant Royston, Heriot arranged to go with her. The occasion was the reception of an embassy from Sweden, come to discuss a possible betrothal of the fourteen-year-old King Gustavus with the Princess Elizabeth. Anne declared that she was utterly opposed to the match, in that her brother King Christian was now again at war with Sweden, however inadvisedly, and such a betrothal would smack of treachery. James apparently saw it otherwise, as an opportunity to play his favoured role of the peacemaker of Europe. Any such wedding would take place over her dead body, the Queen confided—though, of course, the Swedes must not be offended. Fortunately Elizabeth was only twelve, so she could and would hold out against any formal engagement on the grounds of immaturity—which even James could hardly deny. Anne also complained at having to go to Theobalds at all, or anywhere else outside London, for the reception. But James would let nothing—except perhaps the hateful Carr—interfere with his passion for hunting, in season or out. This hunting was assuming the proportions of a national scandal, she averred; indeed there had been many complaints from the Council, the law officers, and in parliament that the King was never available for two-thirds of the year, to sign papers and approve and ratify Acts, without horsed deputations having to go galloping after him through wood and brake. James had even sent parliament an official announcement, by herald, declaring that his health depended upon his regular taking of this sort of exercise, and that it was the duty of all loyal lieges to rejoice heartily that the sovereign retained his health, and to abet him in the pursuit thereof. Indignantly she cited the recent case of a sitting of parliament which could not proceed with its business until it knew whether or no the Crown had given assent to certain legislation—and in the end was reduced to taking the word of Sir Francis Hastings that the Lord Chief Justice had told him that the Lord Kinloss had said that the King was pleased enough with the Bill and it should pass.

Heriot duly sympathised with the Queen and the parliamentarians, but permitted himself a small smile, nevertheless.

The next day, then, he rode in the Queen's train the thirteen miles to Theobalds—to discover on arrival in the early afternoon that James had been away at the hunt for some hours; moreover had left orders that both the Queen and the Swedish embassage should join him in the chase, on arrival. The surprised Swedes had already put in an appearance and had been duly despatched onwards into the wild-wood. In high dudgeon, Anne had to follow—since she was not going to allow any hole-and-corner agreement on her daughter's future to be patched up, as it were between bucks, lacking her own presence. Heriot perforce accompanied her.

It took them two full hours to locate the monarch—although they came across sundry parties of huntsmen, disconsolate or otherwise, who had lost touch with their tireless sovereign, either by accident or design, but dared not return to base minus the King. There was an unending supply of deer, they complained, Salisbury having imported them from far and near—easy enough for him, who was excused hunting on account of his hump-back! The hunt might well go on for hours yet.

They caught up with the Swedish party, presently, still searching for the elusive monarch—to Anne's relief. Soon afterwards they heard the baying of hounds, and apparently coming approximately their way. Infected a little by the exciting sound—for the Queen was a fair huntswoman herself, when the spirit moved a rather indolent nature—she led the way at a canter to intercept.

At the edge of a grassy clearing amidst the scrub they paused, with the hounds obviously not far off and giving tongue loudly.

They were barely halted when three fallow deer, a buck and two does, leapt out from the thickets and raced across the far side of the glade. The Queen, who rather prided herself on her marksmanship, cried aloud demanding a bow. One of the laggard huntsmen gladly spurred forward to hand her his. But it was too late. By the time that Anne had fitted a quarrel and taken aim, the deer had gone from sight.

Then, with the baying and yelping very close, four more deer, all bucks, burst into view, bounding hugely. And behind them came the first of the grey, leaping, slender deer-hounds, only a yard or two at heel.

Quick as thought, Anne raised her bow again. A crossing shot is difficult, with a swift and bounding target, aim-off of the essence. The last buck was the largest of the four with the best head. Automatically she chose it. Twisting in her saddle, she loosed off. The twang of her bow coincided with two unforseen developments. The foremost of the pursuing hounds suddenly leapt high and forward, teeth snapping, for the haunch of the last buck, and the beast, sensing the attack, leapt and twisted away sideways—all in the twinkling of an eye. The arrow transfixed, not the buck but the bounding deer-hound full in the throat, and it fell, writhing while its fellows streamed over it and on after the disappearing deer.

There were exclamations, even a little laughter, from the Queen's party, Anne tutting her annoyance, the Swedes sympathising. Then one of the courtiers behind emitted a cry.

"Christ's Wounds—it's Jewel! Look at the white hind toes!"

Appalled, everyone stared. All at Court knew Jewel as the King's favourite hound, companion of chases innumerable, brought from Scotland. The Queen clapped a gauntleted hand to mouth.

Then the hunt came crashing from the scrub, in full cry, men shouting, horns blowing, horses snorting and steaming, James half-a-head in front, with Montgomery at one flank, Lennox at another, Southampton, Doncaster and Dand Kerr jostling close and young Carr a little way behind. Past the fallen hound they all pounded, without a glance—past the Queen's party likewise—and on after the dogs and the deer. Stragglers followed in ragged order and passed from sight. The glade was empty again.

Almost reluctantly, and frowning, Anne moved her horse nearer to the twitching animal. One of her attendants jumped down, looked at the hound closely, then shook his head. At a nod from the Queen he drew his knife and finished off the poor creature.

"Carry it," Anne jerked, briefly. Picking up the limp body, the man with difficulty slung it over his horse's withers, to mount behind it. In silence they rode on after the others.

They did not have very far to go. In another marshy clearing beside a mere, they found the entire hunt, the hounds milling around, the horses steaming and all the men dismounted—this because the King himself was dismounted and none must remain higher than he. James was more than dismounted. He was busy, bent down, knife in hand, ripping up the belly of a fallen buck and hauling out the entrails with bloodstained hands. For a man who could abide the sight of neither naked steel nor blood, he was extraordinary in his habit of nearly always doing his own gralloching.

The steaming viscera out, heaving and wriggling on the grass seemingly with its own obscene life, the King straightened up, saw his wife and her company, nodded genially, and signed to Robert Carr to come pull off his riding-boots while he leaned on Montgomery's shoulder. Lennox, bowing to the Queen, strolled across to Heriot's side as all save Anne dismounted.

James, boots off, supported now by Montgomery and Carr, stepped gingerly forward and into the heap of entrails and guts and there paddled and dabbled his bare feet and legs in the bloody, slithering mass. He was a great believer in this as a remedy for gout, declaring that it had to be done at once, and in the place where the brute was slain, an excellent remede and recure for strengthening and restoring the sinews.

In the midst of this gory business, James perceived the hound lying across the horse's back. Brows raised, he demanded what this might be?

Amidst a sudden hush, the Queen spoke. "It is the beast Jewel, Sire. Your hound. By an ill mischance it was shot . . ."

"Jewel! My Jewel? Waesucks—shot, you say, woman! My Jewel deid!"

"It was a mischance. The hound leapt forward. The quarrel, aimed at the buck, struck the dog . . ."

"Whae shot it? Whae killed my Jewel? What ill limmer did this to me? I'll teach him to mend his shooting! By God, I will!" Bare and bloody feet notwithstanding, James tottered over unaided to the horse which bore the hound's body. "Och, Jewel—Jewel!" he wailed. "My ain bit tike! Jewel, auld friend!" Tears streaming, the King stroked the rough grey coat.

Anne drew a long breath. "*I* shot it, James," she said. Her voice shook slightly, but she held her head high. "I drew on the buck. But Jewel leapt, and the quarrel . . ."

"*You* did? You shot my Jewel, woman! Precious soul o' God! I might hae kent it! Nane other would hae been sic a fool! Whae said you could shoot at *my* buck, anyway? God save us frae fool women! How dared you to shoot when my hounds were close?"

"How dare *you*, James, bespeak me so!" Anne cried back. "Me, the Queen! Before all these. And these Swedes! How *dare* you, sir!"

It was the King's turn to draw a long breath. After a distinct pause, he spoke in a different tone. "Ooh, aye—I dare, right enough. I can dare mair than that, Annie, see you! I, James Stewart, will dare plenties, when need be. And let nane forget it! But . . . maybe now isna the convenient time, I'll grant you. Aye—we'll put it by, the now." He turned. "My boots, Robin—my boots, laddie." He gave a final pat to the dead hound. "Fare-thee-weel, Jewel, auld friend. You were truer friend to me than many I'd name! Aye—and that's twa guid hounds gone in twa days, waesucks. Jowler yesterday—and now Jewel." His boots pulled on for him, he stamped across for his own lathered roan. Mounting, he called, "We'll awa' back, then. Enough for this day—aye, or any day!" Without another glance at wife or Swedish embassage, he reined round to lead the way back to Theobalds House.

Riding beside Heriot, near but not too near the Queen—who no doubt would prefer her own company just then—Lennox agreed with his friend that this was all very unfortunate. Particularly on top of the Jowler business. Jowler, it seemed, was another of the King's best deer-hounds, and after yesterday's hunt had disappeared. Theobalds had been in a stir over it half the night, with search-parties out and dire threats emanating from the Crown, James asserting that it was no mischance but all some dire malice against himself. Anne had therefore been doubly unfortunate with her arrow. Lord knew what repercussions there might be, now!

However, after a mile or so, a single horseman came trotting back down the long line of tired riders threading the woodlands—James himself. He rode up to the Queen, and tipped a bloodstained finger to his bonnet.

"Och, yon was a pity, Annie," he said. "Aye, a pity. I was maybe a mite hasty. Och, we'll forget it, just. Shall we?"

Anne was stiff. "I cannot forget being miscalled, like some fishwife, in front of all!" she declared. "Especially the new Swedes. If my being a king's wife means so little to you, then recollect, I pray, that I am also a king's daughter and sister!"

"Ooh, aye—you're that, a' right. Or I wouldna hae wed you! And a right unwiselike king to be sister to! To be attacking the same Swedes, in war! A fell fool ploy! And your auld faither was no' much better. I never saw him sober!"

"Sir . . .!"

"Uh-huh. Weel—we'll forget that too, eh? Aye, Geordie—is that yoursel'? Back frae yon troublesome northern realm o' mine! I hear you had your way ower the Hartside nonsense. A deep pouch is fell usefu', eh?"

Heriot blinked. "You did, Sire? Hear? So soon!"

"I hae ears, Geordie! On baith sides o' my heid! And a wheen wits in between! Come and gie me your crack anent Scotland, man. But—nae need to shout it oot for a' this country to hear!"

So, riding close beside the King, through the winding woodland trails, Heriot told all that he considered relevant and important arising from his trip. As ever, how much of it was news to his monarch he could not gauge. He said nothing about the Casket Letters.

James seemed little interested in most of what he told him, but definitely so over the suggestion that the Master of Gray was at present, if not actually co-operating, at least not opposing the Earl of Dunbar, Lord Treasurer of Scotland. "We'll hae to see aboot that," he commented. "Would you jalouse that Doddie Home was a match for Patrick Gray, Geordie? I wouldna like the one to swallow up the other, mind!"

"A match in some respects, Sire, I think. Not in others. In unscrupulousness, yes. In wits, no."

"Ho—so that's the way o' it! You dinna like my guid servant the Earl o' Dunbar, Geordie Heriot?"

"Say that I would not like him to owe me money, Sire. Or anything else! I'd count my life short!"

"Aye—life's a chancy business, is it no'? Short or lang. As it seems yon George Sprott discovered! *Hominis est errare*!"

"That was . . . judicial murder, was it not, Sire?"

"You think so? Your worthy cousin, Tam o' the Coogate, my Advocate, didna so advise me! Maybe you ken the law better? We'll see what Jamie Elphinstone says, shall we? When he arrives."

"Elphinstone? My Lord Balmerino—he is coming? Here?"

"I've summoned him, aye. To gie an account o' his stewardship, just. Holy Writ says 'It is required o' a man that he be found faithfu'', mind. Aye—we maun a' mind it. Mysel'—and even you! Maist times I account you faithfu', Geordie—forby the fact that whiles you canna see mair'n an inch beyond your nose! That's the trouble, eh? The honest are gey apt to be dull in the uptak—and the lads wi' the wits I canna trust! Who'd be a king, Geordie? Who'd be a king?"

"Not me, Sire—thank God! Nor anything other than a simple tradesman."

"A simple tradesman, eh? You?" James looked at him cynically. "And who's the honest man, now?"

They had come to the approaches to Salisbury's huge mansion, and were heading for the stableyards. There was some commotion in front, with shouting for the King. Riding up, James found some of his party in a circle around a forester who held a hound on a lead.

"Jowler!" the monarch cried. "Guidsakes—it's Jowler! And fit as a flea, after a'! Here's a right blessing. Whaur d'you find him, man?"

"Your Majesty," the forester faltered, "I didn't rightly *find* him, as you might say. Three men brought him to the kennels—rough, country fellows. Then ran off. This 'ere paper I found tucked in Jowler's collar." Bobbing a bow he held out a folded paper.

James took it, peering. "What's this, what's this?" he demanded. "Ill writing. Uncouth. You read it, Vicky."

Scanning the paper briefly, Lennox grinned, then schooled his features to a proper solemnity. He read out, "Good Mr. Jowler, We pray you speake to the King (for he hears you every day, and so doth he not us) that it will please his Majestie to go back to London, for els the contry wilbe undoon; all our provition is spent already, and we are not able to intertayne him longer."

There was a snigger from sundry of those well to the rear which stopped quickly at James's scowl.

"What means this?" he asked. "If any ken the meaning o' this screed and perceive wit in it—inform me. Inform me, I say."

None was bold enough to elaborate. Young Carr soothingly declared that it was some bumpkin's half-witted haverings, no more.

"What does it mean?" James said again, ignoring him, eyes narrowed.

Only the Queen dared raise her voice to answer him. "It means, Sire, that the people of this land tire of your so frequent hunting. As indeed do I! Nor just the country bumpkins—for it is to *London* this would have you return. Where your parliament and government frequently require your presence. That is what it means."

The King sat his horse, very still—and Heriot, close to him, saw knuckles gleam whitely in that hand covered in dried blood. He looked, from his wife, slowly round the circle of faces, and back to her—and the silence was a tangible thing. Then abruptly, his features relaxed, he licked wet lips, and chuckled aloud.

"A jest!" he exclaimed. "Sakes—a notable guid jest! I like that—aye, like it! There's wit, here—eh, Jowler! I canna seemly reward thae three limmers, for they've bolted, it seems. But Jowler shall hae double meat for *his* pairt! Aye—see to it. Come, then . . ."

As they rode on, Lennox's glance met Heriot's, and neither smiled.

When they were dismounted, and the horses being led away to the stables, the King beckoned Heriot over to him, turning his back on Carr, who ever hovered nearby.

"Geordie," he whispered, "a diamond, for my Annie. Aye, a fair diamond, set in gold. Och, you'll ken what she likes. We maun keep her happy, I'm thinking!"

* * *

In the months that followed, much that was significant for Scotland, the Scots and their monarch, developed, to build up a new pattern in the governance of that ancient kingdom. The Chief Secretary of State, the Lord Balmerino, duly arrived in England, and after being kindly enough received at St. Albans, and privately questioned by the King, found himself in a steadily deteriorating position, practically a prisoner indeed, having to appear before the English Privy Council strangely enough—and, more strangely still, having to put up with being represented and counselled by none other than Home, Earl of Dunbar, now his chief enemy. There were many charges against him and his regime in Scotland—but the principal one was the old story that, back in 1599, he had so manipulated certain papers for the King's signature that a letter to the Pope, requesting a cardinal's hat for his own cousin, Bishop William Chisholm of Vaison, had been signed and sent. Now, Cardinal Bellarmine was gleefully boasting in various Courts of Europe that King James was sufficiently Papist himself to seek preferment from the Vatican to encourage his Scots Catholics, and this was harming his reputation and efforts as the peacemaker of Christendom. It was a tangled ten-year-old story—for James, in fact, was not the man to sign anything unread, but in violently anti-Catholic England it made a fair stick to beat Balmerino with. The hearings went on for weeks, with the King frequently hiding behind the arras, listening in. Finally, Balmerino made a 'voluntary' confession of treasonable guilt, was deprived of all offices and sent back to Scotland for trial and sentence—although allegedly with a private assurance from James that the worst would not befall him. No reference was made throughout to Robert Logan's estates, debts or the Casket Letters, to the Master of Gray nor even the Gowrie Conspiracy. Dunbar returned North with the prisoner—and took over for himself the forfeited Restalrig estates.

In Scotland a parallel, if slightly less concentrated process had been going on. Spottiwoode, the Archbishop of Glasgow, put before the *Scottish* Privy Council that its chairman, the Chancellor Dunfermline, had been guilty of undermining the authority of the King, Council and Church by numerous misdemeanours, but markedly by encouraging extreme Presbyterian elements of the Kirk to hold an illegal General Assembly at Aberdeen in 1605—the same affair in which the Reverend James Melville had been accused of taking part—to counter the royal rule in Church and State—this, in order to split the godly forces of Reform. This enquiry was also long-drawn and less decisive than Balmerino's in that no confessions were forthcoming; and indeed it all collapsed for lack of evidence.

But it had results nevertheless, for it was now only too clear that the Crown's confidence in the Chancellor was withdrawn. Dunfermline resigned certain offices, though not the Chancellorship, and most clearly was now a marked man.

Balmerino was duly found guilty of high treason and condemned to death, his body to be drawn and quartered. Sentence was, however, to await the King's pleasure—and in fact was never carried out. The former Chief Secretary and Lord President of the Court of Session retired in disgrace and restricted freedom, to private life.

From four hundred miles distance it was not entirely clear what was gained by all this—with Dunbar now apparently supreme in the governance of Scotland, and with the new title of Great Commissioner. Lennox conceived it all to the King's advantage, with the Master of Gray losing heavily, but Heriot was not so sure.

Two further items tended to support his doubts. The Earl of Orkney had suddenly made a strange, secret and unexplained visit to mainland Scotland, was captured and flung into ward in Edinburgh Castle. This seemed to be so unlikely a happening for that tough and savage island despot that it could be explained only by some major betrayal—and his brother-in-law, the Master, was the prime suspect. And very shortly afterwards the old Lord Gray died, at last—and Patrick became sixth Lord and immediately applied for his father's long unoccupied seat on the Privy Council, which the Chancellor promptly granted. Accordingly, to George Heriot, while King James might seem to have swept away Balmerino and largely neutralised Dunfermline, the two Catholic leaders, replacing them with his Protestant minion Dunbar, Patrick Gray was now in a position to sway, if not dominate the Scots Privy Council, with Dunfermline's hands tied, and Dunbar no match for him in wits. He had all Catholic Scotland more or less mobilised and at odds with the King. And he had the King's awkward and dangerous cousin Orkney, with all his menacing potentialities, safely under lock-and-key, to use as he would. The fact that all was done in the King's name was neither here nor there. As a man used to summing up debits and credits, Heriot was not prepared to suggest that James was winning.

Moreover, the King had other matters than Scotland to take up his attention. A distinct and growing lack of popularity with his ordinary English subjects was not a matter to worry James, for whom the popularity or otherwise of God's Anointed held little relevance; but parliament did in some measure tend to reflect popular sentiment, and parliament's grip on the royal purse-strings was as strong as it was infuriating. Young Carr was always on about a suitably dignified landed estate and mansion where he might entertain his beloved liege lord in a fitting fashion, with a park large enough for hunting, of course; and James, on Salisbury's advice, gave the youth Sir Walter Raleigh's estate of Shelbourne. Raleigh was still a denison of the Tower of London—where, however, he was not uncomfortable, had a good suite of rooms and entertained quite lavishly; indeed the Queen on occasion visited him there, and young Prince Henry, who hero-worshipped him, was a frequent caller. Unfortunately Henry was not the only hero-worshipper of Raleigh, and though the man himself had never had any use for parliament or the common folk, both now were loud in their protests at ill done to one of the most distinguished Englishmen alive. Salisbury hated both Raleigh and Carr and it was suggested that he had advised the King to this course in order to infuriate both, having found a legal slip in Raleigh's charter of the estate which enabled it to be confiscated by the Crown. Cecil was ill, and ageing, but not done yet. James was highly indignant when he was booed in London streets.

Then a larger matter loomed. Rebellion broke out in the North of Ireland. This had been a normal occurrence in Elizabeth's reign, and Henry's before her; and both had always put down such revolts with a heavy hand and a sharp sword. But that was not James's way; and by compromise, patience and playing off one faction against another, Protestant against Catholic, he had been able to preserve approximate peace there, under the joint oversight of the Catholic, Irish Earl of Tyrone and the Protestant, English Earl of Devonshire—formerly Mountjoy. Now this happy state of affairs was shattered and James was much hurt. The more so when he heard that Devonshire was putting down revolt in the time-honoured fashion, with vehement fire and sword. He sent immediate commands for the killing and burning to cease—and set himself furiously to think.

It took some time for the fruits of the royal cogitation to become evident, in Ireland as nearer at hand. When George Heriot heard the details of the new statecraft, the King's policy of mercy and wisdom, he was lost in a species of wonder, to put it mildly. It was all so very reasonable, so typically James Stewart. The trouble in Ireland was basically both religious and ethnic. A vast Catholic majority had had superimposed on it an English Protestant aristocracy, with nothing in common, in blood, language or faith, between the two. This had been the Tudor policy; but James decided that it would never work. He was worried, too, that the religious infection might spread to Scotland—for the two Celtic countries had always had close links, the Ulster and Scots coasts being in places little more than a dozen miles apart. Moreover, warfare within his kingdoms damaged his pacific image. So he devised a mighty and noble scheme. The Irish Catholics of the northern counties, particularly the land-owner class, as far as possible were to be moved out therefrom, to the South, and their lands planted with new Protestant colonists, mainly from Scotland and northern England. The deportees would be given land in the southern counties confiscated from rebellious chiefs and earls now in revolt—there was never any lack of empty land in Ireland, however much of it bog, as a result of endless wars, massacres, famines and the like. There, all would be allowed to practice their Catholic religion in peace, government adjusted thereto. The Catholic South. But the fertile North was to be firmly Protestant—no question of that. A Judgement of Solomon.

That was the new policy. But it was the details of implementation which left Heriot, and others, gasping. Somehow Protestant Scots and English must be persuaded to go to Ireland, and to stay there. Only one thing would serve for that—the elementary hunger for land, status, position. The northern counties therefore would be parcelled out into large estates of, say, one or two thousand acres each. Half-a-million acres would be set aside, in the first instance, to start the scheme. These would be sold at very attractive terms, by the Crown, to all Protestant comers. But a more potent inducement, the hereditary knighthoods scheme, would be put into operation. James had found a name for these, since they could by no means be termed knights, and borrowed from English Edward the Third—baronets, or little barons. For a payment of three thousand, two hundred and forty pounds Sterling to the Crown, ostensibly towards the maintenance of the army in Ireland but actually into the royal pocket, the buyers of these Irish estates would receive the title of Baronet of Ulster, would call themselves Sir and their wives Lady, their eldest sons to succeed thereto, and they would bear the Red Hand of Ulster in a badge of augmentation on their arms. They would be responsible for planting the lands gained with Protestant settlers. Ulster would thereafter blossom like the rose, religious warfare would be a thing of the past—and the money would roll in. This was something which parliament could not interfere with, for it had no jurisdiction in Ireland. How much did five hundred times three thousand, two hundred and forty pounds amount to, for a start . . . ?

James Stewart by no means neglected his ancient kingdom of Scotland in his calculations, that year of 1609; but he was scarcely to be blamed if his so active mind tended to be otherwise preoccupied.

22

AT LEAST IT did not stink so badly as on the last occasion. Nor, of course, was the King present in person. But the full panoply of the law was invoked again, and the Parliament Hall in Edinburgh was almost as crowded. George Heriot sat beside his father-in-law to be, no more than an interested spectator.

As on the earlier occasion, nine years earlier, no less, Heriot's bulky and coarsely genial cousin, Sir Thomas Hamilton, Lord Advocate, was the principal actor in the drama, if not exactly the centre of attention. That role was filled, not by the illustrious bench of the King's Lords of Session, as judges, nor yet by the Earl of Dunbar, Great Commissioner, strangely enough clad in the magnificent robes of an English Knight of the Garter, in the throne-like chair, as representing the monarch himself; undoubtedly the focus for all eyes, most of the time, was the accused himself, propped up before the Bar, Robert Logan of Restalrig. The fact that he had been dead now for three years inevitably added a piquancy to the entire proceddings.

The remains, unfortunately, were neither one thing nor another, neither a body nor yet a skeleton. Three years interment is an awkward period, insufficient for all fleshly matter to have disappeared from the bone structure but too long for the least semblance of humanity to have survived. The remaining tissue was in a sort of jellified state, and had come away in places to reveal white bone. Grave-clothing was patchy also, and a new shroud had been wrapped loosely round much of the relic, more to keep all together than for purposes of decency. What was so consistently fascinating however, was the fine head of hair, greying but plentiful, which topped all—except for one patch over the right ear which had come off; that and the wide, gap-toothed grin which the accused maintained. Logan had always been a fleeringly cheerful scoundrel. As has been said, the smell was not nearly so bad as when the Ruthven brothers, Earl and Master of Gowrie, had been tried in the same Court of Parliament in 1600—but then, they had been dead only six weeks, at that time.

As then, Tam o' the Coogate—who had survived a phenomenally lengthy spell as Lord Advocate, indicative of considerable agility of mind and conscience, despite his looks—was concerned largely with the same charges, involvement in the hateful and treasonable attempt on their liege lord his life and person, the Gowrie Conspiracy in St. John's Town of Perth, in 1600. Much new evidence had come to light since then, and since the accused's death by God's just hand, indubitably and undeniably indicting him as in fact one of the prime movers in that shameful stratagem. It was necessary, therefore, that his guilt should be established and made plain to all, conviction of high treason duly pronounced upon him, his estates, lands, properties and goods declared forfeit, his name proclaimed infamous, and all legal rights whatsoever denied to his heirs and assigns. In the name of the King's Majesty and of the Estates of the Realm of Scotland.

There was no counsel for the defence.

Hamilton, sole performer—for Dunbar had played his part, in leaving the judges in no doubts as to their duty beforehand—put on a virtuoso act, with a mixture of righteous indignation, legal nicety and earthy humour. He relied for his case mainly on the signed confessions of the late George Sprott, notary, who, by the implicit faith put in his testimony might have been one of the authors of Holy Writ, no mention being made that one of the charges he had hanged for was forgery. Sundry other letters were produced, sworn to by witnesses as in Logan's own writing. All led to the inescapable conclusion that the former Laird of Restalrig, along with the unnameable Gowries, had been a major instigator in the horrid plot to adbuct their gracious sovereign from Gowrie House, at St. John's Town, and to convey his royal person by boat across the cruel seas to Restalrig's hold of Fast Castle on the Berwick coast, there to constrain him to the plotters' evil wills and purposes, or to His Grace's possible death. Heriot recollected that the dead Gowrie brothers had been convicted of conspiring to kill the King at Gowrie House itself; but this slight discrepancy seemed to occur to neither prosecutor or judges.

There being no defence, no questions and no need for a summing up, when Hamilton had finished, and demanded the sentence as detailed earlier, there was something of a hiatus, not to say anti-climax. The Lords of Session fidgeted and looked uncomfortable, the Earl of Dunbar considered the hammer-beam ceiling and spectators eyed each other or the accused.

The successor of Balmerino as Lord President, Sir John Preston of Fentonbarns and Penicuik, did not trouble to consult his fellow Senators. He declared that all was most indubitably proven as libelled, to the satisfaction of the court, and that the accused Robert Logan was indeed hereby pronounced guilty on all charges, condemned to be hanged, drawn and quarterd insofar as this was possible, and his severed members exhibited above the gates of the cities of Edinburgh, Dundee, Aberdeen, Glasgow and St. John's Town of Perth, his name declared infamous, his heirs deprived, and his property forfeit to the Crown. This for doom. God save the King!

The judges rose, and bowed to the King's representative, who nodded back, stood up—as did all others—and strolled from the chamber; at least thirty-three thousand merks the richer. The accused grinned on.

Heriot caught a glimpse of Patrick, Lord Gray of Fowlis, in an inconspicuous position at the back of the hall, as he queued to get out. As one of Logan heirs general, was this then a defeat for him? He certainly did not look defeated. Probably he had obtained all he could out of his cousin's estate long before this—he had had three years, after all.

Who, then, was this elaborate charade aimed at? James Stewart would know—and perhaps only he.

* * *

The High Kirk of St. Giles, since the Reformation, had been divided into three parish churches for the city of Edinburgh-within-the-Walls—the High Kirk to the east, the largest, the Tolbooth Kirk to the south-west and the Little Kirk to the north-west. This latter was packed full at noontide of the 24th of August 1609 for the wedding of George Heriot, burgess of Edinburgh and Master Goldsmith to the King, to Alison, daughter of James Primrose, Secretary to the Privy Council of Scotland, former Maid-in-Waiting to Her Majesty. This happened to be the parish church of both families. Moreover, Heriot had a personal interest in it, for exactly ten years before he had petitioned the King to have it enlarged and had partly paid for the improvements out of his own pocket. Even so, it was scarcely large enough for this ceremony, despite the use of its flanking side-chapel of St. Eloi, a Popish relic which had been allowed to survive because it was the chapel of the Incorporation of Hammermen of which Heriot was Past-Master. Both families had wide ramifications and all must be invited—however much the principals would have preferred a quiet country wedding over at Culross. Moreover, practically everybody who claimed to be anybody, in Edinburgh, appeared to have made a point of being present—not all, presumably, out of love and admiration. Many of the nobility and gentry also found it expedient to attend, in view of the royal and Privy Council connections, or merely due to the universal pull of great wealth. Some, no doubt, came out of pure goodwill—the Lady Marie Gray, for instance. Although what brought her gallant and splendidly-dressed husband, the bridegroom for one did not care to hazard a guess, as he waited up near the former altar-steps, for his bride. He noted, too, that the Chancellor, the Earl of Dunfermline, was present, with Heriot's cousin, the Lord Advocate. Moreover, Hamilton's father, also Sir Thomas, and brother, Sir Andrew, both Lords of Session under the titles of Lords Priestfield and Redhouse respectively, graced the occasion, though seldom indeed had they had any dealings with their tradesman kinsman. The Primrose family were duly impressed.

Mary Gray was there, with her son John Stewart of Methven, now a boy of almost fifteen, representing the Duke of Lennox, who was on an official embassage to France.

When Alison arrived on her father's arm, Heriot thought that he had never seen her looking lovelier, more piquantly, excitingly alive—nor younger. Her youthfulness once again hit the man as with a physical blow and made him suddenly and heavily aware again of his own years. All in that crowded church must note it. Not that he felt old, or normally ever thought about his age. All that he could say was that his younger half-brother James Heriot, acting groomsman, looked assuredly older than did he—which was a very doubtful consolation.

Alison, dressed in cloth-of-silver, trimmed with white fur, with a falling ruff seeded with tiny pearls—this the gift of her bridegroom—and a long shoulder-train, whatever her age, seemed fully in command of herself and her situation, radiating happiness. When she reached Heriot's side, his doubts and concerns faded wholly in the sheer emanation of her vivid joy and so obvious affection. His own happiness prevailed. They had waited long for this.

They had to wait a little longer, for the minister. There had been a little difficulty over the celebrant. The true incumbent of the Little Kirk was the renowned Master Robert Bruce, a man of towering stature, a former Moderator of the General Assembly and long a friend of Heriot's family. But he had fallen out with King James when he had refused to offer up public thanks from this pulpit on the occasion of the King's notable deliverance from the evils of the Gowrie Conspiracy in 1600, claiming all to have been a fraud. He had been banished, first to Dieppe and then allowed to return to Scotland, but not to venture south of Inverness by stringent royal command. His kirk-session and congregation had refused to accept this fiat, as had the General Assembly, and he was still officially the minister of the Little Kirk of St. Giles. An assistant, Master James Balfour, had been appointed—and Heriot and his bride would have been well content for him to have married them. But this would not do for the King, who considered it proper to take an active interest in the matter. His Geordie was not to be married by any jumped-up assistant, and since Heriot was resolute that he was not going to have one of the monarch's bishops perform the ceremony as James would have preferred, and all but insisted on, they compromised on Master Patrick Galloway. Galloway, now an elderly man and former minister of Perth, was now for long incumbent of the *High* Kirk of St. Giles and Chaplain to the King, a Presbyterian but a king's-man—who, unlike Bruce had preached enthusiastically and at great length at the Cross of Edinburgh on the wonderful delivery of their liege lord after the Gowrie business. Heriot found him little to his taste, an Old Testament prophet type of divine, who nevertheless was notably well aware on which side his bread was buttered; but he could scarcely resist again.

Now Master Galloway delayed his arrival—as James Primrose

had foretold he would, as a matter of policy, always concerned to make a dramatic entry and to show who was master in God's house. Master Balfour was in his position in front of the Communion Table, waiting patiently with the rest. The chatter from the great congregation was sufficiently loud to allow bride and groom to converse easily, without even having to lower their voices, while James Primrose frowned and puffed, and sundry of Alison's sisters, as attendants, giggled behind.

At length Galloway appeared, sweeping in from a vestry door as though blown in by the winds of the wilderness of Sinai itself, long white locks and black Geneva gown streaming, forked beard jutting. At sight of him a suitable silence fell.

Striding, by no means by the shortest route, to the chancel steps, unfortunate relic of Popery, he halted before the bridal pair, head up, not so much as glancing at them. He stood there, so, for moments—and then raised arm and hand high.

"In the Name of the Father, and of the Son, and of the Holy Ghost!" he thundered. There was going to be no doubt about the Deity's involvement in this wedding.

It was at this moment, carefully calculated evidently, that there was a diversion. The great north doors, to the High Street, closed some time before to keep out the town rabble, were suddenly and noisily flung open. All heads turned to stare, and Patrick Galloway, hand still upraised, looked both thunderstruck and ready to call down heaven's thunderbolts.

Two uniformed members of the Town Guard stood within the doorway, and one of them thumped with the butt of his halberd on the flagstones, shouting, "Make passage and silence for His Grace's Great Commissioner, my Lord High Treasurer the Earl of Dunbar, Knight of the Garter!"

Doddie Home came strolling in, with his curious rolling walk, half-a-dozen overdressed young gentlemen in his train. The doors were shut again.

George Heriot did not know whether to groan or grin. This was James's doing, undoubtedly—for he and Dunbar cordially loathed each other, and the Earl would not have shown his heavy-jowled face here had he not been expressly commanded to do so. But it was turning this long-waited-for wedding into a show, another charade like the Logan trial—for some purpose not clear, but which had nothing to do with matrimony he had no doubt.

The entry had a chastening effect on Master Galloway, at least. Quite put off his stride, he frowned, tugged his beard, made a sort of bow to the King's representative, and waved vaguely towards the front of the congregation—where was the only room left in this crowded place, and where the Earl would have installed himself anyway. This inevitably put Dunbar and his supercilious attendants only a foot or two behind the bridal party—to the excitement of the Primrose daughters.

Less than amiably, Galloway swung on Master Balfour and gestured that *he* should proceed with the ceremony meantime. A little flustered, that youngish man made a false start or two before getting under way.

The Presbyterian wedding ceremony was not a long one, and fairly simple. Quite soon Galloway had recovered himself and moved in to take over at the significant stage of the exchange of vows and the fitting of the ring.

Thereafter, having with some speed declared the couple man and wife, he launched into a rousing and almost accusatory address to the pair before him on the duties and dangers of holy matrimony, laying emphasis on the pitfalls rather than the delights and sonorously warning all present of the results and damnations of the sins of the flesh, in some detail. It was at this stage, unhappily, that the noise from above began to become distracting. The old city of Edinburgh, cramped within its walls on its high spine of rock, was notoriously short of space—which was why the lands and closes were so crowded and the tenements so tall. Prison space was in as short supply as all else, and at the Reformation the enormous cathedral-like church of St. Giles had seemed a godsend to the harassed magistracy. The lofty groined-vaulted ceilings soaring into dimness were obviously quite unnecessary for modest and reformed Presbyterian worship, and so timber entresol floors had been inserted above the three churches into which it was subdivided. Indeed, the Tolbooth Kirk was so named for excellent reason, since the Town Council met therein, courts were held and even parliaments had on occasion sat there. It so happened that the garret section above the Little Kirk was used for the incarceration of offending whores, prostitutes and common wantons—and these were not infrequently the most vocal and quarrelsome of the prisoners. A major engagement appeared to have broken out upstairs, and thumps, bangs and shrill invective penetrated the floorboards with ease. With the congregation—

perhaps even the new husband and wife—stretching ears to catch the gist of the disagreement there rather than his own stern words of admonition, Patrick Galloway turned to glare at Balfour and sweep a pointing and commanding finger heavenwards. The younger minister hurried off to see if he could restore order aloft, either by the fear of God or of the Town Guard. Keenly interested, all save Galloway listened on his progress.

By the time that the signing of the register was over, some quiet had been achieved above—but now the congregation itself was stirring and talking. Galloway soon put a stop to that, by striding to the pulpit, banging fist on Bible, and commencing his sermon. The proclaiming and expounding of the Word was considered to be one of the principal planks of Presbyterian worship and no services got off without a sermon—even weddings. Heriot had not really hoped to escape one on this occasion, when he had reconciled himself to Galloway, and now he wondered whether the noise overhead might not have been better left unchecked as a dissuading influence. At least the man was not preaching this time in Latin—as he had done once, at Leith harbour, on the first arrival from Denmark of the fourteen-year-old Queen Anne. He had gone on then for over an hour.

In the end it was probably Dunbar's young gentlemen, rather than the street ladies above that the congregation had to thank for obtaining their release after another half-hour, who, with their undisguised contempt for preachers so infuriated the divine by their cantrips and unabashed teasings of the bridesmaids that he could no longer continue. To the relief of all, he abruptly bellowed Amen at them, hurled a spluttering and angry benediction and stormed from the pulpit and out, an exit even more dramatic than his entry—and without a further glance at the couple he had married.

It was ironical, thereafter, that the first to congratulate the happy pair inevitably had to be Doddie Home, who did so stiffly, formally, before marching out first from the church.

Presently, in the High Street, where a large crowd had assembled, Heriot with an arm round his laughing bride to protect her from the crush, guided her over to the steps of the Cross, amidst cheers. Mounted there, he thanked all who had turned out so kindly to wish them well, declared that he was the most fortunate man in Scotland and announced that free wine, ale and meats would be dispensed for all comers until the evening curfew sounded—this to deafening applause. Then, aided by Alison, he splashed wine, by hand, from a broached cask, over all within range, in the traditional manner and tossed handfuls of placks and groats from a sack for the bairns—and others—to scramble for. A fireworks display would be held, he shouted, at dusk in the park of the Palace of Holyroodhouse, when there would be further refreshment. All were invited—and the Netherbow Port and Watergate would be kept open after the normal closing hour by special and kind permission of the new Provost, Sir John Arnot, here present.

On that happy note a move was made by the entire wedding company, down the High Street and Canongate to Holyroodhouse, which James had insisted was to be the venue of the marriage feast and celebrations, as his royal gift—although Geordie might find it expedient to have some little redecorating and furbishing up put in hand previously, since the place was no doubt in need of it now. Coaches had been hired to convey the bridal retinue and guests down to the palace, but Alison in her lightsome joy would have none of it. The sun shone, she pointed out, they had been cooped up in that church for too long and it was less than a mile of distance. This was the day of days and they would take the crown of the causeway and walk. Her groom was nothing loth.

In the end, everybody walked, in a lengthy narrow procession—for Alison's remark about the crown of the causeway was no mere figure of speech and only the raised centre of the cobbled street was passable for the lightly shod or the fastidious, the wide open gutters at either side being by no means wide enough, for all the waste matter, sewage, household soil and slops, the effluvia of stables, byres, styes and hen-runs, which the good citizens threw therein, with or without the warning cry of "Gardyloo!", in the simple faith that gravitation, evaporation, or speedy decomposition would before long remove it. Mary Gray it was who made the suggestion that a street fiddler should lead them on their way—there were always plenty of these in Edinburgh, though not always sober enough to fiddle walking, or even standing up. They were fortunate enough to find one who was, in a close-mouth; and so, to a jiggling, gay rant, they wound and tripped their way down the long, sloping street, between the canyon-walls of the tall, beetling tenements, hung with washing and folk waving from windows and balconies and shooing out of the way children, dogs, pigs and poultry—although most of the way Alison, on her husband's arm, danced rather than walked, despite her finery, her train wrapped round her like any shawlie. She even constrained the King's Goldsmith to skip a step or two, every now and again, though in highly self-conscious fashion. Once, glancing round rather guiltily after one of these indiscretions, it was to discover, not far behind, the magnificent figure of Patrick, Lord Gray, all in white satin slashed with black, Mary on one arm, Lady Marie on the other, jigging to the lilting melody with entire élan.

So, singing like a lark, Alison, with her love, passed through the Netherbow Port and into the separate burgh of the Canongate, the palace ahead of them.

At Holyroodhouse cooks, bakers, vintners and decorators of various sorts had been busy all day—and indeed for days previously—preparing. The providing of the wedding feast was, of course, traditionally the responsibility of the bride's father, but James Primrose, in the circumstances, had been very happy to bow to the pressure to use George Heriot's deeper purse. No expense had been spared, in consequence, and the ancient palace, though admittedly now somewhat neglected not to say delapidated, at least superficially had not looked gayer since Queen Mary's lively days. Banners, bunting, greenery, flowers were everywhere, hired tapestries and hangings and carpeting covered bare stone and flaking plaster, panelling was repaired and tempera painting was renewed, while instrumentalists played in corners, on balconies and in the pleasance. Even certain repairs had been affected to a leaking roof. King James would have rubbed his hands.

There were actually two feasts, one in the Throne Gallery, set for one hundred and fifty, and one in the open forecourt, not set but supplied for five hundred. There was no very clear distinction between the two, and any such there might be became less so as the day wore on—for this was a prolonged occasion. Not only Heriot and his bride wandered in and out between the two. The Scots were never a very class-conscious race and all sections of the invited guests mingled freely enough—though it would be fair to say that the majority of the trader, craftsmen and apprentice guests did not penetrate up to the Throne Gallery, even though there was nothing to stop them doing so; and indeed many of their womenfolk, in especial, did make a quick foray aloft, just to be able to talk about it afterwards. On the other hand, most of the more aristocratic guests did frequent the forecourt festivities intermittently during the five hours of continuous feasting, for here were the side-shows, the jesters and tumblers and wrestlers, the bear-dancing, cock-fighting, dwarf displays and other delights. Needless to say, the Earl of Dunbar and his minions did not honour this affair with their presence; but Chancellor Dunfermline did, and Tam o' the Coogate—though not his father or brother—as did the Reverend Balfour, a pleasant and not too earnest divine who did not always seem to equate sternness with their Creator.

By no means all the company were in a condition to appreciate the fireworks display when at length that stage was reached—though none complained thereat. Alison, with squeals, let off the first rocket, which burst in colourful radiance against the dark loom of nearby towering Arthur's Seat. With the shapely hill and its crags and all the city's other hills, castle and soaring, serrated skyline as backcloth, the extended display was highly impressive and challenging and the cheers of the watching crowds eloquent. In time, however, even Alison became slightly apprehensive, wondering how much each flash and bang and star-shower was costing.

"Never heed, lass," her new spouse advised her. "Leave me to calculate that. I do not get married every day!" He patted her bottom, in proprietorial fashion, as she ran off to light another.

"An excellent entertainment, Master Geordie. A most notable occasion, for which we are all vastly in your debt," a melodiously assured voice declared at his shoulder, presently.

He turned to Patrick Gray. "Ah, I thank you, my lord," he said. "From you, who are so knowledgeable in these matters, that is more than I deserve."

"I think not. This is altogether a day to remember."

"It will be my joy to remember it, sir."

"Of course, of course. You are, I swear, a most happy man. Your Alison is an enchantment. I do believe that you may be as fortunate in your wife as I am in mine!"

Surprised, Heriot gave a little bow, but said nothing.

They watched a fiery wheel soar and circle, sparking, through the gloaming sky. "You will have put your hand deep in a deep pocket for all this, my friend," Gray observed.

"Not more deeply than the occasion warrants. After all, I have paid for the like times amany, for the King's pleasure. Should I not now do so for my own and my friends'?"

"Well spoken, sir. I do agree. But... I think that you are too kind, at times, to our peculiar sovereign lord!"

"Is it not my duty to serve him? *All* our duty?"

"No doubt. But to serve him and his realm to best effect may demand more, shall we say, discrimination than just giving him all he asks. No?"

"I am a simple tradesman, my lord. Not for me to discriminate amongst the King's wishes."

"Ha—I wonder! And how simple, my friend? Tell me—did that payment to me of nineteen thousand pounds come from your pocket? Or the King's?"

"From the King's. In due course."

"Ah, yes—in due course! I wonder. His Grace is to be congratulated on this simple subject of his, I think! But, Master Geordie—that does not mean that His Grace will necessarily love you the more for it. Nor reward you suitably. Or, perhaps, at all!"

Heriot cleared his throat. "I do not pretend to any nobility of mind, my lord, as of blood—but I do not seek reward from His Grace, I think. I esteem our, our relationship otherwise."

"Said like a very loyal servant. As I was once!"

"I acknowledge that His Grace treated you ill, my lord. I was, and am, sorry. But—he may have had reasons unknown to me. Or even to you! Kings are not as other men. Cannot be."

"An interesting philosophy, sir. I am surprised at your disclaimer of nobility of mind. I conceive you to be all but bursting with it!"

Nettled, Heriot frowned. "Speaking of deep pockets, my lord, you yourself I believe, have been spending largely of late? Or so I hear."

"Ah! You have sharp ears, Master Geordie."

"Say that I have friends, tradesmen friends. In many places. Not all in Scotland. Some even in France!"

"So-o-o! The wind blows from that airt, does it! Interesting, is it not, how universal a language is the clink of gold pieces?"

"Aye. Even from the Vatican itself to, shall we say, the Isles of Orkney?"

Gray was silenced by that for a little—something few men ever achieved. He drew a deeper breath than usual. "You are a man, I swear, after my own heart!" he said then, unexpectedly.

"I find that hard to believe, my lord," Heriot answered, shaking his head. "Since we appear to have such very different . . . persuasions!"

"You think so? Tell me, my friend, if you will, you who so notably support His Sacred Majesty. How much of that support is for James Stewart, the man? And how much for his throne and realm?"

It was the other's turn to take his time. "Both," he said, at length. "Aye, both. I am a leal subject and though I now dwell in London, a true Scot. The realm of Scotland has my devotion. But I do not separate that realm from its monarch. And I have, you might say, an affection for King James, the man—if that seems not over-presumptuous. He is not as other men—but he could not be. He has ignoble qualities, as well as great—but who has not? But he loves peace, instead of war—which is something new in kings, I think. And, in his fashion, he is honest, good-natured, learned, and thinks for his common subjects rather than for his great lords—as few have done."

"But loves neither, to be sure!"

"Perhaps. The more credit to him that he *thinks* of them, then."

"I say he loves only himself—God's Vice-Regent!"

"Not that, no. He is a man who *needs* love, I believe—and can have but little of it. He is a lonely man, for all his favourites and courtiers."

"You are eloquent on his behalf, Master Geordie. He has a better friend in you than he deserves, I say. I would warn you, however—watch him well. He will use you, and discard you, at a whim."

"Not at a whim, my lord. He may discard me—for a king must use men and discard them, since they are the tools of his trade, as mine are tongs and pliers and hammers—aye, and merks and pounds! But with James, it would not be at a whim. Of that I am sure."

"Well—I have warned you, friend. If he turns and rends you, one day, as he has done myself, Balmerino and others—aye, and will do Dunbar likewise, I warrant you—recollect my warning!"

"I thank you. But, since warnings are to the fore, may I do the same by your lordship? King James knows more of your activities and plans than perhaps you think. And if he feels his realm and throne endangered thereby could strike quite ruthlessly. And, it may be, unexpectedly."

"That I have known for years, sir. I seek ever to take my precautions. But . . . so should he! Since you love him, tell him so! But—I thank you for your consideration on my behalf. We will go our several ways, Master Geordie, doing what we consider best for this strange realm of ours. Credit me with some devotion to it, likewise! Now—I have monopolised my host overlong. My apologies!" And with a smile that was kindness itself, he strolled away.

Heriot was stroking his little beard very thoughtfully when Mary Gray came to him. "I have been watching the pair of you, Geordie," she informed him, "talking so earnestly. When Patrick is so attentive, he usually has a reason."

"We were warning each other," the man told her, briefly.

"That sounds . . . direful?"

"I pray that it will not be. For either of us." He smiled. "And you? This is no occasion for such talk. Have you had enough of fireworks?"

"They are very fine. But, yes—I think I have had sufficient of entertainment. Excellent as it is, Geordie. And, see you—there's another who has, I vow!" And she pointed to where Alison, young Johnnie Stewart—not so very far apart in years—and some of the Primrose family were grouped. "Take her away, Geordie. She has had a long day and lived it to the full. But the best of it is still to come, is it not? So be it she is not so wearied as to be unable to savour it properly!"

"M'mmm. You think . . . ? But there is still the dancing. And I am host . . ."

"Not so. You are the *bridegroom.* Have you forgot? I say, forget you are the so responsible George Heriot, for once. You may be *paying* for all this—but is not the bride's father truly the host? Let James Primrose play his part in this, at least. Slip away, Geordie dear—while you may."

"While I may . . . ?"

"Yes. Johnnie tells me that some of the young ones are planning a bedding for you! It may be the custom, but I do not think that either of you would want that . . ."

"By God—no!" he cried, all indecision swept away. "I thank you. I will speak with her. At once . . ."

So, Alison far from unwilling, they did slip away unnoticed into the shadows of the pleasance—or hoped they were unnoticed.

They could have used almost any of the innumerable rooms of

the main palace as bridal chamber, but Heriot was quite content with his own old quarters in the northern conventual wing, and Alison had found no fault. Thither they hurried, and with relief the man shut the outer door behind them, and bolted it.

"Any bedding done tonight we will do without assistance!" he announced grimly.

Her tinkle of laughter did not sound in the least jaded or weary. "I am sure that you are entirely the expert, Geordie!" she said.

He looked somewhat less sure of himself, at that.

And upstairs, faced with the great bed, all ready, and the log fire and candles flickering, they both were constrained to pause a little. Heriot, however, had thought of this, and proceeded to tell the story of his arrival here from London all those years ago, before ever they had met, to be confronted with the large white and active limbs and person of an unknown lady, plus Patrick, Lord Lindores, the Lady Marie's brother-in-law, in this same bed. If the tale was just slightly stilted at the start, he warmed to the telling and before he was finished, they were sitting on the said bed in high hilarity, all tension evaporated. Indeed, the story *was* never finished, for presently the girl had closed the teller's lips with her own, and, almost of their own volition, his hands were busy unclasping, unhooking and detaching her finery—a process at which Alison began to assist enthusiastically, until she changed tactics, to start on him.

He exercised his mastery, however, declaring that one thing at a time was good policy and dutifully she acceded. And, in a little she desisted in her efforts altogether, to give him the satisfaction of removing those last silken garments. Then she stood up slowly, stood back from him, deliberately, opening her arms wide, palms cupped towards him, in a gesture of proud offering and humble giving, both, in all her heart-breaking young loveliness.

George Heriot actually groaned aloud in the extremity of his emotion, delight, joy. Down forward on his knees he sank, to reach out and clasp her white and slender, but sufficiently rounded form about the middle, and to press his brow and lips against her warm, satin-smooth but firm flesh below the small, vigorously-pointed breasts.

"My love, my heart," he whispered. "You are beautiful, beautiful! No man has ever looked on fairer. For long . . . so long . . . I have wanted you. Wanted you thus. Aye, thus and thus and thus!"

"Oh, Geordie, my dear, I am glad, glad!" she exclaimed into his hair. "I feared . . . for long I feared . . . that your need was not so great . . . as is mine! Lord be thanked . . . for this!"

He shook his head against her skin—and the doing of it so affected his lips as to set them trembling, wordless quite.

"Oh—up, Geordie! Up!" Alison cried. "Quickly, I say. We have waited . . . long enough!"

He rose, scooped her up in his arms and carried her to the bed.

23

GEORGE HERIOT would not have chosen to present his new wife at Court quite so soon after their return to London, with much settling in to do at the Exchange premises, the house above the shop to be remodelled and refurbished to a woman's taste, and no urgent desire on the part of either of them for haste in seeking royal recognition—especially as the Queen was said to be in low health and spirits, suffering from arthritis and money troubles and James spending much time away at Carr's new property of Shelborne, in Dorset. But it so happened that Will Shakespeare's new Scots play was now finished and was to have its first showing, naturally before the monarch, at Hampton Court, only four days after their arrival. Needless to say, they both were anxious to see this. Moreover, a summons to attend was awaiting Heriot from James—though no reference was made to his wife. He was not going without her, however—and Alison agreed that putting off the confrontation with the Queen was unlikely achieve anything.

Hampton Court Palace, thirteen miles up the Thames from Whitehall, was neither one thing nor another, as far as James was concerned—not conveniently at the centre of London life, nor yet sufficiently far away to be a useful country house capable of providing the sort of hunting facilities his health was alleged to require. A vast place, built by the unfortunate Cardinal Wolseley and handed over to Henry the Eighth in 1526, James had given it to his children, Henry, Elizabeth and Charles who ran wild amongst its honeycomb of rooms and corridors to their hearts' content—and thus largely kept out from under their father's feet. But it did provide a suitable venue for sundry large-scale activities, where the King and Queen could associate as it were on more or less neutral ground, since it was not officially the Queen's house, although she visited there much. They now lived almost entirely separate lives.

So Heriot and Alison hired a pinnace to take them upriver the dozen miles on a golden September afternoon, amidst a vast deal of other traffic going the same way, a cheerful journey, with the watermen shouting scurrilities at each other, impromptu races, and humble lightermen refusing to get out of the way of great lords' barges and young bloods' wherries. At the riverside palace amongst its terraced gardens, Heriot as usual sought out the Duke of Lennox whom he had heard was now back from the Continent. Ludovick was delighted to see them, made much of Alison, assured them of quarters for the night—but suggested that it might be unwise to seek audience of either James or Anne meantime, for they were having a major quarrel—ostensibly over the old trouble of finance, but all knew that it was really over the insufferable Carr. It was strange how the Queen had shrugged off the succession of earlier favourites but balked so at this one. Later, after the performance, would be the time to see the King. And it would be injudicious to approach Anne, anyway, before Alison had been received by James.

The Great Hall of Hampton Court, with its mighty extent and hammer-beam roof, made an ideal setting for a play-acting, for the accoustics were good, a minstrels' gallery above the stage, with dual stairways there to add dimension and allow for variety of movement. Such was the size of the place that many more could be accommodated than at the Globe or any other playhouse in England. Tonight, as well as all the two Courts, were present the foreign ambassadors, the high officers of state, the judges, many members of parliament, the Lord Mayor, aldermen and sheriffs of the city and other representative notabilities. After all, this was expressly intended to be a representing of Scotland in a new light—new, at least, to the English—and it was important that the highest placed in England should be left in no doubt as to the significance of it all.

Lennox found room for the Heriots beside him, in what they felt to be an embarrassingly prominent position—but which he countered by pointing out that as they were partly responsible for some aspects of the proceedings, it was only suitable that they should be well to the fore. They had a word with Will Shakespeare before the start, who expressed himself as reasonably satisfied with the form the work had taken, with Ben Jonson's scenery and the general arrangements—but was much concerned that the caste were insufficiently expert as yet in the parts and words and would scarce do justice to his dramatic conception.

The royal entrance was delayed, as usual, and the great company, left to entertain itself, was in danger of getting out of hand—as again was not unusual. However, Archie Armstrong, the King's jester, was on hand, and came forth dressed up to represent young Sir Robert Carr and so aped his mannerisms and style to the life that he had the entire audience shouting with laughter and joy—indication of the favourite's unpopularity. When Lennox rather anxiously declared that the good Archie had better take heed, if James got to hear of this, Heriot demurred, remembering what the King had said to him about Carr and his future. He might be none so displeased, since it seemed that it was part of his design that the young man should be unpopular.

The usual blast of trumpets heralded the monarch and Armstrong scuttled off with every appearance of guilt and alarm—but by a round-about route which kept him in view much longer than need be. James came in, leaning on Carr's shoulder—and the youth was over-dressed exactly as had been the jester, all ribbons, bows and jewels, his long, shapely, silk-clad legs on display right up to the bulge of the genitals and buttocks. Shambling beside him, the King looked the more clumsy, his grotesquely padded clothing tarnished, stained and thrown on anyhow. A couple of yards behind, the Queen stalked, frowning, limping a little with her arthritis, magnificently gowned in somewhat too youthful a fashion for her thirty-five years, the Marchioness of Huntly and the Lady Jean Drummond in attendance.

When the royal party were settled, Shakespeare himself again appeared before the still-drawn curtains, dressed in the antique armour of a general of the army of King Duncan of Scots, to bow low to King James and declare that it was his own, Master Richard Burbage's and all the King's Players' great honour to present before Their Majesties and all Their Majesties' illustrious guests the tragedy of ancient Scotland and the King's own remote ancestors, to be entitled *MacBeth*. Hail, King of Scotland!

"Och, man—no' King o' Scotland!" James called out censoriously. "King o' *Scots*, just. I told you before. You maun get the style right, mind. It's a different usage, see you."

The playwright bowed low at this inauspicious start but did not amplify. He signed for the curtains to be opened and disappeared.

A great clash of noise and flashing of lights broke out forthwith, drums beating and rumbling, cymbals clashing, fireworks banging and blazing—to the extreme apprehension of the monarch, who rose from his seat prepared to bolt for safety. However, the drawn screens revealed that it was only a thunder-storm taking place over a moorland scene, backed by realistic mountains, with a ring of ancient standing-stones the sole occupants of the foreground. Remaining standing until he was sure that all was well, James stared suspiciously. Unless he made the bangs himself, he did not like sudden noises.

Three weird and ragged hags entered on the scene, bent, mumbling, tangled of hair, all clawing hands, outstretched arms and darting glances, wary as James's own. The thunder fortunately died away.

"Ha—witches, on my soul!" James cried, into the sudden hush. "Waesucks—right devilish witches, I say! I can aye tell them. Auld, horrid demoniacs. Look there!"

"None so old, Sire!" the Earl of Montgomery's voice rang out from nearby. "See the paps of the one to the side—out-thrust nicely. None so old, I swear!"

"Eh?" The King leaned forward, peering. "I canna just see. Och, I daresay you're right, man Philip. You've the keen eye. Och, well—witches needna be a' that auld, mind. Satan can get at them fell young. I mind one at Dalkeith . . ."

"Pray sit, Sire—of a mercy!" Queen Anne requested. "Or we shall be here all night!"

> Paddock calls—Anon!
> Fair is foul, and foul is fair:
> Hover through the fog and filthy air!

So crying, the witches crept away, and the curtains were drawn to again.

"Short!" James commented loudly. "Aye, maist expeditious. But we're weel quit o' the likes o' them." He sat down, having established his proprietorial interest in the production.

The scene-shifting was not quite so expeditious, for though there was no lack of manpower, the Yeomen of the Guard, pressed into service, were less expert than were, say, the Globe attendants. The next scene, however, could make use of some of the former fittings, since this was also set in heathland, with the same hill background, a tented camp, with painted pavilions of King Duncan and his Scottish lords. His present Majesty called out identifications of the various heraldic devices shown, dwelling rather on the significance of the Lion Rampant, but also hailing Vicky Stewart to note the red saltire and roses of Lennox.

"Lord!" the Duke muttered, to Heriot. "If we're going to have a royal exposition and commentary on all, Anne's right—we'll be here all night!"

The appearance of Duncan and his sons Malcolm and Donald Ban, certainly brought forth further elucidation, but the arrival of a wounded and blood-stained captain to describe how had gone the battle against the rebellious Donald of the Isles had James cupping his ears to listen intently, quickly becoming absorbed in the story. Exclamations of satisfaction, wonder, enthusiasm and displeasure continued to come from him but nothing so prolonged that he should miss any of the serious speaking—to the relief of all concerned. The entry of the Earl of Ross, to announce another victory of the King's forces in far-away Fife, with Sweno of Norway seeking terms and the treacherous Thane of Cawdor dead, ended the second scene amidst jubilation—especially the declaration that the Norsemen were paying ten thousand dollars damages had James cheering loudly.

"Master Will knows his patron!" Heriot whispered.

The King took the opportunity, while the scenery was again being changed, to dilate upon the relationship of MacBeth and Duncan in distant cousinship, pointing out that his right name was MacBoedhe, or MacBeda and that he had some claim to the throne.

The curtains aside, they were back on the empty heath again, with some more bad weather and the three witches reappeared—signal for boos and catcalls from the audience who recognised them as fair game, in view of the monarch's well-known disapproval of the species, with enquiries and wagers as to their ages and physical development. Not a word they screeched was to be heard.

The entry of MacBeth himself and his friend Banquo, to James's vehement shushing—who saw audience participation best confined to himself—produced approximate quiet. Richard Burbage played MacBeth, a noble-looking and battle-scarred warrior and Shakespeare himself was Banquo, his friend. With the latter demanding how far it was to Forres, present Majesty intervened with some geographical information and Lennox took the opportunity to ask who on earth was this Banquo? Heriot admitted that he had never heard of such a character. Possibly he was an invention of Shakespeare's own. Or the King's.

The unfortunate witches therefore again had some difficulty in getting their hailing over, their prophecies anent MacBeth somewhat lost in the general discussion. Montgomery was to be heard declaring that he was not very sure yet where Forres was but if *he* was this MacBeth, he'd have the plumpest one down in her own heather there and then and Forres could wait.

The exchange between MacBeth and Banquo regarding the Thanes of Glamis and Cawdor went rather above the heads of most listeners, and the scene ended.

Furniture was clearly being introduced behind the curtains, during a longer pause, as James announced that he was afraid Master Shakespeare had erred in this of the thanes. MacBeth *was* Thane of Glamis, yes—but the Celtic thane was a lesser rank to that of Mormaor, and MacBeth was in fact Mormaor of Moray. Some elaboration of the Celtic polity followed, with reminders that the actors should really be speaking the Gaelic, the true language of Heaven and Eden both, as he'd explained one time—but belike most of those present would be none the wiser, belonging to neither the one place nor the other!

The scene in Duncan's palace went well, with James concerned that no one should interrupt while a king held the floor. But the change to MacBeth's own castle at Inverness, as Mormaor of Moray, demanded another geography lesson. Moreover Lady MacBeth's appearance drew forth dark allegations from present authority that yon was an ill woman if ever he'd seen one—and he'd seen a few. Though well-bred, mind. You couldn't aye depend on high breeding to produce proper females, like you could with bloodstock horses. If Queen Anne and her courtiers bridled at this sally, the King's own entourage cheered loyally. Scenes five, six and seven, to the end of Act one, therefore, were almost as active off stage as on.

At the interval, refreshments were brought on for all, largely liquid, James thoughtfully sending a good supply back-stage for the performers—which Lennox for one declared a somewhat rash proceeding—with his compliments that they were doing fine, fine, though he had not yet heard one good Scots voice. Thereafter, gazing about him in fatherly fashion, he espied Heriot and Alison, beside the Duke. Banging his tankard on the arm of his chair, to arouse their attention, he beckoned imperiously.

Highly embarrassed and reluctant, the pair got to their feet and made their way through the crush to the monarch's side.

"Aye, Geordie—so you have her, a' safe, sound and whaur she's best kept, atween your legs, heh? Or you between her's! Ooh, aye—and she's looking weel on it!"

Tight-lipped, Heriot bowed but said nothing. He squeezed Alison's arm comfortingly.

James did not fail to notice that squeeze. "Husbandly," he approved. "Aye, a kindly conjugality. And how like you married life, Mistress?"

She curtsied prettily. "Very well, Sire—very well indeed. But then, I have a better husband than most!"

James shot a glance at his Queen. "Hech, hech—pert, eh? I judge you pert, Mistress!"

"I hope not, Sire—but only honest." She turned and dipped low to Anne. "Master Heriot *is* a better husband than most, I do swear!"

"M'mm. You'll hae to watch this one, Geordie," the King said. "Mind, I told you so before. She'll lead you a dance, if you're no' carefu'. I ken the kind!" And he sniffed.

The Queen, who had been prepared to be stiff, smiled graciously instead. "Welcome back to Court, Alison!" she said. "I need not ask if you are well. You bloom, child—you bloom!"

"Your Majesty is most kind. Most generous. I thank you. I have heard that you suffer greatly. Arthritic pains. Yet Your Majesty never looked fairer, more handsome . . ."

"Why, bless you, child—marriage seems to have done you good. In more than your health! Would we all could say as much! My pain is oft grievous, yes. But must be borne. Like other things!"

"Yes, Majesty. You instruct us all in forbearance . . ."

The King banged his tankard. "Enough o' idle chatter!" he commanded. "If there's ae thing I canna be doing wi', it's women enlarging on their bit aches and pains. Forby—you'll be holding up the play-acting, the pair o' you, wi' your clack. Look—I vow they're sweer to be at it again. Back to your seats, Geordie man—and dinna hold a' up."

Bowing away but not overhurriedly, the Heriots moved back to Duke Ludovick.

"Good for you, my dear," Lennox greeted. "Nicely played, I think. You should be safely back in Anne's favour, now."

"So long as I did not overdo it with the King," she murmured.

"I did not really offend him, Geordie?"

"Not you, lass. James does not offend easily. Not over boldness. He'll think the more of you for a bit of spirit. That's what these English do not understand about him. They tend to grovel to their kings, as we do not."

"*You* do not, anyway, Geordie!" Lennox chuckled. "I've never seen less of a groveller than Master Craftsman Heriot, in all my days!"

"Ssshh! The curtain, my lord Duke . . ."

The second act, all at Inverness Castle, went well, with a minimum of royal interpolation, James quite caught up in the drama of it all, and the unfolding wickedness of Lady MacBeth, which so accurately bore out all his own assertions as to the essential baseness of the female nature. He was constrained at one stage to point out loudly, however, in all fairness, that the woman—whose right name was Gruach—had some reason for believing that Duncan had less right to the throne than herself, his cousin, since she represented the elder line. But that, to be sure, did not give her the right to suggest the murder of the Lord's Anointed, the which there was no fouler crime in earth or heaven.

By the time the second interval was over, the refreshments, off-stage and on, were beginning to have their effect. Even a three-act play was really over-long to put before a Court audience of this reign—and this one was reputed to have no fewer than five. Some of the actors, notably the Earl of Lennox, were speaking with increasing thickness—a circumstance which did not fail to rebound on his modern counterpart, in quips and sallies. When he came to the line, "My former speeches have but hit your thoughts", and rendered it, "My former theetches have but shit your sorts", he all but brought down the house—to his own surprise, since his was a comparatively minor part. The rest of his speech went unheard, to the complete demoralisation of the poor man; and Shakespeare himself, who as Banquo had just been slain, had to come back on stage wearing another lord's cloak to pronounce the important finale of the act,

. . . some holy angel, fly to the Court of England and unfold,
His message ere he come,
That a swift blessing may soon return to this our suffering country,
Under a hand accurst . . .

The curtain drew again, James was not too happy about the impact of that. Having missed, through the noise, the fact that the now murdered Duncan had a son at the English Court and he it was who was being thus advised and summoned, the last bit sounded rather as though England were some superior and blest realm urged to come to the rescue of accursed Scotland—which was assuredly not the object of the evening's entertainment. It took the monarch all of the third interval to explain the true situation to a not very attentive audience.

In the circumstances, the so dramatic ghost—and witch-haunted fourth act, with cave and cauldron, scarcely gained the rapt attention and horror it deserved—although there were cheers for the re-appearance of Banquo, however wraith-like. The sudden switch to MacDuff's castle in Fife was lost upon most onlookers, who, having once gone astray were not greatly concerned to return. Even the English Court scene failed to grip or be understood, apart from MacDuff's challenging question, "Stands Scotland where she did?" which received a notably vehement and unanimous answer from a large part of the gathering. And the final line of this act, Prince Malcolm's cry, "The night is long that never finds a day!" was taken up by all, with heartfelt fervour.

The last act, back in Scotland, at Dunsinane, interested Alison and Heriot more than it did most—though that was scarcely the fault of the playwright, who had fulfilled his exceedingly onerous task nobly, nor of Ben Jonson, whose no fewer than seventeen different scenes were a triumph of invention and design, even though none were recognisably Scottish in character. Success in the presentation of dramatic entertainment depends on many factors—and few of the necessary were present at Hampton Court that night. Birnam Wood on the move, admittedly, was a great success, with the entire Court hallooing loudly, as at a buck-hunt; and MacBeth's head, dripping realistic gore and upraised on MacDuff's spear, was cheered to the echo. All, even King James, accepted that as the finish—and so were spared Malcolm's valedictory speech, however hopefully it began, "We shall not spend a large expense of time . . ."

Probably Will Shakespeare was as relieved to see the end as were his audience.

"Think you this piece will serve to endear us Scots to the long-suffering English?" Lennox wondered, as they made their way out in the royal train. "Since that, I understand, was its object."

"I doubt it." Heriot sighed. "Not to this Court, at any rate—which I fear is far beyond conversion. It may serve better with the commonality of playgoers, who have longer wits if shorter pedigrees! Who knows? For there is much good in it. Had we been able to heed it properly, I would have enjoyed it, I think."

"Poor Master Shakespeare," Alison sympathised. "Who would be a playwright. I think it was splendid—or should have been. He was casting his pearls before swine, here."

"It is James I am sorry for," her husband said. "Shakespeare will *know* its worth and will play it to better effect another time. But this was the King's conception, his dream to serve Scotland and the Scots. He will be a sore disappointed man this night—though, I swear, he will never show it. Have a thought for Jamie—even though half the fault was his own."

* * *

The Heriots did indeed go to see the play of *MacBeth* again, some weeks later, when it was performed before a more conventional audience at the Globe, Southwark—and enjoyed it greatly. But now there was another Banquo, for Will Shakespeare had finally done what he had been threatening to do for long—shaken the dust of London from his feet and gone back to his native Stratford, in Warwickshire, there to live the better life. George Heriot asked himself, and his wife, whether the playwright was not the wiser man than he? Alison was young enough still to find the bustle and excitement of the city and Court alluring—but she agreed that a small landed property in green Strathearn, say, near to Methven would make a joyous contemplation. Perhaps in a year or two . . .?

Not that the news from Scotland that winter and spring of 1609–10 was such as to entice exiles home. Trouble was brewing, harshness and uncertainty both were rife in the rule and governance, and rumours of plots, uprising, even armed invasion from abroad, abounded. On the face of it, the struggle appeared to be between Dunbar and the rising tide of Catholicism, but those in the know tended to see it as between King James in London and Patrick, Lord Gray. Dunbar, now to all intents supreme in Scotland, was highly unpopular and known to be feathering his own nest hugely. But against Gray he seemed to be able to achieve nothing, for the latter appeared on the surface to be leading a blameless, innocuous and normal life for a peer of the realm, sheriffing it in Angus, managing large estates there and in Fife, making entirely worthy public appearances in Dundee, Aberdeen, Glasgow and the capital, ornamenting all he touched. But there was little doubt that he, not Dunbar nor yet Dunfermline, was beginning to all but control the Privy Council, as once he had done before. And that a constant succession of unknown visitors, some said to be Jesuits, came and went by night at Castle Huntly in the Carse of Gowrie, Broughty Castle and other of his houses.

Heriot got most of his information from letters sent by Mary Gray to Lennox. And from these, certain significant pointers emerged. For instance, that the Lord Gray had stood security to the Council in no less than twenty thousand pounds, for the captive Earl of Orkney, in order that he should be freed from Edinburgh Castle for a short space—a vast sum to hazard for so apparently small privilege. It was thought that Orkney had been quietly spirited off to Castle Huntly for some important conference—and then as quietly returned to durance vile. Then, only a month or so later, Patrick Gray was again standing surety to the Council, this time for five thousand pounds, for Orkney's younger brother James Stewart, that he should cease importing arms and ammunitions into the Isles of Orkney from France and confine his person to a limited area of mainland Scotland—though that area centred on Angus within Gray's influence and sheriffdom. Again, that same spring, he was standing surety—though only for five hundred merks this time—for Sinclair of Murkill, again not to transport arms and munitions to Orkney. Others, too, troubled the Council with secret and ominous activities—and for all, Patrick Gray, or one of his Catholic friends, nobly stood cautioner. It seemed that he now had almost unlimited funds at his disposal.

King James, as it happened, was also in funds—for the Ulster plantation scheme and baronetcy-selling was going quite splendidly, with good Protestant applicants falling over each other to be involved, from southern Scotland and north-west England especially. Some of the wretched Irish proved a little difficult—as they always did, of course—demurring about being deported southwards; but James thought up an excellent alternative, no fewer than eleven thousand of the most militant males to go to Scandinavia to help the Danes fight the Swedes—at King Christian's expense, naturally, a valuable export. Since James was at the same time working very hard behind the scenes to arrange a peace between the Swedes and Danes, the thing was the more delightful and did no injury to his well-known pacific reputation.

Despite these preoccupations—and the continuing education of young Robin Carr—James did by no means entirely overlook his ancient Scottish realm. He ordered the Earl of Orkney to be removed from Edinburgh to Dumbarton Castle, into much stricter imprisonment, and indeed instructed Tam Hamilton to start gathering material for a trial of his cousin on a charge of high treason. He issued a proclamation that any other of the Orkney Stewarts, legitimate or otherwise, found in mainland Scotland, would be apprehended likewise and held for similar trial—and did indeed collect both the aforementioned James Stewart and an illegitimate brother Edward. He forbade the carrying of arms and munitions of war into any Scottish or Orkney port, under pain of treason. He promulgated new regulations against practising Catholics meeting together—although he emphasised that freedom of worship was still a man's inalienable right, so long as it was done in private. Moreover, the sum of five thousand pounds was to be distributed amongst Scots parish ministers who preached adequately in support of the King's policies, as from Christ's own Vice-regent. And finally, with a sudden edict, he declared that the ancient Scottish Privy Council, with its ninety-one members, including all the Scots Lords of Parliament, had outlived its usefulness and was herewith disbanded and nullified. In future it would consist of only twenty-six members and all appointed by himself. He appointed ten herewith, all carefully chosen, half of them bishops. So Patrick Gray was out, dismissed from the Privy Council for the second time.

For his part, Doddie Home, Earl of Dunbar—who had now added to his responsibilities the offices of Lieutenant of the Border Marches, Keeper of Holyroodhouse, Master of the Great Wardrobe (in England) and Collector-General of Customs as well as Lord High Treasurer and Great Commissioner—did his part. He arranged a General Assembly of the Kirk at Glasgow with himself as Commissioner and the Archbishop of Glasgow as Moderator, which proceeded to deliver practically all central and provincial power in the Church of Scotland to the bishops—and excommunicated the most prominent Catholics. In his other capacity as Borders Lieutenant he hanged no fewer than one hundred and forty of what he named the prime thieves of the Marches, for to discourage envious folk elsewhere as he humorously put it.

The powder-trail in Scotland was nearing the barrel and flash-point seemed imminent.

In all this ferment, life at the English Court went on as usual, indeed all England appeared to be completely unaffected. The great matter here was the forthcoming investiture of Henry as Prince of Wales and the nation-wide celebrations to mark the occasion—one of the principal of which seemed to be the raising of Carr to the dignity of Viscount Rochester and Knight of the Garter.

James Stewart had all—or most—nicely in hand.

24

LUDOVICK OF LENNOX rubbed his hands before the cheerful fire—for it was unseasonably chilly for April—and glanced around the pleasant panelled room.

"You have made a difference in this house, Alison," he observed. "The woman's hand. Would that I had a chamber as kindly at Whitehall."

"You have better at Methven," the young woman reminded.

"Aye. To be sure." He gazed out of the window across the street to the Royal Exchange building with its soaring square tower. "You judge me a fool? Or worse? That I leave Mary there—and my heart with her? To live here at a Court I mislike, aye even despise. She would not come, you know—Mary. Nothing would make her leave Methven."

"I know, yes. She loves Methven. But that is not what keeps her from London. She loves you a deal more, Vicky. She has a clear eye. She knows that her place here could never be aught than that of courtesan, unable to appear with you in your life at Court. An embarrassment and hindrance to you, her own pride the sufferer. She is better at Methven, with Johnnie."

"Aye—say it then, girl, say it! Where *I* should be, too, were I not a weakling."

"No, Vicky—you are not that. You cannot help yourself. You were born to be a duke. Of the royal house. Your place is with the King—must be. Your duty. He relies on you as he does on no other—even though he seems to scorn you often. None other can walk in on him, unsummoned. No other man may call him James. Your influence for good, with the King, is great. There is no other to fill the place of the Duke of Lennox—Geordie always says it. He says the King heeds you and your advice more than he would ever admit."

"You would scarce think it! I am his whipping-boy! Lord save me—the only legitimate near kinsman to His Sacred Majesty! Other than the sons he resents. Ha—but here is Geordie! I hope I have not brought you away from some matter of great moment, friend? Some juggling with pounds Sterling, to buy or sell us all!"

"I was but parading St. Paul's with my fellow-usurers, gossiping away better men's credits!" Heriot assured. "This is a happiness! We see you insufficiently often, Vicky."

"Alas, yes. James uses me as errand-boy ever the more—call it ambassador if he will! I have now been over most of Christendom on his ploys—France, Spain, the Netherlands, Denmark, Sweden. I am new back indeed from the Rhineland, where James would now marry off young Elizabeth to the Elector Palatine, as better for his purposes than Gustavus. He would bring the Empire into his peace-making now. So I traipse and travel—all in the name of peace on earth!"

"A worthy cause, is it not?"

"So I would suppose. Yet I know not one tithe of what he is at, when he sends me, so intricate, so unfathomable are his methods and labyrinths. I fear I have not the wits to be Jamie Stewart's ambassador. But—who has? Save perhaps Patrick Gray!"

"He trusts you, Vicky—as there are few he does. And as he would never trust Gray."

"It may be so. But can *I* trust James? There's the rub! But . . . Gray. That is why I am here, Geordie. I have come straight from a meeting of the Privy Council. I am for Scotland the morn's morn. Would that you were coming with me, again. But," he glanced at Alison, smiling, "that attraction is not what it used to be, I think!"

"I could by no means leave London this week . . ."

"No, no—I did not think you could. I but came to see if I might carry any letters or messages for you, or otherwise serve you, in Scotland."

"You are kind. Will you be gone for long?"

"That depends on . . . fate! My errand this time is an awkward one. I am to bring back the Earl of Dunbar."

"*Bring* back?"

"Aye. Doddie Home's reign is over, I think! James has given him a lengthy rope—of a purpose, I swear—and now he has hanged himself! He is summonded back to London to give account of his stewardship."

"But he comes frequently . . ."

"This time I am sent to fetch him! He will perceive the difference! And I am to bring Tom Hamilton, Dunfermline and Archbishop Spottiswoode with him."

"These too? Are they in trouble also? All these?"

"I think not. They are to act Dunbar's accusers, rather."

"Ah! What has he done, then? We all know the style of him. He is a rogue—but James has always known that he was. And used him, in despite. What has he done, to change that?"

"He has committed the unforgivable sin. He has put his hand in *James's* pocket! So long as it was others he robbed—like Logan or the Catholics—James could use him. You would have thought, as Treasurer and Collector both in Scotland, offices capable of lining his pouch richly enough for any man, he would have been careful not to foul his nest. But, no. He has it seems, been taking his pickings out of James's beloved Ulster scheme. If a Scot wants a share in Ulster now, he has to get it through Doddie Home—at an extra charge! The man is a fool—for it was bound to come to the King's ears in time. I suppose the fact is that he is just a Home Border freebooter at heart, for all his earldom, like the rest of his clan and could not keep his hands off even the King's kye!"

"Aye, James would not like that!"

"How did the King find out, do you know?" Alison asked.

"Oh, yes, we know. A friendly letter, no less—not to James himself but to the English Privy Council, through Lord Chancellor Ellesmere. From Patrick, Lord Gray of Fowlis, no less! Enclosing sworn testimony. Statements from three Angus lairds that they had paid each one thousand pounds Scots, above the required figure, for Ulster lands, signed and sealed."

"Save us! So Gray wins another round!" Heriot exclaimed. "He set a trap—and the fool Dunbar walked into it. Mind, Scotland will be the cleaner lacking Dunbar. But it makes Gray that much the stronger. Who is there now to oppose him?"

"Heaven help me—*myself,* I fear!" Lennox answered ruefully. "Or so James would have it. After I have seen to Dunbar, I have to be the new Great Commissioner for Scotland, to deal with the Kirk—and Patrick Gray!"

"Oh, Vicky!" Alison cried.

"I protested, actually refused, there and then, before the Council.

But James made it a royal command, on pain of treason. What could I do? At least it will mean that I am much in Scotland. Can see more of Mary."

There was silence in that panelled room above the goldsmith's shop for a little, as they all considered the implications of this development.

"Mary . . .?" Heriot demanded. "What will she say? You are to bring down her father!"

"God knows! Only . . . James can make me go, mind you—but he cannot control what I *do,* there. With Mary's sharp wits, we may find a way to weather this storm."

"The King is a *devil!*" the young woman declared.

"I wonder?" her husband said, slowly. "If I was James—which God forbid!—I think . . . I might have done the same!"

"Oh, you ever favour him, Geordie!"

"He has two realms to govern, lass. One of them four hundred miles away."

"Geordie's right," the Duke admitted. "And James has the cleverest man in Europe to master—so he sends me! He can scarcely expect *me* to outwit Gray—so what is he at? Though, to be sure, it may be getting beyond the wits stage. Coming to the sword, at last! And with the sword, it may be, I might shine a little brighter!"

"Oh, no . . .!"

"Is it so bad as that, Vicky?"

"It looks so. Young Robert Stewart, Orkney's bastard and favourite son, has set himself up, in Kirkwall, as his father's appointed representative, indeed proclaimed himself Sheriff of Orkney and Shetland, declaring the Isles to be an independent principality under Udal law. He has taken over all Scots shipping there and announced that he is coming to rescue his father and uncles."

"Rebellion! From the Orcades! Lord—is this to be taken seriously?"

"Who knows? It sounds crazy-mad. But if Gray is behind it—and few doubt that—then it is serious indeed. Shiploads of arms are known to have been sailed into Kirkwall for months past. But not only Kirkwall—there is word of the like all along the east coast of Scotland, from Angus northwards. Especially into the Catholic Gordon lands of Aberdeenshire and Banff. This threatened invasion is not just to rescue Earl Patrick from Dumbarton Castle! It could be the armed Catholic revolt, at last, only making use of Orkney."

"With what hope of success?"

"More than seems likely at first glance. Our peace-loving monarch has maintained no real army in Scotland. Such Scots soldiers as there are, are over in Ulster settling in the planters and ejecting the Irish. Dunbar has divided and weakened the country. And, more important, recollect *who* Patrick of Orkney is—the King of Scots' nearest living kinsman. Nearer than I am. His father was illegitimate, yes, where mine was not, but he was a son of James the Fifth and brother to Queen Mary. And Earl Patrick himself is not illegitimate, whatever else he is."

"Dear God—you mean he might yet become King Patrick the First?"

"Would that be so much more strange than the plot to put the child Henry on the throne in 1603?"

"I can scarce believe all this serious, Vicky."

"Maybe not. But—have you forgotten the Casket Letters, Geordie? What is it James so fears in them? That he himself could be proved illegitimate—or allegedly so! Would Orkney, then, not have a better claim to the throne? And it is believed Gray now holds those Letters. You may not see it as serious—but James does. Sufficiently to have given me a private letter for Patrick Gray. And told me privily I shall receive secret instructions from him before I leave for Scotland. Gray, no doubt, is only using Orkney for his own ends—but that *could* mean Scotland with a new and resident king again. Which many might welcome. James is much concerned. Not so much that he fears for his Scots throne, I think—he believes God will secure him that! But that he, the peace-maker, may have to take the sword to hold that throne. To have to go to war in his own native land, just when European peace seems to be within his grasp."

"And that, I swear, is Patrick Gray's strongest card! If indeed there is a devil here, Alison lass—that is he!"

* * *

Heriot and his wife were conducted through the gardens of Denmark (or Somerset) House, in the golden September sunshine, to the same arbour where once before the man had sat, with the Queen, and handed over to her the jewel which was his first present to Alison. Anne sat there again, amongst the ripe-hanging fruit and turning leafage, and looked notably older than on that other occasion, older and sadder, if not wiser—although she was still but thirty-six.

The Queen was alone and she dismissed the junior Lady in Waiting who had brought them. "My friends," she said, in her guttural voice, heavier even than it used to be, as they made their obeisances, "come and sit by me. It is pleasant here, and the sun warms my aching joints."

"Your Majesty still suffers pain?" Alison asked.

"Bodily pain is the least of my troubles," the Queen said.

"His Highness the Prince of Wales is better, Madam?" Heriot enquired. "I heard that he appeared very well at the ship-launching of the *Prince Royal,* at Gravesend."

"Better, yes—but still less than well. He has grown listless, pale and complains of pains. Both in the head and belly. It is unnatural in so fine, so strong a young man."

"Some passing weakness, Madam. Outgrowing his strength, belike. He is now eighteen, and tall. Often it is so . . ."

"No. That does not come suddenly, as this has done. It is only since his investiture. He has begun to fail. My physicians can find nothing amiss. They have purged and bled and dosed him. They speak, the fools, even of witchcraft! Oh, Master Geordie—I dare speak of this to none. Save perhaps you, my old friend. It could not be . . . it could not be . . . that he is being slowly poisoned?" She choked on the word.

"Your Majesty!" he exclaimed. "Save us—do not . . . never think it! Never that! Here is folly, surely—begging Your Majesty's pardon. A mother's fond fears run riot! The heir to the throne! The most popular figure in the realm . . .!"

"There's the rub! Too popular, I vow! When one is so popular, others less so may seek to pull him down."

"But, Highness—not the King's son?"

"No? If it is the King who most resents that popularity?"

"But—Sweet Mercy! You do not . . . you cannot . . .?"

"James has been turning against Henry for years," she said, in a level voice. "Because Henry prefers *my* company. Is all that James is not—graceful, handsome, strong, noble. And the people love him. As they do not love his father. That James cannot forgive."

"Madam—you cannot, before God, be suggesting that His Majesty would, would . . .!" Heriot shook his head helplessly.

"Not James himself, perhaps. But his minions, it might be. That vicious Carr, or Rochester, as he now calls himself. Who never fails to insult *me*. He, and his governor, Overbury. Would these two hesitate to dispose of my Henry? As they have done with others?"

"Not so, Madam—I swear! Not poison. Not the Prince of Wales!"

"No? Knowing that the King hates him, fears his popularity with the people. James's own mother was deposed, to set *him* up as king. Why not Henry? Moreover, Henry despises Carr, and resents the slights he puts upon me—and shows it."

"There could be ill will, yes. But poison . . .!"

"Carr and Overbury have already used poison, I am told. Powdered glass. Carr learned of it at that she-devil's, Catherine de Medici's Court in Paris. She is dead, but her methods linger on! And now, this latest death. Also to James's advantage."

"What death, Madam?"

"Why, the odious Dunbar. The hateful Doddie Home. Surely you have heard?"

Heriot drew a long, quivering breath. He did not trust himself to speak.

Alison did. "We heard that he had died. Suddenly. While more or less prisoner, in Whitehall. After his . . . examination! Your Majesty thinks it was poison?"

"Half the Court thinks so, girl."

"I cannot believe it, Highness!" the man got out. "Not poison. Or, not at the King's behest. His Majesty . . . is not so. I swear it! I have known him long, been honoured with his confidences. That is not King James."

Anne shook her head. "I hope . . . I pray . . . that you are right. But . . . Carr! That evil youth whom James cherishes in preference to me, his wife, would do *anything*. I am going to Hampton Court, to be with Henry. To watch over him. I must, and shall. God's curse on all unnatural catamites, and those who suffer them!" With an obvious effort, the Queen sought to calm herself and forced her voice to a more even tone. "But . . . I did not summon you both here to speak so, to pour out my woes on you. I have two purposes, Master Geordie, one pleasant, one less so. The first is to offer the appointment of Extra Woman of the Bedchamber to Mistress Alison, here—who was once my Maid in Waiting. And to express my sorrow at the . . . misunderstanding which came between us."

It was Alison's turn to have difficulty in finding words, something which seldom afflicted that young woman. "Oh, Majesty . . . I thank you! You are too good, too kind. I . . . I am greatly honoured. Unworthy. But . . . I fear . . . forgive me, but . . ."

"It will not demand much of you, or your time, girl," Anne said, just a little sharply. "I have attendants amany. I know that you have Master Geordie's house to keep. Aye, and no lack of money! But it is more of a symbol than a task. And will give you the entry to Court again, at will. Not always to be brought by your husband. An *Extra* Woman, I said."

"Yes, Majesty. I understand. And thank you deeply. From my heart. I . . . I will accept, gratefully."

"I, too, Madam, thank you," Heriot said. "It is generously done."

"Good. And now to the less pleasing purpose," the Queen said. She stooped and drew out a quite large leather bag, obviously heavy, from under her seat. "Take this, Master Geordie—and think better of me, the Queen, than I do myself!"

Heart sinking, he took the bag and opened it, guessing something of what was within. The glitter and gleam of diamonds, rubies, emeralds, sapphires and the sheen of gold, glowed in there. He saw a slender crown of gold, inset with pearls and enamel-work, amongst the rest. He closed the bag again.

"I am at your service, Madam," he said flatly. "You wish me to take charge of these? As your Court Jeweller?"

"I wish to *pawn* them, Master Heriot! That is all."

He swallowed. "Not pawn, Majesty! Never pawn . . ."

"Why not? I must have money. I am desperate, man! I have nothing left. I owe *you* what? Eighteen thousand pounds? Twenty thousand pounds? I still owe Herrick. And Gresham. I have not paid any of my household for long. I must have money. James will give me no more. I know that I am extravagant—but, God help me, I am Christian's sister! Daughter of Frederick the Splendid."

"Your debt to me need occasion Your Majesty no concern at this juncture. I can wait . . ."

"You are patient, kind, as ever. But I must have *money*. It is not to be borne that I, the Queen, should be penniless. James is, as ever, away hunting. At Shelborne, this time. He has much money, these days, from the Ulster business—but talks only of asking *parliament* to increase my income. As though those creatures would! I must have it, Master Geordie. Even to pay for my move to Hampton Court."

"How much, Madam?"

"Five thousand pounds. In coin. These are worth . . . more than that?"

"You shall have it tomorrow, Majesty. But . . . never in pawn." He stooped and pushed the bag back under her seat. "Your Highness will keep these safe for me? It will be a loan. On very good security and without interest. My humble duty. And when I have opportunity, I shall speak with the King. He calls me his Fiduciary, his man-of-affairs. I shall make bold to offer His Majesty some fiduciary advice!"

Anne shook her head, wordless.

As they took their leave, the Queen said that Alison at least would not be sorry to be safely out of Scotland, in this troublous time, with all the news from the North grievous. That wicked man Gray was able to twist poor Vicky Stewart round his little finger—thanks to his infatuation with the man's bastard daughter, Mary. Patrick of Orkney was actually issuing proclamations from his cell at Dumbarton. Talk of rebellion and war was on all lips. The only virtue in it all was that Vicky at least would be less harsh on the poor and harmless Catholics than had been the evil Dunbar.

The Heriots made their way back to Cornhill and the Exchange in a state of considerable unease.

25

ONCE AGAIN, ALL the river traffic seemed to be heading for Hampton Court. Blessedly, the May sun shone brightly and the fresh green of the trees was a joy, though there was a cool, easterly breeze—for the day-long festivities were to be held mainly out-of-doors and rain would have been something of a disaster and a move indoors a pity indeed. But the King had assured all that it would be fine weather—his colleague, the Deity and Prince of Peace, would ensure that, in the circumstances—and now the May sunshine did not fail to exact tribute to the Lord's Anointed's close links with the King of Kings, his faith and claims justified. It was in every way a most auspicious occasion.

George Heriot was present partly in a professional capacity and well guarded in one of the royal barges—for he was bringing with him a very valuable cargo of goldsmith-work and plate for the monarch to present to the principal foreign guests, princes, envoys and ambassadors. For months now he had been at work on these—indeed, so large and important was the order that the Earl of Suffolk had, at the monarch's express command, issued a proclamation instructing all mayors, sheriffs, justices, baliffs and constables to aid Master George Heriot, His Majesty's Jeweller, in finding workmen and artificers to enable him to complete his manufacture of these most important gifts and mementos in due time, a task quite beyond the resources of any one workshop or group of craftsmen. When all would be paid for was not stipulated in the said proclamation.

So, amidst the stream of barges, wherries, shallops, pinnaces and yawls, Heriot, Alison at his side and with an escort of scarlet-coated

least his United Kingdom, naturally represented by the largest and noblest-looking lion, its coat gleaming with gold-dust; a nice touch, it remained throughout arm-in-arm with a pure white unicorn, upright and with a long silver horn. This symbolic parade and demonstration was to go on throughout the day, as reminder to all of what they were celebrating.

There was no sign of James himself, so the Heriots and escort, two Yeomen staggering under the weight of the heavy chest, had to go searching the far-flung gardens and pleasure-grounds and then the endless corridors, courtyards and galleries of the vast palace, before finally running the monarch to earth in a disused kitchen of the domestic wing. Here, with the Palatinate ambassador and the new Viscount Rochester, he was busy assembling an elaborate dolls' palace which the envoy had brought as a gift for the Princess Elizabeth from his royal master, the Elector Frederick Henry—and which had come packed in sections and pieces, complete with furnishings, even to miniature pictures, hangings, carpets and tapestries. James was wholly engrossed in this intriguing task, despite the agitation of sundry officials and notables outside. He welcomed Heriot, but showed little interest meantime in what he called his 'kist o' gewgaws'; but insisted that Geordie and his bit lassie, who were sure to have nimble fingers, should come and help with the task of assembly. It seemed that the tapestries were particularly ticklish to hang and the King's fingers blunt. The envoy from Cleves, who had tailed along with them, exclaiming at all, found himself saddled with a stable plus many model horses and coaches and ordered to sort it all out, Carr the while being catechised on the Latin names for all the items represented and alternately slapped and kissed as a consequence of success or failure.

This prolonged and fiddlesome process appeared as though it might well occupy the Crown for much of the day and Heriot took his turn in seeking tactfully to remind Majesty that many illustrious visitors and deputations were waiting, to say nothing of the full and elaborate programme of events devised for the occasion. James tutted all such interruptions away, with the sage counsel that one thing at a time was recommended policy; and Carr, laughing lazily, added that all would wait very nicely, since by God, it must!

For how long the Palatinate dolls' house would actually have detained them, there was no knowing. But in time James's old favourite from Scottish days, James Hay, Viscount Doncaster, turned up in a sort of jocular bad temper, to declare that either Majesty came forthwith to the great dining hall to partake, or all the notable provision he had assembled—at the cost of three manors no less—would be taken to the stables and thrown to the pigs, since that would be all it was fit for. This ultimatum coming at a moment when James had slightly cut his finger with the tiny glass pane of a window-frame, to the effusion of alarming blood, had its effect and a move was made, jewel chest, escort and all.

Doncaster had some reason and right to be thus firm. The King had devised a highly satisfactory arrangement whereby the cost of large and complex entertainments should not always fall entirely upon his own shamefully meagre Treasury. A relay of wealthy individuals were given the privilege of providing the banquets, the entertainers, the masques and scenery and so on—and moreover encouraged to be competitive about it. Hay, although he had come south as poor as a church mouse, being only a younger son, had recently married his second rich wife, this one enormously rich, and was to be created Earl of Carlisle. Today the catering was his responsibility.

On arrival at one of the many great dining halls, the newcomers, heralded at last by a trumpet fanfare, found the Queen, Prince Charles and Princess Elizabeth awaiting them, the former in no genial mood and the place packed with hungry guests, all separated from the groaning tables by a solid line of liveried servitors, cooks and scullions, in the red and white Hay colours. The King beamed on all—as well he might, for it was a most noble company, with a most noble spread laid before them. Hay had done them proud. From the dais at the top end of the great chamber, the royal party—which, purely by chance, included the Heriots, the hairless man from Cleves, the Yeomen of the Guard with chest and sundry other nonentities—could look down on a bewildering array of fare, delicacies, comestibles, viands, savouries, confections and dainties on tables stretching from one end of the hall to the other, piled high as a man could reach, on splendid plate, stands, epergnes, salver-frames and silver wiskets. There were the favoured dishes from every realm and country represented at the gathering, besides as many from stranger lands farther afield, the Indies, Barbary, Arabia, the Caliphate, even from frozen Iceland, meats and sweets formed in the lively shapes and colourings of the animals, birds, fish and vegetables from which they were concocted, cauldrons and puncheons of rare wines and spirits, some actually contrived to be on fire with blue licking flames, a half-sized cow squirting thick cream from its udder and other conceits too numerous to mention.

The King nodded approvingly. "Aye, Jamie Hay—a right comforting provide," he commended. "Your new Viscountess maun hae mair than just double-chins and a noble bum! Yon looks right tasty. Eh, Annie? It's maybe worth having yon Cardinal-man to say a grace ower this lot, I'm thinking. Where is he?"

"Wait, Sire—of your gracious patience," Doncaster intervened, with much boldness. "One moment more—and it please Your Majesties." And he banged a gold ladle on a piece of plate as a signal.

Immediately all was transformed. Like a regiment of maniacs the hitherto so disciplined and motionless line of servants hurled themselves upon the laden tables. Grabbing up the piled dishes and platters of meats and confections, they flung all to the floor at the far side of the tables, in a rain of ruined refections, smashed sweets, damaged delicacies and spilt spirits, spattering the wall-panelling, piling up in heaps, spreading over the floor. On and on the servants went, as though frenzied, while the great company shouted and yelled and groaned, even wept, in pain and fury, until there was not a dish nor sweet nor receptacle left on the line of tables. Pandemonium reigned.

Then, with the enraged guests surging forward and the attendants turned to fight them off, a single trumpet-blast sounded, the hall doors were thrown open, and, led by fiddlers playing a jigging Scots air, in marched a new and seemingly endless regiment of cooks and scullions bearing trays, salvers, platters, cauldrons, flagons, larger and finer model animals, birds and fishes, soups steaming richly, a whole ox roasted, still with its horns and hooves, peacocks with spread tails and a host of similar provisions, to more than fill those emptied tables. And, bringing up the rear, carried by four young pages all in white satin, was a twice-life-sized naked woman, sculpted in sugar, flesh-tinted, nipples coloured, hair contrived, where proper, in gold-leafed toffee tendrils.

The shouting and anger changed to cheering and acclaim. James Hay bowed to the King and Queen and waved and grinned to all the guests, before, with a flick of his hand, dismissing the army of domestics.

"Aye, maist ingenious," James declared, a little breathlessly. "But a fell waste o' meats, man!"

"It is called the ante-dinner, or double-dinner, Sire. As they do it in the Papal States, I understand. With, h'm, improvements!"

"Is that so? Well—we'll no' trouble the Cardinal-man, this time, but just set to—in case you breenge it a' awa' again! You've fair set my belly rumbling."

* * *

When none could eat more and before a similar stage was reached with the wines, James presented his gifts, Heriot assisting and identifying. Clearly he gained much satisfaction from the exercise, especially from the little speech he made, with each item, in the language of its recipient, a feat certainly no other prince of Christendom could have rivalled. Whether all the happy assignees were able to understand the wet and thick-tongued allusions, in the rich Scots accent, was another matter. Of quite a number of the items James asked Heriot the cost, *sotto voce*, in the process, and, when sufficiently impressed, passed on the information like-wise with the gift.

When this was over, a move was made outside, to view the succession of masques, spectacles, tableaux, mimodramas and set pieces in the gardens—although only with reduced numbers of spectators, it is to be feared, strange and exotic liquors having had some equally strange effects, especially on top of some of the more rarified dishes. Some of the entertainments were allegorical, epic, historical or moral, Messrs. Jonson, Jones and Campion having been given more or less a free hand; but others were merely diverting and catered for all tastes. The King's own tastes were catholic, and he appeared to get as much enjoyment out of a piece wherein a lot of little boys disguised as bottles danced and capered round a man in the guise of a great tun, spewing out coloured water as wine, as over an elaborate and erudite charade by Sir Francis Bacon, wherein Peace and Plenty cast their generous offerings before His Pacific Majesty in the shape of a crowned lion, with War, represented by a most loathsome dragon, being continuously stabbed, to the effusion of large quantities of red blood, by a succession of angel-knights with handsome wings sprouting from their shining armour.

As ever, of course, the King began to tire of all this, sooner rather than later and commenced to steer his party gradually towards the large lake where, on an islet, only reachable by two available gondolas, a special pavilion had been erected amongst the trees and stocked with bottles, flagons and playing-cards. Since the gondolas only held four each at most, in addition to the gondoliers, a considerable weeding-out of hangers-on was expeditiously achieved, with Robin Carr instructed, in stage-whispers, whom to include. Some of the most successful gamblers in two kingdoms, more especially the northern one, largely new viscounts but including the English Earls of Montgomery and Southampton, were duly ferried across to the island in relays, whilst Carr was sent in search of the wealthiest known guests, to invite, also in relays, as a mark of especial royal esteem, to make brief pilgrimage to the shrine.

At this stage, George Heriot conceived his duty done and melted away into the shrubbery, to go in search of Alison who had remained with the Queen.

It was early evening, with the thought of the fourteen-mile barge-journey down-river beginning to exercise his mind and Alison about to seek formal permission to leave the Queen's entourage, that Heriot learned that his liege lord had not yet, in fact, finished with him for the day. He learned it from the supercilious lips of Carr, Viscount Rochester, no less, sent in person to find and conduct him to the island. They made a silent journey of it.

Only one gondola survived—the other apparently having sunk without trace—and at both the little jetties and at the pavilion entrance Yeomen stood guard. Within the tent was a picture of chaos. Tables were overturned, bottles, flagons and tankards lay everywhere, playing-cards littered the trampled grass and, amidst all, bodies snored and twitched and grunted. Three men remained upright, all Scots—James himself, at the head of a table, James Hay, Viscount Doncaster, at one side of him and John Ramsay, Viscount Haddington at the other; although admittedly the Archduke Albert of Hapsburg remained approximately in his chair but sprawled helplessly across the swimming table. Beside the three Scots were sizeable piles of specie, gold pieces, rings, jewelled brooches, crosses of knightly orders and, Heriot was interested to note, sundry of the costly gifts he had so carefully manufactured for this day.

The King, beaker in hand, waved genially. "Aye, Geordie—come you. Drink a cup o' wine wi' me. Whaur hae you been hiding yoursel'?" His voice was neither thicker nor more slurred than usual.

"I have latterly been talking with His Highness the Prince of Wales, Sire. In his room."

"You have?" James nodded. "Dutious. Aye, my Annie would send you there. She has a notion our Henry will die, has Annie. Think you so, Geordie?"

Heriot swallowed. "I . . . I do not know, Sire. But—God forbid! I am no physician. He seemed brighter, stronger, I thought."

"Aye, he's bright, all right. Ower bright, maybe, the laddie. I hope he doesna die, Geordie."

"No, Sire. I pray that he will not."

"Aye—you pray. But meantime, come you and sit by me. Here. Johnnie, Jamie—up wi' you. Off! You too, Robin Carr—out! I want a word wi' my Fiduciary. Aye, and you can leave the winnings where they are see you—they'll come to nae harm in Geordie Heriot's care!"

When the other three had bowed themselves out, leaving only the unconscious drunks, James gestured to the three heaps of spoil. "You hae yon kist o' yours, some place? Och, it'll no' need to go back toon! And, here." He dug into a pocket of his padded doublet for a bunch of crumpled papers. "Some notes o' hand, just. There's one for seven hundred pounds frae Philip Montgomery. You'll ken better than I do whether his credit will stand it? But, och—we'll no' can be too hard on the laddie, mind. And here's one for eight thousand, five hundred guilders frae yon fat Dutchman. I dinna ken how much that is—you'll hae to work it out for me, Geordie. You'll see to it a'?"

"Yes, Sire. A, a profitable afternoon!"

"Ooh, aye. Though, mind, a guid head for the liquor is the main thing. Never play the cartes wi' a birling heid! One thing we Scots can teach them, eh? Och, but you dinna play them anyhow, do you?"

"No, Sire. Money is my trade, not my amusement. So I respect it."

"Nae mair'n do I, lad—nae mair'n do I. And dinna sound sae a'mighty smug! Na, na—sit still. Dinna go yet, man. I've news for you. Frae Scotland. Right interesting news."

"Good news, Sire? Or ill?"

"That's maybe a matter o' opinion. You, now—you, I jalouse, hae something o' a shamefu' liking for yon rogue Patrick Gray, hae you no'?"

"Gray? I, I do not rightly know, Sire. I admit he is a very dangerous man. And too clever, by far. But he has his points, too. A, a strange urbanity. His principles may be but ill ones—but he holds to them."

"You think so? He has aye held to treasons, rebellions, plots, subbornings, betrayals. If you can ca' such principles! Piracy, too—wrecking. Hae you heard tell what he and thae graceless kin o' mine in Orkney hae been at? Changing the beacons on the islands that guide the ships, to lure in honest mariners to the rocks. So they can plunder them. For money and arms and gear to raise rebellion against *me!* To pay for French arms. Aye, but the French ships get in safe enough! Devils, they are—just devils! The wet sea! But—och, I've put a spoke or two in that wheel, to be sure."

"There has been talk of this of arms, mercenaries, from France, invasion and the like, for long now, Sire. And little to show for it. Think you it is in truth anything more than a tale? Put out by Gray, no doubt. For his own ends. To alarm, win over faint-hearts, gain concessions perhaps . . . ?"

"Och, aye—it's mair'n a tale, Geordie. I ken fine what's been going on. It's maybe no sae great a matter as has been made out—but invasion was planned, to be sure. Much arms sent. I've a wheen folk wi' sharp ears in France, as well as had Patrick, mind." James shurgged those grotesquely padded shoulders. "But—a' that's done wi'. By wi', man. There'll be nae invasion, now. Nae uprising and fell insurrection in my auld realm o' Scotland. We can a' sleep quiet in our naked beds, now, Geordie. For the man's deid."

"Dead . . . ?" Heriot stared.

"Aye, just that. Deceased. On his way to hell, belike! Mind you, I'll miss him."

"But . . . but . . . you mean the Master? Lord Gray? Gray—dead?"

"Patrick, aye. Verra sudden."

The other moistened his lips and loooked round that shambles of a pavilion, as though for means of escape. "I cannot . . . take it in, Sire!" he muttered. "Patrick Gray! He was, I think, no older than am I. And of excellent health. How—how did he die?"

"It seems to have been fell sudden. The hand o' Almighty God, nae doubt! It aye catches up wi' evil doers, sooner or later, mind. A stroke, they tell me. Aye, a stroke, just."

"Not the stroke of steel! Or bullet?"

"No' so as I've heard tell. In his bed, in his ain house o' Castle Huntly. Ooh, aye—the Lord's ways are wonderfu' and mysterious for to behold."

"The Earl of Dunbar died in his bed also, Sire, did he not—equally mysterious and wonderful! A strange . . . coincidence!"

"So it is, Geordie—so it is. I hadna thought on that. But—a' for the best, mind. Patrick had had his day—like Doddie. Time they moved on, I'm thinking. For the weel o' the realm. Aye—*aut non tentaris aut perfice!*"

There was silence in that tent for a little, save for the snorings and gruntings.

"You seem hard stricken, Geordie—over one o' your lord's enemies!" the King observed presently but not censoriously. "I reckon you had a soft side for the man. So had I, mind—so had I. Or is it Vicky's lassie, Mary Gray, you're consairned for? Or my bonnie cousin Marie. Your sentiments do you credit, Geordie. But . . . the women will get ower it. Like the rest o' us."

"I, I just cannot seem to accept it, Sire. There is something amiss, here."

"You think so? Mind, if it hadna been our Vicky in charge up there, I'd hae let my mind dwell on the thought o' poison, maybe! But, och—Vicky wouldna do sic like a thing. No' wi' Mary Gray in it. And Vicky is a right honourable chiel, you'll agree? Na, na—we can rule out poison, eh? It's just the hand o' God, as I say."

Heriot looked his royal master in the eye, and said nothing.

"Sae that's it, Geordie. That's my news. And a' will be a deal better in Scotland, now—nae doubt o' that. There's no' another Patrick Gray! My Orkney kin will sink like pricked bladders, wi' him gone! So simple a solution, eh? Simple, aye. It gars you think! Waesucks—maybe we're no' simple enough often enough. Aye, well—awa' wi' you, Geordie—and meditate on the ways o' the Lord!"

Abruptly Heriot rose, bowed jerkily and turned to go.

"Dinna forget the gewgaws and the siller, man," James reminded. "Use the Archduke's cloak to bundle it in—he owes me mair'n that, anyway."

With his heavy and awkward bundle, Heriot paused at the tent door as the King spoke again.

"I'm going to miss him, mind. It'll no' be the same without him—no' the same, at all. A guid night to you, Geordie Heriot."

A man in chaos of emotions, George Heriot went seeking his Alison. He wanted to go home.

HISTORICAL NOTE

THE THREE PRINCIPAL actors in this account continued in their various activities for many years thereafter; but although premature death did not strike them down as it had done Patrick Gray, it struck at all three indirectly the following year, 1612, wherein died Henry, Prince of Wales, Jean, Duchess of Lennox, and, after barely four years of marriage, Alison Primrose, in child-birth. George Heriot mourned her for the rest of his days.

James Stewart continued to rule his United Kingdom in his own inimitable way for another fourteen years, dying in his bed after drinking vast quantities of beer to cool himself of a fever, at the age of fifty-nine, having been a king for fifty-eight years. Queen Anne predeceased him by six years, on 9th March 1619—but remained unburied until 13th May, while sufficient funds were found for the funeral. James, who did not like gloomy occasions, did not attend.

George Heriot, who did not remarry, never retired to Scotland after all, though he bought an estate there. He died the year before his monarch—who was still in his debt—and was buried at St. Martin-in-the-Fields, London. He left a huge fortune, a large part of which he donated to his native city to found the great school which still carries his name, based on the example of Christ's Hospital, London, which he had much admired.

Duke Ludovick died in the same year as Heriot, full of honours if not riches, now Duke of Richmond as well as of Lennox. His illegitimate son, John Stewart of Methven, was knighted and appointed Constable and Keeper of Dumbarton Castle—from which Patrick Earl of Orkney was taken to Edinburgh, for execution for treason, in 1615.

On the death of Alison Heriot, her father James Primrose demanded a refund of the five thousand merks dowry money, plus another five thousand in lieu of expenses. Heriot, though disclaiming liability, repaid the first but not the second. Primrose's grandson became the first Earl of Rosebery.